The English Novels
Part A

The Collected Novels of P. C. Wren
Volume 6A

Fiction Titles by P. C. Wren

Dew and Mildew. 1912
Father Gregory. 1913
The Snake and Sword. 1914.
Driftwood Spars. 1916
The Wages of Virtue. 1916
The Young Stagers. 1917
Stepsons of France. 1917
Cupid in Africa. 1920
Beau Geste. 1924
Beau Sabreur. 1926
Beau Ideal. 1928
Good Gestes. 1929
Soldiers of Misfortune. 1929
The Mammon of Righteousness. 1930 (U.S. title: Mammon)
Mysterious Waye. 1930
Sowing Glory. 1931
Valiant Dust. 1932
Flawed Blades. 1933
Action and Passion. 1933
Port o' Missing Men. 1934
Beggars' Horses. 1934 (U.S. title: The Dark Woman)
Sinbad the Soldier. 1935
Explosion. 1935
Spanish Maine. 1935 (U.S. title: The Desert Heritage)
Bubble Reputation. 1936 (U.S. title: The Cortenay Treasure)
Fort in the Jungle. 1936
The Man of a Ghost. 1937 (U.S. title: The Spur of Pride)
Worth Wile. 1937 (U.S. title: To the Hilt)
Cardboard Castle. 1938
Rough Shooting. 1938
Paper Prison. 1939 (U.S. Title: The Man the Devil Didn't
    Want)
The Disappearance of General Jason. 1940
Two Feet From Heaven. 1940
The Uniform of Glory. 1941
Odd—But Even So. 1941

The English Novels

Part A

by

Percival Christopher Wren

BUBBLE REPUTATION
CARDBOARD CASTLE

Edited

by

John L. Espley

Riner Publishing Company
Culpeper Virginia
2020

ISBN
9780999074961

The text of *Bubble Reputation* will be in the Public Domain as
of 1 January 2032 since it was originally published in 1936

The text of *Cardboard Castle* will be in the Public Domain as
of 1 January 2034 since it was originally published in 1938

Introductory Material
Copyright 2020
Riner Publishing Company
rinerpublishing.wordpress.com
John L. Espley
johnlespley@gmail.com

CONTENTS

PREFACE

The English Novels Part A and *The English Novels Part B* by Percival Christopher Wren are the sixth of a multi-volume series, *The Collected Novels of P. C. Wren*. The purpose of publishing this series is to make the novels written by P. C. Wren more available to the reading public. His novel, *Beau Geste*, is usually recognized by most of the book dealers I have met over the years, but his other works are not so easily remembered.

I have been collecting P. C. Wren for over fifty years, and have been working on a comprehensive bibliography for almost as long. The text of the twenty-eight novels was easily obtained from copies in my own collection. For that collection, I certainly need to thank the hundreds of used book dealers I have purchased items from, and I need to thank some by name: Steven Temple, David Mason, Walt Barrie and, especially, the late Denis McDonnell for the advice and help they have provided over the years.

With regard to Wren himself, Mr. John Venmore and Mr. Philip Fairweather, have been very helpful in providing additional biographical information. Both of them are descendants of the late Mr. Richard Alan Graham-Smith, Wren's stepson and executor of Wren's estate.

As it has been over seventy years since the death of P. C. Wren (November 22, 1941), Wren's works have passed into the public domain in the United Kingdom. In the United States, fourteen of the twenty-eight novels are still under copyright. Thanks to information provided by Messrs. Venmore and Fairweather, the heirs to Wren's literary estate, Mr. Danny Adekoya Campbell and Mr. Christopher Oladipo Graham-Smith, were located and permission has been granted to reprint Wren's works.

I also need to acknowledge the help and guidance of my family members: my daughter and son-in-law, Dawn and Andrew; my son and daughter-in-law, Jared and Claudia; and my long-suffering wife, Cathy. Thank you.

In conclusion, I need to thank Percival Christopher Wren for the many years of great enjoyment that his stories have provided. I know that Wren is not a literary or critical success, but, for me, he is one of the great storytellers of the early twentieth century.

John L. Espley
Culpeper, Virginia
February 2, 2020

INTRODUCTION

Percival Christopher Wren is best known as a novelist, publishing twenty-eight novels from 1912 to 1941, the most famous being *Beau Geste* (1924). Wren also published seven short story collections; *Stepsons of France* (1917), *The Young Stagers* (1917), *Good Gestes* (1929), *Flawed Blades* (1933), *Port o' Missing Men* (1934), *Rough Shooting* (1938), and *Odd—But Even So* (1941), containing a total of 116 stories. There were also two omnibus collections, *Stories of the Foreign Legion* (1947) and *Dead Men's Boots* (1949), containing stories selected from *Stepsons of France*, *Good Gestes*, *Flawed Blades*, and *Port o' Missing Men*. All 116 short stories can be found in the five volume collection, *The Collected Short Stories of Percival Christopher Wren.*[1]

Wren was a man of mystery in that the majority of biographical statements about him seem to be more fiction than fact. A typical biography places his birth in Devon in 1885, his education at Oxford, and his career as that of world traveler, hunter, journalist, tramp, British cavalry trooper, legionnaire in the French Foreign Legion, assistant director of education in Bombay, and a Justice of the Peace. Most of the above biography, however, is false or has not been verified.

Wren was born Percy Wren on November 1, 1875 in Deptford, a district of South London on the banks of the Thames. He did attend Oxford University, graduating in 1898 with a 3rd class honours in History leading to a Bachelor of Arts degree. He

---

[1] For further information on *The Collected Short Stories of Percival Christopher Wren* see rinerpublishing.wordpress.com

attained his "M.A." in 1901. In those days, a person acquired a "M.A." after a certain number of years (three in Wren's case) and upon payment of a fee.

After leaving Oxford, he married Alice Lucie Shovelier in December 1899 with whom he had a daughter, Estelle Lenore Wren, born in February 1901, and a son, Percival Rupert Christopher Wren, born in February 1904. Percy worked as a teacher at various commercial schools until 1903, when he and his family left England for India.

From 1903 to approximately 1919, Wren was employed as an educator by the Indian Educational Service (I.E.S.). During that time he published a number of educational textbooks, some of which are still in use in Indian schools today. It was during this period that he started using the name Percival C. and Percival Christopher on the textbooks.

From 1905 to 1915, he also served in the Volunteer Corps (Sind and Poona) in India (see the novel *Driftwood Spars*, which contains a description of a Volunteer Corps), and was appointed a Captain in the Indian Army Reserve of Officers, the 101st Grenadiers of the Indian Infantry, in November 1914. He probably saw action in the East African campaign of World War I (see the novel *Cupid in Africa*, which takes place in East Africa during the War), and resigned from the Indian Army Reserve of Officers in November 1915.[2]

Wren's first novel, *Dew and Mildew*, was published by Longmans, Green in 1912. His first novel of the French Foreign Legion, *The Wages of Virtue*,

---

[2] Most of the biographical information about Wren has been obtained through certificates, documents, and original research at the British Library, Bodleian Library, and the India Office papers. Further information on Wren and his works was obtained during a three week research visit in September 2018 at the John Murray Archives in the National Library of Scotland. Detailed documentation and sources will be cited in the biographical essay to be included in the forthcoming publication, *An Annotated Bibliography of Percival Christopher Wren*.

was written in 1913 and published by John Murray in 1916. One of the many questions about Wren is whether he did serve in the French Foreign Legion. Given the chronology of his documented biography it is difficult to see where he had time to actually serve in the Legion.[3] Wren himself always maintained that he had served and his stepson, Richard Alan Graham-Smith, who died in 2006, "strongly maintained that Wren had indeed served in the French Foreign Legion and was always quick to refute those who said otherwise."[4]

* * * * * * *

The series, *The Collected Novels of P. C. Wren*, is intended to include all twenty-eight novels in seven thematic omnibus volumes. The number of physical volumes will be fourteen, with each thematic volume divided into Part A and Part B. The individual titles will not be in Wren's original publication order, but will instead have a connecting theme such as characters or locale. The seven volumes are:[5]

> v. 1 - The Geste Novels
> > Part A:
> > > Beau Geste
> > > Beau Sabreur
> > Part B:
> > > Beau Ideal
> > > Spanish Maine
> v. 2 - The Sinbad Novels

---

[3] After examining just over half of the available files at the John Murray Archives, it is evident that Wren was consistent about serving in the Legion. The only available time though would have been between 1891, when Wren was fifteen and 1894 when he entered Oxford, shortly before he was nineteen.

[4] wikipedia.org/wiki/P._C._Wren

[5] The order of volumes four through seven has been modified since the publication of volume two.

Part A:
   Action and Passion
   Sinbad the Soldier
Part B:
   Fort in the Jungle
   The Disappearance of General Jason
v. 3 - The Foreign Legion Novels
   Part A:
      The Wages of Virtue
      Sowing Glory
   Part B:
      The Uniform of Glory
      Paper Prison
v. 4 - The Earlier India Novels
   Part A:
      Dew and Mildew
      Father Gregory
   Part B:
      The Snake and the Sword
      Driftwood Spars
v. 5 - The Later India Novels
   Part A:
      Beggars' Horses
      Explosion
   Part B:
      The Man of a Ghost
      Worth Wile
v. 6 - The English Novels
   Part A:
      Bubble Reputation
      Cardboard Castle
   Part B:
      The Mammon of Righteousness
      Two Feet From Heaven
v. 7 - A Mixed Bag of Novels[6]
   Part A:

---

[6] Previous to May 2019 volume seven's title was "The Other Novels".

Soldiers of Misfortune
Valiant Dust
Part B:
   Cupid in Africa
   Mysterious Waye

*   *   *   *   *   *   *

Volume Six of *The Collected Novels of P. C. Wren*, *The English Novels*, contains four novels with a different setting than that of his other novels. The action takes place almost entirely in England, which is why the title of this omnibus edition is *The English Novels*.

*   *   *   *   *   *   *

The English Novels Part A

The English Novels Part A contains two novels, *Bubble Reputation* (1936) and *Cardboard Castle* (1938) which are set in the English countryside in large country manor houses.

Bubble Reputation is the story of Sir Giles Cortenay (known as Bump), the last descendant of an old English family. Due to difficult economic circumstances, Bump has turned the family manor into a country hotel. The main plot is about the mystery of the murder of Bump's granduncle and the search for a great hoard of jewels hidden on the estate by Bump's buccaneer ancestor.

The title, *Bubble Reputation*, comes from William Shakespeare's *As You Like It*, the character Jacque's soliloquy "All the world's a stage" in Act two Scene seven:

Seeking the bubble reputation
Even in the cannon's mouth. . . .

This quotation from Shakespeare's play forms one of the recurring themes of the novel, as the two main protagonists, Bump and his cousin Honor, discuss:

"Bump," she said as he closed the door, "should one read it,

" '*Seeking the bubble—reputation—even in the cannon's mouth,*' with 'bubble' and 'reputation' both nouns and things, interchangeable and all that, or,

'*Seeking the bubble reputation even in the cannon's mouth*' with 'bubble' as an adjective—you know, an adjective is a word entirely surrounded by nouns—'bubble' describing 'reputation.' All bubbly like?" [. . .]

"I should think it means 'Seeking that bubble which men call Reputation; and seeking it in the cannon's mouth of all silly places.' Very funny place to find bubbles, what?"

Bump further pondered the important point.

"On the other hand, of course, it may mean 'seeking the fragile short-lived reputation—for military courage and dash—seeking it in the very cannon's mouth.' Extremely silly place to seek anything at all, if you ask me. In business hours, I mean."

"You don't suppose it's a sort of what-you-may-call-it—a later mistake, misprint . . . ?"

"Interpoliation?" suggested Bump, summoning his literary resources.

"That sort of thing. Yes, 'interpoliation.' Or interpollution. And 'bubble' should be *bauble*?"

"Might be, might be," agreed Bump, "though I wouldn't go looking for baubles either, in a cannon's mouth. The only bauble you'd find there would be a round one, hard and heavy. Impetuous like. [. . .]

"Oh, I only wanted to know. I picked up this copy of *As You Like It* and opened it at the Seven Ages of Man—'how full of quotations Shakespeare is'—and it reminds me of school. We acted the play for a Prize Day do, and the English mistress always used to say to herself, I'm certain, '*Seeking the bubble* —count three under your breath—*reputation*—count three under your breath— *in the cannon's mouth.*' Like that."[7]

Other themes, familiar from his other stories, are such things as psychics and spiritualism. There is also a description of a character suffering from heart problems which is probably taken from Wren's own experiences with heart disease. There are also hints of some resemblances to two of his early novels of India. The Old Contemptibles Club here in *Bubble Reputation* is similar to the Chotapettah Club of *Father Gregory*, and the relationship of Bump and his granduncle is similar to Dam and his grandfather in *The Snake and the Sword*.

Wren's opinion of *Bubble Reputation* is expressed in a newspaper announcement of the publication for the novel:

Temporarily forsaking North Africa,

---

[7] Pages 96-97, herein.

Major Percival Christopher Wren lays the scene of his new novel, "The Cortenay Treasure" [*Bubble Reputation*], to be published on March 31, on the coast of Devon. "Like all my books," he writes to his publishers, Houghton Mifflin Company. "'The Cortenay Treasure' is founded on fact, to the extent that the penny-plain, story of an ancient Devonshire Manor House is twopence-colored in the book. There is a house in Devonshire in which an Elizabethan sea-captain, who fought against the Spanish Armada, undoubtedly did conceal a treasure, in jewels, much as described in the story, and which has never been discovered."[8]

According to the dedication to Viscountess Curzon, Wren finished writing this novel in August 1935. The novel was published in the United States by Houghton Mifflin (under the title *The Cortenay Treasure*) on March 31, 1936, two weeks before the John Murray publication of *Bubble Reputation* on April 15. *The Cortenay Treasure* was reprinted by Grosset and Dunlap in 1938.

The second novel, *Cardboard Castle*, in *The English Novels Part A* is the story of a tutor and the young man he is teaching. The tutor, Henry Waring, is hired because, Anthony Calderton, the teenage son of Lord and Lady Calderton, is considered "different", and remains at the manor house when his parents leave to govern a British colony. When Lady Calderton is taken ill with a "tropical" disease, however, she comes home to recuperate and it is at

---

[8] *Santa Fe New Mexican*, Friday, March 20, 1936, page four, section one.

this point in the plot that the villain, Captain Bertie-Norton, appears. This so-called "old friend" of Lady Calderton is actually her first husband, who everybody thought had died twenty years ago. He now wants Lady Calderton to provide his upkeep and living since he wants to "settle down" after his adventuring throughout the world. He wants to do this without anybody knowing who he really is. The rest of the book is about how Lady Calderton and the tutor, Henry Waring, deal with Bertie-Norton and his demands, and how Henry deals with the teenager who is "mad" about the English Civil War.

This scenario is an "Enoch Arden"[9] theme story that Wren has used before, most notably in *The Wages of Virtue*. But in that novel, Wren has the supposedly dead husband do the honorable act of not disclosing his identity by hiding in the French Foreign Legion. Another example of the villain, blackmailing, a woman for past mistakes, is in the novel, *Spanish Maine*, although in that story, the two were not previously married.

The villain, Bertie-Norton, is vividly described as an Englishman adventurer, but who is also a "bounder." He *might* be based on the first husband, Cyril Graham-Smith, of Wren's second wife, Isabel. Isabel for many years was Wren's secretary and nurse, starting while Wren was in India before World War I. In 1927, Graham-Smith initiated divorce proceedings against Isabel for adultery, and named Wren as a "correspondent". Wren in a letter, dated 23 May, to John Murray wrote:

> "I took this filthy hound's consumptive
> son for a Swiss and Mediterranean tour
> on a specialist's advice, and of course

---

[9] "Enoch Arden" is an Alfred, Lord Tennyson narrative poem about a husband who was thought to be dead, but returns several years later to find his wife has remarried.

his mother went with him. The chivalrous gentleman, instead of thanking me, made it an opportunity for divorce and £1,000 damages—he not having seen his wife for 10 years! He withdrew the damages request directly his counsel found that the case might be defended if he did not. He would never have brought the action if he had expected defence. In each of the hotels he named, Mrs. Graham-Smith and I <u>did</u> stay—and so did her mother, sleeping in the same room! I feel sure you will give me an opportunity of defending Mrs. Graham-Smith when the decree is made absolute. If I said a word now, the King's Proctor would intervene, there would be a re-trial—and she would again be tied to a foul rascal. I greatly regret all this, so far as it touches you, but I was compelled to help one of the best of women—at any cost. When the decree is safe, I intend to libel him in his clubs in India and England."[10]

Other themes in *Cardboard Castle* include Wren writing about child rearing and education as Henry and Anthony interact, and a theme seen in several other novels and short stories is that of "killing no murder", as Henry, his uncle, and Lady Calderton all think that the best solution might be to kill Bertie-Norton.

The writing in *Cardboard Castle* switches viewpoints between chapters featuring the first person perspective of Henry Waring and that of the omniscient third person. Unlike the majority of Wren's novels, there are fewer scenes of adven-

---

[10] John Murray Archive, National Library of Scotland (cited hereafter as JMA), file Acc. 12927/379 CZ27, 23 May 1927.

turous action, but the novel does end on a satisfactory, if not definitive, conclusion. In a letter to John Murray, Wren wrote: "Contrary to my custom I am rather pleased with Cardboard Castle and hope the critics may read it before reviewing it."[11]

Published in February 1938 by John Murray, *Cardboard Castle*, is dedicated to "Dr. William Lyon Phelps, Ph.D., Litt.D., of Yale University", a noted American writer and critic who had some well-received reviews of Wren's writings. The dedication does not appear in the American edition published by Houghton Mifflin in April 1938. There has been no reprint edition of *Cardboard Castle* until this edition by Riner Publishing Company.

*   *   *   *   *   *   *

The original spelling, punctuation, and grammar of the British editions, except for obvious errors, has been preserved as found in the latest editions/printings of the stories during Wren's lifetime (1875-1941). The footnotes, in the novels, are also as found in the original source material.

---

[11] JMA, Acc. 12927/279 F53, 15 September 1937.

BUBBLE REPUTATION

"And then a soldier, full of strange oaths,
Bearded like the pard. Jealous in honour,
sudden and quick in quarrel,
Seeking the bubble reputation even in
the cannon's mouth."

To

<u>THE VISCOUNTESS CURZON</u>

PETWOOD,
August, 1935.

Dear Lady Curzon,
    As I am putting the last touches to this book at your deservedly beloved

PETWOOD

while you yourself are here, I should like to dedicate it to you and to this equally perfect place.

Yours very gratefully,
P. C. WREN.

PART I

I

Old Mr. Mompett was in a bad way. The doctor told Mrs. Mompett so quite plainly, and Mrs. Mompett, who had a poor opinion of Mr. Mompett, told him so, even more plainly.

And Something Else told him so most plainly of all.

"It's me chubes," he said. "Though what chubes has to do with a broken leg, I don't know."

And indeed the connection between bronchial tubes and the femur bone of the thigh is perhaps far to seek. On the other hand, there undoubtedly is a connection between alcoholism and a morbid condition of the lungs, and Mr. Mompett had a very fine taste indeed in old port, ancient brandy, good whisky, and in any other form of liquor that came under the heading of what he termed "real good stuff."

And although Mr. Mompett lay dying in the tiny airless bedroom of a poor cottage, he had been accustomed to the abundant drinking of the best of good stuff for close upon half a century.

"Anythink you fancy?" enquired Mrs. Mompett grimly and with perceptible implication of the fact that such consideration is due to those whose fancies are very near their end.

"No, there ain't. But I'll tell you somethink I don't fancy," wheezed Mr. Mompett, "and that's the sight of your face. If you'll take it away and send young Elbert 'ere, I'll be obliged, Mrs. Mompett."

Mrs. Mompett obliged, and, as she departed from the sick-room, the old man, fumbling with the unclean sheet, and following her with his eyes, muttered,

" 'Bin together now for forty years,'" he mused, "and about thirty-nine and a half too much. . . . Shan't tell *you* what I got to say, Mrs. Mompett."

The door opened and a lad of some sixteen or seventeen years entered.

Mr. Mompett eyed his favourite grandson, tall for his years, well-built and not ill-looking. Perhaps the eyes were a little close-set, the expression somewhat shifty, the mouth a trifle hard, the face somewhat old for its years. If so, Mr. Mompett saw no defect and found no fault.

"Want me, Grandfer?"

"Yes, Bertie boy. I want a word with yer. Give ye a bit of good advice and a—secret. Money in it, I shouldn't be s'prised. And big money, if so."

At the mention of money, the lad shot a quick look at his grandfather, and his manner changed. Closing the door, he pulled a chair up to the bed and seated himself.

"Right. What is it, Grandfer?" he whispered.

"Where's that nit-wit brother of yours?"

" 'Asn't come home yet."

"Good. He's a fool. Don't tell him what I tell yer. Don't tell yer grandmother. Don't tell nobody. Never. Keep it to yerself."

Albert assured his grandfather that he would certainly honour his commands in this respect.

"Now a word of advice, Elbert. And I know what I'm talkin' about. See?

"Get yer legs under somebody else's mahogany, as soon as you can, and keep 'em there. That's all sense in a nut-shell. Let somebody else feed yer and clothe yer. Sleep in somebody else's bed; read yer paper by somebody else's light; and sit and warm yerself in front of somebody else's fire. Ar, and always drink a drop of the very best out of somebody else's bottle and glass. See?"

"No," replied Albert. "Sounds all-right, Grandfer.

How do you do it?"

"Service, my boy. Good service. That's what. Look at me."

Albert looked, without enthusiasm or manifest affection.

"Look at me. Done it all me life. Never paid for anything, and was paid for doin' it. And if I hadn't been so fond of 'avin' a little bit on an 'orse, I should have 'ad a tidy sum put by. As it is, I 'aven't done so dusty."

Albert sniffed non-committally.

"Now listen to me, Son. Wait till you've growed another inch or so, then sit you down and write a nice respectful letter to the old General up at the Hall, saying you are old Mr. Mompett's grandson, and which it was his last dyin' wish that you should go into service there like yer grandfather before you. If your father hadn't been a bl . . . If your father hadn't been a fool, I say, he'd a bin there now, or been a rich man, and as good a gentleman as any gentleman in the land. If he had listened to me. Well, you write this letter, and next day, you put on yer best clo'es and up you go. See?"

"I 'ear," replied Albert. "But I don't know as it's my idea of . . ."

"You 'ear *my* idea, Elbert. You listen to me, for you won't have the chance much longer. . . . Wouldn't you like to be a rich man, a gentleman, as good as any gentleman in the land? Have a butler of yer own?

"Listen. I was in that house, man and boy, for a matter of forty-three years, pantry-boy to butler, and I see three Sir Gileses come and go. Well, three come and two go. There's only the General there now and a kid. . . . And . . ."

Here Mr. Mompett impressively tapped Albert's hand with a soft white forefinger.

"They was all lookin' for somethink."

Mr. Mompett screwed up his eyes and pursed his lips mysteriously.

"And what was it?" he whispered.

"A winner?" hazarded Albert flippantly, in the light of his knowledge that this foolish old man had spent much of his time and most of his money in vain endeavour to spot winners.

"Ar, and you may say so. With odds at about a million to nothing," assented Mr. Mompett. "A winner if you like."

"Well, I 'aven't got any idea of backing winners," objected Albert, making as though to rise. "Hasn't done you much good. No winners for me."

"Then you're a blasted young fool," explained Grandpapa irascibly. "Listen. In that house there is somethink vallyble for the picking up. It is worth hundreds of thousands of pounds—and it'll go in yer trousers' pocket! I heard the talk of it back and forth, for forty years and more. Heard it above stairs at table, heard it below stairs, till I was sick of it, or should 'ave bin if I 'adn't 'ad more sense than to . . . Why, the old General there, now, spends his life tappin' . . . tappin' . . ."

"Tappin' what?" enquired Albert. "Beer-barrels?"

"Tappin' everything. You'd go into the room quiet and catch him tappin' the woodwork, panelling, window-seats and such. He had the tappin' habit like all the rest of the family. Couldn't touch anything without tappin' and listenin'. I've seen him go up the stairs tappin' the big 'and-rail all the way, and come down tappin' the wainscotting. . . . I've watched over a landing and seen him come up the grand staircase tappin' every tread and riser, all the way up. Same with the present kid's father and grandfather. Tap anything. Tap everything. From floor-boards and furniture to chimney-pieces and garden-walls, they would."

"And didn't they never tap the ceilin'?" yawned

Albert.

"Ar, and you can lay to it. Tap the ceilin', says you. All the ceilin's in the old 'All is heavy beams and carved wood mostly; and I'll bet there ain't a square inch of them ceilin's, as you call 'em, that hasn't bin tapped by some of 'em at one time or another."

"Well, what is it?" enquired Albert.

"*Jools.* One of 'em, some way back, hid 'em, and was done in before he could take 'em again."

"Poor feller."

"Yes, you may say so. . . . And before he could tell anybody else where he had hid 'em, too."

"And if them that lives there can't find 'em, who d'you suppose is goin' to?" enquired Albert.

"You listen, me boy. You know young Ted Umpleby?"

"As went for a soldier and just bin killed in Egypt?"

"That's 'im. And what was he before he was fool enough to go for a soldier?"

"Footman up at the Hall."

"That's right. Well, he found 'em."

"*Cor!*" ejaculated Albert, surprised out of the somewhat sardonic scepticism natural to his years and station.

"Then what's all the talk about?" he asked, re-lapsing.

"*Jools,*" replied his grandfather. "'Aven't you grasped that yet? Yes, Ted Umpleby found 'em."

"And where are they now?"

"Just percisely where they was."

Again Albert's eyes lit up, and the settling mists of depression cleared from about his young counte-nance.

"When I say Ted Umpleby found 'em, I mean he found the place where they was."

"Was?"

"Yes—and *is*."

"He never pinched 'em, then?"

"No, nor nobody else. And that's why I'm talkin' to you, Son; why I'm giving you some advice, and tellin' you a secret that's worth money, big money. Make a perfect gentleman of you, as it would of for me, if I hadn't broke me blasted leg. Listen.

"Sir Giles had an idea—that was this kid's father —that the pictures that was left . . . all them in what had bin the proper picture-gallery havin' bin disposed of long ago, for death duties; gamblin' debts; paying off fancy ladies as had got the Baronets where they wanted 'em; and what not. . . . What was I sayin'?"

"Gawd knows," hazarded Albert.

"Oh, yerss. Pictures. Well, Sir Giles had an idea that the pictures in—one o' the rooms—wanted dustin', and I'd got to see it done meself. Got to be flicked over with a feather duster very soft and gentle, so's not to do 'em any 'arm, they not havin' any glass in 'em, and a gentleman being comin' down to see 'em. Going to sell 'em, Sir Giles was, I reckon. And that was how it happened."

"Ar, I can see that!" observed Albert.

"Ho! Can you? . . . Well, after breakfast, I tells Ted Umpleby to bring along the steps and a feather duster, and give the pictures a flick over. And Ted's up on top of the steps, a-steadyin' hisself with one hand against the panelling, up between the pictures, when suddenly there's an 'ell of a crash and down comes Ted and the steps. And when I see what he done, I says, '*Blimey, what 'ave you done, Umpleby?*'. For he had brought down half the panellin'. Leastways, he had brought down a damn great lump of it, big as a cupboard door.

"And suddenly it come to me in a flash. I twigs what he has done. And before he can pull hisself together and see what he's done, I rounds on him.

10

" 'Ted Umpleby,' I says, 'you clod-'opping, 'eavy-fisted, clumsy great 'ound, what 'ave you done? Call yourself a footman? *Foot's* about right!'

" 'I only put me hands against the wall, Mr. Mompett, Sir,' he says, 'to steady meself when I slipped, tryin' to reach that there picture.'

" 'Only put yer hands against the wall! Put yer hands against the wall,' I said, 'put yer leg-of-mutton fists clean through the bloomin' wall and brought down half a hundredweight of panelling. Wouldn't you like to go and put yer feet through a window?' I says. 'You'll bring disgrace on me yet,' I says. 'You can disgrace yerself and welcome,' I says, 'but anythink like this again—and out you goes. I wish I'd never brought you 'ere.'

"And, by gum, that was the biggest lie I ever told," chuckled Mr. Mompett.

"And that's saying something, Grandfer," grinned Albert.

Mr. Mompett smiled at his favourite grandson.

"Albeit, Elbert, I trounced him proper.

" 'Get down below stairs, you blunderin' bullock,' I says, 'and the next thing you smash or so much as cracks, I'll ask Mr. Alstid' (that was the Head-Gardener) 'if he wants a strong lad to carry a wheel-barrer. That's what you'd do, Ted Umpleby,' I says. 'Clumsy great oaf. Carry it. On yer 'ead, you would. . . . Go on,' I says, 'get out of this, while I clears this up 'fore the Guv'nor comes.'

"And then, as soon as he's slunk off, I locks the door and goes to it.

"For I sees what he's done. He's gone and leant his weight against *two* of the knobs of a panel, the one panel in all that house that they had been looking for, all those years. Only, being high up like, they'd missed it. Or else they had pressed only one knob—or two wrong knobs. Young Umpleby had pressed the two right ones—by accident. Out the panel had come, and him not expecting it, and not being ready, it had fell down, leavin' an entrance about four foot by three!

"Up against the bottom of this little doorway, I puts the steps that Ted Umpleby had been using— and there was a regler little room. Well, not to say a room. More like a big cupboard, the sort you can walk into, like one of the old powder-closets those sort of houses have. Yerss, more like a little police-cell, it was, with stone walls. And one of the stones had been taken out and put back. What I mean to say is, it was loose. Hadn't got any mortar round it, and I reckon it never had had. Sort of stone you can pull out whenever you want to."

"And I reckon you wanted," observed Albert.

"Ar! And still wantin'."

"What, you didn't pull it out?"

"No, Boy, I didn't, and for why? It wasn't the sort of stone you could take out with your finger-nails. It was a foot square, and you wanted something in your hand to shift it with."

"What sort of thing?" enquired Albert.

"Well, ask yourself. Something you could shove in a little way, and lever a little bit. Then shove in the other side and lever a bit more, and see if you can get a hold on it."

"Well, hadn't you got a pocket-knife?"

"Ar, but I hadn't got a bloomin' great hunting-knife with a blade six inches long and quarter of an inch thick! Fat lot of good my pocket-knife would've bin. I'd just the very thing in mind, a long flat chisel or screw-driver with a wooden handle. But do anything then and there I could not. For one thing, I was all of a tremble. All of a sweat, I was. . . . Only that stone between me and a fortune! A big fortune! That stone between me and bein' a gentleman for life!

"Well, as soon as I could get me breath and pull

meself together a bit, out I pops, backwards, on to the ladder, picks up the square of panelling—well, not to say square; oblong it was, and pretty 'eavy, too; old black oak and all; with knobs on; heavier than you'd think for.

"And then I sees how Ted Umpleby had done it, and found out what his betters had bin lookin' for since two or three 'undred years. As I say, he'd shoved his hands hard against two knobs at once! Two springs there was in the side of that doorway in the panelling—and the two knobs worked 'em. . . . Well, I'd got to put everythink straight for a start.

"So I gets up the ladder again, somehow, with the panel in me two 'ands, and shoves it back in the hole, the cupboard doorway so to speak. And in it goes with a double click, and fits like a picture into a frame or a door into a door-way, and sets tight.

"And strike me pink if you'd ever have known it was a trick panel. Absolutely like all the rest it was. All the rest being just the same size and shape, and with the same sort of crack running all round, and a knob in each corner.

"Ar, and another thing, tap it as you might, you got the same sound as you got from all the others. Tapping wasn't no good. What you had got to do was to shove hard on two of the knobs at once; and it came outwards. And that was what Ted Umpleby had done—by accident. Like he done everything. . . . I did it again meself, and sure enough it started to come out again, sort of followed me hands as I took them away from the knobs. And all I had to do was to shove the panel back into place, and it clicked again. I tell you I was in a state. All of a doodah and a tremble.

"And that's how I come to break me leg.

" 'Ow? Like a fool I took the steps away meself, and at the top of the stairs, me all of a tremble and a muck-sweat, I was in too much of an 'urry, and I caught me foot in the end of 'em as I was carryin' of 'em, and went headlong down the service stairs. And a man of my build falls heavy, rising seventy."

"Or fallin' seventy," observed Albert.

"Well, there it was. . . . Treated me very well, they did. But I never worked again. Leg didn't seem to jine up proper. Never has. You see, old bones shrinks backwards instead of growin' forwards and knittin' up.

"When I was in 'ospital, young Ted Umpleby comes to see me with some grapes and peaches and stuff out of the hot-houses. Proper upset, he was, when I pointed out to him that it was all his fault. And after I had been so kind and all, repairin' the damage what he had done, and not sayin' a word about it to the Guv'nor. Laugh! You should have seen his silly face when I blamed it on to him. I told him I'd die and haunt him for being the cause of me fallin' down the stairs and breakin' me leg and never fit for work again."

Mr. Mompett fell silent, a reminiscent smile playing about his stubble-fringed loose-lipped mouth.

"Anyways, he never said a word, so far's I could make out, to a livin' soul, not even to his girl what he quarrelled with and went for a soldier.

"Of course, one thing, he never see what he'd done, except knockin' down a great lump of panelling, and his silly self too. Sittin' on the floor holdin' his head where the panel hit him, while I was tellin' him off, he never saw he had uncovered a hole in the wall. Leastwise, he never said he did. Neither he couldn't, either, for he was sitting straight below it; and only too glad to slink off quick when I told him to 'ook it. All he thought of was the damage he had done, and what about it.

"No, me boy, Ted Umpleby never knew what he had done, and now he's dead and gone to Heaven or somewheres. And there's nobody alive, except me, and now you, knows what I've bin tellin' you.

"All them years everybody'd missed that bit of panellin', for all their tappin' and pokin' and pryin' about. Missed it because it was twice the height of a man up above the floor, and if anybody went round the house with a ladder, tappin' every bloomin' panel up to the ceilin', they wouldn't have found nothing. Not by tappin'. Not in that room, anyways. Wood too old and thick, or else all the other panels was stood away from the wall too. And after all their trouble and working it out on paper, which they did do, and readin' up old books and gettin' archie-tex down, it was left for that fat-headed Ted Umpleby to find it. And then not to see what he had found because it was in the act of fallin' that he must have fell against the panelling and shoved hard on the two knobs.

"But *I* see what he had found. I had the sense to know what it was. And then broke me leg, and never walked up a flight of stairs since, let alone climbed a step-ladder. How's that for luck?"

Albert ran his tongue over his lips.

"Who put the jools there?" he asked, "and what was his game?"

"Why, one of them Cortenays came home with 'em from furrin parts, and some of his pals told the Gov'm't, it appears, and when the Gov'm't sends a 'tec down to enquire about it and take a half-share, he sticks 'em in the family hidin'-place, and tells the police to tell the Gov'm't he's put 'em where the monkey put the nuts.

"And they pinched him, and there they still are."

"He didn't tell anybody else? . . . Didn't his wife know?"

"Well, ask yerself, Boy. If I was puttin' a sovereign or two away quiet in a safe place here, should I tell your grandmother? Anyway, it appears she wasn't at the Hall at the time, his wife wasn't, and his son was a baby. No, nobody knew from that day to this, except me.

"Now you go and get me a glass of beer, there's a good boy. And I'll give you a tanner. Damn what the doctor says. Wait till your grandmother goes down the village. And then, to-morrow, we'll have another talk, you and me. Meantime you'll keep your head shut, I know. You're that sort. And whether I live to share it with yer, or not, there's a good time comin', Boy. And you remember all I said. And you get your legs under somebody else's mahogany as soon as you can. And whose mahogany's that, eh? We know, Boy, don't we? We know who's going to be footman up at the Hall, and have a look at the panelling up among the pictures in that there room."

The old man closed his eyes wearily.

"Tell you some more to-morrow, Son," he said. "Tell you just which knobs it is. And which panel."

"Tell me now, Grandfer, and I'll go and get you a glass of beer."

"To-morrow, Son. I've gone all tired," whispered the old man.

Mr. Mompett closed his eyes, and Albert regarded him thoughtfully. Suppose he wasn't alive to-morrow?

II

At the top of the hill Mr. Todding stopped his car, gazed around over the apparently illimitable stretches of moorland, pasture-land, corn-field, yellow sands and shining sea, and decided that this spot would do, would do as well as any, and better than most.

On this narrow second-class road there was practically no traffic at all; on that nice little stretch of grass he could park his car well out of the way of any passing char-à-banc or farm waggon; against that conveniently sloping hedge-crowned bank he could recline; and there, in peace and quiet, he could enjoy his lunch, those neatly-cut and nicely-packed ham sandwiches, tongue sandwiches, beef sandwiches, that generous obtuse-angled wedge of pork-pie, and those two bottles of beer wrapped cool in wet sacking.

And Mr. Todding made it so.

Spreading upon the grass a clean red-and-white check cloth, he laid out the meal that his admirable housekeeper-barmaid had provided for him, and sat himself down beside it. Not greatly given to appreciation of the beauties of nature, Mr. Todding was nevertheless moved to pause and gaze again at the lovely scene that lay before him, hill and dale, moor and vale, meadow and lea, far-distant white-fringed shore and sea, mountains purple-misted on the horizon. What a spot for . . .

The sound of the hoof-beats of a swiftly-trotting horse brought Mr. Todding's eye and thoughts from contemplation of the lovely scene.

Someone in a hurry.

Round the bend of the high-banked road, which

17

was really a lane, came a man in blue uniform riding a sturdy cob. Not a soldier, decided Mr. Todding, though he wore medal ribbons; not a policeman, though the carbine in its bucket fastened to the saddle was such as was carried by mounted soldiers and some police.

On catching sight of Mr. Todding, the man brought his horse sharply to a halt, the while Mr. Todding stared with widely opened eyes and mouth, in one hand a table-knife upraised, in the other a plate bearing the afore-mentioned portion of pork-pie.

"What are you doing there?" asked the horseman curtly.

Mr. Todding continued to stare open-mouthed, considering this question, and a suitable answer thereto.

"Me?" he said at length, meeting the hard stare of this sudden and peremptory person, this inquisitive asker of foolish questions. "Me? What am I doin'? Standin' on me 'ead, learning to swim with me ears. Only that—and mindin' me own business. Why?"

Touching the horse with his heel, the rider moved to a spot whence he could study Mr. Todding yet more closely.

"Where have you come from?" he asked.

Mr. Todding, a bachelor, loved children; and, at home, hanging above his bed, was a picture of a lovely baby—just the sort of fat little chap he would have loved to have had for his own—and beneath the picture was written the curious inscription, *"Out of the Everywhere into Here."*

"Where do I come from?" he said. "Why, out of the Everywhere into 'Ere. . . . Where we all come from."

Leaning over, the horseman made a quick scrutiny of the interior of the car.

"Oh, you did, did you?" he observed, eyeing Mr. Todding thoughtfully. "Well, take my tip and get back there."

The two men exchanged stares, the horseman appraising an individual of whom he felt he should be suspicious, a big burly man with cropped head and clean-shaven face, dressed in loud checks and having in general the appearance of one who might be a professional pugilist, a bookmaker, a publican and a sinner, the sort of sinner with whom the horseman was all too familiar; Mr. Todding considering a person whom he decided he did not like, who was too full of himself, too interfering, a feller who was much too pleased with himself and seemed to think he owned the place but who, nevertheless, was nervous and ill-at-ease.

Mr. Todding, unacquainted with books, was extremely well acquainted with men, and though little given to the reading of print or Nature's infinite book of secrecy, was no mean reader of faces.

Yes, this man, for all his swank and smartness, for all his drilled well-set-up straightness and strength, was frightened. Well, not to say frightened, perhaps, but nervy. His face wore a strained and anxious expression, for all its high colour; and his eyes, for all their clearness, had a hunted—no, haunted—look in them.

"Yes," thought Mr. Todding, experienced observer of men, "for all his top-o'-the-morning freshness, he's tired. I'll bet he doesn't sleep too well."

Removing his gaze from the horseman's face as from something distasteful, Mr. Todding cut himself a noble slice of pork-pie, bit into it hugely, masticated briefly, swallowed prematurely, thrust the not inconsiderable residue into his cheek, and, with reasonable clarity of diction, propounded the question,

"And for why? Ain't I got a right to sit 'ere and eat

me lunch; and then 'ave a nap; and then afternoon tea; and then 'ave a rest; and sleep 'ere all night if I wants to; and 'ave me breakfast before I pushes on, in the mornin'?"

Apparently satisfied as to the *bona fides* of the traveller, the horseman gathered up his reins.

"Plenty of right," he replied. "Sit there till you grow roots, if you want to. Only don't blame me if you get a bump on the dome and your car pinched."

"*Me?*" exclaimed Mr. Todding. "Biff *me* on the napper?" He swallowed hard and fast. "Pinch my car? Why, I'm . . ."

"Yes, you're a wonder," interrupted the horseman. "And there are forty bigger ones in that field up above there."

"Forty . . . ?"

"Yes, forty. Forty-one, to be exact. Life-sentence convicts. Most of 'em murderers too. Man-eaters."

"*Cor!*" ejaculated Mr. Todding.

"Yes, and if some of them knew there was a car down here, all tuned up and waiting and ready, they'd make a dash for it.

"Forty-one of 'em, there are," he continued, "and only two of us in charge; my mate up there in the middle of the field, trying to look all ways at once, and me riding round in circles."

"Yes, he's nervous," thought Mr. Todding. "Makes him chatty-like. No wonder at it."

"Don't know what the authorities think they are doing," continued the warder. "Sending forty-one of them away up here, and me and my mate without a shot between us. And the lags know it. . . . Asking for trouble. That's what it is."

"Ar! If they all run different ways, two of you couldn't do much, could you?" nodded Mr. Todding sapiently.

"No, nor if a couple of them ran different ways, we couldn't follow 'em both, and leave the rest, could we? . . . Forty-one of 'em, and each with something useful in his hands. Why, some of 'em have got sickles. Well, I must be pushing on. And if you take my tip you'll do the same," concluded the warder, as he wheeled his horse about, and rode briskly off.

"Fare thee well," said Mr. Todding, and kissed his hand in the direction of the retreating figure.

"Nervous, that's what he is," he soliloquized, "and don't wonder. Forty-one of 'em, eh, and some with sickles. Well, well; nobody asked him to be a bloomin' warder, did they?"

And, as one who makes up for lost time, Mr. Todding applied himself diligently to the consumption of pork-pie, beef sandwiches, ham sandwiches, tongue sandwiches and beer.

Yes, nervous. That's what the fellow was. Got on his nerves, like the lion-tamers. Daren't turn his back to them. Then he shouldn't be a warder. No sportsman wouldn't. Helping keep pore fellers in quod. And if there *was* only two of them to forty-one, they'd got the whip-hand, hadn't they? Couldn't be far from the big prison. Plenty of warders and police to support 'em. Besides, what chance had the pore fellers got, all dressed up in broad arrows? They couldn't do anything in daylight, even if they got away. And how could they get away —well, stay away—what with alarms and telegraph to all police stations, and this telephoning, too? There'd be a circle drawed round the place in no time.

He was nervous, though, for all he had been a soldier.

Well, well; get on anybody's nerves, living in a prison and then being sent out with forty lifers, any one of which would do you in as soon as look at you, if he thought he could get away with it. The wonder was that more . . .

The sound of scrambling and a heavy thud caused Mr. Todding to turn his head sharply to the left. Between a bush and the bank crouched a man who had evidently just thrust his way through the hedge above, and jumped from the top of the bank, now some dozen feet above his head.

By good luck or previous knowledge or cool observation, he had chosen a spot wherein he would be hidden from the road, between bank and bush and in a dry grass-lined ditch.

Again Mr. Todding stared wide-eyed and open-mouthed. What on earth did the fellow want to shove through that hedge and jump down a twelve-foot bank for, and then lie there, all huddled up, in that ditch behind the bush—and glare at Mr. Todding like that?

Why! Mr. Todding sat bolt upright. Why! Blest if it wasn't one of the convicts, doing a bunk just like that warder had said. Pore feller! Didn't he look bad. Half wild, he looked.

Mr. Todding was a sportsman and proud of it, basing his claim to the title on the fact that he was a bookmaker, a publican, a former professional boxer, and a constant attendant at every form of sporting event, by day and by night, his interests ranging from horse-racing, cock-fighting and pugilism, to such minor games of skill as skittles and shove-ha'penny.

In spite of the fact that he called himself a sportsman because he made the major part of his income from 'following' the alleged sport of other people, he had nevertheless somehow, somewhere, acquired the belief that, save, perhaps, in the matter of one or two such sports as horse-racing, Fair Play is a Jewel; that both sides should have a sporting chance, and that—private interest apart, of course—the good wishes of the true sportsman should be with the weaker party. In a fight, for example, good luck to the smaller lighter man, always provided the other didn't carry your money. In a fox-hunt, good luck to the fox. And, in a man-hunt, good luck to the man.

And, of course, this here was a man-hunt. This pore feller had cut his lucky, done a bunk, and, before long, the big prison that must be somewhere here-abouts, would be ringing bells, firing cannon, telegraphing, telephoning and . . . all that.

How could he get away with it? What a hope! How could he escape unless—unless somebody helped him. Some sportsman. Some sportsman with a car all ready. What was it that fellow had said? A car all tuned up, ready and waiting.

As these thoughts flashed through Mr. Todding's mind, if flashed be not a somewhat violent word to use in regard to Mr. Todding's cerebrations, the convict made a signal to him, crawled forward a few inches, saw the car, and knelt up.

"Sir," he croaked in a harsh, hoarse whisper, "give me a chance. Be a sport, Sir. Give me a lift. Help me to get away, and I can pay you a thousand pounds. Be a sport."

As he spoke, the man crawled nearer, his fierce hungry face bedewed with sweat, his menacing scowl and grim mouth belying the humble entreaty of his appeal.

"I'm a sportsman," said Mr. Todding simply.

And rising swiftly to his feet with the ease and lightness of an athlete, he went to his car.

The eyes of the convict followed him. Rising to his feet and glancing round, the man snatched up an empty beer-bottle, dropping it again as Mr. Todding took a light rain-coat from the car and, turning about, held it up for the man to put on.

"Here, slip into this, quick," he said. "Take my 'at and 'op into the car."

Swiftly the convict obeyed.

Christ! But his luck was in!

This was better than having to fight the chap, knock him out and perhaps have to kill him to get his clothes, and then having to foot it, for he could no more drive a car than he could fly.

He'd do them yet. He'd do them yet, if only the man would hurry.

"Quick, quick," he urged, as Mr. Todding ran to the car, the debris of his lunch gathered up in the red-checkered cloth.

"Quick it is," replied Mr. Todding, and jumped into the driver's seat.

A minute later the car was speeding down the hill; forty life-sentence convicts were toying with agricultural implements and tasks; an anxious warder, perched on a tor, was endeavouring to achieve the impossible and watch them all at once; while another rode round the fields and precincts of the farm, to the harvest work of which, their grudging labour had been allotted.

An hour later, Mr. Todding and his passenger were nearly forty miles away. By the time it had been ascertained that, beyond shadow of a doubt, there were but forty convicts where there had been forty-one, and the alarm had been given, the travellers were over one hundred miles from the scene of the evasion and within a few of Mr. Todding's nice little place, the sequestered but flourishing *It and Miss,* a house frequented almost solely by "sportsmen" who met there to arrange matters, to fix things (and people) and, it was whispered, to proceed sometimes from business to pleasure in the shape of watching some such elevating and ennobling sport as a little cock-fighting or bare-fist pugilism.

Here, Mr. Todding's *protégé* went to earth, and in a suit of Mr. Todding's clothes which fitted him fairly well, soon came to look very much like any other of Mr. Todding's tough sporting colleagues, his shy weekend visitors and retiring resident guests.

As we are all prone to do with those we succour, help, and save, Mr. Todding grew quite fond of the grim man to whom he was wont to allude as his Little Foundling. And anxious as was the latter to lead an unobtrusive, nay, cloistered, life in the back premises of the lonely mountain-side inn, Mr. Todding was equally careful, cautious and solicitous concerning him.

When at length the man suggested that it was time he moved on, Mr. Todding rebuked and reproached him for his impatience, folly—and, indeed, his ingratitude.

"Push off?" remonstrated Mr. Todding. "Whaffor? Ain't you comfortable here? Give yer 'air another week or so to grow, and them bristles a chance to bloom into a proper moustache and beard. . . . Why, you are twice the man you was, a'ready, what with this fresh air and sunshine and good beef and beer. Give yerself another fortnight and you'll be four times. Yer own Governor won't know yer—and that's a joke good enough for the comic papers. Yer own *Governor*. See? You stop 'ere with me. You don't know when you are well off. What's bitin' you? All you've got to do is to lie up an' rest; lie all day on that ledge up there, and watch the road when you feel like it. You are as safe 'ere as if you was in the faults of the Benk of England. Want to find yerself back in stir, do you? If they get you back in the Stone Jug, you won't 'op out again. You wait till you got a good 'ead of 'air and a moustache and whiskers like a sea captain or a beach-preachin' Bible-puncher; then you can talk about pushin' off. . . . Ain't you 'appy?"

"I want to go and find my brother," said the man.

"Brother? Ain't I been a brother to you and a

father and an Uncle and a bloomin' Santer Claws all rolled into one? You don't want to go and get copped and get me into trouble, do yer? I don't know what I'd get for pinchin' you and 'idin' you 'ere. Aidin' and abettin' they'd call it. Always down on bettin', they are, one way and another. Bloomin' 'umbugs. Don't want to get me put away for 'elpin' you, do you? I don't know what I'd get, but I wouldn't be surprised if it was seven years."

"Who's going to accuse you?" replied the convict. "If I were caught near here, you don't know anything about me. You don't think I should give you away, do you?"

"And you wearing my clothes?"

"Well, I broke in and stole them, didn't I? Isn't burglary my trade—according to them?"

"What's yer 'urry?" expostulated Mr. Todding. "Got any objection to livin' like a gent? Such as me. You're safe 'ere as long as you like to stay. The nine days' wonder is over; and twice over. The public's forgot you; the 'ue and cry's died down, and the Police've just about wrote you off as 'avin' got away by sea, which is what you'll have to do eventuerlly. Get you a blue suit and jersey and a seaman's cap, down near some Docks, and get you aboard a tramp steamer or something, and you can 'op it to America or Australia or somewheres."

"It's very kind of you. More than kind," replied the convict. "I didn't know there were gentlemen like you. I'll stop a bit longer, since you're so kind, but I want to go and find my brother. I want to get you that thousand pounds too."

"Get me *what?*" asked Mr. Todding, his eyes opening widely in surprise.

"I offered you a thousand pounds if you'd help me to get away."

Mr. Todding's large face expressed pain, annoyance and disgust.

"Don't talk silly," he said. "What do you take me for? A mug? Wrong again. I lives on 'em. Mugs keep me. In the first place, you 'aven't got no thaousand paounds nor thaousand pence. And in the second place, I'm a sportsman. I've been and defied and defeated the 'ole Might, Majesty, and Dominions and Powers of the Armed Forces of the Crown. See? John Todding, the Old Firm, motter, *Todding Never Troubles You*, weight fourteen stone twelve, versus the Law, weight unknown, and beat it. Beat the 'ole P'lice Force too. That's me, John Todding. And I saved you because I'm a sportsman. You don't think I took no notice of your silly bid of a thaousand paounds, do you? Why, I didn't 'ardly 'ear you say it. Talk sense. Do I look like a mug and a rube and a sucker? Thaousand paounds! . . . Don't believe you got a brother, either."

"Oh, I've got a brother all right. And he's got a thousand pounds—in every pocket of his clothes, and he's got a lot of pockets. I want to go and find him; and when I do . . . you get a thousand pounds."

Mr. Todding studied his man once again.

Suppose he was speaking the truth. Less likely things had happened. Undeniably, Mr. Todding had rescued him in the purest spirit of sportsmanship, but still, a thousand pounds was a thousand pounds and took a lot of earning, even by a man who toiled not nor spun, but, arrayed as the tiger-lilies of the Field, shouted the odds.

From long and amused, rather than bitter, experience, Mr. Todding knew a liar when he met one; and nine times out of ten knew when his friends, and even his enemies, were lying to him; and he was beginning to have a feeling that this man might be speaking the truth. Why, otherwise, should he be so anxious to go away from a place of safety, rest and peace? There might be something in it. Anyway, John Todding wasn't going to do the thing by halves. Unless he simply ran away, which was hardly likely, he would keep him until he was as little like a convict as he could be; fit him out properly; take him in his car to wherever he wanted to go; and leave him to it. If there was a thousand pounds in it, well, that would be very nice; and if there wasn't, well, anyhow, Mr. Todding had shown himself a real sportsman, and had got something of his own back on that detestable, interfering, and objectionable institution called the Law.

Yes, on the Law and its myrmidiums, the Nosey Parker Perlice.

As Mr. Todding eyed him reflectively, the Foundling seemed to come to a sudden determination.

"I'll tell you," he said.

"Closing time in a few minutes," said Mr. Todding. "Come down to my snuggery in quarter of a hower. We shan't be disturbed."

That night Mr. Todding's dumbly taciturn *protégé* found his voice and talked to some purpose.

III

Name? Name of Roger Mompett. Almost forgotten it! I've been a Letter and a Number so long. . . . F. 50. . . . Fifty-fifty they used to call me. Half sane, half mad. There was a "screw," a warder, not a bad chap—for a warder—used to say when I was working in the mail-bag room,

"Well, Fifty, which fifty is it to-day?"

I used to have very bad times when I was fool enough to sit and think about my brother. I used to lose control and throw things about, smash things and hit people. But the prison doctor, who was a clever man and not a bad chap—for a prison doctor—soon spotted that it was genuine, and that I didn't know where I was or what I was doing. Fifty-fifty was having the bad fifty.

It would have been a strait-waistcoat and the triangles not so long ago. It's bromide and an infirmary bed, nowadays.

The wonder is they don't all go mad, from the Governor down to the last-admitted lifer, but of course the officials have their time off and can go right away from the prison; and most of the convicts—well, not most of them, perhaps, but a great many of them—know that they have only got what they asked for; and they sit tight, earn remission of time; and write each day off as it goes.

They've taken to crime because they preferred it to other trades, and they know the conditions. They've sat in on the game against the Law, with their liberty as the stake, and they've lost, and that's that.

But what about those who didn't prefer crime to other trades, and didn't want to sit in on any game

against the Law: those who never thought or intended to do wrong, but broke the Law almost
before they knew it?

There are men in that prison who are no more
criminal than your dog there; men doing a long
stretch for a sudden angry blow; for borrowing what
they fully intended, and wished, to put back; for
giving way to a sudden temptation; for doing something silly, something admittedly wrong—but not
with criminal intent. They are the men who take it
hard. They see themselves in that stone Hell,
branded with that convict dress, reduced to the
level, not only of slaves, but of shameful degraded
slaves, herded with criminals—yet knowing themselves to be honest men; yes, honest, well-inten-
tioned, well-behaved men; good citizens; good parents; good sons; and in no way criminal whatsoever. Guilty if you like, but guilty of one rash, silly,
perhaps unconscious, wrong act. They brood.

They are the sort that go to pieces; go hysterical.
One day, all start screaming together. Perhaps
make a rush, if they are outside. That sort of thing.

And what about the innocent men?

If the normal non-criminal men, who have done
something rash or silly or wrong, take it badly,
what about those who have done nothing at all?

Men who have been 'put away.' Is there any
wonder that they go mad?

It's a wonder they aren't a hundred per cent
mad, let alone fifty-fifty, like I was.

No doubt you are thinking that every old lag
claims to be innocent. If so, you are wrong. Why, a
good many of them are proud of it, proud of the
stretches they've done; proud of the reasons why
they've had to do them. No doubt when they are
out, and have got their chance of a job—those who
want a job—they're innocent victims of some mistake or plot or miscarriage of justice, when they are

telling the tale to an employer or the kind lady who doesn't know a Bill Sikes from an out-of-work who snatched something to get his kids a meal and a handful of fuel. We can quite understand that. Still, anybody with half an eye in his head can tell a habitual criminal when he sees one, especially the sort who has spent two-thirds of his life in prison.

But there aren't so many people can tell an innocent man, and know whether to believe his tale or not.

Here's mine. The tale of F. 50. Fifty-fifty. And I am on the right fifty now. No hallucinations, as the prison doctor called it when I used to see and hear things.

It's rather amusing. What they call the irony of Fate. I got a book from the prison library called *Life's Little Ironies*. I laughed when I read it. I could have told the author a better sample of Life's little ironies than any of his; for, as I sat in my cell, reading that book, I was an absolutely innocent man doing a life sentence for a crime I had never committed, while my own brother, one of the biggest criminals that ever lived, never so much as saw the inside of a Police Court!

And I was in gaol for one of his crimes. How's that for a neat little irony?

Yes, my own brother, Albert Mompett, my own blood brother,—and one better than an ordinary 'own brother,' for he is my twin.

Another of the things I have smiled at, in the days when I could still smile, was accounts of how twins are parts of a perfect whole; how they are more closely akin than any other human beings; bound to understand each other; love each other; be as inseparable and affectionate as they are similar. My brother and I are similar enough, but although I am not much of a hater, I hate him as I never have, and never could, hate anything else on

God's earth—if it be God's earth and not the Devil's.

I don't imagine anybody ever hated anyone or anything more than I hate him, or with as good reason.

First of all, there was my girl.

He was sufficiently like me to impersonate me.

Then he used his money on her. Every penny of it dirty money, dishonest money, stolen money.

Clever? One of the cleverest men who ever lived; both with his brain and with his hands. He could have been Lord Mayor of London if he had run straight, and stuck to honest business. He could have been the world's greatest mechanical engineer, and won a peerage. He could have been another Edison. But he must be a criminal. And, except that he would always have a woman—his audience, his admirer, his slave, his devotee—he worked alone. That's where he was unlike most criminals. No gang for him. No partner.

And there was another way in which he differed from most criminals. Besides working alone, he worked all sorts of different classes of crime. He was a first-class confidence man, and did big business. He was an amazing pen-man and brought off forgeries that would have made him rich for life if he hadn't always spent money faster than he made it. He was a champion conjurer, as good as most professionals, and his speciality was cards. And on top of that he was as good a card-player as ever sat down to a table. So you can imagine the income he made by card-sharping alone, especially at poker, with rich Americans on the trans-Atlantic ships.

Then he was a wizard with skeleton keys and with tools of his own design; and was as good a safe-cracker and jewel-thief as any man in that business.

And to add to it all, he had the most plausible ingratiating address and manners imaginable. Not fulsome and greasy, mark you, but pleasing. He could please and propitiate and attract anybody, man or woman, old or young.

You are wondering how I know all this. Well, he always told me everything. Trusted me absolutely. Was not I his own twin brother? He knew I'd never give him away, just as he knew I would never blackmail him, sponge on him, or touch a farthing of his filthy profits.

That was his weakness and his danger. He must have an audience. He must boast. He must talk about himself. I and his girl were his safety-valves. Every suit of armour has its joint, and every giant has his weak tendon. That was my brother's. And yet he was so clever, so good a judge, that he never made a mistake about the girl. Not one of them ever turned on him, threatened him, told on him. They adored him. He was that sort of man. The worse he treated them, the more they worshipped him. They were that sort of women. There must have been three or four of them in his life at different times, and I've often wondered what became of one of them, who disappeared.

He loved two things, women and wickedness—or rather, wickedness and women, for crime came first with him.

It is curious that we should be twins and so different. Personally I hate all that sort of thing, partly because I have got a bias towards decency and honesty, and don't think there is enough money in the world to compensate one for the loss of one's self-respect; and partly because I know, as all those crooks know, or should know, that that sort of thing can only end one way and in one place, and always does end in one way and one place. Gaol. And very commonly in a special part of the gaol—the condemned cell.

I am not a religious man, and I cannot say that

my experience has given me much reason to be, but I do own and admit my belief, my certainty, that evil courses lead inevitably to an evil end. Yes, bad leads to bad. I don't say that doing the right thing and leading the right sort of life is necessarily going to lead to health, wealth, and happiness, nor even to old-age, security, and roses round the door; but I do say that doing the wrong sort of thing always, without exception, leads to the wrong sort of end.

And my brother is going to learn it, too, some-day.

Now I'm going to find him, get into his house, come face to face with him in the middle of the night; and I'm going to have a talk with him . . . I have got a lot to say.

No, I'm not getting worked up. Not going on to the other fifty. I'm quite calm and cool. I'm just telling you. I'm going to say,

"Well, my dear brother," and he will think I am my own ghost.

I don't suppose it ever entered his head that I'd escape from the tightest prison in England. Nor should I have done, but for the wonderful luck of dropping at your feet, so to speak. God bless you and reward you, Mr. Todding . . .

My twin brother! Yes, through him, I was within a hair's-breadth of being hanged for a murder I never committed.

It's hard to believe it.

Life's no use to me now. I have nothing to live for. What's the good of anything? My girl, whom I trusted like a child trusts its mother; my twin brother who trusted me in the same way. That's what makes it so bad, really, the fact of his always having trusted me so. And then to send me to the gallows, to save himself from hanging.

No; worse than that. He sent me to the gallows so that he should avoid all danger of hanging.

You remember the case, I suppose—old General Sir Giles Cortenay, pretty nearly eighty years of age, killed in the library of Cortenay Old Hall, by a burglar whom he had surprised tackling the safe where the famous Cortenay Treasure was supposed to have been put. Some silly yarn had got into the papers that it had been found at last, and consisted of diamonds, emeralds, rubies, and pearls brought back from the Spanish Main by the Sir Giles Cortenay of Queen Elizabeth's time. It was evident that the old General had tackled the man, and had received a fatal blow on the head with a jemmy. What would have hanged the burglar was the fact that the General, grappling with him, had grabbed him by the coat and clung on. Beside him, on the carpet, was a button with hanging thread and a scrap of cloth. Evidently poor old Sir Giles had used his whole weight and strength in the struggle that tore the buttoned coat open.

And the police came to my bachelor cottage, where I lived alone, the very next day. Hanging in a cupboard was the coat from which the button had been torn. In a corner of the same cupboard were the boots which fitted prints on a garden bed.

I had been out fishing that night, a thing I often did, and could prove no alibi. I was too bewildered to speak, almost too bewildered to think, at first, until it dawned on me that my brother had come to my place in the night, while I was out fishing, and made a complete change of clothes.

He practically laid a trail from Cortenay Old Hall, a few miles away. He had taken a servant's bicycle from an out-house there, ridden straight to my little cottage, left it in the garden, got in at my bedroom window from the roof of the wash-house, and doubtless let himself out by the front door, without being seen, an easy job for him.

At first, I was only angry, seething with indignation that he should have let me in for this. All I accused him of, then, was using me so that he could get away; turning the attention of the police to me while he got out of the country. It never entered my head that he would not come forward and own up, if I were unable to clear myself.

Of course, thought I, by the time I am found innocent and discharged, he will be in a safe place; and if, on the other hand, things go badly with me, he will come forward, confess, and face the music.

That's where I made such a bad impression.

My lawyer must have thought I was half-witted. He got quite angry when I kept telling him that the clothes were not mine, and yet refused to say whose they were. He didn't believe me, of course—particularly when it was shown that they fitted me perfectly.

It was only when I found that I couldn't prove where I had been that night, that I began to feel anxious.

That suit of clothes, and the fact that I was quite unable to prove where I had been that night, made the case about as black against me as it could be. I swore that I was innocent, and did my best to prove it, both for my own sake and because, if I were acquitted, my brother would have no need to confess in order to save me.

But, as the prosecuting Counsel told the jury, and the Judge admitted in summing up, it was a clear case.

I was found guilty, condemned to death, and described in the papers as a very callous ruffian who seemed indifferent to his fate.

I was not indifferent. I was extremely concerned for my brother, in spite of what he had done to me in the matter of my girl—and the fact that I had had nothing to do with him for a long time, because of that.

Well, there it was. I had done my best to save the scoundrel from the gallows. I had tried to prove my innocence without inculpating him, and now he must take the consequences.

You can imagine—or can you—what those three weeks in the condemned cell were like; each day that came and went, bringing no word from him; sitting there wondering if he were already dead, he, the only person who could save me from the gallows.

At the end of a fortnight of an agony of suffering, I decided that either such was the case, or else that he intended to leave me where I was, leave me to pay the penalty for his crime.

I had had enough.

I asked to see my lawyer, and told him everything.

He seemed to think it was a good effort; a surprisingly brainy bit of inventiveness, especially for such a fool as I obviously was; and a line worth trying, even at so late an hour. At any rate, he acted as though he believed me, and did everything he could, started an agitation, got up a petition, interviewed Members of Parliament, and approached the Home Secretary.

The day before the date fixed for my execution, my sentence was changed to one of imprisonment for life.

One gets letters in prison, and one gets news by the grape-vine route.

My brother is alive and well—and wealthy of course—and back in England. I know where he is. I got the news from Tommy Pepper that day I escaped. I think that is why I suddenly pushed my way through that hedge and jumped down the bank.

Well—that's enough about me.

I wish I had words to thank you.

Could this chap, Tommy Pepper, come and see me here? He's pure gold and straight as an arrow. There'd be no risk about it, either for you or for me. He'll help me to find my brother—and glad to do it; for he loves me and he hates my brother nearly as much as I do, and with good reason.

For Tommy Pepper also loved the girl. Tommy Pepper loved her—madly . . . But she loved me . . . Until my brother Albert came along . . . Milly . . .

§2

The man swallowed; fell silent; broke down. His head fell upon his folded arms.

Mr. Todding blew his nose and prescribed hot brandy. With sugar. And lemon.

IV

Mr. Aloysius Slatterthwaite opened the front door of his cottage by the sea, peered out into the thick mist, the sea-fog that had rolled in across the sand-dunes at sunset, and swore. When he had arrived in his sailing-dinghy, three hours ago, the evening had been bright and clear.

And now look at it.

Like being in a different country, with a different climate.

This was going to affect matters considerably. One of those little unforeseen occurrences that cause the best-laid schemes of mice and men to go awry. It meant that Milly would be very late, even if she arrived at all. Certainly she would not be able to find her way to the place in such a fog. She'd have to wait till it lifted. A nuisance.

On the other hand, it cut both ways. If Milly couldn't find her way along the road, on to the track, and along that again, and across the dunes, neither could Tommy Pepper. . . .

What about himself trying to get across the dunes to the track, and following it to the road? Once he got that under his feet, he could make his way along it in the direction of Sandhaven. And if he met anybody at that time of night and in that fog, it would be either Milly or Tommy Pepper. Who else would be along there on a road on which there wasn't another house or other building for nineteen miles? And he would soon be able to make out whether anyone he met was a man or a woman.

Would he be able to strike the road, or would he wander in circles among these cursed sand-dunes, and find himself in front of the cottage again, when the fog lifted? And it would probably lie all night—thick as it was and not a breath of air. It usually did, at this time of year.

Well, anyway, that would be no worse than staying in the house while Milly was trying to find it—and with Tommy Pepper coming in the morning. He must do something. Try to meet her—and avoid Tommy.

That was a thoroughly nasty letter Tommy Pepper had written, and there was no doubt he meant every word of it.

Yes, of course he could make his way to the road, even if he got off the track across the dunes. He'd reach the road sooner or later, if not by the shortest route. It was no great distance away, and he would be on it long before he had begun to walk in a circle. . . .

Doggedly Mr. Aloysius Slatterthwaite ploughed forward in the direction of the road that skirted the sand-dunes as it followed the coast—the wide bay, at one end of which stood the little town of Sand-haven and at the other the fishing village of White-bay Harbour, nineteen miles from it, and sixteen from his very sea-side and week-end cottage.

A few minutes later, after stumbling across tussocks of bents, coarse sea-grass and tough trailing weed-like creeping plants; plodding through loose deep sand and scaling small hillocks; crossing narrow valleys in which his shoes sank deeply, he found firm ground beneath his feet.

The road at last, thank Heaven. And now to turn to the right, keep on it, and walk in the direction of the little railway-station of Sandhaven. Then, if the train had reached the place, and Milly, taking her courage in both hands, had set out, he'd be pretty sure to meet her.

A three-mile walk in the fog. Well, he had faced worse things than that in the good cause, and so could Milly. Just as well that there was no such thing as a station fly or any other conveyance at Sandhaven, or she'd have been tempted to take it. And temptation was the one thing that women could not withstand, as the wise man said.

No, she'd never do a fool thing like that, surely— lay a trail straight from Sandhaven Station to the house on the dunes, the only house between there and Whitebay Harbour, the secret silent house, isolated and apparently unoccupied.

He'd teach her a lesson if she did.

An hour later, Mr. Aloysius Slatterthwaite gave it up. No sound of any distant train, no sign of Milly nor of anyone else. He'd make his way back to the cottage—and look a damned fool if he couldn't find it himself—and call it a day. He'd open a tin or two of stuff and a bottle of whisky, have some supper, a few hours' sleep, and, if the fog had lifted in the morning, push off in the boat again, sail round to Whitebay Harbour, tie up the dinghy, walk to Crochester and get back to Town. A bit of extra trouble, but there was no point in showing his face in Sandhaven, and eventually being identified by some Nosey Parker as the owner of the house on the dunes.

Retracing his steps, Mr. Slatterthwaite, by good luck and good calculation, reached the point on the rarely-used neglected road where the track led from it across the sand-dunes, the ancient smugglers' track that went toward the sea and roughly in the direction of the house which, from time to time, he inhabited as bitter constraint or sad occasion demanded.

And having, with much anxious care and clever reckoning, made his way to the end of the track, set his face in the probable direction of the house, and boldly put forth into the unknown uncharted wastes toward the sea, the fog thinned, lifted, and gave every promise of speedy dispersal and disappearance.

A few minutes later, he saw a light, undoubtedly that which he had left burning in the bedroom, for the guidance of Milly in the improbable event of her reaching Sandhaven, setting forth, leaving the road, crossing the dunes without help of the track, laying a true course, and reaching the house before him.

Plodding heavily up hill and down dale across the miniature mountains and valleys of the reed-grown dunes, Mr. Slatterthwaite drew near to his retreat; opened the gate in the picket fence enclosing the garden, which consisted entirely of uneven sand and coarse bents; and, suddenly, with a swift intake of breath, dropped to his hands and knees. A shadow had crossed the blind that covered the sitting-room window—a shadow which, he felt certain, had been that of a man.

Tommy Pepper?

It could be no-one else.

And in his pocket was the letter he had picked up at the Crochester Post Office that morning, the letter in which Tommy had rashly and foolishly set forth exactly what he was going to do to him, and how he was going to do it.

A nuisance—like this fog—for Tommy would have to be dealt with, once and for all, and he had quite enough on his hands at the moment, without bothering about Tommy Pepper.

What a fuss these fools made about a woman. As if Milly was worth anybody's fuss. And anyway, what's the use of crying over spilt milk—and making spilt blood of it. Couldn't the fools see that the woman who leaves a man is no loss to him?

Damn Milly. He had been a fool to whistle her. He should have known better. . . . *Women!* . . . Well, one lives and one learns, and he had learned about women from her, much as he knew about them already. And to think she had had the nerve, the courage, to threaten him, Aloysius Slatterthwaite! Get even with him if he jilted her, would she? Fix him if he treated her badly, would she? Follow him if he left her, and show him where he got off, eh? Go to Tommy Pepper, would she, and tell him all she knew about Aloysius Slatterthwaite?

Well, those who look for trouble generally find it.

Hell! An idea . . . Had she come, and brought Tommy with her?

No, she'd never do that, surely. She'd have a shot at getting him back before she turned to Tommy and spilled the beans completely.

Yes, that had been all talk. Woman's talk.

They could never see when a man had had enough, and realize that when it was enough it *was* enough, and he was through, finished.

No, she'd certainly have another try to . . .

The shadow fell on the blind again. Yes, it was a man's all-right, and this was where Tommy Pepper got what was coming to him. No-one had seen him arrive, in that fog, and nobody would ever see him depart. Useful place, a sand-dune.

Mr. Slatterthwaite rose to his feet as the shadow moved from the curtain, took an automatic pistol from his hip pocket and, crouching, crept toward the front door.

Softly opening it, he stood listening.

Silence . . . Complete silence.

Had Tommy heard him, and was he listening too? Was Milly in there with him? Or upstairs? Was it a trap? Was Milly to come down the stairs and hold him in conversation while Tommy quietly opened the sitting-room door and shot him?

No, he was getting fanciful, nervy almost. He would bet his life that Milly was all-right. He wasn't going to get rid of her as easily as he had lost one or two of the others, but no woman had ever rounded on him or double-crossed him yet, and Milly wouldn't. Certainly not until she had more cause to do so than she had had yet. The woman didn't live who would ever cease to love Aloysius Slatterthwaite, once he had got her. Milly wouldn't double-cross him. Never. On the other hand one never knew, with women, jealous women especially. She might have . . .

Come, come! This wouldn't do. Nerves. Fancies. It would be time to retire, turn respectable, and sit in the Pump Room at Bath when he started getting fanciful, and having nerves.

Suddenly he raised his pistol toward the closed sitting-room door and shouted aloud, in a deep hearty voice, boisterous and strong,

"Now Tommy, my lad, come on out of that! . . . Come on, Tommy. Out of it!"

The door of the sitting-room was thrown open, and Mr. Slatterthwaite pulled the trigger.

The man staggered back.

Slatterthwaite fired again.

The man crumpled to the ground.

"There we are, Son," observed Mr. Slatterthwaite genially. "Now you've got what was coming to you, eh?

"*Good God!*" he added, as the man rolled over and the light from the lamp fell upon his face. "*Good God!*"

And rising to his feet Mr. Slatterthwaite shrank away from what appeared to be his own corpse.

Mr. Aloysius Slatterthwaite sank into a chair and stared incredulous.

But it was impossible.

It couldn't be.

This fool was safe in prison, doing a life sentence.

He couldn't be lying there.

It was absurd.

He himself must be dreaming, mad.

This must be a nightmare.

It was Tommy Pepper whom he had shot. Not this man!

Tommy Pepper waiting there behind the door, waiting to get him as he had promised in the letter. Tommy and Milly working together. He had meant to shoot Tommy Pepper—not this blazing fool lying at his feet and staring at him with dead eyes. It was Tommy he had meant to get, Tommy lurking in here, and Milly upstairs in the bedroom. Decoy. She was to come to the top of the stairs, and Tommy was to open that door quietly and shoot him in the back while he talked to her. Tommy and Milly!

He sprang to his feet. *Either of them might come at any minute.*

He must do something and do it at once; think clearly and act quickly.

Damn Milly. Cursed silly woman. How could she have been so stupid? But for her, he wouldn't have been here to-night.

How had this fool found the bungalow in that fog? Probably hadn't. Found it in daylight and had lain hidden in the dunes watching it. Crept up as the fog settled down; peeped in at the windows; had seen him go out; gone inside and waited for him.

What for? Had he got a gun?

He'd frisk him and find out.

No.

Well, of all the amazing, unbelievable, impossible . . .

How had he got out of prison? Could they have pardoned him and let him go; and if so, didn't that mean . . . ?

But look, he must have been out for weeks. He

never grew that head of hair, moustache and beard in prison.

What had he come for?

What did he think he was going to do without a gun? He had always been a bloody fool.

Nevertheless, how amazingly like his clever brother the fool was, especially with that moustache and beard. Made the likeness stronger than ever.

The likeness!

Aloysius Slatterthwaite sprang to his feet and laughed and laughed. Hell, what a thought, what a notion, what a brain-wave! Now, Mr. Clever Tommy Pepper—what about this?

With swift practised hands Aloysius Slatterthwaite searched the dead man's pockets, and removed their contents: money, cigarettes, matches, a railway-ticket, handkerchief, a folded piece of paper on which were written memoranda, notes, addresses, figures. That could be examined later.

Quickly he then transferred from the breast pocket of his own coat to that of the corpse, his own wallet, containing cards bearing his own name and a most respectable address; three letters addressed to himself; envelopes containing, one a bill; another, a receipt; and a third, a card of invitation whereon the pleasure of the company of Mr. Aloysius Slatterthwaite was requested . . .

With particular care he also placed in the dead man's pocket a threatening letter wherein one Thos. Pepper expressed his intention of "catching" him at his place by the sea, and so perforating his carcass with holes that he'd be of no further use to himself and of little use to anybody else, save as a sieve. . . .

And having swiftly and definitely arranged matters to his satisfaction, Mr. Aloysius Slatterthwaite carefully cleaned all finger-prints from the pistol and then hid it where the police would inevitably find it.

Then, with steady hand, he clean-shaved his face.

Thereafter he made his way, long ere dawn, to where his sailing-dinghy lay at the water's edge, picked up her anchor, shoved her off, raised the lug-sail, and fared forth upon the slumbering ocean with a favouring breeze which took him safely to Whitebay Harbour, whence he made his unobtrusive way to Crochester and so to London and a new life.

Mr. Aloysius Slatterthwaite was dead. Long live Mr. Henry B. Fielding, recently arrived from America . . . and going back there quickly—his despatch-case bulging with negotiable securities, bonds, cash, and very valuable jewellery.

V

Thomas Pepper, doing his three months "separate," the statutory period of solitary confinement in the local prison, preparatory to being sent to the great prison for convicts sentenced to penal servitude, was at first little better than a lunatic—though a quiet and harmless one.

Possibly he was mentally stunned, and passed the daily twenty-three hours in his silent cell, and the one hour devoted to solitary perambulation in the exercise yard, in a dream condition, a state that was almost one of coma.

Possibly he was buoyed up by an inability to believe that this new amazing condition of life could be long protracted.

Possibly again, he was unable to believe that his friend would fail to step forth and declare himself; to believe that Roger Mompett could calmly accept so great a sacrifice; so costly a gift as his freedom—for which his friend, Tommy Pepper, had almost paid with his life, and was now actually paying so terrible a price.

Undoubtedly, during his trial, the knowledge of his complete innocence had sustained Thomas Pepper, had seemed an infallible protection against the evils that threatened.

Undoubtedly too, the knowledge that each day that passed gave Roger Mompett a better chance of escape, served to make what would have been an unspeakably terrible predicament merely an interesting, if poignant, situation.

Of course Roger Mompett would intervene, would declare himself, when it was seen that he must either do so, or allow his friend to suffer for him.

Even when the almost-worst had happened, Criminal Court history had repeated itself—and he had been found guilty and condemned, without one word from his friend—he had comforted himself with the assurance that, during the next three weeks, Roger would write or telegraph to the authorities, from abroad, assuring them that it was he who had killed Albert Mompett, *alias* Aloysius Slatterthwaite, and offering proof as to his statement.

And then, when hideous and shameful death seemed inevitable, Thomas Pepper had shown his mettle, the incredible depths of his fantastic folly, his idiotic loyalty and half-witted romanticism—by maintaining silence on the subject of his movements on the night when the man said to be Aloysius Slatterthwaite had been killed.

If they caught poor Roger, who himself had been through this, it would be with no help from Roger's friend Tommy Pepper. And if for Roger he must suffer, suffer he would.

The truth would come out, some-day. He had learned at school, and firmly believed, *Great is the Truth and it will prevail.* Sooner or later, Roger would learn what had happened, and would at once set to work to get him set free. Of course he would. Roger was the last man in the world to do what his brother Albert had done to Roger himself.

And again, no man in the world knew better than Roger what the agony was, what the hideous torture was—to suffer thus, innocent, in prison.

So Thomas Pepper, fool, was not as raving a lunatic during his three months' "separate" as he should have been.

Nevertheless, by the time his period of solitary confinement had expired, it was high time that to Thomas Pepper was restored the blessing of human contacts—even if only with hard-faced, rigid-minded warders, and with criminals, be they sane or be they morons, paranoics and abnormal men suffering from prison-induced hysteria, savagery, phantasy, lunacy, vacuity, or homicidal sullenness.

Change of scene was great salvation, and even greater the society, restricted though it might be, of burglars, blackmailers, forgers, incendiaries, pick-pockets, car-bandits, swindlers, coiners, perverts, bogus company-promoters, murderers and other criminals, varying in social type and education from lowest specimens of the Bill Sikes fraternity, to former doctors, solicitors and other men of re-finement, culture and education who had gone astray.

In prison clothing, Thomas Pepper was taken by two warders in a cab from the gaol to the railway-station; by train to a distant part of England; and again by cab to the great Convict Prison in which it was intended that he should be incarcerated for the rest of his natural life.

This, to his surprise, was a place beautifully situated, approached by an avenue of magnificent trees on either side of which were tennis-courts, sports-grounds, club-pavilions and attractive bun-galows—though these, he realized, were not for him and his kind.

Even inside the prison his eye was cheered by the sight of spacious beautifully-kept lawns and gardens.

But these again were not for his delight.

Through further gates he passed, and found himself in a quadrangle of buildings, ugly, threat-ening and sinister, although this was by no means the worst part of the prison precincts, consisting, as it did, of offices and shops. Not shops in which goods are purchased, but in which they are made;

the blacksmith's shop, the carpenter's shop, the boot-making shop; the other buildings being the hospital, the guard-room, store-room and similar excrescences upon the prison proper.

Here too was the block of cells occupied by the obvious mental defectives, the men whom prison had at length, happily or unhappily, driven mad.

There, before Thomas Pepper's astonished eyes, loafed a gang of them, doing no work, talking, gesticulating, laughing vacuously, or standing, sitting, crouching, squatting, and gazing with blank uncomprehending eyes at nothing, the while they thought nothing, did nothing, were nothing.

There in the sunlight, dead though alive, they awaited the physical death whereby they could qualify for decent burial; waited for the other grave wherein, beneath the surface of the earth, they would cease to offend the sight of those who yet moved upon it. Would he be left here long enough to become as one of these?

Again Thomas Pepper was immured in a block of separate cells apart, here to be examined and interrogated; to be inspected by the doctor and classified according to physical condition for Number One or Number Two or Number Three Division of labour; to be paraded before the Governor and receive his warnings as to the consequences of indiscipline or rule-breaking or disobedience of any sort or kind; and to be interrogated by the Chaplain as to his spiritual condition, needs and position.

To Thomas Pepper, after three months of solitary confinement, this was all bright and exciting, a period of thrills and novelties, an emergence into the great world. The world of prison, true, but still, a place wherein men moved and spoke, asked questions, and behaved toward you as though you were not yet quite dead.

Who said prison was a tomb?

Thomas Pepper did, before long; but, even then, these thrilling days were something to look back upon. During them, he received two sets of convict clothing, each consisting of jacket and knee-breeches, waistcoat, stockings, and a cap ornamented with his own private letter and number; a pair of boots, a pair of shoes.

A warder spoke to him and, heavily jocular, if grudging, remarked that they'd be issuing him and his like with carpet slippers next—and therein spoke more truly than he knew, anticipating in his wit, that great prison "reform" whereby convicts were actually given felt slippers!

Having been fitted-out with his nice new livery of death-in-life, he was locked up in a tiny cell furnished with a three-plank bed fixed to the wall; a thin mattress and weary stale bedclothes; a block whereon he might sit or, if the spirit so moved him, stand; a shelf, jutting from the wall, which he could call a table; and a Bible.

High up in one wall, thick opaque windows admitted a little light.

A day or two later, having enjoyed all the aforementioned interviews with warders, Chief Warders, Principal Warder, Chaplain, Doctor and Governor, he was allotted to his future Hall, his Ward, and his own cell—the last-named a much better-furnished home than any he had yet occupied since his conviction. In this was an iron flap-bedstead that let down from the wall, a fixed table, a movable stool, three shelves, a basin, and some cleaning materials.

Quite a home.

Quite roomy too, being ten feet long and eight wide, so that when pacing it, he could get three good steps before turning about to take three more in the opposite direction.

Yes, this was the grand place, for he was constantly seeing people.

There were crowded hours of glorious life during which he exercised, in company—three concentric rings of men walking round, six feet apart, in silence.

One could not speak, save at gravest risk of severe punishment, but it was company nevertheless. A social occasion.

And he understood that, provided he behaved well, as surely he would do, the time would come when he would work in company, work in one of the "shops" that he had seen.

And his screw, or warder, was a nice man, and had once answered a question he had dared in his inexperience to ask—as to whether he would ever get tea with his dry bread for breakfast. He had been accustomed to tea for breakfast all his life, and he missed it badly. Porridge and dry bread was a dreadful change from tea and eggs-and-bacon. And the screw had replied with quite a pleasant speech. Three words,

"After a year."

§2

Oakum-picking was still one of the pursuits and pastimes decreed for the entertainment and occupation of convicts sentenced to penal servitude, and horrible as the work was, it probably saved Thomas Pepper from crossing the border-line, once and for all.

The picking of three pounds of oakum in twenty-four hours was a task that but slowly changed from sheer impossibility to terrible effort, to be achieved with raw fingers and bleeding broken nails. Gradually, however, he had improved until he could make a fair showing, by putting in fourteen hours' good work. And, on the advice of a convict orderly, he always refrained from the folly of wetting his picked oakum to make it heavier, in the foolish hope that the tasking-master would not notice that he had done so.

Sack-sewing, mail-bag making and mending, and such work, with palm-leather and needle, had been better, especially as he had been allowed to do it seated beside the door of his cell where he could see a good deal of what went on in his Hall, a vast building around the sides of which were the cells, tier above tier.

Access to these was obtained by iron staircases and galleries that ran round each tier, the whole enclosed by strong wire netting to prevent suicide by foolish and ungrateful men.

But work in the tin-smith's shop was a vast improvement. For here one could talk. Talking was not permitted, of course, but nevertheless one could and did talk quite freely, it being clearly understood that this great privilege was solely due to the kindness of the screw in charge, and that any man who abused it would be not only a blackguard but something more than a fool.

Thus, when the screw's superior officer hove in sight, every man became dumb, and complete silence fell.

From the tin-smith's shop and soldering work, Thomas Pepper was later transferred to the book-binding and book-repairing shop to which more-or-less educated convicts of good behaviour were generally promoted.

And what interesting conversations had Thomas Pepper with criminals of every sort and kind, some of whom bore famous infamous names, men honoured, respected and admired in the underworld of rogues and criminals, and standing upon a dignity proportionate to the greatness of their crimes.

Here were famous murderers who had escaped

the gallows, among them an ex-officer, one Truman, who, convicted of murder, had been given the benefit of the doubt cast upon his sanity.

Thomas Pepper found him sane enough, abhorred him utterly, and loathed the thought that this man considered him worthy and suitable to be his friend, by reason of the fact that he was a fellow-murderer.

He terrified him by his violence, his hysteria, his fits of terrific passion, and his occasional delusions. Only the understanding kindness of the "screw" kept him from committing insubordinate acts that would have got him into grave trouble.

Frequently he raved about a wrong done him by a jewel-fence, one Gent Jannison who, he said, had swindled him over a cheque, or something of the sort.

It was in this shop that Thomas Pepper saw for a brief space, and from a distance, the man who was probably the most admired of all, the acknowledged aristocrat of that inverted society, the great Knocker Neuson, a long-division man in the grey garb that showed he had already done seven years and had privileges commensurate with his noble seniority—such as freedom to spend a penny a day on luxuries. Yes, the great Knocker Neuson himself, international jewel-thief, the man who could steal packets of diamonds from the strong-rooms of ocean liners, from Hatton Garden jewel-merchants' safes, from guarded Post Office mail-carts, or from any other place of presumed safety for priceless gems.

According to Pepper's informant, one Henry Hyam, a humbler jewel-thief, Knocker Neuson—so called because he had never failed to knock-off any famous diamond, emerald, sapphire, ruby, pearl; any tiara, necklace, or other famous and valuable ornament which he had set out to steal—was a gentleman.

He was a perfect gentleman, rich, educated and vastly superior, who, his sentence completed a year or two hence, would go forth to resume a career of ease and luxury, to live whatever sort of life he chose, in peace and comfort, upon the proceeds of former robberies, or to resume his fascinating and remunerative profession of jewel-knocking, should he feel so disposed.

A very interesting thing about this petty safe-cracker and jewel-thief, his informant, Henry Hyam, was the fact that he spoke of a place well-known to Thomas Pepper, Cortenay Old Hall; and of its famous and fabulous treasure, a treasure which the great Neuson himself was said to intend some day to knock-off.

This Hyam was the cause of great annoyance to the neurotic murderer, Truman, and the cause of many of his most violent fits of passion, by reason of the fact that he professed to know Gent Jannison and to entertain great doubt as to whether the murderer, Truman, did so. According to Hyam, Gent Jannison was far too big a man ever to have come within the murderer's orbit, or to have troubled to cheat him over so small a sum of money as that mentioned.

No, he was not of the type of petty criminal who forged cheques and cheated brother crooks who pledged jewellery with him. He was a master criminal, a king of the underworld, a partner and equal of the great Knocker Neuson himself; and, if the truth were known, the murderer had never set eyes on him, had never had any dealings with him whatever. And who was the murderer, after all, to talk? He might think himself somebody because his trial had been a frontpage affair and he had only escaped the gallows at the last moment on an insanity plea. But he wasn't really a proper murderer.

Then would Truman rage and jibber, pick up a sharp-edged tool and threaten to show Hyam whether he was a murderer or not. The warder would intervene and the quarrel for the moment die down, only to be renewed again when Hyam, talking at the murderer, would expatiate upon the greatness of Gent Jannison, the master criminal of the day, who had never yet been caught, and of Knocker Neuson, the greatest of all jewel experts.

All this was a weariness and a misery to Thomas Pepper, but one day his interest was suddenly and acutely stirred.

"And how does a sneak-thief like you come to know him, then, since he's such a great man?" sneered Truman.

"Because I come from the same part of the world," was the reply.

"London, I suppose. Lots of people come from London. All sorts of cheap can-openers that call themselves safe-experts, like you."

"Wrong again. If you want to know, he comes from a place called Sandhaven, and so do I."

"Does he?" said Thomas Pepper, all agog. "I never heard of him. What's he like?"

"You never heard of him? Don't suppose he called himself Jannison in that part of the world."

"What's he like?"

And Hyam proceeded to give a description of Gent Jannison which set Thomas Pepper thinking.

"Sure he's never been in prison?" he said.

"Gent Jannison? Not he. There's no 'busy' alive who's clever enough to catch him."

"And you are sure he himself is alive?"

" 'Course he is. Why?"

"I only wondered. . . . Came from Sandhaven, you say."

"Yes."

"How do you know?"

"How do I know? I did a job for Knocker Neuson once, and Gent Jannison was with him. I spoke to him, shook hands with him, and not long after, I run into him at a place called Crochester where I had me eye on a good thing. So'd Gent Jannison and Knocker Neuson too. That Cortenay Old Hall place. There's some big jewellery there. My Gawd, there is."

"I know the place," said Thomas Pepper. "This man Jannison hadn't lost half a finger, had he?"

"No, he's got ten all-right, and each of them worth two."

Thomas Pepper sighed.

Why, of course Albert Mompett had all his ten fingers and thumbs.

He was going barmy like Truman.

Yes, life in prison, once one had reached the stage of associated labour and of privileges—permission to attend the monthly concerts and lectures, to borrow four books from the library and change two of them weekly and two of them monthly—was almost endurable. One could almost hope to keep—or rather to regain—one's sanity, especially as, from day to day, and week to week, and month to month, and year to year, one knew that, sooner or later, one's friend Roger Mompett would learn of one's predicament, and intervene in some way.

PART II

VI

Of all the Stately Homes of England, few, if any, are more stately, more fair, more richly endowed with historical incident and interest than Cortenay Old Hall, which stands on one of the loveliest and most favoured sites in England, the densely-wooded hills of its park protecting it from northerly and easterly winds, its ancient grounds and gardens extending to cliff-tops on either side of the vast hand-tended terraced lawns that slope down to the perfect sands of land-locked white-beached Cortenay Bay.

A Saxon thane built the first house on this spot; a Norman knight, Gilles Cœur-de-neige, the Castle of which the ruins still stand; and his descendant, a Sir Giles Cortenay, the present fortified dwelling-house, in the spacious days of Henry the Seventh when the Wars of the Roses, that Civil War to end Civil War, being finished at last, men settled down to live in domestic peace and comfort, to turn their swords into reaping-hooks and their unhomely cheerless castles into beautiful comfortable houses which, while giving a new meaning to the word Home, could still be put into a state and posture of defence.

That Sir Giles Cortenay had succeeded in his object was proven not only by the sheer loveliness of the house, lovely according to the tastes of any period, but by the fact that Cortenay Old Hall had withstood several sieges, and successfully repulsed fierce attacks, both by sea and by land. From behind its moat and grassy ramparts and its stout encircling walls, Cortenays had defied rapacious Kings and a more rapacious Parliament.

In civil wars, religious wars, and foreign wars, it had figured, defying, in its time, two different Cromwells, three Kings who came by land; and defeating and beating off, with pike and carronade, the assaults of Barbary corsairs, Spanish invaders and raiding Frenchmen, who came by sea.

And, as so often has been the way of such British families, from Doomsday Book to these present happy Days of Doom, the strong sons of the house of Cortenay had persisted ineradicable from their Cortenay estate and place and home. In spite of death on the battlefields of England, France and the Holy Land; in spite of death by block and axe on Tower Hill; in spite of attainder and distraint, impeachment and sequestration, siege and assault, outlawry and excommunication, the Cortenays for more than five hundred years had dwelt in Cortenay Old Hall and for over nine hundred years in Cortenay Old Hall and Cortenay Castle.

Antiquarians indeed there were who said that Gilles Cœur-de-neige claimed this particular fief from the Conqueror by reason of the fact that his family already owned it, the Saxon thane who had come thence to support Harold at Hastings having been his "cousin." Had not his ancestor followed Rolfe the Ganger up the Seine into the Gaulish land that was to be Normandy, while that ancestor's brother sailed up the Thames with Hengist and Horsa into the Gaelish land that was to become England?

And so, for a thousand years, in spite of occasional bickerings on such subjects as rights and dues, imposts and taxes, religion and succession, the Cortenays had been King's-men and England's-men, sometimes on the right side, sometimes on the wrong (or losing), Red Rose or White Rose, King or Parliament, James or Monmouth, Catholic or Protestant, royalists and loyalists always; and though Kings might come and Kings might go, Cortenays went on for ever.

In better times or worse, in richer or poorer, in favour or out of favour, always a Cortenay came back, came Home; or else a young Cortenay grew up to take the place of him who never came back from the Crusades, from Crécy, from Agincourt, from Naseby or Marston Moor, from Flanders, from the sea adventure with Drake, Hawkins and Frobisher, from the East Indies, from the West Indies, from the Peninsula, from Waterloo.

And at length—and, according to himself, lowest, least, lousiest, and last—came Bump Cortenay, Keeper of the Inn, Licensee of the Pot-house, Manager of the Hotel—the Cortenay Old Hall (or Arms).

§2

It was Uncle who had given Bump the name that had stuck to him through life, by observing, on the occasion when the boy, having saddled the good steed Banister with a small silk praying-rug, had sat astride it, slid down the broad gleaming rail of ancient polished oak at swiftly accelerating speed, and had shot off the end on to the flagged floor of the hall with tremendous force.

"Gad!" exclaimed Uncle, at first sight of the banister-rider thereafter. "The boy's a living bump!"

Eyeing the contused head, the bruised forehead, swollen nose, blackened eyes and thickened lips,

"Damme! He's nothing *but* a bump!" he said.

And addressing the child in the terrible voice that filled him with scared delight and joyous horror,

"D'ye hear me, Sir? You are not a boy, you're a walking bump—or a limping one."

Uncle had then proceeded to the scene of the

catastrophe.

"Gad!" he had mused aloud—his invariable habit—as he eyed the long and steeply-sloping banister of the last flight of the grand staircase,

"Rode that on a rug, did he—stayed the course and landed here? Ought to be a thruster, if he doesn't break his neck. . . . Might be better if he did, though, poor lad. Well, well. . . ."

Even at that date, Uncle was apparently pessimistic as to the fate and fortunes of the last of the House of Cortenay.

Uncle, who was incidentally Bump's great-uncle, probably had a stronger influence upon the formation and moulding of his character than had any other person, the child's parents both having died when he was so young that they were barely a memory.

In the shadow of Uncle he grew up. He grew up in terror and awe of the fierce old face, the harsh and angry voice, the biting cold contempt, the abrupt unfriendly manner; in deep respect for the mental, moral, and physical uprightness, the proven courage, the brave deeds, the wide knowledge and experience of life and men and places, of adventure and of war; in profound regard for the fundamental kindness, the all-but hidden warmth, the ultimately-friendly helpfulness.

As a very small boy, Bump had confused Uncle with God; as a not-so-small boy he had, perhaps with better reason, confused him with the Devil. In either manifestation, and for many years after these so-conflicting periods, Uncle and Conscience seemed to be reasonably interchangeable words.

It was said that Uncle had had a grand passion, a great love-affair that had gone awry, and that he had eaten his heart out, ever since.

Whether this was so or not, no-one knew for certain, but, on a dressing-table in the General's room, stood a portrait in a silver frame, of a lovely girl; and on it was inscribed,

"D. W. July 15th, 1885."

A governess and then a tutor, to both of whom Uncle rendered life at Cortenay Old Hall a burden too heavy to be borne for long, had taught Bump most of what he had forgotten. Uncle had taught him most of what he knew.

And many boys have worse guides, guardians and exemplars than had Bump in General Sir Giles Cortenay, Crimean and Mutiny veteran, who could not only tell you, on the rare occasions when he felt so disposed, of personal experiences as a Guards' officer at Inkerman and the siege of Sebastopol; as an eye-witness of the charge of the Light Brigade; of the siege of Delhi and the relief of Lucknow.

He could, moreover, tell you of his father's personal experiences in the Peninsular Campaign and at Waterloo; and of his grandfather's personal experiences, frequently retailed to Uncle by his grandfather himself, a soldier who had fought with Clive in India and under Butcher Cumberland in the '45.

Yes, Bump listened by the hour to a man who had listened by the hour to one who had seen Bonnie Prince Charlie on the battlefield, one who had marched on his own feet from London to Culloden.

At times, on days when his gout was not an agonizing torment, Uncle would talk to the boy as to an equal in age, experience and intelligence. At others, he would be taciturn and morose, enigmatic and unpleasant.

At times, his piercing light-blue eyes would glare savagely, and the boy, trembling, would escape from the dangerous presence.

At others, they would soften and warm, and a kind old hand would rest on the boy's shoulder or head as he sat beside the chair in which Uncle nursed his gout, his memories, and his fears of the future—the future of Cortenay Old Hall, and of the very last of the Cortenays sitting there beside him.

But the bad days by far outnumbered the good, and it was with a real if recurrent surprise that Bump discovered that Uncle could laugh. A frosty wintry smile, yes; a brief chuckle, authentic but swiftly suppressed, on rare occasions, yes; but a laugh was an event over which to ponder, a thing on which to speculate.

There was the case of Sir John Moore. Uncle had really laughed over that.

Why?

He had been questioning Bump as usual on the events of the day, and Bump had confessed to crime and punishment. He had grievously offended his governess and been castigated for his offence.

"Uh!" grunted Uncle. "In trouble again, eh? . . . What have you been doing now?" he growled.

"Burial of Sir John Moore, Uncle."

"John Moore? Coruña. Died, and was buried at night. Quite right. You can see his grave to this day, by the harbour. My father helped bury him. He had once been Moore's subaltern in the Fifty-first Regiment of Foot. . . . Yes, it was all just as the poem says. Wonder what became of the sword? The hilt of his own sword clean inside his body. Seven-pounder cannon-ball took him in the ribs. Yes, my father might have written the poem. I can hear him now.

" 'We buried him that night. Fatigue-party dug a grave by the glacis. We'd have brought him home to Westminster Abbey, but the Lord alone knew how long we should be getting to England with the wind still setting as it did. Besides, who was to say they wouldn't have hung the body in chains if we had taken him home, damn them. . . . A great soldier who had done more for his country than most—and with less support. So we buried him on the battle-field, practically; and no time for full military hon-ours or anything of the sort. Between the Devil and the deep sea, we were, literally. And Soult might attack again at any moment. . . . A hurried affair by moonlight, but the grave is marked and the Span-iards keep it up. And well they might. Yes, I held the lantern as they lowered him in . . .' That's how my father spoke of it. Often."

Uncle fell silent.

"Yes," he went on, "the poem wasn't so different from what my father told me. How does it go:

> *"We buried him darkly, at dead of night,*
> *The sods with our bayonets turning;*
> *By the struggling moonbeams' misty light,*
> *And the lantern dimly burning.*

"That's it, I think.

"And what was *your* trouble?" he added sharply.

"That verse, Uncle."

"How?"

"Miss Speight asked me if I understood every-thing, and when I said yes, she asked me questions. She said, 'What does that line mean—*The sods with our bayonets turning?*' And I said they were turning the French out of Spain."

And Uncle laughed, quite unmistakably.

Chuckles, though rare, were more frequent. There was quite a good one for the fairies—in whom Bump believed implicitly.

"Miss Speight says there *are* no fairies, Uncle. She says there never *were* any."

"Oh?"

"There are surely, aren't there, Uncle?"

"There were, certainly."

"Did you ever see one yourself, Uncle?"

"Lots."

"Where, in the gardens?"

"Yes. Vauxhall Gardens."

"May I tell Miss Speight that you saw them there, Uncle?"

And Uncle had chuckled.

And the wintry frosty smile was not uncommon, as when Bump announced that he had that day caught a Painted Lady and enquired whether Uncle had ever caught one.

"Yes—and been caught by one," smiled Uncle.

Uncle had given Bump the education of the youth of ancient Persia—"to ride, to shoot, and to speak the truth."

Incidentally he had also taught him to be what Uncle called a good Cortenay; and, in tale and story, monologue and conversation, had grounded him deeply in the history of his family, as well as in that of his Country, the two stories being, through generation and century, so closely interwoven.

§3

Two Cortenay legends, or rather stories—nay, histories, indeed—interested Bump far beyond the rest.

These concerned the Cortenay treasure and the Cortenay ghosts, with regard to the truth of both of which tales Uncle gave his personal word. He did not merely emphatically affirm his belief in both, he testified to their verity, genuineness, and reality.

There was, and there had been for three hundred years, a Cortenay treasure, a treasure concealed somewhere about the house, the castle, the park or the cliff forts—Fort Raleigh and Fort Drake, which, on either side of little Cortenay Bay, defended it from attack by sea.

There was, and there had been for far more than five hundred years, a ghost that haunted the old castle, the ghost of a Cortenay of the days of the Wars of the Roses, a knight in armour. There was, and there had been since Elizabethan times, the ghost of a Cortenay in ruff, doublet and hose, who haunted Old Cortenay Hall. There was, and there had been since the suppression of the Monasteries by Henry the Eighth, a White Lady who walked along Nuns' Causeway which led across the park in the direction of the ruins of the old House of the Poor Sisters of Mercy.

Those were three established, authentic and well-known ghosts, seen from time to time and from generation to generation, by people who had the gift of seeing what was before their eyes. And such people were surprisingly numerous, and comprised not only members of the family, of the household, of the indoor and outdoor staff, and of the tenantry, but complete strangers who, never having heard of them, would see them and describe them accurately.

And in old letters, some of them centuries old, were references to the ghosts and their manifestations, with speculations on the implied portent of the ghost's haunting and unrest.

Each had its history and its implication, one foretelling by its appearance a death in the Cortenay family, another a disaster of some other kind, and the White Lady a warning of something very notable, whether of good or evil import.

Two great ambitions, among others, were cherished in Bump's ardent youthful mind; the one, the discovery of the Cortenay treasure; the other, an encounter with one of the more important Cortenay ghosts.

The treasure first—business; the ghost second—pleasure.

Endless were Bump's speculations on the subject of the treasure; and none was too childish, too foolish, whimsical, far-fetched or absurd to be given fair hearing and careful consideration by Uncle.

Obviously Uncle was most deeply interested in the subject. Nor in that was he in anywise different from any Cortenay since the days of the notorious half gentleman-adventurer, half pirate, Sir Giles Cortenay, of Santa Maria fame and infamy.

That this Sir Giles had brought home treasure of enormous value—for those days, colossal, fantastic value—was historical fact, its truth as indisputable as that of the siege of Cortenay Old Hall by a regiment of King's pikemen and musketeers, and a troop of the King's horse, not to mention a couple of light cannon—such being the King's answer to Sir Giles Cortenay's flat refusal to part with a half, much less the whole, of the treasure.

"A very wicked man?" mused Uncle. "I don't know, my boy. I wouldn't say that. Not according to the standards of his day. Of course, in these times it would be unthinkable. Piracy, robbery under arms, fire-raising, filibustering, wholesale murder and what-not."

And then with a brief grim chuckle, Uncle had made a reference to something Bump did not understand, something that sounded like,

"Bad as James' Sons' Raid."

"No, in those days, when the King was at war, it was a recognized and proper thing for a gentleman to get the King's permission in writing, fit out an expedition at his own cost, and go and attack the ships of the enemy country, the country itself, or any of its colonies. There was a sort of an understanding, though, that the gentleman-adventurer shared the loot and glory with his Sovereign; and if he took a colony from the enemy, named it after the King or Queen, and handed it over. That's how you find names like Virginia, after Queen Elizabeth;

place-names in various parts of the world like Jamestown, Charlestown, Kingston, Georgetown and so on. . . . Some of the adventurers were Drake, Raleigh, Frobisher, Howard, Grenville and Hawkins; and one of them was Sir Henry Morgan, a gentleman by the standards of his day, who turned real pirate, buccaneer and filibuster. He sacked and burned the city of Panama and, though he had been a pirate, ended his days as a Colonial Governor.

"Well, our man, Sir Giles Cortenay of the treasure, performed a feat very like Morgan's both for courage, endurance, military skill and cruel savagery. But they were cruel savage times, and a man must be judged by the standards of his day. He went to the Spanish Main, all out for adventure, fighting, fun and fame and glory. . . . And of course war was war in those days, when you tackled your man with your sword, hand to hand, and didn't kill him a mile away with a rifle, burn the flesh off his bones with liquid fire, or choke the soul out of him with poison gas. War was a man's game then, a gentlemanly sport, and not a foul and filthy butchery by chemists and armament inventors.

"And the sea venture was a man-to-man affair, begun at a few hundred yards and ended by laying your ship alongside that of your enemy, and boarding with pike and cutlass.

"Mind you, I should think they suffered as much in their own way, in those days, as people do today. Horrible wounds with big soft leaden bullets, iron cannon balls and chain-shot, dirty pikes and rusty cutlasses—and no hospitals, no proper doctors, no anæsthetics or antiseptics. A man didn't get a clean hole drilled through a bone by a hard-nosed bullet in those times, find himself back home in a few hours, with every comfort and attention, and on his feet again in a few weeks. If he stopped a bullet with an arm or a leg then, they hacked the limb off with axe, saw, and knife, and stuck the stump in boiling tar—that sort of thing. . . . Not that we had got very far beyond that stage when I was in the Crimea.

"And then the food and water on those ships, and on foreign service generally. Unbelievable. And the kit and accoutrements. Fancy shoving your way through dense swamp and jungle, dressed in steel and leather, thigh boots and spurs, and with a pike, arquebus and long sword. Incredible.

"Well, this Sir Giles Cortenay, cruising off the Spanish Main, got information, from some pirate or other, that the Spanish plate-train . . .

"What? Did they have trains there in those days? No, my boy, it was a train of mules, each laden with packs of pure gold from the mines in the interior.

"He got the information that the plate-train, the gold convoy, was being diverted from Santiago or Santa Cruz, whichever it was, and taken to the little port of Santa Maria, to be shipped to Spain from there, to avoid the enemy fleets which were lying in wait, off the port from which it was usually despatched.

"Well, he knew that if this were true, the place would be garrisoned, fortified and well protected, from the sea approach. Guard-ships off the harbour too. So what did he do but land miles away down the coast in a creek, make his way inland, bearing south for several days, then west, then north again; and he came upon the city from its southern unprotected land side. D'you follow me?

"With a sudden attack at dawn, he took the place at the double, took it with a rush, had it on fire, and the Dons running for their lives, all before breakfast.

"And if it was a wonderful surprise attack, it wasn't only the Spaniards who were surprised. Sir

Giles Cortenay was just as surprised as they were—to find that he had been fooled, intentionally or otherwise. There had never been a plate-mule, nor the hind leg of a donkey, within a hundred miles of the place. It was quite clear that the Spaniards had put this tale about, while they shipped the annual gold consignment from the usual place, or some other as far as possible from Santa Maria.

"However, according to his letters to his wife, he hanged the pirate, his informant, to encourage others to verify the tales they heard.

"So the capture of Santa Maria by a ship's company of English soldiers and sailors, led by a handful of gentlemen-adventurers, wasn't so much of a deed after all; but what was a real feat of arms was that march. Think of it, boy. It's a most pestilential coast and country; terrific heat; all but impassable mangrove swamps, mountains and rivers, and dense overgrown jungle through which you'd have to hack almost every yard of your way; poisonous insects and snakes; alligators, savages, deadly fevers and what-not.

"And think of the rations they would have. Weevily pantile biscuits as hard as stone and about as nourishing; and stinking rotten junk, horse-flesh and decaying pork thrown into tubs in England, months or years before.

"Think of big heavy steel helmets and breast-plates and thick leather jerkins in that sun and that climate.

"Well, anyhow, they got there, most of them, captured the place—and found they had been done.

"Then—whether by way of rewarding his men, lining his pockets, or gratifying his God, we don't know—Sir Giles Cortenay did what we have again to excuse or condone by viewing it in the light of the standards of his time. He sacked and burned the Cathedral, and, no doubt, as a stout Protestant took credit for the act of 'smoking out a nest of Papistry.' In fact, he says he did, in a letter to the King. His despatches, among the State Papers of the time, can be seen at the British Museum to this day.

"Now, his letters to his wife contain a sort of inventory of the special treasures of Santa Maria Cathedral, one of the oldest and richest on the Spanish Main, especially endowed by pious kings and queens of Spain as a thank-offering for God's guidance and goodness in endowing their country with the immeasurable wealth of the Americas, the great New World discovered by Cristobal Colon and conquered by stout Cortes and Pizarro.

"Well, of the loot of Santa Maria, Sir Giles gave all money, all coined silver, all gold bullion, plate, ornaments and so forth, to his officers and men, as well as all sums paid in ransom and in levy; and for himself kept only jewels. He uses the word 'only' in his letters.

" '*Only*,' mark you. Something of a humorist, especially when one reads the inventory and learns that the altar jewels themselves were worth a King's ransom, let alone that of a few Spanish gentlemen and a small provincial city.

"And these altar jewels, taken from their settings in communion plate, cups, chalices, that sort of thing, and from the marvellous rings, clasps, brooches and other ornaments worn by the images of the Saints, as well as the votive offerings of rich penitents, placed upon or hung about the altar, were only part of the treasure that he allotted to himself.

"The monks, priests, Jesuits, or whoever they were, who were in charge of the Cathedral, had a separate treasury of unmounted jewels. I rather fancy that wealth in this form was exempt from confiscation or taxation by the King or Queen of

Spain. Had it been gold, it would have been the King's, or, at any rate, a very great part of it would have been; so they put their wealth into diamonds and other precious stones.

"Of course there was a certain amount of money, a very considerable amount, and a great deal of gold in the form of altar plate and ornament; enough to make the whole ship's company very satisfied with the day's work and the month's march; but the bulk was, as I say, in the shape of magnificent jewels—and Sir Giles kept 'only' the jewels as his share.

"A considerable proportion of the gems were great diamonds of the first water, and I should think that these were South American stones, specimens of the Brazilian diamonds that became so famous later. Doubtless the Spaniards originally got them from the natives for an old song, and a rough one at that. And probably the emeralds, sapphires, and rubies had come from Spain, gifts, as I say, from the King and Queen. Quite possibly the Pope sent some.

"At any rate, our ancestor—your direct ancestor he was—brought away from Santa Maria some diamonds which he describes as being '*as bigge as the pummil of the hilte of my sworde*,' probably as big as a good-sized walnut and of God knows how many carats weight. There were also some great emeralds, notably one which, as he says, '*is exquisitely cutt and of a perfect flawless clearnesse, and as long as my thumbe*,' and that, I suppose, would be a good couple of inches. Great sapphires there were, too, and rubies which he dismisses as being merely of the size of fine grapes.

"Well, he got home all-right with the treasure, because it was from this house, and probably in this very room, that he made an exact inventory of them, and he didn't have time to do anything about disposing of them, because the King sent messengers riding post-haste from London bidding him come up to Court at once, and bring the treasure with him, full tale, and lay it at his Sovereign's feet, the proper place for it. News of the jewels had got to the Court almost as soon as the stones themselves got to Cortenay Old Hall, and doubtless lost nothing in the telling. So the King wanted the lion's share—which would be roughly a hundred per cent of the total.

"But not a bit of it. They were very troublous times, and Sir Giles decided to make the most of the fact.

"That particular Sir Giles Cortenay knew how to keep money when he had got it. A pity some of his successors didn't. He was not going to part with his loot to the King or anybody else. 'Not one clipt groat's worth,' as he wrote.

"And the next thing he knew was that, since he wouldn't bring it to the King, the King was coming for it—or sending for it.

"So Cortenay Old Hall stood another siege.

"They did the thing properly too.

"The Admiral of the Cinque Ports, or whoever it was, blockaded the coast so that he couldn't get relief or provision by sea, while a very adequate force laid siege to the land defences. There was undoubtedly a certain liveliness. As it happened, Sir Giles had still got several of his excellent gunners who had been with him on the Spanish adventure. And not only them but their guns as well, for directly the royal command was received, the stout Sir Giles knew what the sequel would be, and straightway fetched his carronades, swivel guns, stern-chasers, long-Johns, falconets and the rest of his armament ashore from his ship, which lay in Whitebay Harbour, a few miles away, just in time.

"Of course, there could be only one end to an

affair like that, one man against the State, however full the King's hands might be of bigger things; but it was quite a longish siege, and they had to bring up another regiment of arquebusiers and pikemen by way of reinforcement before the final assault.

"And even then it might have been beaten off, but for the fact that the King's seamen made a landing on the beach of Cortenay Bay, swarmed up in between the two cliff forts, and attacked the position in the rear, while the bulk of the garrison was meeting the main assault from the landward side.

"Well, the King's forces took the place and they killed Sir Giles—a matchlock bullet in the back of his head and any number of dints and dents in his helmet and breast-plate.

"But they never got the treasure.

"He hid it somewhere, at the beginning of the siege, and no-one, not even his wife, knew where. She, poor lady, had an unpleasant time in the Tower of London before she convinced the King that she had no more idea than he had, as to where the treasure had been concealed.

"And when she was released, it wasn't because the King was convinced, but in the hope that she would go straight to where the treasure was concealed, recover it, and start raising money. But although a royal commissioner—or King's spy, or whatever the C.I.D. or Secret Service man of the day was—accompanied her back here, he never had anything to report.

"One can imagine the times they had together, Lady Cortenay and the King's agent, both trying to discover the jewels, and each one endeavouring to do it without the knowledge of the other.

"Well, neither of them did discover them, nor did any other Cortenay from that day to this."

"Did you ever have a treasure-hunt here, Uncle?"

"Did I ever? Did I ever do much else, when I was visiting here in the days of my youth? *And* when I came to live here in my old age. Why, I spend more than half my time, now, thinking of possible places. And I only stopped the actual search when I was convinced that there was not another place in which I could look, and that even if the treasure were in the house I should never find it. It is foolish, of course, because as likely as not he buried it . . ."

" 'Darkly at dead of night,' " whispered Bump.

". . . out in the grounds, gardens, park, cliff forts —anywhere in a space of a few hundred acres. He may have buried it by the roots of some sapling that is now a mighty tree."

"Yes. Wouldn't it be wonderful, Uncle, if he did that, and a great storm arose and blew down a big oak tree, and there, among its roots, was a brass-bound box full of jewels?"

"Very wonderful," growled Uncle. "On the night of your twenty-first birthday—or the day before the mortgage foreclosed. Very wonderful. The mighty storm that saved the House of Cortenay just in the nick of time. The Old Nick of time."

And, looking up, Bump felt fairly sure that he saw the brief wintry smile, though it may have been only the flickering shadows thrown by the fire.

"And did my father hunt for it when he was a boy?"

"When he was a boy and a youth and a man, like every other Cortenay from Sir Giles's day to this."

"There isn't much hope of my finding it, then?"

"No, nor of anyone else doing so, I should say. Your grandfather's great-grandfather, Hell-fire Cortenay, pretty well pulled the place to pieces, looking for it. House hardly recovered from it yet. I suppose some day the marks of his handiwork will be as interesting as those of the big fight on the stairs, when the panelling and the banisters got the sword cuts, pike scratches and bullet marks."

"Why did he make more mess than other people, Uncle?"

"Because he was in more of a mess himself. Wanted the money worse than anybody before or since, until us. He was a noted gambler in a day of noted gamblers, and played at the *Cocoa Tree*, night after night. Once he played against Sir Harry Dashwood, and at the end of twenty-three consecutive hours he had lost thirty thousand guineas—as much as this place was then worth. He came down here and, as I say, pulled the place to pieces: made hay of it. Floors up; panelling spoilt; chimneys knocked to pieces; half the roof off; every conceivable place broken into, searched, ransacked; and he found nothing except one or two interesting concealed cupboards, hiding-places, bricked-up doorways, a secret staircase, and an underground passage from the house to a cave under the cliff. . . . Not a sign of any treasure.

"Then he pressed every man, woman and child he could, into service, and set them digging-up the grounds and gardens round the house; spoilt the flower-beds; ruined the lawns; made dreadful havoc; and found nothing again. I don't see why he should have hoped to, when there were the two forts, the whole of the park, acres of cliff top, a smuggler's cave, and the entire beach available.

"When, at last, he had to give it up, he rode back to London; and the next night he challenged Lord Carrickbridge, one of the maddest gamblers of them all, to stake an even ten thousand guineas on the colour of a card. Sir John Dashwood was to shuffle the pack; Captain Desmond Fitzgerald was to deal the cards face-downward; Sir Harry Bellingham, with his back turned, was to say ' Stop '; and Lord Carrickbridge was to call Black or Red for the last card dealt when the dealer stopped.

"Well, Hell-fire Cortenay won; did it again and won; did it a third time and won; and then gave up gambling, settled down here, and turned religious."

Uncle fell silent, gazing into the fire.

"Treasure-hunting has been more or less of a game here since then," he went on, "though played more wisely by some than by others."

"I shall play it, Uncle," Bump assured the General.

"I'm sure you will, my boy. Good luck to you. You'll need some luck."

§4

And so Bump Cortenay grew up in the nurture and admonition of his great-uncle, and with a gradually increasing knowledge and realization of the hardness of the times, the growing difficulty of carrying on, the ever-waxing fear and probability that he would be the last Cortenay to live at Cortenay Old Hall—indeed the last to own it.

This he regarded as a terrible thing, and lived in the fear and shadow of it, with an apprehension, a dread, and an unhappiness incomprehensible to few who have not been similarly situated. What, in happier circumstances, would have been a quiet pervading joy, an abiding satisfaction and source of gratitude and happiness, became an anxiety, a worry, a grief, and threatened to become an obsession, an *idée fixe*, a heart-breaking, courage sapping misery—a day-dream become a nightmare.

Each time he returned from school, he understood the position better, until, when the day came for him to come home for the last time, he understood only too well: for the General took him completely into his confidence, and fully discussed the painful questions of ways and means.

While the General lived, his pension, annuity

and private income would just keep the wolf from the door, the creditor from the Law Court, the ancient house from complete dilapidation. When he died . . .

The General could only shrug his shoulders and eye his grand-nephew with bleak gaze, his stony face concealing the affection, warmth, sympathy and bitter grief with which his heart was filled.

"One of us has got to make some money, Giles," he said, "and I'm afraid that, like most soldiers, I'm no good at it. It was because I discovered in time, thank God, my undoubted gift for losing money, that I bought an annuity while I had a good lump. And that was long before you were born or thought of. Your father was well off in those days. Another soldier who was a bad business man. Their only financial value is to win and guard the lands in which the capitalist can flourish.

"Talking of which, Honor is coming again, and for a long visit this time. I'm taking her away from school. Got to."

Honor Winter was the orphan daughter of the General's niece Margaret *née* Cortenay, who had married a penniless young soldier who, like Bump's father, had been killed in the Boer War.

"Oh, good," applauded Bump. "She's quite useful—at several things."

"Baiting hooks, you mean, and bowling for you. You'll find her grown up and probably superior, I expect.

"Useful," mused the General. "Be more useful if she were coming into a pot of money instead of precisely nothing."

§5

And then came the terrible, never-to-be-forgotten morning when Bump, roused by screams, sprang out of bed, threw on a dressing-gown, and dashed downstairs to find that a hysterical house-maid, her shining morning face white as death, had discovered Uncle lying on the Library floor, a little pool of blood soaking through the carpet beside his head, an open window and the open safe-door showing what had happened.

Uncle was not quite dead. He spoke once again, as Bump, stunned with horror, stupid with shock, went to raise him. Opening his eyes, he fixed the trembling youth with a glassy stare, swallowed painfully, and whispered,

"*Bubble reputation . . . Bubble reputation . . . in the . . . in the . . .*" and died in Bump's arms.

Strange and curious words to be the last of such a man, no Shakespearean scholar, nor greatly given to studious reading.

Wandering in his mind, of course—decided Bump later, when he could think at all—and possibly his last thoughts as the blow fell and his senses reeled were,

"I have sought 'the bubble reputation in the cannon's mouth,' and here I end at an unknown felon's hand; an old man, dying on a carpet in a comfortable room, after facing shot and shell, bayonet and sword, lance and spear in Russia and India, Egypt and Africa, Afghanistan and China."

Then followed one of the darkest periods of Bump's life, his soul clouded by grief and darkened by hate, grief for the man whom he had loved, hate for the creeping, sneaking, foul assassin who had murdered that brave old soldier.

And to this was added fear, fear of the lonely present, fear of the future that was to see him the unworthy Cortenay who, at long last, lost Cortenay Old Hall.

PART III

VII

It could not be said that Bump's brave effort at saving Cortenay Old Hall was proving a success, except in so far as, after several years, it was still Cortenay Old Hall, its park and grounds intact, and still nominally his.

Like Uncle and most of his forbears, he was not a good business man. It had been comparatively easy, alas, to turn Cortenay Old Hall into a kind of Country Club, a Guest House for gentlefolk in reduced circumstances, but it had not been possible, much less easy, to make it pay. It had not been possible, much less easy, even to make it pay its way.

With the friendly and altruistic help and advice of Messrs. Jackson, Johnson & Jackson, the family Solicitors in Lincoln's Inn Fields, and that of their more-or-less local agent, a gentleman who was, strangely enough, Messrs. Wilkinson, Burt, Wilkes & Harrowby of Sandhaven, he had avoided the worst sort of financial mistakes, pit-falls and disasters.

But what is the use of sound financial advice to a young man who has no finances and a congenital inability to refuse to help an even lamer dog over a stile, to press for a debt, to refuse to believe a hard-luck story, and to harden his heart as and when a business man should.

But for kind Sir Russell Bemmington he must have crashed, failed, been rendered bankrupt, and lost Cortenay Old Hall for ever.

The first paying guests at Cortenay Old Hall had mainly been helpful friends and acquaintances who had come and stayed there instead of going to

Scotland or elsewhere. One or two had brought their yachts into the bay and made Cortenay Old Hall their headquarters for a while. Others had formed shooting-parties, had played golf at Cortenay Abbas, hunted with the Cortenay Moor, boated, bathed or fished, all in due season; and for a time all had gone very well, been very jolly, and financially quite satisfactory.

Most of them had insisted on paying for their pleasures and accommodation at as high a rate as they would have paid at the best hotel they knew. A few, when Bump had blushingly begged them to consider themselves as guests and stay as long as they liked, had taken him at his word. More than one had decided to settle in for life, on those excellent terms.

This first phase had lapsed into the next when strangers, recommended by these earliest guests, had come, seen, and been conquered; had stayed for longer or shorter periods and departed, some expressing great satisfaction and a fixed determination to return, never to be seen again; others paying and departing without comment; a few expressing dissatisfaction, voicing complaints of the absence of central heating and relative paucity of bath-rooms.

Two or three again had departed, leaving unpaid bills, and of this second year's crop there had been one or two limpet-like and determined life-members whose ability and desire to pay had been equally weak.

Then had come the period when wide advertisement had resulted in the house being fairly full for a time, and with guests of a different sort again, folk who, save for those who came for a month's holiday in August, a week at Whitsun or Easter, and again at Christmas, were birds of passage, week-ending, or arriving one day and departing the next, as they motored through the country.

But as Bump soon came to learn, money makes money, and lack of money loses money.

Had he been able to keep his ancient home in first-class repair, to instal the costly amenities that guests demand when paying a good price for accommodation; had he been able to pay a genuine chef, keep a really good cellar, employ an adequate staff of first-class, or at least well-trained, servants, Cortenay Old Hall might have paid as a guest-house.

But in order to attract people to a place which—though admittedly lovely, picturesque, historic, situated in a beautiful part of England, remote yet accessible, close to sea and moorland, mountain, and fishing-river, was nevertheless ill-provided, dilapidated, and lacking in many such important respects as good cooking, service, and winter warmth—charges and prices had to be made commensurate with its draw-backs and deficiencies.

And now, in what Bump, despairing, felt to be the last phase, Cortenay Old Hall was quite definitely the resort, and frequently the only home, of very poor people, the new poor; people to whom its present inclusive charges of four guineas weekly during the winter months, and five in the summer, were its greatest attraction.

Nor did these attractive, nay alluring, charges indicate philanthropy on Bump's part. It was business. Better fifty people averaging four and a half guineas, than a dozen or so paying thrice as much.

And even so, and with a house fairly full, it was a losing fight; and month by month Bump sank deeper and deeper into the debt, not to say the clutches, of kindly Sir Russell Bemmington, late of Calcutta, the ever-watchful friend and supporter who had insisted on coming to the rescue whenever Bump, despairing, had told him that the Hall must soon close; who had insisted on making himself responsible for repairs, improvements and installations; and who seemed only too anxious to thrust money into Bump's reluctant hand. . . .

§2

Kind Sir Russell Bemmington, "late of Calcutta," had first visited Cortenay Old Hall, as a week-ending motorist, in the earlier and palmier days of the venture of the new Guest House; had come again, taken one of the best rooms for a week, stayed for a month, and made himself most agreeable to Bump, to Honor Winter, to Miss Hoping, the housekeeper-manageress, and, at first, to the curiously anomalous person, Richard Rodd. This man was not hall-porter nor head-waiter, not major-domo nor secretary, not barman, cellar-man nor wine-steward, not valet, boots nor butler, yet whose duties somehow seemed to partake of those of all these functionaries, and who manifested at different times in each of these capacities.

His ever-moving hand turned to the work that was nearest; anything that was to be done he found worth doing, and, what was worth doing, worth doing well. In the truest and fullest sense of the word he was a factotum, and Bump was wont to allude to him as his right-and-left-hand man.

A person of unfailing courtesy, illimitable willingness and equable temper, he was famous among the visitors to Cortenay Old Hall; an institution there, and almost universally popular.

With one exception, those who failed to admire him were guests of the less desirable type; those who habitually broke, or endeavoured to break, the few simple rules of the house; those who failed to pay their bills when tardily and tactfully invited; who behaved without decorum in bar, bedroom and billiard-room; who acted in an undesirable manner toward chamber-maid or waitress; or otherwise demonstrated their unfitness for membership of Cortenay Old Hall Country Club, and residence thereat as paying guests, and particularly in the rôle of domiciled members.

The exception was kind Sir Russell Bemmington.

Definitely he did not, it transpired, continue to like Richard Rodd.

And though he did not proclaim the fact, he made no particular secret of it in conversation with Bump, with Honor, and with other residents of his own standing.

This was unfortunate, for if Richard Rodd was a proved and trusted invaluable servant, kind Sir Russell Bemmington was not only the *doyen* of the guests, the senior club-member, and by far the most paying and profitable resident, but he was also by much the biggest creditor on the books of the Cortenay Old Hall Hotel.

For that was what it was, a Hotel, admitted Bump—whether you called it a Country Club, a Guest House or a Blasted Menagerie.

In fact, but for Sir Russell Bemmington, the place would have had to close down, long ago. He it was who had pointed out to Bump that he really must do some painting and paper-hanging, some plumbing and wiring, some re-stocking and renovating; and he it was who, on Bump's pointing out the excellent reason for not doing these admittedly necessary things, had advanced the even more necessary money.

Yes, it would be really very awkward if Sir Russell's curious dislike for Richard Rodd developed to the point of open expression, an ultimatum, a request from the best of all the guests that the best of all the servants should be dismissed.

For apart from his real value, his extraordinary usefulness, his general popularity, and Bump's real affection for him, Richard Rodd was Honor's pet, her find, her *protégé*.

He was, according to Honor, her Illustrated Christmas Number, her Good Deed for All Her Days.

For Honor had found him, literally—and not merely in the sense in which impresarios find talent, just by selecting him from scores of applicants for the post of butler at Cortenay Old Hall Country Club and Guest House.

And moreover, to add to the delightful Christmas Annual Illustration effect, she had actually found him in the gutter; and that nothing of poignancy and poesy should be wanting, she had also found him in the snow.

In the gutter; in the snow; and at Christmas time.

Driving her ancient and battered two-seater from Sandhaven, where she had been on shopping business for the housekeeper, she had come upon a man lying by the road-side, definitely in the gutter, his white face against the muddy road-side bank. And it was beginning to snow—beautifully.

Stopping the car and getting out, she had found that the ragged scarecrow was in a state of collapse, shivering with cold and starvation, or the rigor of some incipient illness. It had been with considerable difficulty that she had helped him to crawl into the car, and, once safely in the seat, he had fainted or passed out, into a state of coma. In that condition she had brought him to Cortenay Old Hall, to the consternation of Miss Hoping, the manageress-housekeeper, of the hall-porter, and of the somewhat supercilious and superior major-domo superintending tea in the hall.

But Bump had, of course, supported her. He

had had the sick man carried to an attic room, restored to consciousness with hot-water bottles, rugs and brandified tea, and had then telephoned to Dr. Bell of Crochester. The latter having diagnosed starvation, exhaustion and exposure, and prescribed nourishment, warmth and rest, Bump had given orders that the prescription be fully administered; and Honor's waif had been fed, clothed and cared for.

Having found him, Honor evinced no immediate desire to lose him. Reluctantly and with a shrinking feeling that the application of the acid test would prove the truth of Miss Hoping's contention as to the inherent worthlessness of all tramps, she found the man a job of work, light work suited to his still somewhat convalescent state. Personally conducting him, one day, to what was known as the wood-yard, she introduced him to a pile of wood and a saw.

That evening, starting out for her usual after-tea walk, she beheld her *protégé* hovering in the near distance, rolling his cap nervously in his hands, and moving from foot to foot, as one preparing to take flight.

'He has had enough, and is wanting cash payment as well,' supposed Honor.

"Well?" she asked, her firm little chin slightly protruded, her plucked eyebrows slightly contracted above her fine eyes. "Well, what do you want?"

"Some more wood, please, Miss."

She was glad she had not said, "How much do you want?"

"Have you finished that lot?"

"Yes, Miss. Hours ago; and been tryin' to get some more. I thought of sawing down a tree."

"We'll take those that have blown down, first."

And accompanying the man to the wood-yard, Honor decided that he must have worked in nowise like a nigger, for what had been a pile of big branches, small trunks, logs, and assorted timber, was now a neatly-stacked pile of uniformly-sawn fire-wood and grate-logs of proper size.

The amazing tramp was not afraid of work.

What he did seem to fear was lack of it, and that a paucity of odd jobs would be the cause of his leaving the place and taking to the road again.

Having sawn wood until there was a plethora of grate-worthy logs, he swept fallen leaves, acres of them, into vast distant mounds which he then removed with the help of a great and ancient wheel-barrow. In fact, he appeared to be in some danger of developing into an under-gardener when Honor, his saviour and patroness, if not patron saint, discovered his indoor usefulness as a handy-man.

Clad in an ancient suit of Bump's and a green-baize apron, he developed into something of a wonder with a hammer, a screw-driver and a pocketful of assorted nails, hooks and screws; and from being an object of some suspicion and contempt on the part of Miss Hoping, changed quite quickly into her most useful and valued employee, as he took up and put down stair-carpets, cleaned windows, re-hung pictures, cured the lameness of castorless arm-chairs, and did quickly, neatly and well, the innumerable odd jobs of a big house, that are otherwise nobody's business, and fall not within the scope and ken of house-maid, parlour-maid, chamber-maid or other.

And from invaluable handy-man, Honor's sal-vaged flotsam of the road developed into valued house-servant who, in decorous if nondescript uniform, did in his time play many parts, a time that began long before dawn and ended not until the departure to bed of the latest reluctant guest.

In the rôle of butler, Richard Rodd could buttle; as a footman could foot it featly; as hall-porter show the desired deportment; as waiter, at tea or table, wait properly; as general servant, serve his master generally and comprehensively, faithfully and well.

No, Bump hardly cared to contemplate Cortenay Old Hall without Richard Rodd, now risen to the undisputed position of chief of domestic staff, and honoured colleague of Miss Hoping herself.

Bump had begun by liking him; had come to approve him; and now did, with regard to him, what he had learned that he could do with but few people. He trusted him implicitly, believed what he said completely, and realized that, should it come to parting with him, he would lose more than an invaluable servant. He would lose a friend on whom he depended for far more than hireling help and service.

It would be in the nature of a calamity if Richard Rodd had to go.

And it would be Calamity itself should kind Sir Russell Bemmington withdraw the light of his countenance from the house, and the support of his ever-ready purse from its tottering fortunes.

But of course it would not come to that. After all, Sir Russell was eminently and essentially a reasonable man, and Richard Rodd a respectful one who would never intentionally give offence.

It was curious that Sir Russell should have let Rodd offend him unintentionally, for the man so obviously meant well; and so well.

Perhaps his quick courtesy and over-willingness had led him into the indiscretion of seeming faintly familiar with Sir Russell, or into being what Sir Russell considered faintly familiar.

And yet the worthy knight was not a touchy man; was not one of those pompous creatures who stand so heavily upon their dignity because they have nothing else whereon to stand. And Calcutta was not a City of Dreadful Knights. Men who won a knighthood in India for their service to Government as well as to the Banks or Businesses they ruled; men who gave freely of their valuable time as Chairmen of Indian City Municipalities, of Indian Chambers of Commerce, of Hospital Committees, and of other Indian Public or Philanthropic Institutions, were almost invariably men of an admirable and excellent class and kind; and, so far as one could tell, Sir Russell was worthily representative of them.

No, he would never push personal prejudice to the length of petty persecution. For that is what it would be if he insisted on Richard's dismissal, or at any rate issued an ultimatum and gave Bump the choice of losing his principal guest or his very best servant.

Both irreplaceable too, for Sir Russell was so much more than guest.

In point of fact, the place could not go on without him, quite apart from the painful fact that it was heavily in debt to him, so heavily that he could, did he but choose to do so, ruin Bump, sell him up, foreclose the mortgage, and turn him out of house and home, the house that had been the home of the Cortenays for a thousand years.

But of course he would never do that.

What an idiotic train of thought. Morbid. And yet nevertheless, idiotic and morbid though it might be, that was precisely what Bump was finding himself thinking, now, between three and four o'clock, almost every morning of his life.

He would start up, frequently from a nightmare; and, for an hour or so, lie awake, his heart sinking, his stomach turning over within him, as he contemplated the future, and the steadily approaching day when he must go.

Go.

The last of the Cortenays to live beneath the ancient roof of Cortenay Old Hall.

God knew he had done his best, and hadn't grudged turning himself from a country squire of broad acres, a landed gentleman, a baronet of most ancient lineage, into a hotel-keeper, a publican, a caterer, a bill-collector, a bell-answering placater of annoyed dowagers, a pacifier of angry motoring road-hogs who had honoured the Hall by condescending to . . .

No, no! That wasn't the way to talk or to think.

Anyhow, he had done his best to fight for the place in the modern way, as his ancestors had fought for it in the old way, the better way; and perhaps things would not look so bad by breakfast time.

That was how it went nowadays in the terrible small hours of the morning.

VIII

Bump looked into the library, that large and lovely old room, in search of Honor, who had breakfasted before him.

Ah, there she was—and what a picture she made, perched on the broad cushioned window-sill, the morning sun casting about her head and her fair curling hair a golden aureole.

"Bump," she said as he closed the door, "should one read it,

" *'Seeking the bubble—reputation—even in the cannon's mouth,'* with 'bubble' and 'reputation' both nouns and things, interchangeable and all that, or,

'Seeking the bubble reputation even in the cannon's mouth' with 'bubble' as an adjective—you know, an adjective is a word entirely surrounded by nouns—'bubble' describing 'reputation.' All bubbly like?"

"Gad, that's queer," thought Bump, rumpling his hair and staring at the girl. "Uncle's last words. And I was dreaming them again last night. Woke up hearing them."

"I don't know, child," he replied. "However, come to me for anything you want to know. I'll always give you an answer. Right or wrong. Spirit of the Guards' Brigade, and all that. I should think it means 'Seeking that bubble which men call Reputation; and seeking it in the cannon's mouth of all silly places.' Very funny place to find bubbles, what?"

Bump further pondered the important point.

"On the other hand, of course, it may mean 'seeking the fragile short-lived reputation—for military courage and dash—seeking it in the very can-

non's mouth.' Extremely silly place to seek anything at all, if you ask me. In business hours, I
mean."

"You don't suppose it's a sort of what-you-may-
call-it—a later mistake, misprint . . . ?"

"Interpoliation?" suggested Bump, summoning
his literary resources.

"That sort of thing. Yes, 'interpoliation.' Or interpollution. And 'bubble' should be *bauble*?"

"Might be, might be," agreed Bump, "though I
wouldn't go looking for baubles either, in a cannon's mouth. The only bauble you'd find there
would be a round one, hard and heavy. Impetuous
like. But ask me anything you want to know, my
child. At any time. Prompt courteous answer. Right
or wrong. Why this research? I'm busy."

"Oh, I only wanted to know. I picked up this
copy of *As You Like It* and opened it at the Seven
Ages of Man—'how full of quotations Shakespeare
is'—and it reminds me of school. We acted the play
for a Prize Day do, and the English mistress always
used to say to herself, I'm certain, '*Seeking the bubble*—count three under your breath—*reputation*—
count three under your breath—*in the cannon's
mouth.*' Like that."

"Just like that," agreed Bump. "Well, it's all very
sad. What *I* came to say was, go and buck-up poor
old Miss Wymper. Wymper born; whimpers still."

"Poor old dear," smiled Honor. "Every day and in
every way she gets whimperer and whimperer and
. . ."

"That'll be enough," interrupted Bump. "What
are we to do about her?"

"How far is she behind?"

"Lost count," was the reply. "She's behind Time
itself, but one can't put her out into the street. Even
if we had a street to put her out into."

"No, you can't," agreed Honor. "And if you could,

you'd have to catch her at high tide."

"What do you mean?"

"One of everything. You'd have to catch her on an On day. Not one of her Off days."

"The girl's mad. She knows not what she says."

"Oh, yes, I do. The poor old dear has exactly one of everything—and she lies in bed while it all goes to the wash. That's why she is in bed now, really."

"Gad! Isn't it awful! And she was a rich woman once."

"It is awful. . . . It's awful for you too, Bump. You can't fill the house with people like that."

"Can't I? I could fill it with people like that to-morrow."

"Yes, but you are not going to. Miss Hoping says that Archie Wilbraham is about a month behind too."

"Yes. We shall have to lose him, I'm afraid. He can always find money to go racing on the Monday but never to pay his bill on the previous Saturday."

"Other way about, Bump. He goes racing on the Monday and therefore can't pay on the following Saturday."

"If Miss Hoping hadn't got a soft spot for him, we should have heard more about it."

"He calls her by her Christian name, Eva. Pronounced Evva, behind her back. Ever Hoping," smiled Honor. "I think I had better tell her, and the soft spot will harden."

Bump went and sat down beside her.

What an attractive kid it was, and how priceless. Best man in the team except . . . Yes, and that reminded him.

"Sir Russell said any more about Rodd?" he asked.

"Yes, in point of fact, he had a growl about him yesterday afternoon when we were playing golf. Richard is undoubtedly getting on his nerves, and he had got it in for the poor chap, good and proper. It'll come to a show-down before long, and I don't know what we shall do. Funny . . . the old boy is not what you'd call vindictive or spiteful, I should say, but he can't stand 'that damned fellow Rodd,' as he calls him, at any price. And he hinted that he wasn't going to, much longer, either."

"What's behind it, Honor?"

"Oh, Doctor Fell, I think."

" 'The reason why I cannot tell,' eh?"

" 'The reason why,' he doesn't tell, anyhow. I asked him, plump out, what he had got against him, and he hummed and ha'd . . . 'Couldn't stand him. Didn't like him. Hated the sight of him! . . .' I asked him whether he had ever found Rodd impudent, disrespectful, or lacking in his duty in any way."

"What did he say to that?"

"Admitted promptly that he disliked his manner intensely; but as to impudence or disrespect, he had never yet met the man who had shown him either of those things, and he hoped, for the sake of the man unknown, that he never would. 'Oh, no; he'd deal with impudence and disrespect all right. *Ha! Hrmmph!* No, he didn't like the feller. . . . He didn't think he was the right man in the right place; and although he was not one to make mischief of any sort at any time, and, still less, one to be the cause of a man losing his job without excellent reason, and all that, he was going to have a serious talk with you about the feller. Very serious.'"

"Yes. A serious talk's what I've been funking for some time," said Bump. "Rather avoiding the old bird accordingly. I simply can't sack Rodd."

"If he goes, I go too," announced Honor with tragic grimace and sepulchral voice.

"Arm in arm. Out in the snow," grinned Bump. "And he'll lay his life's savings at your feet and ask you to take a taxi . . . No. We can't sack Rodd."

"Of course we can't, and we simply can't offend Sir Russell. Though between ourselves, Bump, I'd like to."

"Good Lord! Why?"

"Loves me. Loves me not. Loves me, I'm afraid."

"Good Lord! *You*? Why?"

"Yes, me, and why not?"

"Has he said so?"

"No; and, like you, I'm funking it, and going to avoid the old bird accordingly, in future. I should have been for it, on the golf links yesterday, if I hadn't kept on dragging Rodd in. Red herring. Red rag to a bull, too. I don't know how much he loves me, but, by gum, he hates Rodd all-right."

"Gad! More trouble. Stave it off, Pup, as long as you possibly can. If he proposes, and you turn him down, I suppose he'd go."

"Might. Might hang on for another shot. I get the idea some-whence that he'd hardly think I was serious if I said 'No' to him."

"It would have to be 'No,' I suppose, child?"

"What do you think, Grandpa?"

"Well, he's a rich man. . . . You'd be settled for life, and . . ."

"I should, indeed. Quite settled. Would you like to see me marry him?"

"Why doesn't somebody answer that blasted bell?" cried Bump, springing to his feet. "That's about the seventieth time this week I've answered the damn thing myself. . . . Go and hold Miss Wymper's thumb, there's a darling."

§2

That evening Bump, groomed and sprucely dressed for dinner, was down in the big hall as usual before the other guests assembled for the pre-prandial cocktail, that being one of the daily occasions upon which he played host, tried to keep as closely as possible in touch with each of his established guests, and to make the better acquaintance of new-comers.

It was, he felt, a good custom: and it was a good *quart d'heure*. Nor did the fact that a few wealthier guests improved the shining hour with rounds of cock-tails detract from his or their satisfaction. The bar was, alas, the most paying feature of the guest-house.

As he stood warming himself before the roaring fire—thank God wood cost nothing; and the vast old fire-place had been built for logs—Sir Russell Bemmington slowly descended the grand staircase, that staircase down whose broad balustrade Bump had swooped to shoot headlong into the middle of the hall and earn his nickname.

Dear old Uncle. What a kind good heart that grim old man had denied and hidden.

"Well, young man. Have a cocktail?"

"Oh, later on, thank you, Sir Russell," replied Bump, intending that the knight should call for a dozen, thereby warming the cockles and the cold stomachs of certain poor brethren and sisters, while proportionately enriching the till.

"Oh, damn it all, boy, have a second one later on. What shall it be?"

"Thanks. Dry Martini," and Bump touched the bell.

The service door opened and Richard Rodd appeared.

Bump glanced from Sir Russell Bemmington to his factotum, who was almost literally that, nowadays—his man-of-all-work. For, alas, there was neither butler nor major-domo now, neither head-waiter nor hall-porter.

What a contrast—Sir Russell Bemmington, big,

florid, grizzled, a man of about fifty or so; hale,
healthy, hearty, in the pink of condition; his face
keen, sharp, with quick-glancing beady eyes under
their heavy bushy brows; longish inquisitive nose;
mouth completely hidden beneath its bushy dark
moustache: the servant lean, small and slender; his
lined, craggy features like pale granite; a grey man,
grey-haired, grey-eyed, grey-faced; mouth like a
trap, nose somewhat bent and broken; the face of a
man who had seen and known and borne many
things; sinned and suffered, probably—suffered
certainly. He was gazing not at his master but at Sir
Russell, and the level gaze was not one of love.

To Bump, imaginative and fanciful, it seemed
that the hard eyes, eyes like glass marbles, glinted
with hate, and that the tight mouth tightened the
more. A trick of firelight and a foolish fancy. . . .

"Dry Martini and a White Lady," snapped Sir
Russell curtly, before Bump could speak.

"Yes, Sir," bowed the servant, turning about and
vanishing through the swing-door.

"I detest that fellow. Can't think why you keep
him," growled Sir Russell.

"He's extraordinarily useful," replied Bump.
"Don't know what I should do without him.
Wouldn't willingly change him for three average
servants.

"Why do you dislike him, Sir?" he added. "Anything against him?"

"Only intense—dislike—if that's anything. Natural antipathy, plus . . . well . . ."

"Plus what?" pursued Bump, eyeing his cherished guest, his ever-ready and obliging backer,
friend and creditor, with a puzzled and worried
look.

"Well, I hardly like to put it into plain English.
Hate to do any fellow a bad turn. And, after all, I
can't prove it. At least, I haven't the proof here and

now. But I dare say I could prove it."

"Prove what, Sir?" asked Bump, raising eyebrows in surprise.

"Prove something of which I am perfectly certain —although I hadn't wanted to say anything until I had verified it. . . .

"Well now I have said too much or too little," he added. "But I should have had to warn you, sooner or later, in any case, for I know I'm right."

Bump stared.

Rodd re-entered the hall bearing a tray, which, bowing as he did so, he presented first to Sir Russell and then to Bump.

Lowering his voice almost to a whisper and tapping Bump impressively with a forefinger, Sir Russell Bemmington glanced after the servant as he again vanished through the service door.

"That man's been in prison," said he heavily.

"*What?* Richard? Richard Rodd been in prison?" exclaimed Bump.

"Richard Rodd—as he calls himself—has been in prison," nodded Sir Russell portentously. "Richard Rodd, as he calls himself, has done time. You can bet your boots on that. I'd stake my life on it."

"But . . . but . . . how do you know?"

"By the look of him. You can always tell a convict when you see one. At least, I can . . . I know."

"How?" asked Bump.

"Experience," replied his patron.

"Oh, yes?" said Bump, and realized that his remark, his voice, his expression, had all been— unfortunate, not to say insulting.

"Yes. Experience. I had a lot of it—in India. Took a very great interest in the subject. I'm a J.P., you know. And I was non-official specially-appointed Member of the Calcutta Prison Visiting Committee. Inspected and reported jointly with City Magistrate and all that. Little hobby of mine. Took it up again in England. Prisoners' Aid Society. Concerts and lectures for prisoners; and then meet 'em and help 'em on discharge. Very valuable Society that. Praiseworthy."

"I see, I see," observed Bump, a note of apology in his voice. "Philanthropic work."

"Well, I'm interested. Hobby of mine. I'm not sure that we are not wholly wrong in our Penal System. Wants reform. Different lines altogether. Reclamation and improvement, rather than vindictive punishment. Psychology of crime. A disease. A criminal's mentally sick; quite apart from bad influences in youth; heredity and environment and all that. What nine-tenths of them need is a doctor, an alienist, neurologist, psychologist. What they want is psychology, not stone walls and iron bars and skilly. . . . However, that's beside the point. What I say is that I know a convict when I see one; and that man of yours has done time—and a lot of it."

"Well, if that were so, what he wants is a doctor," smiled Bump, "a neurologist, an alienist. Psychoanalysis. Not the order of the boot from me."

"Yes, yes, that's all very well, my boy; but you don't want a convict about the place. A hospital rather than a gaol, by all means; cured by psychotherapy rather than by penal incarceration; but— cure before employment surely! You don't want to give an unreclaimed uncured criminal the run of a place like this. It's not fair to your guests, not to mention yourself, is it? Jewellery lying about, and money. You'll be having that safe of yours opened one of these days."

"Gad! He won't find much in it," smiled Bump ruefully. "But aren't we going ahead rather fast, Sir? Damn it all, the man has been here quite a while now, and he certainly hasn't pinched anything yet. And he's earned his salary twice over."

"Biding his time, if you ask me, my boy. I should say he had heard about the Cortenay treasure."

"Most people have," laughed Bump, "in this part of the world, anyway."

"Exactly; exactly. If you ask me, I should say he knows as much about it as you do, and a bit more."

"H'm! He could easily do that," laughed Bump again.

"Yes, that he could; and it's no laughing matter either, Bump. You haven't forgotten what happened to your uncle, have you?"

Instantly Bump stiffened, his face hardened, and with a curious gesture he turned his back upon Sir Russell Bemmington, and flung the remainder of his cocktail into the fire-place.

His friend and patron apparently noticed nothing.

"That's what is at the bottom of it, really, I've no doubt," he went on. "What accounts for my feeling of antipathy. The natural antipathy of—well, what shall we say—of the honest man for the crook . . . I don't like him, I don't trust him; and if you'll take my advice, you won't either."

"But I do like him," snapped Bump, scowling at the speaker.

Sir Russell sipped his drink.

"Well, if I were you, I certainly wouldn't trust him."

"But I do trust him," replied Bump curtly.

"Yes, I know you do; and I'm advising you against it, my boy. For you'll rue it. You know nothing about him."

"Nor do you, Sir," interrupted Bump.

"You know nothing about him, I was going to say, except that he was a vagrant, wandering from one spike—I mean casual ward—to the next; an idle, cadging, loafing vagabond . . ."

"Not very idle or loafing now, is he?" interrupted

Bump again. "And I don't think I've ever heard him cadging."

". . . who played the old faint-by-the-wayside trick on Miss Winter, and took her in completely. All credit to her kind heart, but more credit to her heart than her head," proceeded Sir Russell, steam-roller fashion.

"And the result?" asked Bump.

"That I've got the best servant we ever had here, an invaluable man," he answered his own question.

"And the result, from his point of view," continued Sir Russell, "is that he is biding his time. He landed on his feet in a soft job, and has had the sense to stick to it."

"Then what's the trouble?"

"Why, that you've got a man here, in a position of trust, of whom you know nothing whatsoever. As I say, a tramp off the road. He's got the run of the place, and . . . well, I don't like it. For your sake, I mean, my boy."

Bump turned to the fire-place without reply and kicked a log—hard.

"And when you say that I know no more about him than you do, I tell you I know he's a criminal, a . . ." continued the now somewhat pompous voice.

Bump turned swiftly about and faced Sir Russell Bemmington.

"A *what?*"

"A convict. A criminal. Any ex-convict is a criminal, isn't he? The fact that he is an ex-convict doesn't make him an ex-criminal, you know."

"That's a pretty heavy charge to bring against a man—without any real grounds for doing so," expostulated Bump. "Without any knowledge of his previous history, and by pure guess-work . . . Oh, come; really, Sir! Without any knowledge of the facts, any proof whatsoever!"

"Well, my boy, I don't make shots in the dark,

and I don't talk without my book," replied the older man solemnly. "When I say a thing is so, you may be pretty sure it *is* so. And I say that man of yours has been in prison. He's got a prison face. Hasn't he now? Typical broad-arrow mug. Look at his hands too. Criminal hands—and they've been in the stone-quarries for years. You can always spot stone-quarry hands. Another thing, he walks like an old lag. I don't mean as though he has had a ball and chain, gyves and fetters, though he may have done. But he always walks up and down, if you've noticed, when he is on duty in the hall and has got nothing to do. Can't stand still. And does he stroll the whole length of the back of it, from the service door across to that gong? No, he takes four steps each way, always, up and down, up and down, to and fro, to and fro, always the four steps of the same length, and turn about. Hands behind his back, head down."

"Why shouldn't he?" asked Bump.

"No reason why he shouldn't, at all. Every reason why he should—since he has walked up and down a cell for years on end, in just that attitude, just that number of paces."

Bump stared at the speaker in silence and held his gaze.

This was horrible. Beastly.

Sir Russell was a man whose judgment was to be respected, quite apart from the fact that he was also a man whose continued friendship was infinitely to be desired. Was, in fact, absolutely necessary. On the other hand, Richard Rodd had as much right to a fair hearing and consideration as had Sir Russell himself. Yes, damn it all, he wasn't going to listen to things like that behind a man's back, and not give him a chance to clear himself. Much less was he going to listen to things like that behind a man's back, and act on them—and Sir

Russell was pretty obviously leading up to an ultimatum. Having said what he had, he couldn't leave it at that. Nor could Bump.

He took a sudden resolution.

"I shall ask him," he said, "straight out. Send for him and say without any preliminary or palaver,

" 'Have you ever been in prison, because I am told you have. If so, when was it and what for?' And we'll see what he says."

Sir Russell Bemmington frowned at the rug at his feet.

"Suppose he denies it?" he said.

"I shall take his word for it. Believe what he says."

"Then I think you'll be wasting your time, my boy. Of course he'll deny it."

"Well, I shall have given him the opportunity of doing so, at any rate. One owes that much to anybody against whom an accusation like that is brought. It's not right."

"Otherwise," he added, realizing that he was speaking to Sir Russell Bemmington as he had never spoken to him before; realizing with an unpleasant sinking feeling that, judging by Bemmington's heavy frown and pursed lips, he was offending him, "It isn't right, otherwise, is it, Sir? Chap ought to know what is being said, and be given an opportunity of . . ."

"Suppose he admits it," interrupted the older man. "You'd have to get rid of him then, wouldn't you?"

"Well, I suppose so. Depend on what he had done. I mean, depend on . . ."

"Oh, come, come," expostulated Bemmington.

"Well, I mean he might admit having been in prison, but deny having committed any crime."

"He might," smiled the other, cynically. "Probably would. Certainly he would, if he thought you had found out that he had done time. Promptly admit it, and spin a hard-luck story about mistaken identity or circumstantial evidence that made him look guilty."

Bump felt for his cigarette-case.

"Well, do you know, Sir," he said, "I . . ."

"Yes?"

Bump took a cigarette and tapped it on the case, smiling as he put it in his mouth.

"I think I'd believe him."

Sir Russell Bemmington exploded. His snort of indignation might have been that of a peeved rhinoceros.

"Really, my dear chap—you are impossible. And just give this point a thought. If you are quite willing to take a risk for yourself, the risk of having a criminal, an ex-convict about you, have you the right to subject other people to the risk?"

"No, not if there were any actual risk," admitted Bump. "But really, Sir, we are all so poor here that I think it's the last place in the world in which a good up-and-coming criminal would waste his time. Except for yourself and General Botolph-Swales and Colonel Featherston, the rest of us wouldn't be worth holding-up, all in a row."

Sir Russell Bemmington finished his drink, threw his cigarette into the fire, turned upon his foolish young friend, and took him by the lapel of his dinner-jacket.

"Oh, my dear Bump," he growled, "do you *never* give a thought to the Cortenay treasure? . . . It's a magnet, my dear chap, a magnet."

"And has been," grinned Bump, "for over three hundred years."

"And as strong as ever," said Sir Russell Bemmington. "Hullo, here's Miss Cortenay. I mean Winter. Come along, little lady. What'll you have? Sherry or a cocktail? Come along, General, what's yours? Ah, here's Colonel Featherston. Have a drink, my boy?"

In a few minutes, the wide settee-surrounded space about the great old fire-place was crowded with the resident members of the Cortenay Old Hall Country Club, enjoying the kindly knight's hospitality as they awaited the boom of the old Burmese gong.

Anon, Richard Rodd, appearing from the service door, crossed the hall, and smote the gong several times. As its reverberations died down, and the guests trooped through the hall in the direction of the dining-room, Sir Russell laid his hand upon his young friend's arm.

"Believe me, I'm right, my boy. I never make mistakes about those poor fellows. I'm afraid you'll find I'm right, and decide that you will have to part with Rodd."

§3

Late that night, as Bump sat in the office, poring over account-books and bills, and occasionally eyeing with distaste the growing mass of correspondence requiring his personal attention, Richard Rodd knocked as usual at the door, and entered.

"Shall I lock up, Sir?" he said.

"Everyone gone up?"

"Yes, Sir."

"Everyone in?"

"Yes, Sir."

"Right. Lock up, Rodd, and then go to bed. Who's on duty?"

"Olberry, Sir."

"All-right, let him go off."

"Yes, Sir, thank you. Might I have a word with you when you've finished, Sir? Private."

"Why, yes. . . . Come up to my room when you've

been round and go off duty."

"Very good, Sir. Thank you."

What was this? Had Bemmington said anything to Rodd; or had the poor chap by any chance overheard something of what Bemmington had been saying before dinner? He had a rare booming voice, and if Rodd had listened at the service door, he might have heard something of what he said.

Or perhaps it was that Bemmington's manner had been so unfriendly that Rodd felt that he must "speak about it." That's what servants always said when they wanted to make some sort of protest or appeal. They must "speak about it." When they quarrelled with each other, they "had words."

Possibly he had "had words" with one of the staff, and was going to lodge a complaint. If so, he should get every support, for he would be in the right. Always was.

But it wouldn't be that. It was this wretched Bemmington business. Suppose Rodd had decided to forestall Sir Russell and go straight to his employer and tell him all about it. Perhaps he'd forestall Bump too, and tell him all about it before he said anything about this prison business. And what could one do—if it came to that?

Damn Sir Russell Bemmington. Bump didn't care whether Rodd had been in prison or not. At least, yes, he did care. He'd be very sorry to hear that the man was a convicted criminal, an exconvict; but, left to himself, he wouldn't sack him on that account.

Not a bit of it.

A man might be a convicted criminal, a longterm ex-convict, and be no worse than a great many people on whom no shadow of suspicion had ever fallen. Might be a great deal better, in point of fact. Still, there it was. A very nasty stigma. Especially if the trouble had been theft, robbery. Couldn't have a thief about the place.

But suppose it had been theft. Couldn't a man reform? Pay the penalty and start afresh? If he reformed only on the very lowest grounds—the real-ization that crime doesn't pay—still it was reform; and presumably that was the object of prison and punishment.

Surely when a man has been punished, there should be an end of it. The law had judged him, assessed his crime and its deserts—and given him those deserts. It wasn't fair, it wasn't right, to punish him again, keep on punishing him for the rest of his life, dismissing him from every job he got, and penalizing him a dozen times over, for the same offence.

Damn Bemmington. It was a rotten thing to do, trying to shake one's faith in a fellow-creature like this. Especially in a man whom one thoroughly liked and completely trusted; and the worst of it was—Bemmington had succeeded. He had shaken Bump's faith in Rodd because, although he had never noticed it before, he certainly noticed now, that Rodd undoubtedly did have the appearance of a man who had done time.

When one came to think of it, he did have the look of a convict. There was no getting away from it. Not hang-dog; and not exactly what one would call a criminal type; but, well, it was the sort of face one could well imagine seeing behind bars.

Yes, if poor old Rodd went to the staff Fancy-dress Ball as a convict, by gad, he'd look the part.

A curious thing. He had often wondered what Rodd reminded him of, what his appearance sug-gested; and he had thought it was a clean-shaven soldier, and that what he needed was a khaki tunic and cap.

Now he knew it wasn't that, really. It was a convict coat and cap.

A long term in prison would account for the curious skin; the queer colourless complexion, too, that never changed; never showed the slightest flush, whether from heat, exertion, or stress; the grim set look of the thin lips; the general appearance of having been up against it; been through it; the beaten, defeated, and yet defiant look that it had not, even yet, lost.

And when Honor had found him, undoubtedly his hair had been uncommonly short. Regular convict crop.

Bemmington was right. When Rodd was walking slowly, quietly, to and fro, that little ten-foot beat opposite the main entrance, head bent, eyes fixed on the floor, hands behind his back, he did of course remind one of something caged—and used to it; he did remind one of those poor beasts in zoos and menageries, lions, tigers, bears, that eternally went to and fro, the length of their narrow cage, four steps and turn about, four steps and turn about. . . .

Now he came to remember it, he had often wondered what Rodd was thinking of, as he went to and fro like that, in a brown study, always turning about at the same spot at each end of the beat, as though he had come up against an invisible obstacle. Obviously the habit of years. God knew how many years, poor devil. How many times he had noticed it, and wondered at the alert way in which he sprang out of his abstraction the moment a bell rang, or somebody came down the stairs or into the hall.

Yes, it was all too plain, now that Bemmington had spoken of it; and the reason all too clear, now that Bemmington had given it.

Rodd looked like a convict and behaved like one.

Bump rose from his desk and paced his office carpet.

Rot! . . . Rubbish! Bosh! . . .

What idiotic damnable nonsense he was talking —or thinking. What a colossal mountain to make out of a molehill. Sir Russell Bemmington was a silly old fool, and he himself was no better.

A pretty thing if every man on whose face suffering was stamped, seared, branded, so that it bore a look of somewhat hopeless patience, was to be accused of being an ex-convict!

A pretty thing if every man who had a habit of walking up and down on a short beat, in a sort of absent-minded brown study, was to be accused of being an ex-convict!

Pretty thin, bringing a charge like that against a man on the strength of his face and his walk.

Too bad of Bemmington altogether. It would serve him right if Rodd were told that it was he who had said it; told exactly what he had said, and his grounds for saying it.

Absolute rubbish!

And yet it was curious that Rodd should want to speak to him "privately" this particular night, a thing he had never wanted to do before.

Angrily Bump banged down the roll-top cover of his desk, locked it, switched off the light and left the office, locking the door behind him with a key from the bunch that he wore on his key-chain.

Proceeding by the grand staircase to the main landing, and thence by a corridor to the staircase that led to the corridor into which debouched the passage that led to his own bed-sitting room, the room which had once been his nursery, Bump threw himself down in his deep and comfortable arm-chair, flung a log on the fire, and proceeded to fill his pipe.

Confound Bemmington! Why couldn't he let well alone—for well it undoubtedly was. The proof of the pudding was in the eating, and nobody had missed so much as a postage-stamp since Rodd had been in the house. Suppose he had been in prison, suppose he were an ex-convict, what did it matter to anybody so long as he . . .

A knock at the door.

"Come in. . . . Well, Rodd, what is it?"

"If you could spare a few minutes, Sir. I know it is rather late, but I felt I wanted to speak to you, urgent."

"Yes, go on. Out with it."

"It's like this, Sir. Rather a difficult thing to say, but I don't quite know how to, er . . . It's a bit difficult and awkward. I don't like to . . ."

"Take your time, Rodd. And if you really feel you want to tell me . . . Something about yourself?"

"No, Sir. It's about this new man, Olberry."

"Oh? What's wrong? Not up to his work? Lazy?"

"It isn't his work, Sir. It's him."

"Giving trouble?"

"No, Sir. Not a bit of it. He doesn't want to give any trouble. It's . . . well, Sir, between ourselves—the man's been in prison."

Bump stared wide-eyed.

Had he heard aright?

Who had—been in prison?

Not Rodd, then? Olberry? It was Olberry who had been in prison, was it? . . . Prison! Prison! Had they all been in prison—himself included?

"*What?*" he said. "Olberry has been . . . ? *Olberry* or . . . ?"

"Yes, Sir. He's done time—and he's a bad lot."

Bump continued to stare open-mouthed as well as wide-eyed.

"So Olberry has been in prison, has he? It's Olberry now, eh?"

"Yes, Sir. Olberry has been in prison and he's a bad lot."

"How do you know he's been in prison?"

"Well, I had my suspicions of him, Sir, the moment I saw him."

"Yes, but why? . . . Has he got a prison face? A—er—typical broad-arrow mug? Or is it the way he walks—as though he's had a ball and chain on his leg?"

"Well, I don't know about all *that*, Sir."

"Does he walk up and down, as though he can't stand still? Just up and down; to and fro; about four steps each way, and then turn about?"

"Turn about, Sir?"

"Yes, with his hands behind his back and his head down, just as though he had walked up and down a cell for years on end. . . . Just that attitude. Just that number of paces."

Rodd seemed puzzled.

"Well, I don't know about that, Sir."

"Can't one always tell a convict that way?"

"I don't know, Sir, I'm sure. I couldn't say. I've never noticed."

"Oh, I see. It wouldn't be infallible then."

That appeared to be over Rodd's head, for his look of puzzlement deepened.

"Well now, how do you know that he's a—what is it?—'an old lag.' Isn't that it? How do you know that he's an ex-convict?"

"Well, Sir, I do know."

"When you say *know*, do you mean that you suspect it, or that you really know? It's a pretty heavy charge to bring against a man without any real grounds for doing so. Because you know, an ex-convict is a criminal, isn't he? The fact that he's an ex-convict doesn't make him an ex-criminal, you know."

"No, Sir. Well, this man Olberry, as he calls himself, is an ex-convict all-right; and he's a criminal all-right. He hasn't come here for any good; and I want you to get rid of him, Sir, at once."

"But I can't send for him and say, 'Look here, you're an ex-convict and a criminal, and you've got to go at once.' I have no proof that he's anything of the sort."

"No, Sir. No need for you to send for him at all, Give me permission to dismiss him and he'll go all-right. Go like a lamb, he will. Quick."

Bump rumpled his hair in deep perplexity.

What an extraordinary turn of events!

Here was Sir Russell Bemmington asking him to get rid of Rodd on the ground that he was an ex-convict and criminal; and here was Rodd asking him to get rid of Olberry for precisely the same reason. He'd have Olberry coming to him next and asking him to discharge the pantry-boy because he was an ex-convict and a criminal.

Damn it all, was this Cortenay Old Hall or Borstal New Hall, or what?

"Look here, Rodd, you haven't yet told me how you know that Olberry is a crook who's been in prison."

"No, Sir, I haven't, but I do know. And it's gospel truth."

"Don't you want to tell me how you know?"

"No, Sir."

That was interesting. Painfully interesting. Did it mean that Bemmington was right? Did it mean that Rodd had been in prison, and had recognized Olberry as a fellow-convict?

And how could he, in common justice, dismiss Olberry on Rodd's accusation, if he would not dismiss Rodd on Bemmington's accusation?

Well, the answer to that was an easy one. He believed in Rodd. He liked Rodd. And what was more, he simply couldn't afford to lose Rodd, to say nothing of the fact that Honor would never agree to his being discharged.

No, it couldn't be done without Honor's consent,

for Rodd was her property, so to speak.

That was the answer.

But he had said "in common justice," and this wasn't justice at all. Quite the reverse—to ignore the accusation against Rodd for those reasons, and yet to listen to the accusation against Olberry.

Rubbing his head, Bump perpended.

"Look here, Rodd," he said at length. "I can't discharge Olberry on the strength of an accusation like that, unless you tell me how you know the man's an ex-convict."

"Well, Sir, it's a bit difficult. I do know—and I could prove it. I'd be the last to want to get a man out of a job because he had had his little misfortunes, and done time—but . . ."

"Quite so," agreed Bump. "If he had done something wrong, and been punished, that's that."

"Yes, Sir. Quite so. Abserlutely," agreed Rodd with alacrity. "I'm with you every time there, Sir; and if I had happened to learn that this man Olberry had slipped up somewheres, and been put away for a bit, to think it over, I'd have been the first to say, 'Let bygones be bygones, and give him another chance.' But it isn't like that, Sir, at all, with Olberry. He's a bad lot and he isn't here for any good. Let me give him a week's wages and the boot, Sir, to-morrow."

"No," replied Bump. "Proof first. I want proof that the man's been in prison, and that he is what you say."

"Well, there'll be the proof, Sir. He won't appeal to you nor to anybody else. He'll go without a word. Give me permission to dismiss him, and he'll go. Isn't that proof enough?"

Bump scratched his head, looked from the grim eager face of Richard Rodd to that of the clock.

"Well, I won't decide now, anyway. I'll think it over, and tell you to-morrow. Good-night."

"Good-night, Sir, thank you," replied Rodd, and with apparent reluctance, turned and went slowly from the room.

Bump struck a match for his pipe which had gone out during the conversation, but he did not use it. Slowly it burned away as he stared at the flame in the throes of cogitation; for he had been seized of an idea.

Sir Russell Bemmington, so inimical to Richard Rodd and so certain that Richard Rodd was an ex-convict, had been served at table by the waiter Olberry for two or three weeks now. He had had every opportunity of studying not only his face but his hands; to observe not only his physical attitude when in repose—for they also wait who stand and serve—but his gait and perambulatory habits as well. And apparently Bemmington had found no fault in him. Bemmington's suspicions had not been aroused, it seemed. He had seen nothing wrong about the man; or if he had, nothing had been said on the subject. And since he had noticed Rodd so carefully, he must have noticed the other man, surely. Or had he watched Rodd simply because he disliked him so?

What about turning Bemmington on to Olberry and asking him to do a little more smelling-out, exercise his valuable witch-finding faculties a little further, and pronounce upon Olberry too?

Certainly he was not a particularly attractive specimen, but if everybody were to be penalized on that score, there would be a lot of folk in trouble. It might go hardly with not a few of the guests, as well as the personnel of Cortenay Old Hall. What about Colonel Stockling, for example? What about Major Quelph, not to mention old Shelver, and one or two more? If Rodd and Olberry were to be branded as ex-convicts on the strength of appearances, the other three might well be written down as gallows'-

birds, gentlemen though they were—or had been.

Yes, that was the idea. Before he did anything else, he'd turn Bemmington on to Olberry. And then it might be as well to look into Olberry's record, as far as possible. And yet that didn't really seem fair either, for he had never made the slightest attempt to probe into Rodd's past.

What about leaving it to Bemmington? And if Bemmington said,

No, he felt perfectly sure that Olberry was all right, he'd take no further notice of what Rodd had said.

If, on the other hand, Bemmington said,

Yes, by Jove, he was right, there were *two* of them, it might be as well to let Rodd dismiss the man. One suspect would be enough.

Anyway, probably Bemmington wouldn't rest until he had had Olberry on the carpet. Perhaps the Prisoners' Aid Society would know something about him. And of course, "Olberry" would be an *alias.* Then, possibly, Bemmington would start talking about photographs and finger-prints.

Well, well . . . ! And on the whole, damn Bemmington. Why couldn't he let well alone. Then as far as that went, presumably he ought to say, "Damn Rodd—why couldn't *he* let well alone," for Rodd was doing for Olberry precisely what Bemmington had done for Rodd.

An interesting thought! . . . If he said anything to Bemmington about Olberry, and Bemmington decided to pronounce against the man, wouldn't Bemmington at once say,

"Yes, there you are, my boy, what did I tell you? Two of them—and they are in league."

Well, he could checkmate him there by saying,

"Not a bit of it, my dear Bemmington, for it was Rodd who denounced Olberry to me, and asked me to sack him."

But, then Bemmington would cock his eye and wag his finger and say,

"Yes, quite so. They've quarrelled, and when thieves fall out . . ."

Oh, Lord! . . . As if there weren't trouble enough, without . . .

And ruefully again Bump scratched his head.

Sufficient unto the day, anyway—and time to go to sleep.

§4

A couple of hours later, Richard Rodd suddenly sat up in bed; at one moment sound asleep, at the next, wide awake, alert, listening.

Now that he combined with many other duties some of those of night-porter, he slept on a camp bed in a little room opening out of what had been the butler's pantry, a den in which he was advantageously placed for hearing the front-door bell, should any benighted wayfarer arrive or any forgotten reveller return; for watching over the big silver-safe, really a miniature strong-room, the door of which was in the wall opposite his bed; for making a swift occasional tour of the hall, smoking-room, billiard-room, dining-room, ball-room, drawing-room and the rest of the ground-floor premises, should he be urged thereto by fancied smell of burning or sound of movement.

For Richard Rodd preferred to include in the varied list of his duties of night-porter, those of night-watchman and fireman as well.

And in his sleep, he had fancied he had heard a sound, slight but unaccountable and therefore suspicious, though unidentifiable now that he was awake.

What had it been that had disturbed him? A crack, or fall, of a log in the great hall fire-place—

one of those small explosions that occasionally do occur where heavy logs are used as fuel, and smoulder almost throughout the night; the opening or closing of a door or a window; the slight movement of a piece of furniture with which someone had gently collided in the dark; the creak of a stair-tread; a surreptitious foot-step; the click of a latch or catch; the dropping of some small object?

One of these things or something similar. Possibly one of those noises inevitable in an old house of which much of the furniture is co-æval with the rooms in which it stands.

But he doubted it. He did not think that that sort of noise would wake him nowadays, any more than legitimate sea-noises would wake a sailor in a ship, although quite a small sound that was strange and unusual would bring him up "all standing."

Motionless, he listened intently, inexplicably but intuitively feeling that the sound that had awakened him was what he termed a wrong 'un, a noise made by a wrong 'un, in other words. It had fairly knocked him out of sleep, straight up on end; and that did not happen with creaks and groans of boards, stairs, panelling, old furniture or shifting fire-logs.

Could it be that silly old drunk, Colonel Datson, trying to get into the bar again? Hardly likely. The Guv'nor had told him that if he did it again he would have to ask him to go; and when the old boy had said he had been walking in his sleep, the Boss had said, well, next time he'd be walking in his wake. Was he giving the old boy a dig that he'd be having a "wake" before long if he didn't keep off the booze? Quite funny, the Guv'nor was, sometimes.

No, he wouldn't do it again; but there'd be some money in the till and in the diddler too. And somebody might be after that. Olberry . . . perhaps.

Getting out of bed, Rodd put his feet into felt-soled slippers, took his overcoat from a hook, buttoned it over his pyjamas, and felt, in its capacious side-pockets, for his electric torch in the left, and the Popper in the other.

The Popper was an instrument some fifteen inches long, with a knob of the size of a hen's egg at one end and a smaller one at the other, from which depended a wrist-thong of leather. Apparently the instrument consisted of fine wire very tightly woven, but this appearance was deceptive, for, beneath the wire, the knob at either end was a ball of lead, and the stem connecting them was of whalebone of the thickness of a man's thumb.

Noiselessly as a bat, Rodd crept from his den into the pantry, from the pantry into the corridor, and thence to the great hall. There, still as a statue, he stood for some five minutes listening intently. Hearing no sound, he switched on his torch and made a complete tour of the great rooms, shining the light of his torch upon doors and windows. Finding nothing wrong, he returned to the hall and then made an equally careful inspection of the servants' quarters and back premises. No door or window escaped the quick beam of his torch, a glance being sufficient to show that not only was each one closed, but properly fastened.

Opening the inner door of a scullery that looked out on to a small brick courtyard, he illuminated its window. Closed and fastened. Its door. Closed and unfastened, the top and bottom bolts drawn back, the lock turned back.

There it was. He had felt it in his bones.

With pursed lips and contracted brows, Rodd considered the door. An inside job, very obviously. There had been no tool used on that door; and if whoever had got in had been going to use a tool to force an entry, it would not have been by way of that door that he would have come.

No, a clear inside job. Those bolts had been withdrawn and the key turned, since he made his rounds before going up to the Guv'nor's room.

And who had been on late duty?

Olberry, of course.

And Olberry had come and done this job while he, Rodd, was talking to the Guv'nor upstairs.

Had they gone? Was the sound that he had heard the careful shutting of the door as they went out; or had he heard them creep past, under his window? Or was he going ahead a bit too fast? Mightn't it be that Olberry himself had cleared off?

No; why should he? He couldn't get what they were after, he wasn't cracksman enough, the miserable mumper. Pinching pennies out of a blind man's tin would be more in his line.

No, he had let the others in. That was what he was here for. Planted. Planted here for the job. All he was good for.

Very neat. Nice quiet job. The question was—had they got what they came for?

Might not have gone yet.

Who would it be? Bosher Kelly and Jimmy the Goat? They were both out now, and this was the way they worked. Always put somebody inside.

Well, he'd put the damn lot of them 'inside' if they came butting-in on his place. If it was Bosher Kelly they'd be bound to have a look at the safe before they went. Bosher could no more pass a safe than a dog could a lamp-post.

Well, well . . . Pity he couldn't hang it up on Mister Soapy Olberry.

A few minutes later, Richard Rodd, moving absolutely noiselessly on the thick carpet of the corridor, crept to the door of the Library—one of the very few rooms in Cortenay Old Hall that was marked

Private, and strictly kept so, by Bump's order.

The Library contained not only a fine collection of books and the few remaining ancestral portraits by Old Masters, but his private safe and some old muniment chests in which were papers and documents invaluable to members of the Cortenay family.

Pausing and listening for a minute at the door, his torch in his right hand and the Popper dangling from his wrist, Rodd stood silent, tense, straining to hear any sound that might be audible to human sense, as slowly, slowly, gently, noiselessly, he turned the handle.

When it would turn no further, slowly, slowly, gently, noiselessly, he opened the door, and at once realized that his quick hearing had not failed him, for, as he did so, a crack appeared between door and jamb, a faint illumination was perceptible, and he knew that light from an electric torch was turned upon the safe.

Throwing the door open, he switched on all the electric lights of the room, and two men, bending down in front of the safe, sprang round and faced him.

"Why, Henery!" exclaimed Richard Rodd in genial tones, "whatever *are* you doin'?"

§5

Richard Rodd closed the heavy door and, leaning comfortably back against it, folded his arms and eyed the intruders.

So he had been right, had he? Quite right. Except for his guess at the identity of the yeggs. Not Bosher Kelly and Jimmy the Goat, but only Henery the Eighth, so called because his name was Henry Hyam, and Kike Lipsky. A poor lot, just the sort that Olberry would be working for.

Bosher Kelly and Jimmy the Goat would have done the thing properly. Oxy-acetylene lamp and such. Nor would they have been caught this way, like rats in a trap, either. Windows shut and fastened, and the door closed behind them. And hadn't even locked themselves in. . . .

The last attack on that safe had been made, single-handed, by a better workman than the two of them put together. Came in through the window, opened the safe, and got away again. Yes, but like a fool he had done murder, and turned what was only a five-year-stretch job into a hanging matter. And perhaps this pair were just as big fools, though neither of them had made a move to his pocket to pull a gun.

Well, if they weren't armed, for two pins he'd dot the pair of them. Yes, and turn them over to the Police, and Olberry with them.

The nerve of them! . . . Butting-in like this. Who did they think they were—and what did they think they were after, anyway?

"Whatever *are* you doin' of, Henery?" he repeated.

"Me? Shrimpin'," replied Mr. Henry Hyam, *alias* Henery the Eighth Hy-am Hy-am.

"And what's your little boy doin', Henery? Paddlin'?" pursued Rodd, turning the unnecessary light of his torch upon the other man. "What's our Kike doin' of?"

"Carryin' the bucket," growled Henry. "To 'old the shrimps."

"Ain't got many yet, 'ave you?" enquired Rodd.

"Not yet," admitted Henry.

"No, nor ain't likely to," observed Rodd.

"Whatever made you think there was any in these parts?" he continued. "You bin gettin' a bit of misinformation from somebody? That Salvation Army trombone-trumper, Olberry, been leadin' you astray?"

"Olberry? Olberry?" enquired Henry, straightening himself up.

"Yes, Olberry—twice," agreed Rodd.

'Don' know him."

"You don't say? Well, I'll introduce him by-and-by. You'll like 'im. You'll like 'im so much you'll want to take him along with you, all the way back to London. You'll do it, too. And you'll keep him there," prophesied Rodd.

"And you'll keep yourself there too, if you know where's healthy," he added. "And your little boy, Kike, too."

Kike Lipsky acknowledged the reference by spitting.

"Oh, you *dirty* dawg!" reproved Rodd. "Where are yore manners? Disgrace to your country, if you 'ad one. Like you are to your profession."

"Chatty to-night, vasn't you?" snarled the man reproved. "Vat you doin' here, anyvay?"

"He's in with Gent Jannison," said Henry Hyam quickly. "Olberry has done it on us."

" 'Course he has," observed Rodd. "Aren't you the shining lights—to let a fish-faced wooden-legged pick-pocket, like that, fetch you all the way down here? Never said a word about Gent Jannison, I suppose?"

"On'y that he was lyin' up here," replied Henry.

"Then what did you suppose he was doin' that for? His 'ealth?" growled Rodd.

"Cripes! It won't be for yours, when he hears about it," he added.

"Well, 'ow was we to know? That bastard Olberry never told us that Gent Jannison and you was 'ere on this job."

"What job?" growled Rodd.

"Shiners. Olberry said there was a hatful of shiners . . ."

"What, in that tin safe?" sneered Rodd savagely.

"Ar. Olberry said the Cortenay Treasure 'ad been found and been put in. . . ."

"*Olberry* said," snarled Rodd, the cutting contempt of his voice like a whip-lash. "*Olberry* said. You make me tired. You make me sick. *Olberry!* Why doesn't he go back to keeping *cave* for street-corner bookies—if he could get the job again. And why don't you two go back to pinchin' washin' off the hedge. About all you are fit for. Take your Olberry and let him knock at the front door while you sneak shirts off the back garden clo'es-line. . . . *Shiners!* . . . *Here!* . . . And you two ham-fisted plumbers thinkin' you could lift them, if they was. Before Gent Jannison could. You'd show him how, eh? Why, you couldn't open a sardine tin, between you. Not with a patent fool-proof tin-opener. Not without cuttin' y'r fat fingers, bustin' the fish and spillin' the gravy. . . . 'Ere, come on! Clear out. Bung off—before I change me mind. For two pins I'd go and fetch Gent Jannison and let 'im 'ave a look at you. And for less than that I'd ring-up Whitebay Harbour and put you away."

"You vould, vould you?" growled Lipsky.

"Ar! And who'd blame me? Another word out of you, you Hungarian ghetto-louse, and I'll tap you on the dome, you enemy-alien Russian barber's Pole."

"You? *Me?*" whispered Lipsky, as his hand went to his pocket.

"Yes, you, you Buljarian bed-bug."

And Richard Rodd, changing his torch to his left hand, gripped the Popper in his right.

Henry Hyam turned angrily upon his colleague.

"Stow it, you blasted fool," he growled. "Keep that for Olberry—and thank your lucky stars you got the chance. Come on out of this. It's Gent Jannison's lay."

"Yes, you wait a minute, though," growled Rodd. "Stick your faces against that wall, both of you, and put your hands up. Go on, quick."

"Go to it, Kike," growled Henry and, like Hezekiah, turned his face unto the wall, his example grudgingly followed by the growling Kike.

"Now then," snapped Rodd, "I'm going to frisk you, Kike Lipsky, and if your hands come down an inch, by the living God I'll cosh you. Fer keeps."

And with no gentle touch he tapped him on the head with the Popper.

"You keep still, Kike," advised Henry, "unless you want to do a stretch."

"A stretch for his neck," growled Rodd, deftly whipping an automatic from the side-pocket of Kike's reefer coat.

"There's a fool for you," he added. "There's a bone-headed mug. Doesn't know better than to go about with a thing like that on him. And coming on an inside job too, with a red carpet laid down, flood-lighting and a band playin'—pretty near. And he brings a gun so that when he falls down the stairs, or knocks a pile of tin pails off a shelf on to a stone floor, so that a bald-headed pot-bellied country policeman in bed a mile away can't help catching him, he's caught with a gun in his pocket! Sort of silly bastard that'd pull it out too. Ar, and point it at somebody, I shouldn't be surprised."

"Oh, come off it, Potsy," growled Henry.

"Yes, and I'm ashamed of you, Henry," continued Rodd, busy with lightly-moving hands. "Even you know better than to do a thing like that, and I should 'ave thought you'd 'ave known better than to let 'im do it. It's all very well, taking your little boy out for the evenin', but there's no need to let him bring all his toys with 'im, is there?"

Mr. Lipsky made a noise which may have been a remark in Hungarian, Russian, Polish, 'Buljarian' or Yiddish.

"Now then," continued Rodd, stepping back. "Don't forget—if I uses this gun, it's self-defence, and I leaves the Court without a stain on me character and something out of the Poor Box in me pocket too. And let either of you move till I tells you to, and you gets the works, quick. So keep still; don't turn your heads round; and don't let me catch you listenin'."

Whether listening or not, the two cracksmen heard soft sounds of steel upon steel, a click, and the other almost inaudible noises attendant upon the opening of a safe-door.

"Ar! That's all right," announced Rodd a minute later. "You've been and spoke the truth, Henery. It does 'appen that way sometimes. . . . No, the two of you couldn't get inside the safe. Not even with all these gadgets. Not even an ole biscuit box like this. Well, well. . . ."

Rodd closed the safe-door, rose to his feet and eyed his captives.

"All-right. Hands down and turn about. And do exactly what I tell you. You go first, Henery, you 'avin' a glimmerin' of sense, at times. . . . No, you can't take the junk. . . . What, won't be able to earn your livin' without your kit? Takin' the bread out of your mouth? Garn, you couldn't get bread out of a baker's cart with that lot o' rubbish. 'Ardly fit for a plumber's mate to keep to leave at 'ome and go back for. Go on—push off . . .

"Give you back your gun, Kike? No, I won't. Serve you right if I did. Now then, quick march, back the way you came. You can show your torch, Henery, and I'll shine mine on Kike's 'ead—just where I'm goin' to 'it 'im—if either of you makes a mistake."

And a slow silent procession, walking delicately, made its way from the Library to the servants' quarters and an unfastened scullery door.

"Now," said Richard Rodd, as Henery opened the door, "beat it. Get out o' this quicker 'n a bat out of Hell—but take care of yourselves and mind how you go—if you don't want a long holiday. I recommends the milk-train from Crochester. . . . It'll give you plenty of time to wait for our Mr. Olberry. He'll be comin' that way soon. He'll be wantin' his share of the shiners!"

And Richard Rodd laughed softly.

§6

At seven o'clock next morning, Bump's cherished factotum brought him his usual morning tea and a piece of curious, if not disturbing, information. The waiter Olberry had disappeared.

He had gone in the night, without notice given or received.

He had gone, and what was more remarkable, he had gone without a certain small sum due to him in wages.

"Yes, Sir," Richard Rodd assured his master. "His bed has been slep' in. No, Sir, I didn't take it upon me to give him notice. And I give you my word I said nothing at all to him about having informed you that he had been in prison."

"Well, this is most extraordinary, Rodd. You came and spoke to me about him at midnight, asking me to dismiss him or let you dismiss him, and by six the following morning he has—dismissed himself."

"Guilty conscience, if you ask me, Sir."

"What? You think he had an idea that you suspected him?"

"Yes, Sir, I do think he had an idea that I suspected him."

"And he just cleared off before anything was

said. Looks as though he was afraid he might be given in charge."

"Yes, Sir," agreed Rodd. "I think he was. He's gone, anyway. Well, Sir, if you ask me, it's a case of good riddance to bad rubbish."

Sitting up in bed and eyeing the face of the speaker, Bump passed a hand through his tousled hair, in great perplexity.

It certainly was a queer business.

Anyway, Olberry was probably no great loss. It would be a very different matter if it had been Rodd.

Would Rodd also clear off suddenly in this guilty fashion if he knew what Bemmington had been saying?

He had told Bemmington that he would speak to Rodd on the subject, ask him straight out whether he had ever been in prison; but supposing Rodd—whether he admitted or denied the charge—cleared off like this; simply bolted as this fellow Olberry had done?

Anyway, "Never rush your fences" was a good motto. He'd bide his time, think about it, and take this particular fence very carefully.

Meanwhile, what about talking it over with Honor. But then Honor was impulsive, and would want to rush straight off and tackle Bemmington about it, and Rodd too. She'd be highly indignant, and probably say things to Bemmington that were better not said at all.

He must keep it quite clearly before his mind, that if they couldn't afford to lose Rodd, still less could they afford to lose Bemmington.

IX

Unusually depressed in spirit, worried in mind, and anxious in thought, Bump descended the stairs, glanced round the lovely old hall, vast, lofty, panelled and scarcely changed in the least detail since it was first inhabited; looked, as usual, into the office, the billiard-room, smoking-room, lounge, drawing-room and ball-room; and then proceeded to the galleried banqueting hall, now breakfast-, luncheon-, and dining-room for the hotel guests, otherwise the Resident Members of the Cortenay Old Hall Country Club.

His first glance was at his own table in a distant corner. No, Honor was not there, and Bump was distinctly sensible of increased depression.

"Good-morning, Mrs. Wayde," he said, stopping at the first occupied table.

The young and pretty woman looked up from the empty plate at which she was staring with tragic eyes, and relaxed the white-knuckled grip of the empty hand that rested beside it.

"Any news yet?" he asked.

For a second she stared at Bump, apparently uncomprehending, unseeing.

"News?" she said, focussing her tired eyes on Bump's, and obviously bringing her thoughts with an effort to the present and the place.

"News? No, nothing. No offers at all; and we can't keep it going another month. I must fetch Mary from school this week, if I can find the fare. But what to do with her, I . . ."

Bump passed on, gently touching the again clenched hand, as he did so.

Tears coming, poor dear, and he couldn't stand

that.

Rough luck. Comfortably off on a Saturday and ruined on the Monday; practically penniless, and only the newspaper to tell them so, as they sat at breakfast. Just—*crash.*

As if times weren't difficult enough without that villainous scoundrelly swindler failing for millions like that, and blowing his filthy brains out, to escape punishment.

Had to clear out of their beautiful home and come to his Hotel, at four guineas a week, while they tried to sell the house on which they could not pay the property-tax, or keep gardeners to save the lovely grounds from going to a wilderness. . . . And poor Wayde tramping the City, from office to office; and about as much use at earning a living as—yes, as Bump Cortenay himself. . . . What on earth would they do when the last of their little money was gone; their house, a drug on the market, deteriorating to its worth in bricks and mortar and . . .

Well, well, we've all got our troubles. He'd keep the Waydes on at the Hall as long as he possibly could. But he was supposed to be trying to make the place pay, and was up to his neck in debt to Bemmington already.

But as a matter of practical politics, what could they do, where could they go, when they left the Hall? And they weren't the sort of people who'd stay on for long when they couldn't pay, however cordially he invited them to do so.

"Morning, Colonel," he said, passing a neighbouring table.

Colonel Kinloch Grant glanced up.

"Morning, Cortenay," he said, making to rise to his feet. "I say, I'm awfully sorry but I . . . sorry that I . . ."

"Now, now, Colonel, don't. Please don't. Not the

slightest hurry. Make me most uncomfortable."

And laying his hand upon the Colonel's shoulder, he pressed him back into his chair.

Poor old chap! How on earth did he keep so spruce? Keep going at all? Every week of his life his bill was precisely the same—four guineas. Not one farthing spent upon himself for anything whatever. Never a drink—and that, presumably, was why he would never accept one—never a cigar or cigarette; never an 'extra' of any sort or kind; and took his golf by watching other people play. Evidently a fine golfer too, by the excellent advice he gave, and the occasional magnificent shot he made when appealed to by a novice.

One would have thought any Golf Club would have jumped at the chance of getting him as Secretary. A damn shame to write a chap off because he was sixty. But one could hardly blame them for preferring a man of thirty when they could get him at the same price. And God knew officers were going cheap to-day. Perhaps things would be easier for him when his son got through Sandhurst and his daughter left school.

A beautifully-arrayed and handsome young man, with a weak pleasant face, sauntered up.

" 'Morning, Cortenay. 'Morning, Colonel. Either of you want a really good thing for to-day? Hundred to eight outsider, and an absolute cert. It's a job."

"So are you," growled Colonel Kinloch Grant, looking up at him. "Worst job God ever made."

"No, no," laughed Archie Wilbraholme. "Best job ever the Devil made. . . . Can you raise eight pounds, Bump?"

"I could raise my boot," was the reply.

"Because if you can raise eight pounds, put it on Moonbeam in the three o'clock to-day, and you'll get a hundred Jimmy o'Goblins. Price won't shorten. Could you raise four, Colonel, and get fifty; or two, and make a useful twenty-five?"

"I don't put my money on moonbeams—any more," replied the Colonel.

"Well, well, Sir; don't say I didn't try to do you a good turn. Couldn't you do with a hundred, Bump?"

"Look here, my lad, is it an absolute cert?"

"Nothing more certain in this uncertain world."

"Certain as the weather," growled the Colonel.

". . . Simply can't lose. Why, bless my soul, if we could get up a syndicate and raise eight hundred pounds, do you realize that we should make ten thousand? It's a gift."

"How much are you putting on yourself, Wilbraholme?"

"Eight of the best."

"Then it's absolutely certain you'll have a hundred pounds on Monday morning?"

"Can't help it, old bean. Couldn't dodge it if I wanted to. No stopping it. One hundred, marked in plain figures on a pink cheque from Todding the Top-notcher. . . . The Old Firm. *'Todding Never Troubles You. See the Sporting Press.'* One hundred on Monday morning."

"Good," said Bump. "Very good. Then *I* can safely count on being paid on Monday."

"By Todding?"

"No. By you. Little account."

Archie Wilbraholme laughed, somewhat sheepishly.

"Oh, rather! Er—I must be pushing along."

"And to think that damned young fool had the finest start in life a man ever had," grumbled the Colonel, watching Wilbraholme as he swaggered from the room. "Could have looked forward to commanding a Guards Battalion, if not The Brigade. And to be *here* at his age."

Bump winced.

"Next step, Rowton House or the dust-bin," he thought, and turned to find that Lady Grace, who had been watching him with basilisk eye, was beckoning.

" 'Morning, Lady Grace."

"Will you please look at this table-cloth?" was the reply.

Bump put up a monocle and examined the impugned table-cloth with apparent and deep interest, which changed to sad concern.

"Gad!" he said. "Smuts."

"Yes, smuts," replied Lady Grace bitterly. "*And* in the sugar. *And* in the milk."

"Gad!" whispered Bump again. "What can have happened?"

"I can tell you what happened," said Lady Grace. "A puff of smoke happened, and reached as far as my table. . . ."

"Well, you would have it nearest to the fire, Lady Grace."

"That's no reason why I should have it covered with smuts, is it? What I suggest is that you have the sweep; and the sooner the better."

"And the sweeper the . . . sweeper," agreed Bump. "I can't tell you how sorry I am."

"And I can't tell you how disgusted I am. Never in my life . . ."

"No, no; it's terrible . . . inexcusable. The chimney shall be swept at once. I'll do it myself after breakfast if . . ."

And Bump passed on, hating Lady Grace, if possible more bitterly than before.

"Damned old hag!" he thought. "No, no, mustn't say that, poor old dear. Milk of human kindness gone a bit sour. That's all, really. Enough to turn anybody's—er—nature . . . Losing her husband like that. Been far better if he had died."

"Hullo, Critchleigh. 'Morning, Barbara. Merry

and bright, as usual."

Good stuff, the Critchleighs. Kept the flag flying. Go down with it flying too. Die game. If the policeman's job he was after failed, and nothing else turned up, they were going into domestic service as a married couple. Damned lucky employer who got 'em, too. He'd have jumped at the chance of getting them himself; only it wouldn't do. Couldn't see Barbara cleaning fire-places, and Reggie Critchleigh, late Cavalry, in a livery or a green apron. Besides, he couldn't afford to pay the wages they were worth to anybody who wanted whole-hearted, ungrudging service.

Bump reached his table, looked round the dining-room, noted attitudes, demeanours, faces. Fine, war-broken, slump-shattered men and women—defeated, beaten, down, out . . .

"*God!*" said he to himself as he sat down. "*Oh, my kind, loving God . . . !*"

Saturday night was the good time, the high light, of life at Cortenay Old Hall. There was a weekly dance, and to it came non-resident members of the Cortenay Old Hall Country Club, from houses in the neighbourhood; from Whitebay and Sandhaven; from London and elsewhere.

The residents, the four-guinea guests, went gay with a hectic gaiety which Bump found a little more distressing than the quiet courage, the gloom, the patience, the sad anxiety or the depressing misery with which they endured the week.

On these occasions Sir Russell Bemmington was invaluable, a tower of strength and, even better, a fountain of good liquid cheer. With him everyone must drink, and it seemed to give the kindly gentleman real pleasure to lead, here a one and there another, to unburden himself or herself, to pour forth all troubles, make confidence of hopes and fears, and generally to appoint kind Sir Russell Bemmington the Father Confessor.

It was amazing, the things that people told him, and the amount that he learned about their past, their present circumstances, and their future intent. Not a few, indeed a majority, especially of the women, consulted him about their poor investments, told him the story of their losses, and appealed to him to turn them into gains.

And after the dance, the supper, and the general dispersal, when those who had come for the evening had departed; the week-enders, the bridge-fiends, the billiard-addicts and the private-room parties scattered to their respective haunts, the Old Brigade held session about the great fire-place of the main hall, settees, divans and arm-chairs forming a rectangular zareba about it, with an inner supporting line of ancient oak coffin-stools and low tables, for bottles, glasses and ash-trays.

The Old Brigade, known also to themselves as the Old Contemptibles, was a Club within the Club.

To it there was no election, nor was there exactly co-option. When a vacancy occurred—literally a vacancy, for members always occupied the same arm-chair or the same place on the three-seater settees —someone, somehow, by a kind of natural selection or the invitation of a member, occupied it for an evening. In some cases such guests of the Old Brigade never occupied the seat again, sometimes he or she occupied it thenceforth.

Nor was membership of the Old Brigade entirely a matter of seniority. Resident guests of the Cortenay Old Hall Country Club there were who had never dreamed of entering the sacred square about the fire on Saturday nights when the Club was in session—people to whom the atmosphere of the Old Contemptibles was uncongenial, or who were well and rightly aware that their own aura was itself unsuitable and unsympathetic.

Cases there were of guests arriving and finding themselves welcome and popular members of the Old Contemptibles on the very next Saturday night.

Not a few nonentities and members, diffident, nervous and self-distrustful, though glancing with longing eyes at the charmed circle, the squared circle, presenting to the outer world an uncompromising unbroken wall of chair and sofa backs, never summoned the bravery to essay an entry.

Occasionally a bold but unworthy spirit would summon courage to take up position earlier in the evening, and maintain it when legitimate and recognized members of the Old Brigade drifted in from ball-room and bar, card-room and lounge, down from bedrooms and up from gardens, and assembled. But unlike far-famed Mr. Spence, few repeated the offence.

They were not pointedly ignored. Their presence was not sufficiently apparent for that.

No Club with rigid and irrefragable Rules and Regulations set forth in print had orders so unbending and unbreakable as the unwritten laws of the Society of the Old Brigade.

And of course the unelected, uncrowned, but universally chosen and unshakably enthroned king, or rather president, was kind Sir Russell Bemmington.

But, on this particular Saturday night, the Old Contemptibles Club received a shattering shock, one from which it did not quickly recover. For, in the pride of its exclusive eclecticism, its confessed superiority, it was humiliated, brought low, both in itself as a Club and in the persons of each of the proud people, its members.

As usual when the Club was in session, the hall was otherwise empty. Few cared to occupy any of the remaining arm-chairs, settees, divans, and sofas in distant corners of the hall, sitting apart, excluded in outer darkness behind that forbidding rampart of chair and sofa backs.

An ancient grandfather clock with sonorous chime struck midnight, a leaf of the outer double doors opened and slammed, the inner door opened and slammed, and the heavy leather curtain was roughly thrust aside. With raised eyebrows, members turned in the direction whence came this late and noisy intrusion.

Archie Wilbraholme.

Drunk, if one did not misjudge him by reason of the fact that the bow of his white tie was beneath his ear, the stud of his shirt-front missing or in retirement, and his flattened opera-hat balanced precariously upon his head. This crushed hat he removed, as he advanced upon the British square, and the raking fire of its cold, if not hostile, eyes.

"Th' Ol' Brigade," murmured Archie, eyeing the square owlishly. "And *how* old, my God. . . . Th' Ol' Contemptibles. And *how* contemptible, my God!"

The slightly watery yet glassy eye of the speaker fell upon Colonel Kinloch Grant.

"And there you are, Colonel," continued Archie, "and a damn' fine tip that was you gave me this morning! Moonbeam. Moonshine. Moonraker. Moo'n' all night and all day like a damn' cow that's got a pain in its calf. '*Hundred to eight*,' said you. '*Put your shirt, vest, socks and pants on it*,' says you. And what did I do? Put eighty pounds' worth of haberdashery on it, to make a thousand. And what did Moonlight do? Nightlight . . . Rushlight . . . Rush! . . . Light! That's a good 'un. . . . What did he do? Sat down in the middle of the course and scratched his fat head with his off hind hoof. And that's all the thanks one gets for backing him. Eighty pounds that I haven't got. Still, Colonel, you were once a gentleman and I'm ashamed of yourself to see me in such company."

Sir Russell Bemmington rose to his feet.

"Wilbraholme, you're drunk," he intoned portentously. "Drunk!"

"Thank you, Sir Brussell Remington. Thank you, Sir Sprouts. S'russell Sprouts. Says I'm drunk. Well, he ought to know. It's his business, drinking. Hasn't got any other, and never had."

"Look here, Sir," interrupted Sir Russell angrily.

"I am looking, Sir Brussell . . . Sprouts to you."

"Then perhaps you can see . . ." interrupted Sir Russell Bemmington.

"Yes, I can see all-right. And I can see what you are, old cock. I can see what you are not, too. And you are not Sir Russell Bemmington, late of Calcutta. You're not a Sir. Not a Russell. Not even a Bemmington, whatever that is. And you were never in Calcutta in your life. If you were, what's the name of my uncle who was commanding Fort William when you weren't there? . . . Tha's got you! . . . So you sit down and shut up. Too full of yourself, you are. Too full of whisky too. A lill' of you's a lot, and there's too much of you about this place—you and your Old Brigade. The Boozing Boozileers. Think you own the place, don't you—or going to. Think you are the Monarch of the Glen and you're only the Monarch of the Glenlivet. You don't own this place *yet*, you know. Sit down."

Speechless with anger, Sir Russell Bemmington surprisingly obeyed the request of the intoxicated young man.

He sat down.

Incensed and righteously indignant on behalf of her admired friend, Lady Grace spoke up, her head trembling with wrath on her wrinkled neck.

"Go away, you disgraceful, disgusting creature. You should be ashamed of yourself. Go to bed."

" 'Come to bed,' did she say?" murmured the abandoned profligate, turning to her and shaking an admonitory finger. "Now, now, don't you run after me too, Grace Abounding.

"That'd be Grace after Meat," he added, smiling waggishly.

"How's the Family getting on after the start you gave them?" he continued, and, raising his half-crushed opera-hat on high, declaimed:

> "*It gave her Family such a Start*
> *When Lady Grace became a T . . .*"

"Silence, Sir!" cried Sir Russell Bemmington, galvanized into life and activity by what he thought the shameless drunkard was about to say. "Hold your filthy tongue and . . ."

"*Police-woman,*" continued Archibald. "Don't inter-intersperse yourself. I've got to begin again now and run through it from the beginning. I can't walk, but I can run like the Devil. Listen. Sonnet. Lady Grace:

> "*It gave her Family such a Start*
> *When Lady Grace became a . . . Police-*
> *woman,*
> *But Breed is Breed and Race is Race,*
> *And so, to save her Family's face,*
> *She bought the most expensive Beat*
> *On the flood-lit side of Jermyn Street.*

There you are. *Beat.* See? I said she was a Police-woman, Bemmington."

Sir Russell's mouth opened and shut like that of a gold-fish, but, even as is a gold-fish, he was silent and dumb.

"You *puppy*! You're no gentleman, you . . ." began Lady Grace.

"Well, s' far's that goes, my dear, you are no Lady —not with a capital L. . . . They never knighted poor George, you know. . . . They never did. They said to him, '*George,*' they said, '*you've had your day, so we are going to make you a knight,*' and George said, '*Not you. It'd mean making Aggie a Lady,*' and he turned it down flat. They called it a day but he wouldn't call it a knight. So he's still plain George Grace—wherever he is—and you are still beautiful Aggie Grace."

It has to be admitted that the Club listened open-eared to this abominable and unpardonable drivel—until the intoxicated Archie had finished. Then young Mr. Gosling turned and rent him "in high piping Pehelvi" according to Archie, inebriated, eloquent and unpent.

"Well, well! Out of the mouths of babes and ducklings we are convicted. Who spoke to you, you pale pink unpublished poet? You stop gosling and listen to me, Chicken. . . . What? I'm drunk? Go and have half-a-pint of beer yourself and smell like a man, or I'll tell everybody about the gel who keeps you while you write the great Epic.

"*Epic!*" he hiccupped. "*Epic*echuana, more like-ly."

"Silence! . . ." ordered Mr. Gosling.

" ' "*Silence,*" *thundered Mr. Gooseling in a high falsetto squeak,*' " jeered Archie. "All-right, Lamb-kin, I won't tell them who it is week-ends here on your account. Credit account."

Bump, honorary and ex-officio member of the Old Brigade, entered the hall on one of his constant tours of inspection.

Hullo, what was this? The Old Contemptibles in some confusion, eyeing malevolently Wilbraholme the Waster who was apparently treating them to a drunken harangue. He must get him to bed.

As Bump advanced, General Botolph-Swales

took a hand.

"Now look here, my lad, you've said enough," quoth he, rising majestically from his arm-chair. "I'll talk to you to-morrow myself. When you are sober. What you want is a taste of the thin end of a horse-whip, and I'll . . ."

"You, General? You'll *what?* . . ." replied the unabashed and still voluble Archibald. "You'll sit down and you'll shut up, or I'll tell the Mouldy Brigade something about you, you bad old man. . . . Coming here and posing as a bachelor, chasing the girls and making up to the Merry Widows. Bachelor! You with a second wife still alive and seven children."

"*What?* . . . You . . ."

"Yes! A sounder of sons and a gaggle of girls. I know all about you."

Then up spake the General's friend, Colonel Featherston.

"Wilbraholme! You're drunk, and I'm surprised to . . ." he began.

"Not as surprised as I am to see you sober, Colonel. So we're both surprised," interrupted Archibald.

"I say I am surprised to . . ."

"You are surprised to see me drunk and I am surprised to see you sober," was the prompt reply. "Sober! You! Talk about hard times!"

"Old Ladies and Old Gentlemen of the Ancient Brigade, Colonel Featherston is sober," he went on. "Shame. Poor old chap. Something ought to be done about it."

Bump took the drunkard by the arm.

"Hullo, Bumpo! What price your hundred to eight tip? I put on eighty and I'll trouble you to hand it over."

"Come on. Bed-time."

"Old Ladies and Old Gentlemen of the Ancient

Brigade," resumed Archibald, "admonished! I am admonished. And if you've all finished, I will just tell you something. Something that'll surprise you. Something that poor old Bump doesn't know—and jolly well ought to know. There's a pair of prize crooks . . ."

"Will you come to bed?" interrupted Bump, beginning to propel Archibald in the direction of the stairs.

"One moment, one moment, Bumpo . . . I only want to say good-night to the Old Boys and the Old Girls of the Senile Contemptibles, and just mention that I wasn't asleep in the bar when the crooks got their heads together. They thought I was drunk. And I was as sober as two people . . . three people . . . any number of people. And I'll just tell you what that old rip . . . rep . . . rebate . . . reprobate was saying. You all ought to know."

And raising a wavering hand he pointed vaguely in the direction of Sir Russell Bemmington.

"He said . . ."

"For the last time, *will* you come to bed?"

"No, he didn't! He said . . ."

But the painfully interested assembly was not to know what the person vaguely specified had said on the occasion more vaguely specified, for Archibald's knees suddenly gave way, he collapsed upon the cold flags of the hall, and, unregretted, passed out.

Bump touched the nearest bell, and Richard Rodd promptly appeared. Beckoning to him, Bump took Archibald's shoulders, and raised him up. Rodd took his feet and Wilbraholme the Waster was borne from the scene of his downfall and disgrace.

"I'm awfully sorry," apologized Bump as he bore his end of the burden past the back row of the Club enclosure. "Dreadfully sorry. I'm afraid he's been drinking."

"He's certainly been talking," chuckled Colonel

Kinloch Grant, glancing in turn, with a malicious smile, in the direction of Sir Russell Bemmington, General Botolph-Swales and Colonel Featherston whom he detested, and at Mr. Gosling whom he disliked.

The Club, after discussing the character and lack of character of Archibald Wilbraholme, broke up in some slight disorder a session much shorter than was usual.

"I'm awfully sorry, Bump, old chap. I am truly sorry if I made an ass of myself this evening," wept Archibald, an hour later, to that harassed inn-keeper, sitting by his bedside and watching the effect of numerous various and remarkable restoratives prescribed and applied by Rodd.

"An ass of yourself! You made a most offensive beast of yourself."

Archibald wept afresh.

"I can't tell you how sorry I am. Don't chuck me out, Bump. Where the Hell should I go—except to Hell? I'll sign the pledge."

"The Devil was sick," growled Bump. "You'd sign it and keep it—as long as you felt sick."

"Don't talk about it," begged Archibald. "I'll never touch liquor again."

"I've heard something very like that before."

"But I mean it this time. I'll never touch liquor again."

"Well, there's good reason why you shouldn't," growled Bump.

"You mean?"

"That you can't carry it like a gentleman. *In vino veritas* and all that. If a gentleman ever drinks too much—which he doesn't—he still behaves like a gentleman. More so, if anything. If a cad drinks too much, his caddishness comes out. He's just a bigger cad because he's a drunken one—and that was

147

you to-night."

"You think I'm a cad, Bump?"

"You certainly behaved like one. And presumably that's what makes the cad, isn't it? . . . Insulting people like that. Bemmington's furious. Wants you chucked out to-night—this morning, that is."

"Bemmington! Do you know why he's furious? Because what I said was true."

"Well, that only makes it worse."

"But it doesn't, Bump. What you said just now—*in vino veritas.* The man's a humbug, a fraud, a liar. Probably a crook."

"Don't talk such damned rubbish. What you want is another emetic. I'll call Rodd."

"Bump! Bump! For God's sake! Come back! Look here, old chap, I'm as sober as you are, now, and I tell you you've got to watch out for Bemmington. He's a fraud. He'll swindle you."

"Rot! If you don't shut up I'll send for him. Then you can tell him this to his face."

"Right. I'm game. Listen, Bump. If I prove that he's a fraud, will you forgive me this time and let me stay on? If I prove he doesn't know a single word of Hindustani, won't that show he's one sort of a fraud and a liar for a start? And if I'm right in that, you can bet I'm right in the rest of it. He says he lived for years in Calcutta. Says he was a box-wallah there. Well, if he was there for years, it's funny he doesn't know the name of my uncle, Colonel Sir Arthur Lindsay-Dunstone, who was President of the Bengal Club and one of the best-known figures on the Calcutta Turf. Nobody who had been in Calcutta, at the time Bemmington says he was there, could possibly help knowing him, at least by name. And another thing, he doesn't know the meaning of the simplest phrase in Hindustani.

"Why, a tramp-steamer's cabin-boy understands the sort of thing I said to old Bemmington the other day. . . . I was in India a year, you know, A.D.C. to my guv'nor when my guv'nor was a Governor. . . . Conversation in the bar turned on India, and old Bemmington was so amazingly ignorant about people's names that I tried some Hindustani on him. And he doesn't know a word. I just said conversationally,

" *'Bemmington Sahib, kitni baji hai?'*

"He just looked blank and ordered another whisky and soda. Then I said to Rodd behind the bar,

" *'Bemmington Sahib dusra peg nahin mangta. Simkin ap-ko do.* Isn't that it, Bemmington—on me?'

"And he hadn't the vaguest notion that I had been offering him champagne. Of course, Rodd looked absolutely blank and asked what I was saying. I told him Sir Russell Bemmington would explain. But not he. Hadn't the foggiest notion what it was all about.

"Then I gave him a torrent of Hindustani abuse, and it all went over his head. Mind you, I'm not fluent by any means, but damn it all, any seaman down at the Docks knows when you are calling him a *soor ka butcha* or a *bānshūt.* But Bemmington? Not a word. Now what do you make of that, Bump?"

"I don't make anything of it," replied Bump. "Your Hindustani may have been bad beyond comprehension."

"Oh, *bosh!* Look here, Bump—come with me to Colonel Kinloch Grant to-morrow and I'll ask him in Hindustani anything within reason, and I'll bet you he understands me. Or another thing, you ask Colonel Kinloch Grant, who did fifteen years in India, to say something to Bemmington in Hindustani, and I'll bet you he'll confirm what I say—that Bemmington doesn't know a word of it."

"Well, mightn't he have talked Bengali?"

"No, he might not. No Englishman talks Bengali

unless he's some bloomin' pundit of a Government official out for examination-passing rewards. No Englishman talks Bengali in real life—and there's no man on earth who did ten years in Calcutta, or one year either, who doesn't understand Hindustani or remember enough to answer questions like *'Tumhara nam kya hai?'* and such nursery stuff as that. I tell you, Bump, Sir Russell Bemmington has never lived in India."

"Well, just for the sake of argument, suppose he hasn't. Suppose it was a little harmless eyewash and foolish vanity?"

"Rats!" jeered Archibald. "Understand a man pretending he had visited India when he hadn't, but why should he spin a yarn like that—not merely been in India but stayed there for ten years and more? Earned his living there. Prominent business man, widely known and highly respected in commercial and social circles."

"Well, frankly, Wilbraholme, if it's a case of your word against Sir Russell Bemmington's . . ."

"You'd take his, what?"

"Yes."

"Well, don't know that I blame you, Bump, but it needn't be a case of my word against his. What about Colonel Kinloch Grant's word?"

"I'm not going to ask him to trap my friend Bemmington."

"Oh? And you aren't going to take any steps to clear your friend Bemmington of the charge I bring against him?"

"I don't think he needs any clearing from charges you might bring against him, Wilbraholme."

"Then you're a fool, Bump, if you don't mind my saying so. Do you?"

"Not in the least."

"The fact remains you are a fool, whether you

mind my saying it or not. Don't you see that if Bemmington is a fraud and a liar about having lived in India and being an important and prominent man in Calcutta, it's more than probable—in fact it's certain—that he's a fraud and a liar about his having been knighted. If he claims to be a knight and he's not one, isn't that fraud? And if he's a swindler in one direction, isn't he probably a swindler in others? In point of fact, I know he is."

"Well, look here, Wilbraholme, since we are having a little plain speaking, you are accusing of fraud a man who, so far as I know, owes nobody a penny, and certainly doesn't owe me one. Very far from it. Boot on the other leg, as a matter of fact. He's been nothing but a benefactor to me and to Cortenay Old Hall Country Club. But for him it wouldn't be half as . . . inhabitable . . . as it is. That's the accused man. Now what about the accuser? How far are you behind with your weekly accounts? To how many people here do you owe money? I don't know whether you owe Bemmington himself any, and whether that's the reason for your attack on him, but I do happen to know that you owe money all over the place here, and that you spend most of your time betting with what is really other people's money—and losing it."

"Oh, I say, Bump! Really! I only try to do them a good turn and put a bit on a good thing for them."

"Well—we'll call it that, for the moment. But the fact remains. And I don't mind telling you I'd rather have a man here who said he had been in India and hadn't—and who was not only an honest and honourable, but a generous, guest of the Hotel and member of the Club—than a man who said he had been an aide-de-camp in India, and had been—and was a thoroughly unreliable, unprincipled waster and twister. . . . Afraid all that is a bit involved, but do you get the point, Wilbraholme?"

"I say, my dear chap, do leave off calling me that, and call me Archie again."

"Yes, that's all very well—but I strongly object to your coming here drunk and insulting the guests. General Botolph-Swales is livid. Colonel Featherston says he will thrash you to within an inch of your life. And as for poor Gosling . . ."

"Don't say he's going to flap a wing at me."

". . . and Lady Grace. I'm told you insulted her shamefully. Called her a tart or something. If you must insult and annoy people, you might leave women out of it."

"She began it. She insulted me. And I called her a police-woman, which is a high compliment. Whereupon she called me names."

"Probably said you were beastly drunk, which you were."

"Well, I could have told her that."

"Anyway, you'll hear something from them to-morrow. They are all going to . . ."

"Tell you what they are *not* going to do, Bump," grinned Archie. "They are not going to give notice. 'They were never so insulted in their lives,' but they're not going to shake the dust of Cortenay Old Hall off their feet and go where they won't be insulted, are they?"

"No. Why should they? It's you who are going to do that."

Archibald shot up in bed and grabbed Bump by the wrist.

"Oh, my God, my head!" he groaned. "I moved too quickly."

"Yes, and you can move quickly to-morrow morning—out of here."

"No, Bump! No! Don't say that. Give me another chance, Bump. I swear I'll turn teetotal."

"And back no more horses?"

"Only certs, Bump. Only certs."

"Well, you've been doing that ever since you came here. And how much do you owe?"

"I wouldn't tell you a lie, Bump, because I can't. I don't know."

"Anyway, you added eighty pounds to the total to-day."

"Well, yes and no. In a manner of speaking."

"Dud cheque?"

"No, no, Bump! Oh, come, come! *Really!* I mean to say . . ."

"Well, look here, I'll make a bargain with you, Wilbraholme."

" 'Archie,' old chap, 'Archie.' "

"I'll make a bargain with you, Archie; and I'm a fool to do it. You apologize to the people you insulted—I've only heard of about half a dozen so far —and I'll give you a last chance."

"Bump, I solemnly swear . . ."

"So do I. I solemnly swear that I will have you out, neck and crop, first time you get drunk or I know of your betting again."

Archibald beamed and took Bump's hand.

"Oh, thanks awfully, old chap. I knew you'd . . ."

"Yes, and *I* know something," interrupted Bump, rising to his feet. "Don't you bob up so quickly. I'll leave you something to think over. . . . Just after Bemmington came, when I was at the end of my tether, you told me that with a tenner you could make me two hundred pounds. You knew for an absolute fact that Blighdon, that Noble Lord, was running two horses in the same race, one a hot favourite, odds on, and the other a dud called Also Ran, price thirty-three to one—and that Also Ran was to win. By arrangement. Like a fool I trusted you with ten pounds to put on for me, with your bookie. You never went near the race nor made the bet. You went to London. God knows what you did there, but you came back drunk. The yarn you told me was that the favourite was so good that it won against its owner's orders and its jockey's pulling. And I believed you."

"But, Bump . . ."

"Yes, don't say any more, Archie. Referring to the matter weeks later, in conversation with Colonel Featherston, I discovered that there was no such horse as Also Ran in that particular race. You were a common liar and a common thief. You simply stole that ten pounds from me and went on the bend. Good-night—and don't let's hear any more out of *you* about Bemmington."

X

There was no denying that Miss Wymper was queer, uncanny. Had she lived in good King James's golden days she would most certainly have been burned as a witch, for not only was she definitely witch-like in appearance, but in behaviour. True, she did not have a black cat familiar, and had never been seen to ride astride a broomstick, but she was an insatiable reader of fortunes, or perhaps, more accurately, misfortunes.

These she could, and would, foretell by means of the disposition of tea-leaves in cups, by the use of a special pack of cards, by the strange prognostications of her planchette, by dreams, auguries and weird omens.

She was, moreover, an accomplished palmist, and, by studying the lines of the hand, would not only foretell its owner's future but produce disconcerting and sometimes uncomfortably accurate details as to his or her past.

On this point there was no room for doubt. Only time could tell whether her prophecies were false or true;. but, deny them as they might and frequently did, her victims had inwardly to admit that many of her statements as to their past were only too true, alas!

There was the notable case of Miss Aldwen who, arriving on a Saturday and encountering Miss Wymper on Sunday, departed on Monday, wept, honoured and sung by Bump, for she was evidently a person of means, and had announced her intention of spending the whole summer at Cortenay Old Hall Country Club.

Seeing this stranger in the hall, Miss Wymper

had made straight for her, had proclaimed her as psychic, praised the spirituality of her face, seized her hand, and declared that she had suffered greatly. Two noble husbands she had won and lost: with two lovely children she had been blest—only to see them torn from her—when the husbands were given the custody of the respective child. . . .

And albeit Miss Aldwen had denied every single word of Miss Wymper's statement, she had nevertheless re-packed, ordered her car, and departed.

Why?—as Miss Wymper complained—if it weren't true?

At certain seasons—connected with the phases of the moon, according to Lady Grace—Miss Wymper became clairvoyant, could amplify the findings of her palmistry by gazing into her crystal, and could tell fortunes with increased detail and conviction, if not accuracy. As to this last, time alone could prove.

And now Miss Wymper had "taken up" spiritualism and gone all mediumistic.

Unfortunately, from Bump's point of view, she had discovered in Sandhaven a person of marvellous gifts; a medium of remarkable psychic power, transparent honesty, and great willingness to further the cause and practice of spiritualism. Nor, strange to relate, was this newly discovered, but already famous, medium a professional-looking, middle-aged, dubious female, plausible, specious and needy.

Far from it.

The Sandhaven medium was a young carpenter, not educated beyond the ordinary in his walk of life, and obviously quite as much interested in the phenomena of spiritualism in general and his own psychic gifts in particular, as he was in the financial aspect of mediumistic performance.

Nor was he an epileptic invalid; a mental, moral,

or physical freak of any kind; a mute, inglorious Milton; or a musical, artistic, dramatic, or inventive genius. He was just a plain, ordinary, healthy young carpenter; and, in the opinion, not only of prominent spiritualists, but of scientific experts and sharp-eyed, sceptical detectors of fraud, an ingenuous and genuine medium of uncommon parts and power.

He had been discovered, more or less accidentally, by the Pastor of the Chapel he attended, a man deeply interested in Spiritualism; and had quickly convinced this leader in the New Israel that he was out of the ordinary.

Under the good man's auspices, *séances* had been arranged, and had been conducted with such success, such rich harvest of results, that the young carpenter had been forthwith hailed and proclaimed.

A great London newspaper had made a stunt of him, had arranged a *séance* on its own terms and conditions, had sent the most hard-boiled sceptic on its staff, together with a doctor well known for his anti-spiritualistic views, to report without fear, and certainly without favour, upon the proceedings.

The *séance* was arranged precisely in accordance with the terms and conditions laid down by the Editor of the paper.

The reporter and the doctor, frankly sceptical, attended it as hostile witnesses. They came to scoff and remained to admit that they were—puzzled. On the strength of the one *séance* they would not of course admit conversion. But they were forced to confess that, if the affair were genuine, it was amazing; if it were a swindle, it was still more amazing.

And what was the joy of Miss Wymper—on reading a description of the young man and his work in *The Spiritualists' Guide* and *The Psychical*

Research-Light; as well as *The Daily Messenger's* account of his triumphant success in the test carried out by that paper—to learn that he lived in Sandhaven, only a few miles from Cortenay Old Hall.

Promptly she wrote to him, proposing a visit. Quickly she received a reply to the effect that David Jones would be pleased to see her and talk about arranging a *séance*.

It was a success. It was wonderful. According to Miss Wymper it was "thimply marvellouth. Thwarmth and thwarmth of thpirith and motht convinthing manifethtathionth. And Bump thimply mutht mutht come."

And in the end Bump gave way, partly to please poor dear Miss Wymper of whom he was very fond, realizing, as he did, that her fundamental sweetness of nature, broad charity of mind and limpid simplicity of soul were rare and precious things, whether in Cortenay Old Hall Country Club and Guest House or elsewhere; partly for the sake of peace; partly because he was vaguely interested in spiritualism by reason of the astounding things Miss Wymper had told him; and partly on account of a curious hint that she had dropped.

"My dear," she had said when endeavouring to persuade him to accompany her to a *séance* at the house of the young medium, David Jones, so swiftly risen to celebrity in spiritualistic circles, "you never know. You never know what the Spirits may tell you. Suppose they told you something about the great secret, the great desire that is always at the back of your mind. . . ." (What Miss Wymper actually said was, "Thuppothe they told you thomething about the great thecret, the great dethire that ith alwayth at the back of your mind.")

"Eh? What's that?" enquired Bump.

"Why, my dear boy, you know what it is. You

know what is for ever there, just on the threshold of your consciousness—the Cortenay Treasure."

"Oh, that! I'm not always thinking about that, Miss Wymper."

Miss Wymper patted Bump's hand, turned it over and examined his palm—the palm that she was so fond of "reading."

"Well, my dear boy, I am. . . . Oh, the hours I spend, especially at full moon, gazing into my crystal, sitting with my hands on planchette, trying to get into the proper trance-condition for my hand to do automatic writing, trying to fall into slumber or a swoon in which I may force myself to dream— all to get the answer to the question, 'Where is the Cortenay Treasure?'"

"Awfully good of you, Miss Wymper, but . . ."

"Oh, not at all, my dearest boy. You've been so good to a lonely old woman."

"Old? You, Miss Wymper?"

"Old enough to be your mother, Bump, very nearly. . . . And, oh, what wouldn't I give to be able to find it for you! I beg and beg the Spirits to tell me, to write it with planchette or by automatic writing, or to reveal it in a dream or vision; and I gaze and gaze into my crystal, trying to see its hiding-place. Gaze and gaze until almost I go blind. But, so far, nothing. . . . And I can read nothing here on your palm except, vaguely, happiness, success—after much trouble and tribulation. How I pray it will be soon! You are going through the trouble and tribu- lation now, I know, but there is a good time coming. . . . Now don't be foolish. Give the Spirits a chance. You never know. I shall do my utmost, and if you will really put yourself in a receptive frame of mind and help me and Mr. David Jones, I believe we could get in touch."

"Awfully good of you, Miss Wymper, but really . . ."

"Yes, I believe we could get in touch."

"In touch with whom?"

"Why, my dear, with your ancestor. With the very one who hid the treasure. With Sir Giles the Buccaneer, if you don't mind my calling him that."

"They called him 'The Pirate' in those days, I believe. Apparently quite rightly, too."

"Well now, suppose we could get in touch with him. Suppose we could question him, ask him to tell us where he hid the Treasure. Wouldn't it be simply marvellous, unbelievable?"

"Quite unbelievable," agreed Bump.

"Now, now, that's not the spirit in which to approach the matter."

"Not the spirit in which to approach the Spirit, eh?" smiled Bump.

"Not at all the spirit. Not what I call the Cortenay spirit, either."

"And what do you call the Cortenay spirit, Miss Wymper?"

"Why, my dear Bump, what a question! Hope, Faith, Courage. The Spirit of Adventure. The Spirit of 'Let's go and find out.' The Spirit of 'We'll try anything.'"

"Try any drink once, eh?" smiled Bump.

"Now, just to please me. It can't do any harm, can it?"

"No, it can't do me any harm, Miss Wymper; but I can quite understand some people getting a great deal of harm from dabbling in Spiritualism."

"How?"

"Oh, getting all morbid. Going all credulous. Putting themselves in the hands of quacks, liars, rogues and fakers. Gullible fools in the hands of swindling knaves."

"My dear boy, there are swindlers in all professions and walks of life. Not only among professors of new and strange religions, but among the most hard-headed professions. There are swindlers among solicitors, stockbrokers, doctors, mining-engineers, jewellers, builders and contractors, company promoters. . . ."

"*No!*" said Bump.

". . . house-agents . . ."

"*No!*"

"Horse-dealers and racing men . . ."

"Oh, come, come, Miss Wymper! Surely not!"

"Oh, yes, there are; and no doubt there are swindlers among spiritualist mediums too. I am prepared to admit it. Just as there are among psycho-therapists and faith-healers. But David Jones is not a swindler. He's absolutely honest and genuine, and doesn't give *séances* for the sake of the fees. A labourer is worthy of his hire, of course, but there are people who work for the love of work, you know, Bump."

"I do," admitted Bump modestly.

Miss Wymper smiled and again patted Bump's hand.

"You don't, dear boy. You work because you couldn't bear to sit idle and see Cortenay Old Hall go to rack and ruin, or pass into other hands after a thousand years. I think you are wonderful. It is absolutely splendid the way you get down to it and run the place as though you had been apprenticed to the hotel-keeping business. But you don't do it for the love of the work, do you?"

"I loathe it," replied Bump. "Loathe it beyond words."

"Exactly. Well now, you come with me to this *séance,* and we'll see if David Jones can't get in touch with Sir Giles Cortenay and ask him where he hid the treasure. If David Jones can get in touch with him, why shouldn't Sir Giles answer? He has no interest in keeping the treasure hidden now, has he? Of course not. And naturally he'd be only too glad to say where it is; and save Cortenay Old Hall. Well, you are saving it, of course; but what I mean is, naturally Sir Giles, as a true Cortenay, would like you to find the Treasure and restore the Hall, and the Gardens and the Park to their former perfection. And he'd like to see you living as a Cortenay should. He'd like you to marry and carry on the race. Why should you be the last of the Cortenays? . . . Bump dear, why don't you take up Spiritualism?"

"Much too busy. Something else to think about."

"Exactly. Well now, let's find the Treasure and you'll have nothing else to think about, will you?"

"What, nothing else than the Treasure?"

"Nothing else than applying the Treasure to making Cortenay Old Hall perfect, and your life here lovely."

"You're a bit of a treasure yourself, you know, Miss Wymper."

"Then you will come with me to a *séance*?"

"I'll come," sighed Bump.

§2

That night Bump lay awake for a while in bed, and dipped into a book which Miss Wymper had begged him to read, an autobiography of a famous physicist, one of the greatest, if not the very greatest, of all living British scientists.

Not only was he deeply interested, but, before he fell asleep, had to admit that, if not convinced, he was most deeply impressed. It was impossible to avoid the thought,

"If so great a mind as this can, and does, accept the truth of the phenomena of Spiritualism, surely my little mind can do so, or at least can give them its most respectful attention. If he is a believer, who am I to be a scoffer, since the matter is one of research, intelligence and understanding?"

'*Suffice it to say,*' he read, '*that the attempt was successful. I got into ostensible touch with old deceased relatives of whose early youth I knew nothing whatever, and was told of instances which were subsequently verified by their surviving elderly contemporaries . . .*

I took every precaution that I could think of, and the result of the enquiry was conclusive . . .

The genuineness of the mediums having been established beyond reasonable doubt, the only explanation which would evade the spiritistic hypothesis was that the medium in a state of trance had access to the minds of living people. The possibility of reading the mind of the sitter was always allowed for; but when we got information which was unknown to anyone present, it still was usually known to somebody or was recorded somewhere, else it could not be subsequently verified. It was in order to stem this possible utilisation of a hypothetical and unverified faculty of wide-spread telepathy or clairvoyance, that the efforts of the communicators were directed. . . . Indeed, it was a theory that HAD *to be pressed to the uttermost, before admitting the face value of the communications from dead people as a real explanation; for, if that was once seriously established, a portentous step would have been taken. The survival of man would have been demonstrated scientifically, and the power of communication with deceased people established, in spite of the lack of their own bodily organisms . . .*

'*It may be asked whether any residual doubt may reasonably lurk in the mind of an expert about these communications being entirely what they profess to be. I do not think there need be any doubt.*'[12]

---

[12] *Sir Oliver Lodge.*

Bump was deeply impressed.

All very amazing, very interesting, and somewhat disturbing. Well worth examination, anyhow, and deserving of respectful approach with at least an open, enquiring, and unbiased mind.

§3

The Cortenay Old Hall car, known as the Rattlesnake by reason of its physical peculiarities and the viciousness of its nature, drew up outside a modest house, a typical artisan's dwelling, in a back street of the little sea-side town of Sandhaven.

"Here we are," said Miss Wymper enthusiastically, as she stepped from the car, her eager face glowing with the light of faith and hope, and shining with the beams of benevolence and goodwill.

Leading the way, she pushed open a rusty iron gate, of which the squeaking hinges rendered bell or knocker unnecessary. The door was opened by a sad-faced woman, sadly clothed, whose expression, aspect and demeanour proclaimed the fact that she did not hold with such goings-on as these.

"Is Mr. David Jones in?" enquired Miss Wymper pleasantly.

"Yerss. He's *in*," replied the woman, opening the door a little wider.

"Well, we want to see him, please. We have an appointment."

"Yerss, I know," admitted the woman darkly, and led the way into a small front room to which fortunately were added, by the opening of folding doors, the space and amenities of a small back room, the two combining to make an apartment of moderate proportions, adequate at any rate to the holding of a *séance* by about a dozen people.

" 'Ere's two more of 'em," announced Mr. Jones's

landlady, without enthusiasm.

"Good evening, Miss," said Mr. Jones, shaking Miss Wymper's hand. "Good evening, Sir."

Miss Wymper introduced him to Bump without mentioning the real name of the latter, who beheld an earnest-faced, pleasant and intelligent-looking young man, about whom there was nothing remarkable except that he grew small side-whiskers and wore his curly and fluffy hair rather longer than is fashionable among young Trade Unionists. Certainly, had one known nothing whatever about him, the last trade, profession or calling which one would have ascribed to him would have been that of spiritualistic medium.

Nor was there anything in any way unusual about the room, save for the fact that a rather long and narrow table occupied the centre of this combination apartment which ran the length of the little house from back to front.

"Won't you sit down?" said Jones, indicating an inhospitable-looking horse-hair sofa that shrank against the wall. "The Pastor's going to bring his wife. He'll be here in a minute. We got another Reverend coming too, the Reverend Bevans, also bringing his wife. That makes six, and there's two gents coming down from London on the six train. Staying the night at The Dolphin, they are. One of them writes for the papers and the other is a member of the Society. You've met him, Miss," he added, turning to Miss Wymper. "Mr. Lippincott."

"Oh, yes. I'm so glad he could come. He's very keen. Quite a helpful presence at a *séance*. Who's the other?"

"I don't rightly know, Miss, but he'll be all-right, as Mr. Lippincott's bringing him."

"Well, I don't know, Jones. He may be a sceptic whom Mr. Lippincott wishes to convert. I do hope not. I want us all to be In Tune with the Infinite to-night. I do so want to make a convert of the gentleman whom I have brought with me. And what is more, I want him to get in touch with an ancestor who has passed over."

"His father, perhaps?" asked Jones.

"No, another ancestor, a long way back. Three hundred years or so."

"Oh! M-m-m. . . . May manage a control. . . ."

"Tell you what puzzles me," said Bump. "I don't want to say anything facetious or offensive; cast doubt, and all that; but how many people are there alive in the world to-day? Twenty-five hundred million or so?"

"I'm sure I don't know," said Jones.

"No, nor do I. But suppose there were about that, and suppose the world's been going on for a few million years. How many people have died. . . ."

". . . Passed over," murmured Miss Wymper. . . .

". . . since first there were human beings on the earth? The number, even in historical times, say in the last three thousand years, must be beyond human computation."

"There certainly must be a lot," agreed Jones.

"Well now, out of all those millions of billions of trillions, how on earth can you get in touch with one single spirit, one *particular* spirit, I mean?"

"I'm sure I couldn't tell you," replied Jones honestly.

"Oh, I don't think that need be a great stumbling-block," said Miss Wymper. "I think it is the desire, the wish, that establishes the communication; a sort of telepathy; the very fact that you want to get into touch with somebody of whom you are thinking, somebody on whom you are concentrating your whole will-power, thought, wish. That's what does it, I think."

"I see," mused Bump. "There's something in that, of course. Otherwise it seemed to me that you had to imagine a kind of celestial or metaphysical or metaphorical—er—you know what I mean—a sort of telephone; and you just rang up, so to speak, the spirit you wanted. Which strikes one as being a bit absurd, doesn't it?"

"Extremely absurd," agreed Miss Wymper, with faint acerbity.

"Besides, there's another thing, my dear boy," she continued. "We Spiritualists don't regard Heaven as a Better Land, geographically speaking; a glorified illimitable Garden as it were, straight up above our heads on the other side of the sky; a sort of concrete place to which you can—metaphorically, as you say—telephone and ring up some spirit inhabiting that more or less definite geographical enclave. Not a bit of it.

"We regard the spirits as being everywhere about us, around us, in touch with us; and naturally the spirits of our nearest and dearest, the spirits of our friends and relations whom we've loved, are the ones that are most about us, that are about us most. . . . What I mean to say is that, for instance, I am quite sure the spirit of your uncle, the dear General, is with you at the Hall; and the spirits of your father and your mother, the spirits of people who have known you and loved you in this life.

"They still know you and love you in the spirit life, my dear. Why, I should be miserable if I thought that, when I have passed over, I couldn't come back and see you at your house. Come there, where you've made me so happy, and watch you. Watch over you, perhaps. Help you. . . . Isn't that a lovely thought?

"So much better than that silly idea of sitting and twanging a harp and singing Hallelujah. Perfectly ridiculous. Futile way to spend time, let alone Eternity. And just compare it with the idea of those

unimaginative clods of people who believe, or profess to believe, that we die—and there's an end of
us. Never heard anything so absurd in all my life.

"How could there be an end to a *soul*? No, for a
time at any rate, probably as long as we wish to do
so, probably, in fact, until all those we love have
also passed over and come and joined us—we re-
visit the world and the places in it where we have
been happy, where we have loved and been loved.
Isn't that a better idea than sprouting wings and
sitting about on clouds in 'night attire,' and wailing
lugubrious hymns, or of going down six feet into
clay and corruption—and that being the end? . . .
Bosh! . . .

"Why, my dear boy, when I have passed over, if
you come to a *séance* like this, with an honest and
truly psychic medium like Mr. Jones here, do you
think it would take you long to get into touch with
me? I assure you it wouldn't. You just try."

"I will," smiled Bump.

"That's right. Splendid. We'll have lovely talks
together. . . . And you do get the idea, don't you,
how it is that one can get into touch with one single
spirit, one particular spirit, out of all those countless millions of billions of trillions? It's because that
spirit also wants to get in touch with you. It's because there's the bond. It's mutual. Besides—think
of the number of living people who are reached by
an earthly 'S.O.S.' broadcast. May it not be that
every soul that has passed over hears the 'broadcast' when the medium makes his appeal—and that
the spirit whom that particular broadcast concerns
and interests, replies at once? That, too, may be the
reason why you can get into touch with one single
spirit out of the countless millions of billions of
trillions."

"Yes, I see," agreed Bump, still a little dubiously.
"But suppose you wanted to get in touch with a

stranger, one who has no concern or interest in your broadcast, so to speak, a spirit between whom and you there is no bond?"

"Well, there we fall back upon the fact of the *wish*, the desire, the mere fact that you are trying to get into touch. . . . It's a kind of—well, let's use your own metaphor and say it's a kind of wireless telephony. Though telepathy is a better word. And then, of course, there's the medium. What powers the medium has, we don't profess to understand; but personally, I have no doubt that the fact that you can get into touch with strangers that have passed over is due partly to your intense desire to do so, your *will* to do so, and partly to the psychic powers of the medium. Anyway, there it is, it's an established fact that we do get in touch with the spirits with whom we wish to communicate."

"M-m-m . . . Another thing that puzzles me is why there is any necessity for the intervention of a medium," mused Bump. "If my Uncle wanted to communicate with me, why have I got to go and trouble Mr. Jones? Why can't he deal with me direct?"

"Appear before you as an apparition, a ghost, you mean?"

"Well; no, I don't mean exactly that. What about dreams? Why couldn't I exert my will-power, my earnest desire, as you said, as I lie down to sleep, and then get into touch with him in my dreams?"

"I don't know. Nobody knows. But on the other hand, nobody knows what electricity is. We can use it and harness it, but we don't know what it is. Nobody knows why sugar forms one sort of crystal, salt another, and snow another, do they? Nobody knows why man's allotted span is seventy years. Bless me, Bump, what's sleep? Where do we go, so to speak, when we sleep? How are we restored, in the marvellous way that we are restored, by sleep?

And tell me this. How do we come to life again from sleep? Because sleep is a brief death. Our souls go from us, out into the unknown; and infallibly return, each to its own body. How and why? We don't know. But the fact of sleep remains; and we do not deny the phenomenon because we cannot explain it. . . . Dear me, how learnedly I'm talking."

"Very interesting and convincing, anyway," smiled Bump. "Anyhow, I am afraid I shan't be able to get into touch with my ancestor of three hundred years ago because he's fond of me and is still hanging around and watching and all that."

"You don't know. How do you know that he isn't as much at your house as anywhere else? He may, so to speak, live there."

"Do you think so?" asked Bump.

"Well, what does it matter what a foolish old woman thinks? But, for what my theories are worth, I should think that it's only, as I say, people who have known you and loved you, who still haunt your home. When I say haunt, I mean who like to come there and be about you. I should think it is more than likely that all your ancestors come there from time to time, to re-visit the place they knew best and loved best on earth; and I should think that those who knew you are there always. Anyhow . . ."

The groaning of the front gate, followed by the ringing of the bell, disturbed their low-voiced conversation. The door opened, the lugubrious and disapproving landlady announced,

" 'Ere's the Reverends," and four people trooped into the room—a tall grey-bearded man in clerical dress accompanied by a large, moon-faced, buxom woman of some fifty years of age; and a small clean-shaven man in sober dark-grey garments and white bow-tie, with a woman curiously like him, inasmuch as her almost white hair was cropped as short as his, and her thin, ascetic, grey-eyed face was remarkably similar to her husband's clean-shaven, lean countenance, of which the intent expression suggested smouldering fires of fanaticism damped down, discouraged and controlled.

Somewhat clumsy introductions followed, and Mr. Jones observed that only two members of the *séance* were now wanting, and would doubtless arrive quite soon.

"And are you a Believer, may I ask?" Mr. Jones's Pastor, the small clergyman, enquired of Bump.

"No, as a matter of fact I am not," replied Bump.

"Oh, no; he has no reason to be yet," chimed in Miss Wymper, "but I am perfectly certain he's going to be."

"I hope so. I trust so," said the other clergyman. "I don't see how he can fail to become a Believer after attending one of Mr. Jones's *séances*. Facts are very stubborn things."

"Indeed, yes," agreed the other clergyman.

"Seeing and hearing are surely believing, and none are so blind as those who can't see," observed Miss Wymper nervously; and, appearing to consider her own remark, and to find it in some way lacking in accuracy, added, "I mean, who can't hear."

"No. Yes," agreed Bump. "That is to say, I suppose one can hardly expect to *see* anything at a *séance*."

"Hitherto there have been no visible manifestations at any of Mr. Jones's *séances*," replied the Pastor. "No ectoplasmic emanations. Nothing in the nature of a materialization of any sort. . . . But—communications! Amazing!"

"He that hath ears to hear, let him hear," observed the tall clergyman, "and if he will listen with humility and faith, hardening not his heart, he will be convinced."

"Indeed, indeed," agreed his wife.

"There are . . . er . . . there have been . . . materializations—at some *séances,* have there not?" enquired the uncomfortable and unhappy Bump, who was beginning to feel a certain sympathetic understanding of the state of the fish that, haled from the water, lies gasping and floundering in an unwonted element. "Spirits have actually appeared, I mean to say, have they not?"

"It is alleged. It is alleged," replied the Pastor. "But, personally, I have my doubts. . . ."

"Oh? You do doubt . . ." began Bump.

". . . as to whether these ectoplasmic materializations, manifestations, incarnations—I speak metaphorically, of course—were not seen with the eye of faith more than with the eye of the body."

"Let us be content," said the other clergyman, "to proceed step by step, from established fact to further fact, broadening down from precedent to precedent, until we come from the evidence of but one sense to the evidence of two or three; from the auditory to the visual, the tactual and indeed the olfactory."

"Eh? What . . . smell?" enquired Bump in some surprise.

"Yes, yes. Why not? It is credibly reported that in some *séances* held under satisfactory conditions and with the help of a reputable medium, flowers have materialized, flowers which could not only be seen, but smelt and touched.

"And there is one case, reported from France, in which a spirit materialized, was distinctly seen by several, and was heard to speak. Not only this, but the spirit, that of the seeker's wife, who had but recently passed over, bore in her hand a bouquet of beautiful roses. The scent of these roses was perceptible to all."

"And touch, Mr. Braybrook? Could the husband

actually take his wife's hand; kiss her; embrace her?" asked Miss Wymper eagerly.

"No, no," replied the Reverend Mr. Braybrook. "But, none the less, the sense of touch was definitely evoked, appealed to, utilized; for several of the members of the *séance*, if not all, distinctly felt the touch of spirit hands, felt contact with a spirit form, as ghostly fingers were laid upon brow or cheek or hand.

"Yes, in this case, if we may believe the report of the *Proceedings* of the French Spiritualistic and Psychic Research Society, there was, on this occasion, definite, direct, and successful appeal to the senses of sight, sound, hearing, and touch."

Suddenly a deep resonant voice boomed forth from the corner where the Pastor's small wife had ensconced herself,

> *"Oh for the touch of a vanish'd hand*
> *And the sound of a voice that is still."*

"Indeed so. Indeed yes," agreed the Pastor nervously.

"But let me repeat that of such marvels I have as yet had no personal experience; though I have, beyond any possible shadow of doubt, held communication with the spirits of the departed.

"And so, this night, will you," he added, turning to Bump, "if this *séance* be as successful as previous ones have been in this very room."

Again the clamorous gate groaned forth its plangent wail.

"Oh, that'll be the gents from London," said the young carpenter, who had maintained silence, as respectfully he listened to the words of the man who had discovered his gift, urged and helped him to use and develop it, and brought him some measure of success and fame.

The door of the room opened.

"Two more; and that's the lot, ain't it?" announced and enquired Mr. Jones's landlady.

"Ah, Mr. Lippincott. Delighted to see you again, Sir," said the Pastor, rising and shaking hands with that gentleman.

"How do you do, Sir? How do you do? Allow me to introduce my friend, Mr. Marvell, who has come down from London on purpose to attend one of Mr. Jones's *séances*, and to give a full, true, and particular account of it in his famous paper, *The Weekend Journal*."

Sketchy introductions followed.

"I do hope, Mr. Marvell, that you are not a sceptic," asked Miss Wymper anxiously.

"Not at all. I am absolutely neutral. I know nothing whatever about Spiritualism, and I come with a perfectly open mind. Yes, I think I can honestly say that I have no bias whatsoever in either direction, and do really come in the spirit of the enquiring Greek."

"Oh, I'm so glad. It really makes such a difference, you know. It puts us Out of Tune with the Infinite, inevitably; and I'm sure it makes things more difficult for the medium. It increases resistance."

Mr. Marvell smiled.

"Yes? Of whom, to what?"

"Of the Powers of Darkness to the Angels of Light," boomed the deep voice from the dark and distant corner of the room, so suddenly, unexpectedly and accusingly, that Mr. Marvell jumped.

Bump, whose sense of humour was always most active on solemn occasions, was reminded of the family of Lady Grace.

(Why? "*It gave her family such a start . . .*" The wretched Archibald Wilbraholme. Mrs. Pastor had given Mr. Marvell such a start. Come, come, this wouldn't do.)

"Well, I'm sure I shall not intentionally do anything to strengthen the resistance of the Powers of Darkness to the Angels of Light," Mr. Marvell informed her.

"No, no. That's all-right," Mr. Lippincott assured the company. "My friend has come to see, to hear and to report; and you may rest assured that he is entirely unbiased, unprejudiced and—as he himself would be the first to admit—ignorant. On the subject of Spiritualism, I mean. He has come to the *séance* in much the same attitude as a dramatic critic goes to see a play of which he knows nothing whatsoever until the curtain goes up. Are we ready?"

"Yes, we have only been waiting for you," boomed the deep voice of the Pastor's wife.

The Pastor gazed round the assembly.

"Eight of us, and Mr. Jones," he said. "Let us gather round. Mr. Jones will take the arm-chair at the head of the table. I will sit on his right. Will you sit on his left, Mr. Lippincott? And if this lady will sit next to me, and then you, Sir"—indicating Bump—"and if Mrs. Braybrook will sit next to Mr. Marvell and then you"—to his wife—"next to Mr. Lippincott. Or no, perhaps this gentleman would change places with Mr. Lippincott. Yes, that will do nicely. Now I will offer up a prayer and suggest a hymn."

Thereupon the company, closing their eyes, covered their faces with their hands, and reverently bending their heads, sat motionless while the Pastor offered up an extempore prayer. This completed and endorsed by a deep *Amen* from his wife, the Pastor said,

"Let us sing the first verse of the hymn '*Nearer my God to Thee.*' Presumably we all know that hymn, whether we be Dissenters or of the Church of England."

In point of fact, Bump, to his shame, knew neither the words nor the music of the hymn; but, anxious ever to conform, to accommodate, to oblige, he made lowing sounds as accordant as possible with those emitted beside him in the deep diapason of the voice of the Pastor's wife. By the time the last line of the hymn was reached, he felt he was doing quite well.

The singing finished, the congregation again seated themselves about the table, all save the Pastor.

"Now then," said he, in brisk and business-like tones, "if anybody wishes to make any remark or ask any question, will they do so forthwith, and thereafter maintain complete and perfect silence, save when addressed and invited to speak? I shall then lower the gas and the *séance* proper will commence."

"Er, excuse me. This is the first time I have attended a spiritualistic *séance* and I don't know the ritual. Is it against the rules for one to ask a question during the—er—proceedings?" enquired Mr. Marvell.

"Yes," replied the Pastor, "kindly keep questions till afterwards, when I shall be only too pleased to deal with any point. Unless you are addressed, kindly refrain from speech or movement, until I again turn up the light. . . . Anybody else? You, Sir?"

"No, no; I quite understand," Bump assured him.

The Pastor then lowered the gas, which burned inside an incandescent mantle, until only a pin-point of light remained.

Mr. David Jones had apparently gone to sleep, fainted, or thrown a fit. He was breathing very stertorously.

What a quaint idea was this, thought Bump, that people must gather together in greater or smaller numbers and sit round a table in such fashion, before any inhabitant of the spirit-world could enter into communication with any of them.

And again, what a quaint idea that the proceedings must always take place in darkness. Why should that be? What was that text on which the sermon had been preached the last time there was a service held in the chapel at Cortenay Old Hall? Something about men loving darkness rather than light because their deeds were evil.

Well, his deeds weren't particularly evil, and he did not suppose that those of the good folk assembled here were any more evil than his. Probably much less so. Nor would the spirits love darkness because their deeds were, or had been, evil, surely.

What about the spirits of little children?

However, there it was, apparently. One had to come to this sort of queer "parlour," sit round in a circle, turn out the light, and await the pleasure and advent of the spirits.

And then again, what a queer idea was this necessity for the intervention of a medium. Why should this workman, this carpenter, excellent young man though doubtless he was, be necessary to successful communication between Bump and his Uncle or his buccaneer ancestor, or anyone else who had died? Passed over, they called it, without ever using the word 'died.' All very queer and puzzling. Still, people, much more intelligent than he, apparently accepted it as all-right, so he might as well do the same.

And, after all, the explanations given by Miss Wymper were satisfactory. Fairly so, anyway. And of course, what she had said about accepting phenomena as they are, was quite true. There was a time when the telephone and the telegraph would have been regarded as miraculous, and now they were commonplaces. Why not the same with this Spiritualism? And there again, you couldn't telegraph or telephone without wires. And just in the same way, presumably, you couldn't communicate with departed spirits without the medium. The medium was to this spirit-communication what the wires were to telegraphic and telephonic communication. But, hold on a minute, you could telegraph and telephone without wires. There was wireless, of course. Wires could be cut out altogether. Yes, then perhaps the day would come when the medium could be cut out altogether, and one could communicate with the spirit-world freely and direct. And surely it would be better, more appropriate and satisfactory, if he could talk with the spirit of his Uncle in a glorious cathedral, or better still, on the cliff-top at Cortenay, than in this dingy parlour with the help of a young working-man.

Yes, this present method might only be the beginning of things; and communication with the spirits might develop from this as far as communication between human beings had developed from signal-fires to wireless telegraphy.

Suppose he could get into communication with Uncle, wouldn't it be amazingly interesting to talk with him?

Would he have changed much in personality, in views and opinions?

It would be truly wonderful. But then, apparently, so far as one could gather, such communication as human beings did at present have with departed spirits seemed particularly futile and unsatisfactory. Granted that seekers after truth had attended *séances* and been completely convinced that they were in communication with the departed spirit whom they sought, what kind of satisfaction did they get? What sort of information? What sort of useful communication did they establish? It never seemed to be relevant, useful, helpful, or in the least degree satisfying, according to what one read and heard.

Apparently no departed spirit had ever yet given a comprehensible detailed account of conditions of life in the Hereafter.

Still, there again, one might compare all that with the first ghastly and excruciating gramophone records. Just as these earliest musical horrors had progressed to the marvels of the modern wireless cabinet from which proceed music and voices indistinguishable from their originals, so, quite possibly, might these pointless and futile *obiter dicta* progress to complete and soul-satisfying communications and conversations. A man might some day be able to talk with his departed wife by the hour; a wife with her husband; a mother with her child; lover with lover, and . . .

Good God! What was that?

It was a child talking.

What was this? There was no child in the room. Unless one had opened the door and stuck its head in. But no, one would have heard the opening of the door; and besides, the voice wasn't coming from that direction at all; it was from the head of the table, from the arm-chair in which Jones was sitting.

Well, that wasn't Jones's voice, unless Jones was a truly marvellous ventriloquist.

And what was this? There was a woman crying in the room, sobbing very softly, and evidently doing her utmost to suppress and conceal the sounds of her distress. This was very uncanny, very uncomfortable.

The child ceased to talk and the woman continued to weep. Was it the buxom, moon-faced wife of the clergyman, and was the voice that of her own dead child?

How truly dreadful and distressing.

Poor woman—how she was suffering, rent by those terrible sobs. Why did she come and subject herself to such cruel agony?

The Pastor said something, and thereafter silence fell—a silence so prolonged that Bump found himself nodding and had difficulty in keeping awake. He was dozing. . . .

The Pastor spoke again. . . . Miss Wymper replied to him. . . . It was all very dull, now that the child had gone and the poor woman had ceased to sob. . . . Nodding. . . . Dozing. . . .

Suddenly a great powerful voice filled the room, a voice beside which that of the Pastor's wife was small and weak, a voice that suggested Cavalry Captains whose stentorian shout should be heard by galloping squadrons above the thunder of the horses' hooves; a voice that suggested gallant sea-captains whose mighty shout would shame the howling of the winds and the crashing of the waves, out-roar the tempest itself and be heard from poop to fo'c'sle, from truck to kelson, above all other sounds; a great, rich, deep, vibrant voice.

"Ho, ho, kinsman," it boomed now, restrained, quietly thunderous. "You'd have word with me? Then here's a word for thee, though thou art no soldier, seeking the bubble reputation even in the cannon's mouth. In the cannon's mouth, I say."

And with a roar as of distant thunder dying away down a deep canyon, rumbling, reverberating, and echoing as it went, the voice dwindled and departed; and in departing seemed to leave yet, as a whisper in the air, the words again, "*In the cannon's mouth.*"

Bump was aware that he was cold and damp,

wet with a perspiration like a clammy death-sweat.

This was awful, terrible.

This was the road to En-dor, the road down which he would not take another step.

Uncle's last words.

Those dreams from which he had awakened with them ringing in his ears—"*Seeking the bubble reputation in the cannon's mouth.*"

Honor saying those very words again, and asking whether it were the bubble—Reputation—that men sought; or a mere bubble reputation: fame and glory—brittle, fragile and transient as that.

And now this voice, this vast, hearty, resonant voice.

Just the voice one would imagine issuing from the bearded lips of that Elizabethan sea-dog, that buccaneer who sank ships, sacked cities and burned cathedrals.

There was no trickery here.

This man Jones could no more have produced that voice and the delicate voice of that little girl, than he could assume the shapes of the owners of those voices.

Besides, what did he, this utter stranger, this Sandhaven working-man, know of Bump's obsession by this phrase, these meaningless words, this irrelevant line from a Shakespearean play?

How should he know that they were the last words uttered by General Cortenay? No-one on earth knew but Bump himself, for he had never told anyone. How should this artisan know that the phrase haunted Bump as it did?

No, there was no trickery.

But there was something worse than that. There was something occult and *terrifying*.

Never again. Let well alone, and still more, let ill alone.

The Road to En-dor, the oldest road and the craziest road of all!

> *"And nothing is changed of the sorrow in store*
> *For such as go down on the Road to En-dor."*

Seeking the bubble reputation in the cannon's mouth?
Perhaps.
But seeking nothing on the Road to En-dor.

XI

As Bump went from the dining-room one evening, a few weeks later, Miss Hoping intercepted him in the corridor that led to the great hall.

"Excuse me a moment, Sir Giles," she said. "Do you think you could spare a minute to see poor Miss Wymper? She's in rather a bad way, I'm afraid."

"What, worse?" asked Bump anxiously. "Miss Honor told me this morning that she thought she had taken a turn for the better."

"Yes, Sir. She seemed better this morning, but the doctor wasn't satisfied about her heart again, and she had a very nasty turn this afternoon. Almost blue she was, and her lips were quite white. Miss Honor's with her now."

"Oh, I wondered why she was late for dinner. I'll go up, and she can come down and have something while I sit with Miss Wymper."

"Yes, Sir; if you would. The poor lady has been asking for you. Told Miss Honor she had got something to tell you. Something important."

Bump heaved a sigh and returned his unlighted cigarette to its case. Sick people were very sensitive, and he didn't want to offend her by smelling of tobacco-smoke. What could the poor dear have to say? Some nonsense or other, probably.

Still, if it would give her any pleasure or comfort . . .

Lightly he ran up the grand staircase and across the main landing to the corridor leading to Miss Wymper's bed-sitting-room. With a finger-nail he tapped very lightly at the door.

Honor opened it, stepped out, and, closing it

behind her, said,

"I am so glad you've come, Bunny darling. The poor dear is in rather a bad way, I'm afraid; and she has got something on her mind. Something she must tell you."

Bump smiled ruefully.

"I'll hear it. Think we had better ring up Dr. Simpkins again? He was here this morning, wasn't he?"

"Yes, I think I'll ring him up again. She seems so dreadfully weak, and keeps getting heart attacks. It can't do any harm to send for him, anyway."

"Right. And would you mind telling Colonel Kinloch Grant that I shan't be in the billiard-room at eight-thirty as I promised; and Bemmington that I shan't be able to make up his bridge four at nine. Archie Wilbraholme will cut in, with Gosling and the artist bird—Warlock Manningfold."

"Pull yourself together, Bunny. Mr. Manningfold went yesterday."

"Oh, yes. Well, Colonel Featherston . . ."

"Yes, yes, I'll see to everything. Don't worry."

Softly opening and closing the door, Bump tip-toed to where Miss Wymper lay, with closed eyes; and silently seated himself on the chair that Honor had vacated.

"So glad you've come, dear boy," whispered Miss Wymper, opening her forget-me-not blue eyes and holding his with a steady gaze. "So glad you've come. I could not have passed over quite happily, until I had had a talk with you. There are one or two things I want to tell you. One of great importance to me; and one of some importance to you."

"Oh, don't talk about passing over, Miss Wymper," whispered Bump.

"Oh, but I want to, dear. I'd love to. It's the Fifteenth of July, and I'm going to pass over quite soon now; and I'm so happy about it. Do you know,

I've been wanting to go, ever since the General went."

"The General? General Cortenay?"

"Yes, dear boy, your great-uncle. Do you know, I've loved him better than anything in all the world, ever since I was a young girl."

Bump thought back rapidly. If Uncle had been alive to-day he would have been about ninety-five or so. Miss Wymper must be round about sixty-five or so. Yes, there must have been thirty years difference in their ages.

Was the poor dear wandering in her mind?

"Yes, dear boy. Your great-uncle was the romance of my life. Do you know, I fell in love with him when I was seventeen, and he was in his prime. Such a magnificent man; tall, upright, going grey, but oh, such a fine, noble-looking hero, especially to a romantic young girl.

"It was at a lovely ball that I met him. My first— at Lady Richborough's. It was a perfect summer night, the Fifteenth of July; full moon and the marvellous grounds illuminated, and dark shadows thrown by the cedars on the turf and in the shrubberies. . . . You'd hardly think it now, but I was a pretty girl then. Indeed some of the golden lads of those far-off days used to say I was lovely; but that's how young men talked then, when they were making love to a girl. Still, they gathered round me, so I couldn't have been . . . plain.

"But do you know, they didn't interest me. They were so vapid, as I thought then, with their curled, anointed hair and their carefully cultivated whiskers and their lackadaisical airs and graces and foppishness. Why, they used to lisp, and keep on sticking eye-glasses in their eyes and letting them drop out again on to their cravats. Foolish creatures.

"It wasn't sour grapes. They really did run after me, and I really did despise them.

"I wasn't going to enjoy that ball very much, for I was quite heart-whole and nobody interested me.

"Then suddenly Colonel Cortenay appeared, marched straight up to me, either said something or didn't, and I found myself waltzing with him.

"And do you know, Bump, every time I looked up into his face, his eyes seemed to look right through mine down into my heart; and I had to look away, and that same silly heart fluttered and jumped . . . oh . . ."

Miss Wymper groaned.

". . . like it's doing now," she whispered.

"Perhaps you had better not talk."

"Oh, let me talk, dear boy. I just want to tell you before I go.

"And when the dance was over, I clung to his arm, and he led me from the ball-room; across the hall; out on to a few acres of lawn; right across it to where there was a seat under a big over-hanging weeping-willow beside the lake.

"And when we got up to go back—hours later—I felt that I had known him for years and had loved him all my life. He had got my arm tucked through his, and my left hand inside his right, pressed against his breast, and I said to myself,

" 'Darling, I do love you so.'

"And do you know what had happened, Bump? I had said it out loud!

"And he stopped and took my face between his hands and said,

" 'My child, I am old enough to be your father. Now kiss me and forget me.'

"And I put my arms around his neck and gave him a long, long kiss. And then he kissed me, just like that.

"And do you know what he did then?

"He told the butler to send for his groom to bring round his dog-cart—and he drove away. Straight out of my life. And I never saw him again.

"But he never forgot. On that day, July the Fifteenth, he always used to send me a white rose-bud.

"And then he died, Bump. And every year, on that day, July the Fifteenth, I put white roses on his grave."

"Oh, it was you, was it, Miss Wymper, who always put the lovely white roses?"

"Yes, dear. I always laid them there at eleven o'clock at night. . . . I heard the big bell at Richborough House strike eleven just after he had kissed me.

"So you can imagine what it meant to me that one could come and live here in the very house where my wonderful lover lived and died.

"And I have a confession to make, Bump. But I know you'll forgive me. So often, at eleven o'clock at night, I have crept quietly into the Library where he died, and have sat, with my eyes closed, and willed him to come to me. And I'm sure, although I have never seen him, I have got into touch with him. I have known he was standing near me and looking at me as he did that night in the shadow on the lawn at Richborough House.

"And now, Bump, I am going to meet him; and, oh, I am so happy.

"And I have a favour to ask of you, Bump. I wouldn't have dared do it but that you have been so kind, so good to me, a troublesome old woman whom you could never expect to be able to repay your kindness in any way. . . . Just pure goodness of heart, you and dear Honor. . . . I wonder if I dare ask you . . . ?"

"Of course. And be sure I will be only too happy."

Miss Wymper laid a cold and feeble hand upon Bump's.

"It is this, dear boy. Do you think I could be

buried near him? Please, please tell me if you'd rather not. Please say 'No' at once. Just say, 'No. That acre is reserved for Cortenays.' . . . Is it, Bump?"

Furtively Bump brushed the back of his hand across the side of one eye.

"If none but Cortenays had been buried there for a thousand years, it wouldn't matter, Miss Wymper," he said. "You should join them, and they would welcome you . . . when the time comes, that is to say. Many a long year hence, I hope."

"Oh, darling boy. You make me so happy, I do thank you from the bottom of my heart. I am so grateful. And I think he would be pleased, Bump, if he heard you say that. I think he'd be quite glad. He did love me, I know; and he never married."

Bump, sentimentalist, kissed the withered hand that lay on his.

"It's a promise," he said.

"Such a noble man, such a gentle man, dear," whispered Miss Wymper. "If only all men were like you, what a world it would be! Especially for women. You are like him, you know, Bump. And I could give you no higher praise than that, much as I want to do so."

Miss Wymper fell silent.

"I'll go now," whispered Bump. "You've tired yourself."

The white hand closed on his and held it.

"Don't go."

Another long silence.

"And now about you, dear. I'm a selfish old woman, talking about myself and then asking that wonderful favour. Now listen, dear boy. I have made my will, and there's a copy of it in the right-hand drawer of my writing-desk. Messrs. Wilkinson of Sandhaven have got the will. I've left everything to you, Bump. Absolutely everything; for I've not a relation in the world; and although I've lived like a miser here, and often been far behind with my rent, I'm a very rich woman."

"Oh . . . please . . . Miss Wymper . . ."

"No, Bump dear. As I say, I haven't a soul in the world who has the slightest claim upon me or the slightest interest in my affairs; and I leave it all to you. I want you to turn Cortenay Old Hall back into a private house and live here 'happy ever after.' Live here where your Uncle did; and he and I will spend lots and lots of our time with you.

"It's a very lovely and precious thought to me that, whether you find the real Cortenay Treasure or not, I am privileged to be, in a manner of speaking, a Cortenay treasure—one of them—and to be the means of restoring the fortunes of the family into which, had I only been born a quarter of a century earlier, I should have married. For he did love me.

"He fell in love with me that night; and, oh, the kiss he gave me. I can feel it now. . . .

"I've been very clairvoyant just lately, and I know there is such a happy future before you, Bump. Such a future as you deserve; and you are going to find the Treasure. You are, I know. You are going to find the Treasure of Cortenay Old Hall. I know you are. It may not be just yet, not quite soon; and, meanwhile, there is the treasure that I am leaving you. And I am so glad I've been careful of it, and it is really large.

"You will be quite rich, dear boy, whether you find the ancient Cortenay Treasure or not."

"Miss Wymper, you . . . Really, I can't . . . but . . ."

"And I want you, if you will, dearest boy, to put some white roses on his grave and mine, on the Fifteenth of July at eleven o'clock at night, every year. Will you?"

"Miss Wymper, you are going to get better. The doctor is coming presently and I'm perfectly certain . . ."

"So am I, Bump. Perfectly certain. I'm going to pass over to-night; and I am so glad, so thankful. I am going to him, and I feel as I should have felt if I had been going to him fifty years ago. I feel as I should have felt if it were the night before my wedding-day.

"He loved me to the end of his life—and he only kissed me once."

The door opened softly and Honor entered, glanced at Bump, looked at him again, and motioned him to go.

Bump went straight to his room and locked himself in.

That night Miss Wymper died.

§2

So Miss Wymper rested at last beside her lover.

And after the funeral, Bump and Honor, considering it nobody's business but their own, read the copy of the Will which they found in the right-hand drawer of the escritoire in the room which had been Miss Wymper's, and once upon a time, that of General Sir Giles Cortenay, K.C.B., K.C.M.G.

Drawn up by Messrs. Wilkinson, Burt, Wilkes & Harrowby of Sandhaven, it was succinct and to the point; merely stating that Miss Delicia Wymper gave and bequeathed everything of which she might die possessed, to her friend Sir Giles Cortenay of Cortenay Old Hall, and appointed him sole executor of that her will. . . .

"I suppose there are no heirs," said Bump, looking from the will to Honor.

"Well, if there are, the will is clear enough, isn't it?" replied the girl.

"Yes, but I should simply loathe it if I inherited, and then some wretched brother or sister, nephew or niece, or somebody like that, turned up and said it was a burning shame and all that."

"Well, if anybody did come, or write, on the subject, you could see them and . . . act accordingly, couldn't you, Bunny? If it were some member of the undeserving poor who could prove relationship, you could give him what you thought fit, either in a lump sum or an allowance or something like that."

"Oh, I don't know," said Bump. "If the applicant could prove near relationship and great expectations and all that, I'd much rather give them the whole lot."

"You would, my son, wouldn't you. . . . But let's wait until they do turn up. She said most distinctly that she hadn't a friend or relation of any sort in the world."

"I must advertise," decided Bump. " 'Any relation of the late Miss Delicia Wymper, who died on the fifteenth of July at Cortenay Old Hall, will hear something to his advantage by communicating with Messrs. Wilkinson, Burt, Wilkes & Harrowby of Sandhaven.' Something like that."

"Yes. Stick it in every newspaper in England every day for a month and then you'll be satisfied, won't you?"

"Yes."

"Well, I'll tell you what. Before you do anything at all, you go over to Sandhaven and see old Wilkinson, and get probate and all that; and you leave the matter of relatives to him. Tell him to advertise for them; and if any turn up, to satisfy himself as to their *bona fides* and blood-relationship."

"Yes; that'll be best; and whether anyone turns up to claim this legacy or not, we must get her affairs straightened out."

"And I'll tell Miss Hoping to clear the room up. I

suppose she could dispose of anything in the way of clothes and such?"

"Yes, leave all that to her."

"I'd like to keep one or two little personal things. I suppose that would be all-right?" asked Honor.

"Why, of course."

"That funny little brooch she used to wear in the evenings with a 'G' on it in diamonds. Who do you suppose 'G' was?" mused Honor.

" 'G' for Giles, I've no doubt," said Bump. "General Giles Cortenay. Great-uncle Giles."

§3

The gentleman who called himself Messrs. Wilkinson, Burt, Wilkes & Harrowby, of Sandhaven, smiled across his desk at Bump.

"I'm sorry, Sir Giles," he said. "I hope it won't come as anything in the nature of a shock. Naturally it's a very heavy disappointment. I should have liked to have warned you beforehand, but I had my late client's very strict instructions that nothing whatsoever was to be said to you on the subject of your being sole legatee. The simple fact of the matter is that poor Miss Wymper left precisely nothing at all."

It was Bump's turn to smile.

"Do you know, I'm rather glad to hear that," he said. "I should have hated inheriting money from—I was going to say a stranger. . . . She wasn't that, of course, but I had absolutely no claim upon her whatsoever; and I should always have had an uncomfortable feeling that I was doing some rightful heir out of—her estate."

"Estate!" smiled the lawyer. "It was my melancholy business to buy her a tiny annuity, several years ago, with the very last of her money. And that of course died with her. How she lived I don't know, for it was precisely one hundred and fifty-six pounds a year."

"Poor darling," sighed Bump. "And she paid me, alone, two hundred and eight out of her one hundred and fifty-six."

"Did she?" laughed the other.

"Well, as nearly as she could," said Bump. "She used to pay her four pounds a week, for quite long periods, with the utmost regularity."

"And then I suppose didn't pay anything at all, for a period, with the utmost regularity."

"Oh, well," replied Bump. "One couldn't dun her; and she paid when she could. I wish to God I had been able . . ."

"I suppose there's no secret hoard of bank-notes in a trunk or a drawer or anything?"

Bump laughed.

"No, I'm afraid it was a case of nothing but a few old clothes, pitiably few and terribly old. . . . The other was a sort of delusion, I suppose."

"Yes, undoubtedly," replied the lawyer. "She had been quite rich, at one time, you know. Lived on a very spacious scale. Niece of Lady Richborough. Moved in quite distinguished circles. I suppose she took expert City advice, and put all her money into some South Sea Bubble or other. Anyhow, when Cortenay Old Hall was first advertised as a Guest House, she came down here and consulted me. I was horrified at the sort of investments she had been making, and the state of her finances; and most strongly urged her to let me buy an annuity with what was left. And there it is, Sir Giles. She has left you all of which she died possessed, and that is all that there is in the room she occupied in Cortenay Old Hall! . . . I'm sorry."

"Well, believe me, I am glad. I am only sorry she didn't have a better time. Thank you so much. Good-bye."

XII

Honor put her head into Bump's office where he sat at work, his brow corrugated, his hair tousled, his fingers inky.

"Chuck it; and come out for a walk, Bump. You'll go dotty if you stick at it all day like this. Dottier, I mean. Come up on the Cliff till tea-time."

"Righto," replied Bump, throwing his pen into the tray with a sigh of relief.

"Good Lord, look at my fingers. Shan't be a minute."

"Don't stop to wash now, Bump. Put them in your pocket or lick them or something. Come on. Come on out."

Together they ran down the wide stairs, across the hall, and out into the afternoon sunshine.

"Let's go round the kitchen garden, stables, garage, glass-houses, through the orchard, and out that way."

"Not a bit of it. The roofs of the stables are still falling in. The glass of the glass-houses, greenhouses, hot-houses, conservatories and what-not is still all broken, the iron-work still rusty and the paint still peeling. The kitchen garden is still overgrown with weeds; the orchard still in need of pruning, spraying, white-washing, painting and papering. And going round and looking at them won't do the slightest good. Only depress you more. Come on up to the Cliff—and forget it."

"Wants a bit of forgetting," observed Bump, and allowed Honor, who had seized his arm, to lead him across the lawns in the direction of the path that wound down through the Gardens, across the Wood, and up to the East Cliff, on which were the

194

ancient grass-grown ramparts known as Fort Raleigh.

"Gad! the lawns are in a bad way," said Bump, as they crossed the vast tracts of sward four centuries old, that only recently had looked more like velvet than grass.

"Yes, like everything else," said Honor. "But a season's good work would put it all right again. What we want is one of those motor-mowers, isn't it?"

"Yes, that's all," smiled Bump ruefully, "and a man to work it and look after it."

"That's a job I should love," said Honor. "Sit on a motor lawn-mower and puff up and down the lawns all day long."

"Well, if somebody gives me one for my birthday, you shall ride it. Keep it clean and in repair, too."

"Old man Bemmington would give us one, Bump."

"I know he would. It seems to me he'd give us anything. He wants to give us a lot too much. What do you think is the latest?"

"Pull the house down and rebuild it?"

"Pretty well. Next thing to it. He wants to have it completely done up, inside and out. Top and bottom. Wants to bring an architect down here."

"Architects don't paper and paint, do they?"

"No. A gent called '*Builders, Decorators and Contractors*' does that—but he wants to bring an architect because he says he's not sure that the fabric is all right, whatever the fabric may be."

"Beams and things, I suppose."

"Yes. Bricks and mortar and beams, walls and floors, plaster and planks and what-not. He seems to have got the idea that some of the old beams have got dry-rot in them. Says he's quite sure some of the floor-boards and stairs have, in the oldest part, and he wants to have a look at the roof panelling in some of the rooms too, especially the Library and the Banqueting Hall, I mean the dining-room."

"Awfully good of him. He takes a tremendous interest, doesn't he?"

"Yes. Overdoes it a bit, I think. It would cost a frightful lot to do all he wants to have done."

"And he's going to find the money again, I suppose?"

"Yes."

"Oh, Bump! We owe him a frightful lot already, don't we?"

"I do, certainly. You don't mean to say you've been borrowing money from . . ."

"Don't be silly. I only said *we*, because . . ."

"I know, Honor, of course. I was only joking. Yes, we do. A devil of a lot. He almost *owns* us, already. But this isn't a case of sticking any more baths and running-hot-and-cold and radiators and central-heating into a cold wing—that sort of thing. According to him, it's a case of absolute necessity. Saving the house."

"Rot!"

"Yes, dry-rot. And death-watch beetles and wood-worms and worm-wood, and all sorts of funny insects. He's got some powder on a sheet of notepaper. Says it has come down from the roof-beams of his room and that it was caused by wood-beetles boring, and that I really must have an expert to see how bad the damage is."

"Golly! Anybody would think he really owned the place—or wanted to."

"Yes, he certainly takes a wonderful interest in the Hall, and that's the rather uncomfortable feeling that's growing on me."

"What, that he takes an extraordinary interest?"

"Well, rather more than that. What you said. What you hinted at. That he *wanted* to own the place."

"How much do we owe him, Bump?"

"I really don't know. Apart from the cash loans on mortgage that he's made when I've told him that I didn't see how I could carry on any longer, he's never sent me the bills—nor shown them to me—for improvements and repairs."

"I suppose he's paid them, Bump?"

"Yes, must have done, or I should have heard all about it. I don't find anybody anxious to give me much rope. There seems to be quite a wide-spread, as well as well-founded, notion among all creditors —except Bemmington—that if it isn't cash in advance, it must be cash on the nail, and no credit. . . . Oh, yes; I should have had the bills, all-right, if Bemmington hadn't paid them. And the total must be pretty colossal, too. You see, he had the whole roof put right; all that plumbing done; papering, painting and distempering where there's no panelling; a lot of new doors and French windows in place of the ones that were absolutely falling out; new furnaces and boilers . . ."

"Do you still like him, Bump?"

"Yes."

"As much as you did?"

"No. Not quite."

"Why not? Anything definite? Anything in particular?"

"No . . . No . . . But I wouldn't admit it to anybody else. I haven't admitted it to myself before. . . . I don't know . . ."

"I do, Bump. You can divide people, who develop into what are known as friends, into two classes, those who improve on acquaintance and those who don't. There's a certain type of person who, at first, is very—how shall I put it?—extremely well-mannered, very careful as to what he says and does. He is just right, so to speak. Nice and cordial without being familiar. He makes himself charming and attractive and pleasant, and is at some pains to be all that is agreeable. He never jars in the least. And then, as he gets to know you better, this wears off a little. As he gets more familiar with you, he gets more—familiar. You find that the charm, politeness, delightful manners and so on, can be thrown off like a garment. And occasionally are thrown off, and increasingly often."

Bump laughed.

"Yes, and one day he comes out without the garment of courtesy at all."

"And never wears it any more," added Honor, nodding her head wisely.

"Yes, that's one class, and a pretty big one," she continued. "Then there are the rest, who are just like the others at first, but remain so. There's no veneer to wear off."

"Solid oak all through," agreed Bump.

"Yes."

"Wise child. It's a wise child that knows its own friends. And you think Bemmington is veneered?"

"Yes, I do. He's definitely wearing thin with me. Much more 'jolly,' easy-going, familiar."

"Not over-familiar?"

"Well, no. Just familiar. I never liked him much; but I liked him far better at first when he was more careful, polite, on his best behaviour, and not so much at ease."

"Nothing particular? Nothing special?"

"No . . . No . . . I wouldn't say that. But definitely one of those acquaintances whom one couldn't possibly allow to develop into a friend. That's how I feel."

"In fact, the more you know him, the less you like him."

"Bunny, my lamb, you've said it all. You've been delivered of a mouthful."

"Golly, isn't it glorious up here?" the girl added, as they emerged on to the cliff-top and, gazing over the grassy ramparts of Fort Raleigh, beheld the glittering illimitable sea, unmarked, unbroken throughout its vast expanse from where they stood to the far horizon. The emerald green of the grass, the sapphire blue of the sky, and the shaded varying aquamarine of the sea were the only colours; grass, sky and sea the only things to be seen; those and the ancient carronade that some-how had survived the others brought from his ship, the *St. George*, by Sir Giles the Buccaneer.

"Let's sit down and be peaceful, Bump," said the girl, seating herself in a grass-grown embrasure of the rampart.

Bump flung himself down beside her.

"No, I'm sorry to say I don't like him as much as I did," Bump resumed, "and I feel rather ashamed. I try to; but there it is. Almost every time one sees him, one likes him less. And, as you say, he wears the garment of charm more seldom. His manners don't improve, neither does his manner."

"No, it was all 'charm of manner' at first, wasn't it?"

"Yes. It's as though he sat down with you at the banquet of life in correct evening dress, and after the soup, which he ate very daintily, he took off his coat, and after the fish . . ."

"Which he ate with the correct implements," nodded Bump, "he took off his tie."

"You've got it, my dear. Then his collar after the entree; and now, in his shirt-sleeves and braces, he's really comfortable; really is himself again; and eating his peas with a knife."

"He hasn't really annoyed you, has he, Honor? Nothing to . . . ?"

"No. But I'm waiting for it. I don't mean I am always on the defensive or that he is ever offensive.

But he's going to be."

"You mean he's going to propose?"

"Yes, he's certainly going to propose, and there'll be nothing offensive about that. But . . . well, you know—he's familiar. It isn't easy to explain but . . . he paws. Catches hold of one, puts his arm round one. He'll grab hold of me and kiss me one of these days."

"Gad! He had better not," said Bump, frowning at the girl.

"Oh, that's nothing, nowadays. Don't you ever kiss a girl after a dance, Bump?"

"No, most certainly I don't."

Honor laughed.

"Why not?"

"Haven't the slightest desire to, for one reason. What would you do if Bemmington kissed you, or attempted to?"

"Laugh; and tell him not to be an old fool. But don't you worry about that, Bump. I can look after myself and Bemmington too. It isn't that that worries me. Does it occur to you that he's most frightfully interested in panelling?"

"Yes. Why not?"

"On the other hand, why? He's not a man of any taste, or flair for that sort of thing."

"Oh, I don't know. He's very keen on pictures."

"Since when?"

"Oh, I don't know. He had heard that we had got some good ones in the Library, and was very anxious to see them."

"Well, does he know a Rubens from a Van Dyck or a Lely or a Kneller, or any of them from a Gainsborough or a Reynolds?"

"Oh, I think so. It would be by the dress, though, not by the painting."

"That was how he came to be in the Library, I suppose. Looking at the pictures."

"Yes. And he really was concerned about the state of the panelling and the carved roof in that room. Says it is worse, for some reason, than in the others. Worse than any wood-work except the min- strels' gallery and the roof of the Banqueting Hall."

"Well, what is he going to do about it?"

"Wants it all treated."

"He's fond of treating, isn't he?" observed Honor.

"Yes. Well, he wants to treat all that wood-work with some stuff that kills the boring insects. Then he wants all the panelling oiled. Anyway, he's get- ting an expert down here to Go into the Whole Question of the Condition of the Ancient Beams and Panelling of Cortenay Very Old Hall."

"Wonder he doesn't want another one to go into the whole subject of the Very Old Masters of Corte- nay Very Old Hall," said Honor. "Aren't they getting worm-eaten or death-beetle-browed or something?"

"Well, he wants me to have them cleaned."

"Does he really? I say, he has got a nerve, you know, Bump. It's all rather on a par with what we said about his change of manner and manners as he got to know one better. I suppose the first time he saw the pictures he stood with bated breath and then said, 'My God, how marvellous!'; the next time, 'I wonder what they'd fetch at auction, properly advertised in Europe and America.' And on the third visit it'd be, 'Time you had those damn things cleaned, Bump. Want their silly faces washed.'"

Bump laughed.

"Well, not quite as bad as that, but he's worried about them."

"Worried?"

"Well, he thinks that neither I nor my immediate ancestors have taken sufficient interest in them, sufficient care of them. He wanted to know when they were last re-hung and why they are not under glass."

"Well, he should worry! What's it to do with him?"

"No more and no less than the panelling is, but . . . I don't know."

The two sat silent, Honor nibbling a stalk of grass and frowning in deep thought.

"Look here, Honor," said Bump suddenly. "Aren't we getting suspicious-minded and, well, rather ungrateful? Why can't we give him credit for taking the deepest and kindliest interest in Cortenay Old Hall? It seems a bit ungracious, doesn't it, if all he wants is to do us and the place a bit of good with his money. Let's give him credit . . ."

"He's certainly giving us credit," interrupted Honor, "and that's what bothers me, Bump; because I somehow can't get that aspect of him."

"What do you mean?"

"I mean I simply can't see Sir Russell Bemmington as a philanthropist, an altruist. I don't believe he ever gave—or lent—something for nothing in all his life."

"Why should you say that?"

"I don't know. Intuition. I may or may not have any reason at all for thinking so, but I have got a feeling that way. And mind you, Bump, you can *reason* for all you are worth—and be entirely wrong. But what you really *feel* is never wrong, if you know what I mean."

"Yes, I know what you mean. Instinct, intuition and that sort of thing are better than reason, logic and mathematics."

"A lot better. You can prove anything, with figures; and reason can lead you anywhere; but if you've got a real strong *feeling* about something, deep-seated and unshakable, it is bound to be right."

"With a woman," she added.

"Hark at the woman," smiled Bump.

"Yes, you do hark, my lamb; and listen and remember and bear it in mind and act on it and all that. Sir Russell Bemmington never gives or lends something for nothing. I don't like him and I don't trust him."

"Perhaps you mean you don't trust him because you don't like him."

"Or equally perhaps I don't like him because I don't trust him," said Honor. "Anyway, there it is. Don't let him lend you any more money, Bump. I wish to God we could pay off what we do owe him."

"Yes, and then ask him how much the builders' and decorators' and plumbers' and electricians' bills are, and pay those," agreed Bump.

"But how? Well, we certainly shan't save it out of the profits of the Country Club and Guest House," said Honor.

"No, I am only too thankful when it is paying its way. And it wouldn't be doing that, but for Bemmington. I'm afraid I have agreed to his getting this architect chap down, and the panelling specialist, and yet another picture-expert."

"What is a panelling specialist exactly?" asked Honor. "A timber merchant, a glorified carpenter, a cabinet-maker, or what?"

"Well, I understand this chap is an antique-dealer in a big way."

"Yes, I suppose they'd have to know all about keeping death's-head beetles and watch-committees of wood-worms and such things out of antique furniture. They'd have to treat old furniture and such in their ware-houses and store-rooms so that moth could not break through and steal . . . And who's the picture man?"

"Oh, some expert from Brackenridge's. Apparently he tells you whether all's well with a picture, and if that wants treating too. According to Bemmington you've got to treat 'em well and treat 'em often. Apparently small pests get into the wood behind the canvas."

"I suppose they're worth a lot of money, Bump."

"I believe so, but really one couldn't sell those, Honor."

"No, of course not. Almost as soon sell the house itself as the old Buccaneer and his wife and their poor little boy who never saw either of 'em. Not to speak to, so to speak."

"What would you say if Bemmington suddenly made you an offer for one or all of them?" she continued. "The sort of sum that'd pay off his mortgage and all those bills and leave enough over to keep the house going? Perhaps enough to turn it back into a private house and keep it up."

"Tell him not to be funny," growled Bump.

"Would it be so funny, really, though?"

"No, not a bit funny."

"Listen, Bump. You know I lie awake a lot at night, thinking about . . . things . . ."

"You do?"

Bump had a sudden vision of his own four-o'clock-in-the-morning misery when he awoke to visualize ruin; bankruptcy; departure; Cortenay Old Hall in the house-breakers' hands, sold for its value in stone, timber and panelling; the pictures seized and sold at obscure and hasty auction to pay creditors; the Cortenay Gardens turned into allotments; the ancient trees of Cortenay Park felled for timber; a terrible picture, of which the drawing, perspective and colouring improved somewhat by breakfast-time. Could it be possible that this poor kid went through that sort of thing too?

"You do? Wake up at four o'clock in the morning?"

"Well, no. Not very often. I mean, I lie awake thinking before I go to sleep; and I thought out quite a plot the other night, Bump. A dark plot against you, with an accomplice."

"Sir Russell the Bemmington?"

"No. A young and struggling artist. They always struggle. Clerks and people with five rooms and six children don't, of course. Well, the idea is this. I get him down here as a guest."

"Your guest?"

"No, don't be common and unclean. I get him to come down here as a summer visitor."

"I know, a summer boy, with a tennis-shirt collar outside a blazer of a horrible blue."

"Not at all . . . I put him up for membership of the Cortenay Old Hall Country Club, and he comes into residence. And I tell you that I have inspired him to paint. He's going to paint me."

"Might do a bit of useful painting down round the stables and the green-houses."

"Don't interrupt. Well; he finds he can't do me justice."

" 'It's mercy you want, not justice,' " quoted Bump. "Yes, go on."

"And he throws down his brushes in despair."

"On the carpet."

"And I bid him pick them up again and . . ."

"Wipe them on the seat of his trousers."

". . . and go on and do some useful bread-and-butter work."

"Cutting sandwiches?"

"No, some useful bread-and-butter work in the Library. Copy Godfrey Kneller's Giles the Tenth or Peter Lely's Lady Cortenay.

"Then take it up to Town and sell it for five pounds and a ten per cent sale-commission, to Brackenridge, who at once starts an agitation in the daily papers . . ."

"*Is this a genuine Lely? Found rolled up all anyhow in the corner of a dark, damp, and dirty cellar. Miraculously* (as usual) *untouched by rats, toad-*

stools, mould and cockroaches," jeered Bump. "Then a lot of wise old birds squinting at it through quizzing-glasses and giving their verdicts. No two verdicts alike. And in the end a retired pork-butcher or soap-boiler gives a hundred pounds for it, on the off-chance of selling it for ten thousand. And so, in the end, your rake-off is only a tenner."

"Wrong again, Bump. Wrong once more."

"Why, you don't think that your lank, dank young artist sells it to the soap-boiler direct, do you? 'Course he doesn't. It's never like that in the books or on the films. It would be quite contrary to . . ."

"Wronger than ever. . . . Now sit up and listen. When my embryo Michelangelo or Leonardo . . ."

"From Moscow or Soho or Monmartre-oh . . ."

". . . has finished the picture, he gives it that lovely patina that nothing but age—or dirty varnish —can give. Then, when none but the most gifted critic could tell one from the other and would be wrong when he did—we have the new one framed exactly like the old."

"If we cannot get an old frame, we get a new one and give it the patina as requisite," said Bump.

"Yes. Ink it over a bit, and make a genuine antique of it with some cheap gold paint such as the arty-and-crafty use to gild pretty baskets of fir-cones for the parlour fire-place."

"Well, and then?"

"Don't you see? We take down the old picture and hang up the new one."

"I get you, Stephen. A great idea."

"Exactly. Michelangelo then skips to America with the original and sells it to Mr. J. Pierpoint Gould for a hundred thousand dollars, keeps ten per cent rake-off, and everybody is happy. J.P.M. has got a genuine Lely. Michelangelo has got two thousand pounds. And I lay a cheque for eighteen thousand pounds at your feet."

"Aren't I a little surprised?"

"Not a bit—when I tell you it's my moral earnings, and that you've got to close down the hotel and live on them."

"And what about my picture?"

"That's the beauty of it. That's the very essence of the plot. You'll never know. So you are perfectly happy. You are doubly happy. You've got eighteen thousand pounds, and you live and die under the impression that the picture ten feet up on the Library wall is the original Lely."

"I see."

"Yes, and you would see, my dear. On the very rare occasions when you glanced at it, you'd see what you thought was the picture that had hung there for three centuries. A case of where ignorance is bliss. You'd still have your picture and you'd have eighteen thousand pounds."

"I shouldn't have the picture."

"You would while you thought you had."

"Now, no feminine logic. No casuistry. Of course I shouldn't have the picture."

"No, stoopid, perhaps not, in silly logic; but you would in . . . in . . ."

"Don't say in actual fact."

"No, but you would in . . ."

"In theory?"

"Yes, exactly, and in practice. I mean in practical results. You would as long as you thought you had."

"You mean I should get just as much pleasure. Just as much bliss while I was in ignorance?"

"Exactly. You'd think you still had the picture and you'd have all the pride of possession. There you are. I've said it. Pride of possession. Possession, you see. So you've still got it."

Bump lay back and smiled at the heavens.

"Yes, and what about when I came to sell it?"

"Oh, Bump, you'd never do that! You'd never sell one of the pictures, surely?"

"No, I wouldn't."

"Well, there you are, then."

"And when my eighteen thousand pounds came to an end? It would cost that much to get the place straight and . . ."

"Why, I'd do it again. I'd say to you,

" 'Bump, you know how in the old days, the dear dead days beyond recall (thank God), when we had all those poor derelicts and failures living in the Hall at four guineas a week, and how we used to say that we wished we could keep them there for nothing, have them as real guests and keep them there as long as they lived, in safety and peace and freedom from anxiety,' and you'd say,

" 'Yes, I remember. Why didn't we do it, Honor?' and I'd say,

" 'Because we're not damn' fools and the place is not a zoo or menagerie, or an asylum or a workhouse, or an alms-house . . .' "

". . . or a public-house," murmured Bump.

"Yes, and then I'd lay my head on your shoulder, daddy, and remind you of a young struggling artist, long and lank and dank."

"Who stan . . ." began Bump.

"He didn't, except perhaps of paint, sometimes."

"And I'd say, 'Bunny,' " she continued,

" 'Let's have him here again as a guest, as a real guest, let him come and live here and work, give him his chance in life. I'm sure he only wants a chance. Think what we should be giving to the world if we enabled him to work and to paint some great master-pieces that would last throughout the ages and . . .' "

"Yes, yes, I know."

"Well, don't you see? I should send for him and

208

he would copy another picture, and he and I would hang up the changeling, and off he'd go to America again with the Old Master."

"Yes, or with a young mistress; and never come back."

"Bump, don't say such horrible things about my young artist. This time he'd sell it to a really rich American. None of your miserable twenty-million-dollar people, and this time he'd get two hundred thousand dollars, and his rake-off would be four thousand pounds; and on our first Christmas in our new home I'd put a cheque for thirty-six thousand pounds in your stocking."

Bump groaned.

"You haven't done it yet, I suppose," he said. "The few remaining ancestors are still genuine?"

"No, I haven't done it yet, and I don't suppose I shall, now I have told you all about it. But wasn't it a lovely thought?"

"Oh, lovely."

"I'll tell you another lovely thought, Bump. Suppose some Bright Young Thing like myself plagiarized my idea a hundred years ago—and carried it out."

"Oh, well, nobody'd know," Bump reassured her. "The experts would probably certify the copies as particularly fine specimens of the Masters. Haven't got any more lovely thoughts, have you?"

"No . . . What are you staring at? . . . I haven't paralysed you, have I?"

For Bump was gazing wide-eyed and open-mouthed, as though at a ghost, in the direction of the famous old gun that had fought in naval engagements of three hundred years ago.

Rising to his feet, he murmured softly to himself, apparently oblivious of Honor's presence.

"What's the matter, Bump? Lunch? Eaten something rebellious?"

"Nothing. Nothing," replied Bump without turning his head. "Only an idea."

"Suddenly struck you? Too hard?"

Bump walked over to Long John, as the old cannon had been known to generations of Cortenays.

"Aren't thinking of selling him too, are you?" asked Honor, rising and joining him as he stood beside the gun, wrapped in thought.

"You know, that's one of the most interesting things in the whole place, I think," she said, putting her finger on the closed touch-hole. "You can still see where he drove the spike in and rasped it off. Why did he do it, Bump?"

"Yes, why? Just what I was wondering, for the first time in my life. You know the story, of course?"

"I remember hearing Uncle talk to you about it, when we were up here one day; but I'm afraid I was more interested in dolls and such, in those far-off ancient times."

"Well, the story goes that Sir Giles the Buccaneer was suddenly smitten with remorse, one night, towards the end of the siege."

"Bad start for the story," observed Honor.

"How do you mean?"

"Well, if all the tales about him are true, remorse was one of the few things he didn't indulge in."

"Exactly what occurred to me when I had my Great Idea just now.

"On the other hand, they were queer superstitious coves in those days," he continued. "Look at the kings, barons and people, that used fairly to paddle in blood, and then one day suddenly go all pious, and found monasteries and subscribe handsomely to funds for converting the Heathen. . . . So it's just possible. Though I doubt it, and I hope it isn't true, because if so, it upsets my theory, my Great Idea, rather. No—I doubt that, suddenly seized with remorse, he said,

" 'Gad, I've been pooping off that Long John at my own flesh and blood, my own fellow-country-men, my own King, as it were,' or words to that effect. 'The very gun with which I sank Spanish ships, and battered Spanish towns, the gun I fired with my own hand against the enemies of my King, my Country and my God,' or words to that effect. 'Perish the hand that turned that gun against Eng-lishmen.'

"And this time it was deeds to that effect. He wasn't going to do anything to his own hand, so he went and did it to the gun instead. The pet cannon, that was to him what his favourite sporting rifle is to the professional big-game hunter, should never be fired again by him or by anyone else. And as a gesture of shame and repentance that he had put such a gun to such a use, he went straight to it, while the mood was on him, and spiked it. With his own hand he banged a great nail into the touch-hole, and hammered as hard as he could hammer it. And then, when human strength could do no more, he took a rasp and filed the top of the nail off, which meant that the gun was for ever useless."

"And to this day one can see the mark of the nail," said Honor. "I suppose one's steel and the other is iron, or something."

"Suppose again, my child. But, anyway, there's no denying that the gun was spiked. And I haven't the slightest doubt that it was done by Giles the Buccaneer, as the legend goes back to his time, and comes straight from his day to ours. Yes, I firmly believe the story. So did Uncle, who was pretty crit-ical of the family legends. But what I don't believe, for one moment, is the reason.

"Ask yourself," he continued, as Honor stood silent, eyeing the cannon. "Is it likely? The stout old boy got his ship round from Whitebay, and abso-lutely gutted her, brought all her guns, powder, shot, small arms and provisions into the two forts and sent her back. He wasn't worried then about firing his guns at the King's men, and he fired them to some purpose; this one and a score of others. There was no remorse about it. Otherwise, why didn't he spike the lot?"

"Where are they now?" asked Honor.

"Why—they are those iron posts across the stable-yard entry."

"What a shame. Fancy taking historical guns like that and sticking them up on end, as posts. Incredible vandalism."

"Oh, half the old posts about the country are guns of that sort. You see, they were turned from guns into posts at a time when they were just lumber, junk, old iron, of no more interest at that day than last-season's obsolete rifles and guns and such are to-day. Look how we scrap battle-ships, even if they did take part in famous engagements. We don't sentimentalize over the long rifle of last century, now we've replaced it with the short rifle, do we? Well, that accounts for Buccaneer Corte-nay's other guns. But why was this one kept here when the rest were carried away for posts?"

"Just chance, I suppose," hazarded Honor.

"Yes, and possibly because the gun had a name of its own; and on account of the legend. It was the gun that Wicked Sir Giles spiked in a fit of remorse. That probably accounts for its survival here."

He fell silent.

"What exactly is biting you, Bump?"

Bump ignored this.

"I don't believe it. Wish I had brought a walking-stick or something."

"Or your banjo or scooter or 'something'?"

"I'm going back to the Hall. I've got an idea."

"Yes, you said so several times."

"An idea that the Buccaneer didn't spike Long

John in a fit of remorse."

"Well, what then? A fit of temper? What *is* the idea, Bump?"

"I'll tell you when I have . . . It's nothing. It's . . . it's silly. I'll tell you . . ."

"Tell me now."

"No. There's nothing to tell. It's only an idea."

And more than this Bump refused to say.

Nor, passing through the hall, would he stop for tea. Running up the shallow steps of the wide staircase, three at a time, he hurried to the Library, locked the door, and threw himself down in a great old chair.

Of course it was absurd.

He felt excited nevertheless, so thrilling was the notion, in spite of its patent absurdity. Unconsciously he found himself gazing at that place where, beneath the carpet, a stain could still be seen (by those who knew where to look for it) on the old oak boards of the floor.

Uncle's last words.

That first half-articulated word which he had not caught, not understood. And then, clearly and distinctly, the Shakespearean quotation.

Clear and distinct—"*Seeking the bubble reputation . . .*"

And Bump had wondered, a thousand times he had wondered, why Uncle, dying, had, with his last breath, said so curious a thing.

Sometimes the obvious conclusion had seemed that he was wandering in his mind, and that a thought that had often dwelt in it had, for some reason, come to the surface, the reason perhaps being that, as drowning men and other dying men are said to do, the whole of his life had passed in swift review before the eyes of his soul. And he had summed up his soldier's life as a mere seeking of the bubble—Reputation—in the cannon's mouth.

. . . Or, seeking the bubble reputation even in the cannon's mouth.

And sometimes, especially since that dreadful *séance*, he had wondered whether Uncle, in the very article of death, had been clairvoyant—had seen with his mind's eye that which, with the physical eye, he had sought so long and so often—and that the important words were the words he had not uttered—"in the cannon's mouth."

He had died before he could say those words, but what he had said pointed to them, led on to them.

And then the uncounted number of times that Bump had awakened from sleep with that phrase ringing in his ears.

Until recently he had supposed that the phrase that had made so deep an impression upon his mind, had dwelt there and come to the surface in his dreams. Whenever he was disturbed, worried, anxious and afraid; in that mental condition, in short, which might induce nightmare, it had come.

But since the *séance* he had wondered whether, perhaps, all the Cortenays who had lived and died in the last three hundred years, had not been trying to tell him where the Treasure was, that he might use it to save the cradle of their race from destruction, or from passing into other hands.

And again, the curious fact that Honor had asked him how he read that phrase, and whether the real meaning might not be "seeking that bauble men call Reputation, in the cannon's mouth." Seeking baubles in a cannon's mouth. . . .

And then, finally, that great roaring voice that had come from the lips of the medium, a voice that was not the medium's, with a pronunciation and accent that he could never possibly have used when conscious.

"Seeking the bubble reputation even in the cannon's mouth."

It really was amazing, uncanny, disturbing. . . .

And now suddenly, inspired doubtless by the words of that voice of which he had been thinking as he sat gazing at the Buccaneer's cannon, had come the Idea, the magnitude of which oppressed him, the marvel of which thrilled him none the less.

The cannon's mouth!

Of course, Giles the Buccaneer had never had any fit of remorse about defending what he considered his property, against the King. Boldly and joyously as he would have fought against any of the King's enemies, he would equally boldly and joyously have fought against all the Kings and Queens of England, one after the other, if they had, as he considered, made unjust war upon him, tried to take away from him that which was legally his—his anyway, legally or not.

Had he lived in the days of the Great Rebellion he would have been loyalist to the core, and would have given his life, and all that he had, for his King. But had he been one of King John's barons, oppressed, wronged, robbed by the King, he'd have been well to the fore at Runnymede, defending his rights and demanding his dues.

Of course, he had never been seized with a fit of remorse.

By all accounts—and the Cortenay family knew a great deal more about him than the historians and such people did—he did not know what remorse was.

He had spiked the gun all-right; but he had waited until it was quite obvious that the King was going to capture Cortenay Old Hall, was determined to do it, if he had to bring his whole army and fleet against it.

Strange that remorse should only have overtaken him at the end of that long and desperate siege, when the big gun had been banging away all the time, against the King's forces!

No; that was a piece of dramatic eye-wash, and a really clever stroke.

In the sight of his gunners, arquebusiers and pike-men; the sailors from his ship; and the armed retainers of Cortenay Old Hall, who had only to exchange cap and jerkin for morion and breast-plate, to be soldiers, he had staged his little one-man act.

According to the legend and contemporary written accounts, he had done it at night by the light of a lanthorn.

Bump thought of Uncle. Yes, he had done it darkly at dead of night, with a lantern dimly burning.

And while his astounded sailors and men-at-arms had stood about, gaping in wonder at this amazing deed of their stout leader, he had declared himself a sinner, had spoken of the burning of a church and the robbing and slaying of priests; had called himself a traitor, a rebel and, in spirit, a regicide and—as a sign and a token and a gesture of shame, repentance and remorse—had thrust a spike into the breach-hole of the gun and swung mightily upon it with an armourer's sledge-hammer; and, next day, had fought on as desperately as ever—the rest of his cannon still banging forth their defiance of the King, and death to his men-at-arms!

But what of the night? What had he done in the hours of darkness, after the spiking of the gun, and before the active business of the siege was resumed next day?

He had made the rounds, visiting the sentries and the pickets; and, beneath his cloak, he had carried a little leathern bag tied about the neck with a thong. In this purse, this pouch, this poke, had been diamonds *"as bigge as the pummil of the hilte of his sworde; great emeralds, one exquisitely cutt and of a perfect flawless clearnesse, and as long as his thumbe; sapphires and rubies of the size of fine grapes."*

And, as he passed the silenced gun that could never be fired again, he had paused, glanced anxiously around, put the little bag *into the cannon's mouth*, pushed it in as far as he could, and then, with his sheathed sword, thrust it far down beyond the reach of human hand.

Yes, and later on, he would go round the defences again; and, this time, as he passed the gun he would stop, pick up a wad and a handful of earth or a lump of turf and take the sponge or rammer, and thrust it all right down into the breach, until the purse, behind the wad and the earth, was rammed home almost beneath the closed touch-hole, and then he'd withdraw the sponge or rammer or whatever it was, and carry it away with him, laying it beside some other gun.

And then he would laugh mightily.

Safe! His precious treasure was safe where no man would ever think of looking for it.

Clever—and dramatic.

None of his men would ever touch the gun again, for they had seen him put it out of action.

And if the King's men got into Cortenay Hall they'd search the Hall, and never a soul of them would dream of searching the guns that had been thundering at them so long. And if he had to flee the country, he'd get word to his lady wife. Send her a cryptic message. Yes—what was that line in Will Shakespeare's play, that they had seen together in Town at the Globe Theatre with Burbidge starring as Orlando? That was something about the cannon's mouth, something about the soldier cursing and swearing, with a moustache like a leopard's, seeking his baubles in the very cannon's mouth. Yes, how did it go?

"And then a soldier, full of strange oaths,
Bearded like the pard. Jealous in honour,
sudden and quick in quarrel,
Seeking the bubble reputation even in the
cannon's mouth."

Yes, he and his wife Rosalind had liked that play because the heroine's name was the same as hers, and she had laughed and prodded him in the ribs when Burbidge was mouthing that part about 'full of strange oaths and bearded like the pard.' Yes, he'd write that couplet and send it to her and underline the words *'in the cannon's mouth'* . . .

And then, before he had told anyone, before he had written down the cryptic message and had made some confidential servant, friend, or follower memorize it, he had been killed. The secret had died with him, and had been hidden for three hundred years.

Yes, undoubtedly that was what had happened. Knowing how the house would be ransacked, the gardens searched and dug over, he had hidden the treasure in the gun.

And what safer place?

What pictures those two scenes would make. The first one where, play-acting, a famous sailor-soldier—watched by his officers, by a sentry, a gunner, two or three tired men who lay against the ramparts—had flung his plumed hat upon the ground, beat his breast, raised his hands to Heaven, and declared himself a sinner; had cursed himself as impious, a defiler of sanctuaries, a slayer of priests, a rebel, a traitor, a renegade, an outcast; and had sworn that this gun at least should never fire upon Englishmen again, this gun that he himself had laid and fired against the King's enemies. . . .

And then the other picture of the same man, a crafty smile upon his face, thrusting that great treasure into the cannon's mouth. . . .

In the cannon's mouth.

How utterly amazing it all was, this Revelation.

First from his Uncle's lips.

Then a thousand times in dreams.

And then a reminder from Honor.

And, last of all, spoken in the very voice of Sir Giles Cortenay the Buccaneer, at the *séance.*

His very voice.

From beyond the grave, adown the years, across that chasm that divides Eternity from Time, the voice had come to help him, the last of the Cortenays; to tell him where that great Treasure was, the treasure laid up that it might save the cradle of their race.

In the cannon's mouth.

§2

Bump rose to his feet and rang the bell. Having done so, he wondered what exactly he should say when Rodd answered it.

What was it he wanted?

Something at least as long as the gun. A long stick of some sort that he could lay against the outside, and then thrust down the barrel. If the stick went in so far that the inside measurement was equal to the outside, then his theory collapsed. In other words, if he could poke the end of the stick right down to the touch-hole, there certainly wasn't any bag of jewels, any wad, turf and earth inside the gun.

Rodd knocked and entered.

"Yes, Sir?"

"Oh, Rodd, I want something to measure something."

"Shall I measure it, Sir?"

"No, I'll do it. I mean that I want something with which I can measure something."

"A tape measure, Sir?"

"No. Something rigid. A rod or something."

"Well, I can do it for you, then. I'm a Rodd, Sir."

"Yes. Don't be a humorist as well. I've just told you I don't want you to . . . I mean, I want to measure it myself. Look here, have we got a rod about five feet long or so?"

"Yes, Sir. Not marked in inches or anything. Or I've got a yard rule."

"No, it needn't be graduated, and I want something more than a yard long, straight and stiff."

"Broom-handle, Sir?"

"Do very well indeed, Rodd."

"Or, of course, there's raspberry canes. Or what about a billiard-cue, Sir?"

"That's it, Rodd. I'll use a billiard-cue."

"Shall I bring you one here, Sir?"

"No, it's all-right, thanks. I don't want it up here."

How stupidly he had managed that. Why couldn't he have thought of a billiard-cue or a broom-handle himself, instead of sending for the over-worked Rodd. Had he started Rodd wondering what on earth he could be wanting to measure with a billiard-cue? He was certainly looking extremely interested. Or was that just fancy?

What about giving him the impression that he hadn't really sent for him because he wanted a broom-handle, or a raspberry-cane, or a billiard-cue at all? What about doing now what he had promised Bemmington that he would do?

"Yes, Sir. Thank you, Sir." Rodd turned to go.

"Half a minute, Rodd. I'm going to ask you a

question, plump out. And I want you to answer it, straight away; and speak the truth. And I don't want you to take offence. I'll tell you why I asked you, when you've answered."

A change came over Rodd's countenance. He appeared to moisten dry lips with a dry tongue, ere his face set hard, and lost all expression, as his eyes narrowed, and he stared straight into those of his employer.

"He knows what's coming," thought Bump to himself. "I'm very much afraid he knows exactly what's coming."

Anyway, that proved nothing. Bemmington himself might have said something to him. Yes, he knew what was coming. That wasn't a look of ordinary interest and curiosity, bewilderment or puzzlement. He knew what was coming. Damn Bemmington. What good would Bump have done by giving Rodd the opportunity of denying that he had been in prison, as of course he would deny it, and probably quite truthfully?

He had been a fool to listen to Bemmington at all. And he wouldn't have done, if he hadn't been in Bemmington's debt. Damn this poverty. It was a curse that assumed a million shapes, and assailed one from every direction. Why should he hurt Rodd like this? Well, he'd apologize, and assure him that he took his word for it. After all, Rodd's word was as good as Bemmington's.

Of the two men, he preferred Rodd—really.

"Richard," he said, and it was the first time he had called him by his Christian name. "Have you ever been in gaol?"

"Yes, Sir."

Good Lord! Bemmington was right.

Also Bemmington was wrong—for he had been perfectly certain that Rodd would deny it.

The poor chap was being honest about it, anyhow.

Bump wondered if he himself looked as unhappy and uncomfortable as he felt.

Damn Bemmington.

"Oh," he said, "you have? How often?"

"Only once, Sir."

"Oh, only once! What was the sentence?"

"Life, Sir."

"And the charge?"

"Murder, Sir."

Well, now he had done it.

He'd have to ask Bemmington's pardon.

And he'd have to part with Rodd.

On the other hand—well, there are murderers
and murderers. Some people ought to be murdered
and their slayers rewarded.

It was curious how murder had come to be
regarded as the greatest of all sins; the absolute
ultimate crime; the only offence for which, in civilized countries, men were put to death. Surely there
were worse things than killing a man? Especially
some men.

What about killing faith and trust and joy? What
about killing peace of mind? Weren't many back-
stabbing, lying slanderers worse than murderers?
Weren't many blackmailers far worse? And hadn't
what he himself had said to Bemmington been perfectly true?—that whatever a man had done and
been punished for, should be forgotten. He had
paid, and should not be made to pay again, in any
way whatever.

On the other hand, a criminal is a criminal. . . . A
murderer is . . .

"You did murder somebody, I suppose?"

"No, Sir, I did not."

Somehow he had expected that; had both hoped
and feared that Rodd would deny it. He had hoped

he would, because it left a loop-hole. He had feared he would, because . . . well . . . how many people in England are convicted and punished for a murder which they have not committed? For how many innocent people does the Judge put on the black cap?

"And yet you got a life sentence?" he said.

"Yes, Sir."

Then why was he standing there now? Had he escaped from prison? Was Cortenay Old Hall harbouring an escaped convict? A runaway murderer? Or had he served his "life" sentence and been discharged? Because, nowadays, a life sentence meant a definite term of years; twenty, or something like that, didn't it?

"Did you serve your sentence out?"

"No, Sir."

"Escape?"

"No, Sir."

"Then how is it you are free?"

"There was some trouble in the gaol, and I . . . well . . . I stood in with the authorities . . ."

"And your term was shortened as a reward for what you did?"

"Yes, Sir."

"You must have done something pretty useful, then."

"Well . . . I was given a free pardon, Sir."

"A free pardon for a crime you never committed?"

"Yes, Sir."

"How long did you do?"

"Eight years, Sir."

"Were you given a free pardon because there was any doubt in the Home Secretary's mind as to the justice of your life sentence? Or was it simply as a reward for what you did in the prison riot?"

"I couldn't say, Sir. A bit of both, perhaps."

"It was a riot, I suppose? A prison mutiny?"

"Yes, Sir. You could call it that all-right."

"Anybody killed?"

"Yes, Sir."

"Convicts and warders?"

"Yes, Sir."

"And I suppose you risked your life and saved somebody else's—a warder's or other gaol official's?"

"They gave me a free pardon, Sir," replied Rodd doggedly.

"For a crime you never committed, eh?"

Bump rose to his feet. He was going to take Honor's example—and follow his feelings, his instinct, his intuition. . . .

Rodd looked down at the carpet.

"Do I have to leave, Sir?"

Bump extended his hand.

"When prison authorities and the Law give a man a free pardon—for a crime he never committed—I think ordinary decent human beings can do so too. You've paid, anyway," he said. "Shake hands, Rodd. I believe you."

Again Rodd moistened his lips.

"Thank you, Sir," he whispered, looking into Bump's eyes, and took the proffered hand.

"Enough said. Unless you'd like to tell me all about it," smiled Bump. "Some time."

"Some time, Sir," said Rodd. "Thank you."

"Then I shall say no more about it—until you do," replied Bump, and to himself added, "And to Hell with Bemmington."

"Carry on, Rodd," he bade.

§3

Richard Rodd closed the Library door and stood for a moment as though gazing through it.

Again he licked dry lips.

"Yes," he whispered, "I have paid . . . And I'm going to do some more paying.

"Yes, my God, a handsome dividend.

"Thank you, Sir Russell Bemmington."

And Richard Rodd laughed softly.

§4

That evening, one of full moon, Bump, like a thief in the night, crept guiltily forth from his own house, armed with a billiard-cue.

Softly closing behind him the door of the billiard-room which opened on to a shrubbery, he locked it, pocketed the key, and, keeping as much as possible in the darkest shadows, made his way through the shrubbery to the drive, the avenue of great old trees that led from the house to the road. By a roundabout way, and paths on which he would meet no honest person about his lawful occasions, he skirted the Gardens, crossed a corner of the Park and made his way to the cliff-top and Fort Raleigh.

There in the moonlight, pointing out to sea as it had done for centuries, stood Long John, the famous cannon that the Buccaneer's father had brought home with him from his famous voyage to the East; the noted gun, bigger and longer than the ordinary of that day, and cast of a different metal, probably an amalgam of brass, copper, and other metals. Long John the trusty, the unrusting, the chosen guardian of the Cortenay Treasure.

Was it on such a night that Sir Giles the Buccaneer thrust his handful of gems into that cannon's mouth?

No, it would be on a moonless night of black velvet darkness. He would see it silhouetted against the sky as he climbed up the turf of the landward ramp, into the fort. He would make sure that no human eye beheld what he was about to do. In darkness and silence he would place the baubles, that meant more to him than reputation, in the cannon's mouth, and thrust them down the long iron throat.

How amazingly brilliant the moon was to-night. One saw far too little of these glorious nights of full moon. One ought to observe full-moon nights as holidays, holidays from houses and from sleep. It was sheer criminal folly to sleep them all away in stuffy bedrooms.

What was that?

Could there be anybody about here, at this time of night? Surely not.

Had he been followed? . . . Poachers? . . . Precious little worth poaching round Cortenay Old Hall nowadays. An odd pheasant or two. Any number of rabbits, of course. Just possible, on a night like this, that there might be a cottager or an out-of-work fisherman about, setting snares. Hardly likely.

It had certainly sounded as though a dry stick snapped, though.

Anyway, it didn't greatly matter if anyone saw him poking about round Long John.

Yes, it would, though. It would matter very much if he found what he expected, that there was a foot or so of the gun's interior unaccounted for, as it were. If anyone had seen him, and followed him, and realized what he was doing, the treasure might disappear while he went back to the house for tools.

What sort of tools would he want? He should have thought of that before. How would one set about drawing a wad of tamped earth out of a gun, like one would draw a cork out of a bottle? One would want something in the nature of a gigantic corkscrew.

Suppose the Buccaneer had made a real job of it and had cemented the Treasure in?

No, that wasn't likely. He would hardly have the opportunity of secretly mixing cement, bringing it down here, filling up the muzzle of the gun with it and then ramming it down into the breach. He could hardly do that on a pitch-dark night, or expect to do it on a moonlit one without being seen. Nor, for the same reason, could he work by torch-light or with a lantern.

Wait a minute, though. Why couldn't he? The assaults had all been on the land side until the final one, and the garrison would be on the landward walls. There would only be a few sentries on Fort Raleigh and Fort Drake, and watchers on the beach. He could easily send the sentry away from this part of the defences.

But no, it wasn't likely. It wasn't as though he was going to make a sort of safe-deposit of the gun. He had simply thought of it as a temporary hiding-place for the Treasure, outside the Hall—a far better place, too, than a hole in the ground. Disturbed ground leaves traces of disturbance; and, moreover, treasure hidden in the ground is not so easily found again, after a lapse of time, especially by another person.

The Buccaneer would realize how easy it would be to let his wife know where the Treasure was, if he hid it in the gun.

If he dug a hole and buried it, he'd have to give very full directions for its recovery, directions which, whether written or oral, might be followed by the wrong person. By the messenger himself. Yes, if the Buccaneer had to flee the country, or were laid by the heels, there would be a danger of the Treasure being lost altogether, either because nobody knew where it was, or because the trusted person, or over-clever messenger, stole it.

Which, in point of fact, was exactly what had happened. Sir Giles had hidden it, and not a soul had ever known where. Had he hidden it in the earth, in the earth it would have remained for ever.

As it was . . . in the cannon's mouth.

And how wonderfully had the secret been revealed to his unworthy descendant.

Bump emerged from the shadow of the grass-grown rampart. He could wait no longer. If he had been followed, and was even now being watched, so be it. If he found that there was something in the gun, he'd run headlong back and get the crow-bar used for post-planting and fencing.

If he couldn't get the Treasure out himself now, nobody else could—with their bare hands.

Striding up to the gun, his heart seeming to thump audibly, he laid the billiard-cue upon it, the butt covering the touch-hole, the tip end projecting over the muzzle, by an inch or two.

Swiftly he then thrust the cue, butt foremost, into the gun.

It encountered no obstacle, and projected from the gun by the same length as before.

The gun was empty.

Bump withdrew the cue and again laid it along the length of the gun, the toe of the butt exactly covering the touch-hole. This time he snatched the white silk handkerchief from his breast-pocket of his dinner-jacket and tied it about the butt—as though that could do any good.

Again he thrust the cue, butt foremost, down the barrel, and again it projected by the same length.

Obviously the handkerchief touched the end of the gun.

And the gun was empty.

XIII

It was not until Bump's discovery of the hollowness of his theory as to the hiding-place of the Cortenay Treasure that he realized how strong a hold the thought had taken upon his mind; how quickly his great idea had grown into a great belief, strong and firmly seated in his consciousness. In spite of the fact that the wish had been the father of the thought, his disappointment on finding that nothing but the wish remained was overwhelming.

As usual, he told the whole story to Honor, who, again as usual, gave him sympathy and comfort. He then told her of his conversation with Rodd and the latter's amazing confession.

"Do you believe him, Bunny?"

"Believe he has been to prison?"

"No, you ass; of course you believe that. A man wouldn't accuse himself of having been in prison if he hadn't been. I mean, do you believe him when he says he never committed a murder?"

Bump pondered.

"I do and I don't," he said.

"Oh, don't be flabby, Bunny. Don't wobble. You either do or you don't. Where does the 'do' come in?"

"One can't help a sort of feeling that, when a man has been tried for his life on a murder charge, he may get off—and still be guilty."

"A guilty man may get off, but an innocent man won't get on," supplied Honor. "On the scaffold."

"Yes, I know. One can't help feeling that by the time they've done, *everything* has been said; and if the jury brings in a verdict of 'Guilty' the man is guilty. But there have been cases . . ."

"Yes, there have. Many. There have been cases of people, in the condemned cell itself, being reprieved because the real murderer has confessed, or some piece of evidence, like an alibi, has proved the condemned man's innocence."

"Still, one has a sort of feeling . . ."

"Yes, I know. Well, that's the 'do' part of your 'do and you don't.' Now about the 'don't.'"

"Well, we've had Rodd here a long time now. I've come to like him and I don't feel that he's a criminal."

"Exactly. You don't *feel* that he is. It's intuition; and I have the same feeling myself and very strongly. He's not a criminal, and I don't believe he committed a murder. And if he did . . ."

Bump eyed the girl quizzically.

"And if he did?" he said.

"Well, there are some people who ought to be murdered."

"Doubtless; but it would be awkward if Rodd thought so with regard to anyone here, wouldn't it?"

"Well, he won't—unless it were with regard to Bemmington. By the way, did you tell Rodd that it was Bemmington who accused him to you?"

"No; I didn't."

"And didn't Rodd ask who had told you?"

"No; he didn't."

"Then I'll bet he knew. Guessed, anyway. Are you going to say anything to Bemmington about it?"

"Yes, I am. I feel I ought to. He brought the accusation and I refused to believe it, and defended Rodd. I contradicted him flatly and told him I should ask Rodd; and now I think it is up to me to admit to Bemmington that he was right."

"And then?"

"Well, that'll be that."

"No, it won't. Bemmington accused Rodd of

being an ex-convict because he wanted you to get rid of him."

"Why should he?"

"Exactly. It's an interesting point. Why does he hate him so?"

"Well, we've been over all that before; and Bemmington himself isn't very helpful. Sort of natural antipathy, apparently."

"Well, leave it at that. The fact remains; and what are you going to do when Bemmington takes the line that, since he was perfectly right about Rodd, you will naturally dismiss him forthwith or sooner?"

"Tell him I can't and won't . . ."

"Oh, *darling*! I *am* glad. Oh, that's splendid. And if Bemmington . . . Good old Bunny."

Honor clapped her hands together, and her face lit up joyously.

"I *am* glad," she said.

"Yes, that's all right. I've said it and I'm going to stick to it, but . . ."

Honor's face fell.

"Yes, I was forgetting. What are we to do if Bemmington issues an ultimatum? Either Rodd goes or *he* does."

"He'll have to go."

"What, *Bemmington*?"

"Yes."

"But, Bunny . . ."

"Quite so."

"What'll happen if Bemmington says he'll leave the place altogether, and he'll be glad if you will settle up at your earliest convenience?"

"God knows."

"He can't call in the mortgage suddenly or foreclose or whatever they call it, can he?"

"No; not while I pay the interest. Not without proper legal notice. But he can demand payment of all these bills that he has run up, on my account, improving the property."

"Well, he took it upon himself. He gave all the orders, didn't he, to the builders and contractors and painters and plumbers and electricians and people?"

"Yes, with my knowledge and consent. I'm not going to wriggle. I owe him that money as much as though he had handed it over to me in cash."

"Well, what will happen if he turns nasty? Can he bankrupt you, ruin you?"

"Absolutely."

"Look here, Bunny. Do you mean to say that if Bemmington says you must dismiss Rodd, or else he himself will go, sever his connection with the Club, and demand a cash settlement from you—in other words, ruin you and turn you out of the Hall —you will refuse to dismiss Rodd?"

"Yes."

"Even if Bemmington can, and will, bankrupt you and ruin you, you'll refuse?"

"Yes."

"You won't dismiss Rodd whatever Bemmington does?"

"No, I won't."

"Why not?"

"Because I've told Rodd I won't. And because I don't choose to."

"You really mean it?"

"Yes, I do. I've given Rodd my word. I like him. I believe in him. And I'm going to stand by him."

The girl rose from the window-seat and came to where Bump was standing with his back to the fire. Placing her hands upon his shoulders, she raised herself on tiptoe, bringing her face as near to his as she could.

"Bunny, you *are* a darling. . . . I do love you so," she whispered.

"That's all-right," he said easily, and bestowed upon her one of his rare kisses.

"No, I won't sack Rodd," he continued. "He confessed the truth straight out. About having been in prison. He says he didn't commit a murder, and I believe him. Besides, if he did, he has been punished for it.

"And he has been rewarded, too," he added. "He must have done something jolly brave, or else there must have been a pretty big doubt in the Home Secretary's mind, when the recommendation was made and he looked into his case."

"Well, there again, we've only got his word for that," admitted Honor frankly. "But I believe what he says about that too, don't you?"

"Yes, I do. Besides, it can be verified. And, anyhow, I'm not going to be run by Bemmington."

"That's the spirit, Bump. Don't you. Don't you listen to Bemmington. Let him do his damnedest.

"That could be pretty damnable, though," she added.

"Yes; doesn't bear contemplating. Still, we needn't cross that bridge till we come to it."

"Probably he'll only grumble and tell you that you're a fool and that he has warned you. And he'll request you 'not to forget that he did so, when Rodd swindles you.' That's what he'll do, I expect."

"We'll wait and see."

"But you won't give way? You can be frightfully stubborn when you want to, can't you?"

"No, I shan't give way. It's the principle of the thing, apart from any question of Rodd. After all, it's still my place, and while it is, I'll run it. Damn Bemmington."

Honor eyed her cousin thoughtfully.

"I don't think the good Sir Russell will go, or cut up rough, until I've turned him down completely and finally," she said.

"Well, I don't want you to . . ."

"Still, the fact remains. The great man's disposition can still be described as on-coming. Faster and faster. He'll propose now at the first opportunity. Shall I be a schamer, Bump?"

"A schamer?"

"Yes. Sub-tile, artful, cunning, a schemer. Lead him on and head him off. Trifle with his affections."

"No. Put off the evil day as long as you like, by all means, but if and when he proposes, utter a loud cry of 'No.' And do it three times, in both his ears."

"That would be really diplomatic, wouldn't it?"

"No, it wouldn't. And I don't want you to be."

"Why not, Bump?"

"Because you wouldn't for one moment, at your maddest, dream of marrying Sir Russell Bemmington."

"Wouldn't I?"

"Would you?"

"Why shouldn't I?"

"Well, you won't, anyway. 'Nuff said."

"Don't you think he's a suitable—suitor? A fit and proper person? Do you know of one, Bump? I'm getting on."

Bump frowned at the flippant girl.

"Plenty of time," he said.

"I say, Bump, what would you say if my Russell and I rustled into your room, blushing and stammering and confessing our love, and asked for your blessing and . . ."

"Oh, shut up," growled Bump.

§2

"I'll tackle him now," thought Bump that evening as, running lightly down the stairs into the great hall, he saw the man of whom he was thinking, standing dwarfed, big as he was, by the huge, old, high-mantelled fire-place about which so many generations of Cortenays had sat and warmed themselves, from the days of doublet and hose, thigh-high riding-boots, knee-breeches and silk stockings to those of his own more tubular practice.

" 'Evening, Bump. Cocktail?"

"Oh, my turn, Sir Russell."

"Nothing of the sort."

"Then later on, thanks."

"Another one, later on."

And so forth.

As usual, Richard Rodd waited in readiness at *l'heure d'apéritif.*

"I found you were right, Bemmington," said Bump, when Rodd had brought the cocktails, eyeing the older man straitly.

"I'm always right," laughed Sir Russell. "What about?"

"Rodd."

"Oh, yes, of course. I knew I was right. He admits to being an ex-convict? I'm not surprised. At least, I am surprised that he admitted it. I suppose he realized it was hopeless to deny it, as I was on his track."

"I don't know. Anyway, he answered promptly, without any prevarication. He was sent to prison— with a life sentence."

Sir Russell Bemmington emitted a long slow, whistle.

"By Jove, that means murder."

"Yes, he was tried for murder, found guilty and condemned to death. The death sentence was commuted to penal servitude for life."

"Well, then, in a way, it is worse than I thought. You are harbouring an escaped convict. And now that you know it, you are liable yourself."

"He's not an escaped convict. He was pardoned and set free."

"*Says he!*"

"Yes. It's all hearsay as far as that goes—your accusation and his confession."

"Why did they let him go?"

"He was given a free pardon after a gaol mutiny and riot. I suppose his conduct was brought to the notice of the Home Secretary, who then went into his case. . . . A new broom and he swept clean. . . . I think it very strongly upholds Rodd's contention that he is innocent. Never committed a murder at all."

"Don't you believe it, my boy."

"Well, in point of fact, Bemmington, I do believe it. There was obviously a doubt in the mind of the original Home Secretary when he was condemned, or the sentence would not have been changed from Death to Penal Servitude for Life. And again, there was obviously a doubt in the mind of this Home Secretary. Whatever good work Rodd had done in the gaol mutiny, he would not have been set free, I imagine, if he had had a criminal record and had undoubtedly committed some sordid, brutal murder."

"Well, anyhow, damn it all, man, surely there are enough good fellows out of work, without your employing an ex-convict, a man who admittedly has done . . . how long did he do?"

"Eight years."

"Well, there it is. Eight years in quod. Surely there are enough highly-qualified butlers, club-stewards, head-waiters, hall-porters and what-not, out of a job? You don't have to employ a man with a criminal record. What about an ex-service man—with a decoration for bravery, distinguished conduct and that sort of thing—who has been a club-servant? Instead of keeping a tramp picked up in the gutter. He was only there because he had had the good luck to dodge the gallows.

"But you gave him notice, of course, on the spot," continued Sir Russell. "As a matter of fact, you should have sacked him with neither notice nor wages in lieu of it. What did you give him—a week? Better keep an eye on the silver and warn the guests."

Bump waited patiently for the speaker to finish. The more he said now, the less there'd be to say in future, perhaps.

"A week, eh?" rumbled the knight.

"Well, as a matter of fact, I didn't give him notice at all."

"Good Lord, man, why not?"

"Why should I?"

Sir Russell Bemmington eyed the young man in cold surprise.

"Are you being serious? . . . 'Why should you?' Because he's a crook, a criminal, an ex-convict, a murderer."

"Who says so?"

"A British Judge and Jury, for a start."

"Yes, the Law punished him. And now the Law has forgiven him. And I'm going to follow its excellent example. And I'll tell you why."

"Well?"

"Because, in the first place, I believe he's innocent; and because, in the second, if he's not, I don't believe in punishing a man twice for what he has done once; and because, in the third place, if Officialdom can forgive and reward him—so can we."

"Well, I tell you frankly, Cortenay, I don't like it. Nor will the other guests."

"The other guests will know nothing about it."

"H'm! I hope they won't, while he's here."

"Well, presumably Rodd won't tell them; and certainly I shan't. Is there any reason why you should?"

"I'm not sure that there isn't. I think they ought

to know."

"Well, I don't. It's nothing to do with them."

"Well, I think it is."

"Look here, Bemmington. Nobody here has ever found fault with Rodd at all, and he has been in my employ for some time, as you know. Everybody likes him, except you, and I've never heard a word against him from anybody but you."

"Naturally, seeing that they know nothing about him."

"Well, let them go on knowing nothing about him, except that he's a damn' good servant.

"Anyhow, I'm not going to sack him," added Bump firmly, and looking Sir Russell Bemmington in the eye.

"H'm . . . Since you take that line, we'll see."

"Who's we?" enquired Bump with more arrogance than grammar.

"Well, I, then. I. I'll think it over and decide whether I ought not to put it before an informal committee of the Club."

"Well, I hope you will decide not to. I hope you'll be content to leave the matter to me. Will you have another cocktail?"

"No, thank you, Cortenay."

An awkward silence fell.

Suddenly Bump, who was thoroughly, and perhaps unreasonably, annoyed, remembered something that Archie Wilbraholme had said; and even while realizing that he was being childish and petty, willing to wound and by no means afraid to strike, turned about, stirred a log with his foot, and said,

"What years were you in India, Bemmington?" And try as he might, he could not keep from his voice what seemed to him an unpleasant note.

"Eh, what? What do you mean? What's that got to do with Rodd?"

"Nothing whatever, so far as I know. I merely

asked."

"Why do you ask?"

"Well, why not, if it comes to that? I'm not prying, or . . ."

"Prying? I should imagine not. I should hope not. What is there to pry about?"

Bump eyed the speaker closely.

Hullo, what was this? What was the fuss about? Surely this was much ado about nothing. Curious fuss over a simple question. Was it possible that Wilbraholme was right?

But if he were, what did it matter?

"Look here, Cortenay, has that fellow Rodd been saying something about me? Because if so . . ."

"Is it likely I should listen to servants' gossip about you or anybody else, Bemmington? Surely I need hardly say that Rodd has never mentioned your name to me, nor I your name to Rodd."

"Anyway, the sooner you get rid of him the sooner I shall like it, and the better it will be for— the place."

"The better for me, do you mean?" asked Bump coldly.

Sir Russell Bemmington made no reply and, as other guests entered the hall, the subject of Rodd's dismissal was, at that unsatisfactory point, dropped for the time being.

§3

Nor was Sir Russell Bemmington's profound dislike of Richard Rodd lessened by the fact that the latter appeared to grow even, and ever, more ubiquitous. It had been something of a joke among the guests and members that Rodd was Always There, and to bestow upon him such appropriate nicknames as Rodd the Ready; Ram-rod, because he could put anything through; Rodd the Omniscient;

Rodd the Omnipresent; and Rodd the Ubiquitous. There were those, indeed, who called him Rodd the Omnipotent and quoted to new-comers the slogan,

"If you want it done, just mention it to Rodd."

It is said that one can have too much of any good thing save goodwill, but it is probable that no-one at Cortenay Old Hall, save Sir Russell Bemmington, considered that there was too much of Rodd. And in the otherwise universal and unanimous chorus of praise, the only discordant note was the voice of Sir Russell. He alone among the clientele and personnel of Cortenay Old Hall Guest House and Country Club added to the so oft-repeated remark,

"Rodd is always there when you want him," the mitigating addendum,

"Yes, and when you don't want him."

In that lay the head and front of Rodd's offending. He was there when Sir Russell wanted him; there to answer the bell; there at his desk to deal infallibly with telephone and telegram, with letter, message, or order; there at the back of the hall, unobtrusive but inevitably ready to pour the oil of instant service, assistance and politeness upon the wheels of Sir Russell's life in Cortenay Hall; always there when he wanted him, as everybody said.

And he was there when he didn't want him, too.

Not only by day, but actually by night.

For, to Sir Russell's surprise, and indignation indeed, he found, on going down to the Library to get a book, that the fellow was sleeping there!

There was positively no getting away from him.

And when Sir Russell, controlling his wrath, had said, "What on earth are you doing here?" Rodd had replied with an undeniably peculiar note in his voice,

"And the same to you, Sir, if I might say so with all respect."

And when Sir Russell had said that he had come

for a book, the man had replied that he himself must have fallen asleep there reading one!

It had, of course, been beneath Sir Russell's dignity to explain to Rodd that he had Sir Giles Cortenay's full and free permission to use the Library whenever he wanted to do so, and to borrow any book that he might have a fancy to read.

He had nevertheless promised to report the fellow for being there asleep on the sofa in the Library at two o'clock in the morning, a threat which had somehow seemed to leave him curiously unperturbed.

Ever since Rodd's confession to his employer, and the assurance that it did not mean dismissal, he had seemed to serve Sir Russell Bemmington with, if possible, even greater assiduity and care; almost, indeed, specially to attach himself to Sir Russell.

Particularly so, since Sir Russell had brought in his friend Mr. Reginald Minchess, F.R.I.B.A. and A.R.I.B.A., said to be a well-known architect and an authority on the famous houses, the Show Places, among the Stately Homes of England.

Similarly had it been in the case of Mr. Warlock Manningfold, his other friend, said to be a famous art-critic, expert and connoisseur of pictures, the man whose word made and unmade reputed Old Masters.

These three gentlemen, Sir Russell Bemmington, Mr. Reginald Minchess, F.R.I.B.A. and A.R.I.B.A., and Mr. Warlock Manningfold (visiting the Hall again), seemed to find Rodd's attentiveness excessive; to be definitely sure that one could have too much of a good thing—and that here was an example of it.

No matter which room in the house Mr. Reginald Minchess was inspecting, no matter what picture Mr. Warlock Manningfold was considering, there was no escaping Rodd.

During the architect's visit, the nuisance was perhaps greatest, the difficulty of escaping Rodd's kind attentions the most insuperable. Whether seated, side by side, on a settee, and discussing architecture in general and that of the house in particular; whether with the aid of a step-ladder inspecting panelling too high up on the wall to be examined from floor-level; whether, with the help of a ladder, investigating the condition of roof-beams and estimating the extent and danger of the ravages of the death-watch beetle, Sir Russell Bemmington and his architect friend could never be sure of peace and privacy.

Indeed, short of locking the door, which they hardly cared to do, they could not obtain an uninterrupted session of any length.

Had they been Royalty, Rodd could not have been more attentive.

Had they rung the bell?

No, they had not.

Rodd was very sorry. He had been misinformed or mistaken.

Were the steps or the ladder of sufficient height for their purpose?

Yes, they were; otherwise he would have been notified of the fact.

Would Sir Russell come to the telephone?

Could Rodd be of any assistance? These polished floors were apt to be a little slippery for steps and ladders. In fact, he himself had had a nasty fall once.

"In this very room, gentlemen; through the steps slipping. Came down an awful crash."

As he proceeded to embellish the story of his catastrophic downfall, Sir Russell Bemmington broke his frowning silence with a sudden sharp interruption.

"What's that? What? Who fell with the steps?"

"Me, Sir. I did. Came a nasty cropper, I did."

"In this room?"

"Yes, Sir. In this very room."

"What were you doing?"

"Doing, Sir? I was giving the panelling a bit of a polish up."

"Polishing the panelling? That wasn't your work, was it?"

"Well, Sir, anything is my work in a manner of speaking, especially in those days. Very short-handed, we was."

"Did you polish all the upper panelling in the whole house?" enquired Mr. Reginald Minchess, F.R.I.B.A. and A.R.I.B.A., sharply.

"No, Sir. No, not the whole house. Not by any means. Nor will you."

"Look here, my man," began Mr. Minchess, "don't you occasionally forget yourself?"

"Me? No, Sir, never. Nor anybody else either. I got a wonderful memory for faces. No, Sir. I never forget."

"I'm not sure," observed Sir Russell Bemmington, his voice low and quiet, and very hard, "I'm not sure, Richard Rodd, that you don't remember a good deal too much."

"Me, Sir? Oh, no. I don't think that's possible."

"Oh, you don't, don't you? Well, I think it is. And we'll see who's right."

"Yes, Sir, I'm sure we shall. Meanwhile, do let me help you with the steps if you go up 'em. Very slippery floor."

Mr. Reginald Minchess, chin in hand, eyed Rodd thoughtfully.

"Look here, Rodd," he said. "Why were you polishing the panelling in this particular room, and high up?"

"Oh, well, you see, Sir, it's the Guv'nor's room, and I wanted to do it special. And, you see, the panelling had been polished all-right, as far as a man could reach, but above that it was all dull like. See what I mean?"

"Yes, I see what you mean."

"And did you think that any particular part wanted extra careful polishing?" asked Sir Russell.

"No, Sir. No, Sir. Always very conscientious about my work. I polish it all alike."

"Every single panel, eh?"

"And you can lay to that, Sir."

Sir Russell's eyes narrowed and his jaw protruded.

"You are certainly looking for something, Rodd," he said quietly. "Do you know what you are looking for?"

Rodd laughed.

"Do I?" he said. "Do I? And do you?"

"Yes, I do. I do know what you are looking for. You are looking for trouble. See?"

"I hear, Sir."

"The very worst of trouble. And you'll find it. Soon and plenty. I don't know what your game is, but I've got a guess."

"Well, I do know what yours is, and I don't have to guess, Sir Russell," replied Rodd.

"Tell you what, Bemmington," interposed Mr. Minchess. "Isn't it about time we showed this fellow . . ."

The door opened and Bump entered.

"Oh!" said he. "Not finished here yet?"

"Oh, yes, thanks, Cortenay. Thanks very much for giving us permission to intrude in the sanctum. I was just asking Rodd to take the steps away."

"Oh, right. Thanks. I only wanted to get something," replied Bump, making no move to do so and depart.

And with renewed thanks and protestations, Sir Russell Bemmington and his architect friend made their apologetic exit, followed by Richard Rodd carrying the steps.

At the end of the corridor Sir Russell stopped and wheeled about.

"I want a word with you, Rodd," he said, "to-night, late. Come to my room last thing."

"I'll be there, Sir Russell," replied Richard Rodd.

XIV

That night, Richard Rodd completed his duties as usual, saw that all doors and windows on the ground floor were fastened, that all fires had gone out or were in a satisfactory condition of departure, and reported to Bump in his office.

"All-right, Rodd. You go to bed. I'm going up in a minute."

"Thank you, Sir. Good-night, Sir."

And Rodd retired to his own room.

Half an hour later, in rubber-soled shoes, an electric torch in one pocket, the Popper in the other, he made another tour of inspection of the ground floor, and then proceeded by way of the grand staircase to the Library.

In this room, he turned on the lights, glanced at the window-fastenings, the door of the safe, the pictures and the panelling.

"Yes; this is the room all-right," he mused. "This is where Albert Mompett broke in; where he murdered the old General; where Kike Lipsky and Henery the Eighth came poking about with their plumbers' tools; and where Sir Russell Bemmington and the architect are really busy—or want to get busy. I hand it to those two. The other man's very good as the Architect. Almost took me in. Wonder who the Artist was. He had the patter all-right, too. Fine. I wonder why 'Sir Russell Bemmington' has sent him away again. Queer that.

"Yes, this is the room, of course. And it's the panelling or the pictures that interest them.

"Unless it's under the floor. Couldn't be under the safe, I suppose. That's where they are handicapped, poor fellows. They couldn't lock the door and get down to it comfortably in the day-time; and never had a chance at night."

No, and he'd see that they didn't.

Anything that they were going to do, was going to be done with his knowledge and consent, or not at all.

Well, things were moving along, coming to a head, and Bemmington must have come to the conclusion that he couldn't do anything single-handed. Hence the Architect and the Artist. It must have gone to his heart to bring them into it.

Yes, that was the room all-right—and it wasn't likely that he would learn anything by staring at it.

He might learn something from the great Sir Russell, though.

Locking the door behind him, and pocketing the key, Rodd made his way to the floor above, and the big bed-sitting-room, one of the best in the house, occupied by Sir Russell Bemmington.

The door of this room he quietly tried, turning the handle with a motion so slow as to be almost imperceptible. Finding that the door was locked, he scratched gently with his finger-nail until the door was opened.

He entered the room, and its occupant, having closed the door behind him, locked and bolted it.

"You desired to see me, Sir Russell," said Rodd quietly.

"Yes, I want a talk with you. I want to ask you a few plain questions, and to get some straight answers. . . . As a matter of fact, I've had enough of you and your funny ways: more than enough. . . . I want to know what you think you're up to. And I rather think I'm going to show you exactly where you get off, and when."

"Yes, Sir Russell? I'm sorry if I've given you offence in any way."

"In any way? In every way, more likely."

"How, Sir Russell?"

"Well, your manner, for one thing. Look at your manner now.

" 'Yes, Sir Russell' and 'No, Sir Russell' and you've got your tongue in your cheek. And who are you, I should like to know, to have the insolence to annoy me?"

"To annoy you, Sir Russell?"

"Yes, to annoy me."

"How, Sir Russell?"

" '*How, Sir Russell*,'" growled Sir Russell Bemmington savagely. "You follow me about, for one thing. Make a nuisance of yourself. Can't get rid of you. It's almost as though you were spying on me. Why can't you mind your own business—while you've got some to mind?"

Sir Russell Bemmington strode up and down the room, whether in great anger, to work himself up into a state of great anger, or to give the impression that he was in such state.

"Now then, about this morning in the Library. I told you you were looking for something, didn't I?"

"You did, Sir Russell."

"And you didn't understand me. When I said you were looking for trouble, you were surprised. You thought I was going to accuse you of looking for something else, didn't you?"

"Yes, Sir Russell."

"And I told you I didn't know what your game was, but that I could make a good guess. And just as your master came into the room, you had the impudence to say to me that you *did* know what my 'game' was, and that you didn't have to guess.

"Do you call that the way for a servant to talk to a gentleman? It's the first time you've dared to say anything impudent, but your manner has been impudent the whole time. And I'll have neither covert insolence nor open insolence from you or anybody else."

"Is there anything more, Sir Russell?" enquired Rodd quietly, his impassive face expressionless and unchanged, save for the fact that his thin lips seemed almost to have disappeared, his eyes almost to have retreated beneath their beetling brows.

"Yes, there is. A good deal more. If you had made me a handsome apology and told me what you think you're doing and who you think you are, I might have listened and considered it. As it is, you can take it from me that by this time to-morrow you'll be out of a job and out of this house."

Sir Russell Bemmington ceased his pacing, planted himself in front of Rodd, feet apart, arms akimbo, his head thrust forward so that his angry face was within a few inches of Rodd's.

"Who the devil do you think you are?" he growled, "and what do you think you are up to? Who are you and *what* are you?"

"I'll tell you, Sir Russell. That's really what I came up here for," replied Richard Rodd. "I'll tell you who I am and what I am."

§2

Crossing to the fire-place, Richard Rodd, uninvited, seated himself in an arm-chair, the while Sir Russell Bemmington stared in amazement.

"Sit down, Sir Russell," he said, a new note in his voice. "Sit down and listen, while I tell you who I am, what I am, and what I think I am doing. You've had your say. Now listen to me for a change. Take a seat, won't you—or you can damn well stand up, if you prefer to.

"You want to know who I am and what I think I'm up to, eh?

"Well, it's a long story. But you shall know all-right. I won't leave you in any doubt as to who I am, and what I am up to.

"You told Sir Giles Cortenay that I was an old lag, didn't you? Told him I was a criminal, an ex-convict; and that the best thing he could do was to get rid of me as soon as possible or sooner. Sir Giles didn't tell me it was you, and he didn't have to. I knew all-right. What I didn't know was how you had found out—because you had never set eyes on me and I had never seen you, either, until you came here.

"Well, I reckon that was a shot in the dark. You had seen my portrait in the papers, years ago; a bad portrait taken a long time before; and when you first saw me here, you thought we had met somewhere.

"And you knew some of the signs, too, didn't you? I wasn't long out of prison, and I looked like it. You didn't like the cut of my jib; didn't like the way I looked at you; and you caught my eye many a time when you were chucking your weight about and spreading yourself around; and you didn't like it. You caught my eye that time when Mr. Wilbraholme called your bluff about India.

"So instead of coming to a show-down, cards on the table and what about it, you tried to get me the sack. And if Sir Giles had been any other sort of man than what he is, I should have got it. But being what he is, he took my word—and that bit of kindness is going to pay him a million-fold.

"No, you listen to me. Wait till I've finished. I promise you that you are going to hear something interesting.

"Well, you were right. I am an ex-convict. I got a life sentence for murder. For a murder I never committed. And for killing a man who's alive at this moment. Yes. *And standing in this room!* That interest you?

"Yes, I thought you'd sit down.

"Fate's a funny thing, and there's no getting away from it. Works by laws of its own. And one of them is 'Murder will out.' It takes a rather clever man, or a rather lucky one, to commit a murder and get away with it. And then perhaps he hasn't. Not even when it's all forgotten and done with, and ten years behind him.

"No, and not even when somebody else has been arrested for it, and tried and sentenced to death or to penal servitude for life.

"What am I talking about? You'll know in a minute. Ever hear of old Todding? Yes, of course you did. *'Todding Never Troubles You. No Bet too Big or too Small. If you can't Pay you can Owe.'* Well, everybody knows Todding.

"Did you ever stay with him? Ever live in his house? No. You didn't. Of course you didn't, *Sir Russell Bemmington.* You'd have remembered me all-right, if you had.

"You don't know what I'm talking about? No, I'll take my oath you don't. You never said a truer word in your life.

"Another question. Have you ever been in prison yourself?

"No. Of course not. How dare I ask you such a thing? Quite so. Is it likely that Sir Russell Bemmington has ever been in prison?

"Well, as a matter of fact, I know you haven't.

"No, of course you don't know what I'm talking about. You are a very puzzled man, aren't you, *Sir Russell Bemmington*? And even now you don't know who I am, do you?

"No. Then listen to this little tale.

"Over at Sandhaven there were two brothers, Albert and Roger Mompett, twins, alike as two pins outside, and no two things more different than they were inside. One of them, Roger, was a fine chap, straight, honest, one of the best; and he was my friend. The other, Albert, was a rogue. He was a thief and a liar when he was a boy, and grew up to be one of the biggest swine that ever lived. He turned professional crook, and, while he was still a young man, committed a murder, *here in this very house*!

"He had heard the tale that everybody in these parts knows, about the Cortenay Treasure, and being one of the cleverest crooks alive, he thought he could get it where other people had failed. Perhaps he had got hold of some special information. I don't know. Anyway, he broke in here and killed General Cortenay, an old man over eighty years of age. A brave deed.

"Then he went straight off to his brother's cottage, left a stolen bicycle there and his clothes, took a suit of his brother's, and got away.

"His brother, my friend, was taken, tried, condemned—and got the benefit of the doubt. There was a lot of talk about circumstantial evidence; and there was a petition to the Home Secretary. Anyway, he got penal servitude for life.

"About three years later Roger Mompett escaped, with the help of Todding. Todding hid him at his place, and while he was hiding there Roger wrote to me and I went and saw him. Todding never knew his name; only knew him as 'Pore ole Fifty-Fifty,' and left it at that. Roger told me all about it, and I told him what he wanted to know—where his dear brother Albert was.

"And how did I happen to know that? Because of a poor fool of a girl whom Albert had served as he served everybody else who trusted him.

"Poor Milly Harris. . . .

"Well, never mind about her. She little thought what she was doing for me when she told me where Albert Mompett was, and I wrote to him. Wrote what they call a threatening letter—and no doubt it was.

"No, she little knew what she was doing for me."

Richard Rodd rose to his feet.

"Nor what she was doing for you, 'Sir Russell Bemmington'!"

§3

"You wanted to know who I am and what I am, did you, Albert Mompett, *alias* Aloysius Slatterthwaite, *alias* Henry B. Fielding, *alias* Gent Jannison, *alias* God-knows-what, and now Sir Russell Bemmington, late of Calcutta. Very late.

"Well, now you know who I am. I am Tommy Pepper.

"Thomas Pepper, *alias* Richard Rodd, thanks to you.

"That's who I am.

"Now as to what I am.

"*I am your owner. Your sole proprietor.* See?

"You belong to me, Albert Mompett. You are my private property. Anything you think you own you don't own—because it belongs to me. It's my private property. What is yours is mine—and what's mine is my own.

"You don't understand?

"No, I'm sure you don't, but you are going to. Look! *You're a dead man.*

"No, you needn't jump. You are already dead. I murdered you. And I was tried and condemned to death for it.

"At least, you yourself proved that I murdered you; and the jury found me guilty of the murder, and the judge sentenced me to death.

"No thanks to you that I wasn't hanged. I was taken to the condemned cell, and I sat there for a fortnight, sentenced to death, waiting to be hanged.

"Then I was reprieved and given penal servitude for life.

"Now, *Albert Mompett,* since you proved that I murdered you, and I was tried and punished for that murder, *you don't exist.* See?

"There is no such person as you. You are murdered, dead, and buried.

"And since I was caught, tried, condemned and punished for murdering you, I can't be punished again for murdering you again, can I?

"No. The Law can't punish Thomas Pepper a second time for murdering Albert Mompett a second time.

"Doubly, it can't—*because you can't try a man twice on the same murder charge, and because you can't punish a man twice for the same offence.*

"See? I've been tried and punished for murdering you—so I've paid in advance. A cash deal, so to speak, with the Law.

"Only case on record of punishment for murder preceding the crime!

"*Silence!* . . . You hold your tongue. You've been talking all your life. My turn to say a few words now. You listen to me. I can take this gun out of my pocket—belongs to your friend Kike Lipsky, by the way—and I can shoot you dead, now.

"*Sit still,* will you?

"And then I can ring up the Police at Whitebay Harbour, and when they come, I can say,

" 'Clear that away, Inspector, will you, and put it where you like. Time it was buried—because it was murdered nearly ten years ago. Yes, that's been dead ten years. I ought to know, because I was sentenced to death for murdering it, and then sent to penal servitude for life.'

"Then what are the Police going to do about it? Not the fat-headedest village constable is going to arrest me, Thomas Pepper, for killing Albert Mompett whom he killed ten years ago; for whom he was sentenced to swing; and for killing whom he went to penal servitude for life.

"Puts the Law in a bit of a hole, doesn't it?

"Make the Public Prosecutor scratch his head, won't it?

"A bit of a puzzle for Prosecuting Counsel for the Crown, eh?

" *'Here, m'Lud, we have the case of Thomas Pepper, accused of the wilful murder of Albert Mompett. We have had it all before, m'Lud. He murdered him ten years ago, and you sentenced him to be hanged. And now he's bobbed up again. Been and murdered Albert Mompett again, m'Lud. That's twice he's murdered him.'*

"Does put the Law in a hole, doesn't it, Albert Mompett?

"Can't murder a man twice, Albert Mompett.

"And the Law can't hang a man twice, Albert Mompett.

"And the Law can't send him to penal servitude for life, twice, Albert Mompett.

"In fact, the Law can't try him twice, Albert Mompett.

"And lastly, there's no such person as you, Albert Mompett.

"You are dead.

"You are buried.

"I killed you.

"I paid the penalty exactly according to law.

"And I reckon you belong to me. And why?

"*Because I can kill you just whenever I want to, and nobody can say a word against it.* I reckon that makes you my property all-right, doesn't it?

"I can drown a kitten I don't want; or have a dog chloroformed that I don't want; or shoot a horse that's too old to work and no use—and I can do the same with you. If you are no use to me, I can do what I like with you, same as with the kitten or the dog or the horse. There's not a soul alive can raise a finger to prevent me killing a man who doesn't exist; and there isn't a soul alive that is going to lift a finger to punish me for killing a man who doesn't exist, especially as I've been punished once for killing him when he did exist.

"Think it over, and when you've had a good think, and realized you are tight in the trap, let's hear what you've got to say. Something about the Cortenay sparklers, eh?"

§4

The man now addressed as Albert Mompett laughed.

Perhaps it was not a very convincing sound, for the look of bitter contempt on the face of Richard Rodd seemed almost to deepen.

"Makes you laugh, eh?" sneered Richard Rodd, his snarling lips drawn back from bared teeth. "There's a proverb about the one who laughs last, isn't there?"

"Yes, and there's something about laughing on the other side of the face, too," replied the quondam Sir Russell Bemmington. "Look here, I want a drink."

"Devil doubt you. Wouldn't you like to ring for Richard Rodd to bring you one?"

"There's a bottle of whisky in that drawer."

"Devil doubt you. And a gun too, eh? You sit still."

"Now look here, Rodd . . . Pepper . . . why can't we talk this thing over quietly and sensibly, and have a drink while we do it? I admit you've been clever, very clever, and, in point of fact, a good deal too clever. I don't mind admitting freely that you took me in completely. You recognized me, or thought you did, and I didn't recognize you. And that's a thing I shall never be able to understand."

It was Richard Rodd's turn to laugh. A most unpleasant sound.

"Never be able to understand, eh?" he sneered. "You'll never be able to understand why you didn't recognize a man on whom you had never set eyes in your life? The nearest thing you ever came to seeing me, Albert Mompett, was seeing my picture in the papers—

"'Thomas Pepper, the Beach Bungalow Murderer. To be hanged in Porchester Gaol on Saturday next for the murder of Mr. Aloysius Slatterthwaite.'"

"Now, now; listen to me; listen to me, Tommy Pepper," begged Bemmington. "God knows I've listened to you long enough. I tell you, you are being too clever. Look, you talked about cards on the table. Very well, cards on the table. I admit I'm not Sir Russell Bemmington. I admit that our friend Todding would probably recognize me as 'Fifty-Fifty'."

Again Richard Rodd laughed.

"Not all of you, Albert Mompett. *There's a bit of you he won't recognize.*"

"What d'you mean?"

"I'll tell you later."

"I begin to think you are daft, Tommy."

"Would you mind not calling me Tommy," requested Richard Rodd, producing the Popper from his pocket, tapping his palm with it suggestively, and returning it to its hiding-place.

"Well, well, you'll be sorry you took this line by-and-by, T . . . I mean, Rodd. Don't you realize that I and Albert were so much alike that . . ."

"Yes, so much alike that the poor chap's girl didn't know the difference between you."

"Very well, then. If you had ever met Albert you wouldn't have known him from me."

"Quite likely. But I know you now, Albert Mompett."

"Look here, To . . . Rodd, if you prefer that name . . . how can I convince you that *I am Roger Mompett* and that Albert Mompett is dead?"

"You can't. And you can't convince anybody else either, when I produce the proofs that you are not. And apart from that, when did Roger Mompett turn crook? He couldn't do it. He was an honest man, honest and open as the day; never stole or lied or swindled. The worst thing that anybody could ever say about Roger Mompett was that he was fool enough to let his swindling swine of a brother do him down. Twice and more than twice. Until Albert landed him in gaol—like he did me. . . . Just try to imagine my dear friend Roger Mompett assing about as 'Sir Russell Bemmington,' a dressed-up con-man, a swindler, a swell mobsman!"

"Now, now, look here, Tommy . . ."

Richard Rodd's hand went to his pocket.

". . . Rodd, I mean, since you will stick to it. My God, how ten years have changed you!"

"Yes, with eight of them in prison."

"So changed you that you talk like this to *me*, your old pal. Now listen. You know quite well that Albert was murdered, and that your letter threatening to murder him was found in his pocket. If you say you didn't do it, I take your word for it. I can understand you being sore about it and I can understand your blaming me for not coming forward, but I tell you, Pepper, I wasn't in the country, and I never read or heard a word of the trial. Is it likely I wouldn't have come forward if I had known somebody else had been pinched? Now I'll tell you the truth. Listen."

Richard Rodd settled himself deeper in the chair, crossed his legs, rested his elbows upon the arms, locked the fingers of his hands before him, and gazed across them at the plausible and per-suasive man before him.

"Go on," he said. "Go on. There's plenty of time . . . and it will be interesting."

"Of course it will, and God forgive me for not recognizing you sooner. Although I knew that I knew you directly I set eyes on you. But as I said before, you've changed. You've changed beyond rec-ognition in these ten years. Well, that's obvious, isn't it, as I didn't recognize you. No. I didn't recog-nize you."

"And there's a word of truth," growled Rodd.

"You know what Albert did for me," continued Albert Mompett, *alias* Sir Russell Bemmington. "You know how I escaped from prison. You know how Todding, good old Todding, befriended me. You admit that I wrote to you and you came to see me. . . . Damn it all, Tommy, you knew me then, and how I went to look for Albert, knowing where to find him, thanks to you.

"Well, what you don't know, Tommy, is what happened that night.

"I walked straight into the bungalow. Albert opened the sitting-room door, pulled out a pistol and fired straight at me. The bullet must have missed my head and gone out through the open door-way, and that's why the Police found no mark of it. And before he could pull the trigger again, I had knocked his hand up and closed with him. There was a struggle. Some struggle, too, for we were both fighting for our lives—and the pistol went off. That ended it. Although the gun was in his own hand, I had shot Albert."

"Funny it didn't burn his coat, wasn't it?" jeered Rodd.

"No, it wasn't; for the bullet went through two sides of my sleeve first. It was my cuff got the burn mark. And then . . . I don't excuse it . . . I shot him again. Do you blame me? Think of what he had made me suffer! Condemned to death—and then to penal servitude for life! Three years in prison—an innocent man! I was dazed, mad, and when I came to myself, my one thought was to get away."

"Ah? And how did you do it?"

"Walked to Shoremouth—at least, I got a lift most of the way—and did a pier-head jump on to a three-master being towed out of the Docks, bound for Australia. Only too glad to see me, they were, when I jumped down off the swing-bridge; and I never saw land, much less a newspaper, for six months. Driven right out of our course, Southern Indian Ocean. We looked as though we were going to fetch up at the South Pole. . . . Jumped ship at Sydney; made my way to Calcutta, and took the name of Bemmington—I had to take another name, of course—and made good. Did pretty well for myself. When I thought it was safe, years and years later, I came home.

"Then I heard about this place, and thought I'd like to come down to this part of the world for Auld Lang Syne. Had a sort of longing for the countryside that I knew."

"Scene of the crime, eh?" sneered Rodd.

"I don't call it a crime. It wasn't a crime. It was self-defence. And look at the provocation."

"And what about the man who was pinched for it?"

"I didn't know that anybody had been."

"Never gave it a thought?"

"Of course I did. Every day and every night; and I came to the conclusion that if somebody had been hanged for it, the mischief was done."

"And if somebody was still in prison for it?"

"I never thought of that. It didn't occur to me."

"You liar. You slimy, soapy, swindling liar. You god-damned, hell-blistered . . ."

"Look here, look here! What's the good of talking like that, Pepper. You want to know what happened and I'm trying to tell you."

"Yes, you are trying to tell me all-right. Tell me this, first of all. If you are my friend *Roger* and not that stinking, swindling, lying murderer *Albert* Mompett, answer me this. How did you escape from Porchester prison?"

"How did I escape?"

"Yes, how did you escape?"

"Why, Todding helped me. Good old Todding. *'Todding Never Troubles You.'* You know that much, Tom, don't you?"

"I know all-right. Got away in Todding's car, didn't you?"

"Yes, of course I did. As you know."

"And how did you get to the car?"

"Fog, mist . . . usual thing. Made a dash for it—coming back from the quarries—and had the luck to run into Todding."

"Oh, you did, eh? And where did he take you?"

"Why, to his place, of course. You know he did."

"Yes, he ran you straight up to London—because a crowd is the best place to hide in, eh?"

"Why, of course. Where else?"

"Ah, where else? And how much did you promise Todding for looking after you? You remember telling me you were going to get it from your brother and give it to Todding, don't you?"

"Of course I do. . . . Let's see, it was a hundred pounds, wasn't it? A hundred of the best."

"Ah . . . And you remember tramping with me from London to Whitebay?"

"Well, naturally."

"Naturally, eh?"

"And you could prove to Todding, if you were brought face to face with him, that you are Roger Mompett. Or rather 'Fifty-Fifty,' the man he saved."

"Of course I could. Not that Todding would want to make any song-and-dance about having helped me to escape from Porchester Prison, would he?"

"No. But he'd be interested. Wonderfully interested, he'd be."

"What in?"

"I'll tell you what in, *Albert* Mompett. In your left hand."

"What do you mean?"

Richard Rodd laughed unpleasantly.

"You can lie with your mouth, *Albert* Mompett. Not a finer liar alive on the face of this earth—but the third finger of your left hand can't tell any lies, and you can't tell any lies about it, either."

"What d'you mean?"

"What do I mean? I'll tell you, *Albert* Mompett. While Roger Mompett was in prison, he smashed the third finger of his left hand, working in the stone quarries. It did badly, and they had to take it off from the second joint. See? Now then, 'Roger' Mompett, as you call yourself—*how did you grow that finger again*? Eh?

"Now then, come on—how did you grow that finger?

"My God! If only I had known the murdered man was half a finger short, I'd never have gone to gaol for eight years.

"*That was the first thing I looked for, when I first saw you here, Albert Mompett.*

"And when I saw your hand—I knew you!

"I knew Roger hadn't killed you as I thought he had.

"I knew you had killed Roger.

"I knew it was you who had left me to swing.

"And I knew what you were here for. And I waited, Albert Mompett. I bided my time. *And now it has come!*"

§5

Thomas Pepper, *alias* Richard Rodd, stood over Albert Mompett, *alias* Russell Bemmington, and eyed him with a fierce triumphant glare, his face a mask of hate half satisfied, rage suppressed and barely held in leash.

"*He's mad*," thought Albert Mompett, "*mad.*"

The one thing to do was to humour this Rodd. Humour him. Placate him. Obey him while leading him; lead him while obeying him—and, at the right time and place, kill him.

Kill him. This savage animal, this mad dog, must be exterminated.

What cruel luck, what a turn of fate, that brought this upon Albert Mompett now; now at the great moment of his life, the moment for which he had planned and plotted and worked and waited.

Nemesis. Fate.

But Albert Mompett would be no feeble puppet, no broken toy of Destiny, no helpless sport of the mocking and ironic gods. Were his plans to be thwarted, success denied him, the cup dashed from his lips—at the last moment?

Albert Mompett in *Thomas Pepper's* power! In the hollow of his hand. His property as he phrased it. He promised himself a brave five minutes with Thomas Pepper yet. And they'd be the last minutes of the life of Thomas Pepper.

Now, to be very clever and very, very careful.

"You win," he said. "I give you best. You're cleverer than I am. Yes, I'm Albert Mompett. . . . Well? What do you want? What are your terms?"

"Half the treasure," replied Pepper.

"What, and leave me only a half to share with Knocker Neuson? A quarter each?"

"Why should I leave you anything at all?"

"Why should I find it—and give you anything at all?"

"Because if you don't, I'll kill you. Haven't you grasped the position yet? Do I have to say it all again? I can kill you now and send for the police. What can happen to me? I've been punished once for killing you. Yes, and suppose I send for the police without killing you, and hand you over for the murder of your brother, poor Roger Mompett? And for the murder of General Cortenay. And for letting two men—*two* men—get a death sentence and penal servitude for life, you knowing them to be innocent. And for being the damned thieving, murdering crook that you are. And for being in this house with felonious intent—and bringing the convict jewel-thief, Knocker Neuson, here, posing as an architect, to help you. What if I kill you now or send you to gaol for life? What then?"

"Why, then you certainly don't get any of the stuff, do you?" sneered Albert Mompett.

"Now look here, Pepper," he added. "You say, 'haven't I grasped the idea yet.' Well, haven't *you*? We're both after this stuff, and neither of us can do anything without the other. I can't get at it while you keep watch, and you can't get at it until I tell you the secret. And there's nobody alive knows that except me."

"And Knocker Neuson?"

"No. He only knows it's in the house and probably in the Library."

"What did you bring him into it for?"

"Several reasons. It's a two-man job . . . Also I could never go to it at night and be sure of not being disturbed—till old Miss Wymper died. She used to come there nearly every night—at all hours. And stay till all hours . . . You prowl about a damn' sight too much at night, likewise . . . Cortenay comes down there too, occasionally . . . And in the day-time I had to have an excuse for crawling about the panelling and beams, high up, with kitchen-steps and ladders, all over the place. . . . And I had to get the stuff sold in Amsterdam. So I brought him here as an architect and antique expert. That gave us a chance and excuse to mess about with the panelling everywhere. I told him it was probably in the old picture-gallery, kept him guessing, and we pottered around. I saved the Library for the last, so as Cortenay and you and everybody else would get used to the idea of us working here, and so that one day or night we could go to it without being suspected or interrupted."

"And what about the other fellow, 'Mister Warlock Manningfold'? What did you bring him into it for? What's his line of graft?"

"That was a piece of what they call *camouflage.* He's the goods. Genuine picture expert."

"Well, what was the idea?"

"Find out what the pictures are worth. . . . And apparently they are worth just nothing at all."

"Going to pinch those as well, were you?"

"No. No harm in knowing what their value was, though."

"None. And when you get the sparklers?"

"My idea was to give Knocker one big stone at a time, to take over to Holland. When he brought back the money, he'd get his commission and take another—so that if he was going to bilk me, he'd only get away with one sparkler."

"And Knocker doesn't know yet?"

"No; but he's got a pretty good guess that it's a matter of panelling; and there's not much left but the Library."

"Doesn't he know quite well it must be the Library?"

"How should he?"

"Because you killed General Cortenay there."

"Sh-s-sh! Sh! Shut up! What are you talking about, Pepper? Why don't you shout it?"

"I may be shouting it down the telephone before long. Answer my question. Doesn't he know you killed General Cortenay in that Library?"

"No, he doesn't."

"Why did you open the safe that night?"

"Well, ask yourself. Made it like a common burglary, didn't it? Took Henry Hyam and Kike Lipsky in, as well as the police, anyhow."

"Listen, Albert Mompett. If there's any funny business over Knocker Neuson, I'll kill you with no more thought than putting my foot on a cockroach."

"How d'you mean, 'funny stuff'?"

"Why, if while I'm talking to you now, he's pinched 'em and cleared off, and you are going to meet him and . . ."

"Talk sense, Pepper. Think I should give Knocker a chance to get in ahead of me?"

"No, you'd trust him about as far as I trust you. Were you and he going down there again to-night?"

For a fraction of a second, Albert Mompett hesitated.

"No," he said.

"You're a liar; and for two pins I'd batter the life out of you now. You were. What time?"

And drawing his deadly weapon from his pocket, Pepper advanced menacingly upon his enemy.

Albert Mompett flinched. This man was stronger than he. Fierce; savage; relentless; mad; armed. He'd got a gun as well as that black-jack.

"All-right, all-right," he said quickly. "Yes."

"What time?"

"Three o'clock."

"Ah! To-night's the night, eh? Your luck's out, Albert Mompett, eh? And mine's in. Now then. We'll go along to 'Mr. Reginald Minchess's' room next door, and tell him that to-night is *not* the night. And if he puts his head outside of his door, tell him that you and some others will beat Hell out of him—and then hand him over to the Police."

"I say, that won't do. That . . ."

"I know it won't. Tell him what you like, as long as you tell him not to go downstairs to-night."

Thomas Pepper, *alias* Richard Rodd, picked up the dressing-gown that had so recently adorned the honoured figure of Sir Russell Bemmington, and felt in the pockets.

"Empty all your pockets on to that table and leave them inside out. Yes, now your hip-pocket. Turn round. Put your hands up."

Pepper satisfied himself that Albert Mompett had no under-arm holster for a small automatic, and that he was entirely weaponless.

"Put that dressing-gown on, and do exactly as you are told. . . . See this?" and he held the Popper under Albert Mompett's nose.

"I'd as soon bash you with this, as get those jewels. And see this?"

From his left-hand pocket he produced the automatic he had obtained from Kike Lipsky.

"And I'd as soon put a couple of bullets through your stomach as either. Now then. Go to Knocker Neuson's door; call him; and tell him there's nothing doing to-night. And if you want to live a bit longer, be careful. You pass the wrong word to him, and you'll both get it. You first. And if Knocker gets his, well, it's self-defence, see? And nobody better known to the Police than Knocker Neuson. Now then, march. And I'm behind you. . . . Feel this?"

Opening the door and going out into the corridor, Albert Mompett knocked with his ring on the next door, a double knock, a single and a double.

Almost immediately the door was softly opened, and Thomas Pepper, his back against the wall beside the door, heard Mompett's whisper,

"Wash-out. Not to-night. Cancelled."

And the equally cautious reply,

"Why? What's wrong?"

"Rodd. On the prowl. To-morrow night. We'll have to fix him."

Apparently Knocker Neuson was suspicious.

"How do you know?" he asked.

"Saw him. He's in the Library now."

"What were you doing?"

"Went to get the steps, you fool."

"What's he doing in the Library?"

"Oh, counting himself. Eating the carpet! What d'you think? He's on to us, or thinks he is. We've got to fix him. You go to bed. See you to-morrow."

The door closed, and Rodd switched on his pocket-torch.

"Turn round and keep your back to me," he said.

"Knocker thinks I'm double-crossing him," whispered Mompett.

"Fancy that!" replied Pepper. "Down to the Library. Go on. And if you turn your head towards me, I'll smash it."

Arrived at the Library door,

"Stop," said he, "and stand still."

Taking the key from his pocket, Rodd unlocked the door.

"Inside," said he, "and stay there while I get the steps. Don't switch the lights on."

Mompett entered the room, and Pepper closed the door behind him and locked it.

"Let the hound stand there in the dark a bit," said he, as he ran down the stairs. "Perhaps he'll feel the old General's hands on his face—the foul swine."

A few minutes later he returned, carrying a pair of collapsible steps used for inside window cleaning.

He unlocked the door. As he switched the lights on, he saw Mompett standing with his back to him. Placing the steps against the wall, he closed the door.

"Now then," he said. "Go to it. And don't make any mistakes, if you want to go out of this room alive."

"Well, if it isn't there I can't find it, can I? I can't do the impossible."

"Too bad, isn't it? . . . Get on with it."

Taking the steps, Mompett placed them against the panelling in what was the left-hand corner to anyone entering the room.

"Shove your foot against the bottom of the steps," he said. "I've got to push."

Standing on the top of the steps while Pepper held them firmly, Mompett, using as much of his weight and strength as his position permitted, pushed, as hard as he could, each pair of the four knobs that adorned the four corners of every panel within his reach. There was no result.

"Nothing there," he said.

"Perhaps higher, or lower," suggested Pepper.

"No. According to the story, a man standing on an ordinary step-ladder is at the right height. We'll move it."

He descended the steps, shifted them a few feet, and ascended them again.

Once more he pressed, as hard as he could, against each pair of the four small bosses of each of the panels within his reach; and again without result.

Again he descended, moved the ladder and re-peated the process; and again failed to achieve any result.

"He was dusting a picture-frame," he said.

"Who was?" asked Rodd.

"The feller who chanced on the trick of it."

"Well, didn't he chance on the jewels too, then?"

"No, he didn't, or I shouldn't be here, should I?"

"Well, get on with it. You don't go out of here without 'em," growled Pepper.

"And I'm damned if you go with 'em," he added to himself.

Again Mompett's efforts were ineffectual.

He looked down at Pepper.

"How long have these pictures been in the places in which they are now?" he asked. "Any idea?"

"No. How should I know?"

"Wonder if they've been moved in . . . how long . . . thirty years?"

Pepper made no reply.

"Well, we had better move this one."

"Try the other side of it first," said Pepper.

"All-right."

"And then the other side of the next one."

Again Albert Mompett moved the steps and assailed the pairs of panel-bosses on the other side of the picture; a contemporary painting of the Buccaneer, and again without result.

And once more Mompett made essay of pairs of the knobs of the panels between the next two pictures; and the next two, until all the exposed panelling on the left-hand wall had been tested.

"Now we'll try behind the pictures, starting with that one," directed Pepper. "Put the steps close up against the frame, and I'll lift from below. You unhook the chain and ease it down to me."

And with no great difficulty, the portrait of Sir Giles Cortenay the Buccaneer was lifted down and placed against the wall by the door.

This being done, Mompett once more climbed the steps and resumed work.

"Lend me the chisel," he requested of Pepper. "If I hold it in both hands and shove with the handle, I can get more force."

"Lend nothing," growled Pepper. "Use your hands."

And indeed the long chisel with its sharpened end would have made an ugly weapon.

"Well, as you've only got a gun and a life-preserver," sneered Mompett, "perhaps . . .

"My God!" he cried in excitement; for a sharp click followed his pressure upon two of the knobs. And, as he withdrew his hand, the large and heavy panel, some four and a half feet high by three feet wide, was pressed outward and tilted towards him.

"Look out," he called in a hoarse whisper, as, seizing the top of the panel in both hands, he lifted it from the ledge on which it rested, and lowered it to Pepper, who, taking it from him, placed it against the wall.

"Stand still, you, Albert Mompett," warned Pepper. "What's in there?"

"A damned great doll's house! Or a very small room. Or a very big cupboard, cubby-hole, call it what you like. Three stone walls, wooden roof, wooden floor."

"Anything in it?"

"No, nothing at all."

"Worse luck for you, then."

"What d'you mean?"

"What I say."

"I can't find the stuff if it isn't here, can I?"

"No, you can't. But I can give you yours for keeps, if you don't. It'll be the last time you double-cross anybody."

"Oh, talk sense, man! I've found this for you, haven't I?"

"For me, yes, for *me*. . . . Now find something more. If you know this much, know the rest of it. Get a move on."

"Give us your torch. I'm going in."

Handing Mompett the torch, Pepper watched

him enter the aperture, and promptly climbed up and followed.

Evidently Mompett expected to find something in the left-hand wall.

"Now you'll have to give me that chisel. Don't be frightened. I can't do you much harm in here, can I?"

"No," agreed Pepper. "But I could shoot you dead and clap that panel up again, couldn't I?"

Albert Mompett licked his lips and, without reply, held out his hand for the chisel which Pepper gave him.

"What is it?" asked the latter, as Mompett applied the sharp edge of the chisel to the wall. "A loose stone?"

"Just that," was the reply.

And, in a sitting position, with knees drawn up, his back against the opposite wall of the tiny room, Mompett worked at levering a large, loose, dressed stone out of the wall.

'So he knew all about it all the time, did he'? thought Pepper. 'Wonder who told him? . . . Lord above us, how it must have worried him, wondering whether anybody else would chance upon it! I suppose the old General caught him looking for it that night. . . . Yes, it's a two-man job all-right—to do quietly. It must have broken his heart to let Knocker Neuson in on it. As a matter of fact, he wanted to get the stuff without Knocker's help, even now, and without letting him know where it was, for fear Knocker should do him in, on the spot, and collar the lot.

'Yes, what he wanted Knocker for, was to play the architect game all over the place, no doubt. And then Knocker was to flog the shiners, one by one, in Amsterdam, as Mompett handed them over. Yes, that's why he never got them until now.

'Well, better for him if it had been Knocker.'

"It's coming!" grunted Mompett, and, by the light of his torch, Pepper could see that the stone had been worked forward until it protruded from the wall by almost an inch.

Seizing the sides of the stone in his hands, Mompett endeavoured to pull it towards him, and, failing to do so, got to work again with the chisel, using it as a lever only. First on one side and then on the other, he worked the stone forward a hair's-breadth at a time.

"Try it again now," said Pepper.

"Look here," replied the panting, sweating Mompett, drawing his sleeve across his forehead. "Before I work this stone out, you go and put that gun on the table down in the room. See?"

"Anything else?" enquired Pepper.

"How do I know that when I pull the stuff out, you won't shoot me?"

"You don't."

"Look here, Pepper, talk sense. Act like a man that's got some. If you killed me and got the stuff, you couldn't fence it. There's nobody in England would touch sparklers of the size these are, by all accounts. And if there was, you'd get no price for them in this country. And you don't know the ropes with . . ."

"Don't you worry about me. Pull that stone out. Go on. Go on, I tell you. You get a move on. Quick. Out with that stone."

Again seizing the sides of the stone with his hands, Mompett placed his feet against the wall and, using all his weight and strength, heaved, hauled and tugged, working the stone from side to side as he did so.

"It's coming," he said. "It's coming."

And suddenly, with a final effort, he dragged the big stone from its place, letting it down heavily on to the boards between his feet.

Thrusting himself into the hiding-place and almost knocking Mompett over, Pepper shone his torch into the cavity exposed by the removal of the stone.

Save for a small roll of paper or parchment, the recess was empty.

A curious sound, between an oath and a sob, burst from the labouring lungs of Albert Mompett.

"*Christ!*" he whimpered, "*it's gone!*" and put forth a hand to reach into the recess, for the document.

Violently Pepper struck Mompett's hand aside and, reaching in, snatched the folded document, and backed out of the cupboard.

"Stay there," he growled to Mompett who made to move. "Show your head over this ladder and I'll bash it."

Hastily unrolling the stiff ancient document, he saw a few lines of crabbed faded handwriting, angular and irregular, some of the letters, such as the 's,' being of peculiar shape.

With difficulty he read:

"*For my very dere wyfe or my very dere son. Note and ponder. Even in ye cannon's mouthe, seek ye baubles (of Spayne). Ye Thyrde bastarde culverin of 30 hondrede-wt and of boare 5 inche. West Fort. Behind a 10 pounde ball stopt in with claye. Fast binde safe finde.*"

'Well, I'm damned,' thought Thomas Pepper. 'That's it! That's it! Got it, by God. The third bastard culverin in the West Fort. . . . What's a culverin? That'll be a gun, a cannon, I suppose.'

"What is it? What is it?" begged Mompett from above.

"Full directions for finding the treasure, the Cortenay Treasure," growled Pepper, showing his teeth.

"Where is it? For God's sake . . . Where is it?"

"Where you won't find it. Here, put that paper

back in the hole and shove the stone back."

"What?"

"Do as I tell you. Put it back and shove the stone in again."

"Here, Pepper, don't be a bloody fool."

"Don't you, Albert Mompett. You do as I tell you, and be quick about it."

"Well, let me read it, man, let me read it. I might understand it better."

"Ah, you were always the clever one, weren't you, Albert Mompett? You shove it back."

Pepper handed the parchment to Mompett, who held it and glared at him in mingled amazement and rage.

'The West Fort!' thought Pepper. 'That would be Fort Raleigh. Culverin. Bastard culverin. That'd be some of the artillery of those days. The third. But they are gone. There's only one. Good God . . . Where are they gone? Where are they?'

Suddenly he laughed aloud.

The posts! The posts! The old cannon they had turned into posts. Across the entrance to the stable yard. The Guv'nor had told him they were cannon from the Forts.

He had found the treasure for the Guv'nor.

Mompett made to unroll the parchment.

"Put that back," ordered Pepper. "*Quick!*"

Knowing its contents by heart, every word of which was burning into his brain, it would not matter if he never saw it again.

Mompett, open-mouthed, stared insanely.

"Put it *back*?" he whispered.

"Yes. And quick about it."

"But, you fool . . . I . . ."

Pepper's hand went to the pocket in which was Lipsky's pistol.

Mompett closed his mouth, swallowed, and seemed visibly to pull himself together.

He thrust the scroll into the recess.

Well—he knew where it was—and could get it without help next time. He would too—as soon as he had made a plan. Come and get it without any help at all. To-night. As soon as he had got this performing dog where he wanted him.

He'd kill him in his bed this very night, if necessary, rather than let him take a mike out of him like this.

"Now then, back with that stone and get it square and level."

And again Mompett set to work and quickly had the stone back into its place.

Pepper descended the steps, and Mompett thrust the blunt end of the chisel into his trousers-pocket under his dressing-gown. Thomas Pepper would double-cross Albert Mompett, would he, and put a spoke in his wheel!

"Stay where you are and get this panelling back," directed Pepper, as Mompett crawled out backward to the steps. "Hold steady. Right."

And raising the panel in both hands, he lifted it at arm's length and sideways to where Mompett could take it and raise it to its place.

Placing the bottom of the panel upon its ledge, he pressed it into the frame, and with a sharp click it was again fixed securely in place.

"Now the picture," said Pepper.

And raising this in turn and thrusting it sideways, Pepper enabled Albert Mompett to seize the chain by which it hung.

Standing on the top of the steps, and reaching at arm's length, Albert Mompett put the chain over the two hooks and adjusted the picture in position above the panel.

'No wonder that footman, Ted Umpleby, took a toss,' he thought, glancing down to see that Pepper still held the steps.

"That's all-right," he said.

"Come on down," replied Pepper.

"What now?" enquired Mompett as he obeyed. "What's the game? How do we set about getting 'em?"

"We don't," grinned Pepper with a smile that showed his teeth and held no hint of mirth or amusement. "We don't. The Guv'nor's going to get them. And you're going to get what's coming to you —when I've decided what that is."

"Look here, Pepper, did you go barmy in prison?"

"Quite. But I'm all-right again now, thanks."

"Don't you want a big fortune in cash?"

"No."

"What do you want?"

"You."

"And what about the sparklers? Don't you want a share of them?"

Albert Mompett edged nearer to Pepper as he spoke.

"No."

"But what are you going to do, man? What *are* you going to do?"

"Tell their owner where they are, and help him to find 'em. Whose are they?"

"The man's who gets them, aren't they?"

"Yes, and that'll be Sir Giles Cortenay."

"And what share do you think he'll give you?"

"I don't want a share."

"And what about me?"

"You don't exist, Albert Mompett. Haven't you got that *yet?* You're dead. You know it. I murdered you. You yourself proved that. You belong to me. If those sparklers belonged to you, they'd be mine. If this house belonged to you, it'd be mine. But you own nothing, Albert Mompett. They belong to Sir Giles Cortenay. You've made a new place of this house. Spent a fortune on it, haven't you? For yourself, as you thought. That's where you are wrong. It's for my Guv'nor, Sir Giles Cortenay. See? Someone tipped you about the jewels, and you came here to get 'em; and you thought you'd get the whole place and settle down as a country gentleman. *You* . . . you swindling murderer. And what did you find here, as well as the jewels and the grand old house and the estate? *You found me, your owner, your proprietor*, the man who bought you with his life, and then with penal servitude for life. And you're going to find something else. You . . ."

"Listen, Pepper . . ."

This man was mad, raving mad, and he, Albert Mompett, stood in the worst danger in which he had ever stood in his life . . . What a night! Those jewels almost under his hand; and this madman . . . He must settle him, get the paper—and act accordingly.

"Listen, man! Let bygones be bygones. I can make your fortune. I can get the jewels sold for their value! I can make you rich, rich. Why . . ."

And with left hand outstretched, appealing, Mompett edged forward, and with his right hand drew the long, heavy chisel from his pocket.

"Why, I can set you up in . . ."

Suddenly he struck.

"*A-h-h-h-h!*" snarled Pepper, flung up his left arm, and, swiftly and expertly, also struck, the leaden knob of the Popper descending with terrific violence upon Mompett's head.

Albert Mompett fell heavily to the floor.

"There, you dog! . . . At last," panted the triumphant Pepper. "And do you know where you are lying? Right where the old General lay and bled to death after you had smashed his skull. . . . You scum. . . . Murdered an old man of eighty. Sent your brother Roger to the condemned cell. Murdered him when he escaped. Then sent me to the condemned cell for that murder. And you'd have murdered me now. You'd have robbed the Guv'nor of his treasure, and you'd have taken his home and kicked him out. And you had got your filthy eye on a girl whose shoes I wouldn't let you clean. Well, *now* where are you? Not in Hell, I hope. I hope you're not dead, Albert Mompett. Not yet."

Mompett groaned and stirred.

"Good! Now; shall I kill you myself, or have you hanged? Or what about working the evidence so that you get a life sentence? What about letting you rot in gaol like Roger did, and I did; and then picking you up when you come out of prison, still my property, and then killing you when I feel like it."

Albert Mompett opened his eyes.

"No, I think I'll kill you now."

Albert Mompett's glazing eyes turned towards the door which, behind Pepper's back, softly opened and shut.

Pepper wheeled round as a voice that he knew said:

"Not a bad idea, either! . . . Found 'em, have you? And done him in. You don't have to kill him again, you know. . . . Hands up, quick."

And Pepper knew that Knocker Neuson, cool as an icicle, hands in pockets, feet astraddle, a quizzical smile on his lips, held an automatic in the side-pocket of his dinner-jacket.

"*Quick!*"

Pepper sprang, snatching for the Popper as he did so, and Neuson fired.

Pepper collapsed in a heap almost at his feet.

"So I'm Tommy Dodd and Odd-man-out," observed Neuson coolly, bending over Pepper and searching his pockets.

What was this?

Not got the sparklers?

Gent Jannison had still got them, then. From the look of things he would have sworn that Potsy Pepper had lifted them from him. Busted him on the dome and frisked him. Well, Gent Jannison didn't easily let go of anything he had got his hands on.

Leaving the still breathing Pepper, he turned to Albert Mompett and methodically searched him, his frown deepening, his breathing quickening, as it dawned upon him that his search was fruitless.

What had happened? Where were the jewels? One of them must have found them. One of them must have them. They must be here in the room, otherwise why had they quarrelled? Why had Pepper-Potsy killed Gent Jannison? Why had Jannison come to his, Neuson's, room and said it was a wash-out, cancelled, nothing doing that night, and then come down here with Potsy Pepper?

Obviously Gent Jannison had double-crossed him. And, equally obviously, he had tried the same game with Pepper.

But what had they been doing all this time; and why had Pepper laid him out? Pepper wouldn't have done that unless Jannison had got the jewels, or Pepper had learned from him where they were.

Knocker Neuson frowned in anxious thought, and cursed his folly. That came of jumping to conclusions.

Bad luck. Hellish bad luck. Why hadn't he come in sooner, instead of waiting outside the door for them, or one of them, to come out with a hatful of sparklers in his pocket? He had known from Gent Jannison's voice that something was up. He had been excited.

Roughly he shook the dying man.

"Hi! Gent Jannison! You double-crossing dog, where are they?" he growled. "Wake up."

Brutally he dragged Albert Mompett into a sitting position and shook him so that his head lolled and rolled from side to side.

"Where are they, you thief?" he whispered hoarsely.

Flinging the flaccid body back upon the floor, he turned to Pepper.

What about this one?

What a cursed fool he had been to shoot so quickly! Perhaps he hadn't killed him. His eyes were open, but he looked pretty bad. He had got his.

"Where are they? Tell me," he urged. "Cough it up, quick, Pepper-Potsy, and I'll fetch a doctor. Where are they?"

"Fetch the Guv'nor," whispered Pepper.

"What are you talking about? Where's the stuff?"

Pepper opened his eyes and met Neuson's hungry glare.

"Quick!" cried the latter, and shook Pepper, being careful that no blood touched himself. "Where's the stuff? I'll get you some brandy, and I'll fetch a doctor. And we'll share. . . . *Where's the stuff?*"

Moistening his lips, Pepper whispered distinctly,

"Bemmington . . . Slatterthwaite . . . Gent Jannison . . . Albert Mompett. *Him* . . ." and turned his eyes to where Mompett lay. "Double-crossed us. Found it yesterday. Posted it."

"*Christ!*" whispered Neuson. . . . "*Posted it? . . . Gone?*"

He rose to his feet.

So that was it.

Gent Jannison had double-crossed him. Pepper-Potsy had found him out, and had laid him out too.

Pepper had forced him to a show-down. Pepper had known more than Jannison, all along. Pepper had brought him down here to help lift the stuff— and found it gone. Jannison had had to own up that he had posted it away, out of the house. Now where would Jannison have posted it to? God alone knew.

It had been behind some of this panelling. Hence the step-ladder, and the chisel lying on the carpet there.

Well, no good crying over spilt blood. Best thing he could do would be to skip out quick—but not too quick—and go to Jannison's other place. That'd be it. Of course.

Gent Jannison would have addressed the parcel to himself, Sir Russell Bemmington. That'd be it. He'd have addressed it to himself, care of Mrs. Milly Harris, his housekeeper. Well, it wouldn't take Knocker Neuson long to recover the parcel from Milly. Either a well-told tale or a tap on the dome would soon settle Milly. . . .

Yes. He had better go back to bed now, and hear the shocking news in the morning—how Sir Giles Cortenay's house-man, an ex-convict, had killed Sir Russell Bemmington, who had shot him in self-defence. Sir Russell must have come down to the Library and caught the man trying to open the safe or something.

Having carefully polished his automatic with his handkerchief, Neuson again bent over Albert Mompett's body, took his right hand and covered the blued barrel and flat sides of the pistol with Albert Mompett's finger-prints; and then, still holding it with his silk handkerchief, he placed it in Mompett's right hand and disposed hand and pistol upon the carpet.

Well, now the 'busies' could come and make what they could of that.

Good job Potsy Pepper had got a gun in his pocket and a black-jack in his hand. No need to look any further for cause of death. Quite clear to all Scotland Yard that Pepper had hit poor Sir

Russell Bemmington on the head, and Sir Russell had lived long enough to shoot him.

Gent Jannison must have been going to clear out to-night, when Pepper got hold of him.

Well, well! Sad, sad, sad!

And with any luck, Knocker Neuson inherited.

Yes—his best line would be to wait and hear the bad news in the morning, and then catch the nine-forty from Sandhaven. He'd leave his card with the local 'busy,' if he was in the house! Mr. Reginald Minchess, F.R.I.B.A. and A.R.I.B.A. Got to get back to Town. Shocked beyond words.

Of course they were both dead?

Well, Gent Jannison looked the part, good and proper. Cold meat. And what about Potsy Pepper?

Yes, he had crossed the Bar-without-a-Drink all-right.

Again Knocker Neuson scanned the room carefully.

Yes, everything O.K.

Of course the jewels wouldn't be here now, or they'd be in the pockets of one of these two silly swine on the floor there.

Well, all tidy and shipshape. Might as well go to bed. Give the door-handle, each side, a rub up; also the electric-light switch-plate; in case the 'busies' looked for finger-prints there. He had touched nothing else. Must remember to leave the lights on.

And with equal mind and high hopes for the tracking and recovery of the parcel that the wicked double-crossing Gent Jannison had evidently sent off to his female accomplice, Knocker Neuson returned to his bedroom and to bed.

§6

A few minutes after the door closed behind Knocker Neuson, Thomas Pepper opened his eyes.

Slowly and painfully he raised himself on his hand, and looked across at the body of his enemy.

So that dog was dead.

And he had killed him.

Good—if it were the last thing he ever did.

But it wouldn't be.

There was one more thing to do . . .

But he . . .

Ah . . . yes, Knocker Neuson, of course. . . . Well, he had fooled him properly. He'd be off on a wild-goose chase after a registered parcel.

The post! That was funny. That was a good one. Quite a clever joke. The jewels in the *post*.

Yes, but it was a different sort of post, Knocker Neuson. A post that had once been a cannon, this was.

Now to let the Guv'nor know, just in case.

He wasn't feeling too good. Lost a lot of blood, perhaps. If only he didn't feel so cold. And so giddy. And could breathe properly. And get this blood out of his mouth. He'd be all-right then.

Could he get to the big writing-table?

He had got to get to it. He must get to it.

It was a long way, though.

He'd have to get up, somehow.

With a great effort, Thomas Pepper raised himself on his hands and knees.

For a few moments he swayed thus, and then knelt up.

Yes, his head was now on a level with the writing-table. But how far away was it? Within arm's-reach, or half a mile away? No, that was silly. He was in a room. In the Library. It couldn't be far.

He'd be better in a minute.

Yes, the mistake was trying to get up, just here. He must crawl to the table, and then it would be easy to get up—once he had something to hold on to.

Ugh! . . . Hullo, this was bad. . . . He was going very giddy. . . . Couldn't see too well.

Why, what a fool he was. He could do it here. He could write it here. He needn't go all the way to that table.

Kneeling back on his heels, swaying from side to side, he made an effort to take from the breast pocket of his coat, the little shiny-covered note-book in which he jotted down his notes and memo-randa of things to be attended to, each day; mes-sages, orders, times for the car, trains to be met, and so forth.

He must be quick. He was going to faint or be sick or fall asleep or something silly.

Quick. How he was fumbling. The pencil was as big as a pole. No, it was as small as a match. Per-haps if he fell forward . . .

Was he writing? No, this was a nightmare, and the book wouldn't keep still.

Now . . . now . . . come. . . . The bell would ring in a minute. The screw would shop him. He'd get three days solitary on bread-and-water, and no bed, if he didn't pull himself together and get up.

Ah, that was better. Now for it.

With book in one hand and pencil in the other, he poised himself for a moment erect upon his knees, swayed, and fell forward on his face.

One more effort.

Ah, that was better, again. . . . There was the book, steady and firm on the floor, his hand beside it, and the pencil in his hand.

Now then. Now . . . God grant him just one minute. One minute in compensation for those eight years . . .

And with a supreme effort and the last of his strength and mental clarity, Thomas Pepper wrote,

"Sir,

The jewels are found and safe they are in the culverin that was third now one of the posts by the stable yard paper with directions is behind a stone in the cupboard behind the panelling behind the picture by the steps press two knobs and the panel comes out."

There! Thank God. Now he could faint, or sleep —or die. Nothing mattered now. He had put it plainly. He had written it all so clearly.

So Thomas Pepper died knowing that he had left his message.

But as he had written it on the unreceptive surface of the carpet, no-one else ever knew that he had done so.

XV

The following days, of nightmare quality, were a period which Bump Cortenay and Honor Winter long remembered, with horror; and for long strove to forget, without success.

To the local Police it was at once clear that Sir Russell Bemmington had been murdered by Thomas Pepper *alias* Richard Rodd, ex-convict, and that Sir Russell Bemmington had killed his assailant in self-defence.

It is possible that this would also have been the view and verdict of the Coroner, but for the evidence of a woman who—applying to the Police for protection from one Karl Neuson, known to them as Knocker Neuson, international crook and ticket-of-leave man—volunteered to give evidence that would shed illuminating light upon the mystery of the deaths of the two men in the Library at Cortenay Old Hall, and upon their respective characters.

According to this woman, one Milly Harris, unmarried, the dead man, known as Sir Russell Bemmington, was as big a crook as Knocker Neuson himself. If possible, a bigger one.

According to her story, it was because the man calling himself Sir Russell Bemmington was alleged to have forwarded to her a parcel of diamonds and other jewels stolen from Cortenay Old Hall, that Knocker Neuson was threatening and intimidating her, burgling her premises and earnestly, and doubtless truthfully, promising to bump her off unless, within a given period, she enabled him to 'knock off' the said jewels, supposed to have been posted to her, for care and custody, by the late *soi-disant* Sir Russell Bemmington.

This "Sir Russell Bemmington," she avowed, was one Albert Mompett, grandson of a former butler of Cortenay Old Hall. To his twin brother, Roger Mompett, an innocent and admirable man, she had been engaged when a girl in service at a house near Sandhaven, many, many years ago. Of his twin brother, Albert Mompett, indistinguishable from him, she had heard a good deal from Roger.

Before Roger was in a position to marry her, Albert appeared on the Sandhaven scene and, such was his amazing likeness to her *fiancé*, was able to impersonate him.

This he did with such skill and cunning that she was never sure which of the brothers it was who visited her.

Roger, discovering that Albert had undoubtedly impersonated him, was naturally incensed to the point of fury, accused Milly of complicity, and told her that, as Albert was rich and he himself was poor, she had better go to Albert.

This she did, inasmuch as Albert had all the charms and attractions of Roger, and an apparently unlimited supply of cash as well.

Too late she discovered that Albert was not what could be called a marrying man, and definitely was what could be called a rogue, a rascal and a crook, earning his considerable income by every sort and kind of fraud, dishonesty and theft. He was an embezzler, a forger, a confidence-trickster, a most expert safe-opener, a burglar, a jewel-thief and, at length, a murderer.

He it was who entered Cortenay Old Hall, by night, in the belief that he had the secret of the hiding-place of the famous Cortenay Treasure.

With a view to concealing his efforts in this direction, should they prove fruitless, he, without the slightest difficulty, opened the safe in the Library there; and, being surprised and tackled by the aged General Cortenay, killed him, and departed by way of the window through which he had entered.

Not only did he escape successfully, but put an end to the matter in the eyes of the Police and the public, by getting another man convicted of the murder, and thus closing the matter. The victim was his own twin brother, Roger; though, at the time, the witness, Milly Harris, whom Albert Mompett had sent to America with certain valuable and negotiable property, knew nothing of this.

In America he joined her, and later he returned with her to England.

Here he very foolishly treated her as, sooner or later, he had treated everybody else who trusted him—deceived, cheated, and for a time abandoned her, "taking up," as she expressed it, with another woman.

His twin brother, Roger Mompett, escaped from Porchester Gaol during the period of Albert Mompett's infatuation with this other girl. To Thomas Pepper—savage and sore at Albert Mompett who had won, and deserted, the witness—she, Milly Harris, went and told the true story of Albert Mompett's devilish wickedness in the matter of his brother Roger. Roger wrote to Thomas Pepper from his place of hiding. Thomas Pepper went to see him and, aided and abetted and guided by Milly Harris, brought Roger to where he could interview his villainous brother Albert, at the latter's lonely and secret bungalow on the sands near Whitebay Harbour.

Here, Albert Mompett murdered Roger and, having done so, placed evidence upon the body to prove that the corpse was that of the murderer himself; that the dead man was Albert Mompett—murdered by Thomas Pepper.

He then went to America and, on his return,

sought out the witness, Milly Harris, whistled her back—a man, she said, who could whistle a bird from a tree, even though he had just flung a stone at it—took the name of Sir Russell Bemmington, learned with the greatest satisfaction that Cortenay Old Hall had become a Guest House, and devoted his life to the discovery and theft of the famous Cortenay Treasure.

Meanwhile, as she should have mentioned earlier, Thomas Pepper, who had written a very threatening letter to Albert Mompett, had been arrested, tried for the murder of Albert Mompett (whose corpse that of Roger was supposed to be), was condemned to death, reprieved, and given a sentence of penal servitude for life—and this although the "murdered" Albert was alive and well.

This Thomas Pepper, having served eight years of his sentence, was released from Old Marsh Gaol as a reward for the extremely courageous part he had played in saving the life of the Chief Warder, and rendering invaluable help at the crisis of the great convict mutiny.

Being discharged from gaol, he had made his way to London, and had there met an ex-convict who had taken him to a certain quarter of Soho where he had been introduced to a criminal gang, some members of which he had already encountered in gaol; and he had for a time lived in a criminal's hide-out, a sort of thieves' kitchen.

Being precisely the opposite of a criminal by nature and upbringing, he had, as soon as he was able, obtained honest work. In this he had had the experience of all ex-convicts; had been found out for what he was; and been dismissed, time after time, from job after job.

At length, unable to get further assistance from the Prisoners' Aid Society, he had become a tramp, taken to the road, and, making his way to Whitebay

Harbour where he had hoped for casual employment among the fishermen who had once known
him, he had been taken on at Cortenay Old Hall,
and had there been in service when Albert Mompett, calling himself Sir Russell Bemmington, had
arrived and settled-in as a guest. . . .

That much the woman knew from what Albert
Mompett, *alias* Sir Russell Bemmington, himself
had told her when he visited her from time to time
at his hide-out in London; the place that she had
kept always ready for him; the place which was his
accommodation address, whence he could write
and receive letters, interview accomplices such as
Knocker Neuson, and carry on the double life which
so long he had lived, and which he intended to end
as soon as he had located and annexed the Cortenay Treasure.

Now perhaps the Police and the Coroner could
see what had happened that night in the Library at
Cortenay Old Hall.

Undoubtedly Albert Mompett, *alias* Sir Russell
Bemmington, had been endeavouring to steal the
Cortenay jewels from the safe or elsewhere, and
Thomas Pepper, *alias* Richard Rodd, had caught
him in the act, had disclosed his own identity to
Albert Mompett, who had never seen him in the
flesh as Thomas Pepper; and, without doubt, Pepper had struck Albert Mompett down in self-defence, and Albert Mompett had then shot him. . . .

No, the witness, Milly Harris, was not an accessory before the fact, nor an accessory after the fact.
All that she had told the Court was what Albert
Mompett, *alias* Sir Russell Bemmington, had told
her; but she had not the slightest doubt that every
word of it was true.

And, in fact, a great deal of it was proven to be
true.

An open verdict was returned, the case was a nine days' wonder, and Cortenay Old Hall and the Cortenay Treasure were the talk of England.

§2

After the inquest, Bump, touched by the pitiable tragic figure of this Milly Harris, and anxious to learn anything further that he could discover about the late Richard Rodd, got in touch with her before she left Sandhaven, invited her to go to Cortenay Old Hall, and actually went so far as to offer to take her into service there, or otherwise to provide for her.

In addition to his sympathy and wish to learn more about Richard Rodd, there was also the sub-conscious motive of taking the opportunity of knowing more about the man calling himself Sir Russell Bemmington, with a substratum of feeling that this Milly Harris was in some sort the relict and legatee, though not the actual widow, of Albert Mompett, *alias* Sir Russell Bemmington.

Offers of help, Milly Harris declined with thanks. Of independent spirit, she professed to be of independent means and immediate intention of leaving England for ever, and returning to America where in Chicago she had friends and a *pied-à-terre*.

To Honor she unbosomed herself, and laid bare what had puzzled Bump, Honor, the Police, the Court and other hearers of her evidence—her motive and reasons for assailing the character and memory of her late protector, and endeavouring to vindicate that of the man who had died with him.

She had discovered that it was "Sir Russell Bem-mington's" intention not only to obtain possession of the Cortenay Treasure and of Cortenay Old Hall itself, but also to marry its chatelaine, Miss Honor

Winter, the present owner's cousin and a Cortenay by blood. Of his power to do this, he had had no doubt, by reason of the fact that only thus could Sir Giles Cortenay and the girl remain in their ancestral home.

In any case, he was going to acquire Cortenay Old Hall, turn country gentleman, and sever his connection with his past life and his former associates, including Milly Harris herself.

And by the time Milly Harris had said her say to Honor, it was clear that the man who had murdered General Cortenay had died on the spot where his victim had died; that the man who had intended to put Bump and Honor in the position of leaving and losing Cortenay Old Hall for ever, or agreeing to his proposal of marriage, had over-reached himself; that the man who had made Cortenay Old Hall the magnificently up-to-date and beautiful place that it now was, had unintentionally done so, as it now proved, not for his own delectation and possession, but for that of his intended victims.

And in the steel trunk in his bedroom were notes —perfectly genuine Bank of England notes—of high denomination, to the value of upwards of thirty thousand pounds.

And like, in that one respect, poor Miss Wymper, the late Sir Russell Bemmington had no heir, no claimant, relative, business associate, friend; no-one, man, woman or child, who could put in a claim to any lot, part or portion of the estate of the late Sir Russell Bemmington.

And so, to this extent, the Treasury, through the Court of Chancery, was the richer.

§3

Just before he handed over to the Treasury the said Bank of England notes, Bump received confirmation from yet another expert, of what Mr. Warlock Manningfold had privately told him—that the Old Masters in the Library were frauds; copies of the original Van Dycks, Lelys, Holbeins, Reynolds and Gainsboroughs; about a hundred years old, and quite worthless.

Great-grandpapa had been over-busy, first as a speculator and then as a picture salesman . . .

XVI

Cortenay Old Hall Country Club and Guest House had turned the corner, had not only turned it, but was galloping hard along the high road to success.

Not only had the late "Sir Russell Bemmington's" money made the great old house perfect, but the manner of his death therein, and the nine days' wonder that it caused, had advertised it far and wide, and the inevitable boom followed.

Thanks to the large sums spent upon it by the late and greatly lamented Sir Russell Bemmington, the fame of its amenities had spread abroad, and demand for accommodation beneath its famous roof far exceeded supply. Prices had risen accordingly, and had now reached a level which their recipient considered fantastic.

Not every member or guest paid these terrific prices, for, although bills in accordance with the scale of charges were sent weekly to all residents, a few there were—surviving members of the Old Contemptibles Club—who paid what they had always paid, Bump refusing to take one penny more than the old charge, or to permit them to depart.

"No, Colonel . . . No, Mrs. Wayde . . . No," he had said. "Four guineas we said and four guineas it shall be, just as long as you care to stop. Don't like to? Nonsense. It's I who ought to pay you to live here. You are one of the attractions . . ."

§2

"It's a year ago to-day," said Honor, as she and Bump strolled through the gardens.

"So it is, by Jove," replied Bump. "I was think-ing, only the other day, that it must be nearly a year since Bemmington died, and not one single word had we heard from anybody about his estate. He doesn't seem to have had a relation in the world. No-one has produced a will or sent in a bill or any-thing of the sort. It's amazing."

"Yes, and the more I think it over, Bunny, the more certain I am that Milly Harris spoke the truth absolutely. I'm sure poor Richard Rodd caught him in the act."

"What act?"

"I don't know what act, but he was up to some-thing, and Rodd caught him. He used to complain how Rodd followed him about and spied on him. He told me that Rodd used to go into his bedroom and search his belongings, and I used to reply that I didn't believe a word of it. I'm sure she was right. Rodd not only killed him. He killed Rodd. Because Rodd caught him out, or because Rodd knew some-thing about him. Bemmington shot him and, before he died, Rodd killed him—in self-defence."

"And more than self-defence," she added.

"What do you mean?"

"In defence of us, our property, our interests. He was defending you, Bump—and me—in some way."

"What's the girl talking about? Is this some more intuition."

"Yes. Do you know what I believe?"

"All sorts of funny things."

"Yes, and among them I believe that Richard Rodd was defending the Cortenay Treasure in some way. And for us. Bemmington was after it, and Rodd knew it. And so Bemmington shot him. And then Rodd hit Bemmington.

"And a good job too," she added viciously.

"The Cortenay Treasure," said Bump, as they came to the posts that spaced the entrance to the big stable-yard.

"Do you know what I think?" he continued, stopping and leaning against the old cannon, now a post, that had once been the "thyrde bastarde culverin of 30 hondrede-wt," and which still contained the Cortenay Treasure.

"That there is no such thing? I think so myself. I believe the Buccaneer hid it in that Long John cannon, and somebody else found it. There's no Treasure of Cortenay Old Hall," replied Honor.

"Wrong," said Bump. "The girl is wrong—for the first time in her life. Come in here."

"*Bump!* Have you found it?"

"Yes."

"Oh, Bunny! *Where is it?*"

"Here. In this stable. Look!"

And it came to pass that Honor Winter received her first love-kiss in a loose-box.

"I've found it all-right," said Bump, when he had got his breath. "You're it—and I've found you."

"Been a long time," laughed Honor a little shakily, as she recovered herself.

"Not as long as you think. Been waiting . . ."

"Bunny darling, what for? I've loved you ever since—ever since I can remember. When did you fall in love with me?"

"Don't know. When you first came here, I suppose. I've always loved you. But I only seem to have just realized it. Just realized that you are all the treasure I want. Yes, *you* are the Cortenay Treasure, sweetheart. My lovely!"

"Darling Bunny. . . ."

"*Darling* Honor. . . ."

CARDBOARD CASTLE

To

DR. WILLIAM LYON PHELPS, Ph.D., Litt.D.,
of Yale University,

I SHOULD LIKE TO OFFER THE DEDICATION OF
THIS BOOK AS A SMALL TOKEN OF REGARD AND
AS A RESPECTFUL TRIBUTE OF ESTEEM FOR
THE AMERICAN WORLD OF LETTERS IN WHICH
HE HOLDS SO EMINENT A POSITION

I

I am going to tell this story in my own way, because I hold very firmly the belief that one's own way is the best way. And if further reason were needed, there is surely an excellent one in the fact that I know of no other. From which you will gather the undeniable fact that I am not a practised writer; not a trained and experienced novelist, equipped with a classical or even a recognized technique.

But I have a story to tell, and am competent to tell it. Moreover, there is no one else in a position to tell the story as completely and accurately as I can.

§2

No one, not even his parents, knew and understood young Anthony Calderton better than I did, and I very much doubt if anyone understood him nearly as well.

And yet, as will be seen, this may not be saying a very great deal. I knew him because, as his tutor, I spent practically the whole of every day with him for several years. For Anthony being what he was, and I taking the view of my duties and responsibilities that I did, I was not content merely to spend lesson-time with him. In point of fact, I regarded lesson-time as perhaps the least valuable part of the day. Certainly far less important than the leisure time we spent together—talking, walking, riding, reading, pursuing our hobbies and, more particularly, young Anthony's amazing hobby of dramatization.

Doubtless you will at once think—a thing that was often actually said to me—that the boy would be only too glad to get away from his tutor as soon as lessons were over, and that if he worked with me from ten till one and again from five till six, he would see and hear as much of me as he wanted, or more, and be only too thankful to get away from me for the rest of the time.

This, however, was not the case, as it would have been with the normal boy.

But Anthony was not a normal boy.

He loathed my leaving him, as sometimes I was compelled to do, even for an hour, much less for a day or a week-end. He hated saying good night and going to bed; and he knocked at my bedroom door—a quaint little figure with tousled hair and big haunted eyes—in his pyjamas, dressing-gown and bedroom slippers, in the early morning, when the footman brought my tea.

Doubtless you will also think—a thing which, on more than one occasion, was also said to me—that I should have got sick, sorry and tired of the sight and sound of the boy, and been only too glad to leave him to his devices for the afternoon, and again as soon as his evening lesson was completed.

But neither was that the case; for on the rare occasions when Anthony was not with me, I missed him, found myself at a loose end, and much as a dog-lover feels who has to take his usual country walk without his dog.

Not that there was that sort of relationship between the boy and myself; no throwing of metaphorical sticks or stones for him to run after; no benevolent or condescending pats upon the head; no talking down; no sitting upon stiles while the less intelligent animal gambolled about my feet. Nothing of that sort. I merely mean that when he wasn't with me, I missed him so much that the walk was a lonely grind taken conscientiously for fresh air and exercise.

Not only did I miss his company but his conversation; his unusual, remarkable and most interesting thoughts, ideas and fancies—especially fancies—expressed in that somewhat old-fashioned but charming and delightful way that was the result of years of unguided browsing in his father's library, and the reading of books that rarely come the way of boys of his age.

He had had an admirable governess, of whom more anon, whose excellent influence upon his then baby mind had given it a noticeable twist and, in one minor direction, a strange little kink. I think that is the best word, for it would give a wrong impression if I said that she had warped his mind.

And what an amazing and hugely disproportionate effect, not only upon his own life, but upon those of others, was that strange little kink to have.

What she had done, in point of fact, was to give his perfectly sound mind a "King Charles's head"—more than figuratively. To the extent that she had done this, young Anthony departed from the normal, though when he came into my hands, at the age of fourteen years or so, it was some time before I discovered this curious idiosyncrasy which was to have such dramatic and far-reaching consequences.

Now I have already, and before mentioning this peculiarity, admitted that Anthony was not normal.

How difficult it is to say exactly what one means. If there be a true word in the jest that speech is given us for the concealment of our thoughts, there is a far truer one in the statement that speech is a most inadequate vehicle for the exact conveyance of our meaning.

How shall I express the state and condition of Anthony's mentality? Sane but abnormal? Normal enough, but most unusual? A mind so unusual as to be remarkable; and therefore not a normal mind?

Anyhow, what I can say without danger of being

misunderstood, is that Anthony had a beautiful, a lovely mind; that he was brilliantly clever, though I hate the word, for any fool can be "clever"; that he had an acute perceptive brain; that he had a most charming, delightful and engaging nature; that he was infinitely attractive, amusing and intriguing; that he was, with one exception, altogether the nicest, the most lovable personality I have ever known.

Though I am slow in the matter of liking and disliking, cautious in summing up and deciding about a person, I liked him the first time I saw him; liked him very much within a month; soon became exceedingly fond of him; and within the first year of our association, freely and fully admitted that I loved him.

And that was the first time in my life I had admitted such a thing, save for one or two members of my own family.

It is a thing for which I thank God, that Anthony Calderton had wise parents; that his father, albeit a fine flower of the Public School, Sandhurst and Army system, was sufficiently intelligent, broad-minded and perceptive to realize that there are certain rare spirits for whom that system is not suitable; also that his mother had sufficient love, understanding and unselfishness to realize and accept the fact that, greatly as she desired it, Anthony could not and would not go to school.

It must have been a real grief to her, as well as to her husband, that the boy should not follow in the footsteps of his ancestors, sit literally in the seats they had occupied, and emulate their successes or failures in class-room and playing-field.

It was breaking a tradition very dear to them both.

What would have happened to Anthony had his father taken the line that so many soldiers would have taken, and shouted,

"What the Devil! Of course the boy'll go to Eton. Never heard such damn' rubbish in my life. They'll soon knock the nonsense out of him," I shudder to think, especially had such an attitude been encouraged by a high-spirited, never-heard-such-bosh type of mother, with a yelp of,

"*My* son? Of course he'll go; and I shall tell his House Master to stand no nonsense. Put him through it. Make a man of him."

Had such a line been taken with Anthony, it is much more likely that they'd have made a corpse or an idiot of him.

Anthony was fortunate; indeed, he was singularly blessed, in his parents.

Nor, I am glad to say, did he himself, ever, in later life, inveigh against the Public School system simply because it was not the right system for him. He did not proclaim to the world that his was a rotten Public School because it didn't amend and adapt its system to his peculiar requirements; he didn't proclaim, for example, that because he was taught French by an Englishman whose accent was not pure Parisian, the Public School system is an abominable one and stands thereby self-condemned; he did not declare that it is a soul-destroying, character-crushing machine that casts all those unfortunates committed to its care into one uniform mould and, while they are malleable, stamps them with one uniform pattern.

Incidentally I might mention that I heard this view expressed by a visitor on learning that Anthony had been educated by a governess and then by a tutor; and that Anthony thereupon promptly observed that, so long as the mould and the pattern were excellent, admirable and serviceable to their purpose, it did not seem to matter how many people were stamped by it. In fact, the more the merrier.

Such was Anthony's considered opinion; and upon every conceivable subject mentioned by me and other ordinary people in ordinary conversation, he seemed to have a considered opinion, so widely had he read and so incorrigibly was he given to the habit of forming opinions.

At the risk of displaying myself as completely obsessed by the subject of Anthony, I wish to give you a very clear and accurate picture of him, before telling the story in which he played a part so strange, so decisive, so final.

I am describing him at such length because it is important that you should realize not only the fact but the degree, the extent, and the nature of his abnormality.

What is a lunatic, a person who is permanently so "queer" as to be described as insane?

Speaking succinctly and accurately, it is a person who is incapable of distinguishing between fact and fancy.

Personally, I think we sane people are all a little mad; or, to express it otherwise and better, there is some subject on which everyone is more or less mad, generally very much less; and the extent to which we are mad is the extent to which we are unable to differentiate between the facts and our fancies on that particular subject.

Now, how far was Anthony unable to distinguish between reality and make-believe? That was one of the first questions that I asked myself about him; for quite early, indeed by the day after my coming to Calderton, I was struck by his ability to lose himself in the part that he was playing. And Anthony, in spite of all I have said about him, was almost always playing a part and dramatizing himself or the situation.

Doubtless this tendency had been strengthened and increased by the methods followed by his excellent governess who was, very rightly, a great believer in the encouragement of self-expression, and in the use of a child's natural bent and tastes for the furtherance and encouragement of its activities and the development of its abilities. He loved charades, plays, and make-believe, and she encouraged him to act. He had more than the average child's love of dressing-up, impersonation, dramatization—acting, in short—and this had been, as I say, definitely encouraged.

One had to know Anthony well before one knew what he was up to, in what rôle he was behaving; whom he was impersonating, in fact. And one always had a sense of having failed him, of having fallen short of his high expectation and, indeed, trust, if one were stupid, missed one's cue, and responded wrongly, or not at all.

Nor am I in the slightest degree praising myself —indeed I am probably laying myself open to the accusation of being queer and abnormal myself— when I say that Anthony's luck held, at any rate to a small degree, when his parents selected me as his tutor. He would have been nearly as badly off with a bluff, blunt, bulldog-pipe-and-no-nonsense fellow who completely failed to understand him, as he would have been at a Public School with young barbarians at play, and harassed pre-occupied form-masters at work.

The ministrations of the cold bath every morning, sweat run every afternoon, come off that imagination tripe young man, whether Muscular Christian curate or Rugger Blue and recent graduate, would have reduced Anthony to sullenness—no, never that—but to a withdrawn aloofness and a polite, easy, yet incredibly stubborn refusal to conform.

For, though I never found him so myself, I do not deny that Anthony could be very difficult, nor that, quite frequently, he actually was extremely difficult with people who did not understand him, and whom he did not like.

This naturally led to there being two opinions about him, the opinions of those who really knew him, and of those who thought they did; and from this fact arises the implicit commendation that those who knew him best loved him most. Inevitably, the better one knew young Anthony Calderton, the more one loved him—loved his very faults.

For he was no angel-child, no adolescent saint. He had a temper; and, personally, I have no use for anybody who hasn't one somewhere concealed about him or her.

He was impish, and could be exceedingly annoying to people who were fools enough to be annoyed by his little jokes at their expense. These amusingly mischievous tricks were often very carefully thought out and most ingenious; and, in conversation, he would often lead one on to commit oneself to some untenable and indefensible statement or theory. I always found these verbal fencing-matches very diverting, and encouraged them, both for Anthony's amusement and my own. At first I was a little puzzled, but soon came to understand that a series of Socratic questions was leading up to some absurd, whimsical, or fantastic conclusion.

And undeniably Anthony was sly; sly in the way that an elf, a gnome, a fairy, is sly, partly self-protectively and partly for secret and inward amusement, the gratification of a love of subtlety and trickery, a baffling but innocent and harmless deviousness.

And now, perhaps, I have given you a pretty fair idea of the complex character of Anthony Calderton, and equally perhaps, I have completely failed to do so; failed to give you an adequate and faithful portrait of a most delightful and charming boy, attractive, original and engaging beyond the ordinary.

I hope I have not quite failed, for I should like you to be in a position to form your own opinion as to the answer to the question concerning him that even now obsesses, intrigues and troubles me.

§3

I find it less easy to tell you about Lady Calderton; not because she was, like her son, a complex personality—in fact, she was a woman of great simplicity of mind and lucidity of soul—but because I cannot profess to be an unbiased chronicler where she is concerned. Difficult as I find it to speak with impartial just accuracy concerning Anthony, it seems impossible for me to do so with regard to his mother.

I loved Anthony long before I really knew his mother, for Anthony had become the absorbing interest of my life before I saw her daily and came to understand her and know her well.

As with the boy, I liked her from the first, and liked her very much before she again went abroad with her husband, leaving Anthony, and virtually Calderton as well, in my charge.

To obtrude here my purely personal and private affairs for a moment, I was, at the time of my going to Calderton, a somewhat idle, somewhat philosophical young man, blessed or cursed with a modest competence; a dilettante dabbler in the Arts, painting a little, composing a little, writing a little; and an ardent admirer of other arts, in the practice of which I had no ability and in the pursuit of which I had no desire to engage—the dramatic; the poetic; that of sculpture; and so forth.

I had done well on the scholastic side at School

and College, leaving the former with a useful scholarship and the latter with a good degree. But at games I was hopeless, and could do nothing at all with a ball, large or small, save despise it heartily. I hated cricket, disliked both forms of football, intensely detested golf and tennis, and refused to learn to play hockey.

In a vain endeavour to mitigate the contempt which this confession will rightly bring upon me, I claim that a long and successful fight at Prep School, Public School, and College, against the tyranny of the Ball, connotes a certain tenacity and stubbornness of character. In point of fact, a humorous or facetious schoolmaster, in writing one of his annual reports, stated concerning me,

"He is a boy of much character, chiefly bad; a boy of great promise—and small performance; a trying boy who never tries."

But he was one of those excellent fellows who, doubtless rightly, judge a boy by his prowess and performance on the playing-fields, and the value of his contribution to the winning of those cups and pots that so justly are the honour and glory of his House.

Lest you get an even lower estimate of me than I deserve, I would fain add that, in spite of my congenital inability with the Ball, I take a great deal of walking exercise, and think nothing of doing my hundred and fifty miles a week when on one of my frequent walking tours. Also that I am a pretty fair performer with the foil and *épée*, a star pupil of Bertrand's, and more than once a finalist in those interesting early morning encounters in Lincoln's Inn Fields.

Also, I am blessed with an uncle who, on the tacit assumption that I am his heir, sees to it that I do not go to utter moral rack and ruin through my penchant for the idle and contemplative life, my preference for the library rather than the dusty arena, and my inclination to be what he sometimes calls a loafer, sometimes a wretched book-worm, and again, a worthless young man-about-town, according to the severity of his rheumatism.

I visit Uncle in the swiftly dissolving privacies and fastnesses of the Albany for the good of my soul and my pocket; and because, in spite of his insulting tirades, I am very fond of him.

To him I owe it—and for this I am more deeply in his debt than for anything else—that I came to Calderton as Anthony's tutor. In spite of the trite banality of its truism, how endlessly intrusive and attractive is speculation on the immensity of the results that ensue from the smallest acts, events and deeds, the tremendous effects of what are apparently the tiniest causes; as though the dropping of a pin caused thunderous reverberations that echo round the world.

Had not my uncle's man Judd mentioned that the stock of private writing-paper was running low, and had it not been a fine morning, he would not have gone shopping and done what he rarely did— lunched at his Club, the Marlborough, and there encountered General Sir Arthur Calderton, an Eton contemporary and old friend of his; and had not the General mentioned the business that brought him to town, that of visiting a scholastic agency, who might be able to recommend a suitable tutor for his son, I should never have known Anthony Calderton, nor had the privilege and joy of knowing and perhaps helping his mother at a time of direst distress, fear and horror. So slight, so tiny, we may reflect, are the events, the accidents in fact, that change our whole lives and shape our ends.

Wiser, doubtless, is the conclusion that whatever happens was ordained, and was written in the Book of Fate since Time began. (Item, and further reflection for the weak-minded, or such as desire to become so: When *did* Time begin?)

Anyhow, it was 'written on my forehead.'

Uncle rang me up at my tiny though extremely comfortable flat, and bade me dine in Albany with him on the morrow. At dinner he informed me that I was to proceed at my, or his, earliest convenience, by train, to a place called Calderton, where I should be met and driven to Calderton House, the residence of General Sir Arthur Calderton; and should there take up my residence as tutor to his son Anthony.

"High time you had another job, young man," growled my uncle, "and a job in the country, too. Do you all the good in the world. Lucky to get the chance. Lovely place. Incidentally, I told Calderton that he'd be lucky too, so don't let me down."

I agreed at once, for I love swift unexpected ventures and adventures such as this 'leaping-up,' as my beloved sister and I used to call it at home, and doing something unpremeditated and, preferably, silly.

And so, some two or three days later, at four o'clock on a beautiful afternoon, I got out of the train at a little wayside station that bore the name that was to become to me the most important in the world, Calderton, and saw, standing on the tiny platform, an elegant and most attractive female figure.

A primrose by a river's brim, a yellow primrose was to me at that moment. But soon it was something more, for as I languidly superintended the extraction of minor baggage from my compartment and major impedimenta from the luggage-van, I saw from the tail of my eye that she was taking note of me and my mild activities. Evidently she was not proceeding by this train; apparently she was waiting for someone and . . . yes . . . obviously and positively, she was waiting for me. I was almost as surprised as delighted when, approaching and extending a tiny gloved hand, she gave me a smile that immediately won my heart as the writers of books have it.

"Do say you are Mr. Waring," she begged beseechingly, gazing at my face with eyes as clear, confiding and beautiful as human eyes have any need to be.

"I would, in any case," I replied, raising my hat. "I will. I do."

"You am, in fact," she laughed.

"I are," I agreed.

"I'm so glad," said Lady Calderton, and somehow I was then and there, in that moment of our first meeting, more than glad.

How amazing, and how charmingly delightful, that she should have taken the trouble herself to come to the station to meet so insignificant a person as a prospective tutor of her small boy. A mere male governess—though, on the other hand, surely a person of considerable importance, if the physical, mental and moral welfare of the son and heir of an ancient house were to be placed unreservedly in his sole charge.

"I thought I would like to come down and meet you," she said, as we made our way to the big limousine, followed by a chauffeur and a porter, the one not overburdened with my despatch-case and rug, the other bearing kit-bag and suit-case, "so that we can have a talk on the way back. Time is so short and there's so much to tell you about Anthony. He's the dearest boy, but he's . . . different."

Not having met him, I mentally admitted that I was quite certain he was the dearest boy, and that, like every other mother's son, he was different.

And then, glancing at the charming and piquant face beside me, gentle, kindly, beautiful, I softened my heart, and realized that her son might indeed be different. He might well be very different from the average young savage who had so often been my cruel critic and harsh oppressor in my own diffident and difficult school-days.

"Not very strong?" I ventured.

"Oh, healthy enough, but what his father calls 'over-engined for his beam.' He's a queer boy. Simply won't go to school."

"Refuses?" I asked, between admiration of such stoutness and dismay at such defiance. This must either be a young gentleman of remarkable character or else a spoilt brat with whom no one could do anything.

It began to look as though my new job might be no sinecure.

"No, he doesn't refuse. He comes back. Gives it a fair trial and then comes home again."

Runs away from school, in short, thought I. Character again? Or incorrigible disobedience? Or was this one of those examples of the freak education by cranky parents, which is not education at all? No repressions; no coercion; no interference; no —anything. So that, instead of the child growing as some sort of flower, plant, shrub or tree in the Garden of Life, the result is a poor and worthless weed. But obviously there was nothing of the freak, the crank, the doctrinaire fanatic about this particular parent.

"Just comes back," she continued, "and says that it won't do; that he simply can't bear it, and relies on me to have sufficient understanding to refrain from trying to make him return. I know it sounds like a weak indulgent parent, feeble and foolish, on the one hand, and the spoilt head-strong and uncontrolled child on the other; but Anthony's not that, and whatever I may be, I can assure you that his father is not weak and indulgent; neither feeble nor foolish . . . Anyhow, you'll see."

Yes, thought I, in my wisdom, I shall see. The spoilt brat who'll give endless trouble and completely ruin my enjoyment of what should be a delightful job.

And for the rest of the drive from Calderton Station to Calderton House, Anthony's mother did her best to place me *au courant* with the unusual state of affairs, and the ways and nature of what was evidently going to prove a very unusual pupil.

I smile as I look back upon my preconceived ideas.

My first view of Calderton House, in its glorious and almost unique setting, was breath-taking.

Well, thought I, if I couldn't be happy here, were there half a dozen spoilt children to contend with, it would be a pity.

A lovely and historic house; gardens that had been tended with skilful care for centuries; the loveliest part of the most beautiful county in England; a house noted for its library and art treasures, its historical features and—to consider the more mundane things of life, which I am far from despising—its cellar, its chef, its stables, its shooting, its fishing, all highly praised by my uncle, himself a recognized connoiseur.

And as we drove through the park, with its famous chestnut avenue leading from the great gates to the house, I was distinctly conscious, even while admiring the lovely effects of the sunlight slanting through the trees upon the short fine grass and deliberately posing deer, that I was sorry that the woman sitting beside me, her face and voice so filled with a lovely animation, was going away.

Before I had set foot in Calderton House, I realized how different the place would be when she was not in it. Moreover, before I had set eyes on Anthony

Calderton, I registered a determination that if my tutorship were not a success, it would be through no fault of mine—and I was not at that time a person given to enthusiasms.

So little so, in point of fact, that I mentally shook myself, took myself to task, and wondered what was happening to me.

It must be my artistic spirit demonstrating, I decided, on sight of the truly lovely scene on which I gazed—Lady Calderton being part thereof.

Arrived at the foot of the great stone steps that swept in a double flight to left and right of the entrance, Lady Calderton remarked that, at the risk of boring me, she hoped to have a really long talk about Anthony after dinner, and meanwhile, if I would join them at tea on the terrace, I could make Anthony's acquaintance.

I was delighted with my quarters, to which the footman conducted me, a delightful sunny chintz-furnished sitting-room, looking out across the park over the lake to distant hills; and a smaller room, furnished as a bedroom, opening out of it.

Yes, this would do; would decidedly do. Most comfortable, both in summer and in winter, in fine weather and in foul; sun-bathed on fine days, with glass doors opening on to a sunny balcony; wonderfully cosy in bad weather, with curtains drawn and a blazing log-fire in the big fireplace.

Having washed, and given my keys to the rubicund young footman, I retraced my steps to the hall, the centre of the activities of the house, where Jenkins, who looked the Perfect Butler, took me through a big drawing-room to a sunny and sheltered corner of a terrace. Here, in the midst of a circle of deep and comfortable cane-chairs, an inviting tea-table was set.

A tall man, handsome and grey-haired, arose, a pleasant smile lighting up his clean-cut bronzed face. Coming towards me with extended hand, he said,

"Mr. Waring? Delighted you've come. Extraordinarily good luck that I met your uncle at the Club the other day. Known him all my life. Hope you'll be comfortable here."

I murmured my acknowledgments and, almost before I had accepted the cigarette and seated myself in the chair he indicated, I decided that I liked General Sir Arthur Calderton, and that here again my uncle was justified of his eulogy.

Inwardly I smiled to myself, and mentally I rubbed my hands, for all seemed well, and very well. This man and I talked the same language.

He fitted his setting, and went with Lady Calderton, æsthetically, as well as along the Vale of Life. Not that he had gone far down it, for he didn't look a day more than fifty, though he may have been several days more. Some fifteen years older than his wife, I thought.

If only Anthony were as amenable and attractive as his mother thought him, my lines were indeed now cast in pleasant places.

Pleasant! Could one but have foreseen. . . .

"His mother will tell you all about Anthony," continued the General. "I can sum up all I've got to say, by asking you to do the impossible. Anyway, you'll try, I'm sure. What I want is for him to get, here at home, all that he is missing by not going to School, if you see what I mean."

I murmured that I did understand, and would do my best.

"I don't for one moment suppose he will go into the Army, and I certainly shan't put any pressure on him, but I'd like him to go to the Varsity; and I am hoping that, by that time, he'll be sufficiently normal and ordinary to pass in a crowd. Being what he is, he'd have a bad time at a Public School. He has, in point of fact, though a brief one. But at Oxford—at Magdalen or Christ Church, say—I don't see why he should be very different from the average undergraduate, having been in the right kind of tutor's hands for four or five years."

"Nor do I," I agreed. "Nor, moreover, do I see why he shouldn't have an excellent good time, if he *is* a bit different. The Varsity isn't like school, of course, and the chief difference between the two is that, whereas individuality is discouraged at school, individuality and idiosyncrasy are permitted—indeed encouraged—at College."

"Yes, quite so. Quite so. And there again differing from Sandhurst or Woolwich."

"Yes, a man can go his own way, do what he likes, and, indeed, be what he likes, without interference from anybody. Athlete or æsthete, party-thrower or hermit."

"Yes," agreed the General. "Well, I want him to go up, and I want him to lead the ordinary Varsity life among his fellows."

"I understand," I assured the General. "And if he comes back home in the middle of his first term, I shall decide that I have failed."

"Failed?" said the voice of Lady Calderton behind. "Already?"

"No, Lady Calderton," I said, rising and turning to meet her delightful smile. "I was just saying that unless Anthony stays at the Varsity for three years and asks for a fourth, I shall feel that I have failed.

"Failed in life completely," I added, as she laughed.

The smile died from her face and a faintly anxious, deeply solicitous look took its place as, turning, she said quietly,

"Here he is."

A tall slender boy, looking more than his fourteen years, came out on to the terrace, staring hard at me as he approached.

Yes, thought I, definitely different; very highly strung. A fine forehead and not so fine a chin; too small and pointed. Aristocrat; inbred; balanced on a very fine edge. Fine nervous hands. Very good mouth indeed; nothing petulant, greedy, weak or peevish there. Beautiful eyes; too big. Ought to have been a girl. Dressed in a girl's clothes, nobody would use the word 'boyish' about her, him, it.

"This is Anthony," said Lady Calderton, "and I do so hope he will be a credit to you . . . This is Mr. Waring, Anthony, who has so kindly come to look after you and help you while we are away."

The boy shook hands gravely.

"How d'you do," said he. "Do you fence?"

"Yes," said I. "I do."

"Oh, good," he observed. And leaving it at that, turned to the tea-table, and with complete self-possession, became one of the circle, an equal.

As we talked, I eyed him from time to time, always finding, when I did so, that he was watching me with a long considering look, thoughtful, judgmatic. He was not staring rudely, or in the childish manner that is rightly prohibited, but studying me; and, although his eyes left my face directly I looked towards him, I knew that they returned instantly.

I was conscious of a foolish and most unwarranted desire to be approved by this queer boy, and I pondered the problem of what was to happen if I failed to give satisfaction. He might leave school and return home when he decided so to do, but he couldn't very well leave home and the tutor installed there. Or would he, perchance, announce one day that he proposed to join his parents in Montiga, as a tutor-infested home was no longer acceptable?

But behind these idle speculations was a growing belief and assurance that nothing of the sort would happen; that he and I would get on excellently.

Nor should it be for want of the utmost endeavour on my part if I failed to interest, to inspire, and somewhat to mould the young Anthony Calderton.

After tea I returned to my quarters, found that my things had been unpacked, the trunk and suit-cases removed, a large bowl of roses installed, and the rooms looking as though I had inhabited them for years.

What should I do? Seek out Anthony, suggest a walk, and make his better acquaintance; or, treading warily, leave him alone for the present?

There was a knock at my door, and in answer to my call, Anthony entered.

"Hullo," said I, refraining from adding 'old chap' or adopting any sort of avuncular or heavy-father line.

"Hullo," was the reply. "You didn't bring any foils with you, I suppose?"

"No. But I'll soon get them."

This was excellent.

"Had any fencing lessons?" I asked.

"Only from a gym-instructor at school," replied Anthony.

And in cool and quiet comment, added,

"A clumsy lout."

"H'm!" thought I.

"You'll give me lessons, won't you?" he asked.

"Rather!" said I. "More than you'll like, perhaps."

"No, I don't think you'll do that.

"What I really want," he continued, "is to learn to fence very well indeed, and then to have a duel, with real rapiers and sharp points. Father has one, you know. My ancestors'. Charles the First's time. I want to use it in a fight."

This was interesting. Blood-thirsty? Homicidal

destruction-complex? No, not with that face.

"Whom do you want to kill?" I asked, and at once saw that I had said the wrong thing.

"Kill? What a horrible idea. I don't want to kill anybody, nor hurt anybody either. I just want to have a real fencing-match; a proper fight; a duel. I shall dress up as a cavalier and we'd fence by moonlight. Full moon, you know, on a lawn, and I'd throw off my plumed hat and velvet cloak and take off my doublet. Fight in a silk shirt and slashed velvet breeches of the Stuart period. Silk hose and buckled shoes. Take the shoes off, perhaps.

"And you'd do the same, wouldn't you? Only would you mind being a Roundhead?" he asked.

I forbore to simulate tremendous enthusiasm. Only a fool, or rather, a bigger fool than I, perhaps, would 'act' under the steady gaze of those large and level eyes.

I considered the matter.

"Yes, rather fun," I admitted. "Bit dangerous, though, with sharp points."

"Dangerous!" observed Anthony, and the fine lip curled slightly.

After staring out of the window for a few moments, he observed,

"Oh, by the way, Mother sent me to ask if you'd care to go for a stroll with her. She always walks after tea.

"If it's not raining," he added.

Most definitely I would care to do so. I had an idea that it would take me a very long time to see and hear more of Lady Calderton than I wanted to do.

I have never forgotten that walk across the park; the evening; the scene, and the company approaching perfection. And by the time we returned to the house, more than an hour later, I had pretty well made up my mind about her.

I summed her up then as being competent without being clever, well-read without being learned, charming without being insincere, and, as a mother, loving without being foolish.

I gathered the impression that without being weak, vacillating, and over-suggestible, she was anything but strong-minded, firm and determined; not the type of woman of which the best martyrs are made; not the sort that would shine as a militant suffragette or in a crisis; nor one who would suffer in silence, take a strong line and ensue it to the bitter end; or die for an idea.

How far I was right in my assumption as to her probable conduct at a time of crisis, under great suffering, in imminent danger to herself and those she loved, I was to learn.

It is not for one moment to be supposed that I admired her or liked her the less for these reservations. I like a woman to be feminine, and she was, I judged, of the essence of femininity. That Anthony should, to some extent, dominate her, and to any extent get his own way against her better judgment, seemed to me, then, creditable to them both; an attribute to Anthony's clear knowledge of what he wanted, and to her wisdom in compromise.

Wisdom! Had she been a plain, unpleasant, and objectionable woman, I should probably, in the same circumstances, have preferred the phrase "weakness in compromise."

It is axiomatic that whether we realize it or not, we like, and indeed love, people far more for their little human imperfections and weaknesses than we do for their high moral virtues, strength, wisdom and persistence in well-doing.

Anyhow, even on that first evening, I liked this woman exceedingly; and where, perhaps, in the matter of her attitude to her son I might have judged, I forbore—and sympathized instead.

Well, I hope I have now given you some idea of the character and personality of Lady Calderton.

And again, perhaps, I have failed to do so; failed to do her justice; to give you anything approaching a true picture of her wonderful charm, sweetness and true kindliness of nature; of her easy friendliness and the fascination of her simplicity and sincerity.

I never met anyone, whether aristocrat, *nouveau riche*, bourgeois, or of the working-class, less afflicted with conceit, self-importance, aloofness, or air and manner of that stultifying exclusiveness that spoils so many otherwise likeable people.

In short, Lady Calderton was a gentlewoman who was truly gentle, and possessed a face and form that were truly beautiful.

§4

Of General Sir Arthur Calderton, I need not say very much, as, although a most important figure in the drama, he played a small part on the stage.

He was—I fear I must say the words—a great gentleman; a genuine aristocrat; and an ornament of county, military and political society; one of a vanishing race, who served his country without need, or desire, of profit; and though possessed of a magnificent home, more than ample wealth, and all the instincts of a country gentleman and sportsman, he laboured hard and successfully in alien lands and tropic climes *ad majorem patriæ gloriam*, and to the benefit of those he governed.

Able without being clever, forceful without being overbearing, proud without being conceited, strong without being harsh, he was that somewhat rare being, a man at once admirable and lovable. For he was essentially and fundamentally kindly.

It was my good fortune to see a good deal, and to know something, of that truly great man, the late Lord Curzon; and Sir Arthur Calderton reminded me of him, both by similarity and by contrast.

With all Lord Curzon's pride, high sense of duty and inborn aptitude for affairs, he had none of his arrogance of manner, his somewhat pompous aloofness, and but little of his industrious gluttony for work. An easier, more friendly, more human person, with a far greater gift of putting others at their ease, of winning their love, and evoking the best that was in them.

Not only was he lovable, as Curzon was not, but he was endowed with a great gift of loving. This side of idolatry, he undoubtedly adored his wife and son. He had a host of friends, as distinct from acquaintances; and amongst them could be included his subordinates, servants and retainers.

That he could leave behind him the son whom he almost worshipped, was, to me, final proof of his great sense of duty and of service; for as I have said, there was no other reason why he should lead any life but that of a country squire of broad acres.

That he should have left the boy in my charge after so brief an acquaintanceship—for he knew me for less than three months—is the highest compliment I have ever received.

I can only feebly return it by saying that I grew to like him more than I have ever liked any man in so short a period.

§5

And now to tell you about the man calling himself Captain Montague Bertie-Norton.

Wishing not only to be fair to him, as well as to the others, and to draw an accurate picture of him, I will begin by saying that I don't think it is right to call him a villain—by which I mean a downright, unmitigated, blackguardly scoundrel.

No one is all black—nor pure white. We are of all shades of grey, from the palest pearl to the dingiest lead. And some of us again are dappled; and others are like the zebra, streaky. The man who called himself Bertie-Norton can perhaps be judged better by his actions than from my description, but inasmuch as I knew him pretty intimately, I may as well tell you something about him and give you the opinion that I, personally, formed concerning him.

His besetting sin was selfishness, and from this the other sins sprang. I should think one would probably be safe in assuming that never in the whole of his life did he take any step that was not to his own advantage; lift a finger to help anyone but himself; or make any investment of time or trouble that would not show a profit—to himself.

Although he was a "schamer," as our Irish groom said of him, I don't, in justice, think that he spent a very great deal of his valuable time in thinking out schemes for his own advantage and advancement. He hadn't that kind of astute and active mind. Rather was it lazy, somewhat unintelligent, and with a marked preference for the policy of *laisser-faire*. He was not of the stuff of which great defaulting financiers are made, but was an opportunist, and where he saw his opportunity, he took it—at any cost to anybody. He was untruthful, dishonest and unreliable; with a low standard of honour and self-respect. He had done extremely disgraceful things, and was unashamed.

All this I know on the best authority—his own; for if it be, in such circumstances, a virtue, he had the virtue of candour concerning his own misconduct.

So, though not all black, his colour was a very dirty grey. Nevertheless, he had his own standards;

and as he was wont to tell you with a serious air of reassurance, he drew the line. I wonder how many times he assured me that "there he drew the line." A curious "there," but static, standing like a rock in a smooth and oily sea, a very grey sea again.

For example, he said that he had never cheated, and that he never would cheat, at cards; and I believe he spoke the truth—that was in him. He wouldn't descend to the baseness of marking cards. You would never find him with an extra ace. But if I were playing cards with him, I should take note of the position of any mirror that might be in the room. I should watch his dealing with the utmost attention; and I should like his partner to be a man whom I knew.

I am sure that he had never forged, and never would forge, a cheque, under any temptation; but I happen to know that he drew his own cheque upon a non-existent account, for I possess one such document, drawn in my favour—'favour' being a good word in the circumstances.

I am quite sure that he would have neither part nor lot in such turf villainy as "hocussing the favourite." But on his own confession, he had, on more than one occasion, won what he described as a 'pot' of money by participating in the bribery of an amenable jockey, a good puller; he had also done well, he said, in partnership with an inevitably wealthy gentleman whose custom it was to run a hot favourite, odds-on, which was almost invariably beaten at the post by his second string, a very dark horse, odds a hundred to eight.

Finally, he had come before the Stewards, and they had said the sort of thing that such a good sportsman resents.

Staying in the house of a friend, he would undoubtedly keep his fingers from stealing—save such things as any affections that might be lying about. He had only made one marriage, but had unmade quite a few.

He had never murdered man or woman; only killed their happiness, their faith, their trust, their joy in life.

Nor do I think he had ever borne false witness, out of malice, just for the sake of doing such a thing. He was too much of a gentleman to do such a deed wantonly; but when it was necessary to his own convenience, advantage and profit—why, that was another matter.

Of course, if people got in his way, well . . . He himself told me a curious and interesting story of a fellow, even then "doing time," who need not have been, except for . . . But no, Captain Bertie-Norton may have been boasting.

Another thing in his favour. I'm quite sure that when he was a soldier, and presumably in possession of various military secrets of greater or less interest and importance, he would never have sold his knowledge to a foreign power. I don't think there was in the world money enough, or any other acceptable form of bribery and corruption, to have induced him to do such a thing.

No. Captain Bertie-Norton, though pretty much of a bad man, was not the complete villain, for as I have said, he had his own standards of right and wrong, and as he himself proclaimed, he drew the line.

In appearance he was strikingly handsome; in manner, charming; in bearing, urbane; in style, neat, incisive and polished—at times. I make this reservation because he had a defect of style and bearing, a mannerism: and that was a laugh which can only be described as an extremely silly one. It was a flaw in an otherwise almost perfect exterior make-up; and it was as depreciatory, nay ruinous, as a bad flaw in a big jewel. All was well until

Captain Bertie-Norton laughed. One could not but admire his face and figure, form and limb, his fine military bearing, his clipped but musical and pleasing speech, until he laughed. And that fatuous, foolish sound, so suggestive not only of silly self-satisfaction but of weakness and stupidity, spoilt everything.

How I came to loathe it. At first I hated it for his sake. Later, I loathed it for my own. Until I knew him for what, on his own showing, he was, it seemed such a dreadful pity, such a cruel shame, that so fine a *tout-ensemble* should be so disfigured.

It was almost as bad as a squint or a hare-lip.

Nevertheless, it was not very long before I recognized it for what it was—Nature's warning. For surely no one could hear that *crétin* laugh without pausing to consider whether Captain Bertie-Norton could be all that he claimed to be and appeared to be. If I obtrude this mannerism, or, rather, trait, upon your notice, it is because, more than anything else, it indicated the real man, and betrayed him.

Whenever it burst forth, incongruous and jarring, silly and fatuous, one knew that he was complacently regarding some past rascality or contemplating some future one; but, once again, not a piece of cunning and clever villainy that he had thought out for himself. Rather an opportunity that had occurred, arisen gratuitously in his path.

I wish I could make that aspect of his nature quite clear, otherwise what he did would seem too monstrous, too incredible—for a man of his birth and breeding, education and upbringing.

Perhaps I can sum up his character briefly like this.

He would not, and probably could not, hatch some artful plot whereby he could swindle you of a ten-pound note: but if he saw one fall from your pocket as you walked down the road in front of him, undoubtedly he'd 'find' it, and a good home (and a bad use) for it.

And now, is it possible for me to confess that I liked Captain Bertie-Norton fairly well at first, if very ill at last; but even to the last there was something likeable about this charming, easy-going man; this irresponsible, unreliable failure; this utterly selfish and completely callous parasite.

§6

Well, I have, to the best of my ability, given you some idea of the characters of the *dramatis personæ* of this play, which was enacted by real people upon this little corner of the stage of Life. I will tell the story—but in my own way, as I have said—of the terrible drama itself.

Where I was an eye-witness of events and knew of things at first hand, I shall speak in the first person, this seeming to be the more natural and satisfactory method.

Where I only know the facts from hear-say, albeit the indisputable evidence of people concerned, who were actual eye-witnesses, I shall adopt the more usual rôle, omniscient, omnipresent and omnipotent, of the practised story-teller or novelist speaking in the third person. I shall begin thus; and at a date some ten years previous to my arrival at Calderton House.

II

"I didn't know there was such a word as 'unimpeccable,'" murmured Lady Calderton, as she put down the letter and took up her cup.

"Didn't you, my dear?" answered the General, lowering the newspaper which at the moment obscured his handsome clear-cut face.

"No. Did you, Arthur?"

"No," replied the General. "I didn't."

"Well, I don't think we shall do better," observed Lady Calderton, consulting Lady Jane's letter again before looking across the breakfast-table and thoughtfully regarding the newspaper, which once more concealed her husband and hid the loving mocking smile that, as she well knew, played about the corners of his firm mouth.

"Better than 'unimpeccable'?" came from behind the paper.

Always mocking; always smiling at her. Might the day never come when even her most innocent and earnest remark failed to amuse him. Not that her remarks were amusing, of course; nor that she was clever, thank God; but he could always make them amusing—to himself, at any rate.

"No, this Miss Stuart."

"Which Miss Stuart?"

The General dropped the paper and left it unheeded on the glowing scarlet, blue and green of the thick Turkey carpet.

"This one, dear," explained Lady Calderton, raising the letter. "Apparently she is absolutely everything that we want for Anthony. Everything. And is of 'unimpeccable' character."

"Get her at once, my dear," urged the General.

"The sort of governess one so seldom has the pleasure of meeting. I distinctly remember that all the governesses I encountered in my mis-spent youth, were definitely impeccable . . . Never an 'un' . . . We must snap her up."

"Oh, I don't know," mused Lady Calderton. "Good governesses are plentiful nowadays."

"Yes, good ones," sighed the General. "*Le bon Dieu* knows that. But how often does a prospective employer get a firm offer of a guaranteed unimpeccable one? Does Lady Jane mention whether she is also impeachable and maculate?"

"Well, I didn't ask about her Religion," was the reply.

The General's smile again came out from hiding beneath his grizzled clipped moustache.

"She simply said we should be very lucky if we got this Miss Mary Stuart. She was ten years with the Alymer de Warennes, so her religion must be all right. You know how particular Yvonne is. And she is a lady."

"Oh, I wouldn't say that of Yvonne."

"I'm talking of Miss Mary Stuart. Lady Jane says she's a lady."

"She has always behaved like one to me," admitted the General.

"What, Mary Stuart?"

"No, Lady Jane."

Yes, this was proceeding nicely. A conversation according to plan, or at any rate, according to custom. Obviously the General was interested and amused, and all was for the best in the best of all possible *ménages*.

"Yes, dear. Well, she says that this Miss Mary Stuart is a gentlewoman, one of the *nouveaux pauvres*, you know. She says here, 'Her family never thought that . . .'"

"She would sink so low. I know," interrupted the

General.

"Sink? . . ."

"Well, if as you say, she is young, beautiful, pure—or was it poor?—guaranteed unimpeccable, she may as well sink in here."

"When things sink they settle down," added the General, helping himself to marmalade, "and what we particularly want is someone to settle down with Anthony before we go away."

"Yes, I'll write and ask her to come and see me," said Lady Calderton.

"Would you care to interview her too, Arthur?" she added.

"Rath*er*," replied the General. "In view of Lady Jane's unusual recommendation, yes. I wonder if she's beautiful as well as impeachable."

"Lady Jane didn't say that, dear. Her writing is good and it is perfectly distinct. '*Unimpeccable.*'"

"Good enough," smiled the General, passing his coffee cup. "Especially if she's at all good-looking too."

§2

Miss Mary Stuart, so far as her new employers could see, was the Compleat Governess. Apparently perfect. So much so, that General Sir Arthur Calderton said she was too good to last, too good to be true. Such things and such governesses didn't happen to people who, about to go abroad, had to leave their adored only child in the care of a stranger. Most undoubtedly a gentlewoman of definitely pleasing exterior and address, of admirable manner and manners, and obviously of quite sufficient erudition, she proved moreover to be a genuine enthusiast, almost a fanatic, in the pursuit and exercise of her profession.

Her small charge, Anthony, aged four years,

slowly and carefully summed her up, weighed her in the balance and soon found himself wanting, wanting to show her everything he possessed and to give her her choice of it; to tell her all his secrets; to show her all those hidden, and by others undiscovered, places in the park and in the remoter recesses of the house, which were inhabited by friends or by enemies of his; the lovely charming fairies; the intriguing and, on the whole, agreeable, if somewhat uncertain, gnomes; objectionable wolves who pretended to be grandmothers and proved to be neither grand nor mothers; giants whom one could, in the rôle of Jack the Giant Killer, defeat and slay with comparative ease, in broad daylight, *bien entendu*, but which were not so good when the shades of night were falling fast; homes, resorts and meeting-places, of creatures of myth and legend and lore, some completely of his own invention and imagination. Creatures so much more real than uninterested and uninteresting people like nurses, nursery-maids, butlers, footmen, gardeners, game-keepers and other such humans, dull and adult.

Yes, the new governess was a friend, an ally, a really understanding companion, ready to aid and to abet sound schemes, or to show some excellent and comprehensible reason for abandoning them.

Lady Calderton was equally enthusiastic, and thanked Heaven and Lady Jane Hammerley. Within a month of Miss Stuart's coming she told her that she trusted her fully, and that so far as Anthony was concerned, she would not only leave everything to her, but do so without the slightest anxiety.

This she proceeded to do, and with clear conscience and easy mind, accompanied her husband to the distant tropic isle of which he had been appointed Governor, the lovely spot where every prospect pleases and only the climate is vile.

It speaks well for Miss Mary Stuart that Anthony, albeit a most affectionate child, devoted to his mother and adoring his father, missed them but little, nor that little long.

Re-doubling her efforts to make life of thrilling interest, to enter into every game, scheme, plan and idea of the child, she successfully tided him over the first few days of his bereavement; and even sooner than she had expected or hoped, had him talking of his parents without the quivering lip and moistening eye which had accompanied any reference to them, for the first few days after their departure.

The question 'Why did they leave me behind?' was heard no more, nor the other more poignant, more difficult to answer, 'Why did Mother go too?'

Incidentally, Lady Calderton herself would have found that question hard to answer; for when it had come to leaving her only child, she had found herself in a situation even more difficult than those which so frequently beset her innocent and simple mind.

Obviously she could not let Arthur go alone. For one reason she was quite sure she simply could not live without him; and for another, much more important, it was partly because he was married and had a suitable wife to be hostess at Government House, that he had been appointed to the Governorship.

Life without Arthur was entirely unthinkable, and it was a dreadful idea that life could be possible to Arthur without her. That this was so, and naturally so, she quite realized. Nevertheless, it was a thought to put away.

But then, on the other hand, obviously she could not let Anthony remain behind alone. For one reason, she was quite certain that she couldn't live without him. That is to say, she could not live the life which would be expected of her. How could she give her mind to her duties as a Governor's wife when it was at home in England with her only child? She'd be simply distraught. She would be more woolly-witted and foolish than ever, and Arthur would cease to smile at her, at what she said, or rather at what he made of what she said. It was one thing to make fun of her foolishness at Calderton House and quite another to try to do so at Government House, Montiga. What he might find very funny when they were alone together in the delightful comfort of the dining-room at Calderton, would not be at all funny at the dinner-table at Government House, with forty watchful and critical guests weighing her up. He wouldn't be amused. Which would be dreadful, for that was precisely what he had been, from the first day they met on the ship that brought him and her home from India, five years ago.

No, she couldn't go on amusing him if she were eating her heart out; longing for the sight of Anthony's face, the sound of his voice, the feel of his arms about her neck, a longing which would become a yearning, a grief, an obsession.

How could she leave Anthony, in spite of the obvious excellence of this wonderful new governess? Surely a child needed its mother more than a husband needed . . .

No, that was another train of thought she would not pursue. Where would she be if she realized, even suspected, that Arthur did not need her?

And in the end, of course, she had gone; as, all along, she had known that she must go. And some, at any rate, of the bitterness of grief and pain at leaving the child, who had scarcely been out of her sight for four years, was assuaged and ameliorated by the few quiet words her husband had said on the subject, words which showed once again what an understanding and sympathetic nature was his.

"It will be an awful wrench for you, my dear, I know. But the time will soon pass, and—it sounds selfish, I admit, but I need you more than Anthony does. See?"

Whereupon her tears had come, and she had felt better.

"Ever so much more. Couldn't carry on at all, whereas he'll get on fine with the impeachable one," said Sir Arthur, and proved to be right, as usual.

§3

For several years, Anthony Calderton lived almost happily in the shadow and society, the nurture and admonition, of Miss Mary Stuart, kindest and most understanding of governesses, and everything that Sir Arthur and Lady Calderton believed her to be.

All and a little more.

For Miss Mary Stuart, like so many other sane people, had a delightful and savingly mad corner to her well-ordered, disciplined and regulated mind. Her madness to some degree resembled that of a certain Mr. Dick, for upon the horizon of her blameless maiden life there hovered, in rare visions by day and occasional dreams by night, the head of the Martyr King.

When, for some usually inexplicable reason, Miss Stuart was visited by nightmare, she invariably beheld, with an inexpressible cold horror, King Charles's head, held aloft, alive, dripping, while the coarse voice of the brutal executioner boomed forth from beneath his mask,

"This is the head of a traitor."

Whereupon Miss Stuart awoke, bathed in cold

sweat, trembling, and when the nightmare was particularly vivid, screaming.

It is an interesting thought that a picture studied and pondered in her childhood by a Highland girl, and a story oft-repeated with dramatic power and force by an aged Highland nurse, should have changed the fortunes of the ancient English house of Calderton; should so have affected little Mary Stuart that, in turn and in time, she should have so affected a child, a small English boy, that his whole life should have been coloured thereby, and the destiny of his family changed.

As a twig is bent the tree will grow. This, presumably, in spite of the fact that there is nevertheless a Divinity that shapes our ends, rough-hew them as we will.

As an impressionable, highly strung, somewhat neurotic little girl, Miss Mary Stuart had been mere wax in the hands of the aged and dour Scots nurse who had also been her mother's nurse, and who had, in her old age, ruled that Stuart family with a rod of iron.

Herself a Stuart, the old woman was inordinately proud of the established fact that her ancestors, near and remote, had been King's men from generation to generation, and had, in their time and turn, died under Lawrence, Havelock, and Outram in India; under Moore and Wellington in the Peninsula; at Waterloo; and back even to Flodden and Falkirk; that one of them had come South with King James V of Scotland, one of whose sons and grandsons had fought for that King's son and grandson, Charles I and Charles II.

And most sweetly grim, best enjoyed tribute of all, had not her very own great-grandfather died bloodily at Culloden? Had not old Nurse Stuart, when herself a girl, made the then difficult journey from Inverness to Culloden battlefield, and sat her down upon the stone marked with the name, *Stuart*, and wept—reserving a tear to drop upon those other pregnant stones marked respectively *Mackenzie, Macdonald, Maclean, MacPherson*. . . .

And how frequently had she had young Mary Stuart weeping, by the time she had finished that dark tale, picturing the clansmen dying for their rightful King as their fathers had done before them, broken squares and groups of claymore-wielding Highland men dying where they stood, and being buried, by Clans, where they lay.

And the old woman would recite, in her deep musical and indeed beautiful voice,

> *'The Scottish spearmen still made good*
> *their dark impenetrable wood,*
> *Each man stepping where his comrade stood*
> *the instant that he fell.'*

But of all the tales so grimly told to Mary Stuart by the history-and-legend-steeped crone, the piteous death of King Charles I made the deepest impression, an impression strengthened, rendered even deeper and more indelible by a picture that hung in the hall of her father's house, of the brave King standing on a snow-covered scaffold, calmly and courageously facing death at the hands of his . . . murderers—foul, base, black-hearted, treacherous murderers, according to old Elspeth Stuart.

Thus it is not remarkable that Miss Mary Stuart grew up not only a fanatic loyalist and devoted upholder of the monarchical principle, but a Legitimist, a White Rose Leaguer, and an almost worshipping devotee of the Martyr King.

Her favourite holidays were the pilgrimages she made to places historically interesting in connection with King Charles; visits to Carisbrooke, to Whitehall, to Windsor, to Oxford, to the battlefields of the Civil War.

She joined every Royal Stuart Society of which she heard, and annually assisted in the laying of a wreath at the base of the memorial statue of her Hero. Almost her only recreational reading—as distinct from dutiful reading for the improvement of her mind and the widening of her horizon—was historical, and concerned with the history of her hero, martyr and saint.

Not only had Miss Mary Stuart never married a man, she had never even been in love with one; but devoutly and unswervingly, from childhood, she had not only loved, but been in love with, an idealized, an apotheosized Lover, a Stuart figment of her imagination.

In this almost she resembled those nuns who, in their subconscious minds, are spiritual brides of their Lord.

Had all the facts and details of Miss Stuart's curious idiosyncrasy, her little madness, been fully known to her employers, it is doubtful whether they would have been greatly interested. Undoubtedly Sir Arthur Calderton would have experienced no more poignant emotion than a mild amusement, nor Lady Calderton have seen how her loyalty to a lost cause, her Stuart royalism, could have affected Anthony in any way. Certainly in no detrimental manner.

Recommended to them so highly, and appearing to be so obviously the type of person they wanted, Anthony's parents then quickly accepted Miss Stuart, and, as has been said, eventually left the child in her hands with every confidence.

How should they know that there was any special and particular significance in her earnest statement that it would give her particular and peculiar pleasure and gratification to have the training of young Anthony, the moulding of his infant mind and the formation of his character—and creed? The light that momentarily sparkled in her eye, as she made this profoundly truthful asseveration, was taken as a sign and token of her general professional enthusiasm. How should her employers, for one moment, imagine that Miss Stuart saw in the boy, not only a child to be taught, trained and educated as it should be, in all directions, but particularly in one special direction—History; true unbiased History, the history of the House of Stuart, the history of her Phantom Lover?

Nor, had the facts been miraculously revealed to them, was it probable that they would have been greatly concerned by the possibility of the youthful Anthony being briefly biased in favour of any such Legitimist hope as the eventual Restoration—of some descendant of the good King Rupprecht of Bavaria.

It is an interesting reflection, in the mellow light of the wisdom which follows the event, that, had they known, had they objected and acted upon their objection, denying themselves the benefit of Miss Stuart's services, they would have opened the door of the House of Calderton for the entrance of starkest Tragedy.

§4

Now if King Charles's Head lent horror to Miss Stuart's nightmares, and haunted her day-dreams, affecting a mind otherwise sane and sober, sturdy and stable, it was the Wicked Man of the Calderton portrait who haunted that of her charge; a mind, especially at that age, extremely impressionable, sensitive and over-imaginative, the mind of a somewhat melancholy introvert.

Most imaginative children have a bogey, a pet terror of their own devising; a ghost, a goblin, a clutching hand, a terrible and feral beast, a witch; a wicked robber, with gleaming or blood-stained knife; or—still less fortunate—a silent shadow, almost palpable, moving, pursuing, yet unthrown by living object, ineffable, terrible, and, to the stricken childish mind, ghastly beyond description or belief.

To Anthony Calderton, hitherto reasonably unafraid, though definitely inclined to dislike the creakings, crackings and groanings of old furniture and ancient boards, and markedly averse from 'ghosties and ghoulies and long-leggity beasties and things that go wump in the night,' now came a private and personal horror to invade his sleeping-chamber.

With a small boy aged four not very much can be done in the way of biased historical teaching, any more than a great deal can be done in the matter of theology. Incidentally, this latter fact was brought home the more strongly to Miss Stuart, when she discovered that the first of the two prayers taught to Anthony by the nurse or the nursery-maid recently in charge of him, began, quite definitely and distinctly,

"*Gentle Jesus, weak and wild*"; and beyond peradventure of a doubt, contained the line,

"*Pity mice implicitly.*"

This sort of thing would want proper handling. There was a great deal of misunderstanding, misconception and rubbish to be removed, and then proper teaching must take its place. All very difficult, with so young a child.

And as far as historical teaching went, the gradual introduction of King Charles's head to the prominent place which it should permanently occupy in the child's mind, would be a real and splendid starting-point. And again, for that introduction, there already existed a real and splendid starting-point.

For, actually, over the vast marble fireplace in the big drawing-room, hung the original and famous oil-painting of the man known to history as the Great Protector, and to Miss Mary Stuart as the Great Traitor.

Excellent. Here should history begin from a concrete object, the contemporary reproduction in oils of the face and form of one of the protagonists in the greatest drama of English History.

Admittedly the concentric method of teaching history was one of the best, if not the best of all, and Anthony's history should start with this, widen to embrace the Stuart period, spread down to present times, and then begin again with Pictish and Scottish history, leading again, by way of Macbeth, William Wallace and Robert Bruce, to the Stuart Kings of Scotland who added England to their domain.

Now the great drawing-room of Calderton House was somewhat of a *terra incognita* to Anthony. His presence was not requested when it was in use by night, and tea was for him a nursery and school-room occasion.

Nor had he yet formed the habit of studying pictures hung upon the walls high above his head. Picture-books were the proper place for pictures, and in books he looked for them.

But no sooner had the exploring Miss Stuart beheld, with something approaching a shock, and with definite hatred, if not horror, the magnificent portrait of Oliver Cromwell, than she introduced it to Anthony's notice; impressed it upon his mind, brought it into his daily life, and made it a part thereof.

Proceeding to the nursery and receiving him washed, arrayed and anointed, fresh and vernal from the hands of the adoring nursery-maid who prepared him for his morning session with his governess, Miss Stuart led him to the room, haunted and polluted by that evil painted presence.

Seating herself in a deep armchair, straight in front of the picture, she took the child on her lap, and pointing an accusing finger, said,

"That is a Bad Man. A very, *very* Wicked Man. The worst man, but one, that ever lived."

For the sole concession that Miss Stuart was wont to make in Oliver Cromwell's favour was that he ranked second to Judas Iscariot ("second but bracketed with").

"What did he do?" enquired Anthony, eyeing the unattractive wart-infested face of the Great Protector.

"He . . . killed . . . his . . . King," whispered Miss Stuart with bated breath; and then sat silent, considering the portrait with a fierce glare of concentrated hate.

"How?" enquired Anthony, himself a killer of noisy giants, blow-lamp mouthed dragons, deceitful wolves, ever-hungry bears and such undesirable what-nots.

"He . . . cut . . . his . . . head . . . off," whispered Miss Stuart.

"Fighting?"

"No. Oh, no. The poor King was his prisoner. He killed the poor defenceless King, although he was so kind, so good and gentle.

"And brave," added Miss Stuart, divining that the attributes that she had mentioned were not perhaps those that appealed first and most highly to Anthony Calderton.

"Couldn't the King draw his sword and . . ."

"No."

And Miss Stuart did then and there give young Anthony his first history lesson, by telling him her version of the story of the doings of the Wicked Man in the picture.

And on that subject she was eloquent, inspired. At the end of that first long lesson, the first of an endless series spread over several years, the Wicked Man in the picture was firmly established with the Giant Blunderbore, the hypocritical Wolf and the ever-hungry Bear, as a living evil; one of the Powers of Darkness that, in the darkness, grow so powerful; one of the Things to be fought with a sword in the garden by day, and to be hidden from, beneath the bed-clothes, by night. By day, indignation, hatred and vengeance; by night, quaking terror.

So impressive was Miss Stuart's discourse on this almost daily recurrent subject, that ere long Oliver Cromwell was the child's Private Enemy Number One, as it were; ranking before, and far ahead of, Giant Blunderbore in wickedness, malice and power; a terror that stalked by night, making night itself a terror; so that in course of time, young Anthony Calderton was as richly and completely endowed with a Cromwell-complex as was Miss Mary Stuart herself.

And Fate was thorough.

For it was Anthony's *kismet* that he should be taught to ride by a favourite old groom, one Michael Houlihan, a warped and wizened little Irishman who, cleanly spoken and not given to blasphemy, had but one oath, an objurgation picked up from the admired master in whose stables he had first learned his trade as stable-boy, groom and jockey.

As everyone is aware who knows, and what hunting man and race-horse owner does not know, the great Patrick Murphy—whose horses were famous in every Irish hunt and in not a few English, as well as in every Irish Horse Show and on every

Irish race-course, as well as in the Grand National —had but one oath, and, by its frequency, made up for its singularity:

"*The carrse of Cromwell on it*" or "*on ye,*" as the case might be.

How many times had not the stable-boy, groom and jockey, Michael Houlihan, been cursed by the great Patrick Murphy in those terms?

"Phwat? Ye worthless little spalpeen! The carrse of Cromwell on ye."

And in humble imitation of the greatest man he had ever known, Michael Houlihan passed it on to his horses.

"Come over, ye baste. *The carrse o' Cromwell on ye.*"

And in Michael Houlihan, Anthony had a teacher who, if he cared less than nothing for the fate of any King of England, had an inherited, a cherished, an unbelievably bitter hatred of the cruel and savage brute who had been responsible for the appalling slaughters in which Houlihan's ancestors had perished.

Well might people speak of the Curse of Cromwell. When, in all the days of all the world, had a bigger curse been put upon an innocent people? Had not the bloody-minded villain proscribed the Roman Catholic religion? Had he not sold three million acres of Irish land to English adventurers, so that he might use the money for the raising of more troops for the further conquest and massacre of the unoffending Irish?

Had he not herded the priests of God into their own churches and there burned them alive with the weeping women and innocent children who had fled to the sanctuary of their altars?

What need of further oath or curse while human tongue could blister with the words,

"*The Curse of Cromwell . . . !*"

So that, on the subject of the wrongs of Ireland and on Oliver Cromwell, the little old man was as eloquent as was Miss Stuart on those of the Stuart Kings, and on the noble Loyalist lords and ladies persecuted and slain by the Monstrous Regicide.

Illiterate and otherwise ignorant as Houlihan was, he had a remarkably detailed knowledge of the true story of the brutish slaughter of the inhabitants of his native town of Drogheda, after Cromwell had taken it by storm; the tale of the wanton slaying of innocent defenceless men, women, and children; and of the savage martyrdom of the priests. About similar dreadful deeds in Wexford and other scenes of massacre he knew, and to him there was no more bloodstained monster in all history than Oliver Cromwell, the creature whose accursed name ranked even before that of a Pharaoh, a Herod or a Nero.

About Attila and Genghis Khan, Houlihan had never heard, but had he read of their lives and doings, the sinister light that illuminates their names would have paled to the dullest glow beside that which kept the name of Cromwell for ever burning. Burning in Hell.

Between the teachings of the highly educated and very accomplished lady, and those of the ignorant untutored groom, young Anthony Calderton received an ineradicable impression that if the Devil and Oliver Cromwell were not one and the same person, they must be sufficiently similar in evil nature and evil-doing to be indistinguishable; and if they were indeed separate and distinct, Oliver Cromwell was the worse character of the two.

"Was Oliver Cromwell the Devil in human form, do you suppose, Houlihan?" he asked one day, when the groom called down the curse of Cromwell upon his horse which had pecked and stumbled.

"He was that," was the reply. "Indade an' he was.

An' whoilst Oliver Cromwell was trampling the green grass of Oireland and turnin' it black beneath his cloven hooves, Hell had no master."

And so in fear and in hatred of the coarse and cruel face that disfigured the drawing-room, the boy grew; hatred increasing, if that were possible, as fear decreased, if decrease it did. And even up to the time when the slightly unbalanced Miss Stuart took her departure, her duty done; and the savagely vindictive old groom finished his long course, galloped into the straight, and passed the winning-post where even Cromwells cease from troubling and the weary are at rest, Anthony Calderton exhibited, from time to time, signs of the kink, the complex, with which these two people so different, so mutually antagonistic, had independently and unintentionally united to afflict him.

Of this curious obsession his parents continued to know nothing, though of other results of his ten years of training and teaching by Miss Mary Stuart they could not be quite unaware. Admirable as her work in almost all directions had been, it was clear to his mother, and yet more to his father, that what the boy now wanted was masculine society and guidance.

School having proved, for a second and a third time, to be not only a failure but out of the question, Sir Arthur and Lady Calderton determined that, for the next period of their absence abroad, their boy should have a tutor; and strove to assure themselves and one another that the right sort of tutor, working on the right lines, would be, if not as good as School, at least the next best thing.

Hence the advent of Mr. Henry Waring.

III

Yes, as I have admitted, I must confess that I liked Captain Bertie-Norton fairly well at first, though I can honestly say in defence of my powers of intuition, my social instincts and my judgment, that I did not like him very much, did not quite take to him, as they say.

Nor, curiously enough, did Anthony. He wasn't, as a rule, particularly critical or censorious, and I never encouraged him when he was.

Usually, when any new visitor had departed and left us together, if neither of us could commend, we refrained from more than an exchange of a glance and a smile. Eyebrows rather than lips.

But with Captain Bertie-Norton, for some reason, we put our thoughts into words.

"Do you like that chap, Mr. Waring?"

"Do you?"

"Not very much."

"No, nor I."

It must have been the silly laugh that put us both off, I think, for there was nothing whatever wrong with his appearance, manner or speech.

As Anthony and I were sitting on the terrace at tea on a lovely June afternoon, Jenkins brought me a card on which was inscribed, *Captain M. Bertie-Norton*, the name of a Service Club and an address, presumably that of a West End flat.

"I told the gentleman that Her Ladyship was not at home, Sir," began the butler, and I remember that this struck me as an interesting example of understatement, seeing that Her Ladyship was at the other side of the world. "But he particularly wanted to see somebody."

"Do you know him by sight or name?" I asked.

"No, Sir. Never seen nor heard of the gentleman before."

"Where is he?"

"In the drawing-room, Sir. Wouldn't take no for an answer, as you might say, although I told him that neither Her Ladyship nor Sir Arthur was at home nor likely to be. Said he'd very much like to see Master Anthony."

"And you, Sir," added Jenkins.

"Me? I don't know him."

"No, Sir. But he having enquired as to whether Master Anthony was at school or at home, and when I said at home, he having enquired whether he had a governess, I enounced No, that he was in charge of a gentleman."

"Well, I had better see him, then. He may have some business or other."

And pushing back my chair, I rose, asked Anthony to excuse me for a moment, and made my way along the terrace and through a french-window into the drawing-room.

On the hearth-rug stood a tall well-dressed man contemplating with interest the portrait of Oliver Cromwell, painted from life by Sir Peter Lely; a valuable and somewhat famous picture which had been in Lady Calderton's family for generations, her grandmother having been a Miss Fairfax, descendant of one of Cromwell's Generals and stout brother-in-arms.

It was of this portrait that poor little Anthony, as he confessed to me, had lived in abject terror, a terror that returned to him even yet, in nightmares.

As Captain Bertie-Norton turned and eyed me, I suppose I should, if this were fiction, at once have noticed that his eyes were too closely set, his lips too thin, his expression either shifty or cruel. There should have been signs of dissipation about his face, or of seediness about his apparel.

But actually, there was nothing of the sort. If I took exception to anything at all, it was to a stare which was perhaps frank rather than hard, and to a slightly supercilious manner and tone of voice, as he said,

"Good afternoon. May I ask who you are?"

I can also stare and adopt a supercilious manner.

"Good afternoon. You may. I am Henry Waring, tutor to Anthony Calderton. And you?"

"Well, that doesn't matter much" (to you, my worthy fellow, the intonation implied). " 'Point of fact, I am a very old friend, indeed, of Lady Calderton."

"Then doubtless you know that she is at Montiga with Sir Arthur."

" 'Point of fact, I didn't know. Only just got back to England myself. Don't correspond much. Not with anybody."

"No," said I unhelpfully, for it seemed foolish to say, "Can I send her any message?" as presumably the gentleman was quite competent to send his own messages; and equally foolish to observe that I was sorry he had missed her, as he had done so by some thousands of miles and a few months.

There was a perceptible pause during which we eyed each other. Almost warily, I was going to say, and yet there was no need for anything of the sort. I had no earthly reason to suppose he wasn't exactly what he professed to be, a very old friend of the family, and particularly of Lady Calderton.

And yet I had a perfectly groundless and unreasonable feeling that there was something wrong. I should like here to give credit to my fine and perceptive intuition. " 'Point of fact," as Captain Bertie-Norton would say, it was probably nothing more nor less than pique at his attitude and manner of *de haut en bas*. After all, I wasn't a servant, and he knew it.

"Dashed awkward," observed Captain Bertie-Norton to himself.

Again I was unhelpful.

" 'Point of fact, I was going to propose myself for a visit here."

"Yes?" I said, still unhelpful.

"Yes. Ought to have written, but I had somehow got the idea that they were still at home. They were when I last wrote. Let's see. How long ago would that be?"

"Afraid I don't know," I replied.

"Don't know? Don't know when they went away?"

"Don't know when you last wrote," I corrected.

A slight muscular movement was perceptible in Captain Bertie-Norton's cheek, as though a pulse beat briefly.

Good. I had annoyed him as much as he had annoyed me. A childish triumph.

Of course, it was as he said, very awkward, if he had come expecting to receive a warm welcome and an invitation to stay for as long as he liked.

Nevertheless, I was not in a position to invite him to come and stay, even had I the slightest inclination to do so.

"How's young Anthony?" he asked.

"Anthony is very well," I replied.

"Then I would like to see him," announced the visitor, and there was, of course, no reason why he should not do so.

"We are just at tea. Would you care to join us?" I said, without any particular warmth of hospitality.

"Yes," replied Bertie-Norton, without any particular warmth of gratitude.

And turning, I led the way to where Anthony

awaited me.

"Hul-*lo*, old chap. I suppose you don't remember me, do you?" Bertie-Norton greeted the boy as he rose from his chair.

And I can honestly say that I did feel there was a definite note of the *faux bonhomme* in his voice.

Evidently it struck thus upon Anthony's sensitive ear for, although his manners were usually super-excellent, he replied with a cold uncompromising,

"No, I don't," his manner being even less cordial than his words.

"No. No. Of course you wouldn't," agreed Bertie-Norton as he shook hands with Anthony. "Silly of me. Of course you were quite a nipper when I was here before."

"A nipper," murmured Anthony softly, savouring the word.

" 'Point of fact, I don't think you saw me."

And in a manner that would have done credit, or discredit, to a man of experience, Anthony, looking our visitor in the eye, observed,

"I'm quite sure I should have remembered you, if I had ever seen you."

And again the tone and manner added point to the words.

"No. Years ago. Years ago. Well, this is a disappointment. Quite a blow," continued Bertie-Norton a little gustily, as he seated himself in my chair.

"I'm sorry," murmured Anthony, and seemed to imply that our visitor was disappointed because Anthony did not remember him.

"I mean, missing your mother."

"And my father," said Anthony.

"Yes, I was going to propose myself for a nice long stay here. Sort of holiday I used to have here before I went abroad. Silly of me not to write."

"Yes," said Anthony. "But they'll be home next

year. You must write then. I think we had better have some fresh tea."

"No, no. Not for me. Not for me. 'Point of fact, I seldom take tea," Captain Bertie-Norton assured us.

"A whisky-and-soda?" suggested Anthony with adult courtesy.

"Ah! Now you're talking. Just my idea of a good tea. Whisky-and-soda and an anchovy biscuit, followed by—what?" enquired the Captain, heavily avuncular.

"A headache?" enquired Anthony.

"No, a cigar. A whisky-and-soda, an anchovy biscuit and a good cigar, and then it's 'Thank God for my good tea, Amen.'"

And for the first time, we heard Captain Bertie-Norton's irritating silly laugh.

It may be supposed that I was prejudiced against the man for whom I had entertained so sudden a dislike, but had I heard that guffaw without seeing its owner—or perhaps I should say producer—I should have been struck by its blatant inanity, its fatuous silliness.

In justice, I am bound to admit that it accorded but ill with the man's appearance and general style.

I caught Anthony's eye, and our faces remained expressionless.

Robert, our fresh-faced young footman, was hovering near in anticipation of orders for the replenishment of the tea-table. To him I signalled, and as he approached, informed him without comment that a decanter of whisky, a syphon of soda, anchovy biscuits and a box of cigars were required.

Captain Bertie-Norton amplified the order.

"Six biscuits. Butter them with salt butter, and lay three anchovies, *royans à la Bordelaise*, between each pair," he directed.

"Yes, dashed awkward," he observed once again

as the footman departed. " 'Point of fact, I had made all my arrangements accordingly. My flat's let, so without unpacking my stuff, I came straight on down here, expecting to stay."

"Most unfortunate," agreed Anthony. "I am sure my mother will be sorry."

"One thing, there's plenty of room here," continued Bertie-Norton, running his eye along the southern façade of the house which he faced as he sat.

And again I had a, probably foolish and groundless, suspicion that he was seeing it for the first time. Why I should have thought such a thing I don't know, unless his glance had been one rather of inspection than recognition, as it were, and that I had connected it with the look he had cast over the gardens below the terrace, before he sat down with his back to them. That look, I reflected, had surely been one of observation rather than of remembrance.

"Room!" I said. "The house is empty, of course, and Anthony and I lurk in our own corner of it."

"Wouldn't mind lurking with you," said Norton promptly. And, for the second time, we heard the laugh that to me was to become one of the most unpleasant of sounds.

§2

For quite a considerable period Captain Bertie-Norton haunted the neighbourhood, paid us numerous visits and, from time to time, angled for an invitation to come and stay with us. In this he was somewhat shameless, and created situations with which it was a little difficult to deal. After the first visit, he refrained from calling formally, coming to the front door and sending in his name, but established himself as something of a friend of the family, who was, naturally, unknown to the tutorial underling and to the small boy. He would walk jauntily up the drive and, avoiding the steps and terrace of the façade of the house, would cross the lawns and come up through the Italian garden to the south terrace where we had tea, and spent much of our outdoor time.

Towards Anthony he was somewhat heavily avuncular; to me, at first, slightly resentful and inclined to be domineering; later, pleasanter and more friendly, not to say ingratiating.

He had established himself at the Calderton Arms, staying there for weeks at a time, during which periods we saw him almost daily. Then he would disappear for a few days when, according to his own account, business took him to London.

From the first, Anthony was inclined to dislike him, and the more he saw of him, the less disposed did he seem to change his opinion. Nor can it be said that Bertie-Norton went out of his way to cultivate him and make a good impression. That he interested Anthony was undeniable, and I was faintly amused, and faintly shocked at myself, to find that, at times, I entertained a feeling that almost approximated to jealousy. For he could a tale unfold. There was no doubt about it: and as I sat listening to him and watching Anthony's face of rapt attention, I was reminded of Othello and the maiden Desdemona. Nor was the simile far-fetched, Anthony's face being at once the window and the index of a soul as simple, innocent and virginal as that of the hapless girl—or so I thought—as, with widely opened eyes and parted lips, he listened enthralled, with rapt attention to the man's tales of "moving accidents, by flood and field; of hair-breadth 'scapes i' the imminent deadly breach; of being taken by the insolent foe, and sold to slavery."

And then, one day, suddenly realizing that we hadn't had the pleasure of a visit from Captain Bertie-Norton for quite a while, I came to the conclusion that he must have gone away altogether. He had been staying at the Calderton Arms as usual, and I wondered whether my obtuseness in taking hints that he should give up his rooms there and move into Calderton House had been the cause of his departure. I rather hoped it had. But still more I hoped that we had seen the last of him, for, any question of my foolish jealousy apart, I had a sort of feeling that the less Anthony saw of him the better.

I also felt quite sure that if Sir Arthur and Lady Calderton knew him as well as he pretended they did, they would not have been enthusiastically in favour of Anthony seeing a great deal of him. And although Anthony took a dislike to him at first, as I did myself, the boy undoubtedly found him more and more interesting, just as I did. One couldn't deny that he had a curious charm, that a halo of adventure and unusual experience dwelt about him, and that he was definitely and dangerously attractive.

I could foresee the time, if he continued to hang about Calderton House and favour us with so much of his company, when Anthony, from tolerating him would come to like him, to welcome him for his romantic adventurous tales and stories, and so to seek his society.

And that, all question of jealousy apart again, I didn't wish to happen; nor, indeed, did I intend to allow it to happen; for although, as I later learned, the gallant Captain "knew where to draw the line," he failed to draw it where I preferred to see it drawn. He was apt to forget, or to ignore, the fact that Anthony, though tall and older-looking than his years, was only a child, and one of peculiarly and particularly innocent mind. So innocent and ignorant of evil was he, indeed, that, where Bertie-Norton's conversation, remarks and stories were most offensive, they gave least offence and did least harm, for they simply passed over his head. Nevertheless—if evil communications corrupt good manners, they corrupt good morals even more—and I felt that Bertie-Norton was corrupt, through and through.

However, he was gone, and I was very glad that he was gone, and had no desire ever to see him again.

§3

The better I knew Anthony, the more I loved him.

Also the better I knew Anthony, the less I understood him.

Nor did that fact make him the less lovable. Actually it made him the more intriguing, the more attractive, the more worth while, by which I mean the more worthy of study and investigation. Life with him was one long series of little surprises, little discoveries, and an infinity of little amusing, pleasing, or puzzling incidents. And there were times, times without number, when I felt inclined to smack his young head, for subtle impudence, artful little traps, tricks intended to hoodwink me in some way, cunning little plots to bring me to a brief confusion.

How a pompous, insincere or dogmatically omniscient type of tutor would have suffered at his hands!

We had just finished work one morning when he said,

"Mr. Waring, will you tell me the meaning of some words?"

"Yes."

"*Hagiology.* Is it the study of hags?"

"Not unless they were holy hags. Hagiology is the

study of the history of saints."

"Oh, thank you. And what's *eschatology*? Nothing to do with cats, of course?"

"No, nor with chatting . . . It's the study of final things; death; the Hereafter."

"Oh, thank you. And what's *etiology*?"

"Might call that the opposite. The study of beginnings; origins and causes."

"Oh, thank you. Must be awfully nice to know everything, like you do."

"Very nice," I agreed. "Any more?"

"Yes, *bonnance*. What does that mean?"

" '*Bonnance?*' " I asked.

"Yes."

"Sure you've got the word right?"

"Quite sure."

"Well, you've defeated me. I don't know the word, and therefore I don't know its meaning. Are you certain there is such a word?"

"Oh, yes, Mr. Waring. Quite certain. I made it up."

"Good. Now make up a meaning for it, and write the word and the meaning a hundred times."

"Would it do if I apologized?"

"It would not."

"But you win, Mr. Waring. And it was only— fun."

"Oh, quite so. Quite so. You aren't objecting to paying for your fun, are you?"

"What meaning shall I give *bonnance*, Mr. Waring?"

"Its proper meaning. You're the only person who knows it."

And with a sigh Anthony settled to his task.

When he showed up the imposition, it appeared that the meaning of *bonnance* was but brief and easily written, a word of four letters—'Hell.'

It became one of our pass-words, and certainly

none but Anthony and I knew its meaning . . .

Another thing I loved about the boy was the fact that, much as he enjoyed scoring, he equally enjoyed being scored off.

Furthermore, when I had occasion, at a much later date, to take him somewhat sharply to task for adopting an ugly and blasphemous ejaculation much favoured by Captain Bertie-Norton, he apologized, smiled impishly, and appointed the word '*Bonnance!*' as his own private and particular exclamatory oath. As he pointed out to me, I, on the one hand, could find no fault with the word itself, whilst he, on the other hand, could give it any meaning that he liked. A typically Antonian arrangement.

Looking back, it is amazing to realize how swiftly the time passed, how extraordinarily happy we were together, and what pleasure it gave me to know that Anthony was obviously very fond of me indeed. He would not have sought my company so consistently had it been otherwise, nor derived such satisfaction from pleasing me. The fact that I wanted him to do a certain thing was good and sufficient reason for doing it. And it was a fine trait in his character, one which I admired and appreciated, that he liked me not a whit the less for being a pretty strict disciplinarian. He recognized the fact that I did my utmost to be absolutely just and entirely reasonable, understanding and sympathetic. He would have despised me had I failed in discipline as much as he would have disliked me had I been unjust, unreasonable and uncomprehending.

We worked every week-day, and we fenced and walked as regularly as we worked. Most days we rode, and except for the Sabbath, there was never a day when we failed to dress up to greater or lesser degree—sometimes *en grande tenue* and sometimes

only to the extent of Cavalier hat and boots, baldrick, sash and sword—and stage a scene, either
on the greensward beneath the trees or in an old
oak-panelled gallery which made an admirable
setting.

Anthony wrote the scenes, charades and play-
lets, brought them to me for opinion, and joyfully
accepted suggestions for their improvement. We
then learned our respective parts, forgot them or
improved upon them, improvised and gagged. And
when words failed us, drew our swords—a pair of
buttoned foils of fine Italian make—and fell to. And
always the period was Stuart, the theme Cavalier
and Roundhead, and the *dénouement* the downfall
and defeat of the foul Cromwellian.

Personally, so far from life being boring and
monotonous, and time dragging heavily, I never
found the days long enough, nor ever once regretted my acceptance of this post, or wished myself elsewhere.

§4

And, quite suddenly, after what seemed like
several years of this happy busy life, enthralling
and mildly strenuous, came a most unexpected
kind of letter from Montiga, bringing mingled bad
news and good. Lady Calderton, who had suc-
cumbed to the fever prevalent in those somewhat
balefully beautiful islands, a rather virulent form of
malaria, was coming home. Repeated attacks of the
malarial fever had weakened her, and the Government House doctor had told Sir Arthur that he had
no hope of her shaking it off and making a satisfactory convalescence unless she went right away
from the tropics, recuperated thoroughly, and was,
for at least a year, free from any further attacks. It
had accordingly been decided that she should come

back to England, and remain there until Sir Arthur completed his term of office in Montiga and returned.

Though we could have wished that the cause of her home-coming had been any other than what it was, the news filled us with delight. I had not realized that Anthony loved his mother so much, especially in these circumstances of long separation. And although he had talked but little about her, it was evidently not a case of 'out of sight out of mind.' When he read the letter announcing her return, he was transfigured with joy and could scarcely speak for excitement.

My own reaction to the news also surprised me. Far from having any sense of chagrin or disappointment, however faint, at the thought of the inevitable lessening of my authority; far from feeling any sensation, however slight, of jealousy that I should now be taking second place with Anthony, I was delighted. It was the best news that I had had for a long time, and I looked forward with nothing but eager gladness to her arrival. As I say, the nature and strength of my feelings in the matter greatly surprised me. I had liked and admired her exceedingly in the days between my arrival at Calderton House and her departure for Montiga, but I had not realized how tremendously I liked her, how deep an impression she had made upon my mind.

Bright and cheerful as life was, it now took on even brighter hues, and I awoke each morning with the feeling of some happiness impending, some good thing about to come to pass, and throughout the day this little spring of joy bubbled up from my inmost being, and I was not only happy but consciously so. And I was conscious of the reason; of the reason why I found that so often now I lifted up my voice in reasonably tuneful song, whistled merrily, by no means a habit of mine hitherto, and found life one harmonious melody.

When she came, I was relieved and delighted to find that the long sea voyage had worked wonders. She looked perfectly healthy as well as perfectly lovely, and there were no signs of languor, lassitude and weakness. It seemed to me that, unless there were any recurrence of the malaria, brought on by a chill, for example, she ought to make a very quick and complete recovery, if she had not already done so; and I was heartily ashamed of a twinge of fear that she might go back to Montiga instead of remaining at home until Sir Arthur's return.

However, I was able to explain to myself that what I really feared was that she should go back and risk a return of the fever before she had made complete convalescence.

Now began for me a life of almost ideal happiness, even more satisfying and delightful than it had been before her return.

In the first place, she was so appreciative of the way in which I was handling Anthony, and of the improvement that she professed to be able to see in him already.

"He's a different boy," she declared, as we sat alone at dinner a few days after her return.

"In what way?" I asked.

"In every way; both mentally and physically. He holds himself better, he's more upright and alert and active. He looks so much more—normal. Almost the typical Public School boy. He was getting such a weedy little book-worm."

"And mentally?"

"He strikes me as so much happier, brighter; more alert mentally, just as he is physically, and more—there's no other word for it but *normal* again. I used to be so worried about him, but now he really does seem more like the Happy Christian Child, if you know what I mean, instead of the moody little maggot, fanciful and neurotic and queer. It is as though he had been transferred from a hot-house out into the sunshine. I *am* so grateful to you."

"Well, I'm very glad indeed that you form that opinion of him. I had hoped, and indeed thought, that he had improved, but not to that extent."

"Well, you've been with him the whole time, and the change and improvement must have been gradual. I see him suddenly, after all this long time, and, well, he's not the Anthony I expected to see. A different boy altogether. Vastly improved."

"We shall have him wanting to go to school yet," I smiled.

Lady Calderton laughed.

"That I very much doubt, unless you could go with him and be his house-master and form-master too. If you heard how he speaks of you, you wouldn't think there was much hope or fear of his wanting to leave you and go to school."

"Evidently I've overdone it."

"No. As a matter of fact, I'm far more reconciled to his not going to school—now that I've seen him. School couldn't possibly have done him the good that you've done, and it might have caused him infinite harm.

"No, we shall be quite content, in fact only too thankful, for him to go on as he is, until he's ready for Oxford. By the time he's eighteen, if only you'll stay with him, I believe he'll go up to Oxford absolutely fit to take his full share of the corporate life of his College. Not only fit but ready, willing and able. And that's a thing I hardly dared to hope. You don't know how pleased and happy and utterly grateful I am."

And this to me was a very great reward, the greatest reward I have ever had for anything I have ever done.

And what had I done but live a delightful life with a charming boy to whom I was deeply attached?

Life was good. And though I am not superstitious or given to unreasoning foolish beliefs, I felt it was too good; too good to last—even until the time when Anthony could go up to Oxford.

Our day began at seven when invariably he came to my room, made cautious and dramatic entry with much giving of secret knocks, mysterious pass-words and cabalistic counter-signs. He would then have tea with me; propound some new theory; expound some new and brilliant idea for charade or play; talk whimsically of this and that; and endeavour to catch me out with his careful Socratic questioning . . .

"Do you think the earth is round, Mr. Waring?"

"Oblate spheroid, according to the learned. Like an orange that has been sat upon gently, by a lightweight; slightly flattened top and bottom. But still, roughly speaking, round; a ball. So they say."

"Well, then, if you could drive a lift-shaft straight through from London to Sydney, and went down by the lift, do you mean to say that when the lift-gates opened, your feet would be just where the Australian peoples' heads are?"

"It would appear so, Socrates."

"But it's sheer nonsense. Tell me, would you be standing on your head or would they?"

"Neither. We'd both be standing on our feet."

"But you couldn't both be. When you arrived in the lift, your feet would be presented upward."

"Pointing at the Australian sun," I agreed.

"And the lift man in Sydney would be standing on his feet with his head pointing at the Australian sun. Both he and you are standing on your feet yet with your heads pointing in opposite directions. One of you must be upside down, surely."

"So it would appear, Socrates."

"Well then, it's just silly. *Reductio ad absurdum.*"

"And yet the learned men do firmly asseverate that the world is round, a ball, a sphere; and other learned men accept their statement."

"Well, we don't, do we? I mean to say, you don't think that if you arrived at Australia by lift, you'd have to turn yourself upside down, stand on your hands and walk out that way, so that you wouldn't have your head where the Australians' feet are."

"But you would, if you did that, Socrates."

"Well, that proves the earth is flat, doesn't it? Can I have a lump of sugar?"

After eight-thirty breakfast in the schoolroom, we would walk or ride for half an hour, work until eleven, and then fence, either outdoors or in; work again for an hour, and then stroll talking in the park before lunch.

Lunch was a joyous occasion, as we joined Lady Calderton in the big dining-room and ate in state, waited on by Jenkins and Robert.

After lunch we three sat on the terrace, the weather being propitious, for a while, with coffee and cigarette, the remainder of the afternoon being Anthony's until tea-time. Usually, as I have said, it was devoted to play-acting, whether indoors or out.

Indeed, if we did nothing more than go for what the ignorant might suppose was an ordinary ride, we were always busily scouting for hostile cavalry, Roundhead pickets and patrols. Sometimes, on sighting them, we would wheel about and gallop hell-for-leather to take the news back to the main body or the about-to-be-beleaguered castle or town. Sometimes we would charge desperately and put them to flight.

This game undoubtedly gave Anthony a good eye

for country and was in some sort a training for the hunting-field. A policeman of any kind on foot, bicycle, or horseback, counted as a large Round-head force, and many a rural constable must have been sorely puzzled by the behaviour of two horse-men who undoubtedly "acted in a suspicious man-ner."

After tea in the schoolroom we put in another hour's work, had fencing practice and exercise with the punching bag, whereafter Anthony's time was again his own until supper and bed.

And though repeatedly in the early days I offered to leave him to his own devices and set him free to do exactly as he liked and go wherever he would, he never once availed himself of this freedom, nor seemed anything but hurt by the suggestion that I should leave him to himself.

When he had gone to bed, I changed for dinner, went down to the drawing-room, and awaited Lady Calderton's arrival. Together we dined, and togeth-er returned to the drawing-room for coffee; and during the greater part of the time that we thus spent together we talked of Anthony, I telling her of his quaint and amusing sayings and doings of the day, she telling me of his childhood and of her anx-ieties and fears concerning him—from all of which, by the way, she now professed to be entirely free.

In fact, to my infinite satisfaction, it seemed that the boy had turned from a disappointment to a great hope; from an anxiety to a real joy. That she loved him with a great mother-love, deep and wide, was obvious, and having him with her was a great consolation for her separation from Sir Arthur.

Being the woman she was, it was with some slight surprise, and very great pleasure, that I saw how little selfishness and blind possessiveness there was in this deep maternal love, and how wise-ly and carefully she refrained from indulging and spoiling the boy.

I don't think that Anthony ever went to her behind my back, or appealed to her over my head, so to speak; but had he done so, he would have received short shrift. Whenever he suggested something that I vetoed, there was never the slightest suggestion of disapproval, much less of intervention or interference, on the part of Lady Calderton. On the contrary, she invariably consulted me before granting any request made to her, and always referred him to me if he made any suggestion when I was not present. It was her custom to visit him alone for half an hour or so when he went to bed, and it was only natural that if, when talking to her, one of his bright ideas should suddenly occur to him, he should forthwith propound it to her and ask her advice and permission.

It struck me as a most extraordinarily nice trait in her character that, far from being in the slightest degree jealous of my power and great influence over Anthony, she in every way supported it, giving the boy to understand that, so far as his doings were concerned, I was the authority.

And Anthony completely accepting, in fact welcoming, the situation, we three people were about as happy, I think, as three people could be, always excepting the fact that Lady Calderton's cup of happiness would not be completely filled until her husband's return.

It was with a sense of the deepest satisfaction, with a glowing feeling of abiding joy, that I saw her steadily improving in health and spirits, shaking off the remaining effects of the malaria, and taking daily delight in Anthony's quick growth towards normality.

IV

Lady Calderton turned her head as the butler entered with the small silver tray on which lay a card.

People calling already. Well, she wasn't going to see anyone just yet. Too tired. Going to have a thorough rest for ever so long. And she was convalescing from the fever which had pulled her down a good deal.

Without glancing at the card, mechanically she murmured,

"Not at home, Jenkins. You might have known."

"Yes, my lady. Very good, my lady. But the gentleman was very insistent, if I may say so, my lady. Said he was quite certain that you would wish to see him. Name of Barty Norton. Called several times previous, m'lady."

Languidly, Lady Calderton took the card from Jenkins's tray and glanced at it.

Her languor left her as she read the name printed on it and the nickname scribbled beneath.

"Captain M. Bertie-Norton," and in pencil, the word "Wiz" scribbled in writing that she knew.

The colour drained from her face, and the attentive astonished Jenkins thought his mistress was going to faint. He was about to suggest brandy, sal volatile, smelling-salts, when, her hands clenched on the arms of her chair, she suddenly sat erect, her mouth and eyes hardening.

Poor lady. That must have been a nasty turn, and she was looking as he had never seen her look before.

A nasty turn. More of a blow, really. A sort of knock-down blow that had prostrated her. No, she was getting her colour back. Better not to notice, perhaps.

"All right, Jenkins. Show Captain Bertie-Norton in. What's the time? Yes, bring tea at four."

That would give her something to do.

"Very good, my lady," and silently Jenkins faded away, his face impassive, his mind quite unusually active.

Good God in Heaven . . . So *he* was this Captain Bertie-Norton who had been visiting the place!

But it couldn't be. Not Wiz. Wiz was dead. Seventeen years ago. She must be dreaming. But that was exactly as he used to sign letters to her. That was his handwriting. The curious W. Never shaped like a capital, whereas the z never had a looped tail, but was shaped like a capital Z. Somebody impersonating him? One of the very few people who knew that his private nickname had been Wiz? Somebody who knew his signature? But how many people but herself had seen that signature? He had never used it in writing to anyone else, and no one else called him by the name. He couldn't be an impostor.

But the other thought was too terrible to accept for a moment. He had been dead for seventeen years.

Lady Calderton stood up from her low chair as if endeavouring to rise above a flood that threatened to engulf her.

She'd know in a moment.

Feeling giddy, and as though her knees would give way, she sat down again, quickly. It could not possibly be he. Why had he come? What could he want? Here, of all places on earth. Wasn't the world big enough for . . . ?

But of course it could not be. He had been dead for seventeen years and this was . . .

The door opened.

369

"Captain Barty Norton," announced the butler, closed the drawing-room door, and left Lady Calderton face to face with . . . No! That was absurd . . .

In situations of this nature, women are apt to display a courage, self-control and endurance as high as that shown by the bravest of men in situations of gravest physical danger.

Steadfastly she eyed the man who approached her across the big room, the expression of her face a combination of horror and fear as she gazed at him, incredulous.

It was he; he, undoubtedly. Not greatly changed in all those years that she had believed him to be dead. Heavier, thicker-set, and the face older, harder, still displaying its mixture of strength and weakness, intelligence in the upper part, sensuality in the lower; the change showing most in the eyes and mouth, predatory, cunning, ruthless. The face of the type of man who will gain his ends and be not over-particular as to the methods whereby they are gained.

"Well, Katty," he said, extending his hand, and while the mouth smiled, showing gleaming teeth beneath a well-clipped moustache, the eyes remained hard, wary and watchful.

He dropped the powerful and well-kept hand as Lady Calderton made no movement to take it, hesitated for a fraction of a second, then placed the other upon her shoulder and, bending down, kissed her upon the mouth. A quite successful kiss, in spite of the fact that she swiftly drew back as far as her chair permitted, and made a swift futile endeavour to thrust him away.

"Ah," smiled Captain Bertie-Norton, as he straightened himself up.

"*You . . . you . . . you . . .*" whispered Lady Calderton, wiping her lips, and seeming to gasp for air.

"Well," he smiled, "you—what, eh?"

But words failed Lady Calderton.

"Better left unsaid, eh? I quite agree. Well, well, well! Do you know, I see scarcely any change in you whatever, Katty, after all these years. Wonderful.

"Don't seem to hear much change, either," he added, in a different voice. "Well, well, the Return of the Native. Not that I am exactly a native of these parts. 'Point of fact, just as well, eh? Quite incognito. The Stranger's Return. Yes, that's better. Well, well, well! It's nice to find . . ."

"What have you come for? What do you want?" interrupted Lady Calderton, breathing quickly, her hands clenched, her body tense and her face white. "You are dead . . ."

"Come for? Want? To see you, my dear Katty— and for anything I can get. Everything I can get. What do I want? What d'you suppose? A little money to burn, a horse to ride, friends, good company, peace and comfort. I've had enough of wandering, Katty, and more than enough of living from hand to mouth. I want—*security*. Sounds like my old friend MacInstein of MacInstein, Maccabee, and M'Cash. 'No advanth without thecurity.'"

And with an almost physical shock and shudder, a blow that made her nerves cringe, Lady Calderton heard the foolish and fatuous laugh which she had not heard for seventeen years.

"But not that sort of security. I want to settle down; to retire. Retire from the business—of having no business. You know—like the poet says:

'Home is the hunter, home from the hill,
And the sailor home from the sea.'

Had enough hunting—especially hunting in the gutter. Enough of the sea, too, since those swine threw me into it. I'll tell you about that."

Yes, this was Wiz. With her eyes shut she'd have known his voice. Without hearing his voice, had his words been in print, she'd have known they were his. That's how he had always talked when he was nervous.

Nervous? That should be her strength . . . At least to make a pretence of strength. To feign assurance and confidence.

"And how do you propose to get those things—here—from me?"

"Well, surely, that's your business, Katty."

In silence she stared, still almost incredulous, and almost as though stunned by this bolt that had come so suddenly out of the blue; this thunder-bolt from so fair a sky; this lightning-flash that, in a fraction of a second, seemed to have blackened her landscape, to have laid her happy life in ruins about her.

That man standing there, grinning at her, talking, talking, talking. That could not be he. He had died seventeen years ago. She must awake from this nightmare.

The man seated himself in the nearest chair, turning it to face her.

What could she do?

Something she must do. For it was the man whom, as a girl, a fool, of seventeen, she had loved madly—for a little while.

But Arthur, the kindest and dearest of men, who believed in her as he believed in God and the King and the British Constitution?

And Anthony? Why, poor Anthony would be a . . .

Again with a great effort she rose to her feet.

"Where have you come from?" she asked, to gain time, to say something, to learn anything that might be helpful.

Anthony would be a . . .

She sank back into her chair.

"W-e-l-l-l," smiled the man, "that's a vague question, my dear Katty. I've come from the Calderton Arms; I've come from the Calderton Railway Station; I've come from London, and I've come from South America. And to pursue history still further back, I've come from the place that is sometimes described as the safe spot where the birds won't bite you."

"Prison?"

For if he had been in prison once, might he not be put in prison again? But if it were through her that it were done, what wreckage of at least three lives would he leave behind him, in punishment, in revenge.

"Alas!" was the reply. And the fatuous snigger followed. "Yes, I haven't always been as lucky as you, Katty."

"What did you do?"

If he had committed murder, there might yet be a hope that . . .

But what a terrible thought.

"What did I do? What didn't I do?"

And again the laugh.

"Tell you one thing I didn't do, though, Katty. I didn't commit bigamy. But don't let's talk of old unhappy far-off things now, not just in the moment of my return. Let's speak of the bright and shining future. I have sown my wild oats and reaped a few damn wild whirlwinds, I assure you. But that's all behind me, Katty, and I have weathered the storms. I'll tell you some day. When we've got more time. Make your hair curl. Give you a permanent wave, Katty. But for the present, well, I've come into port at last. And a damn good cellar of it, too.

'*Home at last, the harbour past,*

Safe in my—darling's—arms.'"

And again the laugh.

"I say, don't stare at me like that. I'm not a ghost. No, I'm alive all right. Don't be alarmed."

If he laughed again she'd go mad. She'd go mad in any case. Arthur . . .

Arthur was not her husband.

Anthony would be a . . .

She would scream in a minute. She would go mad. She would die.

No, she would not. She would fight like a tigress for Anthony, for Arthur. She would . . .

But what could she do? Find out how far he was safe from the prison he spoke of? . . . Could she kill him? . . . She must be going mad to think such thoughts.

Money? That would be it. That would be what he had come for. But for how long could such a situation last?

Oh, if she could only kill him. One read of such things. One saw such things in plays and films. But this was life, real life. Nevertheless, if she could kill him without being found out, she'd do it as willingly as she would kill a snake.

If only God would strike him dead, as such creatures should be stricken dead—as she had supposed him to be, these seventeen years and more.

What was he saying?

"Yes, safe in port. And meantime, you've been a long while in a pretty snug harbour of your own, eh, Katty?"

"I thought you were dead," she whispered, half to herself.

"I'm sure you did, my dear. So, fortunately, did a good many other people. I was at some pains to give that impression. How long did you mourn me?"

And answering his own question with,

"Not as long as some people did," he laughed loudly.

If he did that again, she'd . . . she'd . . . she'd . . . do something.

What could she do?

She could fight this man with his own weapons. Fight him somehow, for Arthur's happiness and Anthony's happiness. For Anthony was now a . . .

"Yes, there must be quite a few people who'd be interested to know that Montague Ferring-Chevigny was alive," smiled the *soi-disant* Captain Bertie-Norton.

Yes, indeed, there must be. Could she get into touch with anyone who . . . But that was absurd. She was thinking like a ridiculous fool. How could she, Katherine Calderton, wife of General Sir Arthur Calderton, enter into conspiracy with some person or persons unknown, against this . . . this . . . against this man because she feared him, because his continued existence was dangerous to her, threatening the even tenor of her comfortable way, because in fact he was her husband.

It was lunacy, but the whole thing was madness, nightmare.

"Are the police after you?" she asked.

"Not the English police, Katty, thank you very much. I've purged my offence as far as they are concerned. Though I freely admit that there are one or two, indeed three or four, countries in which I am not free to travel, so to speak."

Three or four countries. Now, which were those? If she could find out, would it be possible to inform the Chief of Police of those countries, with the view to extradition proceedings?

But then, of course, he would not be known to them as Captain Montague Ferring-Chevigny. No, nor as Montague Bertie-Norton.

No. That was no good. She'd have to know the

alias under which he figured in their criminal records, and he was probably known by a different name in every country in which he was wanted.

Was that her husband sitting there; alive and well and grinning; and, even in this appalling moment, capable of bellowing with stupid laughter?

It couldn't be. And it was. It was the man she had loved desperately; whose kisses had set her on fire; the man whom, when he was her husband, she had despised and hated as much as she had loved him when he was her lover.

She must do something. She must escape. She must free Arthur and Anthony from this terrible threat, this incredible menace. Anthony would be a . . .

"But aren't you free to travel and to live openly under your own name in this country?"

"Er—no. No. Not quite, perhaps. But don't you worry your little head. You need have no anxiety on my behalf, Kattykins. Why, it must be seventeen years since poor Monty Ferring-Chevigny fell overboard from Alastair Cluny's yacht and his body was washed up on the Perenecque Island beach, days later. Face unrecognizable. Nasty rocky coast. Nasty crabs and cuttlefish too. But clothes and contents of pockets established identity beyond a doubt."

Yes, absolutely beyond any doubt in her mind, as God was her witness.

An idea. A fleeting hope. Of course there would be nothing in it again, when she was able to bring her intelligence to bear upon it and think it out. Yes, she must think. Identity established beyond a doubt. Well now, if this . . . creature . . . had been at such pains to prove his own death, the death of the somewhat notorious Captain Montague Ferring-Chevigny, might he not have done his work too well? Too well for his present purposes? Clever as he was, or cunning as he was, might he not now find that it may have been easier to convince the world and the Law that he was dead than it would be to convince them that he was alive again? Especially if he called her in witness, and said she was his wife—and she declared on the contrary that he was a fraud and a swindler; that though he bore a certain likeness to the late Captain Montague Ferring-Chevigny, he was an impostor, an impudent rogue who should be prosecuted for false pretences and . . .

And what would that do but postpone the catastrophe, the terrible tragedy of . . .

Besides, it would be infinitely easier for him to prove a positive than for her to prove a negative. He'd have no difficulty. Handwriting, photographs, letters, witnesses.

Again, how could she perjure herself, knowing the whole time that he was her husband? Commit perjury? She'd commit murder if . . . But she must put such idiotic and horrible thoughts from her mind. She must be wise and sensible and courageous and . . .

"What do you call yourself now?" she asked.

"My name is Bertie-Norton," he replied gravely, but with what, in a kindlier eye, would have been a twinkle of humour, and what in his was an impish leer.

Thank God he hadn't laughed again.

"And you are known to nobody at all? To nobody in England, except in the name of Bertie-Norton?"

"To nobody in England. To nobody anywhere."

"But someone is bound to recognize you—to accost you in your own name. What then?"

"Depends, my dear, depends. I might just smile and say,

" '*Ferring-Chevigny? Ferring-Chevigny? Who the devil is this Ferring-Chevigny? I'm always being mistaken for him. Must try and meet him some time, and see if I can see the likeness. No, no. Don't apologize, my dear chap. It's always happening.'*

"Or, on the other hand, if circumstances pointed that way, I might go on the other tack.

" *'Well, well, well. Fancy your remembering me. Heard I was dead, did you? Yes, I heard it myself. Report grossly exaggerated, as they say.'*"

Yes, that's what he'd do. And perhaps he'd do both. Establish himself in some part of England as Montague Ferring-Chevigny, returned from the dead. Prove that he was Montague Ferring-Chevigny, that he might have witnesses, should he want them.

No, of course she had been foolish, as usual, in thinking that he had been too clever, and had so completely proved his death that he could never disprove it.

"But what about this part of the country?" she asked, for distasteful and horrible as it was to sit here in conversation with him, she must learn all she could. It would be sufficiently appalling to have to take any step with full knowledge. Whereas, to work in the dark, to act in ignorance, would be far worse—if anything could be far worse.

"Well, I don't suppose there's a soul within a hundred-mile radius of here who ever heard of Montague Ferring-Chevigny, and it's a million to one chance against there being one who knows him by sight. That's the beauty of it, Katty. I can settle down here, in perfect peace and comfort—and security. And if, by any impossible outside chance, I run into somebody who knew me—seventeen years ago, remember—it will be the simplest thing in the world for me to bluff it out. But I am not worrying, and you needn't.

"No, if things go as I want them to, there won't be the slightest danger—*for either of us*, Pussy. You see, if some one-idea-ed, one-way-minded old stick-in-the-mud of either sex saw me at the Hunt, or at one of the big houses about here, or at your dinner-table, or anywhere else, and if the silly geezer couldn't take my word for it that I am not Montague Ferring-Chevigny and never was, that I never saw or heard of any such fellow, well, I've always got you to fall back on, haven't I?

"If you say to him or her, '*My good Mr. or Mrs. Pimpleblossom or Whatnot, I've known Monty Bertie-Norton since I was in the cradle and he was in knickerbockers, and he has certainly been Monty Bertie-Norton all that time. So if he ever was your Mr. Ferring-Chevigny he must have done it very young.*' See?"

And Lady Calderton saw. Nevertheless, she must oppose, struggle, fight to the last ditch.

"And do you for one moment suppose I should do such a thing?"

"Not only for one moment, but for all the moments, Katty. In your own interests. For your own sake. Presumably you don't want it established by your true and lawful husband, Montague Ferring-Chevigny, that General Sir Arthur Calderton is not your husband at all; that you have no earthly right to use his name, to live in his house, to spend his money; and that young Anthony Calderton is not Anthony Calderton at all? He's Anthony Nobody. He is, to put it bluntly, a . . ."

"Stop! How dare you! You vile . . ."

Oh! . . . She must not hear that word; must not think it; must not see it again, in print even. It must never, never be connected in her mind, or in anyone else's mind, with Anthony, her own darling Anthony, who . . .

Lady Calderton may have been weak, foolish and feather-brained. But she was brave.

Once more she rose to her feet and extended her

hand in the direction of a bell.

"Well, Mr.—or Captain, is it?—Bertie-Norton, what a lot of nonsense we've been talking. At our first and last meeting, too. Are you staying long in this part of the country?"

But the man calling himself Bertie-Norton remained seated, adjusted the crease of his trousers neatly along his legs, rested his elbows on the arms of his chair, joined his fingers, and slowly shaking his head from side to side, smiled up into her face.

"No, no, that won't do, sweet Kate. 'Captain Bertie-Norton' undoubtedly to the rest of the world —so long as we can jog along comfortably and quietly—but to you, your very own Wiz."

Her finger touched the button of the bell, but she forbore to press it.

"No, no. It won't do. It won't do at all, Kate. It was a bright thought. Quite bright—for you. But there are, alas, several good lads and lasses who'll believe me only too readily, recognize me only too quickly, if and when the time comes for me to declare myself, to confess my naughty trick with the poor corpse of the sailor that was washed up on Perenecque Island beach, and whom I . . ."

"You wouldn't dare," she interrupted, turning upon him as her hand fell to her side. "It would mean prison for you."

Would he dare do this terrible thing? Could he with impunity establish his identity? He'd hardly do it, if it meant arrest; prison perhaps, for years. Had he killed the man upon whose body were found Captain Ferring-Chevigny's clothes and other 'proofs' of identity?

Was he in danger of extradition for murder?

No, of course not. Pure dramatic nonsense.

No doubt he had come quite accidentally upon the body when bathing from the lonely Perenecque Island beach. Quite probably it was that of some sailor from one of the foreign fishing or pearling or trading boats so frequently wrecked along that coast. He had come upon the dead body and it had given him the idea, the opportunity of escape, of throwing off all burdens of debt, of danger of arrest, of responsibilities; the opportunity of starting life afresh—and, incidentally, of abandoning her, utterly unprovided for, completely alone in the world.

No, in whatever country he was wanted, it would not be for murder. Not his line of rascality at all. It would be for some form of swindling, some base dishonesty, forgery, embezzlement, defalcation; some betrayal of pecuniary trust.

But what did it matter? The position was just as hopeless, whatever he had done, and however badly he might be wanted by the police, whether of this country or any other. For he could utterly wreck her life, lay it in ruins about her, without there being any publicity. He could deal what almost certainly would be a mortal blow to Arthur.

About Anthony she must not think—yet.

Without any question whatever of his past misdeeds and his danger of arrest and prosecution, why, he had only to tell Arthur, to tell her friends and neighbours, the people who made up her world, and he had told the whole world, so far as she was concerned, because one's own little world is the World.

And how could she deny it? How could she possibly do so? When she was able to think clearly, she'd be able to remember a dozen men in various regiments, clubs, hunts, and so forth, whom he could easily satisfy that he was the man whom they had known half a generation ago, the man who had lived and 'died' as Monty Ferring-Chevigny, the bad hat, the dog with a bad name, the man of whom they had said at the time that 'he was the last person whom they would have expected to commit suicide. But still, you never knew, and doubtless he had most excellent reasons.'

And the excellent reasons had transpired later.

Besides, he was the sort of man who'd have press-cuttings, photographs, passports with photographs and names. Yes, quite possibly he'd have a passport bearing her photograph and signature—in his name, Katherine Ferring-Chevigny. Quite possibly he would have their marriage certificate.

No, she was in his hands. And once again her mind was overwhelmed as the dreadful feeling of nightmare horror and numbness returned.

But once again, *no*; this was impossible.

She sank back in her chair.

This dreadful feeling of being stunned, mortally wounded. If only Arthur were here. But no, thank God, he was not.

Anthony . . . Anthony . . .

That stranger sitting there; that hard-eyed, grinning-mouthed utterly detestable creature was her husband.

But no, it was all too absurd. Such things couldn't happen. There was no Law nor Justice, no right nor elementary fairness or decency about it. She had believed him to be dead. Everybody had believed him to be dead. It was accepted as a fact. Accounts of his death had appeared in the papers; something of a scandal; a party of *déclassé* people —fly-blown aristocrats, distinguished *divorcées*, bearers of new but already dingy and damaged titles, British and foreign. And there had been talk of foul play, hints in the baser gutter-rags that he had, no doubt, been knocked overboard during a drunken orgy; or killed and thrown overboard by someone he had cheated and robbed.

Had she not suffered enough then, while that horrible business was in the public memory?

An idea. Of course it was worthless, useless, and futile. Alastair Cluny. As far as she knew, he was still alive.

"Did Alastair know the truth?" she asked.

He grinned.

"He knew just as much as anybody else, and no more. That I vanished from the *Seagull* during the night; no note on the pin-cushion, no anything. Just vanished. And that my body, in a sort of yachting-kit, reefer, white trousers, white shoes, was found in a little cove by Perenecque Island beach. Bit over-matured—not to say high; shop-soiled; but in spite of all—all the crabs and fishes, that is, as well as the rocks—still quite identifiable by the signet-ring, links and yacht-club buttons and the clothes."

Then might not that be in her favour? Might not Alastair Cluny refuse to accept this man's . . .

What was he saying?

"But don't count on that, my dear. I could convince Alastair Cluny in half of two seconds."

And smiling, he hummed beneath his breath,

" '*For a strawberry mark in the middle of the back*
Is all I got from Father.'

"Lots of little things besides that; signature, scar or two, memories."

And again came the laugh, as he added,

"Alastair and I had more than one bit of fun together that nobody knows about, except him and me. And—I blush to mention it—what about the final proof of all?"

"What?"

"Finger-prints."

Yes, it was quite possible that he was speaking the truth; that after he left her and before he 'died,' he might have been in the hands of the police sufficiently long for his finger-prints to have been recorded.

Oh, why, *why* had she been such a fool, knowing what a trickster he was. Fool—though surely that was all she had been. She had done nothing wrong. She had not intentionally committed bigamy. She had had no more reason than anybody else to imagine that he was not dead. But then, how could she ever have been such a ten-times bigger fool as to marry him? But what else is a girl of seventeen but a fool? And it had all been so hurried. He had been on the ship that she had joined at Naples, on her way to a holiday with her people in India. They had been engaged before they had reached Bombay, and married a week later.

Well, there was one thing. She had never deceived Arthur. She had told him everything; and he had accepted the position as she had done, as anybody who ever knew him had done. That he had been drowned while round-the-world yachting with Alastair Cluny and his gang.

But she should have known better. Of course she should have known better. She should never have allowed Arthur to marry her. She might have known.

And now what would happen?

It had happened. She was this man's wife. It was useless to dream of denying it. It had happened. Calderton was not her home; Arthur was not her husband; and Anthony was not his—heir. Anthony could not inherit Calderton. He would have to go— when she went.

What was that? What was he saying?

"So you see, there is not the slightest need for all this skittishness; for there is absolutely no real need for any unpleasantness whatever. So long as you will be reasonable, do the sensible thing, and so long as I get a fair deal out of it, you can carry on in that state of life to which it has pleased you to call yourself."

Carry on in that state of life—so long as he got a fair deal?

"*Blackmail!* A fair deal! You? Why . . ."

It was the *soi-disant* Bertie-Norton's turn to display emotion.

Righteous indignation. A look of genuine anger hardened the face that had been grinning too amiably.

"*What?*" he asked incredulously. "*What* did you say? Blackmail? I was never so insulted in my life! What do you mean? What a horrible idea. You'd offer *me* money? No. I draw the line at blackmail, thank you."

Anger gave way to hard resentment.

"I'm surprised at you, Katty. I really am. You ought to be ashamed of yourself. Have you ever known me do such a thing? Ever had reason to suppose I'd dream of anything so caddish?"

"Then what exactly did you mean—if you meant anything—by saying that so long as I would be reasonable and do the sensible thing and give you a fair deal, there need be no 'unpleasantness'? What do you mean by a fair deal?"

"Well, come! Plain English, isn't it? Fair deal. Live and let live."

And Montague Ferring-Chevigny laughed.

"And live here, too," he added, turning suddenly serious.

"*Here?* Are you mad?"

"Mad? Me? Why? Don't sound balmy, do I? Sounds more as though it's you who are mad. Here am I, come to offer you exactly what I called it—a fair deal—and show you a way out of what might be a damned awkward situation, and you go all

385

melodramatic and talk about blackmail, as if I were a—I don't know what. Why shouldn't I live here? I've got to live somewhere, and preferably somewhere where I'm not known. I don't say I want to *live* in the house. Not all the time, anyhow. But there's no reason why I shouldn't live here or hereabouts, is there?"

"In what capacity?"

"What d'you mean?"

"What I say. Suppose, for one moment, you could live in this county, as Captain Bertie-Norton, or whatever you call yourself. Are you suggesting that I should sponsor you, introduce you, guarantee you?"

"Yes, and a bit more. I'm your old pal; girlhood's friend; home from the Seven Seas and the Ends of the Earth. Been sheep-farming in New Zealand, or ranching in South America, any old thing you like. And having made my pile and had enough of the great open spaces, I've come down here to look round for a nice snug little place, and meantime you are putting me up."

"And do you really think . . . ?"

"Yes, and you had better do some thinking, too, Katty; because I tell you plainly it's either that or the other thing. 'Point of fact, it generally is, isn't it? In this case, it's that—or I get my rights."

"Your rights?"

"Yes. You are my rights. You are my wife. And either I come in with you—or you come out with me."

What did he want? What could she offer him, and what would be the good of offering him anything? It wouldn't affect the situation. It wouldn't change facts. And supposing he meant exactly what he said. How could she possibly live such a life? Live such a lie? She would spend every moment of her life in fear of hearing the first whisper that

Montague Ferring-Chevigny was alive; was not only alive, but visiting the house of his former wife.

Former?

Which would be worse; waiting—or denunciation of this man to her husband?

Husband? Arthur wasn't her husband.

And what had she done to Arthur . . . and to poor little Anthony?

It was unthinkable. It was impossible. And it was stark staring fact. There he was, sitting grinning at her, and in a moment he'd laugh. Not laugh at her, but just laugh at nothing, or rather, at the terrible *impasse*. Laughter for him and death for her.

Death, of course. For what would life be like?

What did he want? What could she give him, to go right away to the other end of the world and stay there? Yes, and for how long would he stay? And what an existence—waiting for him to return; waiting to receive a letter with some threat or outrageous demand; waiting for the day when she should pick up the newspaper and catch sight of a paragraph telling of the discovery and arrest of the notorious Captain Ferring-Chevigny who was supposed to have died long since.

A silver-chimed clock struck four. They'd be bringing tea in a minute. Should she tell Jenkins to show her visitor out, and then give him instructions never to admit him again?

What good would that do? What could she possibly gain by antagonizing him? And surely it would be far better for her to know where he was and what he was doing and what he was proposing to do. And what would that be? She must make him state it clearly.

"Listen," she said. "Just now you said that you drew a line. You drew it at blackmail. Well, suppose I apologize to you for using that word and . . ."

"All right, all right, my dear! No offence meant; none taken," smiled the man. "Ugly word."

". . . but, at the same time, I say that I'm willing to help you, if you are in trouble. I am willing to give you the largest sum of money that I can possibly raise, in return for your going right out of my way; right out of my life, and never coming near me again; never writing to me—but being, as you've been for the last seventeen years, dead, so far as I am concerned."

As she spoke, Captain Bertie-Norton uncrossed his legs, drew his feet in, placed his hands upon the arms of his chair as though about to rise.

"Look here, Katherine," he said, in a low and serious voice, "will you please understand that I have my self-respect as much as you have, and as your husband . . . as Sir Arthur . . . has. I wouldn't dream of uttering a threat under any circumstances, nor even of hinting at one, but I don't think you are very wise to insult me. I don't think you'll gain anything by it."

In silence they stared at each other for a long moment, he dignified, forbearing, reproachful; she agonized, despairing.

"You won't take money to go away again?"

"I most certainly will not; and if you suggest such a thing again, I shall . . . well, I shall be more than offended."

"Will you tell me exactly what you do propose?"

"I've told you. I propose to live here—or hereabouts. I propose to enjoy life; do myself well; and have a thoroughly good time. The Exile's Return—to all that makes life worth living. I'm going to live . . ."

"On what?"

"Oh, well—what shall we say—on my wife's bounty. I don't like putting it in those words, but that's really what it comes to. I know that the majority of men support their wives. I supported mine to the best of my ability in the old days; but there are lots of fellows who are fortunate enough to have a wealthy wife—and don't complain. I'm a proud man. I admit it. But I really don't see why I should be too proud to take the goods the gods provide."

"You know perfectly well that, if such a thing were feasible, if it were thinkable, and I were fool enough and wicked enough to agree to it, you'd be living on my husband's money."

"I wouldn't, Katty," and again the dreadful silly laugh seemed to fill the big room, "that's just what I wouldn't be doing. Any more than I am now," he added.

"You are a 'proud' man. You 'draw the line.' You find the sound of the word blackmail unbearable—but you propose to come and live here on Sir Arthur Calderton's money and . . ."

"Oh, my dear girl, why must you split hairs and wrangle over straws. You have plenty of money, and you'll always have plenty of money wherewith to be able to help me to jog along. And please don't suggest or even imagine that I should—what shall I say —put the screw on. Damn it, I draw the line somewhere. You let us come to what I call a sensible arrangement, and give me a fair deal, and you can take my word for it, there will be no trouble from me. It would never enter my head to ask you to increase . . . improve the . . . well, you know what I mean. And I should never ask you for lump sums, or do anything that would embarrass you financially. Put it clean out of your head. All I want is a decent . . ."

"Decent!" whispered Lady Calderton.

"Well, say reasonable, moderate amount of help from my wife. Nothing wrong with that, is there? You help me and I'll help you, and we'll all be happy together. Don't you see that we are partners; married partners?"

Lady Calderton rose to her feet—and at that moment the door opened. The footman bearing a great silver tea-tray entered, shepherded by the butler.

Tea was set and the servants departed.

And once more, Mrs. Ferring-Chevigny found herself pouring out tea for her husband.

§2

How incredible life could be. How could she possibly be doing this, sitting here, giving tea to this man? To keep up appearances before the servants —which must be done, at any cost, until the end came—so long as this monstrous thing was a secret, she must play her part in keeping it a secret.

She remembered that on the rare occasions when he did drink tea, he took lemon, and neither sugar nor milk. What a thing to remember at such a time.

Of course it must be a dream, a dreadful nightmare from which she would wake, the very worst nightmare that she had ever had. She or anyone else in this world, surely.

She must wake up.

If only she could do so, find herself alone, say,

"I've been dozing. Well, how lazy I am. Disgraceful," and thrust the memory of that horror from her mind.

And meanwhile, she passed her husband a cup of tea in which floated a thin slice of lemon.

"Thank you, my love. Quite like old times, eh? I see you remember. Well, well, isn't this nice? Cosy, eh? When does your—when does the General come back from Montiga?"

"In December."

And though aware of the folly of it, could not refrain from adding,

"You are in no immediate danger."

"Nor, incidentally, are you, my lass."

And the voice lost some of its false pleasantness.

"It's you who are in danger, isn't it? It is not I who've committed bigamy. I have no reason to fear the return of the General, have I? Does he know, by the way?"

"Know what?"

"That you were—what shall we say—*the* Mrs. Ferring-Chevigny."

"Of course he does."

"And how soon he's going to know that you are still *the* Mrs. Ferring-Chevigny depends entirely on you. And as I've said, there is no earthly reason why he should ever know."

"Of course he must know," she replied, trying to make the statement sound convincing; trying to seem fearless and utterly contemptuous; trying to pour tea into her cup with a steady hand.

"Oh, well, that's all right, then. We know where we are."

Was there a note of disappointment in his voice, a hint of chagrin and annoyance, as though he were thwarted and angered?

Probably not. Doubtless the wish was father to the thought. Montague Ferring-Chevigny would have his opportunist plans cut and dried to meet whatever situation might arise from this interview.

"Well, that's all right, then," he repeated. "I'll go and see him soon after he returns. Round about Christmas, eh? Merry Christmas. Of course he'll want proof that I am whom I profess to be, but you'll be able to support me there, won't you?"

She stared at him in silence, her white face distorted.

"Yes, I shan't want any further proof, since you'll

bear me out when I tell him that I am your husband."

With trembling hand, she raised her cup but
found herself unable to drink, unable to speak.

Helping himself to a sandwich, leaning back in
his chair and crossing his legs comfortably,

"What line will the General take, do you suppose?" he asked conversationally. "You know him
better than I do."

Yes, what line would poor Arthur take? He
would, of course, and as usual, do what he considered right. And there could hardly be any question
as to what was right. Certainly none in the eyes of
the Law.

She was this man's wife.

Arthur would never get over it. Not only the horrible publicity and scandal, the front-sheet news,
but the blow. Because he loved her. He really did
love her. She was part of his life. It would be like an
amputation, a terrible operation from which he
would never recover. How could they separate now,
after all these years of practically perfect happiness? There might be no such thing as the perfect
marriage, but no two people on this earth had ever
lived together more happily than she and Arthur.

But General Sir Arthur Calderton could not and
would not go on living with another man's wife.
How could he, once the fact became generally
known? How could he indeed, being the man he
was, if he alone knew it; even if no one in the whole
world except he, she, and this man knew it?

And how could she possibly carry on life without
Arthur and Anthony?

There was one thing, no power on earth could
make her go back to this man.

But where could she go, then? Where could she
go? This was her home. Arthur was her real husband, whether she were legally married to him or

not. Anthony was her son. Why should Arthur's life be ruined and Anthony's too—and her own—because this poisonous scoundrel had played this trick all those years ago, and had now returned from the dead, as it were?

Once again, what wrong had she done?

Why, because he chose to do such a thing as that, and to do it in order to escape pressing difficulties, great danger, duns, the police, scandal, should Arthur and Anthony and she receive the punishment? And such a punishment. One that would be the death of their happiness. And of more than their happiness. It would kill Arthur. It would kill her. And it would spoil Anthony's life.

People who so cleverly proved themselves to be dead should be considered dead, and not allowed to return to the life, the position, the rights that they had voluntarily forfeited. Why should this criminal come back to his place in society and drive an innocent boy out of it—resume his life and destroy Anthony's?

But wasn't she taking too tragic a view of it, if that were possible? Of course, Arthur would look after Anthony and keep him with him as long as he lived; but he couldn't legally bear Arthur's name nor inherit Calderton. Why, he'd have no legal existence at all.

And was this horrible and terrible creature speaking the truth when he said that she had committed bigamy? Had she, by committing bigamy, put herself in danger of punishment by the Law, in danger of imprisonment?

No, there was Justice as well as Law in England; and that would be too utterly unjust.

"Yes, it'll be interesting to see what line the General will take," he continued.

"*That* you'll find out for yourself in December," she replied, in the hard cold voice that scarcely seemed to be her own. "I don't think that whatever line he takes will be a pleasant one for you."

"You don't, eh?"

"No, I don't. Why should it be? Why should he and our boy and I suffer, and you go scot-free?"

"Why? For obvious reasons. I disappear. I return. No law against that, is there? I seek out my wife. Commendable, surely. Admittedly, I have been away a long time, but that's my misfortune, not my fault; and if you and everybody else chose to think I was dead, well, I'm not responsible for the conclusions to which people jump."

Oh, why did she sit here talking to this creature? What possible good could come of it?

She could bear it no longer.

She must bear it.

"By the way, I wonder if you've got such a thing as an anchovy biscuit, Katty. Delightful tea, I'm sure, and it was very nice of you to remember that I take it with lemon, but you know what I really like at this time of the day, don't you, old girl?"

She stared at him, again incredulous. What was he? The shallowest puddle of filthiest water that was ever splashed upon unfortunate passer-by; or the deepest, darkest, most dangerous ocean in which victim was ever drowned?

How could he babble about the wretchedest trifles when the happiness, the lives almost, of three people hung in the balance; when he was about to destroy three harmless and innocent fellow-creatures who had never done him the slightest injury of any sort or kind? Was this a braying, trampling ass, or was it a dreadful monster?

Again, she could bear it no longer. She was suffocating.

She must bear it. She must fight.

Yes, that was better. She could still speak, dry as were her tongue and mouth. Drier than ever before in her life.

"What do you suppose you'll gain by going to my . . . by going to Sir Arthur Calderton, and telling him that you are my husband?"

"Well, well, one never knows. In the troubled waters, just under the waterfall, is a good place for fishing. And there'll be a blooming Niagara when I tell him, eh?"

And at the thought of the promised Niagara, Captain Ferring-Chevigny laughed heartily, the sound causing his wife almost to shudder with disgust and horror.

"But why talk about what I'll *gain*? Right's right, isn't it, all the world over? You are my wife still; and, let me say, Katty, a damned attractive woman still. Why shouldn't I claim my rights?"

Lady Calderton rose to her feet, making a semi-conscious and ineffectual movement with her hand towards the bell.

No, she must hear him out. She must know the worst; know all that could be learned; she must fight. For Arthur's happiness. For Anthony's. What would be the best thing to do, that they . . .

"Do you really suppose, for one instant, that it would ever enter my head to go back to you?"

"Well, where else would you go? Can't stay here, now, can you? Can't go on living in sin with Arthur after Monty's come back. Can't stay on at Calderton if I demand restitution of conjugal rights and all that. Don't see what else you are going to do but return to me."

As she stared at him in horror, she was conscious of the cunning look that came into his eyes as he added,

"But there's one thing I ought in fairness to mention at once, so that you get it quite clear in your mind from the first. I don't want the boy. Definitely you can't bring him along, too."

Yes, she was right. She knew it intuitively. He didn't want to go to Sir Arthur. He didn't want her himself. He had been disappointed when she had said that of course her husband must know. He didn't want him to know. Probably it was the very last thing that he wanted.

Naturally, in spite of his horror and indignation, whether real or simulated, at the introduction of the word 'blackmail' (and was it real or simulated; and did he himself know which it was?), what he really wanted to do was to benefit by the situation. Literally to trade upon it, turn it to his own account, use it for his own ends.

He wouldn't face the word 'blackmail,' accept a lump sum, and go away. He drew the line. Much too honourable a gentleman. But he'd live "here or hereabouts" for the rest of his life.

Yes, Montague Ferring-Chevigny ran true to form. Opportunist. Selfishness incarnate. A man who'd stoop to most forms of rascality, but who drew the line. Drew the line at being an honest rogue. Declining to call his muddy spade a spade— but seizing the treasure he had dug up with it.

No. No blackmail for Monty Ferring-Chevigny. Only the destruction of a woman's happiness; and the certain ruin of the lives of three innocent people.

But even so—what then? Suppose she could have bought him off. Suppose he had gone to the uttermost ends of the earth and never been heard of again, it would still be for ever on her conscience. But why conscience? She had done no wrong. And if not on her conscience, it would be on her mind. For ever on her mind that Arthur was not her husband; that Anthony was not Anthony Calderton; that he was a . . .

But now she was being selfish, surely. What did it matter if she were for ever and perpetually oppressed by that dreadful load, not of sin, not of guilt, but of knowledge—provided it could be kept from Arthur and from Anthony? Of course, she must fight. She must accept the situation, and for their sakes make the best of it. That was what she must do. She must put her husband and her son first; put everything else aside; meet this man on his own ground; stoop to his level; and fight and strive, plot and plan, for the happiness and safety of her husband and her son.

What was he saying—"Why not be reasonable?"

Yes, she must be reasonable. There was a chance, a hope, so long as it was to this man's interest to keep the secret, that the secret could be kept. She must see that it *was* to his interest. That it was well worth keeping. For, strike whatever attitude he might, draw whatever line he might choose to draw, the fact remained that his own interest was his one criterion.

"And what exactly do you mean by reasonable?" she heard herself asking.

"Exactly what I have said. And if you can think of anything more reasonable, for Heaven's sake say so. 'Put it clearly once again?' It is so simple that there's nothing to put. Simply a matter of 'as you were.' Carry on precisely as usual, and nobody a penny the worse."

"And you a penny the better. To what extent?"

"My dear Katty. I leave it to you. Don't let's get sordid about it. No damned haggling, please. As I said, all I want is just to live in peace and quiet, in comfort and security, instead of like a damned sea-gull scouting for offal—and the nearest land a million miles away. All I ask is that you treat me as a wife ought to treat a husband when he's down on his luck. Mind you, if I struck it rich, put a packet on another Signorinetta at a hundred to one—my god, think of a thousand on Signorinetta at a hundred to one!—or got on to some really good thing in the City; you know, gold shares artificially forced down to twopence-ha'penny and kicking about the market, and you get the tip to buy all you can lay your hands on as the mine's really a bonza —anything of that sort; I'd scorn to touch a penny of even my own wife's money. And I shall try, of course. Keep on trying."

Yes, he'd certainly do that on every race-course in England, and with Arthur's money. But what of that, if it were to save Arthur's happiness, his very life, perhaps. Arthur would crack up, age, get a stroke, die, if this thing came suddenly upon him out of the blue. The kindly proud man whose life had been so honourable, so blameless.

"Very well," she said. "I'll be—reasonable. Just as long as you are, and no longer."

Captain Monty Ferring-Chevigny sprang to his feet, beaming.

"My dear," he said, "I knew . . ." and made a movement as though to take her in his arms.

This time, Lady Calderton's finger reached and pressed the bell-push.

Captain Ferring-Chevigny laughed, and at the sound, Lady Calderton seemed again to shrink as the knuckles of her clenched hands shone white.

"Well, well," he said, "plenty of time for that sort of thing. And the little financial details later, eh? We'll . . ."

The door opened and the footman entered.

With one last call upon her reserves of strength and courage, Lady Calderton rose to her feet, smiled, extended her hand.

"Well, good-bye, Captain Bertie-Norton," she said. "It's so nice to have seen you again. Good-bye."

And smiling, easy and debonair, the caller took his departure.

V

And thus, suddenly as on a sunny morning a cloud will arise, spread, cover the sun and turn a warm, bright and delightful day to a grey, cold, dull one, blighting not only the landscape but the mind of the beholder, so, with equal suddenness and equally marked and disastrous effect, a cloud of gloom descended upon Calderton.

At dinner one evening, Lady Calderton had been her usual cheerful and happy self, laughing merrily at little incidents that had occurred during the day, at quaint conceits and jests of Anthony's, and apparently without a care in the world.

At dinner the next evening, she was a different woman. It is no idle form of words, no exaggerated *façon de parler*, when I say she was like one who had received a mortal wound.

She had not come to lunch, and I had not seen her at all that day until she appeared in the drawing-room before dinner—looking like a ghost. I was so concerned, so shocked, that as I rose from my chair, I stared in amazement, probably open-mouthed.

"Why, what's the matter?" I cried. "Are you ill? Can I . . ."

"No, no. Sit down, Mr. Waring," she said, and sank into a chair. "I'm not . . . ill. I've had . . . some bad news. I don't feel very . . ."

"Let me ring for your maid, and . . ."

"No, no. Please don't fuss. I'm quite all right. I . . . I don't quite know . . ."

And then she lay back in her chair so still, so silent, with closed eyes, that I thought she had fainted; so white, so motionless, I almost thought for a moment that she might be dead. I was, I think, more horrified, more shocked, than ever I had been in my life.

As I rose to my feet to ring for her maid to bring water, ice, brandy, sal volatile, anything that might help, and with thoughts of telephoning for Stanton, the Calderton doctor, she opened her eyes.

"Don't ring," she said.

"But you are ill. I must . . ."

"I'm not ill, and no one can do anything for me—unless perhaps it is you."

"Lady Calderton, I'd do anything on earth . . ."

"Yes, I feel sure you would. Do sit down. I want to think."

And again she closed her eyes.

I suffered badly during the silence that followed, in spite of the warm, deep pleasure that her words had given me.

Suddenly she opened her eyes and sat up.

"I shall tell you everything," she said, "because I know you will not repeat a word of it to a living soul, until I ask you to do so."

"Thank you, Lady Calderton," I replied.

Jenkins entered and announced dinner.

"We'll go in to dinner," she said, "and afterwards I'll tell you."

It was terrible, sitting at table with a ghost, the wraith of an almost mortally stricken woman who but a few hours before had radiated happiness, contentment and peace. It was like being at table with the corpse of a person one loved, a cold dead body that yet, in strange robot fashion, moved mechanically.

And after dinner, in the drawing-room, when we were finally alone, she told me a tale that seemed at one and the same time to turn me cold with horror and to make my blood boil with rage and indignation; a dreadful story of neglect; desertion; and then, of an incredibly heartless, wicked swindle, whereby a girl still in her teens found herself a widow, and whereby the same girl, now a woman in her thirties, found herself still the wife of the man who had married her when she was seventeen, found herself the mother of a boy who was not her husband's child, the "wife" of a famous man and County magnate of ancient lineage and high repute, who was not her husband.

The days that followed were sheerly dreadful; life a nightmare, through which one walked aware yet incredulous; aware of a horror unspeakable, a calamity immeasurable, and yet unable to believe that such a thing could be.

How I played my part with Anthony while driven to distraction by fear of what might happen to his mother, I don't know. For, realizing that she was in no sense of the word a strong woman, a woman of tenacious will and powerful character, I lived in hideous fear, fear that, early one morning, a hysterical maid would run shrieking through the house, screaming that her Ladyship was dead. Braver and stronger women than Lady Calderton have taken sleeping-draughts before now; draughts from which there was no waking. The fear so grew upon me that I—at the risk of putting into her mind a thought that might not yet be there—begged her to give me her promise that she would never increase the prescribed dose of the sedative that Dr. Stanton had given her; begged her to assure me that she would never, for one moment, consider the coward's way of escape from trouble.

"But I am a coward," she said, "and there are times when I feel I can't, absolutely *can't*, face this thing. Can't sit and wait and wait for the blow to fall."

"But Sir Arthur and Anthony?"

"Sir Arthur who is not my husband. Anthony who is not . . ."

"Anthony is your son and he worships you. Sir Arthur is your husband and he worships you, and Anthony is his son. The fact that during all those years that foul dog was not really dead . . ."

"Yes. All right. I'll promise. Of course I'll promise. It would be a dreadful thing to do. Poor Anthony."

Wrung with pain, an agony of sympathy, I took her hand in both of mine and spoke to her as man to woman, equal to equal.

"Listen. I do give you my most solemn promise, my absolute assurance, that we'll find a way out of this. If only you'll have faith and patience and hope, I'll help you—somehow. You and Anthony and Sir Arthur."

She was silent for a moment as her eyes filled with tears and her lips trembled.

"I *will* have patience," she said. "I'll *try* to have hope. Faith in you I have already."

§2

When I do get a bright idea, which is not, I'm afraid, very frequently, it is usually upon waking from a good night's sleep.

Perhaps the brain is fresh and rested—if the brain ever rests. Perhaps it is because the subconscious mind has had its way during the sleep of the body, and has pushed a thought up into the conscious mind.

Usually when this happens, the thought is something in the nature of a solution. I suppose this again is because the unconscious mind works independently of the conscious, and is sometimes able to present it with the results of its labour. This would appear to be the explanation of the way in which certain fortunate people find poems, stories, plots, and rolling periods of rhetoric, coming into their unexpectant and otherwise empty minds.

Anyway, waking as usual to instant consideration of the appalling problem that occupied my thoughts almost exclusively, the idea suddenly occurred: Why not consult my uncle?

All too frequently when I am suddenly visited by a bright idea, its brilliance begins to dim as soon as I consider it, and grows duller in proportion to the attention it receives. But, now and again, one of these bright thoughts grows even brighter in the light of the mild beams of my intelligence. So it was with this one.

I would consult my uncle.

Had I not done this often, and with invariably satisfactory results, from comparatively early childhood? At Prep School, Public School, at College, and since leaving College, I had, when in serious trouble, or what at the time had seemed to me to be serious trouble, summoned up my courage, screwed it to the sticking-point, and taken it straight to Uncle. And never had I had cause to regret doing so. For if he could not solve the problem, smooth away the difficulty or get me straight out of the trouble, he could and did give wise advice. Moreover, he could give courage, and it is wonderful how obstacles decrease as courage grows. And whenever it had been a matter of help that was needed, help had always been forthcoming.

I don't say it had always been easy. He wasn't the sort of man whom one lightly approached, smiling more or less sheepishly, with a tale of folly, stupidity or wrong-doing. One got one's medicine; and, giving another shade of meaning to the metaphor, one had to take one's medicine too, for Uncle had a tongue like a rasp when he chose to use it as such, an instrument of infinite variety, now golden, now steel; a pointed probe, a razor-edged knife; a cross-cut file, harsh and cruel, but cruel only to be kind, for there was no real cruelty-for-cruelty's-sake in the hard-seeming cold man. One could only tell one's tale beneath the steely stare of his watchful eye, blurt it all out, make what faltering explanation one could, and then wait, with what appetite one might, for what was to come.

And whether he flayed me for my folly or grunted a word of sympathy for undeserved suffering or bad luck; whether he made no comment whatsoever, good or bad, he always *did* something about it, so to speak.

He was a very wise man. He knew his world. He had seen and heard a wonderful lot in his time, was a mine of experience and a most admirable mentor for youth; or for anyone else, man or woman, young or old, so far as that went, if they had the good sense or good fortune to go to him for advice and assistance, or the advice that often is the best of assistance.

Now, of course, I couldn't go to him with a terrible tale of his old friends, Sir Arthur and Lady Calderton and of Captain Ferring-Chevigny, whose name, incidentally, he would almost certainly remember. There was nothing of the club-gossip about him, and I should defeat my purpose if I began to blurt out the dreadful scandal. He would stop me.

He'd say he wished to hear no more, and would look at me in a manner that would make me feel, quite rightly, that I had sinned against the Code, and forfeited his good opinion.

I knew, of course, that had I done so, and he had heard me out, the secret would have been as safe as if I had never spoken.

But the point was that he wouldn't have spoken. He'd have been angry with me. Angry with Fate too, and if I hadn't failed altogether I should have made a mess of the whole business.

I should have to walk very warily, be diplomatic, and not only lay the whole case before him without naming any names, but in such a way that he would think the better of me, and a great deal about my story.

Yes, where there seemed nothing whatever to be done, here was something to do. Where everything seemed hopeless, here was a ray of hope. I would enlist my uncle's help, ask his advice—and make a supposititious case of it. He would understand, sooner or later, and supply the names himself.

He'd understand—and I thanked God that I had just sufficient understanding to understand him.

I would ring him up at the earliest possible moment. Or to be more accurate, ring up my old friend Judd, his man-servant—for Uncle Walter would have nothing to do with the telephone. He knew that one was installed in the pantry, and was not averse from benefiting from its usefulness; but countenance it further he would not. I believe I am right in saying that never in his life had he placed a receiver to his ear or his lips to a mouth-piece.

Yes, I would ring up Judd and tell him to ask Sir Walter whether it would be convenient for me to lunch with him this very day, and if not, for him to make an appointment with me.

So, when Robert brought me tea, I bade him tell Lady Calderton's maid that Mr. Waring would be glad if he could see Lady Calderton when convenient. She would understand that I wanted to speak with her more or less urgently, and would either come along to the schoolroom where Anthony and I would be at work, or send for me to her morning-room when she came downstairs. She always

405

breakfasted in her room, and was generally down-stairs between nine and ten. If I got away by ten, that would give me time to reach the Albany by lunch-time.

While I lay thinking, I heard Anthony's secret knock at the door. Pass-words, signs and secret knocks had all recently been changed, as it was supposed that there was a Roundhead spy in the house.

A loud knock, two soft ones, a loud knock, a soft one and a loud one. Yes, I must remember. He'd be seriously annoyed with me if I used the wrong word or sign.

"Who's there?" I called, and a sepulchral voice, evidently from a mouth at the keyhole, replied,

"Confusion."

"To his enemies," I responded, taking my cue.

And Anthony entered, gracefully cast the end of an imaginary cloak across his shoulder, laid his left hand upon the hilt of an imaginary sword, and strode to my side.

"All is well, Sir Henry," quoth he.

I wished I could agree with him.

Robert arriving with the tea, our conversation fell to lower levels.

I gave the man my message and, as he departed, informed Anthony that I should be going away for the day.

His face fell, the Cavalier nobleman or Stuart king promptly becoming a disappointed boy.

"Oh, I say. What, all day? Must you really?"

"Afraid so. I must go up to Town," I said, and as the boy looked at me, I saw in his eye that curiously 'ageing' look again. As I said before, I cannot describe it, but the effect was as though the soul of a much older person peeped out through the child's eyes.

And though what he actually said was merely,

"All right, I'll look after Mother," which meant anything or nothing, it quite definitely seemed to me to mean something. Completely unspoken between us, and almost completely *not* understood between us, was the implication that, I being away, his mother might be in need of some sort of help, assistance and protection. It was the merest nuance of expression, both of voice and of face; it was the slightest shadow of a suggestion of a hint, the merest nothing—and yet that nothing was a reality, so to speak.

And for the merest infinitesimal fraction of a second, I realized that the boy fully understood the situation. Most uncanny. Most disturbing. Had he been 'listening'?

And then, of course, I was perfectly certain that I was imagining, and imagining the most arrant nonsense. Of course, the child knew nothing, and that old wise understanding look that came into his eyes, momentary and fleeting, was the merest meaningless phenomenon, part and parcel of what one called his 'old-fashionedness.'

The boy knew absolutely nothing at all . . .

Or did he?

"Yes, rather. I'll leave her in your charge, and when I return, I shall find that all is well; the draw-bridge up, the portcullis down, sentinels posted and the flag flying."

While he and I were breakfasting, a message came to the effect that Lady Calderton would be in her morning-room at nine-thirty; and, after giving Anthony enough work to keep him employed for most of the morning, I went to see her, taking a short cut from the schoolroom along a corridor and down what had once been a secret staircase, a long steep flight of stairs completely enclosed by panelling, that led to a secret door in the panelling of a wall in the hall below . . .

Once again, I was shocked, though scarcely surprised, at the change in her. Each day seemed to me to find her more haggard, worn and weary than did the previous one.

"Good morning, Mr. Waring," she said, giving me her hand; but there was warmth and friendliness in the words, the hand-clasp, and the expression of her face. It was a look that promoted me, made me more than employee, more than tutor to her son, however well approved in that capacity. It gave me the rank of friend, and it also gave me the feeling, inexpressibly gratifying, that she was coming to regard me as a person upon whom she relied, and from whom real help might possibly come.

"I want my 'afternoon-off to-day, please, your ladyship,'" I said facetiously, trying to speak lightly, and as though cheerfulness were still possible.

She looked at me enquiringly.

"I want to run up to Town," I said, and was ashamed that I was pleased at being unable to deny that her smile died away as the look of anxiety returned.

"Going to desert . . . Calderton . . . for the day?"

"Yes, if you don't mind. I've left Anthony some work and shall be back this evening."

"Be back to dinner, if you can," she said.

And I quite understood that she did not wish to dine alone with her thoughts, her fears and agony of mind.

"Yes, I'll be back before dinner. I want to go and have a talk with my uncle."

"Sir Walter Waring? A talk?" she said.

"Yes. May I? No possible harm could conceivably come of it, and I should mention no names."

She studied my face anxiously.

"I know my husband has the greatest admiration for him."

"Yes. It's mutual. They saw a great deal of each

other when they were younger. He is the wisest person I know, and discreet and reliable as an archangel. Two archangels. And as silent as the tomb."

"As two tombs," she smiled courageously. "Look, Henry . . ." and I felt a surge of pleasure, nay of joy, as, for the first time, she called me by my christian name, ". . . I'll leave it to you entirely, for I rely upon you absolutely. It seems a terrible thing that anybody else should know, but that's an idiotic thing to say. The whole world will know soon. Do what you think best."

She 'relied upon me absolutely.' That was something worth hearing—even if it were only because I was the sole person upon whom she *could* rely.

"Thank you. I'm perfectly certain that nothing but good can come of it. I'll just find out that my uncle can see me, and I'll start at once. I'll take the small car and drive myself. If I might suggest it, refuse to see anybody to-day. Don't be at home to anyone at all."

"No, I will never see him again, if I can help it, except in your presence, until my husband . . . until Sir Arthur . . . returns."

A few minutes later, I had got Judd on the telephone and a reasonably cordial invitation to lunch at the Albany.

§3

"Well," said my uncle, fixing me with a stare of his piercing blue eyes, a look that always deflated me a little, made me feel younger without in any way rejuvenating me. "What is it now? Debts and duns? Wine and women? Horses and cards?"

And although no smile lit up the bleak countenance, this I understood was to be taken as jocularity.

Well, better that and a frosty stare from a man of

understanding and a fundamental kindliness, than horrid jocund laughter and fulsome welcome from one who would be a broken reed in time of trouble.

"Well, sir," said I, "nothing much in the way of cards. It has been *Snap* and *Beggar my Neighbour* chiefly, of late. Not much in the way of wine. The boy and I drink barley-water. Horses I have neglected, though everything I have fancied has won, unbacked by me, at good prices. Duns don't get as far as Calderton, and as to debts, well, while you are so good to me . . ."

"That leaves women," snarled Uncle, and made the noise that may be spelt *Hrrmph!*

I sat silent.

"Trouble with a woman? What do you come to me for? Godfather? Money?"

"It is trouble about a woman. One of the nicest, sweetest, finest women who ever . . ."

"She always is," snapped Uncle. "They always are. What do you want?"

"I want you to listen to a story."

"*Hmph!*" grunted Uncle, and prepared to listen with the closest attention. He spoke no word, and never took his eyes from my face, while I told him everything—except names.

And when I had finished the supposititious story which he knew quite well to be a real one, he sat silent while I glanced about the familiar room in which I had first sat as a Prep-school boy in joyous expectation of half a crown and high hopes of half a sovereign.

"That's damned bad," he said at length, stretching out a well-kept hand for the cigar-box that lay on a low table beside his chair. "Shocking business. Have a cheroot. Good gad! Poor lady. And it isn't blackmail, eh?"

"No, not clear-cut, deliberate lump-sum blackmail."

"The man's a 'gentleman,' you see," I added.

"Yes, I've no doubt there's a special corner of Hell for gentlemen of that type. He wouldn't take a lump sum, however big?"

"Well, I suppose there's a figure that would tempt a man like that, but there are two difficulties there. The lady in the case couldn't find a really big sum, and the gentleman draws the line—at blackmail."

"H'm. What does he really want, do you suppose? His wife?"

"No. Not *qua* wife, anyhow. I think he has had a very thin time, somewhere or other, and has probably got away from something very unpleasant, by the skin of his teeth. He's gone to earth, and to mix metaphors a bit, he's gone to earth on velvet, and wants to stay put. I should think he's entirely without resources; been living by his wits from hand to mouth, and now wants to sit pretty for the rest of his life. I shouldn't be surprised if he reached England two jumps ahead of some foreign police, nor, in point of fact, if he reached his wife's part of the country three jumps ahead of the English police."

"And apparently thrown 'em off the scent?"

"Yes. He has been unmolested, and so far as he knows, unshadowed, for some months now, so, unless he has the worst of bad luck and somebody spots him, he seems to be safe there."

Noticeably my uncle forbore to inquire where "there" was.

"Do you actually know that the police are after him?"

"No, but one gathers that impression. He has certainly had a good deal to do with the police in some part—or several parts—of the world, but whether the English police want him, or whether he's liable to arrest and extradition, I don't know."

"So all he wants really is the run of his teeth, pocket-money, and a position in society, for the sake of a good time plus such safety as respectability gives?"

"Just about that, I think."

"But doesn't he realize that he's a damn sight worse than a blackmailer? That, so long as he's within a thousand miles of his wife, the wretched woman must live in fear and trembling of discovery?"

"I don't know what he realizes, Sir. I don't think he gives his wife's fear, anxiety, horror, agony indeed, a single thought. What he wants is to live like a member of County society, in good standing. And that's that."

"Just a hog, eh?"

"Yes. A human hog, with all the sensibility, sensitiveness, honour and chivalrous feeling of a hog. And with the swinish, insensate swinishness of a dozen hogs," I growled.

"And what line does the unfortunate woman take, poor soul?"

"Well, she is living in a kind of waking nightmare. She's like a person stunned. Scarcely able to realize what has happened. I suppose there is a pain so great that it defeats itself. Fear, horror, grief, so great that they only numb. So far as she can think and plan at all, her one idea is to spare her husband and son; to save them, if possible. Naturally, she doesn't actually welcome social ruin for herself, but I believe she'd do anything, suffer anything, for the sake of the others. You might say, that her one idea is protection for her husband and child."

"For her reputed husband and the illegitimate child," murmured Uncle Walter.

"A boy or a girl?" he enquired, shooting a sharp glance at me.

"A boy. Only son. Heir to a wonderful old place, of which he'd have been about the fifteenth owner in the direct line."

"So the line ends, eh? No heir. The boy is the son of the reputed husband, of course? Not of the real one?"

"Oh, yes. Born a couple of years after the supposed and accepted death of the first husband."

"Where is the man now? I mean in relation to the family?"

"Hanging about in the neighbourhood. Stays at the village inn occasionally. Disappears and returns. Comes up to the house a good deal."

"How does he propose that she should explain him to the reputed husband when he returns to England?"

"Leaves that to her. She can say what she likes, do what she likes, provided she keeps him on velvet."

"Keeps the pig in clover, eh? And the problem is how to get him out of the clover before the husband returns, and keep him out. *And* shut his mouth."

"Yes. Some problem. That's why I came to you, Uncle."

My revered relative blew a long, slow cloud of cigar smoke.

"What's your interest in the matter, Henry?" he asked, examining the ash of his cigar.

"That of *any* decent person who knew the circumstances. I should like to help this most unhappy and unfortunate lady—not to mention her son and husband—and I should like to put a spoke in the wheel of a damned rogue."

"Quite so."

A long silence followed, and my eye again roved over the comfortable room with its valuable ancient shabby furniture, its air of quality, its atmosphere of solidity and worth, of good cigars, good wine,

413

good leather and good service. Table and other wood surfaces like dark glass; beautifully polished silver and brass; something old-established and permanent in a changing world wherein . . .

"It seems to me," said my uncle, withdrawing his thoughtful gaze from the cheerful fire, "that there are several solutions to the problem, all unsatisfactory; some more so than others. Personally, I'm for the straight thing, the perfectly clean potato. Always have been, and hope I always shall be. I believe in the truth, the whole truth, and nothing but the truth. But that's all right as far as one's own private affairs are concerned. One's own personal conduct. But it's a different thing where another person is involved; especially a woman. Very easy to say she should tell her reputed husband everything, and take the consequences. The consequences are more to him and the boy than they are to her. So we'll put aside the high and noble truth-at-all-costs-to-anybody line of action and try something a little more useful and practical. And practicable.

"Now the second solution is the elimination of the actual husband; and, so far as I can see, he can only be eliminated by purchase; by counter-attraction, so to speak; by arrest; or by death.

"As to purchase, you say he is not a blackmailer, and anyhow there isn't money enough.

"As to counter-attraction, what I had in mind was something that would take him to the other side of the world. Find him a job or send him on a wild-goose chase, treasure-hunt, gold-mine, valuable concession, that sort of thing.

"As to arrest, that would be all very fine, provided he would keep his mouth shut. But suppose we set the best private detective agency to work, to find out that he is wanted, and where, and by whom, and the police ran him in—would he squeal, do you suppose?"

"I haven't the slightest doubt he would, if he had any idea that it was through us, his wife's friends, that he had been pinched. He'd have a good deal to say about bigamy. Sell his life-story to the gutter-press and get a bit of his own back, as he would express it."

"And suppose he had no reason whatever to suspect his wife, or you, of having any hand in it; suppose he thought that the police had tracked him down without any outside help?"

"Then I don't think he'd say a word," I replied. "I think he'd have sufficient decency and self-respect to keep his mouth shut; and I think he'd also argue that he'd be a fool to queer his own pitch. He'd look for a bright to-morrow and a sweet by-and-bye, when, having finished his time and purged his offence, he could return—to the clover and the velvet."

"I see. Like the blackmail idea. Too much of a gentleman to do it—and the bribe not big enough. In this case, too much of a gentleman to squeal—and a silly waste of a valuable secret."

"I think you've got him about right, Sir."

"So even if we could get him arrested, and put him away, it's only a postponement, and the poor woman would be on tenter-hooks until he came out —and one day turned up at her house, grinning."

"Laughing, in this case, Sir. He has a laugh. I could kill him for it."

"We're coming to killing now," said Uncle. "The fourth aspect of the elimination idea, and by far the best, is the death of the gentleman. If he could only die, what a happy issue out of all our afflictions."

"By the way," he interrupted himself. "That's an idea. Suppose it is a hanging matter that he's wanted for. That would suit us nicely, wouldn't it?"

"Perfectly," I agreed, "and unless he knew that

we had any hand in the matter, he'd go to the gallows with his mouth shut."

"Getting quite dramatic, aren't we?" said Uncle. "Well, that's too much to hope for, I suppose. But we'll certainly try to find out. Meanwhile, suppose he's not wanted on a capital charge in any country with which we have reciprocal extradition treaties, that idea is no good to us. No elimination by that method. And so we come to a third solution of the problem.

"Could he be frightened away? Is he that sort of chap?"

"I'm inclined to doubt it. It would certainly have to be something pretty terrifying that would frighten him off. He's very pleased with himself, you know. Talks about having come into port after having weathered some pretty dangerous storms. It would take a lot to frighten him out of the port and make him put to sea again."

"Yes, I suppose so. Is he a really stout-hearted knave, do you suppose? Some of them are. Plucky as any of the hero class."

"Well, I've no actual means of knowing, one way or the other, but he certainly gives me the impression of being quite tough."

"One of the bull-dog breed gone wrong, eh?"

"Yes, I should say that once he's got his teeth in, it would take a lot to make him leave go, but you never know. Conscience doth indeed make cowards of us all, though I shouldn't think he goes in much for conscience," I said.

"Depends on what you mean by conscience. I don't imagine that there is a department of his mind or soul or what-not that registers repentance and remorse and wakes him up in the night—that sort of thing. But the dirtiest dog and the most devious crook has got something that takes the place of conscience, if it's only memory of misdeeds that may yet come home to roost. Something rather different from what one usually means by conscience, that attribute which is creditable, and the more highly developed and sensitized, the more creditable. Bit of a misnomer to use the word in the case of a man like that. So what shall we say— consciousness of crime, perhaps?"

I listened in silence as Uncle Walter paused in his rumination.

"Well, call it what you like. It probably exists and it might be useful," he continued. "Yes, I think we'll explore that avenue later on—if we don't think of something better. Rather a pleasurable pastime, eh, frightening the fright-merchant?"

The grandfather clock ticked audibly as I thought of that threatened home; of a distraught and terrified woman; and of the boy over whom this cruel doom impended.

"Anyway," said my uncle suddenly, "there are one or two things that we can do. What's more, we'll certainly do them. What's more still, there is a chance of success. And so we'll toy with the ideas of leading him away; of frightening him away; and of eliminating him altogether."

And my uncle's jaw closed with something of a snap.

Silence again in the mellow old room with its portraits of long-dead Waring generals, admirals, and of a youngster who, as a boy of seventeen, was killed at Waterloo with a sword in his hand.

"Duelling was a damn' silly custom," said my uncle, breaking the silence in which the only sound had been the gentle ticking of the beautiful old clock, inexorably measuring off the minutes of men's troublous little lives.

"When it degenerated into a silly business, that is. But it had its uses, y' know. Had its points. Good sharp rapier points sometimes—for people like our resurrected friend . . . Nice to have him out on a shady lawn at five o'clock on a June morning, eh, Henry?"

"Yes, Sir," I agreed idly, wondering what sort of a swordsman, if any, our Mr. Bertie-Norton might be.

My uncle eyed me quizzically.

"I don't speculate, Henry, but I'm now talking speculatively. I'm not a fool, but I am now talking foolishly; just talking nonsense to myself. Wouldn't it be funny if this Mr. What's-his-name was the sort of chap who would respond correctly to a smack in the face, or a nasty insult? Wounded honour. I'm quite sure he's a man of honour—of that sort. The satisfaction of a gentleman. A gentleman. You are pretty good with the small-sword, aren't you?"

"So-so. But it's more probable that our friend rough-houses when annoyed. Considers the point of the jaw more than the point of honour. Besides, supposing he were a funny man who had been in foreign parts long enough to absorb the *duello* idea, there would be a frightful fuss if such a thing hap-pened in England, wouldn't there? . . . In all the papers . . . *Duellist in Court.*"

"Not exactly a court of honour," smiled my dour relative. "The Old Bailey. Manslaughter. Seven years at least."

"I could take it."

The old man shot me a sudden penetrating glance from his hard blue eyes.

"*O-h-h-h,*" he said quietly. "H'm. Like that, is it?"

And I thought the eyes' blue stare softened a little, and that the faintest suggestion of a smile hovered about the firm still-handsome mouth.

"Of course," he continued, "things do happen of which the Police hear nothing. Such a thing might happen in a sequestered corner of a big estate, in parts of which no one sets foot from year's end to year's end. Especially to a gentleman who had been at great pains to avoid the lime-light. Almost the daylight, one might say. A gentleman known to have died seventeen years ago, a Mr. What's-his-name who hasn't got a genuine name that's trace-able. He'd never be missed. Sad. We all like to be missed."

"But all this is idle speculation," he continued, "and, as you know, I don't speculate. Shall we have a glass of sherry?"

My uncle touched the bell and the admirable Judd entered, an obvious telepathist, for on a heavy silver tray he bore a fine old decanter and two sherry glasses. These he filled, and faded from the room.

"And then there's 'accidents,'" mused my uncle, sipping. "Suppose this poor friendless fellow—who really has no existence whatever outside his own suit of clothes, so to speak—suppose he met with an accident. There are hunting accidents, shooting accidents, swimming, motoring and boating acci-dents."

"All sorts," I agreed. "People fall out of trains, and even out of aeroplanes. Some fall over cliffs. Even fall out of bed. But although I would risk my precious life in a duel with him—provided it was swords—and take the consequences, I don't think I could commit a murder."

The astute man opened his eyes wide in grave surprise, if not in shocked astonishment.

"What a mind you have, Henry!" he said. "Dreadful. Not only given to harbouring the crudest criminal ideas, but . . . Of course you were joking. Nevertheless, there *are* accidents."

We applied ourselves to our sherry.

"Now, you've certainly given me something to employ my leisure time, something to think about, and I shall think about it a lot."

And pursing his lips, he nodded his head slowly.

His look of determination, air of power and of wisdom, gave me a foolish and unwarrantable, but nevertheless comforting, feeling of hopefulness that Uncle would do something in this case in which there was nothing to be done.

"Any particular hurry?" he asked.

"No, beyond the need for shortening the period of a woman's agony—a time of ghastly suffering and suspense."

"Yes. Yes. Quite so. What I meant was, though, is there any particular date after which hope's hopeless and help's helpless?"

"No. I don't see what can happen until the husband—the reputed husband—comes home."

"And even then the real husband won't tell him, provided things are going as he wants them?"

"No. But *she* might. There's a point beyond which a woman cannot bear that sort of thing, and simply must tell somebody," I said.

"Well, she's told you. And directly she tells her husband, the game's up. He's not the sort of man, I take it, to sit down with the situation, so to speak. Actually to sit down, cheek by jowl with the real husband, at table with the innocently bigamous wife and illegitimate child."

"No . . . no . . ." I mused. "And of course, as I said before, her one idea is to prevent harm coming to him and the boy."

"In short, to prevent their knowing."

"Yes. But how long could she keep it up? How long could she stand the strain of so false a position? She is not a very . . ."

"Well, anyway, there's no immediate hurry, is there?" interrupted my uncle. "No 'date by which,' as I said."

"No."

"Good. Now don't say a word about the business while we are at lunch. I can't eat and think too. Not if I'm to enjoy my food and digest it. Then, after lunch, we'll smoke a quarter of a cigar together, and then I'll say good-bye, for I take my nap. And I wouldn't miss it for the Prince of Wales or the Archangel Gabriel . . . And if the Death Angel calls between two and four, he'll find me asleep, and I hope he won't wake me."

And we referred no more to the matter that was uppermost in my mind, and, I believe, in his.

After an admirable lunch, most deftly served by the swift and silent Judd, we returned to our arm-chairs, and my uncle asked how I was getting on with my job, what I thought of Anthony and wheth-er I found life at Calderton as interesting as he had prophesied.

"It is quite as interesting as you prophesied, Uncle," said I, meeting and holding his eye.

"Ah, that's good," said he, swirling his '48 brandy round and round in the balloon glass as he warmed it between his hands. "Excellent. I shouldn't be surprised if I were to come down and see you there, soon. Damn nuisance, Arthur being abroad so much. I don't know where I enjoy myself better than there.

"Except here. Except here," he added, and sipped his brandy.

After a little more desultory conversation, he put his glass down and rose to his feet.

"Well, good-bye, my boy. I'll think that matter over."

And as we shook hands, he held mine for a second longer than usual, and smiled his brief illuminating smile and said,

"If Katherine knows that I know, give her my kind love and deepest sympathy, and tell her I am certain, I positively am *certain*, that all will be well. Good-bye, Henry."

And I returned to Calderton enheartened and

hopeful—quite illogically, as I realized, for what hope was there?

VI

Captain Montague Bertie-Norton, almost daily a visitor at Calderton House, could not have been a gentleman of what was once termed sensibility. He must, on the contrary, have had what Mr. Henry Waring alluded to, both before his face and behind his back, as the hide of a rhinoceros. For, in lieu of other welcome he made his own, and made it a warm one. Having invited himself to lunch, to tea or to dinner, or indeed for the day, he, figuratively speaking, met himself, shook hands with himself right heartily, bade himself walk in and take not only his ease but anything else that he fancied.

His hostess firmly refusing to let him live in the house, refusing to see him when he called; the apparently all-powerful tutor regarding him with cold unsmiling dislike, patent and almost palpable; the son of the house tolerating him only for his wonderful stories—he yet came and continued to come, made himself at home, and appeared to notice nothing unpleasant in the social atmosphere. If the said atmosphere was strained, Captain Bertie-Norton was not. Not the faintest evidence of strain appeared upon his smiling countenance nor lessened the volume or frequency of his long and loud guffaw.

Having dropped in at tea-time, he would saunter to the terrace without going through the house, drop into an easy chair and mention to the attendant footman that he thought that perhaps, on the whole, he would have his—usual, the usual being whisky-and-soda, anchovy biscuits and a cigar.

Calling in the forenoon, he would, when handing hat, stick and gloves to the same young man, just mention casually that he would be in to lunch.

Arriving in the evening, in what is prettily termed immaculate evening-dress, he would whisper to Jenkins that a bottle of the '84 port would do him nicely. Yes, and talking of the '84, was there a bottle of the '48 open, the old and bold and dark brown brandy?

A gentleman with a way with him, and by no means clumsy or unhandy with his tips.

VII

I'm afraid that my influence on Captain Montague Ferring-Chevigny, *alias* Bertie-Norton, was not a good one, for I encouraged him to drink and to brag. And in both pursuits, to do him justice, he needed a little encouragement, particularly with regard to the former. I think that at one period of his life he must have been a pretty useful drinker, though I shouldn't think he was ever a drunkard. Nowadays, for some reason or other, he was moderate in the use of alcohol, not to say abstemious; but, left alone with a decanter of old port, a box of cigars and a good listener, he would drink glass after glass, become loquacious, and then boastful, bragging of his great and numerous successes, all due to his own cleverness.

To be quite fair to him, he was not, when sober, a braggart. Only when wine had loosened his tongue would he boast. Nor, when he was blowing his own trumpet and loudly sounding his own praises between blasts, did he extol his courage, nerve, skill and endurance as some men do, nor tell of hair-raising adventures, terrific feats, or marvellous experiences.

It was always of his cleverness that he boasted; only of the successes due to his astuteness and cunning.

In the cold light of morning or the mellow light of afternoon and evening, he was cautious; and, doubtless with excellent reason, reticent.

One could well understand that he, with so much to hide, was well advised to think before he spoke. But *inter poculos* he was different—garrulous, self-revealing. Ale is another man. And wine is yet another. *In vino veritas*: and I think that, by the time the two-bottle decanter needed replenishing, the man was telling the truth—as he saw it. More *vinum*, more *veritas*.

§2

"Damn good wine," he observed that evening, holding up his third or fourth glass to the light. "I love a glass of vintage port. One of the good things of life; one of the things I came home for. Can't get it abroad, you know. By gad, what filth one drinks when one is abroad. I don't mean France or Germany, Spain or Portugal, Austria or Hungary. (Ever taste real Hungarian Tokay, the *Essence*, as they call it, grown in the late Emperor's own vineyards?) No, I mean Asia, Africa, Australia, America. Especially South America. *Aguardiente*. Ever hear of it and *tequila* and *pulque*? They're the stuff to get you going."

"And where did you get them? Mexico?"

"Yes. And that's a damn good country to get into and a better one to get out of. Not so easy either, sometimes. Had some good sprees there. Great friend of old Obregon at one time. Sort of financial adviser to him. Might say I advised the whole financial system. Put through some wonderful deals too."

Then came the horrible laugh, inane, fatuous, self-satisfied.

"Concessions. Any number of American prospectors after oil and what-not. Lots of capital behind some of them too. I came a cropper, though. Sold one concession twice. Damn nearly got out of the country with the bullion, too. But old Obregon was a downy bird. Just got away with a whole skin, and lucky to do that. Skipped to Boruela. Now, that's a country, if you like; and it's run by the cleverest man in the world. The very cleverest, bar none. By gad! He's a great lad, old Gil Vicente Romez. He's the Devil in human form. Ever hear of him?"

"No, I'm ashamed to say I never heard of him."

"No, I didn't suppose you ever had, and that's part of the cleverness. Do you know that, for a quarter of a century, he's been the most perfect Dictator the world has ever seen?"

"No, I don't know it."

"Well, I'm telling you. Dictators! All the others are timid little constitutionalists compared with Romez. Any one of them is like a four-year-old child playing cup-and-ball, trying to get the ball into the cup, while Romez is like Atlas with the Ball on his shoulders. The world."

"The world?"

"Well, his world. And he has defied and defeated the rest of it. Do you know that he *owns* Boruela. And every man, woman and child, every town and village, every mountain and river, every mine, farm and estate—as much as any Englishman owns his house and dog and back garden—and a damn sight more so. An Englishman could go to prison for torturing his dog to death. Romez has never been to prison and never will, though he has tortured ten thousand men and women to death. Real torture. He *owns* the country, man. There's nobody dare whisper a word; and if anyone did, he'd whisper his next in a gaol that he'd never come out of. And believe me, they are *some* gaols. Charnel-houses of lingering awful death. I shudder, even here and now, when I only *think* of them.

"And he's clever, mind you. There's more statesmanship, more knowledge of the art of government in the little finger of Gil Vicente Romez than in all your modern Napoleons and all their gangs rolled into one. And he's ten times richer than the whole lot put together. Yes, including all the Tsarist loot in the Kremlin.

"And in spite of that, he has turned a national foreign debt of a hundred and fifty million bolivars and an international debt of seventy million into an exchequer balance of a hundred million."

"And how has he done it?" I inquired.

"Oh, oil, cattle, coffee, cotton, what-not—and his own system."

"What's that?"

"Why, rooking the foreigner and taking a private rake-off on every last Government deal. Give you a single example—and it was yours truly who put him up to it. All sorts of stuff comes from the interior, of course, down to the coast. So what does the old bird do but draw a line *inside* the country, parallel to the coast, right across Boruela between the source of supply and the ports, with a chain of Customs barrier-posts on every road crossing the line. And you've got to stick to the roads in that country.

"Very well. Every damn thing, every head of cattle, has got to pay a heavy duty when it crosses the line. If it is his own goods, Romez pays up like a man. Takes the money out of his left-hand trousers pocket as tax and puts it in his right-hand trousers pocket as revenue. Costs him exactly nothing. But what about the rest of the people—and especially the poor old foreigner? He leaves him just about enough to make it worth his while to carry on. And he plays that sort of game with every product of the country. Clever! He's superhuman."

"And you got the better of him?" I asked.

"Oh, now and again. Now and again. Overdid it, though. I got the better of him one time, and he got the best of me. Everything I *had* got. And I saw the inside of one of his lovely gaols. My oath, they are as far below the worst gaols in the world as he is far above the best Dictators. You simply wouldn't believe me if I began to tell you some of the things I have seen in that El Libertador prison. Pretty name, isn't it, *El Libertador*? The Liberator. By gad! Some of them were glad to be liberated . . . by death.

"Yes, a humorous lad . . . El Libertador! . . . Like his own name. What do you think that is? *El Benemerito!* I gave him that. At least, we decided it would be a nice one, and I put up a couple of good Congress men to propose and second it. Carried with acclamation. *El Benemerito*, the Well-Deserving. Lord, if he is to get what he deserves, when the time comes, the Devil will be hard put to it to think up a good one."

"You got out of the prison, though," I observed.

"As you brightly observe, I got out of the prison."

"Bit of luck, eh?"

"Luck? It was more than luck. You don't get far with luck alone, my lad. Luck and judgment and ability. Romez was clever, but I beat him to it."

"You wouldn't care to go back there, then?"

Ferring-Chevigny laughed, emptied his glass, put it down with a bang.

"Go *back*? Back to Boruela?" he said. "Why, I'd sooner be . . ."

Words seemed to fail him.

And for a moment, words failed me, too. I glanced down and toyed with the walnut-shells on my plate, afraid that he might see a change of expression on my face, a light that I felt must have come into my eyes.

I never did much talking on these occasions. Only just enough to show him that he had an attentive and deeply interested audience; just a "Yes" or a "No" or a "Quite so," or an appropriate question, to keep him going.

But at the sight of his face and the sound of his voice when he could find no words to describe his horror of the idea of returning, I'm afraid I became inattentive. Certainly I missed something of what he was saying. For it seemed to me that chance had played right into our hands—the chance of his happening to commend the port leading to a dissertation on drinks, thence to the *tequila* of Mexico, thence to Boruela—and had given me a weapon.

Uncle Walter had, among other possibilities, considered that of frightening him away. He had considered the question of the man himself being in any danger, and had spoken of frightening the frightener. There might be nothing in it, but no stone must be left unturned, no "avenue unexplored."

Nothing on earth would induce him to go back to Boruela where, presumably, some terrible fate at the hands of this monster awaited him, eh?

I'd keep him on the subject for just as long as I could keep him awake and talking.

". . . Yes, absolutely the very finest Dictator in the world. There's no doubt about it. Why, it is estimated that at least three times as much is spent on his own private and personal Secret Service as is spent by any Department of State except his War Office.

"And not only inside the country, mind you. If anything, it is better organized abroad than at home, and that's saying something. It is a colossal international spy-system covering the whole of Europe and all North and South America. Absolutely incredible, the number of Secret Service agents he has got, and the amount of money that's spent on Secret Service.

"And mind you, although it is national in theory, and paid for out of national revenue, it is his own. It is as much his own as the domestic service of his private palaces. Every capital city in Europe and America has got a headquarters-bureau and a splendidly organized and wonderfully efficient spy-system.

"And from the capital, they cover the ports, the other big towns and, in fact, the whole country; London, Paris, Berlin, Rome, Madrid, Lisbon, Brussels, Moscow, Amsterdam, all the lot are centres for their own countries."

"But why?" I asked, and now my question wasn't merely mechanical, a noise to show him I was awake and listening, for I was listening with all my ears, my hands shading my eyes, as I watched his face.

"Why? Ask yourself, man. How many prominent Boruelans do you suppose have fled for their lives to all parts of Europe and America? How much money do you suppose is sent to them by their friends and well-wishers, who'd give their last *bolivar* to see a reasonably hopeful invasion of the country? Why, there'd be revolution and armed rebellion from end to end. Why, a revolutionary army would spring up from the ground in every province in the country. Everywhere. And the garrison of every town, every one of them, would be besieged. The nation would rise, almost as one man, with no other weapons but their machetes—if they got such a lead as an armed invasion would give them."

"Then why don't they do it without one?"

"Ask yourself, again. Romez, as I've told you, is the perfect Dictator, and as any good Dictator can, he rules absolutely against the will of the people. And he can do it indefinitely because, not only has he seized the machine, but he has perfected it. The Machine of Government, of which the army, the police and the spy-system are, what shall I say, the invaluable, inescapable, inexorable, incorruptible engine.

"For one thing, between seventy and eighty of

his most important subordinates are his own relations, and every official in the country knows that if Romez falls, he falls. And Romez's system sees to that. They are the first people the populace would hang if they didn't burn them alive.

"That's why there is no fear or chance of rebellion from within. They just can't do it. They are crushed. Why, a whisper against not merely Romez but against any one of his officials, would cost a man his liberty; and when you lose your liberty in Boruela, you lose your life soon after. They don't take it from you. You just lose it, unless you are amazingly tough and strong.

"No, that's the only thing he's got to fear, a successful military invasion by a powerful revolutionary army of exiled patriots. And, by gad, there must be enough of them, alone, to make a fair-sized army, for they bolt in thousands every year. Hence the foreign spy system."

"And there's actually such an organization here in England?" I asked, trying to control my voice and speak naturally. "With headquarters in London?"

"You've said it," replied Ferring-Chevigny, as he hiccupped and apologized.

Was he sufficiently under the influence of Bacchus to have laid aside his guard? If I pursued this line of questioning, would he shut up like an oyster, not only refusing further information but regarding me with suspicion?

I must risk it. The opportunity was too good, the subject having been introduced, indeed pursued, if not laboured—by himself.

"Well, well," I yawned, "one lives and learns. Fancy that. Here in peaceful England. Secret Service agents, spies, revolutionaries, wicked villains and what-not."

"And not so what-not, either," he answered in a slightly offended, not to say bellicose, tone. "Funny-stuff to you perhaps, but real enough to anybody they were after."

"What, here in England? Do you mean to say that this what's-his-name—Romez—could interfere with anybody *here*?"

"You try, my lad. Try it for yourself. Chuck up ushering and go into the gun-running business. See if you can charter a little tramp steamer and load her up with a cargo of rifles and ammunition for Boruela, either in an English port or Rotterdam or anywhere else—and see how you get on. Not that you'd get as far as Rotterdam."

"Who'd stop me?"

"You try it and see. You'd find it a very different story from trying to get rifles into the Riff country . . . Spain . . . Ulster . . . Mexico . . . Brazil . . . any-where that didn't bring you up against the Romez organization."

"Really, that's most interesting."

"I'll say it is," growled Ferring-Chevigny, and poured himself another glass of port. "You let a whisper get abroad in the market that you are out to get rifles for Boruela, and see what happens to you. But say good-bye to your best girl and wind up your other *affaires* first."

"Really, you amaze me."

"I could amaze you. Damme, I could curl your hair and stunt your growth, if I told you some of the things I've seen in that country. Incredible. And not only concerning Boruelan nationals either."

"It's marvellous that nothing of this is known in Europe," I observed, endeavouring to give my tone the right shade of doubt and incredulity to lead him on to further asseveration, without offending him.

"That's where old Romez's cleverness and power come in again. Complete censorship; perfect con-trol of the Press. Why, if any editor in Boruela, with the best will in the world, published something that

Romez didn't like, he'd never publish anything again. And his home town would be without a newspaper for quite a while.

"No, not a word concerning the real state of affairs gets outside the country—except word of mouth from runaway Boruelans. And who's going to listen to them? Not that they'd have a chance to talk for long. Who's going to take any notice of renegade rascals who have fled from their country's justice? No; what with owning the Press at home, and a system that looks after runaway squealers abroad, there's not much of 'The Truth about Boruela' gets to Europe—or anywhere else."

I could scarcely control my excitement, and feared that it might show in my voice, as I strove to lead him on, keep him talking.

"And his organization in England now. Would that be in connection with the Boruelan Legation?"

Ferring-Chevigny smiled.

"With what else? *Sub rosa*, of course. Legation and every Consulate in the country . . . No, there's not much known about Boruela—outside Boruela."

He fell silent and suddenly laughed.

"Laugh! Gad, how I laughed when His Holiness the Pope conferred an order upon the pious President El Benemerito, the Well-Deserving, and made old Romez a Cavalier of the Holy Order of Piana. Really very funny. I wonder what sort of a man His Holiness thinks Romez is. Give him a bit of a shock if someone told the Pope that Romez has only been married once but has got a hundred and seventeen children! Mothers and children doing well. Yes, a hundred and seventeen little Romezes carrying on the good work. Talk about a well-rooted oak, eh? Yes, and he has had decorations and high Orders of Merit from France, Holland and Belgium. Shouldn't be surprised if we gave him one. You can do wonders with oil."

"Oil?"

"Do you know, my lad, that when the Great War ended, Boruela had never produced a single barrel of oil, and that to-day she's the second biggest oil-producing country in the world? By gad, that was a racket, and I was in on it, too. It was I who gave old Romez the National Reserve tip, as well as the survey notion."

"What was that?"

"Well, I had seen how Mexico had muddled her oil business instead of handling it so that she'd be the richest nation in the world. Selling concessions outright and getting about a penny in the pound for herself. Penny in the hundred pounds, more likely.

" *'Look here, Gil,'* said I. *'You put the concession up to auction and when you grant it to the highest bidder, make a law that after a certain time—and you can make it a damned uncertain time, if you like —half the concession reverts to the State. See? Otherwise to Mister Gil Vicente Romez. And before very long, you'll have one-half of the oil in your pocket. Sounds messy, but* pecunia non olet, *as we used to say at school.*

" *'And another thing, old son,'* said I, *'when you've sold the concession, keep a royalty and a damned good one. Check up at the ports on every barrel—and see what good luck will send you. You'll be ten times as rich as the ten richest men in the world put together. And that on your oil alone.*

" *'And another thing,'* said I, *'you make the blight-ers who are after your oil make a perfect Ordnance Survey of the whole country—at their own expense. That'll be useful to you, too, one day. Other things than oil.'*

"By gad, the amount of my own little rake-off from the oil racket would make you sit up. It doesn't bear thinking of—what I left behind in Boruela. I should have got it out to Curaçao, to the

Bank of Holland, while I could."

"No chance of getting it now?" I asked.

"Is there a chance of getting it? Like Hell there is. Just as much chance as you'd have of recovering a five-pound note from the heart of a furnace."

"You can't go back; and nobody would send it to you?"

"Go back? *There?* Dangerous enough here! And as for getting any money sent out of the country . . ."

And again he laughed.

"Nor bring it, I suppose?" I said.

"Huh! Boruelans who get away with money don't bring it to other people."

He fell into a musing silence.

"It's certainly a country one doesn't hear much about," I observed.

"Yes. I've told you why."

Ferring-Chevigny sat glum and silent, and I was afraid that he might be wondering whether he had said too much in telling me why.

I must go and see Uncle to-morrow and lay this story before him. If only I could get a little more, some details as to exactly whom and what he feared in England.

"Yes, and what you say quite accounts for it. But, you know, I marvel that a man like Romez isn't assassinated—by the son or father or husband of some victim who . . ."

Again Ferring-Chevigny laughed.

"Take a clever man to get him. When he goes out, he buzzes along in a bullet-proof car at seventy an hour, surrounded by a bodyguard of gun-men on motor-bikes. However, few people ever see him, except those who live on and by and through him; people to whom his death would be the worst sort of calamity.

"And, of course, his palaces are absolute barracks. Before he had come into full power and quite consolidated his position, his enemies occasionally used to have a try, but they never had a chance. Romez saw to that. He used to treat 'em to the *gusana* and the *grillos*, and let it be known that henceforth anybody who annoyed him in that way —never mind whether they took a pot shot at him, plotted, disobeyed an order, or whispered a single word of disparagement—would get the same."

"What are they?"

"*Gusana* and *grillos*? Well, the *gusana* is a fly, I believe it is an indigenous fly, pretty well confined to Boruela, as a matter of fact."

"Poisonous sting?" said I intelligently.

"Well, no. It doesn't sting you, so much as bite; and when it has had its nibble, it lays eggs in the hole. And these eggs hatch into worms and maggots and they've got the exploring urge or itch. Itch is the word for it, by gad! They explore, inland and up-country and so on, until the person who has been bitten by the *gusana* fly is riddled through and through with the maggots. They eat him alive, in fact. That's where the *grillos* come in. They are seventy-pound irons, and if you've got a pair on your ankles and a pair on your wrists, you can't do much about the *gusana* fly when he's buzzing round in hundreds, making provision for his young, home-building all over your back, because, of course, you haven't any clothes. You just sit in this cell, which has been occupied, and never cleaned, since the Spaniards came there—three hundred years ago. You sit in almost total darkness —just enough light to see what you look like, and enough black beans and stinking water to keep you alive. Old Romez's pet research scientists estimated that on the whole, that is the slowest and nastiest death a human being could suffer. No, they don't assassinate Romez much."

Ferring-Chevigny fell silent, staring into the depths of the wonderfully polished table in front of him, pondering and remembering; and, judging by the look on his face, his thoughts were not pleasant.

"Yes, I could tell you some things," he continued, "but I won't waste my breath, for you wouldn't believe them. Even to me who saw them, it is almost incredible here, that such things are going on to-day. To-day, mark you, in these prisons, in Caibo, Boledo, Paracay, or Puerto, any of them. There are torture-chambers, real going concerns, working in full blast, and not only inflicting the tortures that the Spaniards inflicted on the Indians, but improved ones, the fine product of three centuries of progress.

"There are no atrocities nor tortures more terrible anywhere in the world, and there never were, than those that have been committed in these places, and are being carried on at this moment as we sit here. And no one knows!

"No wonder you are inclined to take it all with a grain of salt. But you needn't. Why, his Public Works alone is a thing that would disgrace the most degraded savages. He started his Public Works when the prisons were full, when there were so many tens of thousands of rotting, slowly dying skeletons and parodies of humanity in his prisons that there was no room for any more.

"He suddenly laughed at breakfast one morning, looked round at his staff and solemnly announced his slogan,

" 'Unity, Peace, and Work for All.'

"By the way, poor old General Peñaloza died, walled up in a tiny cell with a hundred and sixty pounds of *grillos* and about a hundred and sixty pairs of *gusana* flies, simply for saying to a friend in a Caibo Club,

" '*Unity, Peace, and Work. Unity in suffering, Peace in the grave, and Work on the public roads.*'

"Yes, it was the public roads that solved the problem of the prisons. He sent instructions to all his Governor-Generals, Senators, Mayors, and what-not, to supply him with a labour force—of all the people whom they didn't like. And he set them to work to drive a magnificent wide road clean through swamp and jungle from nowhere in particular to nowhere at all; and on that road, these people whom his officials didn't like—which meant anybody in any way connected with someone who might be suspected of being anti-Romez by reason of his wrongs and suffering—died like flies, in thousands.

"Why? Starvation. Malaria. Exposure. Dysentery. And in these chain-gangs were some of the best men in Boruela; men of gentle birth and breeding; old men; youths; foolish young students who had talked as the students always will, whether in Russia, France, Spain or—Boruela.

"Yes, they got Unity all right; Peace before long, and Work all the time, as they crawled in thousands through the jungle, leaving this road behind them. And not a tent nor a hut among the lot of them. Not the slightest protection whatsoever against tropical rain or sun, against mosquitoes, or anything else. I know. I've been along those roads in El Benemerito's own car.

"And I'd be in one of those gangs, too, unless I was in one of the prison cells, if he could lay hands on me now."

VIII

Sir Walter Waring of the Albany and the Marlborough Club, albeit known to his friends and acquaintances as a dry old stick, had, in the days
when sparks and blades were fashionable, been
equally well-renowned as a bright young spark and
a mettlesome blade. And though in his present
fifties the spark might be dulled and the blade a
little rusted, the one was not quenched nor the
other broken. Thus, after dinner on the day of his
nephew's visit, as he sat gazing into the fire, smoking his cigar, he could not forbear to wish that he
were twenty or thirty years younger.

Yet, as he asked himself, what could he have
done? What could he have done that young Henry
could not and would not do? It was very well to rage
furiously against this infernal fellow, Ferring-
Chevigny; to talk threateningly and imagine all
sorts of fine plans for putting a spoke in his wheel;
but what, in point of actual practical fact, could one
do? He was the unfortunate lady's husband, and
nothing could alter that, except his death. No, there
was no getting away from it. Just as long as he was
alive, he was her husband. And he was very much
alive. Nor, in the twentieth century and in England,
could anything be done about it. All very well to
babble about duels, accidents, "liquidation," that
sort of thing, but it was the sheerest nonsense.

And even supposing that, like so many men of
his generation, Sir Walter Waring imagined himself
to be a far finer fellow than the young men of the
rising generation, how could he demonstrate it?
Being a wise man and a knowledgeable, he had no
illusions on the subject, and entertained not the

slightest doubt that young Henry was as good a man as he had been at Henry's age.

Still, something must be done—for it was intolerable. One of the finest fellows he had ever known. One of the very nicest women. And a really charming and delightful boy. And to set against the happiness and welfare of that trio, the "rights" of this infernal runagate gaol-bird. The state of the Law was damnable that allowed a man like that to sham dead for the best part of twenty years and then turn up and wreck lives and ruin families. If ever murder was justified . . .

But murder never was.

Surely there must be some bribe that would buy the fellow off, even if he did object to the word 'blackmail' and pretend to take a high-and-mighty line when it was suggested.

Would he be able to do any good by going down to Calderton and seeing the fellow? Would it be possible to frighten him away with some sort of bogey? Would a man like that be amenable to threats of any kind? Probably the sort of chap who'd call one's bluff, when one told him that, if he didn't clear out of England within a given time, something most devilishly unpleasant might occur. And what would be the good of it? Would he be any less her husband if he were living on the Riviera or in Timbuctoo or at the Antipodes?

It was maddening that, however much one pondered the subject, whatever line of thought one followed, one sooner or later came to absurdity, ridiculous melodrama or sheer fantasy. You cannot, at this time of day, call a man out and kill him. In the first place he wouldn't come out, and in the second place he might kill you. You cannot, at this time of day, hire bravos in the good old Borgia style, and do him in. You cannot go up to a hale and hearty Briton 'sitting pretty,' acting absolutely within his rights, and frighten him off with threats of danger and death. And when you are driven back to the old, old Danegelt idea, to bribery and blackmail, the man is still alive and still her husband, and the position unchanged. And it is you who are doing the inverted blackmail, as it were—*asking* him to be a blackmailer.

Still, something had to be done, and the first thing was to get Ferring-Chevigny away from Calderton. That would in no wise affect the facts, but it would ease the situation for the poor lady. Wherever he was, he'd be her husband, but life would presumably be a little more bearable for her if he weren't on the doorstep.

What about getting an introduction to Sir Rodney Blake, Commissioner of Police, and asking him to find out whether the English police had anything on one Captain Montague Ferring-Chevigny, *alias* Captain Montague Bertie-Norton? But then, those would not be the names under which he'd be known to the police, if known he were. Of course they wouldn't.

As Ferring-Chevigny he had wiped himself out, in that yacht case at Perenecque Island, nearly twenty years ago; and as Bertie-Norton he'd have started afresh when he returned to England just recently. Besides, one had got to be most devilish careful in a case like this. Walk very warily indeed, if one weren't going to do the very thing that must not be done—give the whole show away. It would be a nice thing if, by way of being helpful, he was the cause of the news being published abroad that the late unlamented Ferring-Chevigny was anything but late and even less lamented. No, he must keep away from the police.

What about one of those private detective agencies, run by former members of the C.I.D.? There were one or two quite famous Yard men who had retired and gone into business on their own.

But there again, one would have to give names. One would have to set them on the fellow's track; and, sooner or later, they'd place him, spot him for whom he was. And then how many people would be in the secret? So far, no living person knew but himself, young Henry and Lady Calderton; and he mustn't do anything to enlarge that circle.

Or would it be worth while going and seeing her, to get her permission to tell one other person, the renowned John Nichols, until recently one of the Big Five? . . . But there again, it wouldn't stop at John Nichols. He must have a staff who'd know what he was doing; he must employ other detectives, male and female "watchers," as they called them; a secretary and clerks. It wasn't to be expected that John Nichols could do the whole business single-handed, trace out this fellow's past, find out something actionable, tax him with it, threaten arrest, and frighten him away.

No, it wouldn't do. One was helpless, absolutely impotent, and, if the worst happened, the blame would really lie with that devilish ass, the Law. Ferring-Chevigny might be a damned scoundrel, but it was the Law that allowed him to be one; allowed him still to be her husband; allowed him to walk grinning into Calderton House and lay the House of Calderton in ruins.

But he'd do something, as sure as his name was Walter Waring. He'd do something—even though it looked as though there were nothing else for it but plain common murder . . . Murder most foul . . . Murder most righteous and commendable. Nothing else for it, if Arthur and Katherine and young Anthony were to be saved.

By gad, how true it was that evil begets evil. For here sat he, Walter Waring, plotting, or at any rate imagining, the doing of deeds of which he otherwise never would have dreamed.

He dreamed on.

There came a discreet tap at the door, and Sir Walter Waring's soldier-servant entered.

"Mr. Henry on the 'phone, sir. Will you speak to him?"

"No, I won't," was the reply.

"No, sir. He says he's coming up to see you to-morrow morning. Proposes himself for lunch. Very urgent that he should see you."

Sir Walter nodded, and Judd withdrew.

Well, that was to the good. He'd have one or two ideas to suggest to young Henry, and it looked as though Henry had got something interesting to suggest to him. Not a bad boy, Henry, for all his messing about with poems and paint-brushes, instead of playing cricket. He might pose flabby, but to do him justice, he didn't act flabby. He had got guts. Mustn't let him overdo it, in the matter of this damned scoundrel. Perhaps it had been unwise to talk to him about duels and accidents, but he had got his head screwed on the right way, and would be no more likely to do anything really silly than to do anything dirty.

Still, one had to remember that there was a woman in the case, a devilish attractive woman, too; that young Henry was something of a romantic, and had an undeniable streak of quixotry in his make-up. No, if anybody was going to run any risk of getting into trouble over Montague Ferring-Chevigny, it must be old Walter Waring. And he was damned if he'd sit by and see this thing happen without doing the utmost that was in his power to prevent it.

And there you were, once again, back at the starting-point. Nothing but the man's death could prevent it . . . Round and round . . . Vicious circle

. . . Only two facts clear, the fellow's death the only solution, and his early removal from Calderton the only relief, however temporary.

They must watch the time, too. Time was valuable. Anything that could be done must be done before Arthur came back, for the situation could not then be long hidden from him. Therefore get the man away, and hope that something might happen to him . . . *Make* something happen to him.

To think of the number of people who are killed annually on the roads of Europe. Tens of thousands of them. And the tens of thousands of people who die of influenza and other diseases. Think of the people killed in ship-wrecks, train-wrecks, aeroplane crashes, motor smashes. But this scoundrel goes on his way rejoicing, grinning, happy.

Accidents . . . An accident to Captain Montague Ferring-Chevigny?

§2

"Yes, my boy, I think there's a gleam of hope there," said Sir Walter Waring to his nephew, after lunch next day, as they sat on either side of the fire in the cosy Albany room.

"Definitely. I don't know anybody at the Boruelan Legation, and if I did, I should have a certain delicacy about proposing to make him my bully. Couldn't very well go up to the Boruelan *chargé d'affaires*, for example, and say,

" 'There's a renegade Englishman who's very badly wanted by His Excellency the President of the Republic of Boruela, and who is most particularly not wanted by myself and certain of my friends. Pray pinch him. Shoot him up. Knock him down; drag him out; kidnap him; ship him off to Boruela, like we used to ship our English criminals and other unfortunates to Barbadoes and Jamaica, the

445

Vexed Bermudas and the Dry Tortugas.'

"Quite possibly the Secretary might say,

" *'Si, si, Señor. Ciertamente! Seguramente! Conplacer! Congusto!'* and get on with it. But it isn't a thing I'd care to do—set those South American gentlemen on to an Englishman, with the view to his being done in, or most painfully done down in some way."

Henry Waring agreed that it would be an unpleasant task, the memory of which might leave a disagreeable flavour on the palate, but . . .

"Yes," agreed Sir Walter, "there's the 'but.' Unpleasant flavour or not, it would be ten thousand times more unpleasant to look back for the rest of our lives on what we might have done and didn't do, by reason of a scruple. We were brought up to despise—what shall I say—treachery; stabbing in the dark; though that's putting it strongly. Say, working behind the other fellow's back, handling anything but the clean potato. But . . . And there's your 'but' again."

And the older man fell silent.

"By gad," he said suddenly. "I've got an idea . . . Cipriano! That's it. That's what I'll do. Absolute *deus ex machina.*"

"Who's he, Sir?" inquired Henry Waring.

"Why, he's the Argentine Ambassador to Paris. He was at Oxford with me. I stayed with him in Buenos Ayres when I went round South America. I met him at the Duke of Miraflore's place when I was in Spain; and he has undertaken to come and see me next time he's in London. I'll hop over to Paris. Damme, I'll go to-morrow."

"What will you tell him?"

"What'll I tell him? Why, that—that—he'll be doing me a real good turn, for which I shall be deeply indebted, if he'll put his *cher collègue* of Boruela wise to the fact that there's an *échappé* from Boruela making himself a nuisance to the British authorities at a place in England called Calderton. I suppose we might call General Sir Arthur Calderton a 'British authority,' and although he doesn't know it, this fellow is certainly making himself a nuisance to him. We'll palter with the truth to that extent, and I'll make it quite clear, in a quite devious manner which will appeal to Cipriano, that if it happened that his Boruelan colleague in Paris communicated with his own *cher collègue* in London on the subject, the latter might be extremely grateful to him . . . Yes, I'll make it quite plain to Cipriano, without mentioning a single name except that of Bertie-Norton. If the English branch of the Boruelan Secret Service people move in the matter at all, they'll very soon find out who Bertie-Norton is. And if the fellow has been telling you half the truth about his doings in Boruela and how badly he's wanted there, I should certainly think that they'd take prompt action. Anyway, it's worth trying."

"By Jove, yes!" agreed Henry Waring. "I should say so. On his own showing, he's very badly wanted, and they are the sort of people of whom the saying is true, that if you want a thing badly enough, you'll get it. They want him badly and they'll get him all right."

"And what precisely might you mean by 'get him'?" inquired Sir Walter, suddenly relapsing into his more frigid and formal manner, the spark of his enthusiasm apparently expiring.

"Well, I haven't exactly visualized anything. If they assassinated him, I shouldn't go into mourning; nor if they kidnapped him and ran him out of the country. I . . ."

"Should they do that and run him as far as Boruela, I think we might safely write him off, eh?"

"Yes, but what I really had in mind, and what is

the most we can hope for, I suppose, is that he'd soon find out that they were after him—and clear out of his own accord. Without the wish being father to the thought, I really do think that he's in mortal terror of the Boruelan Secret Police and Secret Service agents."

"Yes. Doubtless with good cause. There's a chance. There's a hope. What would actually happen, I imagine, is that Cipriano would go and see his friend the Boruelan Ambassador, who would certainly mention the matter to the chief agent of their Secret Service in France. He'd send a man with a code message to the Boruelan Secretary in London and he would pass the information on to his Secret Service people here, and tell them to get busy. If, once again, what Ferring-Chevigny has told you is true, it would be quite a feather in the cap of the person responsible for tracking him down and doing—whatever they do to defaulting fugitives and enemies of the Republic of Boruela.

"Supposing the worst happened, I suppose his blood would be on our hands, in a manner of speaking," mused the younger man.

"Nasty manner of speaking, too," growled the elder man.

"His blood on our hands," he mused. "Well, one can wash; one can wash."

"Yes, Sir. I wash mine daily, whether they want it or not," smiled Henry Waring.

IX

It was during this period that I lived in that condition of puzzlement, that state of wonder at myself which has ever since been a cause of puzzlement and wonder.

For at one and the same time, I so detested Montague Ferring-Chevigny that I could scarcely speak civilly to him; nay, could scarcely bear to remain in his presence. And yet, at the same time, I found myself almost liking him for brief periods. When he was talking, telling me and Anthony, or telling me alone, late at night, tales of his amazingly hectic past in North America, Mexico, Peru (where he made a determined and prolonged effort to recover the treasure buried by the Jesuits before their expulsion), in Brazil, up the Amazon, gold-seeking; in every one of the five Continents; and, most particularly, of his last adventures in Boruela, I listened as breathlessly as did Anthony himself, feared to break the spell and the flow of reminiscences by a question, greatly regretted the fact when he fell silent, and almost joined with Anthony in begging for more.

And when I use the term 'amazing,' I don't for one moment mean incredible. They were amazing experiences and adventures and they were not incredible. They bore the stamp of truth, and I believed every word he said.

The local colour was so obviously accurate, the details so full and interesting, the characters and doings of the people of whom he spoke, whether they were Dictators or aboriginal savages, were so consistent and convincing.

Had he been the lawful husband of anyone but

Lady Calderton; had his errand been other than the monstrous and abominable thing that it was; had his presence at Calderton not cast a shadow that was as the shadow of death, I should have liked him.

I confess that I should have liked him very much indeed, and thoroughly enjoyed his company. Admitted that he was a rogue, a scoundrel, and his life one long series of misdeeds, punctuated by periods in prison; admitted that he was an utterly unprincipled adventurer, he still was an adventurer in the better, as well as the worse, sense of the term.

To one who was not suffering—as I was, through Lady Calderton's suffering—from his rascality, he could seem something of a laughing cavalier, a debonair swash-buckler, a soldier of fortune, whose courage and resolution were as high as his morals and principles were low. Had I met him elsewhere and known nothing about him save what he himself told me, I should have been reminded of Claude Duval, the gentleman turned highwayman; of Robin Hood, the noble-born outlaw, cut-purse and cut-throat; possibly of D'Artagnan. Certainly of those charming, care-free Sicilian, Sardinian and other brigands, so popular with those whom they did not rob and detain. Because, apart from this present unspeakable villainy, the things he had done were no worse, and many of them a good deal better, than those that are done in what is called Big Business, things done by men who, by doing them in America, become multi-millionaires, and in England, tread that narrow path of financial glory that leads but to the House of Lords or gaol.

And, as he so often remarked, he knew where to draw the line. Undoubtedly there had been opportunities from which he had shied away in distaste for their abomination.

Nevertheless, beneath a very pleasing exterior,

and behind the façade of an officer and a gentleman of great charm, he was a foul man. No, murderous as I felt towards him, I'll be honest; he wasn't a foul man. He was a man who might have been a fine one, but who did foul things; for verily I believe that he had no conception of the wickedness of what he was now doing, no appreciation at all of the unbelievable horror of the situation that he had created, no notion of the insupportable suffering that he was causing his wife.

Is a man to be tried, condemned and cast into hell, the hell upon earth or the Hell of the Hereafter, because he lacks imagination? That, I think, was the greatest lack of this man who was lacking in so many of the qualities that go to make a decent human being, not to say a gentleman. He was almost devoid of imagination, and he could not begin to understand that his presence at Calderton, his very existence in this world, was destruction and death and damnation to this happy and united family into whose midst he had thrust himself.

Inasmuch as the man from time to time interested me, charmed me, and opened windows upon a world into which I had not so much as peeped, I like to think that, had he been able completely to grasp and understand what he was doing, what agony he was causing, what ruin he was threatening, he would have "drawn the line," would have faded away with an earnest and convincing promise that nothing on earth would induce him to return; would have departed, bitterly regretting that he had done irreparable evil to at least one person, an innocent woman, even if he now went away and were heard of no more.

But no, he could not see it. And perhaps that is one of the main differences between the criminal and the non-criminal person.

Nor was it through any fault of mine that he failed to see the light; through anything being left unsaid by me; anything that he didn't understand.

"Look here," I said one night when he sat late in my room, as he was fond of doing, before returning to the inn where he had established himself, "you said just now that you didn't agree to the assassination of Colonel Pedro Garcia, because you draw the line at that sort of thing."

"Yes, of course I do. Don't you? I have killed plenty of men, but I've always done it face to face and man to man, gun to gun or what-not, but I've never shot anybody in the back or connived at it."

"No, you 'draw the line' at that; and yet you are doing a far worse thing here. Personally, I should consider to be less of a reptile than you, the Spanish Indian half-breed whom Romez hired to murder a man he couldn't 'get' any other way."

"Here! Here! My good Waring. You looking for trouble?"

"No, I'm trying to prevent trouble. Incidentally, perhaps—though quite incidentally—to you."

"Suppose you mind your own business."

"Precisely what I am minding. Lady Calderton—having no one else to protect her—has made it my business."

"What are you going to do?"

"Oh, you'll see. You'll see. But first of all, I'm going to do something simple and easy. Something that may save the most awful and ghastly trouble for everybody, including yourself. I'm going to appeal to your better nature."

Captain Ferring-Chevigny yawned.

"Since there are things at which you draw the line, things too foul even for you, why don't you draw the line here and now? Since you draw it at creeping up behind a man and stabbing him in the back and in the dark, why not draw it at creeping up behind a woman and stabbing her in the back?"

"What are you talking about, my good idiot?"

"I'm talking about the filthy cowardly crime of shamming dead—to save your own dirty hide—for seventeen years, and then suddenly coming to life and announcing to your wife, whose shoes you were never fit to lick—that she has committed bigamy; that she is not the wife of the man she loves and has lived with, for all those years; and that her only child is illegitimate, a bastard who cannot inherit his father's name. If you don't draw the line short of that, you are the rottenest cad and cur of whom I've ever heard or read. You haven't the decency, self-respect or common manhood of one of your jungle savages. You are not a man, you are a louse."

And I added, as coldly as I could, and with as steady a voice as I could compass,

"And you are a louse on which I'll put my heel, before you shall get away with this."

And I gripped the arms of my chair hard, as Ferring-Chevigny's fatuous guffaw assailed my ears.

I stared at him, livid with the rage that I strove to suppress.

"What's biting the boy?" smiled Ferring-Chevigny, and the smile was no grimace, no deliberate sneer intended to annoy. He was genuinely amused.

"Now look here, Waring. Don't go mad and bite me. Whenever a dog has gone mad and bitten me, 'the dog it was that died.' I can quite sympathize with your feeling as the butted-in-upon boy-friend, but I don't want to queer your pitch. I'm not queering your pitch. I mean, damn it all, Waring, live and let live. I don't take any high moral tone with you. What's between you and my wife is your business—

or perhaps Sir Arthur Calderton's. Not that I am threatening you. God forbid. There's nothing of the spoil-sport, much less the blackmailer, about me. You and Lady Calderton . . ."

"Listen," I interrupted, "I've borne a lot from you, and for Lady Calderton's sake I'll bear a lot more—because I know it won't be for long. But if you are as clever as you think you are, you won't make that particular innuendo again. One expects a grunt from a hog, but unless you are pure hog and pure fool too, you won't utter that particular grunt once more."

"No?"

"No. And one can get another note out of a hog, you know. One can get a squeal. Ever heard a hog having its throat cut?"

Again Ferring-Chevigny laughed; and again it was a laughter of genuine amusement and not merely a noise signifying contempt. I did amuse him, and I felt that, in point of fact, I was, compared with him, young, inexperienced and foolish.

But I was sincere, and if there is anything that I believe, it is that sincerity counts—nay, that it is invaluable, is all-important; that the truth is great and will prevail; that right eventually must defeat wrong; and that, well, "somehow good . . ."

"I know I must seem very funny, Ferring-Chevigny," I said, "sort of, what shall we say, melodramatic and . . . Trying to sound tough, eh? Sort of penny-dreadful melodramatic; but I'm speaking quite seriously and soberly now; and I'm going to tell you something that I want you to believe. I give you my word it's the absolute truth. Will you believe me?"

"Why, sure, Sunny-Boy. Shoot," smiled Ferring-Chevigny quite kindly.

"Why, just that," I said. "I want to give you my solemn word that—but for the fear of making bad worse—I *would* shoot you, like the dog you are, rather than let you ruin Lady Calderton's life and wreck Anthony's; not to mention Sir Arthur's."

"Spoken like a little man. I'd get up and pat you on the head, only you'd think I was going to smack you, Sunny-Boy . . . Now you've got that off your little chest, just listen to me . . . What's all this talk about wrecks and ruins, death and damnations and dirty dogs? Where do you get all that stuff? You've been reading books, you know. That's your trouble. *East Lynne. Maria Marten in the Red Barn. The Body on the Line.* Addled your young brain. Now, since my wife has seen fit to put you wise on the situation, I'll take it upon me to put you a bit wiser still. And, in the first place, for God's sake drop this red-ruin, blackmail, blue-murder, pink-rats and pure-white-lily stuff. I haven't the slightest desire or intention of doing your girl-friend the very slightest harm in the world. You are barking up the wrong tree, boy; and all het-up about what hasn't happened and isn't going to happen. Damn it all, you talk as though I had come with a bloody great bomb to plant in the middle of Calderton House. Where do you get the notion? You've been listening to a hysterical woman talking tosh and tripe and twaddle. Dash it, man, I'm Eugene Aram."

"Eugene Aram? Well, thank Heaven for that. He was hanged," I said.

"Eh? Don't talk bosh. Upon my word, I begin to think I'm in a lunatic asylum. I mean the man who came home and saw his wife sitting happy on the knee of another man. I forget whether the latter was the new husband or the tutor. Anyhow, the husband took one look through the window, uttered the deepest groan he had got, and tottered on. Wasn't it Eugene Aram who took the knock?"

"No. It was Enoch Arden."

"That's the sportsman. I knew there was a knock

in it somewhere. I mean I'm Enoch Arden—only I don't totter on. I just sit down. Enoch couldn't have been as tired as I am. I stop. Just sit down in the front garden. And when Mrs. Arden opens the door to put the cat out, I merely mention that I'd be awfully glad of a glass of water and a crust of bread. Where's the harm to Mrs. Arden or to the second Mr. Arden or to the tutor? All I want to do is what old Caspar did. You know, his work was done and all he wanted was, beside his cottage door, to go on sitting in the sun. And didn't give a curse that by him sported on the green somebody else's little by-blow, Wilhelmine. Why, damn it, Waring, Enoch Arden is one of the Good Men of Poetry, not to mention History. Now, this is where I want you to get not only wise but a damn sight wiser. I am Enoch Arden—practically. The only difference is that Enoch toddled on, and I'm not toddling just yet. I'm sitting pretty. Well—what's the trouble, then? Why all these wicked words like *reptile* and *louse* and *dirty dog*? Why these awful threats about shooting-up poor old Enoch Ferring-Chevigny?"

I gazed at the man in the wonder and puzzlement of which I have spoken, for he was in earnest.

"Well, go on. What's the difference between Enoch Arden and Enoch Ferring-Chevigny?"

"I wonder if it's possible that you don't understand the difference between Enoch Arden and you? If you don't, how can I tell you? How shall I put it, except that Enoch Arden was a decently unselfish man, what is called a gentleman, in fact; whereas you are a selfish, self-seeking blackguard who doesn't begin to have the glimmering of an idea of what a gentleman is.

"As you've pointed out, Enoch Arden passed on. You didn't. Enoch Arden would have died sooner than let his wife know that he was alive. He'd have died sooner than have turned up, wrecked her happiness and ruined her life. And Enoch Arden, mind you, hadn't pretended to be dead for his own selfish ends. But when you discovered that your wife was married, what did you do? Stepped straight into the middle of her life—and killed it. And you'll kill her. And if you do, I'll kill you—and feel that I've done at least one useful and meritorious act in my life."

"Loud cheers, Sunny-Boy. I like you when you talk like this. Almost makes me feel I'm back among real men again . . . But you aren't being a bit helpful, you know. You can't think straight. Can't keep to the point. It must be this love, or something. Now, will you just try to let a little light in on my dull mind. Just tell me. So long as nobody except us three—you and I and she—knows a word about it, who's a penny the worse?

"Nobody knows. Nobody is going to know—so far as I'm concerned, at any rate. And presumably neither you nor she is going to shout about it. Very well, then, where's the trouble? Life goes on precisely as before. Sir Arthur Calderton comes home on leave, and she is completely free to go with him to his next job or back to Montiga, or whatever it may be. I'm not demanding any conjugal rights. I've not said one word about blowing the gaff and making trouble. It's you who are doing that. You are making the fuss, not I. Damn it all, man, she is my wife, isn't she? And ninety-nine men out of a hundred would make her toe the line, too. Fairly hold her up to ransom. Yes, and the second Mr. Arden, too. And, mind you, if I were that sort of man, I've got him in a cleft-stick, pretty neatly. He's a very rich man, and I imagine he'd pay handsomely to prevent the scandal. Also to keep the boy. To keep him as his legitimate heir, I mean. Can't leave entailed estates to a little Master Wrong-side-of-the-blanket, I believe. Yes, he'd be in a bit of a hole if I was one of those blackmailing swine, wouldn't he? But I draw the line at blackmail, Waring, and I'll thank you to get that. Get it into your fat head and keep it there . . . I don't know what you take me for, and I don't know whether you judge others by yourself, but I can assure you that nothing is further from *my* mind than blackmailing or trouble-making or wrecking peoples' lives, or any other such damn nonsense. Lot of melodramatic bilge.

"Fact is, you are jealous, Waring. That's what is the matter with you. And let me tell you, I don't think you show up at all well. If you ask me, you're a damned little dog-in-the-manger. Devil admire me! What do you think you want? You're sitting pretty. You're getting it both ways. Whereas I'm not to be allowed to exist, according to you. I ought to be shot—and you are going to shoot me! Well, shut both eyes tight, and put both your forefingers round the trigger, listen for the hell of a bang, and then see if you haven't shot the canary . . . I'll have another drink, if you'll touch the bell."

"Time you were going," I said, "in more senses than one."

"How can I go in more senses than one, Sunny-Boy?"

"I don't know. But I do know how it can be time you went, in more senses than one."

Again Ferring-Chevigny laughed.

"What they call veiled threats, eh? You'll get me all nervous if you go on like that, Waring. Now, don't do it, boy. Drop it. And try to see sense. You talk about selfishness. Drop some of your own damned selfishness and try to see somebody else's point of view, for a change. Anoint my soul! Any-body'd think you were the husband; or Sir Arthur Calderton—instead of his employee. I don't want to blow my own trumpet, but damn it all, man, can't you recognize a bit of magnanimity when you see it?

I'm not bearing the slightest grudge against Katherine. Nor against Sir Arthur. Why, I'm not even bearing malice against you—and surely I might be excused if I thought,

" '*Well, I'll wring* that *bird's neck, anyhow*' . . .

"I not only act magnanimously but I show every possible consideration. I might say I act with the utmost delicacy. I have taken every possible care to remain incog, to come secretly and tread warily.

"Can't you grasp that everybody in this country who ever heard my name, knows that I'm dead. Dead as a damned door-nail. And forgotten as though I had never lived. I come back as silently as a shadow—to find my wife has not only got a husband and a son, but a 'tutor' as well, and all I say is,

" '*Right, I make no complaint. I merely suggest that my lawful wife gives me a much-needed leg-up and helps me round a difficult corner. Tides me over for a while. I don't want much and I may not want it for long, but I do think that in return for my complete forbearance I can expect a little help.*'

"And what do I find? Here are you, with absolutely no legal status whatsoever, damning and blasting me, and insulting me for all you are worth, and talking about shooting me up! It's funny, in a way. So are you, Waring. Damn funny, really. What do you know about Miss Christabel Hardacre?"

"Very little, except that she's a hard-riding sportswoman. Hunted the hounds during the war."

"Rich woman, isn't she?"

"I've never asked her."

X

The gentleman known here and there, but not everywhere, as Señor Diogenes Barrios, awoke with a piercing scream from a very terrible nightmare. He had been dreaming that he was back in the Old Homeland; and that, having committed an indiscretion, he was going to be kept dangling about, as the Police Sergeant used to say, in the happy village in which Don Diogenes had had the good fortune to be born. Kept dangling about on a meat-hook; from a tree; by the dusty wayside; in the blistering sunshine. And if he were alive by evening, that was his good fortune, and showed that he was a favourite of the Saints. And if he were dead, that was just too bad. Or perhaps not so bad.

Anyhow, the nightmare had been unspeakably horrible.

Señor Diogenes Barrios raised himself from the lumpy surface of his straw-stuffed palliasse and looked round his attic room wherein there was no beauty—for certainly there was none in the eye of the beholder. Very sordid, very fusty, very frowsy, wholly unworthy of occupation by a young gentleman rejoicing in the euphonious title of Don Diogenes Barrios.

And he must have been reckless last night, for his suit, his one-and-only but excellent suit, lay crumpled, undignified, where it had been thrown upon the dirty floor. The suit over which he usually spent an industrious *quart d'heure*, turning the trousers inside out; wetting the creases very carefully with his face-rag, soaping them skilfully with the edge of his long-lasting, almost immortal, cake of soap; re-turning them and folding them with the utmost care, and laying them reverently beneath the palliasse that, in his very slumbers, he might do good, as his weight aided the pressure of the mattress in ever more sharply defining the creases of the admirable trousers.

The coat he would hang upon a pair of beautiful wooden shoulders that had once been the property of no less a person than a Secretary of Legation.

The waistcoat he was wont to damp and "iron" with the smooth base of a heavy water carafe.

And there lay the suit, not only having been denied this care, but having been positively maltreated. There would be balls of grey fluff upon the underside of those creased dishonoured trousers; on that of the coat which had gathered grace and shapeliness from the wooden shoulders that had once been the property of a Secretary of Legation.

He must have been mad last night. But what self-respecting *caballero* did not at times risk, nay court, the divine madness sent by Bacchus? Still, it was damn silly to go and get drunk the night before he had to go to the Legation.

And with a groan, Señor Diogenes Barrios fell back upon his grey and greasy pillow, and stared at the sloping ceiling which, close above his aching head, presented him with the familiar map of the basin of the Amazon, a river that rose just above the door, flowed across the ceiling, receiving numerous tributaries, and debouched into the wallpaper so near that he could put a finger into its estuary. It was unwise to do so, however, as the estuary was apt to widen unduly, and become a somewhat alarming delta.

Well, anyhow, with an immaculate and well-creased suit or a creased and dishevelled one, he must be at the Legation, according to orders.

What could they be wanting? It wasn't pay-day, worse luck; and he wasn't conscious of any shortcoming or wrong-doing. He had sent in his reports, faithfully and regularly, upon every one of his clients, as he termed, with pleasant humour, the innocents, the suspects, the worse than suspects, and the already condemned, whom it was his business to shadow, and whose movements it was his pleasing duty to report.

And he hadn't been faking, either. That is to say, not unduly; not more than usual. A *caballero* must have a night off sometimes; and if the infamous Señor Ramon had not been visited by, and closeted with, the yet more infamous Don Diego, there was no great harm in saying that he had, and giving chapter and verse, time and period. Lots of interesting if imaginary details.

But, *Madre de Dios*, it would be most awkward if, when he reached the Legation, he were to be confronted with his detailed and documented account of a day in the life of the infamous Señor Ramon, and informed that the gentleman had committed suicide on the *previous* day; had been picked up by the British Police on misinformation received; or indeed liquidated at the urgent request of the Dictator.

Still, he had never had any bad luck of that sort, and had never been threatened with punishment.

No, thought Don Diogenes Barrios, as he drew a venomous-looking cigarette from a somewhat battered package that lay beside the bed, lit the black Boruelan tobacco and deeply inhaled the acrid smoke; no, he wouldn't be here if he had. They only punished once.

Why should he worry? He could honestly flatter himself that he was useful; very useful. They couldn't deny it; and they'd allow so useful a man as himself a little latitude if he did make such a mistake as to report the daily activities of an already dead man. Probably it was another job—

though hitherto the job had come to him, so to speak. Orders and directions had been given him without his having to attend at the Legation in person. Sometimes in the dark corner of a cinema; sometimes at the Anarchist Club; sometimes in the little secret room behind Mother Viega's kitchen; sometimes sitting in the middle of the great stretch of nice green grass in one of the parks, where no eavesdropper could come within a quarter of a mile without being seen for what he was.

Well, he'd soon know; and, having finished his cigarette, the Señor rose from his bed, and set about the business of doing whatever his skill, loving care and remorseful solicitude could do for the evilly-entreated suit.

Having done his best, Don Barrios permitted himself to do perhaps a little less than his best in the matter of washing; but it cannot be denied that he passed the face-rag over his more salient features, and naturally got his hands wet in the process. But any lack of energy in this direction was compensated by the almost excessive labour that he lavished on his hair, anointing it with pungently scented oil and brushing it straight back from his forehead, with an almost savage industry.

And when he had finished, none could deny that this, his crowning glory, was effulgent, sleek and glossy beyond praise. Quite beyond. It was as though a close-fitting skull-cap of black satin adorned his shapely head.

Between collars he hung in doubt. There was one, immaculate as new samite, the white flower of a blameless laundress; and there was another which matched the chaste mauve shirt with its alternating plum and gooseberry stripes, but which no amount of careful licking at the edge or sponging at the back could, by the most generous standards of judgment, make into a really clean collar.

The white one it must be; and who should find
fault? Did not the Secretaries of Legation themselves wear white collars? That they wore them with
white shirts, black ties or black cravats, black coats
and white-edged black waistcoats, was neither here
nor there—unless one were being pedantic, and
then of course it was there. But what South American gentleman of all the inmates of all the Embas-
sies of South America would cavil at a white collar
because it was worn with a mauve shirt of plum
and gooseberry stripe, and a suit of pleasing pur-
plish hue?

Having dressed, Señor Barrios descended the
uncarpeted stairs that led from his eyrie to the
delicatessen shop of Señor Alphonso Alvares and
the Soho slum of which that shop was an amenity.

Looking up from her seat behind the counter,
Señorita Concepçion Alvares eyed Don Diogenes
with warm approval. A most handsome young gentleman with his natty purple suit, yellowish velour
hat, yellowish brown shoes and pretty socks that
matched the pretty tie of palest pink, green-barred.

"Early, Don Diogenes!" she murmured, looking
up through her long black eye-lashes and shaking
back her long black curls. "Important business, one
would say."

"Most," replied the Señor with an airy wave of
his cane. "At the Embassy."

"Have you had any breakfast?"

"Yes, yes, most ample, thank you," replied Señor
Barrios, who had scraped out the residuary contents of a sticky tin labelled *Coffee and Condensed
Milk*, a compound sweet and bland, and which,
followed by a draught of water, gave for a few
minutes a pleasing illusion of *petit déjeuner* or
post-prandial coffee.

"But for the love of the Most Pure and Most
Illustrious Mother of our Lord Jesus Christ, give me

a fag, Concepçion."

Turning to the shelves behind the counter, the girl reached for a packet, the while Don Diogenes reached swiftly for a sausage-roll, slipped it into his pocket with his left hand, and, as the girl turned back, extended his right for the cigarettes—a packet of ten real American Giraffes.

"On me," whispered the girl, to whom the *delicatessen* of New York East Side were not alien corn . . . .

Choosing a seat in the Park, Señor Diogenes Barrios sat him down and munched his sausage-roll, lit a cigarette, and kept his eye upon the time.

Having finished and rested from his labours, he arose, and strolling steadily in the direction of Queen's Gate, arrived, by somewhat circuitous approach, before the imposing portals of a very fine house which stood back from the broad clean pavement of a street of similar mansions; a street incredibly proper and correct; the sort of thoroughfare through which none but the most respectable could be expected to pass, and only on the most reputable business.

A semi-circular drive joined the house with this road; and, from the drive, a flight of snow-white steps ascended to the great front door.

As he turned in at the first of the two gates, a man lurking in a glorified sentry-box stepped out and confronted him, a man in a green and gold livery, a livery at once dignified and impressive.

Fixing upon Don Diogenes the hard stare of a pair of cruel eyes that looked out from his face of a swarthy prize-fighter, the man raised heavy eyebrows in silent question, the effect being not a little deterrent and discouraging, not to say insulting. For though the grim mouth remained firmly shut, a mere slit in the sallow craggy face, the raised eyebrows indicated quite distinctly that here was no

465

necessity for the effort of speech, no need for the wasting of the spoken word upon so insignificant an intruder. Had the guardian of the outer portal opened his mouth, or one small corner thereof, and said,

"Where do you think you are going, miserable little dog?" the visitor might have felt less insulted.

However, Señor Diogenes Barrios had a spirit of his own, a clear conscience, and an excellent excuse. And he, too, without the use of speech, made insulting reply. Taking from his breast pocket a card which bore nothing but a number and a signature, he held it up before the forbidding face of the dark-browed Cerberus, thrust it closer than was necessary, and then, ranging himself beside the man, pointed to the figures, to the first letter, the second letter, the third letter, and the others, one by one, until each separate letter had been touched.

Had he said,

"It's no good my showing you this, my good fool, for of course an ignorant oaf like you can't read," the insult would have been no clearer.

Swinging his cane and wishing he had the courage to whistle, Señor Barrios marched past the surly official; mounted the great white steps, raised his hand to the great golden, or perhaps brazen, knocker; and was somewhat disconcerted to find it snatched from his hand as the door swung open to reveal a man arrayed in green morning-dress piped with yellow, a black and yellow striped waistcoat, and a shining dress-shirt, wing collar and white bow tie. And magnificent black side-whiskers in the Spanish fashion.

To him also, but with more respectful gesture, Don Barrios showed the card; whereupon the man glanced contemptuously at the Señor, closed the door behind him, and turning, pointed towards yet another functionary, clothed in solemn black. This man sat at a table on which were neat piles of sorted letters, a large ledger, pens, ink and paper.

Across the great flagged hall marched Señor Barrios, bowed to the major-domo, butler, hall-porter or whatever he might be, and again held out the talismanic card.

And the third, perhaps, of the insults with which he had been received by these pampered under-lings was the grossest of all, for the man at the table, though looking straight before him, was evi-dently able to see right through the *caballero* with-out actually seeing either him or his extended card.

Deep in thought, and adding sums of money in a semi-audible Spanish voice, he continued to dis-regard the early morning visitor to the Embassy.

Well, on the fellow's head, on his silly bald fat head, let it be, thought Don Diogenes Barrios, as he regarded the heavy-featured face before him, pom-pous, self-satisfied and smug, redeemed only from utter insignificance by flat and perfectly trained side-whiskers that, venturing out from the safety of his ears, made their way across his vast cheeks, each ending courageously in an upward-pointing tip.

Noble whiskers. They had probably earned him his job, thought Diogenes. Better than the foot-man's. Badges of the highest rank of flunkey.

And Diogenes coughed gently, deprecatingly, presented the card a little nearer to the face of the thinker, and awaited results.

Uncomfortable as he felt, he had no real fear of these underlings. What could they do? They had not the ear of such people as the *Chancelier d'Am-bassade*. They had nobody's ears, save their own ugly cabbage-leaves. They could give themselves airs, but nobody else gave them any.

"Señor," he murmured softly. "Doubtless the

instructions of the Privy Councillor, Señor Rafael José Albarado, are not worthy of your consideration, but the fact remains that I . . ."

The man at the table, with the appearance of seeing even better and further through the body of Diogenes, counted with a slightly increased rapidity, and stroked one of the beautiful flat and forward-pointing whiskers that seemed painted upon his sallow cheek—and a soft voice at the *caballero's* ear bade him step this way.

Turning, and seeing a fourth man rapidly departing in the direction of a closed door, Diogenes followed him, feeling that on the whole, the thinker had won, for certainly there was no conceivable evidence that he had been for one moment aware of his visitor's existence.

The bastard must have pressed a bell-push underneath his desk, Diogenes thought resentfully, and promised himself that, in the extremely unlikely event of the opportunity ever presenting itself, he'd press something into *him*.

Opening the door, and waiting for Señor Diogenes Barrios to pass through into the corridor, the man led the way up a flight of service stairs to the floor above, and along another corridor to a door on which was painted in gold letters upon a little black oblong, the words *State Councillor Albarado*.

Knocking and listening intently for answer, the man who, as Don Diogenes now noticed, was arrayed in a complete morning-suit of dark green with brass buttons, whispered,

"Stay there, you," opened the door, entered, and closed it behind him.

Outside this door, in the dingy ill-lit corridor, Señor Diogenes Barrios waited, with sinking courage and mounting apprehension.

What did they think he was? And what was this place? A prison, or only a huge trap? That made four men who had had to handle him before he had even reached this grandee's door, if one counted the fat slob at the table. Not that he had handled him much, but undoubtedly there were four of them between him and the street, and doubtless four more as well. And added to the *caballero's* apprehensions was an unpleasant feeling of claustrophobia.

Which way should one run? There were more stairs leading up at the far end of the corridor. If one sprinted . . .

The door opened. The messenger reappeared, and, with curt gesture of his thumb, bade him enter. As Diogenes obeyed, the man closed the door behind him, and left him alone in a vast sunny room with Don Rafael José Albarado, *Chancelier d'Ambassade.*

This gentleman, a person of undoubtedly different type from those whom Diogenes had hitherto encountered, looked up from the letter that he was writing, favoured the *caballero* with a flashing smile that displayed perfect little teeth beneath a perfect little moustache, clipped, trimmed and curled, and studied him with cold relentless eyes.

"So you are D.B.6, are you?" he said, and the *caballero* bowed gracefully in answer.

"And the author of these interesting reports," continued the Councillor, drawing a wire basket towards him and taking from it a blue cardboard file containing papers.

"H'm," he observed non-committally, flicking them over with some contempt. "And pray, my good Señor D.B.6, do you imagine that any one of these alleged reports is of the very faintest interest or value whatsoever?"

And as Diogenes maintained a respectful silence, the Councillor shot a sudden look at him, and with a sound suggestive of the cracking of a whip-lash, added,

"Answer."

"To be honest I do, Your Excellency," admitted Diogenes. "They give an exact and faithful account of the movements of the men whom I have been instructed to watch; and some of them have been obtained at the risk of . . ."

"The cost of half a bottle of bad *vin ordinaire* or half a pint of filthy British beer, eh? Not much other risk than the loss of those, I imagine."

And he eyed his visitor with a look of slightly wondering contempt. This was his speciality, and he had acquired it in Boledo, cultivated it at Madrid, practised it in Berlin and perfected it in London. There was probably no one in the whole personnel of his country's Diplomatic Service who was his equal at the production and use of that stare which, without the use of language, expressed complete unbelief, utter distaste, and the profoundest contempt, just faintly tinged with pity.

"What do you suppose we pay you for, my good creature?" he asked.

And again as with the hiss of a whip, the ensuing silence was broken by the word,

"Answer."

"For . . . for work, Your Excellency. For taking serious risks, running into great danger; keeping a constant and watchful eye upon the movements of the suspects."

"Yes. That is what we pay you for; and unless you want a free trip Home and free quarters (free is a rather amusing word in that connection, isn't it?), free quarters, I say, in one of the lower cells—they contain a foot of slime, you know, and you have to sit in it—at San Carlos, you are going to earn your pay."

The smile died away from the pleasant mouth of the *Chancelier d'Ambassade* as, with a sudden frowning stare of his cold and calculating eyes, he shot at the uncomfortable Diogenes the sudden question,

"Where is Mr. Sherry?"

"Excellency, my information is that Señor Xeres has not yet . . ."

"Your *information!*" growled the Councillor with a contemptuous sneer. "Like the rest of this 'information' here, you twittering twerp."

He flicked the file that lay before him as though it were a noxious insect.

"Now, my friend, I'll give *you* some information, and I'll give you some instructions; and if you value your job, not to say your freedom, I recommend you to pay careful attention. Listen.

"Mr. Sherry, as he used to call himself—Señor Xeres, as you call him—is in England; and the Boruelan Government doesn't want him in England. Understand? Where it does want him is in Boledo, somewhere in the neighbourhood of the Rotunda. Now, if you could get him there, or anywhere else in Boruela, you might come here grinning and with your tail up as though you expected a bone. And you'd get a bone, too—or a bonus. A gold one. But there's not much hope of your being clever enough to get him *there* . . . Anyway, you've got to get him away from where he is, and as far away as you can. And to do that, you'll have to frighten him—badly. Can you manage that much?"

Señor Diogenes Barrios smiled brightly.

"I'll undertake to promise that he will start travelling, quite soon after I get in touch with him . . . If he does not, he'll meet with an accident and . . ."

But there was no answering smile upon the lips of the *Chancelier d'Ambassade*. On the contrary, his heavy black brows drew together over his reptilian glittering eyes.

"Listen, once again, *hombre*. The man who was known in Boruela as Sherry is to be frightened away from the place where he is at present hiding. Just repeat that to yourself until it penetrates your brain and effects a lodgment, will you? I said nothing of 'accidents.' What will happen to *you* will not be an accident, if you exceed your instructions, or if you fail to carry them out. Mind, if you were clever enough to help him to meet with a genuine accident, well, that would be just too bad—for him. And very nice for you. But don't forget what country you are in. And remember what happens in the case of 'accidents' here.

"You go and commit a murder, and leave a trail that leads straight to the front door of this house, and you'll have most excellent cause to wish you had never been born. Very well, there's your information.

"Sherry's in England, in hiding. And he has got to be frightened out of England. If he met with a genuine accident on the way, well, the worse for him and the better for you, as I say. But if you bring one shadow of suspicion on you, and so on us, you'll be badly in need of a hiding-place yourself. So go and frighten him—to death if you can—but out of England, anyhow . . .

"Very well, there are your instructions.

"Now you will go and see the First Secretary, Señor Ignatio Cedeno, and he will give you fuller details and further instructions. *Adios*, my dear Señor—er—what-is-it? Yes, Diogenes Barrios."

And with a charming smile of the mouth and a cold forbidding stare of the eyes, the *Chancelier d'Ambassade* sped his parting visitor.

As the door opened in answer to the bell that Diogenes had not seen him ring, he added,

"And do take care of yourself. I should be so sorry to hear that you had got into any sort of difficulty."

Without instructions from the *Chancelier*, the

messenger, having closed the door of the room, led the puzzled and uncomfortable Diogenes along the same corridor, up the flight of stairs that he had seen at the end of it, along another corridor, and again halted at a big door on which also was painted in black letters on a gilt oblong, the name and official title of the occupant.

This gentleman proved to be more urbane, better informed, and altogether more agreeable than the *Chancelier*.

"Ah, yes," said he, looking up from his desk as the messenger approached, followed by Diogenes. "Thank you," and as the man retired, seemed to hover on the brink of inviting his visitor to sit down. But on the brink he halted, resumed his writing, and apparently forgot all about the matter.

After standing for several minutes admiring the magnificent marble fire-place, and wondering how and why it was that one man should sit in a padded armchair at a beautiful desk while another stood humbly beside it, Diogenes was suddenly recalled from abstract and idle speculation to immediate realities, as in a pleasant, quiet voice, the First Secretary suddenly began to speak.

"Go to-morrow to Euston Station and take a single ticket to Calderton. I'll write it down. There, from the station, to the village inn *not* called the Calderton Arms. Find a humbler one, a pot-house, a little wayside *posada*, a *pulqueria*; take a room and tell what story you like. Play whatever rôle suits you best and in which you find yourself most at home; a hungry artist; a cheap professional photographer making picture-post-cards; a publisher's agent's hack doing that part of the country for the illustrations of the guide-book of their famous series. If you prefer it, you can be an—er—what do they call it—hiker; or a fisherman, though I don't suppose you know the jargon and technique of the sport.

"Perhaps you had better be a seedy and needy commercial traveller, in what, shall we say, barber's-shop hair-oil, perfumes and scented soap—whether on holiday or on business.

"Anyhow, keep there, stay there, continue to stay there, and be as inconspicuous as possible. It won't matter in the least if you are inconspicuous to the point of furtiveness, so that you give the impression that the furtive inconspicuousness is intentional; and that you have some good reason for wishing to attract notice.

"If the gossips in the bar regard you as a bit of a mystery and speculate as to whether you are lying low for a bit, if not actually in hiding, that would be all to the good.

"Now then, having done that, discover a man calling himself Bertie-Norton. He visits the mansion, Calderton House. He's your man. None other than our friend Mr. Sherry, late of Boledo and Paracay, Bolivar, Caibo—and Boruela generally.

"Now, Mr. Sherry seems to think he can settle down in peace and quiet in his peaceful quiet country. In spite of what he did, and what he tried to do, to our country. Well, it's going to be your job to disabuse him of the idea altogether. He's certainly going to realize that he's not as far from South America as he thinks he is. And that even if he were, he wouldn't be safe. He has been kept on the run, all over the two Americas as well as over Europe, and you've got to start him on the run again.

"But, mind, there's to be no rough stuff of any sort. We don't want the British Police in this; and although they are the most unobtrusive police in the world, they are on the spot quicker than any others, when there's trouble.

"So there's to be *no* trouble; no arrest; no inquest—either on you or on him.

"What you have to do, is to get him away from there; and the further you get him, the better, especially if it's out of England. And if at the furthermost point, anything happened to him, well, so much the better again.

"But there must be no sort or kind of bother in this country, for if there were and you survived it, you wouldn't do so for long. In any case, as you know, we repudiate you, of course; but if there were trouble, we should do more than that. It is you who would be endeavouring to get as far away as possible—and you'd fail.

"However, don't let's talk of such unpleasant things."

And the First Secretary sighed deeply in ready if anticipatory sympathy.

"Well," he continued more brightly, "I shall hope to see you again, Señor D.B.6, to hear your report from your own lips. And I shall expect you to be able to tell me that Mr. Sherry has departed, in haste, for what he fondly imagines to be an unknown destination. When he reaches it, someone else shall look after him. Unless, of course, he meets with an accident there or *en route*, and departs not only for an unknown destination but for a better or, at any rate, another, world . . . Now as to expenses . . ."

XI

"What's to be the end of it? And when will it come? If this goes on much longer, I begin to think I shall almost welcome the—end," said Lady Calderton, as we sat in the drawing-room awaiting the arrival of our Captain Montague Ferring-Chevigny, who had telephoned to say that he would have the pleasure of dining with us this evening. He had been away on his own urgent private affairs for a few days, and had given us a breathing-space—an unspeakably anxious and miserable time of suspense and fear, but a breathing-space, a rest from his eternal guffaw, smiles and small-talk.

There we sat and there we waited, absolutely impotent, defenceless, entirely in this man's hands; entirely at his beck and call, save in one or two minor matters on which he had given way before Lady Calderton's absolutely final refusal to do as he wished.

She would not, for example, consent to his coming to live in the house. Nor would she agree to seeing him alone again. Nor would she fall in with his suggestion that she should invite various people whom he named and whom he wished to meet at her table. If people dropped in at tea-time when he was there, we had no choice but to introduce him; or if people were lunching and he suddenly arrived just in time for the meal, as quite frequently he did, again he had to be introduced.

And this sort of thing was far from being the least of Lady Calderton's troubles and daily trials at this time, for it had to be done naturally and easily, so that there might be nothing in the slightest

476

degree unusual, much less suspicious, about the manner of his introduction. At the same time, she was most anxious to avoid any appearance of vouching for the new-comer, of sponsoring him in the least degree, or of endeavouring to launch him in County society. And this was the occasion of bitter complaint on the part of Ferring-Chevigny, and of acrimonious accusation.

Inasmuch as Lady Calderton invariably rose and left us when he began this sort of complaint, whether we were at table or not, he soon learned to make me his lightning-conductor, to make his complaints to me, and to bid me see to it that Lady Calderton 'came to heel,' as he was pleased to describe it.

So there we sat and waited for him, and Lady Calderton wondered aloud how much longer she could bear it.

"I don't know how much longer it's going on," I said, "but I'm perfectly certain that it won't be for very long, and that there is every reason to hope."

"Hope? For what? So long as he's alive . . ."

Yes. So long as he was alive. That was the thought that was for ever at the back of my mind, and for ever striving to push its way to the front.

"Well, he won't live for ever, and I feel perfectly certain that he won't live in this part of the world much longer. As I told you, my uncle has a plan, and something will come of it."

"Grateful as I am, both to you and Sir Walter, I don't see what good can come of any plan. I can't see a gleam of hope. The very fact that the man is alive, wherever he may be, makes any plan useless. Suppose he went to the absolute ends of the earth and remained there for the remainder of his life, the facts are the same."

"Yes, but the position isn't."

"So long as he's alive . . ." whispered Lady Calderton.

And I realized with a little cold pang of horror that she too had the same thought at the back of her mind. It was inevitable. Also that the thought at the back of her mind, as in my own, was for ever striving to push its way to the front.

So long as he was alive . . .

Nothing on earth but his death could alter the position. His death now would put the hands of the clock back seventeen years, to the time of his supposed death.

"It would alter the position," I said again, "very materially—completely, in fact—if he were at the other side of the world and were never heard of again. Life would go on as before, and everything be again as it was."

"While I knew he was alive? While I feared, every time that a door opened . . ."

The door opened and Ferring-Chevigny entered.

"So sorry if I'm late," he smiled, flashing his excellent teeth. "Who said a glass of Amontillado?"

A footman entered with a large silver tray on which were decanter and glasses. Lady Calderton declined the offered wine.

"Sherry, sir?" said Robert, taking the tray to Ferring-Chevigny.

"For God's sake, don't call it that," he said abruptly, pouring himself a glass.

"No, sir," replied the stolid Robert.

"Why not call sherry what it is?" I asked, for the sake of making conversation, my usual and somewhat difficult task when we three were together.

"Because I hate the word," was the curious reply.

"Damn fine wine, though," he added, smacking his lips. "One good thing that comes out of that accursed country."

"Accursed country? What's wrong with Spain?" I

asked.

"Spaniards," was the reply, and Jenkins announcing dinner, we made our way into the dining-room, as curious a procession of three as went in to dinner in England that evening.

It was terribly difficult to keep up appearances before the servants, or rather, it was an anxious and nerve-racking business to remember that this must be done. I don't know whether Jenkins had any suspicion that anything was wrong, but it was impossible to tell. Not that it mattered very greatly, for he was absolutely devoted to Lady Calderton, had the greatest admiration and respect for Sir Arthur, and would, I think, have lain down his life for Anthony.

He had been at Calderton House for some forty years, from the days when he was an apple-cheeked page or pantry-boy, and had been taught his work by his own father, who had himself been butler to the late Sir Arthur Calderton. In point of fact, there had been Jenkinses in Calderton village for as long as there had been Caldertons in Calderton House. And that was going back somewhere in the direction of Doomsday Book.

Although Lady Calderton had firmly refused to introduce Ferring-Chevigny as her brother, a course which he had suggested, I rather fancy that Jenkins suspected him to be a relation of hers; a brother or a cousin, possibly a bit of a detrimental, not to say a ne'er-do-well; and perhaps the black sheep of the Fairfax family.

However, I always did my best, when servants were present, to keep the conversation light and natural, easy and flowing. For my, more or less, successful efforts in this direction, poor Lady Calderton was deeply grateful, since she herself, not unnaturally, found it practically impossible to behave as though nothing whatever was wrong, as though she were as light-hearted, happy and care-free as she had been before he came, and as though no cruel weight of misery crushed her spirit. She found it all-but-impossible to address a remark to this incredible death's-head "guest," well-nigh impossible so much as to eat in his presence . . .

A pause in the conversation, a miserable hiatus, one of those dreadful gaps which it seems impossible to fill; Lady Calderton looking like a ghost toying with the food upon her plate; Ferring-Chevigny enjoying his food and wine, taking his ease as though at his inn; I racking my brains for something more to say, and finding nothing. It had all been said, every topic exhausted, every last word uttered, silence growing longer and deeper, Jenkins and Robert standing like graven images.

I must say something. What was I saying? What had I said?

"So you've been having some good sport, eh?"

Just as though anything had been said about sport. Just as though Ferring-Chevigny would appreciate kind inquiries as to what he had been doing during his recent absence from Calderton.

Putting down his glass, he shot a quick look at me.

"Sport?" he said, and laughed his smug guffaw. "Might call it that, too. Yes. Good hunting."

"Had some good hunting, eh?"

"Oh, you might put it like that," he smiled.

"Which pack?"

"Well now, I wouldn't really say I was hunting with a pack. Doin' a little lone-wolf huntin'. All on my own."

This wouldn't do. This would sound queer to Jenkins and Robert, if they were listening, which probably they were not. Doubtless Jenkins was sufficiently occupied in watching plates and glasses, and Robert in watching Jenkins, as a well-trained sheep-dog does its shepherd.

Another awkward silence.

Ferring-Chevigny emptied his glass.

"Met a friend of yours, Kathie," he said as he put it down.

"Yes?"

"Sent her love to you. Coming to see you one of these days. Something about the Annual Charity Ball, or some such doings. Christabel Hardacre."

"Yes, she runs a charity ball every year. For the County Hospital."

"Wants you to have it here, this year."

"Yes. It's always held here when we are at home."

"So Christabel said. She'll be descending on you one day soon. I told her I should be staying here."

Lady Calderton gave him a cold questioning look, with faintly raised eyebrows.

"Here or hereabouts," he smiled. "I told her I should be seeing her when she came over. You'll let me know when she comes, won't you?"

"Why?"

"Oh, we are great old pals, Christabel and I. I like her. Damn fine woman."

"She's certainly a very fine horsewoman."

"You know her, Waring?" he asked.

"I've met Miss Hardacre," I said, and, turning to Lady Calderton, added,

"She dropped in once or twice at tea-time, to ask about you, and to see Anthony."

"Yes, she always looks in when she's over on the Calderton side of the county. Comes and stays with us sometimes."

"You know her well?" said Ferring-Chevigny.

"I've known her for a good many years."

"Like her?"

"Yes. We haven't very much in common, as I don't hunt; but no one could help liking her for her honesty, good nature and cheeriness."

"Wonder she has never married," mused Ferring-Chevigny. "Unhappy love-affair or something?"

"I have heard her say that the more she sees of men the better she likes hounds and horses," replied Lady Calderton coldly.

And this seemed to amuse Captain Montague Ferring-Chevigny, for not only did he laugh his famous laugh, but from time to time chuckled irrepressibly thereafter.

XII

Captain Ferring-Chevigny emerged from the door of his inn, snuffed the lovely morning air, and gazed around upon the peaceful and beautiful rural scene with the deepest satisfaction.

How utterly and perfectly English. England might be a good country to get out of, but it was a damned good country to return to, say what you will. No country in the world like it. In fine weather, *bien entendu.* On a day like this. But as for the winter, or worse still, the spring—as the poet says— 'Oh to be out of England now that Spring is here.'

Well, thank God that Montague Ferring-Chevigny was under no compulsion to get out of England. Never again.

And as he was wont to do, quite frequently these days, the Captain burst into tuneful song:

> "*Safe at last, the harbour past,*
> *Safe in my f-a-a-ther's home . . .*"

Not exactly 'father's' though, he mused, nor precisely brother-in-law's—though that might be a good line for Katty to take. Monty the long-lost black-sheep brother whom the family never mentioned. Arthur's new brother-in-law. But perhaps she wouldn't like to produce an unknown brother all sudden-like. However, that was her affair, not his. Queer relationship and situation altogether. But a very nice one. Very nice. Yes, this would do for Uncle Monty quite beautifully.

And Uncle Monty strode forth across the road and the stile, and took the field-path that led in the direction of Calderton House.

Do very nicely indeed, British climate included. He'd hunt in the winter with two or three packs, and be very snug on non-hunting days, whether at Calderton House or the Calderton Arms; and February and March he could spend down the Riviera way, having a flutter at the tables on brother Arthur's money. Monty at Monte, what? Pity it would have to be Arthur's money, but there it was. Since his own was for ever lost in Boruela, he couldn't help himself. A gentleman can't live without pocket-money, even with the run of his teeth, and all found.

Then in the summer, England would be good enough; and perhaps a run up to Scotland in the autumn. Grouse and salmon in due season.

Yes, that would do beautifully. Well, well, he had seen a peck of trouble. Pots of it. And now it would be a case of pots of money. Flesh-pots; potting the red; plucking the pigeons; dealing the cards—from the bottom of the pack; and . . .

Hullo! What was that?

The sense of smell is the one most immediately connected with the faculty of memory. Neither sights nor sounds, flavours nor the sense of touch, call up a mental vision as quickly as does an odour, whether it be wood-smoke, bringing instantly a vision of African and other camp-fires; a whiff of jasmine, recalling an Eastern jungle glade, heavy with the scent of flowering trees; the scent of hay bringing to mind a June day in England's pleasant countryside. And what Captain Ferring-Chevigny smelt brought him to a sudden stop, and the happy look of pleasure and contentment, even as he halted in his stride, was replaced by one of anxiety, not to say alarm; his smile by a quick, deep frown.

For, from the other side of the hedge by which he walked, came a faint but unmistakable odour that he knew too well—a mixture of the smell of a Boruelan cigarette and of a perfume, happily unknown in England. How many hundreds, thousands, hundreds of thousands, of times had he smelt that beastly scent, whether used as a body-perfume for the dominance of even less agreeable odours, or as hair-oil. And mingled, too, with that peculiar acrid smell of a *pitillo* of black tobacco, wrapped, not in rice-paper but in straw-husk.

It cannot be said that Ferring-Chevigny's face paled nor that his hand trembled; but it was obvious to the man watching through the hedge, that if the big Englishman were not actually frightened, he was most certainly perturbed.

And that would do for the present.

Stepping quietly back into the long grass that grew up close to the hedge on his side, Señor Diogenes Barrios turned and walked quickly away, unseen, in the direction opposite to that in which his quarry was proceeding.

Yes, he flattered himself, that was a very good start. Undoubtedly Señor Xeres had got a whiff of the *pitillo*. And of the good strong perfume.

He had got it all right, and it had given him a bit of a jar; and mentally the *caballero* made out his report, stating how, having observed that Mr. X was in the habit of taking the field-path opposite the inn, he had discovered a suitable spot in the high hedge bordering that path, had secreted himself there, and that the breeze, being in the right direction, had allowed the perfume of black Boruelan tobacco and of strong scent to be wafted to the nostrils of the man who was passing within a yard of where he crouched concealed; of how the man had stopped, sniffed, looked as though he had seen a ghost, and had undoubtedly got his first intimation of the fact that—he wasn't as far from South America as he thought he was.

And in the main, the *caballero's* report would be

accurate, for Captain Ferring-Chevigny had undoubtedly received a shock. As the over-familiar
whiff reached his nostrils (and, in fact, the spot
fairly reeked with the scent from the sodden handkerchief, the oiled hair and the smouldering cigarette) he saw a lightning-swift procession of South
American scenes—railway-carriages and stations,
cinemas, hotels, shops, cafés, streets, market-
places, bars, and an army innumerable of swarthy
men, each of whom wore a 'gent's straw boater,' a
black suit or a white cotton one, a cummerbund,
pointed shoes, anointed locks and a perfume-
drenched handkerchief, and smoked a Boruelan
cigarette.

And he saw swarthy faces that he hated, and
one that he feared beyond telling.

Turning sharply towards the hedge, he peered
into it, endeavoured to see through it, thrust at it
with his stick in a vain attempt to make a hole,
found it was impossible, and became more and
more conscious of the distinctive odour, as familiar
and unmistakable to him as that of a slum in the
Chinese native quarter is to the missionary who
dwells among the Celestials; as that of a fried-fish
shop is to an East End costermonger; or as is that
of the tap-room of his village pot-house to the yokel.

He must be imagining things . . . But, thrusting
closer to the hedge and sniffing industriously, he
realized, quite correctly, that the perfume, the
odour, the *stench*, was unmistakable.

Yes, that was a cigarette from Capadare, and its
smoker was a Damned Dirty Dago—for thus, mentally, did Captain Ferring-Chevigny allude to all the
millions of the Spanish-Indian inhabitants of South
America.

Returning to the path, he ran to a gate some two
or three hundred yards distant, vaulted lightly over
it, and hurried back along the other side of the

hedge. Having arrived in the neighbourhood of the place opposite to where he had encountered the disturbing smell, he stopped and sought carefully forward, with eye and nose, like a questing hound.

Yes, yes, there it was—definitely. An alien and pungent offence to the glorious morning with its almost-imperceptible delicate odours appropriate to the sweet and wholesome countryside.

Yes, and there was the actual spot; there where the long grass was disturbed. There where it was flattened. A man had sat there; had crouched in under the hedge; had smoked a cigarette, and exhaled the filthy perfume of his hair and handker-chief.

Suddenly, with such feelings as those that disturbed the breast of Robinson Crusoe on beholding the strange footmark, Ferring-Chevigny saw two cigarette-stubs lying on a broad dock-leaf, affronting the day with their chewed ugliness and their beastly smell.

Now then, had all this been premeditated, cut-and-dried? Had he been intended to smell those familiar odours? To do exactly what he had done, even to the finding of the cigarette-butts?

He was inclined to think so, for those cigarette-ends had not been flung idly down, just anywhere. They had been laid on that dock-leaf; laid there for him to find—as he had done.

Or was he imagining things? Was that too far-fetched? Might not some seaman, with foreign cig-arettes in his pocket, have sat there, smoked a couple and passed on? And might he not have laid them on the big broad leaf with some idea of avoid-ing a fire? He might have had bad luck at some former time; had unintentionally set light to the dry undergrowth in some wood where he was resting; might even have set fire to a hay-rick, and got into bad trouble.

But what seaman, foreign or other, passed through Calderton? And more conclusive still, what wayfaring seaman, tramping between ports or to his home from a port, anointed himself with that stinking stuff?

No, it wouldn't do. *They were after him.*

And gripping his stick, Ferring-Chevigny gazed about him.

The fellow must have been here quite recently. The cigarette-butts were cold, but a man had been smoking there a few minutes before. Which way had he gone? Back towards the inn or on in the direction of Calderton? He couldn't have gone across the field, or he'd still be in sight.

Perhaps the best thing would be to stand and watch for a while. He might come into view on the far side of the opposite hedge, across the field there, as he went up the green hill that rose about half a mile distant, its sides scarred with clumps of gorse, rabbit-holes and little winding sheep-paths. Yes, he'd watch a while.

And as he did so, Captain Ferring-Chevigny was aware that the glory of the morning had departed, its beauty dimmed, as though a slight cloud had obscured the sun, throwing a thin blighting shadow on the lovely scene.

Was it one of those clouds no bigger than a man's hand that—how did the quotation go? Anyhow, he was being a fool. This England, this Calderton, this haven-under-the-hill, this great compensating stroke of luck, this success-at-last, were not the insubstantial fabric of a dream to be dissipated and dissolved by an odour, the mere smell of a Damned Dirty Dago.

Yes, it was indeed time he retired from all dangerous business. His nerve was going, if he could be frightened by a smell. And with a short and angry laugh, Captain Ferring-Chevigny turned on his heel and in leisurely manner resumed his walk in the direction of Calderton.

But his day was spoilt.

XIII

Without troubling to knock at the door, ask permission to enter, or in any way announce himself, the admirable Captain Montague Ferring-Chevigny walked into my sitting-room that night, as I sat, smoking the last pipe of the day, deep in thought before the delightful but really unnecessary fire.

Without greeting, I steadfastly regarded the gentleman in a way that quite failed to make him feel uncomfortable.

"Hullo! Got such a thing as a whisky-and-soda about? Or a brandy-and-soda. And a cigar," he asked, unabashed.

"I've no whisky; I've no brandy; and I don't smoke cigars."

"And don't swear, don't gamble, and never cock an eye at a lass, eh? Well, well, well! . . . What about taking steps to get some liquor?" he added.

"It's just on eleven. I'm not going to start ringing bells and . . ."

"I should, if I were you. Wiser. Much wiser."

And giving me a pleasant smile, he pressed the bell-push, turned the other arm-chair round to face the fire, seated himself and grinned ingratiatingly.

"Don't feel like bed yet," he said, and fell silent.

Robert knocked and entered.

"D'you want whisky or brandy?" I asked, addressing the uninvited guest.

"Brandy. Bring a bottle and a balloon glass. And a box of cigars."

"Soda-water, sir?" inquired Robert.

"Good Lord, man, no. Liqueur brandy. The old and bold. Did you ever see anybody put soda-water in old brandy, in a balloon glass?"

"Yes, sir," replied Robert.

"My condolences," growled Ferring-Chevigny, and Robert departed.

"No, don't feel a bit like bed," he continued, "and I don't mind telling you, my lad, that I'm uneasy."

"You amaze me," I said.

"Yes, I amaze myself a bit. The fact remains, though."

"What's making you feel uneasy?"

"Oh, shadows o'er life's pathway cast. Coming events casting shadows before them, too. I get these hunches, nowadays. I'm not superstitious, you know, but I've got a sort of a premonition."

"Of what?"

"Coming events," he grinned. "If they do come, it'll be 'draw stumps' for yours truly. Stir stumps, too."

This was extremely interesting. For surely the sooner and the further he went away, the better. He'd be just as much of a menace, but not as much of a nuisance, or rather, a curse, an incubus.

"Feel as though someone were walking over my grave," he said. "Walking over it! Running round and round it in circles; dancing on it; damn well digging it."

"An unpleasant feeling," I observed.

"Yes. Silly expression, if you come to think of it. 'Walking over your grave'—before you've got one. I suppose it means walking over the place where your grave is going to be. More sense in the expression 'somebody digging your grave.' Well, that's how I feel to-night . . . Perhaps because I've seen so many poor devils digging their own graves."

"Digging their own graves?"

"Yes. That was one of El Benemerito's little jokes. What he called a labour-saving device. Make a chap dig his own grave. Then stand with his back to it. If he fell neatly into it when the firing-squad shot him, that was good joss, sign of luck. For El Benemerito, of course. If he was particularly annoyed with the about-to-be-deceased, he'd pot him himself with his revolver, at ten paces; and if he had potted him straight into the grave, he was frightfully pleased. Like a good shot at billiards."

"Would he do that with you if you fell into his hands?" I asked.

I think Ferring-Chevigny shivered or shuddered slightly.

"No. If he were going to kill me, it wouldn't be until I was more than ready to be killed. And I've no doubt that, when he had finished with me, I should have to dig my grave and then get into it."

"Alive?"

"Yes. Alive. It's one of my nightmares. Seen it done more than once. On the last occasion, El Benemerito gave me a nasty look, as much as to say, 'I've got my eye on you too, my lad.' I found he had, and stood not upon the order of my going. I'm still going, in a manner of speaking."

Robert entered with the brandy and cigars, opened the ancient bottle, and Ferring-Chevigny half filled the balloon glass with the '48 brandy.

Before Robert had closed the door behind him the glass was empty and replenished.

"Ah! That's better. Like milk. I'll say Arthur keeps a cellar. Sure you won't have some?"

"Quite sure, thank you."

"Good. Going to bring your Anthony up a non-smoking teetotaler, who'll neither swear, gamble, nor cock his eye at a lass, too, eh?"

"Well, I shan't urge him to smoke, nor ply him with drink."

"Nor swear in front of him, eh?"

"Nor behind him."

"What's wrong with swearing?"

"Nothing, that I know of."

"Why not, then?"

"Matter of habit, I suppose."

"Wonder how one forms the non-swearing habit."

"A distaste for ugliness might have something to do with it," I observed. "Ugly words, ugly noises, ugly loss of temper, and so on."

"I see. And how did you acquire the non-smoking habit?"

"I haven't."

"Why not a cigar, then?"

"Prefer a pipe."

"And the non-drinking habit?"

"Don't like alcohol; and like still less its effects on me."

"But you'd cock an eye at a lass if not at a glass, eh? And we could give the lass a name, couldn't we?"

I looked him in the face and contrived to hold his gaze, and without any change of countenance, I believe.

He looked away while I still stared at him, and he gave vent to his fatuous laugh.

"Well, well. Joke's-a-joke. No offence. I come to praise Cæsar, not to bury him. So don't burrow into yourself. Come to the surface again."

Another draught of brandy. And this time he filled the big glass completely.

"Yes, I've come to talk to Cæsar, not to annoy him. You are doing fine, and the boy is a credit to you. Damn nice boy and a little gentleman."

"He's a gentleman," I agreed.

"Mind you, he's a queer youngster. Not everybody's cup of tea. If I had a boy of my own, I don't know that I'd want him to be exactly to Anthony's pattern."

"No, I imagine not," I said.

"No."

Leaning back in the chair, his legs stretched straight in front of him, face upturned to the ceiling, he inhaled deeply, and slowly and luxuriously breathed forth the blue fragrant smoke.

"Gad, it must be very nice to have a nipper of your own. Your very own boy, to bring up and teach and train, like you do a dog."

"Just like that," I murmured.

"Yes, I'd like a boy of my own. Handed over to me when he was old enough to be some good, y' know. Blow his own nose and do up his own buttons and that. Take him ratting, blood him, teach him to shoot and to ride. Make a good scrapper of him."

Silence.

"I'd have made a good father, y' know."

And turning his head, he looked me in the eyes, and if ever a man were sincere and speaking what he believed to be the truth, it was Captain Montague Ferring-Chevigny at that moment.

Another silence which I forbore to break.

"But they're queer cusses, you know. Talk about women being kittle cattle! Children have got 'em skinned a mile. God knows women are unaccountable enough, but they are nothing to children."

Another silence.

"I met the nicest boy I ever knew, on a ship. I'll tell you about him. And what's a damn curious thing is, that Anthony reminds me of him, although he'd got what I'd call more guts to the square yard than Anthony has. More of a character; more to say for himself; and not so hoighty-toighty. No damned Little Lord Fauntleroy stuff about this other boy. More like a human kid, if you know what I mean . . . I'll tell you.

"I got jolly fond of the little beggar. I'd have liked to adopt him, only they weren't that sort of people. And if they had been, I had nowhere to stow him when I landed. Could have left him at school, I suppose, but there's the holidays; and suppose his fees didn't roll up one term . . . Anyhow, that's idle speculation, for the parents were wealthy people, and the boy was the apple of their eye. Not that he was spoilt, mind you. Not a bit of it. The mother was very kind but firm, and the father was very firm but kind.

"There was a girl, too. Nice little kid, and though they treated them both absolutely alike, the boy was number one. There was no doubt about it. Not that the girl realized it; for, if anything, they were more indulgent—no, indulgent is not the word really—more demonstrative, shall I say, with her than with the boy.

"Well, they were the only kids on the ship, and great favourites with everybody. If I remember rightly, they came on board at Havana, Cuba. No, it wasn't. It was Hamilton, Bermuda, where the parents had been visiting. Governor, or O.C. Troops, or somebody like that. Very good-class people. So, you see, the kids weren't tropical born and bred. They had been taken for this voyage and visit to Bermuda, for a trip, for the good of their health. What I mean to say is, it wasn't a case of temperamental spoilt brats brought up by black servants; kids with livers; given to ungovernable rages; lacking in discipline and self-control and so on. One has seen that sort of brat, American, from Panama and Philippines way; and English, coming home from India. No, these were absolutely normal, healthy, hearty English kids, well bred, well educated, and damn well brought up.

"Well, now, I developed a regular soft spot for the boy. I liked the little girl enormously, but it was the boy who filled my eye. Gad, if he had been for sale I'd have paid a good price for him. For a nicer, more attractive boy I never saw. And your young Anthony reminds me of him. Now then, what price this?

"One afternoon, lovely day, pretty hot, everybody lying about in deck-chairs and those long Madeira cane things, whole ship quiet, I woke up from an afternoon snooze, mouth like the bottom of a parrot's cage, and thought I'd better go and have a drink. I got up, walked along the boat-deck, down the companion and on to the promenade-deck. That was quite empty. On the sunny side. Everybody was round in the shade on the port side—except for the two kids. The little girl was standing at the top of the companion that led from that deck down to the main-deck, a very steep, narrow flight of steel-plated steps. The ship was steady as a rock, and the girl was looking at something—I couldn't see what—down below.

"Just as I got sufficiently far down my companion-ladder to see her, the boy came out from the smoking-room, and then, with his back to me, he crept on tiptoe, in his rubber-soled shoes, towards the girl.

"I supposed he was going to shout 'Bo!' in her ear, or something of that sort, and I was just beginning to think it might be a dangerous thing to do—to startle her suddenly, as she was standing at the top of the steps—when he stretched his hands out in front of him at arms' length, fingers upward, then crouched, drew them back, and shot them forward with all his strength, taking the girl square in the small of the back and knocking her, head over heels, headlong down that steep flight of iron stairs.

"It was the most deliberate thing I ever saw in my life.

"And it was deliberate, cold-blooded *murder*. Yes; the poor little kid landed on her head and fractured her skull and broke her neck as well."

"Good God!" I whispered.

"Yes . . . That's what I said," continued Ferring-Chevigny. "It all happened in a flash. I suppose that between the time I saw her on the promenade-deck and the time she landed on her head, there couldn't have been more than five seconds. I had only just stepped off my ladder on to the deck, as the boy did it; and as they were twenty or thirty yards away, I couldn't do anything. Hadn't time even to shout. I was too astounded. It wasn't until he had thrust, that I realized what he was doing. Never dreamed of such a thing, up to the very moment that she shot headlong off the deck.

"Now what do you make of that?"

"Well, if it was deliberate . . ." I began.

"My dear chap, take it from me. I've just told you I've never seen anything more deliberate in the whole of my life. The boy walked out of the smoking-room door, happened to look to the left instead of the right—in which case he'd have seen my feet coming down the companion—saw the girl, and immediately his demeanour changed. His action changed. Instead of walking, he crept on tiptoe. He crouched as he crept. Then, as I've told you, he stuck his hands out as though to measure his distance, drew them back to his shoulders, and shot them forward, as though he were going to burst a door open or knock a wall down. No sort or kind of suggestion or possibility of *accident*. And it wasn't as though he were playing one of those damnable practical jokes that boys get up to. Wasn't as though he had intended to give her a little shove forward with one hand and quickly grab her back with both. One has seen fools do that at the edge of a quay or a precipice. You know, grab hold of somebody and pretend to push them forward, and then pull them back. No, he simply took his time, judged his distance, and used all his strength and skill to knock his sister flying headlong from one deck to another . . . 'Was it *deliberate*?' Huh!"

"Well," mused I, "since it was deliberate, I should

think it was a sudden surge of homicidal mania."

"Homicidal, all right," growled Ferring-Chevigny. "But you never in all your life saw a boy with less signs of mania of any sort. Absolutely bright, happy, normal boy. Normal as I am."

"And he had always appeared fond of the girl, had he?" I asked.

"Oh, absolutely. They played around together all day long. Never apart. Never a sign nor a sound of a quarrel of any sort. He was the leader in their games, of course. But he didn't want to play at anything, or do anything, without her. It was always 'we' when he told his mother what he was going to do, or wanted to do. Can 'we' go up on the bridge? Can 'we' have a line and fish over the side? Can 'we' have my soldiers out? . . . No, they were the best of pals."

"Something in the subconscious mind, then, I suppose," said I. "Jealousy, of which the conscious mind was utterly unaware. When he did it, he was what the latest jargon calls 'in the grip of the unconscious,' and didn't know what he was doing."

"Didn't know, me foot!" jeered Ferring-Chevigny with less than his usual courtesy. "Of course he knew what he was doing. If ever a murderer in this world knew what he was doing, that one did."

"What a ghastly thing!" I said, turning the conversation from the psychological aspects of the tragedy and the workings of the unconscious mind. "More especially for the boy himself. Worse for him than for the poor parents."

"Shockin'! Shockin'!" he agreed. "Poor devils. Daughter killed. Son a killer—though they never knew that, unless he has confessed it, since. But anyway, daughter dead, and son homicidal. Shockin' tragedy."

And indeed it seemed to me that I could think of nothing more terrible that could happen to a devoted father and mother than that their only son should kill their only daughter. Better far if the children had fallen overboard together and both been drowned.

And then I thought of another tragedy, close at hand; the equally dreadful, possibly more dreadful, tragedy for which this man was wholly, solely and entirely responsible.

With difficulty I controlled myself and bit back the words that came to my lips as I watched him sitting there, half drunk, pitying these strangers and this other boy, while my Anthony . . .

"What did you do?" I asked, for the sake of saying something—and to keep myself from saying something else.

"I ran down to where the child lay, picked her up, rushed to the Surgery and handed her over to the ship's doctor. He sent for the parents and broke it to them that she was dead."

"You told the parents how it happened?"

"No, I didn't."

"Why not?"

"Well. Bad enough for them as it was. Bad enough when they only thought it was an accident."

Surprising. A piece of consideration and decency that somehow one hardly expected from this man. One would have supposed that he'd have blurted out full details. He went up in my estimation, a thing which, as I have admitted, he was annoyingly wont to do, from time to time.

"And the boy?"

"He didn't say anything, either."

"Did you say anything to him?"

"Not a word. Why should I? If he knew what he had done—well, he knew. If he didn't know, why tell him? Why rub it in?"

"Exactly. It would have been a most cruel thing to do, if he didn't know."

"Yes. And whatever I may be, I am not a cruel man," quoth Captain Montague Ferring-Chevigny, with complete sincerity.

Quite so. So long as his private and personal interests were not involved, he was not a cruel man. Not wantonly cruel, like his friend Gil Vicente Romez. But Self was his god, Selfishness his religion. And in his religion, he was a fanatic.

"No. So far as I was concerned, nobody ever knew that the death of the child was deliberate murder."

"And that boy reminds you of Anthony, does he?" I asked.

"No. T'other way about. Anthony reminds me of that boy."

"Did you ever talk to him about the—er—death of his sister?"

"Yes. Frequently. I didn't bring up the subject, of course, but the poor kid could never keep off it."

"Did he seem terribly grieved by the loss of his sister—who, incidentally, was his inseparable companion and playmate?"

"No. That's the queer thing. He didn't blubber, from first to last, so far as I know; and he certainly didn't seem depressed, much less bereft and broken-hearted. The parents fairly went to pieces, but the boy seemed—what shall I say—more interested than, well, shocked or dazed, or overcome with grief. In fact, there was nothing of that sort at all."

"You say he couldn't keep off the subject of the girl's death. What sort of line did he take?"

"Well, two or three. He was undoubtedly deeply interested in the subject of death itself. Death simply *as* death. Then he got on to the question of the survival of personality. Not in those terms, of course, but in childish language. Would she go to Heaven? Would he see her there? Would she change at all? Suppose he lived to be an old man, would she remain a girl of twelve? Then he'd fairly tie me up with questions about predestination, fate, kismet, that sort of thing. Not in that kind of language again, of course, but—

" 'Why does God allow accidents? Could anything have saved her? Why did it happen to her and not to me? Did God know, from the moment that she was born, that she'd die at the age of twelve by breaking her neck?' That sort of question."

"But nothing about the actual event itself?" I asked.

"Yes, I was coming to that, for however the conversation about her started, and whatever line he followed, he always came to that point, invariably. *How could it have happened?* And I can tell you, Waring, it was one of the strangest experiences of my life, and that's saying something. Real psychology and all that. To sit in a deck-chair and have that kid stand beside you, his great innocent eyes looking straight into yours, and saying, as bold as brass, *or* as innocent as milk,

" *'How did it happen?'* "

"And you got the impression, in fact conviction, that the boy was absolutely honest, in earnest, genuine—in fact, innocent as milk, and not bold as brass?" I asked.

Ferring-Chevigny took another drink of brandy and refilled the big glass, incidentally emptying the bottle. By the time he had done the same for his balloon glass, he'd have drunk the whole bottle of old brandy. But he hadn't turned a hair. He was now, to all appearances, as sober as when he came into the room. If the brandy had had any effect at all, it had made him a little more eloquent and fluent, stimulating his mind and his memory. Doubtless other and different effects would follow.

"Well," he said, pursing his lips and taking another cigar, "sometimes most certainly yes, and sometimes just possibly no. When he leant up against me, chattering about her, not light-heartedly but, as I say, rather with great interest than with deep concern, I felt he must be innocent. When he asked such a question as whether I didn't think that burial at sea wasn't very much nicer than burial in the clay of a churchyard, and that sort of thing, I'd wonder. And when he turned to me to say,

" 'What *could* she have been doing? Do you think she was running, and perhaps looking behind her, and simply ran right into the opening of the companion?'; and as he looked me in the eyes and I looked into his, just as though I was trying to read something, read his mind, his very soul, as in point of fact I was, I'd just answer, 'I wonder. I greatly wonder.'

"And, by gad, it was the truth. I did wonder. Hardly left off wondering—whether the boy was a monumental liar and a homicidal lunatic, or whether, when he did it, he had been completely unconscious of what he was doing."

"There have undoubtedly been such cases," I said. "Men have escaped the gallows and been set free through the defending counsel taking that line and persuading the jury that the murderer simply did not know what he was doing at the time; had no recollection of having done it, and was not responsible for his actions."

"Yes. Quite so," agreed Ferring-Chevigny, "but did he get off because of his ignorance of what he was doing, or because of the ignorance of the jury? Get off through the cleverness of his counsel, or the helplessness of the judge to go against the jury's verdict?"

"Of course, there's somnambulism," I mused aloud, "and there's delirium, temporary insanity, that sort of thing."

"Yes, and a dozen other doodahs," observed

Ferring-Chevigny, "but the lad wasn't exactly sleep-walking when he sauntered out of the smoking-room, looked along the deck, saw his sister, and fairly stalked her like a cat stalking a sparrow, was he? And he was about as delirious as you are now. He was in perfect health. And as for temporary insanity, the same applies. He was just about as insane as you or I . . . No, it was murder. Conscious or unconscious, that is to say. What I mean is, he went up to the girl and killed her as intentionally as I pick up this glass and drink."

And Ferring-Chevigny suited the action to the word. He had finished the bottle and reached the top of his form, the apex of his intelligence, clarity of memory, and lucidity of argument.

"And generally you decided in favour of inno-cence? What about when you had faint doubts?"

"Why, I got that sort of uneasy feeling when he stared at me a second too long, when he opened his eyes a fraction too wide, when he looked too damned good to be true—as he sometimes seemed to do.

"And then again, he came it too often. Harped on it too much, because, as I have said, he never brought up the subject without that eternal 'What happened? What caused the accident?' and some fresh suggestion such as, 'Perhaps she tripped at the top of the steps and fell down them.'

"One day he actually took me to the spot to show me how there was not only a grooved steel plate on each wooden step, but one at the top, on the deck itself, and as it was about three-eighths of an inch thick, the edge of it did offer at least a tiny stum-bling-block—conceivably just high enough to catch the toe of a little shoe."

"A case of 'methinks he doth protest too much,' eh?" I mused.

"Yes. At times I was inclined to feel that he

rather over-did it. And when I thought that, I wondered whether he was reassuring himself that it was all-right; that no one suspected anything; that he had got away with it all right; and that I and everybody else took the view that it was an accident."

Ferring-Chevigny fell silent, picked up the empty bottle, and looked at me. For a moment I thought he was going to suggest ringing for another bottle, but he put it down, yawned widely, and threw the butt of his cigar into the fire-place.

"Yes, by gad," he said, "interesting is the word. Amazing to listen to that lad, watch the changing look of his eyes and the play of expression on his face, and speculate as to whether he was a cunning and callous young murderer or an innocent little chap who was merely—queer. Like young Anthony."

I let this last remark pass in silence, realizing that it might only have been uttered to annoy, or at any rate to draw me, and get a rise.

"I should like to have been present when he was told what had happened," I said, "to see how he carried it off, then. That must have been the real test, I should think, as to whether he was innocent and ignorant of what he had done, or cognizant and guilty."

"Yes, you'd think so, wouldn't you? But it wasn't," said Ferring-Chevigny. " 'Point of fact, I was there. After the surgeon had sent for the parents and they had realized that the child was dead, the mother's one idea, when she came round from her fainting-fit or collapse, was that the boy shouldn't see the girl as she was; that he shouldn't get a shock; that he should be told carefully and properly. Someone must break it to him gently.

"And I offered to do it. I was in the Surgery, of course, when they came, and I stayed in case I could be of any sort of help, for it looked at first as though the mother would have to be carried to her cabin. The husband wasn't much good, and the doctor was—well—occupied.

"But they declined my offer and said they'd rather tell him themselves.

"And here's an interesting point. At that very moment, the Surgery curtain was pulled aside and in walked the boy. I got between him and the surgeon's bench on which the girl's body was lying, and said,

" 'Hullo! What d'you want here?' And it must have been a trick of light, for sunshine was reflected from the water through the porthole on to the white ceiling, moving and flickering, you know. But I seemed to see a look come into the boy's eyes, and disappear again, if you know what I mean.

"And that sudden look of guilt or fear or knowledge or whatever it was, that came and went like a flash, coupled with the fact that he had come to the Surgery then, gave me the wrong idea. Until he spoke, I thought he had come to give himself up; come to confess; come to tell the whole truth about how it happened. But as he looked me straight in the face with his clear innocent gaze, and said,

" *'What's up? Is anything the matter?'* I twigged at once that I was wrong. He was going to brazen it out —and if that were so, I wasn't going to give him away. Or conversely, he knew nothing whatever of what he had done—and I wasn't going to tell him or anybody else.

"So you see, he had his line from the very first, whether premeditated or not. And his line was that he knew nothing whatever. But I made a mental note to ask him when we were alone, why—since he knew nothing whatever—he had come to the Surgery! A queer place for a kid to go to in the middle of the afternoon.

"And as we stood grouped there, the surgeon bending over the little girl, the father supporting the mother, and I getting between the boy and the bench, the mother broke down and burst into the most awful flood of tears and sobbing, and calling to the dead child. Probably saved her life that she could cry. Then,

" *'What's up?'* said the boy again. *'What's happened? What's the matter?'*

"And I thought the best thing I could do was to clear him out of it. So I said,

" 'Here, come along with me, son,' and took him by the hand and more or less dragged him out of it and up on deck.

"Then in spite of what the mother had said, I did tell him. It seemed to me that, having come into the Surgery and seen for himself that there was some hell of a bad business on, it would be perfectly idiotic to pretend that there was nothing whatever wrong.

"And do you know, it was only when I began to tell him, that I realized that there was no need; remembered that he knew more about it than anybody; that it was he who had *done* it.

"So there I was, breaking it to him gently, just as though it was ghastly news that must be given to him with as little shock as possible. And, by gad, that kid could act—or else it was a marvellous case of one of your psychological flap-doodles."

The speaker paused and took a third cigar, lit it and settled back again in his chair.

"Mind you," he resumed, "in spite of the fact that he had turned up at the Surgery so *à propos*; in spite of that look of knowledge, of cunning, and of guilt that I may or may not have seen on his face; and in spite of the fact that I had seen him deliberately knock that poor kid down the stairs, I decided that, on the whole, he was innocent! Innocent of intention, that is to say, and that his *'How on earth could it have happened?'* was genuine."

"By the way," I asked, "how did he account for visiting the Surgery in the middle of a hot afternoon, visiting an out-of-the-way place presumably three or four decks down below where he usually played with his sister?"

"Oh, he had an answer pat enough. He had heard the steward, the surgeon's dispenser, in point of fact, tell his father and mother that the doctor wanted to speak to them at once, in the Surgery. He had thought that something must be wrong and that he would go too. He had never seen inside the Surgery.

"And he confessed—or with damnable cunning invented—that he thought perhaps there might be sweets in the Surgery like there are in the chemists' shops.

" 'You know,' he said, 'black currant jujubes, cough drops, barley sugar, acid drops, lemon drops, that sort of thing.'

"And as he said it, it all sounded perfectly plausible. Just the sort of thing a kid would do. Often wanted to go into the Surgery; hadn't had the nerve; but here was a first-class opportunity, mother and father going down there."

Silence.

"No, there was nothing to that idea of yours of how important it might have been to note the way in which he took the news when he was told what had happened. For he took it perfectly. Absolutely naturally. Though I admit that some kids might have been more distressed than he was. But there, you never know. One kid'll be broken-hearted when its father or mother dies, and another will promptly ask if it'll have nice new black clothes for the funeral. Something of that sort.

"Yes, it was a queer business, and I don't know

to this day whether that kid was a callous little murderer or a blameless and pitiable innocent."

Again my visitor yawned cavernously. The brandy was taking effect.

"Wha' 'bout a spot o' bed?" he mumbled. "Yarning for hours. What started me tellin' you 'bout that boy? Oh, I know. Young Anthony reminds me of him."

And closing his eyes, he began to breathe heavily.

A minute or two later, he was asleep and snoring.

So Anthony reminded him of the wretched child who had killed his sister.

Why?

Or was it simply untrue; and had he merely remembered the young murderer, simply because he had happened to be speaking of another boy; of Anthony?

How had the subject arisen?

Thinking back, I remembered that he had said something to the effect that Anthony, though a nice boy and a little gentleman, was a queer youngster, and not everybody's cup of tea. Then, that he would like to have a boy of his own, though they were kittle cattle and unaccountable. And then he had begun to tell me about a particularly unaccountable sample of the kittle cattle; one who had been all that a boy should be; one who had pleased and attracted him enormously—and had suddenly committed a murder. Why should Anthony remind him of such a boy?

Probably because, in spite of what he had said, Anthony really appealed to him as much as the other boy had done. Yes, that was what had reminded him of the young fiend—or poor unfortunate—whichever he might be.

Or had he told me the story of this other boy

simply to annoy me, to prick the bubble of my 'fatuous satisfaction with what I had made of Anthony'—as he would call my pride in him.

The devil of doubt and incipient anxiety gnawed at my mind. Could it really be that he saw something in Anthony that reminded him of a peculiarity, an abnormality, in the other boy; something of which he had not told me?

But why shouldn't he tell me, especially if he thought it would hurt and annoy. Possibly because he didn't wish to admit that his young friend fell short of perfection: for would the committing of a mere murder, *en passant*, by an admired young friend, constitute a flaw in his character as judged by the approving and lenient eye of Captain Ferring-Chevigny?

But wasn't this very definitely a case of Much Ado About Nothing? Why should I worry because the man professed to be reminded of a homicide by some kind of resemblance between this boy and Anthony? I was being fanciful and foolish.

Realizing this, I was nevertheless annoyed and perturbed, as I stared at the snoring sleeper opposite to me, his empty bottle beside him, two of his cigar-butts stinking in the ash-tray between us, another adorning the hearth, their ash liberally besprinkled over his clothes and the carpet.

I wondered if he would be surprised into speaking the truth if I roused him suddenly and shot a question at him as he awoke. I had either heard or read somewhere that that was one way of getting at the truth that was in a person's mind. Probably he'd be too annoyed to answer at all. However, I'd try.

Leaning forward towards him, I suddenly bawled at the top of my voice,

"Hi! You!" and succeeded beyond my expectations. For he jumped as though he had been shot.

He had certainly spoken the truth when he had said that he was uneasy and apprehensive. Definitely he was nervy. And as he shot up in his chair, I continued almost without a pause after my shout,

"Why does Anthony remind you of that boy on the ship?"

And instantly he replied,

"The queer look that comes into his eyes. As though he peeped out at you from ambush, if you know what I mean. A look of wisdom, as though he knows a damn sight more than he says. So he does, too. As though he always has something up his sleeve. So he has too. Deep young beggar . . . Got *me* taped, I do believe."

And leaning back he yawned again and said it was time he went to bed, as he thought he could sleep now. I don't think he had any idea that he had just been asleep, and imagined that my question had followed immediately upon his last remark, his last words, "Young Anthony reminds me of him."

I rose to my feet, as I did not propose to discuss Anthony. I had learned what I wanted to know, and was none the happier for the knowledge. For I felt that in the moment of waking, Ferring-Chevigny had spoken the simple truth, and had not been talking to annoy me.

Anthony had reminded him of the boy on the ship—and for the reason that he gave.

What made me the more unhappy, resentful and angry, was the fact that I could not contradict him about that aspect of Anthony. I had, of course, noticed it myself, from the first; had observed it very frequently; and had given it a very great deal of thought.

It was remarkable and discomfiting that this man should have described it so accurately—the look the boy sometimes had of knowing more than he admitted, meaning more than he said; what, indeed, I have referred to already as the 'ageing' sort of look that came into his eyes, as though the brain of an adult, endowed with wisdom, knowledge and understanding, were behind the face of a child. It was indeed, in Ferring-Chevigny's own words, as though Anthony peeped out at you from ambush; from where he hid behind his own boyish façade.

And though my mind was at the moment obsessed with Anthony, I could not help realizing, once more, how complex a character Ferring-Chevigny had; how intricate was the network of his thoughts and fancies; how various and contradictory the aspects of his mind.

How could a man be so observant and so blind; so intelligent and so stupid; so sensitive in some ways, so callous in others; so acute and yet so blunted? From the way in which he spoke, he undoubtedly had felt a very genuine disinterested affection for this boy on the ship; and yet, up to that moment, I would have sworn that he was utterly incapable of loving anyone but himself, of considering anything but his own interests.

Quite obviously, again, he had noticed this peculiarity of Anthony's; yet, up to that moment, I had felt certain that no one, no one whomsoever, had remarked it.

I studied his face. He was wide awake enough now.

"And the boy on the ship had that sort of look, had he?" I asked, without admitting or denying that Anthony had any such idiosyncrasy.

"After the murder, he had," was the prompt reply. "And no doubt about it. It was one of the things that made me say just now that, although most of the time I thought he was innocent and ignorant of what he had done, a small part of the time I doubted it; what made me—just now and again—wonder whether he was a callous and cunning young killer or a poor little chap who was absolutely innocent of evil intention; and only queer, like young Anthony."

He stared, unseeing, at the fire.

"I couldn't swear, of course, that there was nothing of the sort before the murder, but I rather think I should have noticed it if there had been. It may have been there. It may have been—without my seeing it. Of course, I wasn't what you might call *studying* him before he killed his sister. I was only enjoying him, so to speak. He took me out of myself and I loved playing with him; listening to him chattering with the little girl; giving him rides on my shoulder all over the place; and telling him yarns. He loved a good tale . . .

"But after I had seen him deliberately kill the little girl, I naturally sat up and took notice. I couldn't have liked him more—well—loved him more, I might say; but I noticed him more, studied him, so to speak. Watched his face when he was discussing the accident. And then it was that I saw in him what I see in Anthony; that oldish *knowledgeable* sort of look, if you know what I mean."

I did—only too well. And I had had enough.

"I'm going to bed," I said.

"About time too," agreed Ferring-Chevigny. "I can't sit here all night listening to *you*."

XIV

Next evening, Captain Ferring-Chevigny, with a pleasant good night to the footman who opened the big double front doors and let him out, stood on the wide flagged balustraded space from which the great flights of steps curved, left and right, down to the drive below.

A most lovely evening for a stroll. No moon yet, but the stars were glorious. Almost like the sort of night one got in the tropics. Perhaps it would be as well to go back to the inn by way of the main avenue, as the moon wasn't up. Couldn't miss one's way in the dark, with gravel underfoot; and there would be someone at the lodge to let him out if the gates were locked.

Lovely place. Lovely evening. Lovely life . . . One of Arthur's cigars before he set off. And taking out his cigar-case, he bit the end from a cigar with one nip of his sharp front teeth—something characteristic in that action—lit the cigar, exhaled luxuriously, descended the steps and started on his way.

Yes, it was a bit dark, here in the drive, but you couldn't have a magnificent chestnut avenue like this without a certain tunnel-like effect.

However, darkness by night was delightful shade by day; and if it were suggestive of a tunnel, it had its compensating advantages. One couldn't lose one's way in a tunnel.

And whistling softly to himself, he confidently made his way along the avenue, glancing up between the trees, from time to time, at the starry sky.

Well, things were going very nicely. He had just about got Katherine where he wanted her; and by the time Arthur came home, she'd be much more than willing to meet her Monty much more than half-way. Like all other women, she knew on which side her bread was buttered. Naturally, she wasn't going to be such a fool as to spill the beans when his and hers were inextricably mixed in the same pot—which they most undoubtedly were. But even if she did get an attack of high-and-mighty conscience—or, what was likelier, a *crise de nerfs* and got the wind up—she'd still realize that she couldn't do him any harm without harming herself still more.

No, she'd be held back at the last moment, whatever sort of panic or religious throes she might get into—by the realization that there were four of them, all in the same boat. *Of course* she wouldn't scuttle the boat in which were her precious Anthony, her Arthur, and what is more, herself, even for the pleasure of drowning her own lawful husband.

Naturally it was all right, and he wouldn't have been thinking such foolish thoughts but for that queer little experience. Like the title of a short-story thriller by Robert Louis Stevenson—*The Incident of the Scented Dago and the Capadare Cigarette*. But that came of having things on one's conscience, or in the hole where one's conscience used to be, or ought to be. Some local yokel—good rhyme that, local yokel—had bought him half a pint of the ghastliest hair-oil, to impress his girl; or had knocked off a bottle of civet-cat scent in the ring-game at the Fair, and drenched himself with the muck.

And as luck would have it, the same bold lad, on a cheap return trip to some mighty city, had seen a packet of unfamiliar cigarettes in a tobacconist's window, and had bought them, to impress the other corner-boys. *Stinkadores colorados*, marked *Brazilian Cigarettes as smoked by the South American Millionaires*. That's what it was.

Yes, but what should such a lad be doing crouching under, and into, a hedge on a lovely spring morning?

On the other hand, why shouldn't he? Besides, it might not have been a local sheikh at all; it might very well have been a tramp, who had also been to the Fair; and, among the loot he had pinched when he crawled in under the back of a tent, might have been a bottle of the scent they sell at Fairs, and a packet of the cheapest foreign cigarettes, proper god-awful *cigarillos estrangeros* some gypsies had got hold of. And he might have been under that hedge all night, wakened up in the morning, and smoked some of the filthy fags for breakfast.

Yes, and, by gad, he might very well have drunk the scent that he had pinched.

These people thought nothing of drinking methylated spirit and furniture-polish; yes, and cheap commercial eau-de-Cologne if they could get it. What was that Red Biddy stuff they sell in the port slums but coloured eau-de-Cologne, methylated spirit and crude alcohol?

Why, there were a dozen explanations for the smell that had brought Boruelan scenes so vividly to his mind. He had been a fool to . . .

"*Buenas tardes! Como le va, Señor Xeres?*" suddenly and softly called a voice, apparently from the depths of the big rhododendron shrubbery in which the chestnut avenue ended.

Captain Montague Ferring-Chevigny was a brave man and, in many a tight place and dangerous crisis, had displayed physical courage of a high order—but, as he admitted, his nerves were not quite what they had been, for the period spent in the Rotunda Gaol had done them no good at all—and undeniably he jumped.

And as he realized that the voice spoke in Spanish, he had that extremely unpleasant sensation caused by the apparent complete turning-over and stopping of the heart. That *Como le va* was definitely South American. A Spaniard would have said *Como esta usted* or *Y como lo pasa usted*. Yes, this was a message from the other side of the world. From Boruela . . . And now what?

"With *El Brujo's* compliments and hopes that you will enjoy life in Hell as much as you did in the *El Libertador* prison," continued the voice.

A short ugly laugh.

A quiet "*Que divertido, eh?*" and a terrific

Bang . . . !

Shot, by gad!

No, he wasn't. And with a swift and mighty bound, he leapt for the blacker darkness of the shrubbery on the opposite side of the drive.

"I see you, Señor Xeres," cried the mocking voice, in Spanish, as he crashed into the bushes.

And instantly there followed another tremendous

Bang . . . !

He could see him, could he? Well, he'd have damned good sight if he saw him now.

Captain Ferring-Chevigny flung himself upon the ground in the pitch-black darkness behind and beneath the friendly cover of one of the great and thick old rhododendron bushes which formed the long continuous bank that was one of the June beauties of Calderton. Here he lay, recovering breath and swiftly considering his next move.

And that had better be no move at all, until the would-be assassin compelled one.

What would the swine do? He could see well enough to shoot, and he must have seen, as well as heard, him dive into the rhododendrons. Perhaps he'd wait a while and come in after him. If so, the Dago would get his. Let him come within reach of Señor Xeres's long arms, and he'd find his ankles seized and himself on the flat of his back and Señor Xeres on top of him, with his hands at his throat, almost before he knew what had got him. And before he could use his gun, too.

The damned murdering swine must be able to see in the dark. They could, those half-Indian fellows, like cats. And what was more likely was that he had been lying flat on the ground at the edge of the gravel under a rhododendron bush; and, looking upwards, he would clearly see a passer-by, silhouetted against the sky. Well, two could play at that game. He himself, after a while, would edge forward until his head was out from under the bush, and he'd see what he could see. If he kept as still and quiet as a dead mouse, he'd see the Dirty Dago against the sky as he crossed the road. He'd almost certainly hear him on that gravel, too, unless he was wearing sneakers.

And, supposing he didn't come straight across the drive to the right spot, one might be able to stand up in the shadow and fairly spring on him as he stepped on to the grass.

He'd go armed after this—if there were an 'after this'—and he had been a fool not to do so always. But one didn't expect this sort of thing in England. Certainly not away down in a rural back-of-beyond like Calderton. Disgusting. A damned shame and a disgrace to the police. He'd make a row about it. Write to the papers and complain . . .

Well—there was no doubt about it; they were after him. And a wave of despair, of weakness, almost of nausea passed over him as he realized that the game was up, and that he was no safer in the depths of the country than he had been in the heart of London; perhaps less so.

'The compliments of El Brujo,' eh? The high-souled, self-sacrificing, devoted Liberator; the second and even greater Bolivar, father of his country; the good and noble El Benemerito, *alias* Old Brujo, the Witch-doctor. *El Benemerito* in his privately owned Press, which was the sole press of Boruela; and *El Brujo* in every town and village of his privately owned country. Officially the Well-deserving; privately and secretly the Witch-doctor; the smeller-out of enemies; the relentless wholesale slayer, who, by the help of his Secret Service, was the omniscient, omnipotent, omnipresent punisher, the least of whose punishments was death.

'*The compliments of El Brujo*' here, in rural England, in the very park of an English county magnate, himself a ruler, the Governor of a British Crown Colony.

Yes, El Brujo's arm was long.

Well, it hadn't quite reached him yet.

Or had it?

Only the darkness had saved his life. It was a marvel that that first shot hadn't got him. Probably missed his head by the fraction of an inch.

El Benemerito's killers didn't usually miss. And of course, the second shot had been literally a shot in the dark. Simply fired at a noise, the sound of his bursting into the rhododendron clump.

Captain Ferring-Chevigny rested his head upon his hands and was amazed, indeed shocked, to find that he was almost on the point of tears. Positively, given a little self-encouragement, a little self-pity, he would have broken down, sobbed, burst into tears and blubbed like a child. It was too bad, too damned bad, after all he had done and suffered; to have come into port like this, into safe anchorage in the beautiful little haven-under-the-hill—only to find that it was a goddam death-trap.

However, that line of country was no good to any rider. Self-pity is the bottomless pit-y, and the beginning of self-pity the end of self-help, the beginning of self-destruction.

But oh, the true pity of it. The cruel pity of it. Enough to drive a man mad. In clover, on velvet, and then—shot up. Shot clean out of the clover and off the velvet.

For he must go, and go while the going was— well—while there was any going at all.

Anyhow, he had had a lovely rest; and this time he'd set off on his travels with a full pocket, and what's more, Katty would have to keep it well lined. It was no more than a wife's duty to help her husband when he was in trouble.

Duty? It was her privilege. And the only help unfortunately that she could give him now would be financial—and that wasn't his fault. He'd have been content—'point of fact, only too thankful—to settle down in peace and quiet, with the run of his teeth and a horse and a bottle and a cigar; and beyond that, he would have accepted only a little pocket-money, mere chicken-food.

But now it would have to be cash instead of kind; instead of kindness too, if he had to put the screw on. But it wouldn't come to that. She'd be only too damned glad to see him go, and only too damned anxious to help him get away and provide him with the means of staying away. But the cruel pity of it. To have to 'take to the heather' again; to be on the run again; to 'take to the mountains' like a damned peon turning bandit in Mexico.

Where had he better go? Other side of the world, perhaps. Australia or New Zealand. Probably be safer still if he got well into the middle of Africa.

Yes, go there to escape El Brujo's killers—and die of malaria or dysentery; be eaten by a lion, taken by a crocodile, trampled by a rhinoceros, gored by a buffalo, or some damned thing!

That sort of life was all right when you felt like it. All right when you were young, but he had had enough of roughing it. More than enough of the jungle and God's great wide open spaces. Great wide open green Hell, more likely!

No, something civilized would be better. Australia perhaps. One could have quite a good time at Sydney. Or, of course, there were some pretty good spots in the South Sea Islands where one could do oneself uncommon well. Honolulu and Waikiki Beach, Hawaii and Samoa, Tahiti, places like that; and he'd like to see Perenecque Island again. No, perhaps that might be a bit risky, although it was seventeen years since his body was found there.

Perhaps Papeete would be best, Tahiti being French. Better than the Hawaiian Islands as they were American; or the Fijis which were British.

Yes, one could hide best in a great crowded town like Sydney, or on a tiny island. Surely he'd be safe enough in such a place, even from El Benemerito. Granted they cast what must be pretty well the biggest net in the world and the finest-meshed, even so they'd never spot him under an assumed name in a place like Papeete. Yes, that would be the best. The French know how to live, and there would be all sorts of fun there. And with what Katherine could easily allow him, he could do himself proud.

Meanwhile, how to get there? There'd be two great dangers; one—that he'd be killed between Calderton and Southampton or wherever he sailed from; the other that he'd be traced to the ship or seen going on board. El Benemerito had his men at every European port from which ships sailed, and they kept close watch on all who entered and left the country.

Yes, if he were seen boarding a ship for the Panama Canal, they'd be on the look-out for him at Colon and Panama. They'd get him for a certainty when he changed ships for the South Sea Islands. Of course, he might hop across to France and get a

French boat direct to Papeete—if they didn't see him at Dover or Calais, Southampton or Cherbourg, and put a spoke in his wheel—or a knife in his gizzard.

Anyhow, he had got to go, and he might as well have a run for his money, as sit here and 'take it.'

But what a nerve, shooting him up, actually here in Calderton! What an organization; what an Intelligence Service. If he hadn't thought he was safe anywhere else in England, he might have supposed he was safe in the depths of this particular county. And if he weren't safe in a rural inn and a country lane at the back of beyond, he might reasonably have thought he was safe in Sir Arthur Calderton's own back garden.

And he could have sworn that he had shaken them off, that he hadn't been followed down here. Why, coming down from London, he had walked for hours, he had cycled for hours, he had made four different railway journeys of it, he had been the first out of the train at Calderton and had sat on that seat on the platform until there hadn't been a soul in the place except himself and the ticket collector.

It was amazing. And what was more, it was terrifying.

Yes, Papeete next stop. And meanwhile, what? It would be madness to try to get to the Calderton Arms to-night. This damned gunman had only got to wait somewhere in sight of the inn where his quarry would be bound to pass close to him.

The best thing to do would be to get back to the house. That would be it. Lie up at Calderton House for a bit, and then get away in broad daylight, and in company too. Even one of El Brujo's killers would hardly assassinate him deliberately and openly, with people looking on. You can't do that sort of thing in England and get away with it. No, they didn't stand for that sort of thing here; and the foreign killers know it. He'd make the tutor fellow come to the station with him and see him off. Bring young Anthony, too. And there'd be the chauffeur. And he'd travel third class in a compartment with several other people. Damn it, he'd make the tutor come to London with him.

By gad, why not go the whole hog and make the tutor see him safe on board the ship? And he needn't go by train at all, so far as that went. Go by car, straight from door to door. Get in at Calderton House and get out at the foot of the gangway. And remain indoors at Calderton House until he had booked his passage, got his ticket, and made all arrangements.

Of course, he could point out to the tutor and Katherine that it was entirely up to them; that since they were so anxious to get rid of him, they could damn well *get* rid of him; see him safe out of the country. It would be the simplest thing to make it perfectly clear that his safety was their own. Yes, and he'd give Katty a fair deal. Provided she did her best to help him with cash and the loan of her boy-friend, he'd do his best to make things easy for her; make everything all right for her, in point of fact. He'd fade away as quietly as he had arrived, and no one a penny the worse—except Arthur, in the matter of his pocket, and he'd never know it. Katty would take damn good care of that. . . .

Meanwhile, how to get back to the house? He couldn't lie here till daylight. On the other hand, he could. Perhaps it would be the best thing to do— though it would look a bit queer if he knocked-in at dawn; came home with the milk. Start the servants talking, and there was no need to do that. The less he was talked about the better, here, there, or anywhere else.

Besides, who was he that he should lie on his belly under a bush all night long because one of that damned witch-doctor's killers was out to get him?

No, he'd wait another half-hour or so, then wriggle forward, stick his head out and watch for the gunman to cross the drive and come looking for him, and if he got half a chance, he'd jump on the swine's back, gun or no gun, and strangle the life out of him.

Who would it be? The voice sounded unpleasantly like that of El Benemerito's own private thug, Juan Torillo, his bodyguard, body-servant and right-hand man, or devil.

But it would hardly be he, for Romez would scarcely pay even his old friend Señor Xeres the compliment of sending Torillo all the way to England to get him. Besides, Torillo was a full-blooded Carib Indian and would be unable to get along in England or in any other European country, except Spain.

What was more likely was, that the Well-deserving had sent for half a dozen of his brightest young men and said,

"Get you down to Caibo, take the next ship to Colon, and pick up the first mail-boat to England. Stay there till you've got the good Señor Xeres, and don't come back till you have."

But how on earth, once again, had they traced him to Calderton?

After lying motionless and silent for what seemed to him to be the better part of an hour, Ferring-Chevigny edged gently and slowly forward, inch by inch, on his hands and toes, until, his head protruding from beneath the leaves of the great rhododendron bush, he could see the stars, the tree-tops silhouetted against them, and the gravel road a faintly outlined blur amidst the greater darkness.

Here again he waited, half fearing, half hoping,

to see a black figure between him and the starry sky. For it needs cold courage to attack, unarmed, a man who, concentrating every sense and nerve and faculty, advances with his finger upon the trigger of an automatic pistol.

Nevertheless, such was Ferring-Chevigny's disappointment and grief, chagrin and rage, that had his enemy come within his reach, he would have seized his ankles to jerk him from his feet, or flung himself at him, low, in a flying rugger tackle.

But nothing moved.

There was no sound, and, having buttoned his coat, turned up its collar and tucked his cuffs inside his sleeves, that no gleam of white linen might betray him, he rose, with infinite precaution, to his feet, and crouching low, crept softly along the grassy verge of the drive in the black shadow of the shrubs.

Arrived at the beginning of the chestnut avenue, he turned aside from the edge of the gravel road, on to the wide turf of the park, and, his nerves overcoming his discretion and self-control, ran for his life in the direction of the house.

In his own hiding-place opposite to that of his quarry, Señor Diogenes Barrios heaved a sigh of relief, as he pocketed his automatic, rose to his feet and brushed himself down.

That had been a little too exciting. Distinctly unpleasant, not to say nerve-racking, lying there armed with nothing better than an automatic loaded with blank cartridge. A nice thing if that damned great Englishman had caught him. Like all the rest of his beefy tribe, the English brute would have a knowledge of *pugilato, le boxe,* yes, boxing, and would have given Señor Barrios a frightful hiding if he had been able to lay hands on him.

Carramba! They didn't want much for their

money, up at the Embassy!

XV

Things took a turn for the worse, if that were possible, when our Captain Montague Ferring-Chevigny announced that henceforth he proposed to live at Calderton altogether.

What prevented the situation from becoming absolutely unbearable was his assurance that it might not continue for very long. Had we been able to place any real reliance upon his word, the assurance would have made his visit almost welcome. As it was, we could only hope, hope for the best, and do, from hour to hour and day to day, what seemed to be for that best.

I had, as usual, sat in the drawing-room for a while that evening, talking with Lady Calderton on the subject that obsessed our minds, the only subject of which we could possibly talk or think; and, having succeeded in making her take a little more hopeful view of the situation, had persuaded her to go early to bed. I had then gone up to my room and thrown myself down in my armchair to have a last pipe before turning in. I had just got my pipe alight and going well when there came a tap at my door and Jenkins entered, a little hurried and perturbed.

"Excuse me, sir," he said, speaking somewhat more quickly than usual, "but the gentleman has come back. Had a sort of heart-attack or fainting fit. Just managed to get back to the house, and had time to ring, before he collapsed. When Robert opened the door, he was lying against it. Very bad, he seems."

No such luck, thought I, but, putting on a hypocritical look of concern, sprang to my feet and said,

"That's bad. I'll come at once. Perhaps we ought to ring up Dr. Stanton.

"Or have you done so?" I added, praying that he had done nothing of the sort. For I felt in my bones that this was another of Ferring-Chevigny's tricks. He had been well enough when he had left the house an hour or two ago. Besides, if he had had a seizure, a stroke, or a heart-attack, all that time ago, it would have been at the inn or close to it. Surely he hadn't been lying at the bottom of our main entrance all this time?

Thus thinking, I followed Jenkins by the short cut down the formerly-secret staircase into the hall.

On a huge oak chest lay Ferring-Chevigny, a cushion beneath his head, his eyes half closed, the eyeballs rolled back so that only the whites showed. His lips were parted and distended in a kind of fixed grin, displaying his even teeth. His colour was bad, and beads of moisture stood upon his forehead. Apparently breathing had ceased. He certainly appeared to be in a bad way, and I wondered whether the cold sweat could be that of death. Frankly I hoped it was.

Did I commit murder in my heart, not only in hoping this, but in deciding that I would not tell Jenkins to ring up Dr. Stanton and ask him to come as quickly as he could? The moralist might so argue—and he is quite welcome to do it.

"Brandy, I think, Jenkins," I said, "and if you've got any ice, we'll put some on his forehead and wrists. If there's any strong ammonia, that might be useful, too."

"Her Ladyship has some smelling-salts, sir, but . . ."

"Plain strong ammonia would be better, I think," I said grimly. "There's some in my bathroom."

I'd be damned if I allowed him to get anything of

Lady Calderton's for the fellow's benefit.

Directing the gaping Robert to fetch the bath ammonia, Jenkins departed in search of brandy. As his footsteps died away along the flagged corridor that led to the servants' quarters, Ferring-Chevigny's eye-balls returned to their normal position, the eye-lids opened widely, the mouth relaxed, and he raised his head.

"Good Lord!" he whispered.

"What?" I asked sharply.

"He's gone for the *cooking*-brandy!"

"And some ammonia," I added.

"Well, you can drink that, Waring. Listen—with both ears. You've got to get me to bed. Right here. I've come to stay for a bit. I have just been shot up. Here in the drive. I must stay in the house—in hiding—or they'll get me."

"What d'you mean?"

"Just what I say. Have a room got ready, and I'll go to bed at once. I'll stay in bed all day to-morrow, too—perhaps the next day as well—and I'll be too ill to leave the house for some time. How long I don't know, but it will be as long as I think fit. Let my wife know, and she can tell the servants what she likes. Got to keep up appearances, I suppose—and I've done my part. It's up to her now. I'm going to lie doggo here until . . ."

Suddenly he fell back and resumed his cataleptic trance; nor, when Jenkins handed it to me, could I force any of the cooking-brandy between his clenched teeth. Nevertheless, the ammonia worked wonders, if only by suggestion; for, uncorking the bottle, I bade Jenkins take the unfortunate gentleman's handkerchief, press it firmly across his mouth, while I raised his head, closed one of his nostrils, and pressed the bottle hard against the other.

It proved unnecessary. Again the eyes became

normal, the mouth relaxed, a deep sigh was audible and the patient spoke.

"Where am I?" he whispered.

"Not where you ought to be," replied I promptly.

Ferring-Chevigny eyed me straitly.

"Not at the inn? . . . Good Lord, no. Calderton . . . What's happened? Oh, I remember. I say, old chap, I'm afraid I shall have to ask for a bed. I'm in for one of my bad goes . . . Always begin like this. Heart-attack . . . Rigor . . . Malaria . . . If you and Jenkins would give me a shoulder each, I think I could get upstairs. I'll lie down on your bed if I may, while they get one ready, eh?"

And so Captain Ferring-Chevigny came into residence at Calderton.

§2

To do him justice, I must say that on the whole he behaved well, though whether this was due to the fact that he was badly frightened and very anxious as to his future, I don't know.

When I visited him in bed the next morning, ostensibly to see whether he had everything he required, but actually to try to discover his plans, I found him definitely subdued and inclined to self-pity.

"What did I tell you?" he said. "Thought I was drawing the long bow, didn't you, when I told you about El Benemerito's intelligence-organization— how it was the best in the world, and even better in foreign countries than at home? I told you he could strike equally surely, if not equally quickly, in London or in Boledo. Well, what price striking in Calderton? Right here, in Calderton Park. How's that for a long arm?"

And he proceeded to tell me how someone had

emptied an automatic at him at a few feet range; how by skilful ducking and dodging, turning and twisting and zig-zagging, he had escaped being shot, by drawing his assailant's fire until the pistol was empty and then rushing at the spot whence the flashes had come, and put the cowardly ruffian to flight. Then without waiting for the assassin to reload his pistol, he had run back to the house.

"I told you they were after me, didn't I?" he said. "Well, they all but got me to-night. I marvel there are no bullet-holes in my hat or clothes."

"The sooner you get away from here the better," I observed, "now that it is obvious that they know where you are."

"You've said it, brother. If I stay here, they'll get me. I can't spend the rest of my life inside the house, and if I could, our Arthur might object."

"He might think it strange," I agreed with somewhat heavy sarcasm.

"Yes, I'm not going to do anything in a hurry, though. I'll go as soon as the coast is clear, if ever it is—and I'll take you with me."

"What d'you mean?" I asked, making little effort to hide the unbounded satisfaction that his words gave me. For come what might, surely the first thing was to get rid of the man, get him as far away as possible, get a rest, a breathing-space, and then hope for the best.

"What do I mean? What I say. When the going seems good, we'll go together, you and I and the chauffeur and anybody else we can think of, and you will see me safe on board the ship. I'm not going to set foot outside this house after dark, and I'm not going out in daylight until I go for good; and I'm not going until two or three hours before my ship sails. And you are going to take care of me; stick closer to me than a brother sticketh, and get me safe out of the country. See? . . . They won't shoot me up in broad daylight and in good company, because they don't want to hang in England for killing me, any more than they want to do so in Boruela for not killing me. So you are going to chaperone me, my lad."

"Why should I?"

"Don't ask silly questions. You get me safe out of the country, and you and the girl-friend will be safe here *in* the country. Arthur too. And our beloved young Anthony."

I eyed the man without comment.

"For I shan't squeal," he continued, his spirits visibly rising as he planned his escape. "Don't you be afraid. I'm no spoil-sport. You both do your best for me, and you won't find me ungrateful."

"Do you mean that Lady Calderton will absolutely never see or hear anything of you again— provided we get you safe out of England now?"

"Absolutely," he replied. "Obviously I can't come back here, can I? This place is no good any more as a hide-up. God's curse on the swine—they've queered this pitch for me."

"Yes," I agreed heartily. "Your life won't be worth a minute's purchase if you show yourself outside . . . They must be determined beggars to come right into the park here."

"Yes, by gad, what did I tell you? They stick at absolutely nothing. El Brujo is one of those who say to a man 'go' and he goeth, 'come' and he cometh. And he doesn't cometh back until he hath done what he was told to do. Wonder how many of them there are."

"Well, there's one thing," I assured him. "If three or four of us start out together in a fast car in broad daylight, and go straight to the ship, you'll get on board safe enough. They can't do anything. And once you are on board, you'll be all right."

"You'd think so, wouldn't you? But I rather

fancy I'll book two passages on two ships, say one from Liverpool and one from Southampton, and I'll start out towards Bristol. And if we are followed by another fast car, which we can't shake off, we'll go through some town like Winchester, and as we suddenly turn a corner, I'll jump out and nip into a shop, almost without stopping our car. Then you buzz on, and they'll follow you, and the laugh will be on them. I'll lie low for a time in Winchester, or wherever it is, then get a taxi or a hired car or something, to Southampton. Oh, we'll fool them all right."

And again his spirits obviously rose.

"And where will you go?"

"Haven't decided, but probably . . ."

He paused and eyed me speculatively.

"Probably where you won't know that I've gone," he continued, and uttered his irritating silly laugh. "If you don't know you can't tell, can you? All you and Katty need know is a bank address, and the only address of mine that bank will have will be a branch of the Singapore and Sydney Bank, Shanghai way or Bangkok; and the only address that branch bank'll ever have will be—the one I give them."

"Excellent," I agreed. "I assure you I haven't the very slightest desire to know where you'll be."

"That's all right then, because you wouldn't if you did, if you know what I mean. Now I'll tell you what you can do. You go for a walk. Take young Anthony with you, and tell that bright-eyed boy to see if he can spot the winner, in this case something foreign-looking—in the ice-cream merchant or organ-grinder line. He'll probably be small, stocky and swarthy. Black moustache and eyebrows, black hair: that sort of brute. As I say, the kind of thing you used to see pushing an ice-cream barrow or with a smaller edition of himself on his shoulder, or on his barrel-organ. Might be two or three of them, of course; and they might be got up as gentlemen—save the mark!—South American tourists doing England. But I doubt it. More likely something in the tramp and pedlar line. And what I want you to do—though you mustn't take the holy boy in with you, of course—is to go into the pubs and make kind inquiries.

"This assassin certainly wasn't staying at the Calderton Arms, but he might have gone there now. He may be at the Red Lion. And there's a stinking little beer-shop just outside the village. I don't think it has even got a name. He may be there. Don't march in and say,

" 'Have you got a bloody-minded, yellow-bellied Dago who brandishes a thundering great automatic pistol staying here?' "

"No?" I inquired, with the heavy sarcasm that always seemed to pass him by.

"No. You can look at the registration book at the Calderton Arms before trying the Red Lion, for they are bound to make him sign it if he goes there, and you needn't expect to find something like Señor Cascara Sagrada y Oompara Tarrara, because he won't use his own name, or anything like it."

"No?" I inquired again.

"No. He won't use his own or any other foreign-sounding name. You look out for 'Mr. John Thomas' or some such name as that, written in a foreign hand—pointed, spidery, and with something funny about the loops and curves. They can't disguise it. You can have a Dago, clever as the devil at disguises, but can he disguise his handwriting so that the fact that it is foreign doesn't stick out a mile? No, he can't. Well, having spotted some foreign-looking handwriting, you say you've come to call on Mr. John Thomas. And if they say he's out, you say you'll wait for him, or make an appointment. Anyway, you get face to face with him and see whether he's a sallow, greasy-faced Dago-looking bastard."

"And if he is?"

"That's all I want to know. You simply say that he is not the John Thomas you are looking for, the old pal who was at Oxford-and-Cambridge College with you. Something of that sort."

"Quite," I observed, in a manner that should have annoyed him.

"Well, 'point of fact, I don't suppose he's there. When you are sure he isn't, go to the Red Lion. Before you go in, tie a coloured handkerchief round your neck, turn up your coat-collar, pull your cap down over one eye, drop your Oxford accent and, in as Cockney a voice as you can manage, ask the blowzy woman behind the bar, or the dirty-shirted pot-man, whether there's a vacant doss for the night. If they say no, ask them if they are full, and so find out if they've got anybody staying there. If they say yes, ask to see the room, and then inquire whether they haven't got something better, and find out, that way, whether there's anyone staying there. If somebody is, then it's up to you to get a sight of him.

"Same sort of game, or more so, at the anonymous pot-house. If you draw a blank at all three, then go from door to door in the village and say you are a Census Officer, and particularly want to know if they've got any lodgers, and that anything they say will be twisted into evidence against them, so they'd better speak the truth because it is a Government job and a hanging matter if they tell lies. In fact, go through that cursed village with a fine tooth-comb and find out where my free-shooting friend (or friends) is staying."

"What then—if, and when, I've located him and . . . ?"

"Why, then it's up to you," he interrupted, "to

find out 'if and when' he goes away for the day, or for good, so that I can make a bolt for it, while the coast is clear. That's where the power of the purse and the beauty of bribery and corruption come in. You promise the old woman, or whoever it may be, a quid, if she lets you know. If she has got the intelligence to go to the Post Office and use the telephone, to send a message like 'The cuckoo has left the nest,' or 'Pratztank and Widdelrat have boned the baby,' then she can ring you up here. Or if it's just some plain B.F., that couldn't use a telephone, say you'll pass the house at ten every morning and if there's a card in the window or a jerry hanging on the knocker, that's a sign and a token that the foreigner has gone . . . I'll leave it to you."

"Thank you," I replied gratefully.

"Anyhow, you find out if there's a Dago staying at Calderton; how many of him there is or are; and lay water-tight plans for finding out when they are going away, either temporarily or for good."

"I'll do that—and will take the liberty of doing it in my own way. Anything else?"

"Yes. You can tell our girl friend I want to see her."

"If you wish to speak to Lady Calderton, you can get up and dress; and I've no doubt she will see you in the drawing-room, this afternoon."

"Is that so now? Well, it doesn't suit me to get up and dress and wait till this afternoon. So you can hop it, my lad, and bring my wife here. At the double."

"Look here, Ferring-Chevigny, do you want me to help you?"

"Do you want me to go? What's more, do you want me to keep my mouth shut?"

Yes, he still held the whip hand. And with sinking heart I realized that as long as he lived he'd hold the whip hand.

As long as he lived . . .

Need that be very long?

Why shouldn't I kill him? He'd never be missed, for, legally, he didn't exist. He had 'died' seventeen years ago.

For a man who could laugh that awful laugh of his; a man who could be such an utter fool as to be a criminal; a man who could be so smugly self-satisfied, and do and say such stupid things, Fer-ring-Chevigny could be, as perhaps I have indi-cated, acutely observant, and could exercise his undeniable powers of intuition pretty accurately.

Sitting up suddenly, and pointing a finger straight at my face,

"I say, Waring," he said, "I'm putting all my cards on the table, in front of you. I'm trusting you absolutely. I'm relying on your sense of honour, your honesty, your decency, and the fact that you are a gentleman. I trust you implicitly . . . You wouldn't give me away to these Dagos? Get me done in, so that you and the girl—so that you and Lady Calderton—I mean . . . so that Sir Arthur and Lady Calderton—could live happy ever after?"

To this I made no reply whatsoever.

"I rely on you, Waring, and I trust you to do nothing against me—behind my back."

To this also I made no reply.

"I know when I'm dealing with an honourable man. I am in your hands, Waring—and you can play either the gentleman or the Judas Iscariot."

To this also I made no reply.

If he were absolutely safe so far as I was con-cerned, there was no reason why he should know it. It was no business of mine to give him any sense of comfort and security. And there was another thing. Who had the first claim on my 'decency'? Lady Calderton or this blackguardly schemer?

And inasmuch as his death would be her salvation, why should I lift a finger to prevent it?

And from that it was but a short step to the question—Why should not I encompass his death? If one of the two had to die—and I was perfectly certain it would mean death to Lady Calderton—why should it not be he? Why should it be the innocent woman rather than the scoundrelly man? In principle, I am against murder, but there are worse things than murder. And this man threatened a worse thing. His very existence implied it.

And I thought of a famous phrase, a title of some Tudor pamphlet, "Killing no Murder." Was it a murderous act to kill this reptile that had crept into this house?

And his talk of my being an honest man, an honourable man, a decent man, a gentleman; his talk of trusting me implicitly, relying on me absolutely—what was that but trickery and cunning, a base appeal to my vanity, on the presumption that I was vain and proud of my alleged honour and impeccability? It wasn't as though he had trusted me with a simple child-like and genuine faith—as Anthony did. It was Anthony who trusted me, trusted me to do the right thing as surely as he trusted the sun and the moon and the stars to shine. This man trusted nobody, me perhaps least of all. And his putting me on my honour was but one of the tricks of his trade.

Again he seemed almost to read my thoughts, or perhaps he took my silence for dissent.

"But it is also a little bit of the 'Trust-in-Heaven-but-keep-your-powder-dry' wisdom, too, you know, Waring. I do trust you. I know you are incapable of a dirty trick; but I'll put just a little bit of reliance on the fact that no one does the dirty on me and gets away with it. If I'm shot here, or anywhere else in England for that matter, or if I am kidnapped—and they are quite competent to kidnap the strongest man alive, and take him wherever they want him— if, I say, I am shot or kidnapped here, I shall blow the gaff all right."

I eyed him in silence.

"And don't you think," he added, "that if I am shot in the back of the neck and haven't any breath for blowing the gaff, it therefore won't be blown. If anything happens to me so that I am not heard of for a given period, a letter goes automatically from my bank to General Sir Arthur Calderton. See? I should be awfully sorry for that to happen, and as you are rightly thinking, it won't do me any good— but it'll do you and the girl friend a hell of a lot of harm, and their beloved Anthony too, not to mention Sir Arthur. And that's why I've so rigged it up that my life will be very precious to you, Waring. Therefore you'll keep me alive and healthy and happy and free to come and go. Especially *go*. See?"

Was he speaking the truth? Somehow I didn't believe it; but it was an uncomfortable thought. As I've said before, I want to be just to the man— though I've never in my life hated anybody as I hated him; and, in fact, I've never hated anybody but him—and to be quite fair, I don't think he had done anything of the sort. Selfish he was, selfish beyond belief, cruel, heartless, and base in many ways; but, as he himself so often said, he drew the line, and I don't think he was meanly vindictive. Not to the extent of deliberately planning a posthumous vengeance like that. Certainly he would have sacrificed any of us and all of us, to further his own interests, but I believe he wronged himself in pretending that he had planted any epistolary bombshell, fused and ready to be hurled in ignorance by his bank, in the event of his death or disappearance. As a matter of fact, I doubted whether he had a bank.

"Well, now we know where we are," continued Ferring-Chevigny. "You get down to it and locate the Dagos, and I'll have a talk with Katty. Send her up."

And as I was about angrily to refuse, he added,

"And don't forget, my good ass, that we must keep up appearances. Bear in mind that I'm damned ill, and that I can't fall into the house half dead at midnight and prance about the drawing-room next afternoon in rude health, can I? She can come here, secretly, a damned sight better than I can go there. Anyway, send her."

And in completest agreement with what I was miserably thinking, he grinned and made the motion of one who cracks a whip.

XVI

Lady Calderton entered the room in which her husband lay in bed, and, closing the door behind her, said,

"Mr. Waring brought me your message, and I've come to hear anything you may have to say.

"And I pray God it may be the last time I see your face or hear your voice," she added.

Captain Ferring-Chevigny laid down his newspaper, laughed, and extended the hand of friendship.

"Now, Katty, my dear, don't be hard. Don't be bitter. Let's part friends, since part we must."

"What did you wish to say to me? If there's nothing new, I'll go."

"Well, there's a lot new. Come and sit down here. Come along, I say. Quite like old times, isn't it? Do you remember when you used to bring me my breakfast in bed? Always would take the tray from the maid at the door, wouldn't you, Katty?"

"If you've anything to say, will you please say it at once?"

"Well, since you won't be pally—and in point of fact, it's unwise of you, as well as unnecessary, to take this sort of line—I'll make the position clear. No doubt the boy friend has put you wise to the fact that I've got to clear out. Got to go while the going's bad; and you and he have got to help me—especially he. As you can't do much except lend him to me and spur him on, you make it quite clear to him that it's his job in life to get me safely out of England with a whole skin—and a shut mouth."

"Naturally I shall do everything I can to help you to get out of England."

"Devil doubt you, my love. And as you might have known, I'm going to do the right thing by you. Can't make an honest woman of you, Katty, or I would. But you can take my word for it, I'm not going to make trouble. I draw the line at that sort of thing. 'Point of fact, it looks as though you are going to have your kind wish, and never see my not unhandsome face again, nor hear my not unpleasant voice."

"Where are you going?"

"W-e-l-l-l, least said soonest mended, and fewest questions fewest lies, and all that. In other words, if you don't know, you can't tell, can you? At any rate, I'm going where you won't be troubled by me. As I say, you won't see me nor hear me, nor get any letters. Provided you do your wifely part, and I get letters, that is. All I want is a letter from you once a quarter; and that only a few figures and a signature. On a cheque. Unless, of course, you'd like to write and tell me all the news . . . Oh, for the Lord's sake come and sit down. Don't stand there staring. Come and sit on the side of the bed. For old times' sake, Katty. The good old times."

"How much do you want me to send you? How can I possibly do it without it becoming known?"

"That's your trouble, my dear. No, don't let's say trouble. Let us say it's your pigeon . . . And surely that's where the boy friend will come in useful. Anyway, you've got to get me the wherewithal, and I'll leave the means to you. You get it safe into the Singapore and Sydney Bank. And honestly, Katty, I don't want to put you to any inconvenience. Arthur's a rich man; and some husbands would insist on making a real good touch in the circumstances, a real good killing, but I'm not that sort of man. As you know, I draw the line at . . . at . . ."

"At what?" inquired Lady Calderton.

"Well, at anything—what shall we say—wrong,

improper, unreasonable. Blackmail, as you are good enough to call it, for example."

"What do you call it?"

"Well, if you will have it defined in words of one syllable, I call it right and proper assistance given by a wife to her husband. What do you call it? You are my lawful wife. I'm your lawful husband. And it is your right and duty, and should be your privilege, to help your husband when he's in trouble. Any objections?"

"How much do you want?"

"Katty, you really are a bit—er—businesslike, not to say harsh and sordid. Damn it all, you needn't make things unpleasanter for me than they are. You don't suppose I like having to depend on my wife for a little while, do you? I can assure you that when I am on my feet again, I shan't trouble you. You can keep your money and be damned to it."

"How much do you want?"

"Well, within limits I am willing to leave that to you. Within reason, I say. Do get it into your head that I don't want to inconvenience you, though in the circumstances an unprincipled man would bleed you white . . . What about a thousand a year until I'm straight? That's reasonable enough, surely."

"So that, every three months, I am somehow to scrape together two hundred and fifty pounds, and pay it into this bank, am I? And how do you suppose that I'm going to do that without my husband knowing?"

"Your *husband* will know, duckie," and a loud guffaw seemed to envelop and drown her in a surging sea of sound. "Your husband will know all right, and believe me, he'll know if you don't send it . . . What you mean is, how are you to do it without the good Sir Arthur Calderton knowing. Once again, that's your affair, *if* it is in any way difficult. But, once again—the boy friend—I've got an idea that he's a lad with Great Expectations as well as great present enjoyments. Hasn't he got a Rich Uncle? Doubtless the boy friend'll be able to help, any time when you couldn't lay your hands on the right amount just at the moment . . . And as to my getting away, could you manage a hundred?"

"Yes, I can give you a hundred pounds to help you to get away.

"I'd give a million if I had it," she added.

"Oh come, come! Drop it, Katty. Don't be so bitter. Do you know what 'bitter' is the comparative of? Bitch. Don't you be one. You be a good girl. Come on. Drop it and be matey. Kiss and be friends. Yes, literally. I mean it. Come here. Come on."

"Listen," said Lady Calderton, retreating towards the door. "I understand that you are in danger; that an attempt was made on your life last night."

"Right again, my love, right as usual. It was."

"And that you've taken refuge here because you daren't show your face outside in daylight, and still less dare to go out in darkness."

"That's the situation. Nice state of affairs, isn't it, in Merrie England?"

"Then hadn't you better bear it in mind, and remember that your safety, your life, are in my hands, just as much as my happiness and social safety are in yours?"

"Exactly. Quite. We are quits. What are you driving at?"

"I'm suggesting that you behave and talk as though you realized that you are here on sufferance, that if I were to let anger and indignation and resentment get the better of me, I could . . ."

"Yes, my lass, and so could I. You try anything of

that sort, and see where you'll be! . . . Really, Katty, I'm ashamed of you. I wonder you aren't ashamed of yourself. A nice way to talk, after what I've just said to you—that the last thing in the world I want to do is to make any trouble. All I want to do is to go . . ."

"Now that your life is in danger!"

". . . go away quietly, I was going to say, without causing any trouble to you or to anyone else. Yes, and showing you every consideration, instead of trying to wring the last penny out of you that I could get."

Captain Ferring-Chevigny folded his arms upon his broad chest, and regarded his wife steadily, as much in sorrow as in anger.

"I really feel hurt," he said.

The woman stared at him, almost in wonderment, almost incredulous, amazed that such a man as he could exist; yet more than half convinced that he was in earnest, that the point of view that he expressed was genuine.

For some seconds they eyed each other in silence, her look of contemptuous wonderment met by his glare of irritation, annoyance and disappointment.

Why couldn't the silly woman meet him halfway, let by-gones be by-gones, and accept the situation?

Why couldn't she join forces with him for their mutual safety?

Suddenly his brow cleared. He sat up and held forth appealing open hands.

"Come on, Kathy, let's be friends. Let's work together. Surely our interests are identical. Surely to God it would be wiser to help each other, than to hinder. Smoothness is always better than friction—and especially at a time like this. Let's get together. Kiss and be friends. Come on. After all, you are my wife, and I've got my conjugal rights, haven't I? Even if I've waived them out of consideration for the situation you've brought about. Come on, old girl . . . Partners . . . A man wants a little love in his life, doesn't he? And you are . . ."

"Listen. If there's anything you wish to say that must be absolutely private between us, say it now, and I'll undertake not to repeat it. For I'll never speak to you again alone. I'll never be in the same room with you again, except in the presence of a third person."

"The boy friend, eh?"

"Yes. Mr. Waring. Or the butler. Or a groom—with a dog-whip in his hand and . . ."

"And that'll be enough, I think. You're a fool, as you always were . . ."

"I was, indeed."

". . . a fool, as you always were, as well as a bigamist. You want me for an enemy, do you?"

"Infinitely rather than as a friend. And please remember that I could, at any moment, turn you out of this house and that I'm sorely tempted to do so."

"And queer your own pitch! And your husband's. And your son's."

"No, it's for the sake of my husband and my son that I'm standing here talking to you alone, now—for the last time. I'll do my best to help you to get away, and I'll do my best to pay you a thousand a year to keep away. And to keep silent . . . And although I'm a fool, I have sense enough to realize that you've no wish to lose the income that you'll get from me—for the time being. How long it will go on, I don't know. There are limits to what I can bear, and it's quite possible I may break down under the strain—and tell my husband everything. And you'll be dealing with a man then. Not with a foolish woman."

Captain Montague Ferring-Chevigny sat up straight and suddenly.

"I say, Katty! You'd never ruin yourself by . . ."

"Ruin myself, or *you*, do you mean? Think over what I've just said, keep it well in mind—and get out of this house as soon as you can. Meantime, say to Mr. Waring anything you have to say; make with him any arrangement you have to make. I'll never see you again."

"No need, so long as I see your signature on a cheque," replied the Captain as the door closed.

"There's a bitch for you!" said he to himself as he took up his newspaper, and turned to the Financial columns.

§2

That same afternoon, Anthony Calderton had a bright idea.

He would go riding with his beloved friend and tutor, but with a difference. Instead of being Captain of the King's Bodyguard, and scouting with a Troop of Horse in search of the Roundhead picket-post that was said to have been established during the night within a few miles of Calderton House, he would be a lone scout, and Mr. Waring, instead of being the King's Troop of Horse, should be an Ironside patrol.

He would give him a quarter of an hour's start, and then ride out in search of him. When he saw him, he would blow a blast on his bugle, but if, on the other hand, Mr. Waring saw him first, the latter would blow his whistle. That would be a splendid idea and quite a new game. It would be frightfully thrilling to ride along behind high hedges, peeping through or over them; to hide in spinneys and coppices; to reconnoitre farm-yards and buildings and hay-stacks; to stand up in his stirrups and peep over sky-lines; the whole time feeling that he was in great danger himself, because the enemy was doing exactly the same thing.

Having fully explained the idea to the receptive Mr. Waring as they sat on the terrace after lunch, fixed general direction and the boundaries beyond which he must not ride, and asked him to be sure to remember to take the big police whistle, he went in search of his bugle, a somewhat tarnished and battered instrument from which he could produce one long and piercing note, plaintive and mournful but far-carrying.

"Sir Anthony wound his horn," he said aloud, and tucking his lips into the mouthpiece, distending his cheeks and blowing with all the strength of his lungs, he 'wound.'

"He blew a blast right woundily," he remarked. "Now would that be 'woundily' like a wound, or 'woundily' like wounding (no, winding) up a watch?

"Anyway, he'll hear that, if I catch sight of him; and it will be his death-knell . . . Golly! That's an idea . . . If he hears the sound of my silver-tongued clarion, no, brazen-voiced trumpet—I'll have my trumpeter riding at my sword-hand—then he's to fall off his horse, dead. In other words, dismount. Likewise, if I hear the shrill menancing—or is it menacing—shriek of his fatal whistle, then I fall from my horse, dead . . . Yes, that'll be splendid."

A few minutes later, Henry Waring, with a word of comfort and assurance to Lady Calderton, went and took the whistle from where it lay with dog-collars, leashes, whips and odds-and-ends in a drawer in an old bureau in the hall, and departed to the stables . . .

"Now, it's a quarter to three, Sir. I'll start at three o'clock and the general direction will be eastward, won't it? Then as the sun comes round to the west, I shall have it behind me."

"Shouldn't be surprised, my son."

"Then I shall be able to spot you better, with the sun on you, and you'll be able to see me silhouetted against the skyline."

"Dismounting allowed?" inquired Waring.

"What d'you think?"

"Make it much more difficult. I could tie my horse up, in a coppice somewhere, and climb up a tree and spot you miles away."

"Yes. So you could. Right. No dismounting in the game, until I hear your whistle or you hear my bugle, eh? And the one that hears is defeated, and falls dead."

"Yes." And trotting across the gravel square before the stables, on to the springy turf, Henry Waring cantered across the park and out of sight.

A quarter of an hour later, Anthony Calderton rode down the drive, through the great gates and out on to the road, along the grassy margin of which he would be able to get a good gallop.

As he turned on to the wayside grass, a man rose from a stile on which he had been sitting, raised his hat of yellow velvet velour, bowed from the hips, smiled with a flash of bright white teeth beneath bright red lips and a little black moustache, and held out a letter towards the boy.

"Egg-scuza me, sair," he said with an exaggerated foreign accent, "but would you pliz be so ver' kindly as to give this letter to the *caballero, gentilhomme,* who stay at Calderton House?"

"What, Mr. Waring?" replied Anthony Calderton, eyeing the brilliant mauve envelope.

"No, sair. Ze other *caballero* who stay there leetle while. *El Capitan*—er——"

"Captain Bertie-Norton? All right. But why not post it? Or take it up to the house yourself?"

"Sair, pliz. It is ver' important it reach him, and I am not writing English post-address so good. And sure, if I go up to the *casa—ze castillo*—perhaps the major-domo say, '*You getta der Hell outa dis.*' Sair, pliz."

"Oh, all right. Give it here," said Anthony, bending towards the man as his horse reared and sidled away. "I'll see he gets it."

"Sair, I t'ank you."

"Pooh! How it stinks," thought the boy as, with a kindly nod to the man, he put the letter in his pocket and gave his impatient hunter its head.

And it came to pass that Anthony Calderton's bright idea did his mother invaluable service, and very promptly rid Calderton House of a loathed and detested presence. For, that night, undressing and emptying, as was his wont, the contents of his pockets on to his dressing-table, he found the sealed mauve envelope which, in the absorbing interest of his scouting for the Roundhead patrol, he had quite forgotten.

Smiling his side-way secret smile, he put the letter under a book that lay on his bedside table, completed his preparations for the night, and got into bed. . . .

"What do I smell, darling?" asked Lady Calderton a little later, when she paid her usual bed-time visit.

"Smell, Mother?" asked the boy innocently. "Is it like sulphur? Because just now the lights in the chamber burned blue and with a stamp of cloven hooves and a fierce waggle of a barbed but prehensile tail, the fiend . . ."

"No, darling, not a bit like sulphur. More like
. . ."

"I know. Mice. Exactly like three blind mice. Smell how they run. I saw three pink-eyed . . ."

"More like some sort of barber's hair-oil or cheap scent. You haven't been having your hair cut?"

And Lady Calderton sniffed the boy's hair,

rumpling it fondly.

"I think you must have brought the smell in with you, darling. Don't muck my hair about. I've just brushed it. Tell me a tale about Montiga. You know, Voodoo and papaias or papalois; or how the son of a white planter defended the old colonial house near the sugar-cane plantation, the planter's house in which lay his aged mother; defended it from the attack of ten thousand rum-maddened negroes armed with machetes and—what-not."

"Afraid I wasn't there, just at the time, my son."

"No, darling. But you can imagine it."

"I'm sure you can imagine it a great deal better. I'll tell you about the crabs that get the great green coco-nuts down from the tops of the palm-trees."

"Or what about the great black-bearded pirates that get the doubloons up from the holds of the merchant-ships?"

"You tell me."

"Right. Would you like Captain Teach, Black-beard, Sir Henry Morgan, or . . ."

And artfully spinning out his story, he detained his mother as long as possible.

"Ask Mr. Waring just to look in, last thing before he goes to bed, to see if I'm asleep, won't you, Mother?" he said, as Lady Calderton departed.

That would establish the fact that he was sound asleep, whether he were or not, and would wake him up if asleep he were . . .

Opening the door, some hours later, and letting in a shaft of light from the corridor, Henry Waring glanced at the humped figure in the bed, whispered 'Good night, Anthony,' in case the boy were lying awake, softly closed the door and went along to his bedroom.

As the door shut, the boy sat up in bed, turned on the light of the shaded lamp that stood on the small table beside him, and looked at his watch.

Half-past eleven. Give Mr. Waring a quarter of an hour or so, and it would to be all right. Better make it twelve o'clock, perhaps. Yes, he'd have a read till then. Twelve o'clock was a fine time for dark nocturnal deeds when church-yards yawn and graves give up their . . . No, that was an unpleasant thought.

There was a story—that had been carefully kept from his ears by parents, governess and tutor, and carefully poured into them by nurse-maids, grooms and footmen—a story about a ghost that walked in Calderton House. A lover, or some such silly thing. He had been flung down the secret staircase and had broken his neck.

What a pity that the secret staircase had been brought to light and uncovered, and was now merely a short cut from the hall to this landing. If only he had discovered it, as he had one or two other secrets, he would have said nothing about it at all. He'd have kept to himself the door in the panelling down in the hall, and the one in the panelling on the landing too. As it was, some silly ass had taken away the door this end, at the top, and as often as not, the one at the bottom was left open. Nothing secret about it whatever.

Did the ghost walk on some particular night, the anniversary of the man's death; or at full moon; or just when it thought it would, or what? Probably it was all bosh; but it would be frightfully interesting to see it 'walk,' especially if it were dressed in the Stuart style. Some people said it was dressed in helmet, breast-plate, jerkin, sword and high riding-boots. A parlour-maid had told an under-nurse, whom he had heard telling the head-nurse, that she had distinctly seen it walk along the corridor towards the head of the steep narrow staircase, where it turned about, glared at her, and vanished backward down the steps; and then she heard a crash and a cry.

True, old Nannie's comment had been, "The little liar!" but it made a good story. He'd write it all out one day.

Golly, what a crash a man in armour would make if he went headlong from the top of those stairs to the bottom. Stairs nearly as steep as a ladder against a wall. He'd crash on the stone floor and up against the panel-door, almost without touching the steps. Most satisfying. Probably burst the door open and roll right out into the hall. It would be rather fun to see the ghost do it. Provided it *did* do it, that is to say. Did its stuff properly, without any nonsense. It would be too awful for words if, instead of turning round and falling backwards headlong down the stairs, it turned round and just came for you instead. One would simply scream one's head off.

Probably the girl was, as Nanny said, a little liar; but on the other hand, it didn't sound like the sort of story that a Calderton village girl would make up —especially the turning round and looking towards her before falling backward down the stairs. There was one thing that didn't ring true though, and that was the ring of the armour, so to speak. How could the ghostly armour of a ghost crash on the little stone square at the bottom of the steps? A ghost hadn't weight and solidity. If you struck a ghost with a sword, you wouldn't hear your sword clash on its helmet or breast-plate, surely? On the other hand, one was always hearing tales about 'ghostly footsteps.' There was the ghost at Mardingley Castle, that tramped up and down the picture-gallery that used to be a banqueting-hall. Any number of people had heard it. Then there were ghostly sighs and groans, and stairs that creaked under the weight of a ghost. So if you could hear a ghost walk, or sigh, presumably you could hear it fall? . . .

There was twelve o'clock striking from the clock-tower over the stables.

Anthony Calderton got out of bed, put on his felt-soled bedroom slippers and his dressing-gown, slipped the strongly scented, highly coloured letter into his pocket, took a small flat pocket-torch from a drawer in his dressing-table, switched off the bedside light, opened his door with the utmost care, and crept along the dark corridor, from time to time switching on the light in the tiny bulb of his pocket-torch.

Near the head of the once-secret stair he stopped by a door in a deep recess. The handle of this he turned with the utmost caution, tried the door and found, as he expected, that it was locked.

Smiling to himself, he then shone the light of his torch upon the right-hand panelling of the deep recess, reached up and, placing the fingers of his right hand upon the protruding ledge of a panel, pulled hard. The panel, with a faint click, moved downward half an inch, and had he not raised the other hand that held the torch, to support it, would have fallen forward. Placing the panel on the floor, the boy reached inside the aperture thus disclosed, pulled back a stout brass bolt and pushed upon the door of which the small removable panel formed a part. This door, or hinged panel, some six feet high by two feet wide, opened inward, and disclosed a passage which was the space between the thick heavy panelling of the room itself and that of the corridor.

Creeping along this, with his light throwing a small wavering beam before him, the boy stopped where a small wooden peg stuck out from the rough wood-work on his left, withdrew from its setting an imitation knot in the wood, applied his eye to the hole, and peeped into the room.

All was well. The room was in darkness save

where, through the high narrow mullioned windows, the pale weak light of a setting moon shone
into the room.

The foul traitor Roundhead spy slept.

Now to place the terrifying missive where he
would see it when he woke. See it, pick it up, and
discover that he was unmasked, his real character
known, and that this chance of escape was given to
him by the son of his Cavalier host and intended
victim; given him because he loved him, or rather,
had loved him until he had accidentally discovered
who and what he was. Between love and duty his
heart was torn. Duty cried that he should denounce
him, have him seized and cast into a dungeon, and
there lie in chains until his father returned. But
love forbade. How could he deliver to shameful
death this man whom he had adored? David and
Jonathan . . . But when he found this letter and
read the stinging words that he had written, how he
would burn with shame; how he would slink away
and . . .

Hullo, what was that? Only a snore or a snort or
something, as the villain Roundhead spy tossed
and turned, his evil mind haunted by terrible
dreams.

Now for it.

But suppose Captain Bertie-Norton woke up
and caught him. What an ass he would look. No,
he'd just say,

'Oh, I say, a fellow gave me this to give to you to-
day. Awfully sorry I didn't bring it along before.'

Captain Bertie-Norton might think it a bit funny
that he should bring it in the middle of the night,
like this, but he couldn't do anything about it,
could he?

And drawing back two more brass bolts, one at
the top of a panel and one at the bottom, he slowly
and gently opened the second panel-door and

stepped into the room.

He knew his way about this particular bachelor guest-chamber pretty well, as he had often used it for his own private diversions, plays and games, his private stronghold, ever since he had been shown the secret entrance by Miss Stuart. She had read about it in the old book *A Historie of Calderton Castle*, hunted about until she had discovered it, and then shown him the trick of it. Jolly decent of her, and great fun they had had, playing Cavaliers and Roundheads with this as the secret room.

The beauty of it was that the bedroom door, of heavy solid oak, was self-locking, and unless he knew the trick and moved the catch back, a person entering and closing the door behind him was locked in, whereas anyone inside, hearing some-body coming, could go through the panel into the narrow passage, out by the panel in the recessed doorway, and so down the secret stairs to the hall and freedom.

Having tiptoed into the room, the boy stood still and silent, looking round and making sure that no chair, stool, or other obstacle stood between him and the dressing-table where he proposed to place the letter.

As he did so, another of his bright ideas entered his ever-active mind. What a joke to put it on the vile Roundhead spy's pillow, actually beside his head.

Yes, his breathing was regular and heavy enough, and if the man did wake up it would be all right. He could say his little piece and apologize.

Yes, and then slip away in the darkness and disappear through the panel! Golly, that would puzzle him.

Tiptoeing towards the bed, the boy placed his torch behind him, switched it on and, by the dim diffused light, saw an excellent spot for the placing of the letter. A few seconds later, he was out of the room, the panel closed behind him, the deed accomplished.

Returning to his bedroom, he lay awake a while, elaborating a magnificent story of how the daughter of a great Cavalier house warned her vile false lover of her discovery of his shame, and, while bitterly ashamed also—of herself and her too-merciful deed —allowed him to escape.

Splendid. He'd tell Mr. Waring all about it, some day, and show him the trick of the room, too. It would be a bit of a wrench to part with the secret, share it with somebody else, but he'd do it. Yes, it would be rather a jolly thing to do, and Mr. Waring would understand, and perhaps like him all the better for it.

§3

Captain Ferring-Chevigny awoke next morning at his usual hour of seven, yawned heavily, gazed round the lovely room, into which the sunlight streamed, making it bright and cheerful, in spite of the dark panelling and low and heavily-beamed ceiling.

Suddenly he sniffed audibly, turned his head in the direction whence came the penetrating scent, saw the mauve missive, and realized suddenly the import of its odour, its cheap foreign paper and spidery foreign handwriting. He shot up in bed, recoiling from the letter, as though it had been the deadliest of serpents waiting upon his pillow.

God in Heaven! How had it come there? The self-locking door was bolted, as he had left it last night. The casement windows were shut and fastened on the inside. Only the small upper panes, too narrow to admit anything much bigger than a cat, were open. No human being could reach down from the ventilation panes to the fastening at the bottom of the tall windows. No, they could not possibly have been opened from without.

The ancient fireplace was small, and there again nothing much larger than a cat could have made its way from the chimney into the grate, nor was there the slightest mark or indication of any disturbance.

As he glanced about the room like a trapped animal, his face paled, his eyes distended more wildly, his hand shook as he took the letter . . . They had been in the room while he slept! One or more of them had stood over him. They had had him absolutely at their mercy. Why was his throat not slashed from ear to ear? Why had not a Spanish knife been driven through his heart?

Endeavouring to moisten dry lips, he opened the letter with trembling fingers.

Yes, a letter from El Brujo, or purporting to be from him. A letter saying that the Dictator of Boruela was delighted to learn that his dear lost son-in-law had been found, assuring him that he would never be lost again, and bidding him wait peacefully and patiently for that which would soon and surely come to him. A terrible letter in that vein of sinister playfulness which signified the most terrible mood of that superhuman man, who ruled as a god a population of three million helpless and defenceless souls.

Why had they not killed him in the night? Obviously because their instructions were to torture him for a while, make his life a living death of suspense and fear, play cat-and-mouse with him, until almost he would welcome death; the death they had in store for him.

Or was it—dreadful thought—that they had instructions to bring him back alive; to kidnap him; drug him by way of his food and drink, or by forcible injections, as they had done with thousands of hapless girls? Better death, any death, than be taken back and be delivered to the mercy of El Brujo.

One of those two things it must be. Either cat-and-mouse torture till they killed him here in England; or surveillance and relentless pursuit until opportunity arose for his being knocked on the head, kidnapped, and taken in some Spanish or Boruelan ship and, in the rôle of a sick man, back to Boruela.

But how in the name of miracles had they got into, and out of, that room with its locked and bolted door, its fastened windows, forty feet above the ground, and its narrow chimney down which quite obviously not so much as a sparrow had come that night?

That was almost as unnerving as the dreadful fact that there, there on his pillow, lay a letter from El Brujo. Not written by him, of course, but written for and on behalf of him by the chief of his secret police, that organization from which no enemy was safe in Europe or the whole continent of America.

It had been placed there, doubtless, by the same man or men who had shot at him the other night. Had they deliberately aimed to miss, obeying their instructions to put him to the torture of fear, suspense and terror, before killing him?

Yes, undoubtedly. Otherwise why had they not murdered him last night when they could have done so with the utmost ease and impunity? But that was not their way. Not El Brujo's way. What satisfaction would he get from knowing that the man who had swindled, robbed and unforgettably injured him, had died without knowing what had killed him and who had killed him?

That was not El Brujo's way. His idea of punishment was a period of the utmost horror and suffering that his devilish ingenuity could inflict, a period prolonged to the limit of human endurance. And then, when come it must, the slowest death that he could make his victim die.

And he had thought he was safe here, hidden in Calderton House. Perfectly safe, so long as he had the wisdom and patience to remain within its four walls.

Well, he knew better now, and his one chance was to escape at once, escape so suddenly, swiftly, and secretly, that they would be thrown off the scent. It must be done in such a way that they would suppose him to be still here in Calderton House. The longer they thought that, the better his chance of getting away, far away to some place where El Brujo's secret writ did not run, if such a place there were.

If only he could get out of the country without their knowing it; get on board a ship while they thought he was still here, here in Calderton House, he might win out yet. Surely somewhere he could find some refuge, once he had thrown them off his trail, broken the scent, as a fox might do by swimming a river.

Rising from his bed, thrusting his feet into slippers and throwing on his borrowed dressing-gown, he unfastened the bedroom door, set back the self-locking catch and went along to the bedroom occupied by Henry Waring.

"Look here," he said, bursting into the room. "Do you know anything about this? . . . Send the kid away. I want to speak to you. Look sharp, I say. Matter of life and death."

Anthony Calderton, glancing at the mauve envelope, and eyeing the haggard face of the obviously excited and troubled man, smiled secretly.

"Will you excuse us a moment, Anthony?" said Henry Waring, his raised eyebrows and almost shrugged shoulders seeming to apologize to the boy for the crude and peremptory manners of the visitor.

And with a cold, "Certainly, Sir," the boy departed to his bedroom where, in an ecstasy of secret glee, he rolled upon his bed.

"Look here," gabbled Ferring-Chevigny, as the door closed. "You are one of these damned 'men of honour,' aren't you?"

"It's a phrase I don't much like, and never use," replied Waring.

"Well, you call yourself a gentleman, don't you?"

"No. If other people ever do, I raise no objection."

"Look here, Waring. I'm in earnest. For God's sake don't be funny. Matter of life or death. Now then. Cards on the table; straight dealing and plain truth. Do you know anything about this?"

"I have never, to my knowledge, seen it before."

"Look here, man. Plain yes or no. This is a letter written in Spanish. It's from—them. I found it on my pillow when I woke this morning. Now, do you know anything whatsoever about it? Anything at all?"

"I know nothing whatsoever about it," replied Waring. "Nothing at all."

"You don't know how it got there?"

"Listen, Ferring-Chevigny. I'll see if I can make it plain. I've never seen—or smelt—the thing before. I've never heard any sort or kind of reference to it. I know nothing whatsoever about it. I haven't the faintest notion of how it got into your room. I tell you, man, I know *nothing whatsoever* about it. Is that clear?"

"Right, Waring. Thank you. I'll take your word for it. Now then, look. You know that trick door to the room I am in. Well, I'm one of those people who like their bedroom door fastened; and as trick doors may have more than one trick, I bolted it when I went to bed, and I had to unbolt it when I let myself out this morning—as well as fastening back the self-locking latch. No one came in by that door during the night. That's that . . . You know those tall narrow windows between the stone mullions."

"Well?"

"I particularly carefully fastened those before I went to bed last night, and they were securely fastened this morning. The only ventilation was through the little hinged panes at the tops of the windows. Three of them. And there's no cat alive that could walk up those windows and get through them, let alone a human being. The chimney is nothing more than a pipe that joins the big main shaft that goes up from the great hall fire-place. If a cat could come down that narrow bedroom chimney, it's as much as it could do; and there wasn't the faintest sign of any disturbance; no fallen soot, no mark of any kind. Not so much as a bird came down it . . . Now then, how did a man get into that room during the night and put that letter on my pillow? And mark you, Waring, I'm by nature and habit and training, as light a sleeper as there is in this world. The slightest noise would have wakened me. Now then, how was it done?"

"I haven't the very vaguest idea," replied Henry Waring. "And at the moment, I cannot think of anything; any possible solution.

"Supposing I had been going to play a trick upon you," he continued. "How could I have got in, since you had bolted the door; and the window and the chimney being out of the question?"

"Damn it, man, it's impossible. It's impossible," chattered Ferring-Chevigny. "It's absurd. Damn it, there isn't a trap-door in the floor or in the ceiling! And if there were, how the hell could the people break into the house? How could they break into the house and use the trap-doors, if there were any? How should they know what room I'm in? It's impossible; and yet if there's one thing on this earth that is certain, it is that that letter wasn't in that room when I went to bed—much less lying beside my head, on the pillow."

"It's utterly amazing," agreed Henry Waring. "It's fantastic. It is impossible."

"It's a damned miracle! My God, you'd think that they had got the sort of powers those Indian Yogis are supposed to have; and could levitate things. No, 'project' things, don't they call it? Make 'em materialize just where they want 'em to. It's utterly incredible. It's . . . I tell you, Waring, I'm frightened. And I've got the guts to admit it. I'm terrified. Not so much because of what they can do to me, as because of what they've already done. It's miracle-mongering. Damn it all, it makes being shot-up, the other night, just nothing at all. I mean, anybody can be shot-up, and anybody who can get hold of a pistol can do some shooting-up. Not that you'd expect it in a quiet corner of Merrie England. But these . . ."

"We'll go down and have a look at the windows from below," said Waring. "Just to see whether there are any footmarks, or whether a ladder was planted under your window."

"You can go. I'm not going out of the house until I go for good—and that'll be damn soon. But you won't find any marks there. Suppose they could have brought a forty-foot ladder, what then? The windows were fastened. They couldn't have opened 'em, and still less could they have got out again and fastened them on the inside after they had done their job!"

"No," agreed Waring. "Same thing, I suppose, applies to the roof. Still, I'll get up there, through an attic skylight, and just see whether there are any sort of marks on the coping or leads above your window. If they had got up there and lowered a man down by a rope, which of course is absurd, there are bound to be marks in the dirt and dust, scratches on the lead, and the evidence of where a rope had rubbed on the more-or-less mossy or weathered stone at the edge."

"Thanks. But of course that's quite absurd. Suppose a man had been lowered down, he's not coming through a little hinged pane eight inches square, is he? Nor going out through it again, leaving the windows securely fastened on the inside. It's absolutely——"

"By the way, here's an idea," interrupted Waring. "I don't see how it could possibly be done, but just suppose a man got into the house, say while we were at dinner, found his way upstairs and—again incredibly—knew or discovered the one room, out of dozens of rooms, that is your bedroom. Suppose he hid himself in a wardrobe or under the bed and stayed there until . . ."

"Oh, my good ass," groaned Ferring-Chevigny, "I was never out of the room the whole of yesterday, not for five minutes. Don't you realize that I was in the room myself, lying there in bed, the whole day? Of course, a man couldn't march into the house, and of course he couldn't come up to this floor, and of course he couldn't know which was my bedroom. And suppose he did, there was I lying in bed waiting for him. No, that won't do.

"And I'll tell you what's a damned disturbing thought, too," he continued. "They've got an accomplice in the house, planted here. Must have."

"Oh, but that's absurd. You don't imagine that Jenkins or Robert are people of that sort, do you? You don't suppose that the housekeeper is, or the cook. Typical old 'faithful retainers.'"

"What about some Calderton wench that they've got hold of?"

"Rubbish. The head parlour-maid has been with the family for donkey's years, and comes from London, I believe. The second parlour-maid is her sister; and the house-maids and kitchen-maids are simple and decent local girls, who'd as soon think of being criminal accomplices of strangers as of cutting their throats."

"But damn it, man, there's got to be some explanation and——"

"I'll tell you what there has got to be," interrupted Waring, "and the sooner the better. Departure, flight, escape. I've no cause to wish you anything but ill, but I assure you I don't want you murdered here. Not in the house. You are trouble enough alive, Ferring-Chevigny. You'd be even more trouble dead. Disposal of your body, for one thing . . . You must *go*."

"Yes, you're saying something, for once. I'm off, and I'm going to-night, and you've got to help. Tell you what. You and that damned kid are for ever playing your dressing-up games, and mucking about with wigs and whiskers and what-not. Suppose you rig me up with a beard and moustache, some sort of wig, and a hat and overcoat that I've never worn, and you drive me to . . ."

"Southampton?" suggested Waring.

"Southampton! South Hell! We'll start for Tilbury. We'll turn off for Hull; we'll double back in the direction of Bristol; we'll break north and go to earth in some God-forsaken hole, until we are certain we're not followed—some place like Broadway in Gloucester, where these foreigners would be as conspicuous as black-beetles on a table-cloth; and when we are sure we've shaken them off, we'll nip up to Glasgow, and there I'll get a ship for—wherever I decide to go. Now then, which would be better—to go in broad daylight at eleven o'clock in the morning, trusting to disguise, or to slip out at three o'clock at night, in darkness?"

"What about going in daylight, dressed up as a woman?" suggested Waring. "Golden wig; sporting hat with a feather, and a long coat with a skirt under it."

"And bloody great boots," growled Ferring-Chevigny. "And what about the servants?"

"Well, then, what about going in the middle of the night, or rather the small hours of the morning, dressed as a woman?"

"No. I'll trust to a beard, moustache and that light cap and overcoat of yours. That's it. And, by gad, if they are on to us, we'll give them a run for their money. Stop the car in a lonely place, if necessary, and wait for 'em and shoot it out. Nothing I'd like better. What I can't stand is this letter-on-the-pillow miracle stuff. It has got me beat. Let's go to-night."

"To-night it is," replied Henry Waring, getting out of bed.

XVII

How can I attempt to describe the effect on our minds, resultant upon Ferring-Chevigny's departure? To say that a cloud lifted does not begin to describe it. It was like the glorious dawn of a bright and peaceful day after a long black night of storm and danger and terror. It was as though the ship of our fortunes emerged from a dense enveloping fog—after days of gloom and horror throughout which the siren wailed its note of disaster and despair—into glorious sunshine, with an azure sky above and a smooth blue sea around us, a sea whose little white-topped waves were playful, and upon which glittered the happy smile of a benignant sun. It was like waking to peace, comfort and security from a shattering nightmare. It was like the condemned man's reprieve.

Yes; but unfortunately, it was only reprieve, not pardon; not like the pardon that sets him free for ever, free to walk out from the death-cell and the shades of the prison house, into God's good sunshine and sweet air. Only a reprieve for poor Lady Calderton; for while he was alive he was a danger. Nay more, his life was her death; his existence the ruin and destruction of her peace, welfare and happiness, and of those whom she loved far more than she loved herself.

Nevertheless, he was gone. We had a breathing-space, and—he might never be heard of again. That, perhaps, was too much to hope; but the blow had not fallen, and there was a chance that it might not fall. Nay—there was a chance that it might fall on him, instead of upon her.

And at times, when I came to that point repeatedly reached in my unceasing reflections, I had something like a sense of shame that I had not caused the blow to fall on him. I, in a more gallant age, or had I been a more gallant man in this age, would have taken it upon myself to set her free; would have found it not only a source of pleasure and of pride, but a plain and simple duty. And then the cold breath of common sense would whisper that two wrongs never made a right; that noble aims and ends do not justify violent and evil means; that nothing, nothing in Heaven or on earth or in hell, excuses *murder*.

And having so decided, chivalry promptly would contradict conscience.

The effect upon Lady Calderton of his departure was marked. Not only did her health and spirits visibly improve; not only was it obvious that she breathed more freely and experienced a great relief and lightening of her insupportable load of misery and fear; but at times, and for brief periods, she was almost her old self. She was less tense and tragic, less crushed and crippled in spirit, as the immediate danger receded to form the background of her thoughts, instead of filling and holding her mental stage completely.

He had gone; and though it was anything but a case of 'out of sight, out of mind,' it tended greatly to become one of 'out of sight, not permanently and perpetually in mind.' Nevertheless, there was no day on which she did not spend a part, sometimes longer and sometimes shorter, in talking the position over with me.

One gleam in the darkness, and a cause for some thankfulness, was that he had gone before Sir Arthur's return from Montiga. If the strain of actually seeing the man, added to that of the knowledge of his existence, was almost greater than she could bear, and had brought her very near to breaking-point, what would it have been if he had remained permanently in the neighbourhood, and had continued to visit the house when Sir Arthur was at Calderton?

That dreadful situation had not arisen, and immeasurably bad as things were, she had been spared from suffering something even worse.

§2

"That I could not have borne," she said as we walked in the park, one day. "It would have been unthinkable, impossible. There can hardly be another man alive who'd dream of such a thing, much less suggest it—and fully intend to carry it out."

"It's incredible," I agreed, "and perhaps the most incredible thing of all is the fact that it really didn't seem to strike him as anything out-of-the-way. When I used to try to give him some idea of the poisonous foulness and utter villainy of such an idea; or, another time, of the ludicrous impossibility and farcical tragedy of such a position, he only uttered that awful laugh and asked what there was to make a fuss about. . . ."

(And I forbore to add that on one memorable occasion he had informed me that he considered that I had a definitely dirty mind. And he had talked as though I accused him of proposing that Lady Calderton should live there in sin—with two husbands and a lover!)

"When it seemed that he could and would settle down here," said Lady Calderton, "living in the neighbourhood and in our circle, introduced, guaranteed and sponsored by Sir Arthur and me, I used to feel that it was not only an impossible thing for me to allow, but a thing I would not do, even if I could. Night after night, and every night of my life, I thrashed it out, again and again, till I thought I should go mad: and always I came to the same conclusion—that it was a thing I could *not* do, a state of affairs I *could* not dream of permitting.

"And then I was faced with the alternative. And that was worse, far worse. It was the end of everything for my husband, my boy, and myself. And then, at that thought, in a worse panic, if possible, I would decide that I must go through with it, for their sake; must play my part to the end.

"But how could I? How *could* I?" she turned to me with piteous appeal.

"You couldn't. And you haven't got to. He's gone. It's another of those cases of the calamities from which we suffer most being those that never happen to us. He's gone, and you'll never see him again. All we've got to do is to send the money regularly; and not only will you never see him again, but you'll never hear from him; never have any reminder of the fact that he's alive, beyond sending the money four times a year.

"And what's more," I added, "it needn't be four times a year. And you need have nothing whatsoever to do with him or his money. I'll send it. And you can settle up with me just whenever convenient. . . . What I mean is this. I'll see the man is paid promptly and regularly, and in such a way that no one could possibly ever connect the payment with you. You don't come into it at all."

"Henry . . . my dear . . . I . . ."

"Not in any way at all. Just when it's convenient to you to settle up with me, we can adjust things. It might be extremely difficult at one moment for you to find a considerable sum of money, and at another time it might be perfectly simple. Now, if you'll just let me . . ."

"I wish I could even begin to thank you. I . . ." She took my arm and a warm glow of happiness and pride suffused me from head to foot.

"I wish you wouldn't try to thank me. You don't thank people because you are giving them tremendous pleasure."

"You are a *friend*, Henry, and I shall always . . ."

"That's all I want to be, and if reward were needed . . ."

"And when I think of all you've done for Anthony, and now you . . . How can I . . . ?"

"Well, I don't want to talk like a lunatic and suggest the impossible, or I'd say, 'Now forget him. Leave all the rest of this business to me and put it right out of your mind.' . . . You can't do that, of course. It's wholly impossible: but you can get it further and further to the back of your mind, and gradually come to realize that, not only is the immediate danger past, but that it may never arise again."

"But he's alive, and while he's alive . . ."

"Yes, I know. But have you looked at it like this? He has been alive the whole time! During all those seventeen years of peace and happiness he was alive. He's no *more* alive now than he was then."

Lady Calderton smiled sadly.

"Yes, my dear boy, but I didn't know it."

"No, but it ought to be some sort of a help if you think of it like that. You neither saw nor heard anything of him for seventeen years, and you may neither see nor hear anything of him for another seventeen years. And in that case, there's no reason why you shouldn't be as happy in the future as you were in the past. . . ."

"Nearly as happy," I added lamely.

"Waiting for him to come back; wondering when he'll walk in again, grinning, and . . ."

"But he won't!" I assured her. "If ever a man in this world had a fright, Ferring-Chevigny had one. He'd as soon go to Boledo itself as come here—

where he thought he was absolutely safe. That was the real blow, you know—that they should have traced him to Calderton. Found him out. And so quickly. When he thought he had put them off the scent, once and for all; escaped for good; and was going to live happy ever after in this distant and secluded spot. Why, after this shock, he'd feel infinitely safer in London than he would here—and he'd go in terror of his life even there. He'll never set foot in England again. When you must think of him —and I know you must, of course—think of him as a figure in a nightmare from which you've awakened; think of the whole thing as the horror of a dream that is past. Forgive me for waxing eloquent, but I feel as . . . as . . . as joyous as a bubble in a glass of champagne. And I want you to feel the same. The cork's blown out and the bubbles can rush out to the surface and . . ."

I forced a merry laugh.

"And burst," said Lady Calderton.

§3

The months passed; and our sense of safety, peace, and hope grew steadily.

Until . . .

Among many memorable Calderton mornings, the one of which I am about to tell stands out more clearly in my memory than any other. It should have been a Friday, the thirteenth of the month, a grey and gloomy morning, infinitely depressing, or perhaps one of those red-sky mornings that are shepherds' warnings, oppressive, stifling, electrical, with portent of thunder and storm.

On the contrary, it was a lovely day, one of the ten fine days of the English year, fresh and exhilarating, the sort of day on which it is a joy to be alive.

It was Anthony's birthday, and therefore a holiday. The boy was bubbling over with happiness and excitement, delighted beyond measure with his presents, of which mine had apparently taken his fancy most. Having discussed the matter with his mother, and found that she had no objection, I had given him a genuine seventeenth-century rapier, one which might well have been used by one of Rupert's cavaliers in the great charge at Naseby. It had a Toledo blade, made by the famous Andrea Ferrara, which was much older than the hilt to which it had been fitted somewhere about 1625. A light, delicate, and lovely thing. To handle it was a pleasure to a sword-lover; and to a boy like Anthony it was a joy merely to contemplate it and to consider its historical associations.

So, on that fair morning, he was happy; joyous, as only the young can be; and I was happy with him—and determined to shake off, if only for that one day, the gloomy and apprehensive thoughts from which my mind was never wholly free.

At dawn he burst into my room incoherent with gratitude and joy, holding the sheathed rapier (I had had a new velvet silver-tipped scabbard made for the beautiful blade that had outworn so many sheaths) as though he could scarcely believe that it was real.

"I *say*," he said, time after time—and had nothing to say, adequate words failing him.

"What shall we do to-day?" I asked as I sipped my tea, and he sat on the side of my bed gazing at the sword with shining eyes, as might a young Galahad at a visionary Grail, a young mother at her first-born. A wonderful thing, imagination, and the gift of romantic idealization! A piece of old iron—and a boy transfigured.

"I'll tell you what I want to do, first of all," he answered, smiling at me shyly, "because it's my birthday and we have known each other for a long time. I'm going to call you Henry, if I may."

"Why, of course," I agreed, inwardly delighted, and feeling strangely proud and complimented.

" 'Mr. Waring' is rather formal, isn't it, between such—friends—if I may call us that?"

"Yes. And I'm glad you've waited well, before suggesting it."

"Oh, rather! I hate people who rush anything of that sort, don't you . . . Henry? Bad as people who paw you."

"What else would you like to do to-day?"

"Well, for a start, let's go for a jolly long walk, shall we—Henry?"

But the walk was not jolly and was not long.

For, as we left the main gates of the park and turned on to the country road that led through Calderton up on to the hills, we rounded a corner and suddenly came almost face to face with the last person in the world I expected to see, and most certainly the last person in the world whom I wanted to see—Captain Montague Ferring-Chevigny!

Perched on a stile, eupeptic, gay and debonair, he sat and viewed the smiling country-side with the eye of kind indulgent favour. Also ourselves.

As we turned the corner past a great leaning and projecting tree-trunk and came full upon him, he gave us, after one swift, sharp glance, a bright, kind smile, and with upraised hand that held a cigarette, waved us an airy benediction.

"*Buenos dias, Señores,*" he laughed. "*Como esta usted? A donde va usted?*"

I stared in utter amazement, open-eyed if not open-mouthed, scarcely able to believe the evidence of my senses.

Ferring-Chevigny here! Sitting on a stile in broad daylight, close to Calderton village! It *couldn't* be. And yet it was.

I felt physically sick with chagrin, disappointment and fear; and the fear was as real as though I
were in danger of my life, so identified were my
feelings, my hope and anxiety, my faith and my
dread, with those of Lady Calderton. My sympathy
was so strong in the matter of this terrible danger,
that my mind was one with hers; and this renewed
threat, this revived danger, frightened and horrified
me as it would have done her, had she, instead of I,
come face to face with the man—a thing she might
well have done had he entered the park a little
earlier.

"Struck dumb with admiration, eh?" he jeered.
"Both of you. Hearts too full for words. Never mind
—the shock of joy never kills. Cheer up."

"*You!*" I gasped stupidly.

"You've guessed it, first time."

"But . . . but . . ."

"Quite so. 'But where are the hordes of assas-
sins, peeping from behind every tree,' eh? . . . Don't
you read the papers?"

"No," I replied truthfully, and in point of fact, we
scarcely saw a newspaper at Calderton. And had I
studied several papers daily with the utmost care, it
was hardly probable that I should have seen the
announcement of the return to these shores of Captain Montague Ferring-Chevigny, under that name
or any other.

"Well, well, well! Then I can tell you a piece of
news, and you can join in my rejoicing."

Had he gone mad and, in his madness, somehow found his way back to Calderton?

No, he was sane enough. As sane as he was
spruce and debonair, merry and bright and self-
satisfied and complacent.

Leaning forward, he placed the ferrule of his
smart cane against my breast and, marking em-

phasis with gentle thrusts, cried jovially,

"He's *dead!* . . . He's *dead!* . . . He's *dead!*"

For one dreadful second I could think only of Sir Arthur Calderton.

Sir Arthur dead—and this man his illegal heir, by reason of his being Lady Calderton's husband?

"Who's dead?" I said stupidly.

"Who, you fool? Who but His Excellency, the President of the Republic of Boruela; El Benemerito, the Well Deserving: El Brujo, the damned old witch-doctor! Dead, I tell you. Dead as a door-nail. By this time he's probably President of his newly founded Republic of Hell."

"President Romez dead?"

"The bright lad has grasped it. Yes, *dead.* Dead and damned—and I'm a free man. Understand? Free to come and go. Especially to come, eh, Sunny-Boy?"

I stared in horror, still mentally half stunned, and only beginning to realize the implications of what he was telling me. And suddenly I grasped the awful connotation. He was free and safe—free to live in England.

"*Dead,*" he babbled, "and Boruela is one vast living howl of joy, from end to end. Delirious with joy and the delight of hanging, drawing, and quartering every Romezite in the country. There isn't an official of the Romez *régime* left alive by now, except the few who are praying for death. There isn't a prisoner in a gaol or a flunkey in a palace. The mob has sacked and looted and burned the lot. In every town and village, the Romezite mayor or policeman and what-not, is hanging on a lamp-post or a tree—where he hasn't been burned alive in his own house. By gad, I'd like to know what they did to those of the Romez Royal Family that they laid their hands on. But I'm afraid the majority of them must have skipped when they realized the old man was for it. Skipped out on his ocean-going yacht—that lay perpetually ready, with steam up, in Caibo harbour. They'll all be off to Curaçao and the two million pounds they've got in the Bank of Holland. Gad, I hope the Boruelan navy had its little fire alight, its steam up, and its little keel off the mud. I'd give half what's coming to me to hear that it had got between the yacht and Curaçao, found a shell that would fit its gun, steamed up close enough to hit the yacht and blow it out of the water, with all the hundred and eighteen sons and daughters of El Benemerito. And their husbands and wives and children, all his brothers and sisters and their sons and daughters *and* their sons' and daughters' husbands and wives and children; all his cousins and uncles—in short, the whole damned lot that ruled Boruela for him. Gad, that'd be a piece of news that'd make me believe in a just God. To think of that lot all struggling for dear life among the sharks would make me laugh for a week."

And Ferring-Chevigny laughed merrily in happy and hopeful anticipation.

Suddenly a light flickered across the black despair of my mind.

"Why, then," said I, "if he's dead as well as all his family and officials, down to the last village policeman, you can go back. You can go back and get your money!"

The laugh stopped short and the smile died instantly on Ferring-Chevigny's face, his thin mouth hardened, and his eyes narrowed as they stared into mine.

"Go *back*? Back to Boruela? I? My good fool, the mob want me worse than any of them. Why, up to the time that Romez got wise to my game and rounded on me, I was One of the Boys; Romez' right-hand man, and about as popular out there as a tax-collector—or as St. Michael in Hell."

And Captain Ferring-Chevigny laughed again.

"Back to Boruela! *I?* Why, I shouldn't even have time to be hanged comfortably on a street lamp-post. They'd hang me on the landing-stage. Unless —what is more probable—they'd give me a taste of the *gusanas* and the *grillos* first. Like I did so many of them, when I was top dog . . . Yes, it's their turn now."

I understood. And the glimmer that had lightened my gloom died down. While Romez was alive, he had not dared to return for fear of punishment, dreadful vengeance, for some unforgettable and unforgivable offence against the Romez Government. Now that Romez was dead, he dared not return, for fear of the possibly more awful vengeance of the men whom he had oppressed and injured when himself a servant of that Government.

No, he could not return to Boruela—but he could live here in England without a care in the world.

With Romez would fall every official and office-holder of the Romez Government. Every man appointed by Romez would have to leave his post and return home, or what was more probable, become an exile for the rest of his life. Every chief of police, uniformed or secret, every spy and agent, every official of his Secret Service, would, by the death of Romez, become an execrated fugitive, a price on his head, and his life not worth a minute's purchase. To have had any official connection whatsoever with the late Romez Government, that vilest, biggest and most powerful tyranny of all time, would be a death-warrant. Returning, such men would be torn to pieces by the infuriated mob; by the people who, from the highest to the lowest, had suffered and trembled, ground down and terrorized, for a generation.

Thus, Captain Montague Ferring-Chevigny

577

would not have a Boruelan enemy left in England.

Nor would the new ambassador and his staff be concerned with him. They would know nothing about an English refugee from Boruela, who had fled from the wrath of that foul villain, the late Dictator. The name Bertie-Norton would convey absolutely nothing to them; and in his chosen corner of the green and pleasant land of England, "Captain Bertie-Norton" could live in peace, take his ease, and fear nothing from the successors of a *régime* that had vanished as completely as a loathsome nightmare—the dread nightmare that it was.

"So here we are again, Sunny-Boy," grinned Ferring-Chevigny, "all set fair and sitting pretty. This time it's a real case of 'Home is the sailor, home from the sea, and the hunter home from the hill.'"

I felt a very definite pain through my heart, as well as a dreadful sinking of the stomach. All our work undone; our hopes wrecked; the cup dashed from our lips—and even if that cup had not exactly contained the healing waters of life, its draught had been as the Waters of Lethe, calming, soothing, giving a measure of forgetfulness.

This was defeat.

I stared at him stupidly, feeling hopeless and helpless.

Anthony, who hitherto had stood by in silent and polite patience, yawned a trifle ostentatiously.

Yes, the boy had heard quite enough, and the sooner we moved on, the better. In his present mood, Ferring-Chevigny might say something that I should not like Anthony to hear; something that might require a good deal of explanation.

"Well," said I lamely, "I shall be seeing you again later, I suppose."

"By gad, you will," replied Ferring-Chevigny with a kind of grim jocularity. "I'll look in at about teatime. How's Katherine?"

"Lady Calderton is very well, thank you," I replied. "Her health has improved a good deal recently," I added with meaning.

"Good. Let's hope it will be maintained," was the callous reply.

And Anthony and I walked on.

"I don't like that man," he said, as we got out of ear-shot.

"No, nor do I."

"I don't want to be censorious," continued the boy, using one of the long words of which he was rather fond, and which made his conversation quaint and amusing, if elderly-sounding for so young-looking a boy, "but I think he's rather what they call a bounder, don't you, Henry?"

"Yes," I agreed. "Undoubtedly he bounds."

"Why does he refer to mother as Katherine, and come back here again? I thought he had gone for good."

"Well, I think he presumes on having known her when she was a child, and when they called each other Katherine and Monty. And as for coming back here again, I suppose this is his favourite part of England. He evidently likes the hunting, shooting and fishing. And the society, of course—beginning with your parents' circle."

"Y-e-s-s," replied Anthony thoughtfully, and, I fancied, a shade doubtfully.

"Some people come back to the Quorn country when they retire from active life abroad, some to the Pytchley, others to the Whaddon Chase, the Fernie, the Beaufort. I know a chap who, because he hunted with the Bicester when he was an undergraduate at Oxford, went and lived in the Bicester country when he came back from India and left the Army."

"Yes," said Anthony again, and I felt, as so frequently I did, that he had left something unsaid.

That was one of the many ways in which he was so different from other young people of his age. He didn't often chatter; didn't say everything that came into his mind, without stopping to think. He gave you the feeling that, though he might be as innocent of duplicity and *arrière pensée* as a baby, he yet had unchildish reservations; and that, although he certainly thought what he said, he by no means always said what he thought.

"Does Mother like him?" he asked.

"Not much, I fancy," I replied, as casually as I could. "No, I don't think she has very much use for him, really."

"No. No. I should imagine not. He must have changed a good deal since she knew him as a boy."

"We all change, you know," I observed sententiously.

"Yes," agreed Anthony, and, looking up at me with his puckish smile, quoted,

> " '*Change and decay in all around I see;*
> *O Thou, who changest not, abide with me'*

. . . meaning you."

"Indulging in a little mild blasphemy?" I asked, endeavouring to strike a happy medium between flippancy and heavy tutorism.

"Not at all. He is a bit of a changed and decayed gentleman, isn't he?"

"I thought he looked pretty fit physically, and definitely prosperous."

"Sartorially," added Anthony, savouring the word.

"Well, where does the decay come in, then?"

"Morals and manners."

"What do you know about his morals?"

"Nothing. And not much about his manners, except that I don't admire them. What I meant was, he must have changed since Mother knew him as a boy, and I think it has been in the direction of decay, don't you?"

"Perhaps."

"But what I'm driving at, Henry," he said, slipping his arm through mine, "is that I don't want you ever to change. Not the least little bit. Especially towards me. And I want you to abide with me. Always."

"I shan't change towards you, Anthony," I assured him, and permitted my arm to give his hand a slight pressure against my side. "And I shall abide with you until you go to Oxford."

"You'll go up with me; and come and see me every term, won't you?"

"I will. That's a promise."

"And you'll spend all the hols with me, especially the summer?"

"They call them vacs, as a matter of fact; and the summer one, the Long. And I've no doubt we shall meet."

"Meet! But I want you to be here; and I want us to go away together for the Long. Travel."

"Well, we'll see about that. Your father and mother may have other views."

"Other . . . elephants!" he scoffed. "You know perfectly well that they wouldn't be happy unless I were with you."

"And suppose I had other views for my own vacations, and wanted to . . ."

The boy's face fell visibly—almost audibly, so great and sudden was the change from smiling happiness to blank disappointment, distress. I had almost said horror.

Obviously my careless words had given him quite a shock, and I hastened to reassure him.

What a sensitive soul it was. How unarmed and unprotected.

"I was only joking," I laughed. "Of course, I'll come down here every vac, and if you still want to do it, we'll travel in the Long. See the world. Do a bit of yachting—*not* at Cowes. Go to Scotland and have some good fishing. Do a bit of stalking."

He brightened up again.

"That's a promise, Henry?"

"It's a promise. And no doubt you'll make friends of your own age at Oxford; and if so, we'll take them too, eh? Make up reading-parties; go for tramps in the Black Forest; go to Switzerland for the winter sports; all sorts of doings."

And talking so, I kept him off the subject of Ferring-Chevigny with whom, the whole time, one half of my mind was most painfully concerned.

Pretending to be troubled by an extrusive nail in my shoe, I curtailed our walk. I must see Lady Calderton before Ferring-Chevigny visited the house, and prepare her for the shock of his coming.

I'm afraid Anthony found me dull and abstracted and sadly lacking in the proper care-free holiday and birthday spirit, though I did my best, and endeavoured to receive with rapturous approval his suggestion that we should respectively dress up in full war-paint as Cavalier and Roundhead, and fight a desperate duel.

In fact it was I, I believe, who improved upon the idea, to the extent of suggesting that not only should we be Cavalier and Roundhead, but actually King Charles the First and Oliver Cromwell in their proper persons, and *en grande tenue.*

Fortunately for the furtherance of this admirable scheme, Anthony now had a pretty complete Cavalier outfit of plumed hat, slashed doublet, wide lace collar, baggy velvet breeches, high soft boots and big round Mexican spurs; and there was in the house an ancient but well-preserved pair of vast and heavy square-toed Cromwellian boots and a coat of the period, for me.

These were believed actually to have belonged to Oliver Cromwell himself. Hanging in a corridor there was, moreover, a trophy of arms consisting of a lobster-tail helmet, distinctively Ironside; a breast-plate; and a pair of heavy, ugly, basket-hilted cavalry swords that might well have been worn by Cromwellian troopers.

Yes, with genuine Cromwell stuff and with appropriate armour and weapons, I could put up a passable Great Protector impersonation, worthy to compete with Anthony's more finished representation of the Martyr King.

And of this I talked while of Ferring-Chevigny I thought.

On reaching home, I went to Lady Calderton's morning-room, and did my best to break the ghastly news to her as gently as possible. It was not a pleasant task, but it was one that had to be done; and I was the person to do it. I should have been guilty of cruelty and cowardice if I had left her to meet Ferring-Chevigny, unwarned and unprepared. After what she had gone through, and especially after the dawn of hope, the hope that she might never see or hear from him again, the shock would have been positively dangerous.

"Well, Henry," she said, turning from her writing-desk as I entered the room, "why so solemn?"

"A little bad news," I said, "and I hate being the bearer of bad news—to you."

"Anthony . . . ?"

"No, no. He's absolutely all right. We've just had a walk, and he's now unearthing the Cromwellian kit to make me a foeman worthy of his steel in the great duel that . . ."

"What's wrong, Henry? Tell me, quickly. Something about—that man? Is he . . . ?"

I nodded without replying.

"Threatening to write the sort of letter that would cause . . ."

"No."

She rose to her feet.

"Don't say he's coming . . ."

I nodded again.

"Yes. I'm afraid that's it."

"Coming back here?"

She sat down suddenly.

"Don't imagine that things are worse than they are. There's nothing new, really."

Her face went white, her eyes seemed to grow larger, and suddenly she looked ill, haggard, almost old, as intuition told her the truth.

"He has come back," she whispered.

"Well, we'll get rid of him again," I replied with a false heartiness and forced cheerfulness. "We did it once and we'll do it again. Don't take it to heart too much. Believe me, I . . ."

She dismissed this with a quiet,

"I know you'll do your best, Henry," and added, "Is he coming to the house?"

"He's sure to do that."

"To live here? I won't . . ."

"No, no. That's out of the question. He shan't do that. But he'll want to see you, and . . ."

"Why has he come? I thought he was afraid of another attempt on his life. He was frightened."

"Yes. But he isn't afraid any more. His enemy is dead, and the organization that threatened him is broken and scattered. His enemy's worst enemies are in power now, so he is perfectly safe."

"Then he'll stay here. Live here. Be here when Arthur comes home."

"Somewhere in this part of the world, I suppose," I admitted.

"But no. I don't believe it," I contradicted myself stoutly. "We'll get rid of him. I'll go and see my uncle again and he'll think of something else."

She buried her face in her hands.

My heart sank. What could one say? Words were so futile. What *could* I say? I must say something.

"Look. Please, please don't despair. Don't give way. We've got to fight; defeat him; get the better of him; and I'm perfectly sure we can."

She looked up at me.

"Thank God you are here, Henry. You're such a tower of strength. How *can* we get rid of him?"

"I won't pretend that I have a plan yet, but do believe me when I say that my uncle and I will think of something. We'll *do* something. We'll get rid of him—and before Sir Arthur comes."

And then in my misery, anxiety, pity; my yearning to say something, do something, I blurted out incoherently,

"Do something! I'll *kill* him, if . . ."

She looked up.

"Don't talk like that, Henry. It's too . . . too . . . awful. It's playing with fire. It's hypocritical of me, I know, but, oh, please, please don't put anything like that into words—for I've had that kind of thought myself. A man like that ought to be killed, but to think about it *is* playing with fire. It'll turn from preposterous nonsense into a possibility, a temptation, and in time, a reality . . . I cannot express myself properly . . . an obsession. Don't . . . don't *say* it . . ."

"No," I said. "I won't. I was talking wildly. But a poisonous scoundrel like that who, for his own ends, pretended for so long to be dead, ought to be dead. Why should he, again for his own ends, come to life to kill the happiness of people whose shoes he is not fit to clean. I'd kill him with my bare hands if . . ."

"Yes, *if*, Henry. If it weren't murder, and if no one in the whole world but you and I could know. I'd kill him myself to save Anthony and Arthur if . . ."

I tried to smile.

"If it weren't murder, and if no one in the world could know—and the other 'ifs,'" she went on wildly.

"It wouldn't be on one's conscience in the least," I said.

"It would be a righteous act. In the circumstances, he *ought* to die. He ought to be killed, and a just God would . . ."

"Well, we'll have to leave him to a just God," I interrupted, somewhat horror-stricken at the turn the conversation had taken, and the trend that fear and terror had given to her thoughts.

It was all very well for me to talk airily about wringing the fellow's neck, but it was a very different thing to hear this gentle, sweet, and kindly woman talk in such a strain. And once again my blood boiled and my mind seethed with impotent rage, as I thought of that callous and selfish hound, completely self-satisfied, greedily grinning and stupidly guffawing.

If ever there were a case of 'killing no murder,' surely this was one. And when one compared Montague Ferring-Chevigny with Anthony Calderton: with Sir Arthur Calderton, and with this woman; his killing seemed something more than 'no murder,' a righteous and excusable act, an act that needed no excuse. A necessary deed, and rather than that this unthinkable thing should happen to these three people—to this dear and blameless woman, to my Anthony—I would do it myself. And I would . . .

Amazing how one's thoughts run away with one when one gives them rein, like horses that must be for ever ridden on the curb, lest they bolt, and galloping headlong, carry their rider to destruction.

Well, mine should not. Neither should those of Lady Calderton. But what if hers were more unmanageable than mine; her hands too weak upon the curb-rein. Suppose that she, in her ungovernable fear for her child and husband . . .

And there went my thoughts again.

Nevertheless, if this man Ferring-Chevigny drove us too far . . .

Oh, stop thinking, cried I to myself. Stop being a fool, and remember who you are and where you are.

I must see my uncle again.

"That's what I'll do," I said aloud. "I'll run up to Town and have a talk with my uncle."

"Yes, but don't go now. Not to-day. I don't feel I can . . . Wait till I've seen him again. I want you to be present. Did he say what time he would come here?"

"At tea-time."

"Well, we'll see him, and find out what he proposes to do."

"And tell him what we propose to do," I said.

"What can we do but accept his terms? But I'll never willingly see him alone again."

"No, I wouldn't. I'd make him say anything he has got to say in front of . . ."

"In front of you, Henry. There's no one else, and there's no one whom I'd prefer—while Arthur's away. And Arthur is the last person in the world before whom . . . I mean, when he says it to Arthur, that's the end of everything. What should I have done if you hadn't been here, or if you had been a different sort of person! To give you all this worry and . . ."

"If you only knew the joy it gives me to be able to help you. I thank God, too, that I am here: and there's nothing I wouldn't do, nothing I won't do . . . And about his coming this afternoon. There's one thing I'd like to suggest. Let's put up a pretence of—how shall I express it—having something up our sleeves, so to speak. A man like him must have all sorts of uneasinesses and anxieties. I feel quite sure, from the things he has let drop in unguarded moments, that the late Romez was not his only enemy. I shouldn't be at all surprised if he weren't just as badly wanted in one or two other countries. Mexico, for example. I don't suggest that the Mexicans are going to be of use to us in the way that the Boruelans were, but there may be others who want him, beginning with the English Police. We don't want to put up a bluff that he's going to call, but at the same time, I think it would be a mistake to take meekly what's coming to us, so to speak; to let him ride rough-shod over us, as though we are completely at his mercy."

"As we are," said Lady Calderton.

"Yes, but he's not to know it. We'll be a bit stiff-necked and also mysterious. Try and puzzle him a little and have him guessing, and if you agree, I'll go and lunch at the Albany again to-morrow."

§4

That afternoon, I got another surprise from the incalculable Anthony who had given me so many.

On returning from our walk, he had spent the rest of the morning in dressing up, arraying himself in his really rather beautiful Cavalier garb, combing and brushing out the wig, arranging its long curls to his satisfaction, and manufacturing, with *crêpe* hair and spirit gum, a magnificent moustache and Vandyck beard.

I imagine that, when he had finished, hung his new sword in the slings of his baldrick, and clapped his great plumed Cavalier hat upon his head, he was a completely accurate impersonation of a young gentleman of quality, of the days of Charles the First.

After lunch, faithful to my promise, though inwardly cursing the uncomfortable things the while, I put on the equally accurate Cromwellian outfit that he had assembled from wall and old oak chest; the lobster-tailed helmet, thick heavy breast-plate, sword and spurs from the trophy that hung on the corridor panelling, the impossible jack-boots, buff jerkin, heavy horseman's coat, gauntlets and knee-breeches from one of the attic trunks in which the dress-up kit was kept.

By special request, indeed definite directions (this being his birthday and he Master of all Ceremonies and Lord of Misrule), I was to descend the secret staircase that led down into the hall, leave the house by the "postern gate," an inconspicuous iron-sheathed, nail-studded door that gave on to a shrubbery, make a detour, and approach the house, by way of the main drive, at the head of an imaginary troop of dismounted Ironsides.

By the main entrance, at the top of the left-hand flight of steps leading from the drive to the pillared porch, Sir Anthony Calderton, Captain of the King's Own Bodyguard, was to confront me, and declare that the King was not hiding in Calderton House. When I refused to take his word, ordered him to stand aside and permit me and my men to enter, he was to bid defiance to us all, draw his sword, and prepare to sell his life dearly while the King made his escape by another postern gate at the rear of the house.

Hot and heavy work after luncheon, especially to one who, his mind preoccupied with tragic realities, must play his part satisfactorily and whole-heartedly, make impassioned though extempore speeches, take his cues correctly, and bear himself like a man and an Ironside, albeit a crop-eared boor. Yes, that was the phrase, I believed:

"A curse on the crop-eared boor who sent me and my standard on foot from Marston Moor."

I must have played my part well, for undeniably Anthony played his too well.

The unrehearsed encounter opened excellently, and we mouthed our impromptu lines, and with complete satisfaction established each the other respectively as crop-eared boor and Man of Blood with long essencéd hair, the latter phrase coming happily to my mind from school-days, as I ground my teeth and muttered beneath my breath,

"And the Man of Blood was there with his long essencéd hair."

And after due prolongation of the desirable preliminaries and a shout of "In the name of the Parliament, stand aside, Sir Anthony," answered by a high-pitched cry of "Back, dog. Advance at your peril," we drew and fell to.

So far, so good. But what I had not realized was that the loyal and faithful defender of his King was still wearing the very real rapier that I had given him that morning. Whether Anthony actually realized it, I didn't know. I don't know now, and I am not sure whether Anthony himself knows. Anyhow, he drew the keen-edged, sharp-pointed sword and attacked me with the utmost fury.

He wasn't playing. He *was* Sir Anthony Calderton, selling his life against hopeless odds, dying that his King might live.

I was but one of a troop and the staircase must be held at all costs while the King got to horse. No matter that the "staircase" was a great flight of steps a dozen feet in width. No matter that half the troop had but to run round to the other flight of steps, go up and take him in the rear; no matter anything at all, save that, here before him, was a Roundhead soldier, a Cromwellian rebel, nay,

Cromwell himself—even as no doubt Sir Anthony Calderton became, while he fought, the spirit of loyalty to the Stuarts and then the Stuart King himself; Charles the King fighting Cromwell the Traitor.

I have said he attacked me with the utmost fury. It is a form of words that here is not an exaggeration. He became a fury, and as I parried and riposted, guarded and cautiously thrust, he went mad before my eyes.

Ira furor brevis est; he was temporarily insane, and my growing discomfort quickly changed to anxiety and alarm. My weapon, apart from any question of my extreme carefulness in its use, was not dangerous, a heavy basket-hilted thing, genuine of the period, but of the poorest quality, fortunately blunt, and square-pointed.

There was no fear of my scratching the boy, and I saw to it that my point never rose to the level of his face, or went anywhere near it. What I did fear was that he'd give me an incapacitating wound, or accidentally do me an injury about which he would be heart-broken when he came to his senses.

And yet accident was hardly the word, for he was doing his utmost to run me through, straining every nerve and sinew to kill the enemy of his King. Whether I am a good teacher of fencing or not, Anthony was certainly a most apt pupil, with a natural gift for that magnificent art and exercise, and he was now fencing with real skill. Luckily I knew all his tricks—as I had taught them to him—and contrived to parry them as they came, but it was an extraordinarily difficult thing to fight entirely on the defensive—attack being always the best defence.

What worried me as much as the fear that a wild thrust or cut might reach my face and do damage that Anthony would regret as long as he lived, was the realization that he was, for the time being, insane.

That word again. How I hate it: because it is as misleading as it is inevitable. Perhaps it is better to say that he was mad, and qualify it by the words "with rage." Surely the sanest person can be mad with rage upon occasion? He was beside himself. Perhaps that is the best expression I can use.

A curious phrase, but apt, inasmuch as Sir Anthony Calderton, the Cavalier Captain of the King's Guard, stood beside the boy Anthony Calderton. And for the moment, the spirit with which they were both infused, the spirit that enfilled and informed them both, was concentrated in the one, the desperate hero, desperately dying in the royal cause.

Anyway, the boy had gone *berserk*, and no actual cavalier in actual battle at Marston Moor or Naseby ever attacked real Roundhead with a more desperate ferocity.

For a little longer, I defended myself and then began to retreat backwards down the steps, still desperately assailed and sore beset by the Cavalier captain. Anxious as I was to put an end to it before anything untoward happened, I was also loth to be a spoil-sport, stop the play, and, by throwing off pretence and disguise, exert my authority in my proper person and rôle of tutor.

Arrived at the bottom of the steps, Anthony's rapier ringing on mine and occasionally on my helmet and breast-plate, I suddenly bethought me of a way of escape and of playing 'possum as well as Roundhead. With a cry of anguish followed by a deep groan, I sagged at the knees, collapsed, dropped my sword and fell at Anthony's feet.

"So perish all the King's enemies," panted the boy, wiped the, happily imaginary, blood from his sword upon the sleeve of my jerkin, raised it till the hilt was against his lips, sheathed it—and that particular play was finished.

As I sat up and smiled at the now perfectly normal Anthony, someone crossed the gravel towards us from the shade of the trees. Glancing round and seeing who it was, Anthony went up the steps and into the house without further speech.

"By gad," said the voice of Captain Ferring-Chevigny, as I rose to my feet. "Is that a boy or a wild beast? Upon my soul, I thought he had done you in."

§5

There is little need to dwell upon the misery of the days that followed. Ferring-Chevigny again established himself at the Calderton Arms, or, at any rate, with that inn as his headquarters, as he came and went a good deal, disappearing for days at a time, returning suddenly and remaining for longer or shorter periods.

When staying at the Calderton Arms, he spent most of his time at the house, made himself one of the family, and behaved as though he were not only a relative of Lady Calderton, but a most welcome and privileged guest.

To the butler, the footman, the head groom and the head chauffeur, he made, in pleasant but authoritative manner, such requests as he saw fit to make, and these they accepted as orders.

Although I, of course, refrained from doing so, I should very much have liked to talk about him to the faithful Jenkins, and to hear what he and the staff thought about our visitor. I expect I should have found the general opinion to be that he was undoubtedly a "one"; that Lady Calderton never knew what he would do next, and that she was quite as glad to see him go as she was to see him come; that, albeit a perfect gentleman, he was a bit of a lad, a gay spark, must have been an anxiety to his mother, and no doubt was a bit of an anxiety to poor Lady Calderton. Had these worthy folk been in the habit of using such expressions, they'd probably have called him an *enfant terrible*, if not a *mauvais sujet*. Doubtless in the servants' hall they discussed him, but I don't think that for one moment there was the slightest suspicion of there being anything wrong, of there being anything to conceal, much less that ghastly tragedy impended.

More and more people called as it became known that Lady Calderton was better and was seen about in her car and on horseback; and there was a certain amount of entertaining.

To do Ferring-Chevigny justice, he behaved circumspectly, his manner, when we were alone, being unprovocative, and, when we had guests, that of a very old friend of the family who had returned, after many years abroad, to take up life again in England, and probably in this county and this particular part of it.

On the surface all was well, and beneath the surface life was tragic horror, a long-drawn agony of suspense as we miserably awaited the day when someone should recognize him; something should happen, such as the arrival of detectives from Scotland Yard; some breath of scandal should suddenly arise and poison the air; and awaited what was worst of all, because inevitable, the return of Sir Arthur Calderton, when the blow must surely fall.

"I couldn't possibly do it, Henry," said Lady Calderton. "How could I? How could I let that man cross the threshold when Sir Arthur is in the house? How could I possibly remain silent, even if he did?"

"He'll remain silent all right," I said. "Why should he spoil his own game? As a matter of fact, that's the last thing in the world that he wants. He's perfectly happy, and his idea is for things to go on exactly as they are."

"But how can they? How can they? How could I introduce him to Sir Arthur? How could I let him sit at table with him? Such appalling deceit and . . ."

"It's that or the crash," I said. "I don't see how you can possibly allow it, as you say; but it means the end of everything, directly you tell your husband."

"Oh, if only I were one of those strong women with perfect self-control . . . But how could any self-respecting woman do such a thing? I feel I cannot possibly bear the . . . And then I think of Arthur and of Anthony and . . . Oh, what can I do? What *can* I do? Give me your advice, Henry. Help me."

"My advice is this," I said. "Wait. Bear it as long as you possibly can. Certainly until Sir Arthur comes. One never knows what might happen. I might even yet be able to shame him into . . ."

"But he'd still be alive. And while he's alive, the position . . ."

"Yes, I know. But I say *wait*. Easy to advise, I know; but be patient and be brave, and wait till the last possible minute. Wait and hope. Remember we got rid of him once. My uncle's plan worked and, but for the death of that man Romez, we should never have seen him again. And Romez wasn't the only enemy. His were not the only police that Ferring-Chevigny is hiding from, I'm quite sure. Likely as not our own police want him. Wait till the last moment. Wait at least until Sir Arthur comes. It would be the greatest folly to despair yet, and give in. I have tremendous faith in my uncle, and still more in the eternal justice of things. My advice is—wait."

"I'll go on as long as I can, Henry," she said.

"After all, he might die," she added.

"Yes," I agreed, meeting her gaze. "He might die."

§6

Meanwhile, what was an undoubted help, by reason of its being a distraction and a piece of work into which she could plunge, was the organization of the annual Charity Ball. This was a big County affair which every year brought in a very considerable sum of money for the local hospital, inasmuch as there were no expenses at all, the County magnates taking it in turn to be host, to give the ball in their own houses and to bear all costs. To limit the numbers within reasonable bounds, the tickets were extremely expensive. Everybody who was anybody went, and the affair was one of the big County social-occasions of the year.

XVIII

"Fancy dress again this year, I suppose," said Lady Jane Thyrleby, as the Ladies' Committee of the Hospital Charity Ball sat in session at a table in the library at Calderton House.

"Oh, yes, rather," agreed Miss Christabel Hardacre. "Much more fun."

"More of a draw, too," observed the Dowager Lady Bramlingham, in her deep contralto.

"Yes, I think so," said Lady Calderton, from the chair. "It's more of a draw, as you say, and it also helps to keep it a little on the exclusive side. We don't want more people than we can possibly accommodate."

"Oh, we shan't have that, my dear," said Lady Jane Thyrleby. "We have never yet been really overcrowded, and this is by far the biggest house in the County. If we had a full band in the musicians' gallery above the hall, and things did get a bit crowded in the ballroom, the band would be perfectly audible in the drawing-room as well as in the hall."

"Oh, yes," agreed Lady Calderton. "You hear it all over the house. Anyway, it's what we've done before, isn't it?"

"Yes, darling, but we have never been quite so ambitious, have we? Five hundred tickets seem an awful lot."

"No, I think not," mused Lady Bramlingham. "There wouldn't be more than three hundred people dancing at once, and the ballroom and the drawing-room would take a hundred couples each, not to mention the hall."

"Right, then," said Christabel Hardacre. "Let's

settle on that. Five hundred tickets, fancy dress, and a full band. If Lady Calderton approves."

"What'll you do about supper, dear?" asked Lady Jane.

"Oh, I'll leave all that to Holroyds. I thought they did everything splendidly when it was at your house."

After the conclusion of the business, the Committee adjourned to the drawing-room for tea, and departing one by one, as Jenkins announced their cars, left Miss Christabel Hardacre alone with Lady Calderton.

"I told my man not to come round till five o'clock unless he were sent for, Katherine," she said. "I wanted to out-stay the others and have a talk with you."

"Very nice of you, dear. I was hoping for a word with you alone. How is everything?"

"Katherine, I want your advice."

Lady Calderton smiled.

"What do they say about advice, Christabel? It's the only thing we give too freely, and the one thing we ask for and never take."

"Perhaps it isn't advice I want. Perhaps it's . . . shall I say, encouragement. I think I want a push in the direction in which I want to go."

"Why, Christabel! Good news?"

Heavens above, the poor woman was blushing. Surely Christabel Hardacre wasn't going to . . . Surely not *Christabel!* What did Arthur say the men called her? 'The Hard-boiled Virgin.' Poor Christabel, with her too-golden hair, weather-beaten horse face, mannish ways, and general utter lack of desirability, from the masculine point of view.

In spite of her wealth, in spite of her forth-right out-spoken honesty and good-heartedness, in spite of her fine sportsmanship and general popularity, there had never been a suggestion, never the faintest whisper of anything of the sort. Who could it be?

Well, if he were the right man, he'd be a lucky man. If he were some hard-riding bluff and jolly squire who lived for horses and hunting, it might turn out splendidly. Mannish and *gauche* she might be, with much of the speech and manners of her own grooms; hot-tempered and sharp-spoken she might be; narrow, limited and bucolic; with hardly an idea beyond sport; the stables her spiritual home; she nevertheless had a heart of gold. She was kind, charitable in every sense of the word, and loyal; a friend dependable and true as steel. What if she were a joke—'Ard-faced Aggie; Leathery Lou; Horsey Hannah and a hard-boiled virgin to the haw-bucks and the half-sirs. She might be a joke, but she was a good joke, a good woman and a good sportsman.

And as she sat blushing and twiddling her fingers, she said,

"That's what I want to consult you about, Katherine. There's no one whose opinion I value more. Nobody alive whom I admire more . . . Would you think I was an old fool?"

"Don't be silly, Christabel. You know you are not old, and I know you are not a fool. Who is it, my child? Anyone I know?"

"My dear, I met him here."

"Here? Not Mr. . . . ." No, it couldn't be. It couldn't possibly be. Why, Henry Waring was ten years younger than Christabel Hardacre.

"Yes. I met him here. Long ago. I was passing the lodge gates and I thought I'd just look in and see how Anthony was, and drop you a line about him. And riding up the drive I met him."

"Anthony?"

"No."

"Mr. Waring?"

"No. Captain Bertie-Norton. He raised his hat and I asked him if he knew whether Anthony was in, and he stopped and talked to me. He stroked my horse's neck and smiled up into my eyes and . . . and . . . now he . . . I believe he is going to ask me to marry him!"

If Lady Calderton lay back in her chair and for a moment closed her eyes, Christabel Hardacre did not notice it.

Lady Calderton sat up.

"Has he actually *proposed* to you?"

"*Actually?*" Miss Hardacre sat up very straight. "And why not? Do you consider that I am too old for a man to . . ."

"When I said 'actually,' I meant . . . I meant . . . 'definitely,' Christabel. Please don't misunderstand me. Let me say it again, dear. Has Captain Bertie-Norton in so many words asked you to marry him, or do you mean he's showing signs of . . . ?"

"Katherine dear, Captain Bertie-Norton is going to ask me to marry him. He has told me he is going to *ask me something* at the Ball; and that if my answer is what he *prays* it may be, he is going to tell everybody, 'tell the world,' as he said—announce it, in fact."

Lady Calderton stared incredulous, white-faced. Christabel Hardacre rose to her feet.

"Well!" she cried. "Is that all you've got to say . . . ? What's the matter?"

Lady Calderton still stared in silence, in horrified incredulity, apparently stricken dumb.

"What the devil . . . ?" began the offended spinster. "Well . . . !"

And she was at a loss for words.

The two women stared at each other in silence, the one white-faced, shocked beyond speech; the other, red-faced, glowering, too angry for words.

Miss Hardacre recovered first.

"Oh, so *that's* it, is it?" she said. "Well, well, well! I'd never have believed it. *You* of all people. With an excellent husband, not to mention an admirable tutor!" . . .

And the incensed and insulted Miss Hardacre marched from the room and out of the house.

XIX

Before dinner on that day of the ladies' Ball-Committee meeting, while Captain Ferring-Chevigny and I sat in the drawing-room, moodily sipping sherry, and eyeing each other with mutual disapproval and distaste, Jenkins came with a message that Lady Calderton would not be dining downstairs.

"No, sir," he replied to my question. "Her maid did not say that her Ladyship was ill. Merely that she was tired after the committee-meeting and had retired, and that a tray was to be sent upstairs . . . Dinner is served, sir."

It was an awkward and unpleasant meal, for I was hating Ferring-Chevigny fiercely. Not only for what he was, for what he had done and was doing, and for what his very existence foreboded, but especially for his manner. So small an addition to wrongs and villainies so colossal, but it was almost the last straw, threatening to break down my endurance, and my self-restraint.

"Huh! Shirking it, is she? Well, she can't run away much longer. There's got to be a show-down," he sneered as we drank our soup.

"And I wonder how *you'll* come out of a show-down," I growled.

"Might be a show-up, you mean," he laughed.

"Precisely. And you aren't hiding here because you are particularly anxious for lime-light."

"Don't you worry about me, Sunny-Boy," was the reply. "I appreciate it, you know; but you are over-solicitous."

And the servants entering with the next course, we stopped our snarling.

Dinner finished, Ferring-Chevigny took it upon himself to tell Jenkins that we would have coffee served at table.

"We'll go up to your den afterwards," he said to me, as the servants left the room. "I want a talk with you, since her delicate-minded Ladyship funks it.

"Perhaps it's as well, too," he continued. "I'll get the idea into your head clearly enough, and I haven't the slightest doubt you'll get it into hers. She'll enjoy listening to you, Sunny-Boy."

After three glasses of port and a cup of coffee, Ferring-Chevigny picked up the brandy decanter and one of the balloon glasses that Robert had left on the table.

"Come on," said he, "let's get up to your room where we can be private . . . Bring the cigars."

"Now, my lad," said Ferring-Chevigny when he had half filled the big glass, lit a cigar and made himself comfortable in my armchair, "I want you to listen to what I've got to say. Listen carefully, for you've got to put it fully and accurately before my wife. And I hope that she'll give me credit for the consideration and forbearance that I'm showing."

I sat and watched the man, without comment.

"First of all, it is not pretended that she's desperately fond of me, is it? No, and I think I can quite truthfully say that, having got along without her for seventeen years, I can hold on for another seventeen . . . Now then, we parted, and parted for good, when Captain Montague Ferring-Chevigny died. We parted still more, and parted for even better, when she married Sir Arthur Calderton. So, on the whole, you might say that now, seventeen years later, we are, on the whole, pretty damn well parted, eh?

"Good. That's point one.

"Lady Calderton, wife of Sir Arthur Calderton,

mother of Anthony Calderton, the heir, châtelaine of this noble castle, is, well—just that.

"Captain Montague Bertie-Norton is nothing in her young life. And doesn't want to be. She had never even heard his name until she came back from Montiga. What does it matter to her or to him or to you or to anybody on God's earth, if he happens to be a reincarnation? Nothing at all. It doesn't matter if, in his previous life, he was Peter the Great, or Sam Small, or the King of the Cannibal Islands, or a silly soldier-man who was drowned off Perenecque Island beach, does it? Not a bit.

"Well now, why should these two utterly unconnected, independent, unentangled people interfere with each other in any way at all?"

"Precisely," I agreed, as he not only paused for an answer but sat awaiting one, his curious light eyes staring compellingly into mine. "Precisely what I've asked you. What on earth do you want to come here for at all, since you realize that? Why come here, after seventeen years, and interfere?"

"You know perfectly well why I came here; and we don't want to go into all that again. Needs must when the devil drives. The devil drove me here, and he damn well drove me out again. Well, the devil's dead. What's that tag young Anthony was spouting the other day out of *The Closet and the Hearth* or what-not—the bloke with the cross-bow: '*Courage, mon ami, le diable est mort.*' Gerard was his name, wasn't it? Anyway, *my* devil's dead, and here I am again."

"Yes, here you are again, and pointing out how utterly unnecessary it is for your life and Lady Calderton's to . . ." I began.

"Now, don't interrupt, Sunny-Boy. You listen to me. Here I am again, I was going to say, *but*—and the Hell of a fine 'but' it is—*but* the situation is absolutely changed. Man cannot live by bread alone, as you may have heard in the course of your learned researches; and all I wanted was just a modest pat of butter with my bread. You know, 'A jug of wine, a loaf of bread, a pat of butter' and I can make my own 'Paradise enow,' even in this little wilderness. I was going to say, even in this bloody hole, but I think the original is 'wilderness,' isn't it?

"That was all I asked. Modest enough, surely, and nobody a penny the worse. Careful, kindly, considerate I was, making no sort or kind of upset or disturbance, never a thought of blackmail—and now here comes the reward of virtue. Some reward too, Sunny-Boy! As far as I can make out, about twenty-five thousand a year. Think of it!"

"I could think of it better if I knew what you were talking about," I said, as Ferring-Chevigny again interrupted his monologue and beamed upon me.

"Twenty-five thousand jimmy-o-goblins, *per*. A very neat lump sum for a lad who has been up against life in the rough, and seen hard times. A very neat lump sum indeed, but this is *per annum*, Sunny-Boy. How's that for the reward of virtue?"

"You've inherited twenty-five thousand a year?"

"Going to, in a manner of speaking."

"Then you'll be leaving here?"

"Leaving this immediate neighbourhood. Not going to tear myself away altogether, but I'm certainly 'going away,' in a manner of speaking—with your kind help, Sunny-Boy. You put it neatly and concisely and clearly to the girl friend, and show her the all-round beauty of the scheme, the perfect solution of everybody's problems and difficulties and troubles, and you'll be doing your bit. Helpful ever—especially to the girl friend. Your favourite rôle in life, Sunny-Boy.

"And *my* rôle? I shall *roll* in money," continued Ferring-Chevigny, as he emptied his glass and took another cigar.

"And you won't find me ungrateful," he added. "The day it comes off, I shall write you a nice little cheque.

"Why, bless my soul," he grinned, pausing in the lighting of his cigar, "I'll guarantee you the job of tutor to all the little Ferring-Chevignys. I mean Bertie-Nortons. One down, t'other come on. I mean, one gone on to school and t'other come up to the school-room. Job for life for you, Sunny-Boy. If we haven't left it too late!

"Now then, be serious a minute. Brass tacks. You've just agreed with me that there's no earthly reason why Lady Calderton and Captain Montague Bertie-Norton should be anything to each other whatsoever, except good friends. They knew each other as youngsters, and the friendship has been revived. Nothing more to it than that. Nothing whatsoever. Very well. Captain Bertie-Norton, thinking of settling down in this part of the world where he has got friends and someone to introduce him to the County, has met a woman after his own heart, a fine open-air, hard-riding, sporting lass, and he has fallen in love with her! Ack over tock, which is Boruelan-Spanish for head over heels. *'And the lady?'* you ask. Well, she's what you might call distinctly on-coming. I haven't definitely proposed and demanded a definite answer, yet, but she knows. *She* knows! And she's all of a doodah. All het-up and girlish. And you can take it from me that it's not going to be a case of 'decline and fall.' No—she'll fall without a thought of declining."

"Fall?" I said, still uncomprehending. "Who?"

"Be your bright self, Sunny-Boy. Be your age. I'm going to marry Miss Christabel Hardacre—and nobody on this little round earth is going to stop me."

Once again I stared at this amazing man, incredulous.

"*Marry* Miss Hardacre?" I said stupidly.

"Yes, and put an end to what you must admit is a somewhat galling situation."

"Galling?"

"Yes. To my pride. You may not be able to understand such feelings, but I assure you I don't like having to live on my wife's bounty. (Which reminds me that quarter-day falls on Wednesday. Make a note of it.) Although it is perfectly right and proper that a man and his wife should share and share alike, it being quite immaterial whether the source of income is actually his or hers, the present circumstances are a bit unusual. Lady Calderton lives, of course, upon Sir Arthur Calderton's money, and feels no more discomfort in doing so than Sir Arthur Calderton would feel in living on his wife's money if she were a rich woman. But it isn't quite the same thing with me, is it? Because, in a manner of speaking, the help that she gives me comes out of Sir Arthur's pocket. I mean, you could argue that way if you liked. No need to, of course, because by the time she has got it, it is hers; absolutely hers. And whatever share of it her lawful husband gets is *his* fair share of *her* own money. Still, I don't like it, Waring. And, as I say, this marriage, admirable from every point of view, is all the more so by reason of its putting an end to what I have just called a galling situation."

"But . . ."

"But me no buts, Sunny-Boy. Unless it's a butt of malmsey for a wedding-present. Just keep quiet, and I'll tell you what you've got to do, and that's easily told. You see the girl friend as soon as possible, and put it to her that here's the solution. It lets us both out. She rests assured that there never can nor will be a word out of me to upset the seventeen-year-old applecart; and I escape from the present humiliating situation of being her pensioner or whatever you like to call it.

"And be particularly careful to point out to her that from now, henceforth and for evermore, I'm just as much in her power as she is in mine. I could no more threaten her with exposure—not that I ever have or ever would do such a thing—than she can threaten me. I should be queering my own pitch, just as much as hers, if ever I said a word about— auld lang syne."

I eyed him in silence, feeling that nothing that I could say could adequately express my feelings; that nothing that I could say would penetrate the shell of his conscienceless egotism; that no words would have any result whatever. Comment, expostulation, would have as much effect upon this man as would the throwing of water on a stone.

Ferring-Chevigny poured out more brandy, drank and lay back in his chair.

"Neat, eh?" he smiled. "Pretty. The ideal solution . . . 'And they all lived happy ever after.'

"Naturally Katherine will jump at it when she grasps the full beauty of it; gets all the implications. She's fully and finally rid of a spare husband; and I am fully and finally settled in life. She has no need to send any more cheques; and I've no need to accept any, either. Sir Arthur Calderton and our beloved Anthony stay put; and Miss Christabel Hardacre knows joy at last, her life a path-way of roses without a thorn. And Sunny-Boy Waring remains sitting pretty."

Ferring-Chevigny fell silent.

"We'll announce it at the Ball, I think," he said. "Create quite a sensation."

He yawned loudly.

"Well," he said, rising to his feet. "Tell the girl friend just as soon as you like. Only fair to let her know that all's well now, and she need not worry any more . . ."

§2

I shall be believed when I say that I didn't sleep that night. When Anthony came to my room in the morning, I told him to go along and see his mother, and say that Mr. Waring would like to speak to her when she came downstairs.

Soon after breakfast, Robert came to the school-room with a message—Lady Calderton's compliments, and she'd be glad if I could spare a minute to speak to her in her morning-room.

Thus, with the dreadful final and fatal avalanche impending, did we keep up appearances.

She looked like a ghost, and my heart bled for her. That's a silly expression, perhaps, but I can truthfully say that literally it ached.

"You are not looking too well, Henry," she said, smiling as I entered. "I believe you feel the strain almost as much as I do."

"Had a bad night," I said ungraciously, "and I've got some bad news."

I was too savagely angry, too desperate, in my sense of impotent futility, to be careful and diplomatic.

"He now proposes to end the situation—which is galling to his manly pride—by deliberately committing bigamy, you and I being accessories before the fact. We are not only to connive but to congratulate."

"Christabel Hardacre," whispered Lady Calderton.

"You knew?" I said in surprise.

"She told me herself, yesterday evening."

"That he has proposed to her?"

"That he's going to. She wanted my advice, poor soul. And then changed that to 'a push in the direction in which she wished to go.' Dear God! Is the man sane?"

"No," I replied. "He's not. It's diseased egotism. He . . ."

"Henry, this is the end. I must tell her. I must tell her at once."

"You said nothing when she spoke to you yesterday?"

"I . . . No, I told her nothing. I made no confession, I mean. But I was . . . stunned. All I could say was, '*Has he actually proposed to you?*' And poor Miss Hardacre thought I meant, '*Does that fine handsome man want to marry a middle-aged spinster like you?*' Or something of that sort. I must have merely gaped at her. And she, poor dear, immediately jumped to the conclusion that I simply could not believe such utterly incredible news. She was perfectly right, of course. I could not believe— that he was serious . . . I can't, now."

"He is, though," said I. "Absolutely serious; and he honestly cannot see any objection. Thinks it's a splendid way out of the *impasse*."

"But it makes things just twice as bad as they were before."

"Not in his opinion. Not from his point of view. He requested me to point out to you that, after marrying her, he would be as much in your power as you in his; that you could rest assured that you were safe for the rest of your life; and that Sir Arthur and Anthony would be safe too. Also, that you would henceforth be entirely free from the awkward, distasteful, and possibly risky task of keeping him supplied with money."

Lady Calderton buried her face in her hands.

"Well, this is the end, Henry," she said, in a quiet, dull voice, resigned and dry.

I would have preferred that she had burst into tears and sobbed without restraint. As well she didn't, perhaps, or I should have been unable to refrain from comforting her in the way in which any human-hearted man must comfort a woman in such circumstances. And where Lady Calderton was concerned, I was all too human.

"Don't say it," I begged. "It isn't the end. It isn't."

"What can we do? I've thought all night long."

"So have I," I replied, "and there are two things; two ways, courses, possibilities. Suppose I, or you, go to Miss Hardacre and tell her that Captain Bertie-Norton is not what he appears to be; that that is not even his right name, and that he's a married man."

Lady Calderton looked up.

"Wouldn't she at once tax him with it? Being the downright, straight-riding, out-spoken woman that she is, I think she'd immediately do that. And wouldn't that be the end?" said Lady Calderton.

"No. I don't think it would. He'd simply deny it."

"And then?"

"Then it's up to us to convince her. And there again, I believe both I and my uncle could help. We could go to her independently, and tell her that we know that the man calling himself Bertie-Norton is an adventurer, living under an *alias*, and a married man.

"You see, directly you tell her that you know him to be a married man, she'll want some sort of proof," I continued. "Supposing I then go and see her, and assure her that not only do I know this man's real name, which is not Bertie-Norton; but that I *know* him to be married, and that his wife is alive. Then, when torn between indignation on behalf of her *fiancé* (who is still stoutly denying it) and fear that there may be something in it, she wants further proof, I'll take her up to see my uncle at the Albany. That'll be better than bringing him down here. If there's anybody on this earth who could convince her, it's Sir Walter Waring—the more so because he'll be speaking the absolute truth, though not the whole truth. By the time he has told her that he *knows* that the man calling himself Bertie-Norton has a wife living, and moreover that he'll intervene—forbid the banns, don't they call it—she'll be convinced."

"And the second course?" asked Lady Calderton, her face unanimated by any gleam of hope.

"Why! Call his bluff! Tell him that if he really proposes to marry Miss Hardacre and she accepts him, you'll tell her the truth."

"Do you suppose that that would stop him?"

"I do."

"And don't you suppose he'd be vindictive, vengeful and . . ."

"No, I don't. He's far too wily to lose both the substance and the shadow. He's not the man to say, '*Well, you've done me out of the chance of twenty-five thousand a year, now I'll do myself out of the thousand I have got.*' Don't you see, he's what he calls 'sitting pretty,' as it is, and he sees a chance to sit prettier still. But if he can't have the 'prettier,' he's not also going to lose the 'pretty' surely! No, I firmly believe that he'll drop the idea."

"I don't. You don't know him. Not as well as I do, Henry," she smiled sadly. "When he's in pursuit of something he wants, he's like a steam-roller. There's no stopping him. There's no holding him. And nothing matters. Nor do I for one moment believe that he will suppose we are in earnest. I don't think he could imagine anybody doing the right thing simply *because* it is the right thing to do. He just simply couldn't visualize anyone doing what he'd call 'queering their own pitch.' If you assure him with all the vehemence and force of which you are capable, that I'll tell my . . . tell Sir Arthur . . . the truth, wreck his life, ruin Anthony's life, ruin myself, rather than let him marry Miss Hardacre, he simply won't believe it. If I see him myself and say that the moment I know that they are going to be married I will tell her he is my husband, he'll merely laugh that ghastly laugh of his, and ask me whether I really am such a fool as to suppose he's such a fool as to believe it."

We sat and eyed each other in silent misery.

"It's the end, Henry," she said, "and whatever happens, and however long I survive it, I shall always be grateful to you . . . Far, far more than grateful and . . ."

"Then will you do me a favour?" I begged.

"I will."

"Will you promise me not to tell your husband, nor Miss Hardacre, nor anybody else, without consulting me first."

"I will, Henry. I promise you faithfully that I'll confess nothing without telling you first. But you do understand, don't you, that I must and I will do whatever may be necessary to prevent this unforgivable crime . . . That poor woman . . ."

"Of course I do. Of course. It has got to be prevented at any cost. But I do thank God that you didn't tell Miss Hardacre why you were so utterly incredulous. Up to this moment, nobody on this earth knows except my uncle and I, and—there's always hope. While there's life there's hope, and while nobody knows but ourselves, there is no need to despair."

"Henry, what hope is there? This unspeakably wicked idea of . . ."

"I don't know what hope there is. But I do know that I've still got it. Hope—and faith too. And what's more, a plan. And I'm not talking idly, in a feeble attempt to comfort you."

"You really have a plan? Something possible?"

"Believe me I have."

"What is it?"

"I don't want to tell you."

Lady Calderton rose to her feet.

"Henry! *No. No.* Not that! I won't have it. It was easy enough to talk. But now . . . I won't hear of it."

"You haven't heard of it," said I brusquely. "I'm only asking you not to despair. I'm only saying that I have not only hope, not only faith, but a belief. So long as you keep your promise to me . . ."

"I'll do that, my dear."

". . . and admit nothing, confess nothing, without telling me, we shall defeat him—and save Anthony, not to mention yourself and your husband."

Lady Calderton sank back into her chair.

"Words fail me to tell you how grateful I . . . How I thank God that you . . . that you . . ."

"By the way," I interrupted, "you know Miss Hardacre pretty well. Suppose the worst came to the worst, and other things failed, could she be trusted? With a secret like that?"

"If I went to her and told her that he was my husband? I don't know . . . I don't know. Anyhow, I should have a terrible feeling that . . . How can I put it? That an avalanche was growing and growing and slipping and . . ."

"I know. I know. It's as though the stone he had flung into the placid pool of your life was making ever more and ever-widening circles."

"Yes, I should feel that all the world knew, that everyone was whispering, was looking at me . . . You see, I had to tell you. I don't mind your knowing a bit. I wanted you to know. Then, as your uncle is practically a recluse at the Albany, and we hardly ever see him, it didn't seem to matter that he knew. Of course, I realize, too, that he's as solid and silent as a rock. But it would be awful for her to know as well. Here, in our own corner of the county, in our own circle."

"I understand," I said. "It would be most painful for you to meet her, and terribly difficult to be natural, knowing that she knew. You'd never be able to forget it."

"*To forget it!*" whispered Lady Calderton.

"As a matter of actual fact, and if the worst came to the worst—not that it will—do you think she'd keep the secret?"

"I don't know. And that's the dreadful part of it. If she gave me her solemn promise to tell no one, I believe she'd keep her promise. But how do we know what her attitude would be if I went to her and said, '*You can't marry this man; he's my husband.*' She might even refuse to believe it. Do you know that her last words to me, as she marched out of the room yesterday, were to the effect that it was a pity that I, with a perfectly good husband and a perfectly good 'friend'—*you*, Henry! —couldn't bear to see my other 'friend,' Captain Bertie-Norton, carried off by another woman!"

I forced a smile, and indeed there was an element of comedy in this ghastly tragedy, as there so often is—just as tragedy lurks beneath the surface of so many human comedies.

Lady Calderton, jealous that her *friend*, Bertie-Norton, should be carried off by Christabel Hardacre!

"She might completely refuse to keep anything secret," she continued. "She's a good-hearted woman but . . . she *is* a woman. And I believe she's really in love with him. And when a woman of her age falls in love, it's apt to be serious. She may behave like a tigress and blame me for the whole thing."

"But surely it would be hardly reasonable."

"*Reasonable?* As I've just remarked, she's a woman, Henry."

"But wouldn't her anger be against him?"

"Quite probably not. She'd be literally mad with

615

rage, with thwarted love, with a kind of jealousy, and, a long time before she'd see in him the scoundrelly bigamist who has tried to marry her for her money, she'd see in me the woman who has intervened and wrecked the romance of her life! I may be wronging her, but . . ."

"Anyway, it won't come to that," I replied with an assurance that I was far from feeling. "No, we are making too much of it. We thought at first that he had done the impossible, and made matters worse than they were before; but he hasn't really. He'll understand that we simply won't for one moment contemplate the bare idea of permitting, much less being accessories to, a foul crime like this, and he'll abandon the idea."

"He won't, Henry. He won't. Apart from what you call his diseased egotism, he's mentally lacking. Lacking in a sense of right and wrong. For him, there *are* no such things. There's only what is expedient and what is not. My fear—and indeed, my belief—is that he'll go on with it until we simply have to intervene and prove to her that he's already married. And then the truth will come out."

Again she buried her face in her hands.

"It must come out, Henry. And I've nearly got to the point where I shall say, '*The sooner the better.*' If it weren't for Anthony and Arthur, I wouldn't bear it another day. I'd shout the truth from the housetops, to put an end to this . . . this . . ."

"But it *is* for Anthony and Sir Arthur," I interrupted. "And you won't give way. You'll fight to the very last. And you'll keep your promise to me."

"I'll keep my promise to you, my dear," she said.

I turned away and hurried from the room.

I too was rapidly coming to the point where I could bear it no longer—could bear Ferring-Chevigny no longer; could bear the fact of his existence no longer. And before this awful thing happened to the woman whom I loved infinitely better than I loved my life, something should happen to the good Montague Ferring-Chevigny.

I returned to the schoolroom. With one half of my mind, I carried on my work with Anthony; and with the other half, I planned and schemed and plotted—ways of killing Ferring-Chevigny.

It was the only way out. It must be done—and it must be done in such a manner that there should be no scandal at Calderton. He had staged his own death once, as Ferring-Chevigny. I would now stage his death as Bertie-Norton. As Bertie-Norton he had come here out of the blue, and as Bertie-Norton he should go away again—into the darkness. I had once told him that he was a foul insect on which I would set my heel, and the time had come now for me to do it. I would do it with as little compunction as I would crush a scorpion or kill a snake.

Murder?

Killing no murder. The killing of a creature unfit to live, to save three innocent people, one hair of the head of each of whom was ten thousand times worth his vile carcase.

Freely and, indeed, unashamedly, I set it down in black and white, that I had already killed Ferring-Chevigny in my heart, and was a murderer in intent and purpose.

Thou shalt not kill? No, thou, Ferring-Chevigny, shalt not kill these innocent people from whom you have received no harm; and from one of whom you have received the ultimate kindness.

Clever man, you die! I'll plot and I'll plan, I'll scheme and I'll intrigue and contrive, till I get you where I can kill you without danger of discovery; and, a thousand times more important, without danger of there being the least shadow of connection between the dead Bertie-Norton and Lady Calderton.

So amazing are the workings of the human mind that I actually found myself whistling, under my breath, a line from an idiotic popular song which I had not heard, and of which I had not thought, from my childhood. What was it I was whistling? Why should it have come into my mind?

An extraordinary psychological phenomenon of association of ideas. *'After the Ball.'*

Yes, let him do as he threatened, let him force our hands by proposing matrimony to Christabel Hardacre and announcing it at the Charity Ball—and he would have signed his own death-warrant.

§3

Yes, he would have signed his own death-warrant. My mind was made up, and I felt the better for the fact. I was almost gay. I was fey. And that afternoon, Anthony must have found me grimly jocular.

As usual he responded. He was mildly facetious; and then he waxed confidential.

"I say, Henry, I've been thinking over that quotation," said he. "We read it wrongly. Shakespeare didn't mean,

> *'There is a divinity that shapes our ends,*
> *Rough-hew them as we will.'"*

"Oh?" said I. "Expound."
"Why, obviously, what Shakespeare meant was,

> *'There is a divinity that shapes our ends*
> *rough,*
> *Hew them as we will.'"*

"Shapes them rough, eh?" I smiled.

Poor little chap. Providence was shaping his ends 'rough,' with a vengeance. To-day, heir to an ancient house and a great estate; to-morrow, a nameless bastard, heir to nothing, not even to a name.

No, it should not be. I would prevent it. I would myself have the courage to shape a better end for him than that.

And again I told myself that Ferring-Chevigny should die before he committed this vile crime. I would kill him myself, without compunction and without pity.

What was that? What was the boy saying?

"Why does my mother fear Captain Bertie-Norton?" he said, repeating the question that I had only subconsciously heard.

"*Fear* Captain Bertie-Norton?" said I in feigned astonishment.

"Yes, she's afraid of him; and she hates him."

"What *are* you talking about?"

Anthony put his hand through my arm.

"I say, Henry," he said, "the foul Roundhead spy has some hold upon the brave wife of the Cavalier nobleman who is away at the wars."

"Yes, that's all right for play-acting, old chap, but what nonsense were you talking about Lady Calderton and Bertie-Norton?"

"*Ah!* . . . I know something."

"What maggot have you got in your brain now?"

"*I know* . . . I overheard."

"Good Heavens! You don't mean to tell me you've been eavesdropping on your own mother, when she was talking to a guest?"

"Eavesdropping? Oh, no. I was spying. I'm the King's own special Secret Agent. He has sent me to Calderton Castle to watch a Roundhead spy who

has got into the house in the guise of a—guest . . .
Well, I once went to spy on him in his room. I had
an idea for giving him an awful fright. A ghostly
voice behind the panel. But when I looked through
my spy-hole, I saw that mother was in the room,
and she and the Roundhead spy were quarrelling. I
don't mean that exactly, but I heard her say,

" *'I pray God it may be the last time I see your
face or hear your voice.'*

"And the spy laughed rudely and said something."

"And you stayed and listened, eh?"

"Well . . . no. I came away as soon as I felt sure
about the Roundhead spy . . . And I'm quite certain
that my mother hates him."

I suppose that at any other time this would have
been a staggering blow; but now it was not. It
scarcely troubled me, for mentally I deflected it
from myself to fall upon the coffin of Montague
Ferring-Chevigny. It should drive in the last nail.
Had my resolution needed strengthening, which it
did not, this would have strengthened it, made me
yet the more determined that I would do what I now
conceived to be my simple duty.

No. Enough blows had fallen. Only one more
should fall. And on him, this time. It should be the
last; final and fatal; and the sooner it fell, the
better; before the boy learned anything else.

Had Anthony heard more than he admitted?

Did he know more than he professed to know?

It was possible, if not probable. I knew he would
never for his own ends tell me a direct lie; but he
loved reservations, perfectly harmless deceptions,
and a sort of unchildlike, though innocent, diplo-
macy. It is difficult to explain, as I have already
said; but though you loved and admired the boy
and knew that he loved and admired you, you
always felt that you would never quite understand

him, never quite get to the bottom of his mind. For not only did he remain unpredictable and a little enigmatic; but his mind, albeit wayward, whimsical and amusing, had an inner citadel, an impenetrable fastness into which he would, at times, retire and be alone.

Whenever that happened, he was baffling, elusive, and difficult—but nevertheless still delightful, intriguing, and charming.

How much did he know?

Well, it would be my fault if he ever knew any more.

"Well, old chap," said I to Anthony. "A game is a game, but eavesdropping is a very dirty one."

And,

"Ferring-Chevigny," said I to myself, "you've lived long enough. I only hope you haven't lived too long."

§4

It was from this moment that I set to work, seriously, carefully, and methodically, to plan the best means of killing Montague Ferring-Chevigny, with the minimum risk of causing scandal at Calderton and danger to Lady Calderton's secret.

I must kill him in such a way that I should not be suspected; and in such a way that if I were actually caught and convicted, no motive should be even imaginable.

EPILOGUE

"Mr. Waring," announced Judd, soldier-servant and invaluable factotum to Sir Walter Waring, as he opened the door of that gentleman's Albany sitting-room.

Sir Walter Waring permitted himself sufficient display of pleasure and interest, not to say emotion, to rise, take his nephew's extended hand, press it warmly, and hold it for a few seconds longer than usual.

"By Jove, I'm glad to see you, my boy!" he said, "and that's a thing I say to very few people nowadays."

"Glad to see me, Sir, or to hear my tale?" smiled Henry Waring.

"Well, since you ask, to hear your tale, which I can't very well do without seeing you, can I? . . . So you broke his neck, eh? . . . Good . . . Did you snap it across your knee, and then hide the body behind the panelling at the bottom of the secret staircase, or what? How did you do it? . . . No. Don't tell me. Don't tell me a word till we've had lunch and are settled for the afternoon. Then tell me all about it. By the way, *are* you going to tell me the truth, or would you rather not?"

"I'll tell you the truth, Sir, the whole truth, and nothing but the truth."

"Good. After all, you trusted me with Katherine's secret, so I'm sure you feel you can trust me with your own. Shan't blackmail you, Henry. On the contrary, I'm going to write you a cheque for a thousand pounds, before you go. Can you find a good home for it?"

"The very place, Uncle Walter. It's awfully kind of

622

you; but why?"

"Little token of—er—what shall we say, esteem, not to say admiration and approval."

Sir Walter Waring sat down again in his arm-chair.

"I suppose you are safe enough? Once there has been an inquest and a verdict of Misadventure, it would never be re-opened?"

"Oh, I'm safe enough," smiled Henry Waring.

"And no possibility of blackmail by anybody?"

"No. None whatever."

"Neat. Very neat. Very nicely done. And just in the nick of time, too. You did him in before he could announce his engagement, eh?"

"There was no announcement, Sir. The poor fellow was cut off in the midst of his bridal schemes and other sins."

"How did you . . . ? No, don't tell me till we've got the place to ourselves and, as we used to say at Whist, 'a clean hearth and the rigour of the game.' And we'll have those. We'll treat this story worthily, Henry. Give me something to think about for the rest of my life, as I sit here alone . . . I'm proud of you, my boy. I don't mind saying I envy you. Wish I had done it myself. So I would, at your age."

"Uncle, you do me too much honour. Wait till you've heard the story and you'll withdraw the compliments. Probably call me a fraud and tell me I'm not worthy," expostulated Henry Waring.

"How's Katherine?" interrupted Sir Walter.

"Like a person who's making a splendid recovery from an almost fatal illness. She's reviving. Coming back to life. She's going to be happy again. And married again, of course, very privately, when Sir Arthur returns. But she can hardly believe it all yet."

"No, she must be like a condemned man re-prieved and let out of his cell, the night before the hanging . . . Poor soul, what an experience! Still, she'll value peace and security and happiness at their real worth after this, eh?"

"She will. Every time she looks at Anthony, I can see her thanking God."

"And not a breath, not a whisper, not the faintest shadow of a suspicion! The fellow called Ferring-Chevigny killed himself pretty effectually seventeen years ago, and Bertie-Norton was killed pretty effectually a month ago. And all that Arthur at present knows is that some poor fellow of whom he has never heard, had the bad taste to go and break his neck at the Charity Ball at Calderton House!

"Death by Misadventure, eh?" he continued with a chuckle. "That Coroner, Dr. Stanton, seems to have been—er—what you might call helpful, wasn't he?"

"Yes. Yes. Certainly he did his duty, like an honest official, but he has a terrific admiration for Sir Arthur and Lady Calderton, and he was out to spare them all he could," replied Henry Waring.

"Devilish lucky he was at the Ball and on the spot," observed Sir Walter.

"Yes, Dr. Stanton as good as told the jury that he knew all about it because he was there when it happened; that, as a doctor, he could tell them the *cause* of death; and as an Officer of the Crown he could tell the police the *method* of it. Nothing for it but 'Death by Misadventure.'"

"Do you think he had any inkling of the truth?"

"What truth, Sir?" inquired Henry Waring, regarding his uncle quizzically, with raised eyebrows.

"Of how he met his death. I mean, met his—er—misadventure."

"He was perfectly certain of the truth."

"*Oh, yeah?*—as they say elsewhere. And had he any inkling of the previous truth that led up to that truth?"

"Who shall say, Sir?"

"Well, you might, for example. Putting it bluntly, do you suspect that he suspects?"

"Suspects what, Uncle?"

Sir Walter smiled frostily.

"I shall have to wait for the story, I see," he said. "Still, I think I might let you tell me that much."

"Ease my mind, you know, my boy," he added, with his thin-lipped sardonic smile. "Does he, or does he not, suspect *you*?"

"He does not. Most emphatically and most certainly he does not."

"Does he suspect anybody else?"

"If so, he hides it well."

"So that there is not the slightest danger that you might have to come forward, some time, and make a confession—because somebody else was in danger?"

"No. There is not the slightest fear that I shall ever have to do anything of the sort," replied Henry Waring.

"Then everything is absolutely straight; absolutely squared up; finished, wiped out and settled."

"Yes, the whole thing is over and done with. It was a nine-days' wonder and talk, of course, about the sad affair; largely because the unfortunate man was in fancy dress, and met his death at a ball. But it is past and forgotten now, and the incident closed."

"Thank God," said Sir Walter Waring earnestly. "I've some faint notion of what you and Katherine must have been through, for I haven't had too good a time, myself. It has hardly been out of my mind for a minute since the day you came and told me about it. It has affected my sleep. Worse still, it affected my palate; and neither my wine, my old brandy nor my cigars, were the same. When we had managed to have him frightened off, I began to get better, though he was still at the back of my mind; and when he returned, it was a real shock. It made me ill, Henry. And now I know that he's dead, and you are not in the slightest danger, well, as I say, I thank God. And . . ."

"Lunch is served, Sir," announced Judd.

"Now, my boy," said Sir Walter Waring, heaving a sigh of relief as Judd retired with the coffee-tray, leaving the two men in armchairs on either side of the sitting-room fire-place, a low table, furnished with liqueur brandy and cigars, between them. "Now let's have it. The whole story."

Henry Waring smiled at his uncle.

"Right, Sir.

"As I told you when I was up here just before the ball, things were looking about as bad as they possibly could. He simply would not, and probably could not, believe that if he proposed marriage to this Miss Christabel Hardacre, and announced their engagement, we should throw in our hand: that Lady Calderton would write to Sir Arthur telling him the truth; that she would show the letter to Miss Hardacre, and put an end to the whole dreadful situation.

"He simply laughed. (Incidentally, thank God I shall never hear that laugh again.) Simply laughed, and asked me what I took him for, that I should try such a childish bluff. He then disappeared from the neighbourhood for a time, and returned to the Calderton Arms just before the ball. He invited himself to dinner the night before it, and told me that he was coming to the ball. I did my best to dissuade him, and painted him a pretty good word-picture of himself as I saw him. One might as well try to stick a pin in the back-side of a rhinoceros. He didn't take me as seriously as he would have done a mosquito. I had told him that if he came to the ball, he'd regret it, and . . ."

"No one heard you threaten him, I suppose?" interrupted Sir Walter Waring.

"No, we were alone in my room, late at night. He was in a queer mood. I had never seen him quite as —what shall I say—self-satisfied, insolent, uplifted, and domineering. And now I haven't found the *mot juste*. He was absolutely triumphant. He saw himself successful at last, victorious over all difficulties; and he was utterly beastly, far worse than he had ever been. Sober enough, but drunk with success; proud and conceited and overbearing. He was ὑβρις personified.

"Well, I didn't see him again, after he swaggered out of my room that evening, until late on the night of the ball.

"Jenkins came and said that Captain Bertie-Norton wanted to speak to me: that he was up in my room, and it was urgent.

"Of course, not knowing what devilry the swine might be up to, or contemplating, I left the ballroom and went up to see what he wanted.

"What he did want was some sort of a fancy-dress. He knew we had got plenty of stuff up in Anthony's play-room, and he wanted me to rig him up, so that he could join the other guests. I thought it best to humour him, and was wondering what to suggest, when suddenly he said,

" '*I know. Give me that Roundhead trooper's kit you were wearing the other day. We are about of a size.*'

"Well, that was simple enough. And one's whole attitude to the man, in those days, was one of 'anything to keep him quiet.'

"So it didn't take me long to run upstairs and bring down the lobster-tail helmet, buff jerkin, breast-plate, velvet breeches, high boots, sash, baldrick and sword, that he had recently seen me wearing when I was play-acting with Anthony.

" *'That's the stuff to give the troops,'* said he, and quickly dressed himself as an Ironside soldier. The kit fitted him well, suited him admirably, and made an excellent fancy-dress.

"Having duly admired himself in the mirror, he clattered off downstairs, and joined in the fun.

"What happened next I didn't know, till Lady Calderton told me some time afterwards.

"One assumes he went to the buffet and over-quenched his thirst. No doubt he was pretty hot in his buff jerkin and breast-plate. Anyway, he sought Lady Calderton out, and began to pester her. I didn't think that that man could really add one more grain to the mountain of his offences. But he did. For he actually began talking—though in plain English—of his *droits du seigneur*, his *droits du mari*, rather; in fact, his conjugal rights. Can you believe it? He must have been more-or-less drunk, of course. Anyhow, he was more-than-less amorous, and Lady Calderton simply had to—well, escape. Luckily there was no scene. It happened during an interval between dances; most people were making for the sitting-out places or the buffet; and he spoke quietly—as well he might. She walked across to the main staircase, he following her, and when she turned on to the second flight, out of sight of the hall, she ran as fast as she could to her bedroom and locked the door.

"Our gentleman, finding it shut in his face, banged on it with the hilt of the heavy sword he was wearing.

"There was the stage set. A dimly lit corridor, a man in fancy-dress hammering at a locked door with a sword.

"This I had from Lady Calderton, as I said.

"Now to go back a little while.

"Young Anthony, as a great treat—and his mother could refuse him nothing in those days, of course—had been allowed to come to the Ball and stay up till midnight, with special extension if I thought he wasn't over-tired.

"Now see the hand of Fate, Sir."

"At twelve o'clock Anthony said he wasn't really tired, but that he had had nearly enough, and what about another half-hour. Right, said I, and at half-past twelve I gathered him in and went up to his room with him. He was dressed as Charles the First, by the way, and a wonderful young Cavalier he looked.

"I helped him off with his kit, saw him into bed, and stayed and had a chat with him, as of course he was a bit excited; (and it was *then*, just as I came out of his room, that Jenkins came to me with the message of which I told you, that Captain Bertie-Norton wanted to speak to me).

"Well, an hour or so later, at about two o'clock, I went upstairs, and I went for two or three reasons. I thought I would have a look in on Anthony and see if he had settled down all right. As you know, he's of a nervous temperament and very excitable. I wanted to get my cigarette-case—and this may, of course, be fanciful, but I honestly think Fate had got the business thoroughly in hand, and that I had a kind of *prompting* to go upstairs. Anyway, I went.

"As I got to the top of the stairs, I was suddenly aware that Bertie-Norton was there, that he delivered a terrific bang on Lady Calderton's door with the heavy hilt of the old sword that he was wearing, that he stepped back, shook his fist at the door and was going to take a run at it as though to burst it in.

"In stepping back three or four paces, he came to the head of what used to be a 'secret' staircase that leads down at right-angles, and from the top of which the panelled door has been removed.

"Also, I was aware of the fact that as he struck the blow and stepped back, Anthony's door opened; that Anthony came flying along the short corridor and uttered a loud cry; that as he did so, Ferring-Chevigny turned towards him with his back to the staircase; that, like a young tiger, Anthony leapt, thrust with both hands, and sent Ferring-Chevigny flying headlong down the steep narrow staircase, and that he fell with a crash on the flagstone at the bottom.

"The impact stopped Anthony's rush, and without a glance downward, he turned about, walked back to his room and shut the door.

"The whole thing hadn't taken longer than the time required for me to go up the last half-dozen steps of the staircase.

"As I stepped on to the landing, there was nobody. There was nothing. Lady Calderton's door was shut; Anthony's door was shut; and I was alone in the now silent corridor."

"Silent?"

"Yes, not a sound came from the secret stair. No sound of a man getting to his feet and coming up again. Complete silence. I hurried down the steep, narrow, panelling-enclosed stairs and struck a match. There lay Ferring-Chevigny—dead. He had landed on his head and broken his neck."

Sir Walter Waring sat erect in his chair, his cigar cold between his fingers, an amazing sign of his rapt and enthralled interest.

"Good Heavens!" he whispered. "So the *boy* killed him?"

"The boy killed him," said Henry Waring.

"Intentionally?"

"That I don't know, and probably never shall

know. I don't imagine he'll tell me; and I most certainly shall not ask him.

"Uncle, you and I are the only two people in this world who know how Ferring-Chevigny died."

"Unless young Anthony does," said Sir Walter.

"Let's assume that he doesn't," said Henry Waring. "For Heaven's sake, let's pretend that he doesn't, anyway."

"Sleep-walking, perhaps," suggested Sir Walter Waring.

"I told you I'd tell you the truth, the whole truth, and nothing but the truth," replied Henry Waring. "I told you the boy uttered a cry as he rushed along the landing. What he shouted was '*Bonnance!*'"

"'*Bonnance,*' did you say?"

"Yes. It was a word he had invented, a kind of oath, kept for special occasions. Now, does a sleep-walker select a word and shout it aloud . . . ?"

"Recognizing a special occasion?" said Sir Walter. "I don't know, Henry. I'm not an alienist, not even a psychologist. I don't know whether a sleep-walker would do such a thing. I don't know whether a sleep-walker recognizes a special occasion, selects the appropriate word and shouts it aloud. I don't know whether a sleep-walker runs swiftly, makes a violent effort, thrusts a big heavy man down a flight of stairs, saves himself from falling, and then turns about and walks back to his bedroom and gets into bed, still sound asleep and unconscious of what he has done."

"I suppose you went along to his room pretty soon?" he asked.

"Yes. As soon as I had assured myself that Ferring-Chevigny was dead, I went to Anthony's bedroom."

"Well?"

"He was in bed and asleep."

"Sure he was asleep?"

"No. I'm not sure; but I'll tell you what I tell myself, and what I'm going to tell myself—until Anthony tells me something different, which he never will do. It's this.

"Anthony Calderton, excited by the Ball, his fancy-dress as Charles the First, late hours and perhaps a glass of champagne, fell into a troubled sleep, and dreamed. He awoke and got out of bed, or else he got out of bed without waking. He opened the door, and there he saw before him, in the flesh, his lifelong *bête noir*, bogey, monster of horror and terror incarnate—Oliver Cromwell himself. (I've told you about the Oliver Cromwell neurosis that Miss Stuart contrived to give him.)

"He saw Oliver Cromwell, not only standing there in the flesh, but beating down his mother's door. So, in somnambulistic trance, or if you like, in a waking dream, he rushed at his enemy, and, as Fate would have it, *as Fate had willed it and arranged it*, his enemy was standing at the top of those stairs. He flung him down them, and, as the dream faded, Anthony walked back to his bed; or again, still walking in his sleep, he returned to his room, lay down and dreamed on.

"That's how I intend to see it, Uncle Walter."

"I understand, Henry . . . And you'll never say a word about it to the boy?"

"Never a word. I'll never mention the name Bertie-Norton to him as long as I live."

"And of course Lady Calderton knows nothing of this?"

"Absolutely nothing. All she knows is that Bertie-Norton was found dead at the bottom of those stairs, and that Dr. Stanton came to the conclusion that he had tripped over the great spurs he was wearing, and fallen headlong from top to bottom . . . If anybody thought that the poor gentleman had had just a drop more champagne than he could comfortably carry down the steep flight of stairs, they were too well-bred, well-mannered, or good-natured, to say so. No, said they, he must have wandered up the main staircase and started to come down by the secret one, which was a short cut to the hall. He knew his way, of course, as he had stayed in the house once, when he was taken ill after dinner there . . ."

"Anthony wasn't at the inquest, I suppose?" asked Sir Walter.

"Oh, no. No, there was no earthly reason to call him."

"And has he made no reference to the matter?"

"Not one single word. It's just as though he had heard nothing whatever about it."

"H'm," mused Sir Walter Waring. "That's a little strange, isn't it?"

"No, Uncle. No, *please*. Anthony was walking in his sleep or actually living a nightmare."

Sir Walter Waring rose to his feet, stared at his nephew a while, and then laid his hand upon his shoulder.

"Undoubtedly, Henry," he said, and patted his nephew's shoulder gently ere he withdrew his hand.

"Anyhow," he said brusquely as he turned away, "he killed Montague Ferring-Chevigny. And that, my boy, is a very strange and wonderful thing, when you come to think of it."

NOTE

Anthony Calderton became my closest and most intimate friend. Never once did he say a word to me concerning the events of that amazing night.

Nor did I to him.

Incidentally, it is an interesting fact that neither did he ever again mention Oliver Cromwell to me—nor dress up as King Charles, nor take part in any play, charade or enactment concerning Stuart times and the days of Cavalier and Roundhead.

Never once.

Available P. C. Wren Titles
from
Riner Publishing Company

The Collected Short Stories

Volume One: ISBN 9780985032609
Volume Two: ISBN 9780985032616
Volume Three: ISBN 9780985032623
Volume Four: ISBN 9780985032630
Volume Five: ISBN 9780985032647

The Collected Novels

Volume One: *The Geste Novels*
    Part A: ISBN 9780985032678
    Part B: ISBN 9780985032685
Volume Two: *The Sinbad Novels*
    Part A: ISBN 9780692639382
    Part B: ISBN 9780692639429
Volume Three: *The Foreign Legion Novels*
    Part A: ISBN 9780999074909
    Part B: ISBN 9780999074916
Volume Four: *The Earlier India Novels*
    Part A: ISBN 9780999074923
    Part B: ISBN 9780999074930
Volume Five: *The Later India Novels*
    Part A: ISBN 9780999074947
    Part B: ISBN 9780999074954
Volume Six: *The English Novels*
    Part A: ISBN 9780999074961
    Part B: ISBN 9780999074978
Volume Seven: *A Mixed Bag of Novels*
    Part A: ISBN 9780999074985
    Part B: ISBN 9780999074992

Further information can be found at
rinerpublishing.wordpress.com

2 February 2020

www.ingramcontent.com/pod-product-compliance
Lightning Source LLC
Chambersburg PA
CBHW032250020726
47495CB00001B/41